THE MODERN LIBRARY
OF THE WORLD'S BEST BOOKS

CITIES OF THE PLAIN

CITIES OF THE PLAIN

BY

MARCEL PROUST

TRANSLATED BY

C. K. SCOTT MONCRIEFF

THE MODERN LIBRARY · NEW YORK

Random House IS THE PUBLISHER OF

THE MODERN LIBRARY

BENNETT A. CERF · DONALD S. KLOPFER · ROBERT K. HAAS

Manufactured in the United States of America

Printed by Parkway Printing Company   Bound by H. Wolff

MARCEL PROUST

(1871-1922)

A NOTE ON THE AUTHOR OF "A LA RECHERCHE DU TEMPS PERDU"

"I don't think there ever has been in the whole of literature such an example of the power of analysis, and I feel safe in saying that there will never be another."—Joseph Conrad.

The world of fashion in which Marcel Proust spent his youth and early manhood saw nothing of him during the last thirteen years of his life. A victim of chronic illness, he barricaded himself in his apartment, swathed himself like an Egyptian mummy, drew his shutters and curtains to exclude the light, and there recorded his chronicle of things past. Son of a distinguished physician and an heiress of a rich Jewish family, Proust had his first training under the guidance of the Roman Catholic Church. An association in the 1890's with some of the aesthetes of that period resulted in the publication of a review, to which Proust contributed some juvenile prose and verse. Thereafter the fashionable Faubourg St. Germain became his sphere, and it was there, among the illustrious and well-born, that he assimilated those fragments of gossip and family history which were later transmuted into a world in itself—the world of A La Recherche du Temps Perdu.

BIBLIOGRAPHY

LES PLAISIRS ET LES JOURS (with a preface by Anatole France (1896))

DU CÔTÉ DE CHEZ SWANN (1918) (SWANN'S WAY (1923))

À L'OMBRE DES JEUNES FILLES EN FLEURS (1918) (WITHIN A BUDDING GROVE (1924))

LE CÔTÉ DE GUERMANTES I (1920) LE CÔTÉ DE GUERMANTES II (1921) (THE GUERMANTES WAY (1925))

SODOME ET GOMORRHE I (1921) SODOME ET GOMORRHE II (1922) (CITIES OF THE PLAIN (1928))

LA PRISONNIÈRE (1923) (THE CAPTIVE (1929))

ALBERTINE DISPARUE (1926) (THE SWEET CHEAT GONE (1930))

LE TEMPS RETROUVÉ (1928) (THE PAST RECAPTURED (1932))

TRANSLATOR'S DEDICATION

To

RICHARD and MYRTLE KURT

and Their Creator

Pisa,
1927.

CONTENTS

PART I

CITIES OF THE PLAIN

PART I

Introducing the men-women, descendants of those of the inhabitants of Sodom who were spared by the fire from heaven.

La femme aura Gomorrhe et l'homme aura Sodome. Alfred de Vigny.

THE reader will remember that, long before going that day (on the evening of which the Princesse de Guermantes was to give her party) to pay the Duke and Duchess the visit which I have just described, I had kept watch for their return and had made, in the course of my vigil, a discovery which, albeit concerning M. de Charlus in particular, was in itself so important that I have until now, until the moment when I could give it the prominence and treat it with the fulness that it demanded, postponed giving any account of it. I had, as I have said, left the marvellous point of vantage, so snugly contrived for me at the top of the house, commanding the broken and irregular slopes leading up to the Hôtel de Bréquigny, and gaily decorated in the Italian manner by the rose-pink campanile of the Marquis de Frécourt's stables. I had felt it to be more convenient, when I thought that the Duke and Duchess were on the point of returning, to post myself on the staircase. I regretted somewhat the abandonment of my watch-tower. But at that time of day, namely the hour immediately following luncheon, I had less cause for regret, for I should not then have seen, as in the morning, the footmen of the Bréquigny-Tresmes household, converted by distance into minute figures in a picture, make their leisurely ascent of the abrupt precipice, feather-brush in hand, behind the large, transparent flakes of mica which stood out so charmingly upon its ruddy bastions. Failing the geologist's field of contemplation, I had at least that of the botanist, and was peering through the shutters of the staircase window at the Duchess's little tree and at the precious plant, exposed in the courtyard with that insistence with which mothers " bring out " their marriageable offspring, and asking myself whether the unlikely insect would come, by a providential hazard, to visit the offered and neglected pistil. My curiosity emboldening me by degrees, I went down to the ground-floor window, which also stood open with its shutters ajar. I could hear distinctly, as he got ready to go out, Jupien who could not detect me behind my blind, where I stood perfectly still until the moment when I drew quickly aside in order not to be seen by M. de Charlus, who, on his way to call upon Mme. de Villeparisis, was slowly crossing the courtyard, a pursy figure, aged by the strong light, his hair visibly grey. Nothing short of an indisposition of Mme. de Villeparisis (consequent on the illness of the Marquis de Fierbois, with whom he personally was at daggers drawn) could have made M. de Charlus pay a call, perhaps for the first time in his life, at that hour of the day. For with that eccentricity of the Guermantes, who, instead of conforming to the ways of society, used to modify them to suit their own personal habits (habits not, they thought, social, and deserving in consequence the abasement before them of that thing of no value, Society—thus it was that Mme. de Marsantes had no regular " day," but was at home to her friends every morning between ten o'clock and noon), the Baron, reserving those hours for reading, hunting for old curiosities and so forth, paid calls only between four and six in the afternoon. At six o'clock he went to the Jockey Club, or took a stroll in the Bois. A moment later, I again recoiled, in order not to be seen by Jupien. It was nearly time for him to start for the office, from which he would return only for dinner, and not even then always during the last week, his niece and her apprentices having gone to the country to finish a dress there for a customer. Then, realising that no one could see me, I decided not to let myself be disturbed again, for fear of missing, should the miracle be fated to occur, the arrival, almost beyond the possibility of hope (across so many obstacles of distance, of adverse risks, of dangers), of the insect sent from so far as ambassador to the virgin who had so long been waiting for him to appear. I knew that this expectancy was no more passive than in the male flower, whose stamens had spontaneously curved so that the insect might more easily receive their offering; similarly the female flower that stood here, if the insect came, would coquettishly arch her styles, and, to be more effectively penetrated by him, would imperceptibly advance, like a hypocritical but ardent damsel, to meet him half-way. The laws of the vegetable kingdom are themselves governed by other laws, increasingly exalted. If the visit of an insect, that is to say, the transportation of the seed of one flower is generally necessary for the fertilisation of another, that is because autofecundation, the fertilisation of a flower by itself, would lead, like a succession of intermarriages in the same family, to degeneracy and sterility, whereas the crossing effected by the insects gives to the subsequent generations of the same species a vigour unknown to their forebears. This invigoration may, however, prove excessive, the species develop out of all proportion; then, as an anti-toxin protects us against disease, as the thyroid gland regulates our adiposity, as defeat comes to punish pride, fatigue, indulgence, and as sleep in turn depends upon fatigue, so an exceptional act of autofecundation comes at a given point to apply its turn of the screw, its pull on the curb, brings back within normal limits the flower that has exaggerated its transgression of them. My reflexions had followed a tendency which I shall describe in due course, and I had already drawn from the visible stratagems of flowers a conclusion that bore upon a whole unconscious element of literary work, when I saw M. de Charlus coming away from the Marquise. Perhaps he had learned from his elderly relative herself, or merely from a servant, the great improvement, or rather her complete recovery from what had been nothing more than a slight indisposition. At this moment, when he did not suspect that anyone was watching him, his eyelids lowered as a screen against the sun, M. de Charlus had relaxed that tension in his face, deadened that artificial vitality, which the animation of his talk and the force of his will kept in evidence there as a rule. Pale as marble, his nose stood out firmly, his fine features no longer received from an expression deliberately assumed a different meaning which altered the beauty of their modelling; nothing more now than a Guermantes, he seemed already carved in stone, he Palamède the Fifteenth, in their chapel at Combray. These general features of a whole family took on, however, in the face of M. de Charlus a fineness more spiritualised, above all more gentle. I regretted for his sake that he should habitually adulterate with so many acts of violence, offensive oddities, tale-bearings, with such harshness, susceptibility and arrogance, that he should conceal beneath a false brutality the amenity, the kindness which, at the moment of his emerging from Mme. de Villeparisis's, I could see displayed so innocently upon his face. Blinking his eyes in the sunlight, he seemed almost to be smiling, I found in his face seen thus in repose and, so to speak, in its natural state something so affectionate, so disarmed, that I could not help thinking how angry M. de Charlus would have been could he have known that he was being watched; for what was suggested to me by the sight of this man who was so insistent, who prided himself so upon his virility, to whom all other men seemed odiously effeminate, what he made me suddenly think of, so far had he momentarily assumed her features, expression, smile, was a woman.

I was about to change my position again, so that he should not catch sight of me; I had neither the time nor the need to do so. What did I see? Face to face, in that courtyard where certainly they had never met before (M. de Charlus coming to the Hôtel de Guermantes only in the afternoon, during the time when Jupien was at his office), the Baron, having suddenly opened wide his half-shut eyes, was studying with unusual attention the ex-tailor poised on the threshold of his shop, while the latter, fastened suddenly to the ground before M. de Charlus, taking root in it like a plant, was contemplating with a look of amazement the plump form of the middle-aged Baron. But, more astounding still, M. de Charlus's attitude having changed, Jupien's, as though in obedience to the laws of an occult art, at once brought itself into harmony with it. The Baron, who was now seeking to conceal the impression that had been made on him, and yet, in spite of his affectation of indifference, seemed unable to move away without regret, went, came, looked vaguely into the distance in the way which, he felt, most enhanced the beauty of his eyes, assumed a complacent, careless, fatuous air. Meanwhile Jupien, shedding at once the humble, honest expression which I had always associated with him, had—in perfect symmetry with the Baron—thrown up his head, given a becoming tilt to his body, placed his hand with a grotesque impertinence on his hip, stuck out his behind, posed himself with the coquetry that the orchid might have adopted on the providential arrival of the bee. I had not supposed that he could appear so repellent. But I was equally unaware that he was capable of improvising his part in this sort of dumb charade, which (albeit he found himself for the first time in the presence of M. de Charlus) seemed to have been long and carefully rehearsed; one does not arrive spontaneously at that pitch of perfection except when one meets in a foreign country a compatriot with whom an understanding then grows up of itself, both parties speaking the same language, even although they have never seen one another before.

This scene was not, however, positively comic, it was stamped with a strangeness, or if you like a naturalness, the beauty of which steadily increased. M. de Charlus might indeed assume a detached air, indifferently let his eyelids droop; every now and then he raised them, and at such moments turned on Jupien an attentive gaze. But (doubtless because he felt that such a scene could not be prolonged indefinitely in this place, whether for reasons which we shall learn later on, or possibly from that feeling of the brevity of all things which makes us determine that every blow must strike home, and renders so moving the spectacle of every kind of love), each time that M. de Charlus looked at Jupien, he took care that his glance should be accompanied by a spoken word, which made it infinitely unlike the glances we usually direct at a person whom we do or do not know; he stared at Jupien with the peculiar fixity of the person who is about to say to us: "Excuse my taking the liberty, but you have a long white thread hanging down your back," or else: "Surely I can't be mistaken, you come from Zurich too; I'm certain I must have seen you there often in the curiosity shop." Thus, every other minute, the same question seemed to be being intensely put to Jupien in the stare of M. de Charlus, like those questioning phrases of Beethoven indefinitely repeated at regular intervals, and intended—with an exaggerated lavishness of preparation—to introduce a new theme, a change of tone, a "re-entry." On the other hand, the beauty of the reciprocal glances of M. de Charlus and Jupien arose precisely from the fact that they did not, for the moment at least, seem to be intended to lead to anything farther. This beauty, it was the first time that I had seen the Baron and Jupien display it. In the eyes of both of them, it was the sky not of Zurich but of some Oriental city, the name of which I had not yet divined, that I saw reflected. Whatever the point might be that held M. de Charlus and the ex-tailor thus arrested, their pact seemed concluded and these superfluous glances to be but ritual preliminaries, like the parties that people give before a marriage which has been definitely "arranged." Nearer still to nature—and the multiplicity of these analogies is itself all the more natural in that the same man, if we examine him for a few minutes, appears in turn as a man, a man-bird or man-insect, and so forth—one would have called them a pair of birds, the male and the female, the male seeking to make advances, the female—Jupien—no longer giving any sign of response to these overtures, but regarding her new friend without surprise, with an inattentive fixity of gaze, which she doubtless felt to be more disturbing and the only effective method, once the male had taken the first steps, and had fallen back upon preening his feathers. At length Jupien's indifference seemed to suffice him no longer; from this certainty of having conquered, to making himself be pursued and desired was but the next stage, and Jupien, deciding to go off to his work, passed through the carriage gate. It was only, however, after turning his head two or three times that he escaped into the street towards which the Baron, trembling lest he should lose the trail (boldly humming a tune, not forgetting to fling a "Good day" to the porter, who, half-tipsy himself and engaged in treating a few friends in his back kitchen, did not even hear him), hurried briskly to overtake him. At the same instant, just as M. de Charlus disappeared through the gate humming like a great bumble-bee, another, a real bee this time, came into the courtyard. For all I knew this might be the one so long awaited by the orchid, which was coming to bring it that rare pollen without which it must die a virgin. But I was distracted from following the gyrations of the insect for, a few minutes later, engaging my attention afresh, Jupien (perhaps to pick up a parcel which he did take away with him eventually and so, presumably, in the emotion aroused by the apparition of M. de Charlus, had forgotten, perhaps simply for a more natural reason) returned, followed by the Baron. The latter, deciding to cut short the preliminaries, asked the tailor for a light, but at once observed: "I ask you for a light, but I find that I have left my cigars at home." The laws of hospitality prevailed over those of coquetry. "Come inside, you shall have everything you require," said the tailor, on whose features disdain now gave place to joy. The door of the shop closed behind them and I could hear no more. I had lost sight of the bee. I did not know whether he was the insect that the orchid needed, but I had no longer any doubt, in the case of an extremely rare insect and a captive flower, of the miraculous possibility of their conjunction when M. de Charlus (this is simply a comparison of providential hazards, whatever they may be, without the slightest scientific claim to establish a relation between certain laws and what is sometimes, most ineptly, termed homosexuality), who for years past had never come to the house except at hours when Jupien was not there, by the mere accident of Mme. de Villeparisis's illness had encountered the tailor, and with him the good fortune reserved for men of the type of the Baron by one of those fellow-creatures who may indeed be, as we shall see, infinitely younger than Jupien and better looking, the man predestined to exist in order that they may have their share of sensual pleasure on this earth; the man who cares only for elderly gentlemen.

All that I have just said, however, I was not to understand until several minutes had elapsed; so much is reality encumbered by those properties of invisibility until a chance occurrence has divested it of them. Anyhow, for the moment I was greatly annoyed at not being able to hear any more of the conversation between the ex-tailor and the Baron. I then bethought myself of the vacant shop, separated from Jupien's only by a partition that was extremely slender. I had, in order to get to it, merely to go up to our flat, pass through the kitchen, go down by the service stair to the cellars, make my way through them across the breadth of the courtyard above, and on coming to the right place underground, where the joiner had, a few months ago, still been storing his timber and where Jupien intended to keep his coal, climb the flight of steps which led to the interior of the shop. Thus the whole of my journey would be made under cover, I should not be seen by anyone. This was the most prudent method. It was not the one that I adopted, but, keeping close to the walls, I made a circuit in the open air of the courtyard, trying not to let myself be seen. If I was not, I owe it more, I am sure, to chance than to my own sagacity. And for the fact that I took so imprudent a course, when the way through the cellar was so safe, I can see three possible reasons, assuming that I had any reason at all. First of all, my impatience. Secondly, perhaps, a dim memory of the scene at Montjouvain, when I stood concealed outside Mlle. Vinteuil's window. Certainly, the affairs of this sort of which I have been a spectator have always been presented in a setting of the most imprudent and least probable character, as if such revelations were to be the reward of an action full of risk, though in part clandestine. Lastly, I hardly dare, so childish does it appear, to confess the third reason, which was, I am quite sure, unconsciously decisive. Since, in order to follow—and see controverted—the military principles enunciated by Saint-Loup, I had followed in close detail the course of the Boer war, I had been led on from that to read again old accounts of explorations, narratives of travel. These stories had excited me, and I applied them to the events of my daily life to stimulate my courage. When attacks of illness had compelled me to remain for several days and nights on end not only without sleep but without lying down, without tasting food or drink, at the moment when my pain and exhaustion became so intense that I felt that I should never escape from them, I would think of some traveller cast on the beach, poisoned by noxious herbs, shivering with fever in clothes drenched by the salt water, who nevertheless in a day or two felt stronger, rose and went blindly upon his way, in search of possible inhabitants who might, when he came to them, prove cannibals. His example acted on me as a tonic, restored my hope, and I felt ashamed of my momentary discouragement. Thinking of the Boers who, with British armies facing them, were not afraid to expose themselves at the moment when they had to cross, in order to reach a covered position, a tract of open country: "It would be a fine thing," I thought to myself, "if I were to shew less courage when the theatre of operations is simply the human heart, and when the only steel that I, who engaged in more than one duel without fear at the time of the Dreyfus case, have to fear is that of the eyes of the neighbours who have other things to do besides looking into the courtyard."

But when I was inside the shop, taking care not to let any plank in the floor make the slightest creak, as I found that the least sound in Jupien's shop could be heard from the other, I thought to myself how rash Jupien and M. de

Charlus had been, and how wonderfully fortune had favoured them.

I did not dare move. The Guermantes groom, taking advantage no doubt of his master's absence, had, as it happened, transferred to the shop in which I now stood a ladder which hitherto had been kept in the coach-house, and if I had climbed this I could have opened the ventilator above and heard as well as if I had been in Jupien's shop itself. But I was afraid of making a noise. Besides, it was unnecessary. I had not even cause to regret my not having arrived in the shop until several minutes had elapsed. For from what I heard at first in Jupien's shop, which was only a series of inarticulate sounds, I imagine that few words had been exchanged. It is true that these sounds were so violent that, if one set had not always been taken up an octave higher by a parallel plaint, I might have thought that one person was strangling another within a few feet of me, and that subsequently the murderer and his resuscitated victim were taking a bath to wash away the traces of the crime. I concluded from this later on that there is another thing as vociferous as pain, namely pleasure, especially when there is added to it—failing the fear of an eventual parturition, which could not be present in this case, despite the hardly convincing example in the *Golden Legend*—an immediate afterthought of cleanliness. Finally, after about half an hour (during which time I had climbed on tip-toe up my ladder so as to peep through the ventilator which I did not open), a conversation began. Jupien refused with insistence the money that M. de Charlus was pressing upon him.

"Why do you have your chin shaved like that," he

inquired of the Baron in a cajoling tone. "It's so becoming, a nice beard." "Ugh! It's disgusting," the Baron replied. Meanwhile he still lingered upon the threshold and plied Jupien with questions about the neighbourhood. "You don't know anything about the man who sells chestnuts at the corner, not the one on the left, he's a horror, but the other way, a great, dark fellow? And the chemist opposite, he has a charming cyclist who delivers his parcels." These questions must have ruffled Jupien, for, drawing himself up with the scorn of a great courtesan who has been forsaken, he replied: "I can see you are completely heartless." Uttered in a pained, frigid, affected tone, this reproach must have made its sting felt by M. de Charlus, who, to counteract the bad impression made by his curiosity, addressed to Jupien, in too low a tone for me to be able to make out his words, a request the granting of which would doubtless necessitate their prolonging their sojourn in the shop, and which moved the tailor sufficiently to make him forget his annoyance, for he studied the Baron's face, plump and flushed beneath his grey hair, with the supremely blissful air of a person whose self-esteem has just been profoundly flattered, and, deciding to grant M. de Charlus the favour that he had just asked of him, after various remarks lacking in refinement such as: "Aren't you naughty!" said to the Baron with a smiling, emotional, superior and grateful air: "All right, you big baby, come along!"

"If I hark back to the question of the tram conductor," M. de Charlus went on imperturbably, "it is because, apart from anything else, he might offer me some entertainment on my homeward journey. For it falls to my lot, now and then, like the Caliph who used to roam the streets of Bagdad in the guise of a common merchant, to condescend to follow some curious little person whose profile may have taken my fancy." I made at this point the same observation that I had made on Bergotte. If he should ever have to plead before a bench, he would employ not the sentences calculated to convince his judges, but such Bergottesque sentences as his peculiar literary temperament suggested to him and made him find pleasure in using. Similarly M. de Charlus, in conversing with the tailor, made use of the same language that he would have used to fashionable people of his own set, even exaggerating its eccentricities, whether because the shyness which he was striving to overcome drove him to an excess of pride or, by preventing him from mastering himself (for we are always less at our ease in the company of some one who is not of our station), forced him to unveil, to lay bare his true nature, which was, in fact, arrogant and a trifle mad, as Mme. de Guermantes had remarked. "So as not to lose the trail," he went on, "I spring like a little usher, like a young and good-looking doctor, into the same car as the little person herself, of whom we speak in the feminine gender only so as to conform with the rules of grammar (as we say, in speaking of a Prince, 'Is His Highness enjoying *her* usual health'). If she changes her car, I take, with possibly the germs of the plague, that incredible thing called a 'transfer,' a number, and one which, albeit it is presented to *me*, is not always number one! I change 'carriages' in this way as many as three or four times, I end up sometimes at eleven o'clock at night at the Orleans station and have to come home. Still, if it were only the

Orleans station! Once, I must tell you, not having managed to get into conversation sooner, I went all the way to Orleans itself, in one of those frightful compartments where one has, to rest one's eyes upon, between triangles of what is known as 'string-work,' photographs of the principal architectural features of the line. There was only one vacant seat; I had in front of me, as an historic edifice, a 'view' of the Cathedral of Orleans, quite the ugliest in France, and as tiring a thing to have to stare at in that way against my will as if somebody had forced me to focus its towers in the lens of one of those optical penholders which give one ophthalmia. I got out of the train at Les Aubrais together with my young person, for whom alas his family (when I had imagined him to possess every defect except that of having a family) were waiting on the platform! My sole consolation, as I waited for a train to take me back to Paris, was the house of Diane de Poitiers. She may indeed have charmed one of my royal ancestors, I should have preferred a more living beauty. That is why, as an antidote to the boredom of returning home by myself, I should rather like to make friends with a sleeping-car attendant or the conductor of an omnibus. Now, don't be shocked," the Baron wound up, "it is all a question of class. With what you would call 'young gentlemen,' for instance, I feel no desire actually to have them, but I am never satisfied until I have touched them, I don't mean physically, but touched a responsive chord. As soon as, instead of leaving my letters unanswered, a young man starts writing to me incessantly, when he is morally at my disposal, I grow calm again, or at least I should grow calm were I not immediately caught by the attraction of another. Rather curious, ain't it?—Speaking of 'young gentlemen,' those that come to the house here, do you know any of them?" "No, baby. Oh, yes, I do, a dark one, very tall, with an eyeglass, who keeps smiling and turning round." "I don't know who' you mean." Jupien filled in the portrait, but M. de Charlus could not succeed in identifying its subject, not knowing that the ex-tailor was one of those persons, more common than is generally supposed, who never remember the colour of the hair of people they do not know well. But to me, who was aware of this infirmity in Jupien and substituted "fair" for "dark," the portrait appeared to be an exact description of the Duc de Châtellerault. "To return to young men not of the lower orders," the Baron went on, "at the present moment my head has been turned by a strange little fellow, an intelligent little cit who shews with regard to myself a prodigious want of civility. He has absolutely no idea of the prodigious personage that I am, and of the microscopic animalcule that he is in comparison. After all, what does it matter, the little ass may bray his head off before my august bishop's mantle." "Bishop!" cried Jupien, who had understood nothing of M. de Charlus's concluding remarks, but was completely taken aback by the word bishop. "But that sort of thing doesn't go with religion," he said. "I have three Popes in my family," replied M. de Charlus, "and enjoy the right to mantle in gules by virtue of a cardinalatial title, the niece of the Cardinal, my great-uncle, having conveyed to my grandfather the title of Duke which was substituted for it. I see, though, that metaphor leaves you deaf and French history cold. Besides," he added, less perhaps by way of conclusion than as a warning, "this attraction that I feel towards the young people who avoid me, from fear of course, for only their natural respect stops their mouths from crying out to me that they love me, requires in them an outstanding social position. And again, their feint of indifference may produce, in spite of that, the directly opposite effect. Fatuously prolonged, it sickens me. To take an example from a class with which you are more familiar, when they were doing up my Hôtel, so as not to create jealousies among all the duchesses who were vying with one another for the honour of being able to say that they had given me a lodging, I went for a few days to an 'hotel,' as they call inns nowadays. One of the bedroom valets I knew, I pointed out to him an interesting little page who used to open and shut the front door, and who remained refractory to my proposals. Finally, losing my temper, in order to prove to him that my intentions were pure, I made him an offer of a ridiculously high sum simply to come upstairs and talk to me for five minutes in my room. I waited for him in vain. I then took such a dislike to him that I used to go out by the service door so as not to see his villainous little mug at the other. I learned afterwards that he had never had any of my notes, which had been intercepted, the first by the bedroom valet, who was jealous, the next by the day porter, who was virtuous, the third by the night porter, who was in love with the little page, and used to couch with him at the hour when Dian rose. But my disgust persisted none the less, and were they to bring me the page, simply like a dish of venison on a silver platter, I should thrust him away with a retching stomach. But there's the unfortunate part of it, we have spoken of serious matters, and now all is over between us, there can be no more question of what I hoped to secure. But you could render me great services, act as my agent; why no, the mere thought of such a thing restores my vigour, and I can see that all is by no means over."

From the beginning of this scene a revolution, in my unsealed eyes, had occurred in M. de Charlus, as complete, as immediate as if he had been touched by a magician's wand. Until them, because I had not understood, I had not seen. The vice (we use the word for convenience only), the vice of each of us accompanies him through life after the manner of the familiar genius who was invisible to men so long as they were unaware of his presence. Our goodness, our meanness, our name, our social relations do not disclose themselves to the eye, we carry them hidden within us. Even Ulysses did not at once recognise Athena. But the gods are immediately perceptible to one another, as quickly like to like, and so too had M. de Charlus been to Jupien. Until that moment I had been, in the presence of M. de Charlus, in the position of an absent-minded man who, standing before a pregnant woman whose distended outline he has failed to remark, persists, while she smilingly reiterates: "Yes, I am a little tired just now," in asking her indiscreetly: "Why, what is the matter with you?" But let some one say to him: "She is expecting a child," suddenly he catches sight of her abdomen and ceases to see anything else. It is the explanation that opens our eyes; the dispelling of an error gives us an additional sense.

Those of my readers who do not care to refer, for examples of this law, to the Messieurs de Charlus of their acquaintance, whom for long years they had never suspected, until the day when, upon the smooth surface of the individual just like everyone else, there suddently appeared, traced in an ink hitherto invisible, the characters that compose the word dear to the ancient Greeks, have only, in order to convince themselves that the world which surrounds them appears to them at first naked, bare of a thousand ornaments which it offers to the eyes of others better informed, to remind themselves how many times in the course of their lives they have found themselves on the point of making a blunder. Nothing upon the blank, undocumented face of this man or that could have led them to suppose that he was precisely the brother, or the intended husband, or the lover of a woman of whom they were just going to remark: "What a cow!" But them, fortunately, a word whispered to them by some one standing near arrests the fatal expression on their lips. At once there appear, like a *Mene, Tekel, Upharsin,* the words: "He is engaged to," or, "he is the brother of," or "he is the lover of the woman whom we ought not to describe, in his hearing, as a cow." And this one new conception will bring about an entire regrouping, thrusting some back, others forward, of the fractional conceptions, henceforward a complete whole, which we possessed of the rest of the family. In M. de Charlus another creature might indeed have coupled itself with him which made him as different from other men as the horse makes the centaur, this creature might indeed have incorporated itself in the Baron, I had never caught a glimpse of it. Now the abstraction had become materialised, the creature at last discerned had lost its power of remaining invisible, and the transformation of M. de Charlus into a new person was so complete that not only the contrasts of his face, of his voice, but, in retrospect, the very ups and downs of his relations with myself, everything that hitherto had seemed to my mind incoherent, became intelligible, brought itself into evidence, just as a sentence which presents no meaning so long as it remains broken up in letters scattered at random upon a table, expresses, if these letters be re-arranged in the proper order, a thought which one can never afterwards forget.

I now understood, moreover, how, earlier in the day, when I had seen him coming away from Mme. de Villeparisis's, I had managed to arrive at the conclusion that M. de Charlus looked like a woman: he was one! He belonged to that race of beings, less paradoxical than they appear, whose ideal is manly simply because their temperament is feminine and who in their life resemble in appearance only the rest of men; there where each of us carries, inscribed in those eyes through which he beholds everything in the universe, a human outline engraved on the surface of the pupil, for them it is that not of a nymph but of a youth. Race upon which a curse weighs and which must live amid falsehood and perjury, because it knows the world to regard as a punishable and a scandalous, as an inadmissible thing, its desire, that which constitutes for every human creature the greatest happiness in life; which must deny its God, since even Christians, when at the bar of justice they appear and are arraigned, must before Christ and in His Name defend themselves, as from a calumny, from the charge of what to them is life itself; sons without a mother, to whom they are obliged to lie all her life long and even in the hour when they close her dying eyes; friends without friendships, despite all those which their charm, frequently recognised, inspires and their hearts, often generous, would gladly feel; but can we describe as friendship those relations which flourish only by virtue of a lie and from which the first outburst of confidence and sincerity in which they might be tempted to indulge would make them be expelled with disgust, unless they are dealing with an impartial, that is to say a sympathetic mind, which however in that case, misled with regard to them by a conventional psychology, will suppose to spring from the vice confessed the very affection that is most alien to it, just as certain judges assume and are more inclined to pardon murder in inverts and treason in Jews for reasons derived from original sin and racial predestination. And lastly—according at least to the first theory which I sketched in outline at the time and which we shall see subjected to some modification in the sequel, a theory by which this would have angered them above all things, had not the paradox been hidden from their eyes by the very illusion that made them see and live—lovers from whom is always precluded the possibility of that love the hope of which gives them the strength to endure so many risks and so much loneliness, since they fall in love with precisely that type of man who has nothing feminine about him, who is not an invert and consequently cannot love them in return; with the result that their desire would be for ever insatiable did not their money procure for them real men, and their imagination end by making them take for real men the inverts to whom they had prostituted themselves. Their honour precarious, their liberty provisional, lasting only until the discovery of their crime; their position unstable, like that of the poet who one day was feasted at every table, applauded in every theatre in London, and on the next was driven from every lodging, unable to find a pillow upon which to lay his head, turning the mill like Samson and saying like him: "The two sexes shall die, each in a place apart!"; excluded even, save on the days of general disaster when the majority rally round the victim as the Jews rallied round Dreyfus, from the sympathy—at times from the society—of their fellows, in whom they inspire only disgust at seeing themselves as they are, portrayed in a mirror which, ceasing to flatter them, accentuates every blemish that they have refused to observe in themselves, and makes them understand that what they have been calling their love (a thing to which, playing upon the word, they have by association annexed all that poetry, painting, music, chivalry, asceticism have contrived to add to love) springs not from an ideal of beauty which they have chosen but from an incurable malady; like the Jews again (save some who will associate only with others of their race and have always on their lips ritual words and consecrated pleasantries), shunning one another, seeking out those who are most directly their opposite, who do not desire their company, pardoning their rebuffs, moved to ecstasy by their condescension; but also brought into the company of their own kind by the ostracism that strikes them, the opprobrium under which they have fallen, having finally been invested, by a persecution similar to that of Israel, with the physical and moral characteristics of a race, sometimes beautiful, often hideous, finding (in spite of all the mockery with which he who, more closely blended with, better assimilated to the opposing race, is relatively, in appearance, the least inverted, heaps upon him who has remained more so) a relief in frequenting the society of their kind, and even some corroboration of their own life, so much so that, while steadfastly denying that they are a race (the name of which is the vilest of insults), those who succeed in concealing the fact that they belong to it they readily unmask, with a view less to injuring them, though they have no scruple about that, than to excusing themselves; and, going in search (as a doctor seeks cases of appendicitis) of cases of inversion in history, taking pleasure in recalling that Socrates was one of themselves, as the Israelites claim that Jesus was one of them, without reflecting that there were no abnormals when homosexuality was the norm, no anti-Christians before Christ, that the disgrace alone makes the crime because it has allowed to survive only those who remained obdurate to every warning, to every example, to every punishment, by virtue of an innate disposition so peculiar that it is more repugnant to other men (even although it may be accompanied by exalted moral qualities) than certain other vices which exclude those qualities, such as theft, cruelty, breach of faith, vices better understood and so more readily excused by the generality of men; forming a freemasonry far more extensive, more powerful and less suspected than that of the Lodges, for it rests upon an identity of tastes, needs, habits, dangers, apprenticeship, knowledge, traffic, glossary, and one in which the members themselves, who intend not to know one another, recognise one another immediately by natural or conventional, involuntary or deliberate signs which indicate one of his congeners to the beggar in the street, in the great nobleman whose carriage door he is shutting, to the father in the suitor for his daughter's hand, to him who has sought healing, absolution, defence, in the doctor, the priest, the barrister to whom he has had recourse; all of them obliged to protect their own secret but having their part in a secret shared with the others, which the rest of humanity does not suspect and which means that to them the most wildly improbable tales of adventure seem true, for in this romantic, anachronistic life the ambassador is a bosom friend of the felon, the prince, with a certain independence of action with which his aristocratic breeding has furnished him, and which the trembling little cit would lack, on leaving the duchess's party goes off to confer in private with the hooligan; a reprobate part of the human whole, but an important part, suspected where it does not exist, flaunting itself, insolent and unpunished, where its existence is never guessed; numbering its adherents everywhere, among the people, in the army, in the church, in the prison, on the throne; living, in short, at least to a great extent, in a playful and perilous intimacy with the men of the other race, provoking them, playing with them by speaking of its vice as of something alien to it; a game that is rendered easy by the blindness or duplicity of the others, a game that may be kept up for years until the day of the scandal, on which these lion-tamers are devoured; until then, obliged to make a secret of their lives, to turn away their eyes from the things on which they would naturally fasten them, to fasten them upon those from which they would naturally turn away, to change the gender of many of the words in their vocabulary, a social constraint, slight in comparison with the inward constraint which their vice, or what is improperly so called, imposes upon them with regard not so much now to others as to themselves, and in such a way that to themselves it does not appear a vice. But certain among them, more practical, busier men who have not the time to go and drive their own bargains, or to dispense with the simplification of life and that saving of time which may result from cooperation, have formed two societies of which the second is composed exclusively of persons similar to themselves.

This is noticeable in those who are poor and have come up from the country, without friends, with nothing but their ambition to be some day a celebrated doctor or barrister, with a mind still barren of opinions, a person unadorned with manners, which they intend, as soon as possible, to decorate, just as they would buy furniture for their little attic in the Latin quarter, copying whatever they had observed in those who had already "arrived" in the useful and serious profession in which they also intend to establish themselves and to become famous; in these their special taste, unconsciously inherited like a weakness for drawing, for music, a weakness of vision, is perhaps the only living and despotic originality—which on certain evenings compels them to miss some meeting, advantageous to their career, with people whose ways, in other respect, of speaking, thinking, dressing, parting their hair, they have adopted. In their quarter, where otherwise they mix only with their brother students, their teachers or some fellow-provincial who has succeeded and can help them on, they have speedily discovered other young men whom the same peculiar taste attracts to them, as in a small town one sees an intimacy grow up between the assistant master and the lawyer, who are both interested in chamber music or mediaeval ivories; applying to the object of their distraction the same utilitarian instinct, the same professional spirit which guides them in their career, they meet these young men at gatherings to which no profane outsider is admitted any more than to those that bring together collectors of old snuff-boxes, Japanese prints or rare flowers, and at which, what with the pleasure of gaining information, the practical value of making exchanges and the fear of competition, there prevail simultaneously, as in a sale-room of postage stamps, the close cooperation of the specialists and the fierce rivalries of the collectors. No one moreover in the café where they have their table knows what the gathering is, whether it is that of an angling club, of an editorial staff, or of the "Sons of the Indre," so correct is their attire, so cold and reserved their manner, so modestly do they refrain from anything more than the most covert glances at the young men of fashion, the young "lions" who, a few feet away, are making a great clamour about their mistresses, and among whom those who are admiring them without venturing to raise their eyes will learn only twenty years later, when they themselves are on the eve of admission to the Academy, and the others are middle-aged gentlemen in club windows, that the most seductive among them, now a stout and grizzled Charlus, was in reality akin to themselves, but differently, in another world, beneath other external symbols, with foreign labels, the strangeness of which led them into error. But these groups are at varying stages of advancement; and, just as the "Union of the Left" differs from the "Socialist Federation" or some Mendelssohnian musical club from the Schola Cantorum, on certain evenings, at another table, there are extremists who allow a bracelet to slip down from beneath a cuff, sometimes a necklace to gleam in the gap of a collar, who by their persistent stares, their cooings, their laughter, their mutual caresses, oblige a band of students to depart in hot haste, and are served with a civility beneath which indignation boils by a waiter who, as on the evenings when he has to serve Dreyfusards, would find pleasure in summoning the police did he not find profit in pocketing their gratuities.

It is with these professional organisations that the mind contrasts the taste of the solitaries, and in one respect without straining the points of difference, since it is doing no more than copy the solitaries themselves who imagine that nothing differs more widely from organised vice than what appears to them to be a misunderstood love, but with some strain nevertheless, for these different classes correspond, no less than to diverse physiological types, to successive stages in a pathological or merely social evolution. And it is, in fact, very rarely that, one day or another, it is not in some such organisation that the solitaries come to merge themselves, sometimes from simple weariness, or for convenience (just as the people who have been most strongly opposed to such innovations end by having the telephone installed, inviting the Iénas to their parties, or dealing with Potin). They meet there, for that matter, with none too friendly a reception as a rule, for, in their relatively pure lives, their want of experience, the saturation in dreams to which they have been reduced, have branded more strongly upon them those special marks of effeminacy which the professionals have sought to efface. And it must be admitted that, among certain of these newcomers, the woman is not only inwardly united to the man but hideously visible, agitated as one sees them by a hysterical spasm, by a shrill laugh which convulses their knees and hands, looking no more like the common run of men than those monkeys with melancholy, shadowed eyes and prehensile feet who dress up in dinner-jackets and black bow ties; so that these new recruits are judged by others, less chaste for all that themselves, to be compromising associates, and their admission is hedged with difficulties; they are accepted, nevertheless, and they benefit then by those facilities by which commerce, great undertakings have transformed the lives of individuals, and have brought within their reach commodities hitherto too costly to acquire and indeed hard to find, which now submerge them beneath the plethora of what by themselves they had never succeeded in discovering amid the densest crowds. But, even with these innumerable outlets, the burden of social constraint is still too heavy for some, recruited principally among those who have not made a practice of self-control, and who still take to be rarer than it actually is their way of love. Let us leave out of consideration for the moment those who, the exceptional character of their inclinations making them regard themselves as superior to the other sex, look down upon women, make homosexuality the privilege of great genius and of glorious epochs of history, and, when they seek to communicate their taste to others, approach not so much those who seem to them to be predisposed towards it (as the morphinomaniac does with his morphia) as those who seem to them to be worthy of it, from apostolic zeal, just as others preach Zionism, conscientious objection to military service, Saint-Simonism, vegetarianism or anarchy. Here is one who, should we intrude upon him in the morning, still in bed, will present to our gaze an admirable female head, so general is its expression and typical of the sex as a whole; his very hair affirms this, so feminine is its ripple; unbrushed, it falls so naturally in long curls over the cheek that one marvels how the young woman, the girl, the Galatea barely awakened to life, in the unconscious mass of this male body in which she is imprisoned, has contrived so ingeniously by herself, without instruction from anyone, to make use of the narrowest apertures in her prison wall to find what was necessary to her existence. No doubt the young man who sports this delicious head does not say: "I am a woman." Even if—for any of the countless possible reasons—he lives with a woman, he can deny to her that he is himself one, can swear to her that he has never had intercourse with men. But let her look at him as we have just revealed him, lying back in bed, in pyjamas, his arms bare, his throat and neck bare also beneath the darkness of his hair. The pyjama jacket becomes a woman's shift, the head that of a pretty Spanish girl. The mistress is astounded by these confidences offered to her gaze, truer than any spoken confidence could be, or indeed any action, which his actions, indeed, if they have not already done so, cannot fail later on to confirm, for every creature follows the line of his own pleasure, and if this creature is not too vicious he will seek it in a sex complementary to his own. And for the invert vice begins, not when he forms relations (for there are all sorts of reasons that may enjoin these), but when he takes his pleasure with women. The young man whom we have been attempting to portray was so evidently a woman that the women who looked upon him with longing were doomed (failing a special taste on their part) to the same disappointment as those who in Shakespeare's comedies are taken in by a girl in disguise who passes as a youth. The deception is mutual, the invert is himself aware of it, he guesses the disillusionment which, once the mask is removed, the woman will experience, and feels to what an extent this mistake as to sex is a source of poetical imaginings. Besides, even from his exacting mistress, in vain does he keep back the admission (if she, that is to say, be not herself a denizen of Gomorrah): "I am a woman!" when all the time with what stratagems, what agility, what obstinacy as of a climbing plant the unconscious but visible woman in him seeks the masculine organ. We have only to look at that head of curling hair on the white pillow to understand that if, in the evening, this young man slips through his guardians' fingers, in spite of anything that they, or he himself can do to restrain him, it will not be to go in pursuit of women. His mistress may chastise him, may lock him up; next day, the man-woman will have found some way of attaching himself to a man, as the convolvulus throws out its tendrils wherever it finds a convenient post or rake. Why, when we admire in the face of this person a delicacy that touches our hearts, a gracefulness, a spontaneous affability such as men do not possess, should we be dismayed to learn that this young man runs after boxers? They are different aspects of an identical reality. And indeed, what repels us is the most touching thing of all, more touching than any refinement of delicacy, for it represents an admirable though unconscious effort on the part of nature: the recognition of his sex by itself, in spite of the sexual deception, becomes apparent, the unconfessed attempt to escape from itself towards what an initial error on the part of society has segregated from it. Some, those no doubt who have been most timid in childhood, are scarcely concerned with the material kind of the pleasure they receive, provided that they can associate it with a masculine face. Whereas others, whose sensuality is doubtless more violent, imperiously restrict their material pleasure within certain definite limitations. These live perhaps less exclusively beneath the sway of Saturn's outrider, since for them women are not entirely barred, as for the former sort, in whose eyes women would have no existence apart from conversation, flirtation, loves not of the heart but of the head. But the second sort seek out those women who love other women; who can procure for them a young man, enhance the pleasure which they feel on finding themselves in his company; better still, they can, in the same fashion, enjoy with such women the same pleasure as with a man. Whence it arises that jealousy is kindled in those whc love the first sort only by the pleasure which they may be enjoying with a man, which alone seems to their lovers a betrayal, since these do not participate in the love of women, have practised it only as a habit, and, so as to reserve for themselves the possibility of eventual marriage, representing to themselves so little the pleasure that it is capable of giving that they cannot be distressed by the thought that he whom they love is enjoying that pleasure; whereas the other sort often inspire jealousy by their love-affairs with women. For, in the relations which they have with her, they play, for the woman who loves her own sex, the part of another woman, and she offers them at the same time more or less what they find in other men, so that the jealous friend suffers from the feeling that he whom he loves is riveted to her who is to him almost a man, and at the same time feels his beloved almost escape him because, to these women, he is something which the lover himself cannot conceive, a sort of woman. We need not pause here to consider those young fools who by a sort of arrested development, to tease their friends or to shock their families, proceed with a kind of frenzy to choose clothes that resemble women's dress, to redden their lips and blacken their eyelashes; we may leave them out of account, for they are those whom we shall find later on, when they have suffered the all too cruel penalty of their affectation, spending what remains of their lifetime in vain attempts to repair by a sternly protestant demeanour the wrong that they did to themselves when they were carried away by the same demon that urges young women of the Faubourg Saint-Germain to live in a scandalous fashion, to set every convention at defiance, to scoff at the entreaties of their relatives, until the day when they set themselves with perseverance but without success to reascend the slope down which it had seemed to them that it would be so amusing to glide, down which they had found it so amusing, or rather had not been able to stop themselves from gliding. Finally, let us leave to a later volume the men who have sealed a pact with Gomorrah. We shall deal with them when M. de Charlus comes to know them. Let us leave out for the present all those, of one sort or another, who will appear each in his turn, and, to conclude this first sketch of the subject, let us say a word only of those whom we began to mention just now, the solitary class. Supposing their vice to be more exceptional than it is, they have retired into solitude from the day on which they discovered it, after having carried it within themselves for a long time without knowing it, for a longer time only than certain other men. For no one can tell at first that he is an invert or a poet or a snob or a scoundrel. The boy who has been reading erotic poetry or looking at indecent pictures, if he then presses his body against a schoolfellow's, imagines himself only to be communing with him in an identical desire for a woman. How should he suppose that he is not like everybody else when he recognises the substance of what he feels on reading Mme. de Lafayette, Racine, Baudelaire, Walter Scott, at a time when he is still too little capable of observing himself to take into account what he has added from his own store to the picture, and that if the sentiment be the same the object differs, that what he desires is Rob Roy, and not Diana Vernon? With many, by a defensive prudence on the part of the instinct that precedes the clearer vision of the intellect, the mirror and walls of their bedroom vanish beneath a cloud of coloured prints of actresses; they compose poetry such as:

I love but Chloe in the world,
For Chloe is divine;
Her golden hair is sweetly curled,
For her my heart doth pine.

Must we on that account attribute to the opening phase of such lives a taste which we shall never find in them later on, like those flaxen ringlets on the heads of children which are destined to change to the darkest brown? Who can tell whether the photographs of women are not a first sign of hypocrisy, a first sign also of horror at other inverts? But the solitary kind are precisely those to whom hypocrisy is painful. Possibly even the example of the Jews, of a different type of colony, is not strong enough to account for the frail hold that their upbringing has upon them, or for the artfulness with which they find their way back (perhaps not to anything so sheerly terrible as the suicide to which maniacs, whatever precautions one may take with them, return, and, pulled out of the river into which they have flung themselves, take poison, procure revolvers, and so forth; but) to a life of which the men of the other race not only do not understand, cannot imagine, abominate the essential pleasures but would be filled with horror by the thought of its frequent danger and everlasting shame. Perhaps, to form a picture of these, we ought to think, if not of the wild animals that never become domesticated, of the lion-cubs said to be tame but lions still at heart, then at least of the negroes whom the comfortable existence of the white man renders desperately unhappy and who prefer the risks of a life of savagery and its incomprehensible joys. When the day has dawned on which they have discovered themselves to be incapable at once of lying to others and of lying to themselves, they go away to live in the country, shunning the society of their own kind (whom they believe to be few in number) from horror of the monstrosity or fear of the temptation, and that of the rest of humanity from shame. Never having arrived at true maturity, plunged in a constant melancholy, now and again, some Sunday evening when there is no moon, they go for a solitary walk as far as a crossroads where, although not a word has been said, there has come to meet them one of their boyhood's friends who is living in a house in the neighbourhood. And they begin again the pastimes of long ago, on the grass, in the night, neither uttering a word. During the week, they meet in their respective houses, talk of no matter what, without any allusion to what has occurred between them, exactly as though they had done nothing and were not to do anything again, save, in their relations, a trace of coldness, of irony, of irritability and rancour, at times of hatred. Then the neighbour sets out on a strenuous expedition on horseback, and, on a mule, climbs mountain peaks, sleeps in the snow; his friend, who identifies his own vice with a weakness of temperament, the cabined and timid life, realises that vice can no longer exist in his friend now emancipated, so many thousands of feet above sea-level. And, sure enough, the other takes a wife. And yet the abandoned one is not cured (in spite of the cases in which, as we shall see, inversion is curable). He insists upon going down himself every morning to the kitchen to receive the milk from the hands of the dairyman's boy, and on the evenings when desire is too strong for him will go out of his way to set a drunkard on the right road or to "adjust the dress" of a blind man. No doubt the life of certain inverts appears at times to change, their vice (as it is called) is no longer apparent in their habits; but nothing is ever lost; a missing jewel turns up again; when the quantity of a sick man's urine decreases, it is because he is perspiring more freely, but the excretion must invariably occur. One day this homosexual hears of the death of a young cousin, and from his inconsolable grief we learned that it was to this love, chaste possibly and aimed rather at retaining esteem than at obtaining possession, that his desires have passed by a sort of virement, as, in a budget, without any alteration in the total, certain expenditure is carried under another head. As is the case with invalids in whom a sudden attack of urticaria makes their chronic ailments temporarily disappear, this pure love for a young relative seems, in the invert, to have momentarily replaced, by metastasis, habits that will, one day or another, return to fill the place of the vicarious, cured malady.

Meanwhile the married neighbour of our recluse has returned; before the beauty of the young bride and the demonstrative affection of her husband, on the day when their friend is obliged to invite them to dinner, he feels ashamed of the past. Already in an interesting condition, she must return home early, leaving her husband behind; he, when the time has come for him to go home also, asks his host to accompany him for part of the way; at first, no suspicion enters his mind, but at the crossroads he finds himself thrown down on the grass, with not a word said, by the mountaineer who is shortly to become a father. And their meetings begin again, and continue until the day when there comes to live not far off a cousin of the young woman, with whom her husband is now constantly to be seen. And he, if the twice abandoned friend calls in the evening and endeavours to approach him, is furious, and repulses him with indignation that the other has not had the tact to foresee the disgust which he must henceforward inspire. Once, however, there appears a stranger, sent to him by his faithless friend; but being busy at the time, the abandoned one cannot see him, and only afterwards learns with what object his visitor came.

Then the solitary languishes alone. He has no other diversion than to go to the neighbouring watering-place to ask for some information or other from a certain railwayman there. But the latter has obtained promotion, has been transferred to the other end of the country; the solitary will no longer be able to go and ask him the times of the trains or the price of a first class ticket, and, before retiring to dream, Griselda-like, in his tower, loiters upon the beach, a strange Andromeda whom no Argonaut will come to free, a sterile Medusa that must perish upon the sand, or else he stands idly, until his train starts, upon the platform, casting over the crowd of passengers a gaze that will seem indifferent, contemptuous or distracted to those of another race, but, like the luminous glow with which certain insects bedeck themselves in order to attract others of their species, or like the nectar which certain flowers offer to attract the insects that will fertilise them, would not deceive the almost undiscoverable sharer of a pleasure too singular, too hard to place, which is offered him, the colleague with whom our specialist could converse in the half-forgotten tongue; in which last, at the most, some seedy loafer upon the platform will put up a show of interest, but for pecuniary gain alone, like those people who, at the Collège de France, in the room in which the Professor of Sanskrit lectures without an audience, attend his course but only because the room itself is heated. Medusa! Orchid! When I followed my instinct only, the medusa used to revolt me at Balbec; but if I had the eyes to regard it, like Michelet, from the standpoint of natural history, and aesthetic, I saw an exquisite wheel of azure flame. Are they not, with the transparent velvet of their petals, as it were the mauve orchids of the sea? Like so many creatures of the animal and vegetable kingdoms, like the plant which would produce vanilla but, because in its structure the male organ is divided by a partition from the female, remains sterile unless the humming-birds or certain tiny bees convey the pollen from one to the other, or man fertilises them by artificial means, M. de Charlus (and here the word fertilise must be understood in a moral sense, since in the physical sense the union of male with male is and must be sterile, but it is no small matter that a person may encounter the sole pleasure which he is capable of enjoying, and that every "creature here below" can impart to some other "his music, or his fragrance or his flame"), M. de Charlus was one of those men who may be called exceptional, because however many they may be, the satisfaction, so easy in others, of their sexual requirements depends upon the coincidence of too many conditions, and of conditions too difficult to ensure. For men like M. de Charlus (leaving out of account the compromises which will appear in the course of this story and which the reader may already have foreseen, enforced by the need of pleasure which resigns itself to partial acceptations), mutual love, apart from the difficulties, so great as to be almost insurmountable, which it meets in the ordinary man, adds to these others so exceptional that what is always extremely rare for everyone becomes in their case well nigh impossible, and, if there should befall them an encounter which is really fortunate, or which nature makes appear so to them, their good fortune, far more than that of the normal lover, has about it something extraordinary, selective, profoundly necessary. The feud of the Capulets and Montagues was as nothing compared with the obstacles of every sort which must have been surmounted, the special eliminations which nature has had to submit to the hazards, already far from common, which result in love, before a retired tailor, who was intending to set off soberly for his office, can stand quivering in ecstasy before a stoutish man of fifty; this Romeo and this Juliet may believe with good reason that their love is not the caprice of a moment but a true predestination, prepared by the harmonies of their temperaments, and not only by their own personal temperaments but by those of their ancestors, by their most distant strains of heredity, so much so that the fellow creature who is conjoined with them has belonged to them from before their birth, has attracted them by a force comparable to that which governs the worlds on which we passed our former lives. M. de Charlus had distracted me from looking to see whether the bee was bringing to the orchid the pollen it had so long been waiting to receive, and had no chance of receiving save by an accident so unlikely that one might call it a sort of miracle. But this was a miracle also that I had just witnessed, almost of the same order and no less marvellous. As soon as I had considered their meeting from this point of view, everything about it seemed to me instinct with beauty. The most extraordinary devices that nature has invented to compel insects to ensure the fertilisation of flowers which without their intervention could not be fertilised because the male flower is too far away from the female—or when, if it is the wind that must provide for the transportation of the pollen, she makes that pollen so much more simply detachable from the male, so much more easily arrested in its flight by the female flower, by eliminating the secretion of nectar which is no longer of any use since there is no insect to be attracted, and, that the flower may be kept free for the pollen which it needs, which can fructify only in itself, makes it secrete a liquid which renders it immune to all other pollens—seemed to me no more marvellous than the existence of the subvariety of inverts destined to guarantee the pleasures of love to the invert who is growing old: men who are attracted not by all other men, but—by a phenomenon of correspondence and harmony similar to those that precede the fertilisation of heterostyle trimorphous flowers like the *lythrum salicoria*—only by men considerably older than themselves. Of this subvariety Jupien had just furnished me with an example less striking however than certain others, which every collector of a human herbary, every moral botanist can observe in spite of their rarity, and which will present to the eye a delicate youth who is waiting for the advances of a robust and paunchy quinquagenarian, remaining as indifferent to those of other young men as the hermaphrodite flowers of the short-styled *primula veris* so long as they are fertilised only by other *primulae veris* of short style also, whereas they welcome with joy the pollen of the *primula veris* with the long styles. As for M. de Charlus's part in the transaction, I noticed afterwards that there were for him various kinds of conjunction, some of which, by their multiplicity, their almost invisible speed and above all the absence of contact between the two actors, recalled still more forcibly those flowers that in a garden are fertilised by the pollen of a neighbouring flower which they may never touch. There were in fact certain persons whom it was sufficient for him to make come to his house, hold for an hour or two under the domination of his talk, for his desire, quickened by some earlier encounter, to be assuaged. By a simple use of words the conjunction was effected, as simply as it can be among the infusoria. Sometimes, as had doubtless been the case with me on the evening on which I had been summoned by him after the Guermantes dinner-party, the relief was effected by a violent ejaculation which the Baron made in his visitor's face, just as certain flowers, furnished with a hidden spring, sprinkle from within the unconsciously collaborating and disconcerted insect. M. de Charlus, from vanquished turning victor, feeling himself purged of his uneasiness and calmed, would send away the visitor who had at once ceased to appear to him desirable. Finally, inasmuch as inversion itself springs from the fact that the invert is too closely akin to woman to be capable of having any effective relations with her, it comes under a higher law which ordains that so many hermaphrodite flowers shall remain unfertile, that is to say the law of the sterility of autofecundation. It is true that inverts, in their search for a male person, will often be found to put up with other inverts as effeminate as themselves. But it is enough that they do not belong to the female sex, of which they have in them an embryo which they can put to no useful purpose, such as we find in so many hermaphrodite flowers, and even in certain hermaphrodite animals, such as the snail, which cannot be fertilised by themselves, but can by other hermaphrodites. In this respect the race of inverts, who eagerly connect themselves with Oriental antiquity or the Golden Age in Greece, might be traced back farther still, to those experimental epochs in which there existed neither dioecious plants nor monosexual animals, to that initial hermaphroditism of which certain rudiments of male organs in the anatomy of the woman and of female organs in that of the man seem still to preserve the trace. I found the pantomine, incomprehensible to me at first, of Jupien and M. de Charlus as curious as those seductive gestures addressed, Darwin tells us, to insects not only by the flowers called composite which erect the florets of their capitals so as to be seen from a greater distance, such as a certain heterostyle which turns back its stamens and bends them to open the way for the insect, or offers him an ablution, or, to take an immediate instance, the nectar-fragrance and vivid hue of the corollae that were at that moment attracting insects to our courtyard. From this day onwards M. de Charlus was to alter the time of his visits to Mme. de Villeparisis, not that he could not see Jupien elsewhere and with greater convenience, but because to him just as much as to me the afternoon sunshine and the blossoming plant were, no doubt, linked together in memory. Apart from this, he did not confine himself to recommending the Jupiens to Mme. de Villeparisis, to the Duchesse de Guermantes, to a whole brilliant list of patrons, who were all the more assiduous in their attentions to the young seamstress when they saw that the few ladies who had held out, or had merely delayed their submission, were subjected to the direst reprisals by the Baron, whether in order that they might serve as an example, or because they had aroused his wrath and had stood out against his attempted domination; he made Jupien's position more and more lucrative, until he definitely engaged him as his secretary and established him in the state in which we shall see him later on. "Ah, now! There is a happy man, if you like, that Jupien," said Françoise, who had a tendency to minimise or exaggerate people's generosity according as it was bestowed on herself or on others. Not that, in this instance, she had any need to exaggerate, nor for that matter did she feel any jealousy, being genuinely fond of Jupien. "Oh, he's such a good man, the Baron," she went on, "such a well-behaved, religious, proper sort of man. If I had a daughter to marry and was one of the rich myself, I would give her to the Baron with my eyes shut." "But, Françoise," my mother observed gently, "she'ld be well supplied with husbands, that daughter of yours. Don't forget you've already promised her to Jupien." "Ah! Lordy, now," replied Françoise, "there's another of them that would make a woman happy. It doesn't matter whether you're rich or poor, it makes no difference to your nature. The Baron and Jupien, they're just the same sort of person."

However, I greatly exaggerated at the time, on the strength of this first revelation, the elective character of so carefully selected a combination. Admittedly, every man of the kind of M. de Charlus is an extraordinary creature since, if he does not make concessions to the possibilities of life, he seeks out essentially the love of a man of the other race, that is to say a man who is a lover of women (and incapable consequently of loving him); in contradiction of what I had imagined in the courtyard, where I had seen Jupien turning towards M. de Charlus like the orchid making overtures to the bee, these exceptional creatures whom we commiserate are a vast crowd, as we shall see in the course of this work, for a reason which will be disclosed only at the end of it, and commiserate themselves for being too many rather than too few. For the two angels who were posted at the gates of Sodom to learn whether its inhabitants (according to Genesis) had indeed done all the things the report of which had ascended to the Eternal Throne must have been, and of this one can only be glad, exceedingly ill chosen by the Lord, Who ought not to have entrusted the task to any but a Sodomite. Such an one the excuses: "Father of six children—I keep two mistresses," and so forth could never have persuaded benevolently to lower his flaming sword and to mitigate the punishment; he would have answered: "Yes, and your wife lives in a torment of jealousy. But even when these women have not been chosen by you from Gomorrah, you spend your nights with a watcher of flocks upon Hebron." And he would at once have made him retrace his steps to the city which the rain of fire and brimstone was to destroy. On the contrary, they allowed to escape all the shame-faced Sodomites, even if these, on catching sight of a boy, turned their heads, like Lot's wife, though without being on that account changed like her into pillars of salt. With the result that they engendered a numerous posterity with whom this gesture has continued to be habitual, like that of the dissolute women who, while apparently studying a row of shoes displayed in a shop window, turn their heads to keep track of a passing student. These descendants of the Sodomites, so numerous that we may apply to them that other verse of Genesis: "If a man can number the dust of the earth, then shall thy seed also be numbered," have established themselves throughout the entire world; they have had access to every profession and pass so easily into the most exclusive clubs that, whenever a Sodomite fails to secure election, the black balls are, for the most part, cast by other Sodomites, who are anxious to penalise sodomy, having inherited the falsehood that enabled their ancestors to escape from the accursed city. It is possible that they may return there one day. Certainly they form in every land an Oriental colony, cultured, musical, malicious, which has certain charming qualities and intolerable defects. We shall study them with greater thoroughness in the course of the following pages; but I have thought it as well to utter here a provisional warning against the lamentable error of proposing (just as people have encouraged a Zionist movement) to create a Sodomist movement and to rebuild Sodom. For, no sooner had they arrived there than the Sodomites would leave the town so as not to have the appearance of belonging to it, would take wives, keep mistresses in other cities where they would find, incidentally, every diversion that appealed to them. They would repair to Sodom only on days of supreme necessity, when their own town was empty, at those seasons when hunger drives the wolf from the woods; in other words, everything would go on very much as it does to-day in London, Berlin, Rome, Petrograd or Paris.

Anyhow, on the day in question, before paying my call on the Duchess, I did not look so far ahead, and I was distressed to find that I had, by my engrossment in the Jupien-Charlus conjunction, missed perhaps an opportunity of witnessing the fertilisation of the blossom by the bee.

CHAPTER I

M. de Charlus in Society.—A physician.—Typical physiognomy of Mme. de Vaugoubert.—Mme. d'Arpajon, the Hubert Robert fountain and the merriment of the Grand Duke Vladimir.—Mmes. d'Amoncourt, de Citri, de Saint-Euverte, etc.—Curious conversation between Swann and the Prince de Guermantes.—Albertine on the telephone.—My social life in the interval before my second and final visit to Balbec. Arrival at Balbec.—The heart's intermissions.

AS I was in no haste to arrive at this party at the Guermantes', to which I was not certain that I had been invited, I remained sauntering out of doors; but the summer day seemed to be in no greater haste than myself to stir. Albeit it was after nine o'clock, it was still the light of day that on the Place de la Concorde was giving the Luxor obelisk the appearance of being made of pink nougat. Then it diluted the tint and changed the surface to a metallic substance, so that the obelisk not only became more precious but seemed to have grown more slender and almost flexible. You imagined that you might have twisted it in your fingers, had perhaps already slightly distorted its outline. The moon was now in the sky like a section of orange delicately peeled although slightly bruised. But presently she was to be fashioned of the most enduring gold. Sheltering alone behind her, a poor little star was to serve as sole companion to the lonely moon, while she, keeping her friend protected, but bolder and striding ahead, would brandish like an irresistible weapon, like an Oriental symbol, her broad and marvellous crescent of gold.

Outside the mansion of the Princesse de Guermantes,

I met the Duc de Châtellerault; I no longer remembered that half an hour earlier I had still been persecuted by the fear—which, for that matter, was speedily to grip me again—that I might be entering the house uninvited. We grow uneasy, and it is sometimes long after the hour of danger, which a subsequent distraction has made us forget, that we remember our uneasiness. I greeted the young Duke and made my way into the house. But here I must first of all record a trifling incident, which will enable us to understand something that was presently to occur.

There was one person who, on that evening as on the previous evenings, had been thinking a great deal about the Duc de Châtellerault, without however suspecting who he was: this was the usher (styled at that time the *aboyeur*) of Mme. de Guermantes. M. de Châtellerault, so far from being one of the Princess's intimate friends, albeit he was one of her cousins, had been invited to her house for the first time. His parents, who had not been on speaking terms with her for the last ten years, had been reconciled to her within the last fortnight, and, obliged to be out of Paris that evening, had requested their son to fill their place. Now, a few days earlier, the Princess's usher had met in the Champs-Elysées a young man whom he had found charming but whose identity he had been unable to establish. Not that the young man had not shewn himself as obliging as he had been generous. All the favours that the usher had supposed that he would have to bestow upon so young a gentleman, he had on the contrary received. But M. de Châtellerault was as reticent as he was rash; he was all the more determined not to disclose his incognito since he did not know with what sort of person he was dealing; his fear would have been far greater, although quite unfounded, if he had known. He had confined himself to posing as an Englishman, and to all the passionate questions with which he was plied by the usher, desirous to meet again a person to whom he was indebted for so much pleasure and so ample a gratuity, the Duke had merely replied, from one end of the Avenue Gabriel to the other: "I do not speak French."

Albeit, in spite of everything—remembering his cousin Gilbert's maternal ancestry—the Duc de Guermantes pretended to find a touch of Courvoisier in the drawing-room of the Princesse de Guermantes-Bavière, the general estimate of that lady's initiative spirit and intellectual superiority was based upon an innovation that was to be found nowhere else in her set. After dinner, however important the party that was to follow, the chairs, at the Princesse de Guermantes's, were arranged in such a way as to form little groups, in which people might have to turn their backs upon one another. The Princess then displayed her social sense by going to sit down, as though by preference, in one of these. Not that she was afraid to pick out and attract to herself a member of another group. If, for instance, she had remarked to M. Detaille, who naturally agreed with her, on the beauty of Mme. de Villemur's neck, of which that lady's position in another group made her present a back view, the Princess did not hesitate to raise her voice: "Madame de Villemur, M. Detaille, with his wonderful painter's eye, has just been admiring your neck." Mme. de Villemur interpreted this as a direct invitation to join in the conversation; with the agility of a practised horsewoman, she made her chair rotate slowly through three quadrants of a circle, and, without in the least disturbing her neighbours, came to rest almost facing the Princess. "You don't know M. Detaille?" exclaimed their hostess, for whom her guest's nimble and modest tergiversation was not sufficient. "I do not know him, but I know his work," replied Mme. de Villemur, with a respectful, engaging air, and a promptitude which many of the onlookers envied her, addressing the while to the celebrated painter whom this invocation had not been sufficient to introduce to her in a formal manner, an imperceptible bow. "Come, Monsieur Detaille," said the Princess, "let me introduce you to Mme. de Villemur." That lady thereupon shewed as great ingenuity in making room for the creator of the *Dream* as she had shewn a moment earlier in wheeling round to face him. And the Princess drew forward a chair for herself; she had indeed invoked Mme. de Villemur only to have an excuse for quitting the first group, in which she had spent the statutory ten minutes, and bestowing a similar allowance of her time upon the second. In three quarters of an hour, all the groups had received a visit from her, which seemed to have been determined in each instance by impulse and predilection, but had the paramount object of making it apparent how naturally "a great lady knows how to entertain." But now the guests for the party were beginning to arrive, and the lady of the house was seated not far from the door—erect and proud in her semi-regal majesty, her eyes ablaze with their own incandescence—between two unattractive Royalties and the Spanish Ambassadress.

I stood waiting behind a number of guests who had arrived before me. Facing me was the Princess, whose beauty is probably not the only thing, where there were so many beauties, that reminds me of this party. But the face of my hostess was so perfect; stamped like so beautiful a medal, that it has retained a commemorative force in my mind. The Princess was in the habit of saying to her guests when she met them a day or two before one of her parties: "You will come, won't you?" as though she felt a great desire to talk to them. But as, on the contrary, she had nothing to talk to them about, when they entered her presence she contented herself, without rising, with breaking off for an instant her vapid conversation with the two Royalties and the Ambassadress and thanking them with: "How good of you to have come," not that she thought that the guest had shewn his goodness by coming, but to enhance her own; then, at once dropping him back into the stream, she would add: "You will find M. de Guermantes by the garden door," so that the guest proceeded on his way and ceased to bother her. To some indeed she said nothing, contenting herself with shewing them her admirable onyx eyes, as though they had come merely to visit an exhibition of precious stones.

The person immediately in front of me was the Duc de Châtellerault.

Having to respond to all the smiles, all the greetings waved to him from inside the drawing-room, he had not noticed the usher. But from the first moment the usher had recognised him. The identity of this stranger, which he had so ardently desired to learn, in another minute he would know. When he asked his "Englishman" of the other evening what name he was to announce, the usher was not merely stirred, he considered that he was being indiscreet, indelicate. He felt that he was about to reveal to the whole world (which would, however, suspect nothing) a secret which it was criminal of him to force like this and to proclaim in public. Upon hearing the guest's reply: "Le duc de Châtellerault," he felt such a burst of pride that he remained for a moment speechless. The Duke looked at him, recognised him, saw himself ruined, while the servant, who had recovered his composure and was sufficiently versed in heraldry to complete for himself an appellation that was too modest, shouted with a professional vehemence softened by an emotional tenderness: "Son Altesse Monseigneur le duc de Châtellerault!" But it was now my turn to be announced. Absorbed in contemplation of my hostess, who had not yet seen me, I had not thought of the function—terrible to me, although not in the same sense as to M. de Châtellerault—of this usher garbed in black like a headsman, surrounded by a group of lackeys in the most cheerful livery, lusty fellows ready to seize hold of an intruder and cast him out of doors. The usher asked me my name, I told him it as mechanically as the condemned man allows himself to be strapped to the block. At once he lifted his head majestically and, before I could beg him to announce me in a lowered tone so as to spare my own feelings if I were not invited and those of the Princesse de Guermantes if I were, shouted the disturbing syllables with a force capable of bringing down the roof.

The famous Huxley (whose grandson occupies an unassailable position in the English literary world of to-day) relates that one of his patients dared not continue to go into society because often, on the actual chair that was pointed out to her with a courteous gesture, she saw an old gentleman already seated. She could be quite certain that either the gesture of invitation or the old gentleman's presence was a hallucination, for her hostess would not have offered her a chair that was already occupied. And when Huxley, to cure her, forced her to reappear in society, she felt a moment of painful hesitation when she asked herself whether the friendly sign that was being made to her was the real thing, or, in obedience to a non-existent vision, she was about to sit down in public upon the knees of a gentleman in flesh and blood. Her brief uncertainty was agonising. Less so perhaps than mine. From the moment at which I had taken in the sound of my name, like the rumble that warns us of a possible cataclysm, I was bound, to plead my own good faith in either event, and as though I were not tormented by any doubt, to advance towards the Princess with a resolute air.

She caught sight of me when I was still a few feet away and (to leave me in no doubt that I was the victim of a conspiracy), instead of remaining seated, as she had done for her other guests, rose and came towards me. A moment later, I was able to heave the sigh of relief of Huxley's patient, when, having made up her mind to sit down on the chair, she found it vacant and realised that it was the old gentleman that was a hallucination. The Princess had just held out her hand to me with a smile. She remained standing for some moments with the kind of charm enshrined in the verse of Malherbe which ends:

> "To do them honour all the angels rise."

She apologised because the Duchess had not yet come, as though I must be bored there without her. In order to give me this greeting, she wheeled round me, holding me by the hand, in a graceful revolution by the whirl of which I felt myself carried off my feet. I almost expected that she would next offer me, like the leader of a cotillon, an ivory-headed cane or a watch-bracelet. She did not, however, give me anything of the sort, and as though, instead of dancing the Boston, she had been listening to a sacred quartet by Beethoven the sublime strains of which she was afraid of interrupting, she cut short the conversation there and then, or rather did not begin it, and, still radiant at having seen me come in, merely informed me where the Prince was to be found.

I moved away from her and did not venture to approach her again, feeling that she had absolutely nothing to say to me and that, in her vast kindness, this woman marvellously tall and handsome, noble as were so many great ladies who stepped so proudly upon the scaffold, could only, short of offering me a draught of honeydew, repeat what she had already said to me twice: "You will find the Prince in the garden." Now, to go in search of the Prince was to feel my doubts revive in a fresh form.

In any case I should have to find somebody to introduce me. One could hear, above all the din of conversation, the interminable chatter of M. de Charlus, talking to H. E. the Duke of Sidonia, whose acquaintance he had just made. Members of the same profession find one another out, and so it is with a common vice. M. de Charlus and M. de Sidonia had each of them immediately detected the other's vice, which was in both cases that of soliloquising in society, to the extent of not being able to stand any interruption. Having decided at once that, in the words of a famous sonnet, there was "no help," they had made up their minds not to be silent but each to go on talking without any regard to what the other might say. This had resulted in the confused babble produced in Molière's comedies by a number of people saying different things simultaneously. The Baron, with his deafening voice, was moreover certain of keeping the upper hand, of drowning the feeble voice of M. de Sidonia; without however discouraging him, for, whenever M. de Charlus paused for a moment to breathe, the interval was filled by the murmurs of the Grandee of Spain who had imperturbably continued his discourse. I could easily have asked M. de Charlus to introduce me to the Prince de Guermantes, but I feared (and with good reason) that he might be cross with me. I had treated him in the most ungrateful fashion by letting his offer pass unheeded for the second time and by never giving him a sign of my existence since the evening when he had so affectionately escorted me home. And yet I could not plead the excuse of having anticipated the scene which I had just witnessed, that very afternoon, enacted by himself and Jupien. I suspected nothing of the sort. It is true that shortly before this, when my parents reproached me with my laziness and with not having taken the trouble to write a line to M. de Charlus, I had violently reproached them with wishing me to accept a degrading proposal. But anger alone, and the desire to hit upon the expression that would be most offensive to them had dictated this mendacious retort. In reality, I had imagined nothing sensual, nothing sentimental even, underlying the Baron's offers. I had said this to my parents with entire irresponsibility. But sometimes the future is latent in us without our knowledge, and our words which we suppose to be false forecast an imminent reality.

M. de Charlus would doubtless have forgiven me my want of gratitude. But what made him furious was that my presence this evening at the Princesse de Guermantes's, as for some time past at her cousin's, seemed to be a defiance of his solemn declaration: "There is no admission to those houses save through me." A grave fault, a crime that was perhaps inexpiable, I had not followed the conventional path. M. de Charlus knew well that the thunderbolts which he hurled at those who did not comply with his orders, or to whom he had taken a dislike, were beginning to be regarded by many people, however furiously he might brandish them, as mere pasteboard, and had no longer the force to banish anybody from anywhere. But he believed perhaps that his diminished power, still considerable, remained intact in the eyes of novices like myself. And so I did not consider it well advised to ask a favour of him at a party at which the mere fact of my presence seemed an ironical denial of his pretensions.

I was buttonholed at that moment by a man of a distinctly common type, Professor E——. He had been surprised to see me at the Guermantes'. I was no less surprised to see him there, for nobody had ever seen before or was ever to see again a person of his sort at one of the Princess's parties. He had just succeeded in curing the Prince, after the last rites had been administered, of a septic pneumonia, and the special gratitude that Mme. de Guermantes felt towards him was the reason for her thus departing from custom and inviting him to her house. As he knew absolutely nobody in the rooms, and could not wander about there indefinitely by himself, like a minister of death, having recognised me, he had discovered, for the first time in his life, that he had an infinite number of things to say to me, which enabled him to assume an air of composure, and this was one of the reasons for his advancing upon me. There was also another. He attached great importance to his never being mistaken in his diagnoses. Now his correspondence was so numerous that he could not always bear in mind, when he had seen a patient once only, whether the disease had really followed the course that he had traced for it. The reader may perhaps remember that, immediately after my grandmother's stroke, I had taken her to see him, on the afternoon when he was having all his decorations stitched to his coat. After so long an interval, he no longer remembered the formal announcement which had been sent to him at the time. "Your grandmother *is* dead, isn't she?" he said to me in a voice in which a semi-certainty calmed a slight apprehension. "Ah! Indeed! Well, from the moment I saw her my prognosis was extremely grave, I remember it quite well."

It was thus that Professor E—— learned or recalled the death of my grandmother, and (I must say this to his credit, which is that of the medical profession as a whole), without displaying, without perhaps feeling any satisfaction. The mistakes made by doctors are innumerable. They err habitually on the side of optimism as to treatment, of pessimism as to the outcome. "Wine? In moderation, it can do you no harm, it is always a tonic. . . . Sexual enjoyment? After all it is a natural function. I allow you to use, but not to abuse it, you understand. Excess in anything is wrong." At once, what a temptation to the patient to renounce those two life-givers, water and chastity. If, on the other hand, he has any trouble with his heart, albumen, and so forth, it never lasts for long. Disorders that are grave but purely functional are at once ascribed to an imaginary cancer. It is useless to continue visits which are powerless to eradicate an incurable malady. Let the patient, left to his own devices, thereupon subject himself to an implacable regime, and in time recover, or merely survive, and the doctor, to whom he touches his hat in the Avenue de l'Opéra, when he supposed him to have long been lying in Père Lachaise, will interpret the gesture as an act of insolent defiance. An innocent stroll, taken beneath his nose and venerable beard, would arouse no greater wrath in the Assize Judge who, two years earlier, had sentenced the rascal, now passing him with apparent impunity, to death. Doctors (we do not here include them all, of course, and make a mental reservation of certain admirable exceptions), are in general more displeased, more irritated by the quashing of their sentence than pleased by its execution. This explains why Professor E——, despite the intellectual satisfaction that he doubtless felt at finding that he had not been mistaken, was able to speak to me only with regret of the blow that had fallen upon us. He was in no hurry to cut short the conversation, which kept him in countenance and gave him a reason for remaining. He spoke to me of the great heat through which we were passing, but, albeit he was a well-read man and capable of expressing himself in good French, said to me: "You are none the worse for this hyperthermia?" The fact is that medicine has made some slight advance in knowledge since Molière's days, but none in its vocabulary. My companion went on: "The great thing is to avoid the sudations that are caused by weather like this, especially in superheated rooms. You can remedy them, when you go home and feel thirsty, by the application of heat" (by which he apparently meant hot drinks).

Owing to the circumstances of my grandmother's death, the subject interested me, and I had recently read in a book by a great specialist that perspiration was injurious to the kidneys, by making moisture pass through the skin when its proper outlet was elsewhere. I thought with regret of those dog-days at the time of my grandmother's death, and was inclined to blame them for it. I did not mention this to Dr. E——, but of his own accord he said to me: "The advantage of this very hot weather in which perspiration is abundant is that the kidney is correspondingly relieved." Medicine is not an exact science.

Keeping me engaged in talk, Professor E—— asked only not to be forced to leave me. But I had just seen, making a series of sweeping bows to right and left of the Princesse de Guermantes, stepping back a pace first, the Marquis de Vaugoubert. M. de Norpois had recently introduced me to him and I hoped that I might find in him a person capable of introducing me to our host. The proportions of this work do not permit me to explain here in consequence of what incidents in his youth M. de Vaugoubert was one of the few men (possibly the only man) in society who happened to be in what is called at Sodom the "confidence" of M. de Charlus. But, if our Minister to the Court of King Theodosius had certain defects in common with the Baron, they were only a very pale reflexion. It was merely in an infinitely softened, sentimental and simple form that he displayed those alternations of affection and hatred through which the desire to attract, and then the fear—equally imaginary—of being, if not scorned, at any rate unmasked, made the Baron pass. Made ridiculous by a chastity, a "platonicism" (to which as a man of keen ambition he had, from the moment of passing his examination, sacrificed all pleasure), above all by his intellectual nullity, these alternations M. de Vaugoubert did, nevertheless, display. But whereas in M. de Charlus the immoderate praises were proclaimed with a positive burst of eloquence, and seasoned with the subtlest, the most mordant banter which marked a man for ever, by M. de Vaugoubert, on the other hand, the affection was expressed with the banality of a man of the lowest intelligence, and of a public official, the grievances (worked up generally into a complete indictment, as with the Baron) by a malevolence which, though relentless, was at the same time spiritless, and was all the more startling inasmuch as it was invariably a direct contradiction of what the Minister had said six months earlier and might soon perhaps be saying again: a regularity of change which gave an almost astronomic poetry to the various phases of M. de Vaugoubert's life, albeit apart from this nobody was ever less suggestive of a star.

The greeting that he gave me had nothing in common with that which I should have received from M. de Charlus. To this greeting M. de Vaugoubert, apart from the thousand mannerisms which he supposed to be indicative of good breeding and diplomacy, imparted a cavalier, brisk, smiling air, which should make him seem on the one hand to be rejoicing at being alive—at a time when he was inwardly chewing the mortification of a career with no prospect of advancement and with the threat of enforced retirement—and on the other hand young, virile and charming, when he could see and no longer ventured to go and examine in the glass the lines gathering upon a face which he would have wished to keep full of seduction. Not that he would have hoped for effective conquests, the mere thought of which filled him with terror on account of what people would say, scandals, blackmail. Having passed from an almost infantile corruption to an absolute continence dating from the day on which his thoughts had turned to the Quai d'Orsay and he had begun to plan a great career for himself, he had the air of a caged animal, casting in every direction glances expressive of fear, appetite and stupidity. This last was so dense that he did not reflect that the street-arabs of his adolescence were boys nc longer, and when a newsvendor bawled in his face: "*La Presse!*" even more than with longing he shuddered with terror, imagining himself recognised and denounced.

But in default of the pleasures sacrificed to the ingratitude of the Quai d'Orsay, M. de Vaugoubert—and it was for this that he was anxious still to attract—was liable to sudden stirrings of the heart. Heaven knows with how many letters he would overwhelm the Ministry (what personal ruses he would employ, the drafts that he made upon the credit of Mme. de Vaugoubert, who, on account of her corpulence, her exalted birth, her masculine air, and above all the mediocrity of her husband, was reputed to be endowed with eminent capacities and to be herself for all practical purposes the Minister), to introduce without any valid reason a young man destitute of all merit into the staff of the Legation. It is true that a few months, a few years later, the insignificant attaché had only to appear, without the least trace of any hostile intention, to have shewn signs of coldness towards his chief for the latter, supposing himself scorned or betrayed, to devote the same hysterical ardour to punishing him with which he had showered favours upon him in the past. He would move heaven and earth to have him recalled and the Director of Political Affairs would receive a letter daily: "Why don't you hurry up and rid me of that lascar. Give him a dressing down in his own interest. What he needs is a slice of humble pie." The post of attaché at the court of King Theodosius was on this account far from enjoyable. But in all other respects, thanks to his perfect common sense as a man of the world, M. de Vaugoubert was one of the best representatives of the French Government abroad. When a man who was reckoned a superior person, a Jacobin, with an expert knowledge of all subjects, replaced him later on, it was not long before war broke out between France and the country over which that monarch reigned.

M. de Vaugoubert, like M. de Charlus, did not care to be the first to give a greeting. Each of them preferred to "respond," being constantly afraid of the gossip which the person to whom otherwise they might have offered their hand might have heard about them since their last meeting. In my case, M. de Vaugoubert had no need to ask himself this question, I had as a matter of fact gone up of my own accord to greet him, if only because of the difference in our ages. He replied with an air of wonder and delight, his eyes continuing to stray as though there had been a patch of clover on either side of me upon which he was forbidden to graze. I felt that it would be more becoming to ask him to introduce me to Mme. de Vaugoubert, before effecting that introduction to the Prince which I decided not to mention to him until afterwards. The idea of making me acquainted with his wife seemed to fill him with joy, for his own sake as well as for hers, and he led me at a solemn pace towards the Marquise. Arriving in front of her, and indicating me with his hand and eyes, with every conceivable mark of consideration, he nevertheless remained silent and withdrew after a few moments, in a sidelong fashion, leaving me alone with his wife. She had at once given me her hand, but without knowing to whom this token of friendship was addressed, for I realised that M. de Vaugoubert had forgotten my name, perhaps even had failed to recognise me, and being unwilling, from politeness, to confess his ignorance had made the introduction consist in a mere dumb show. And so I was no farther advanced; how was I to get myself introduced to my host by a woman who did not know my name? Worse still, I found myself obliged to remain for some moments talking to Mme. de Vaugoubert. And this annoyed me for two reasons. I had no wish to remain all night at this party, for I had arranged with Albertine (I had given her a box for *Phèdre*) that she was to pay me a visit shortly before midnight. Certainly I was not in the least in love with her; I was yielding, in making her come this evening, to a wholly sensual desire, albeit we were at that torrid period of the year when sensuality, evaporating, visits more readily the organ of taste, seeks above all things coolness. More than for the kiss of a girl, it thirsts for orangeade, for a cold bath, or even to gaze at that peeled and juicy moon which was quenching the thirst of heaven. I counted however upon ridding myself, in Albertine's company—which, moreover, reminded me of the coolness of the sea—of the regret that I should not fail to feel for many charming faces (for it was a party quite as much for girls as for married women that the Princess was giving. On the other hand, the face of the imposing Mme. de Vaugoubert, Bourbonian and morose, was in no way attractive).

People said at the Ministry, without any suggestion of malice, that in their household it was the husband who wore the petticoats and the wife the trousers. Now there was more truth in this saying than was supposed. Mme. de Vaugoubert was really a man. Whether she had always been one, or had grown to be as I saw her, matters little, for in either case we have to deal with one of the most touching miracles of nature which, in the latter alternative especially, makes the human kingdom resemble the kingdom of flowers. On the former hypothesis—if the future Mme. de Vaugoubert had always been so clumsily manlike—nature, by a fiendish and beneficent ruse, bestows on the girl the deceiving aspect of a man. And the youth who has no love for women and is seeking to be cured greets with joy this subterfuge of discovering a bride who figures in his eyes as a market porter. In the alternative case, if the woman has not originally these masculine characteristics, she adopts them by degrees, to please her husband, and even unconsciously, by that sort of mimicry which makes certain flowers assume the appearance of the insects which they seek to attract. Her regret that she is not loved, that she is not a man, virilises her. Indeed, quite apart from the case that we are now considering, who has not remarked how often the most normal couples end by resembling each other, at times even by an exchange of qualities? A former German Chancellor, Prince von Bülow, married an Italian. In the course of time, on the Pincio, it was remarked how much the Teutonic husband had absorbed of Italian delicacy, and the Italian Princess of German coarseness. To turn aside to a point without the province of the laws which we are now tracing, everyone knows an eminent French diplomat, whose origin was at first suggested only by his name, one of the most illustrious in the East. As he matured, as he grew old, there was revealed in him the Oriental whom no one had ever suspected, and now when we see him we regret the absence of the fez that would complete the picture.

To revert to habits completely unknown to the ambassador whose profile, coarsened by heredity, we have just recalled, Mme. de Vaugoubert realised the acquired or predestined type, the immortal example of which is the Princess Palatine, never out of a riding habit, who, having borrowed from her husband more than his virility, championing the defects of the men who do not care for women, reports in her familiar correspondence the mutual relations of all the great noblemen of the court of Louis XIV. One of the reasons which enhance still farther the masculine air of women like Mme. de Vaugoubert is that the neglect which they receive from their husbands, the shame that they feel at such neglect, destroy in them by degrees everything that is womanly. They end by acquiring both the good and the bad qualities which their husbands lack. The more frivolous, effeminate, indiscreet their husbands are, the more they grow into the effigy, devoid of charm, of the virtues which their husbands ought to practise.

Traces of abasement, boredom, indignation, marred the regular features of Mme. de Vaugoubert. Alas, I felt that she was regarding me with interest and curiosity as one of those young men who appealed to M. de Vaugoubert, and one of whom she herself would so much have liked to be, now that her husband, growing old, shewed a preference for youth. She was gazing at me with the close attention shewn by provincial ladies who from an illustrated catalogue copy the tailor-made dress so becoming to the charming person in the picture (actually, the same person on every page, but deceptively multiplied into different creatures, thanks to the differences of pose and the variety of attire). The instinctive attraction which urged Mme. de Vaugoubert towards me was so strong that she went the length of seizing my arm, so that I might take her to get a glass of orangeade. But I released myself, alleging that I must presently be going, and had not yet been introduced to our host.

This distance between me and the garden door where he stood talking to a group of people was not very great. But it alarmed me more than if, in order to cross it, I should have to expose myself to a continuous hail of fire.

A number of women from whom I felt that I might be able to secure an introduction were in the garden, where, while feigning an ecstatic admiration, they were at a loss for an occupation. Parties of this sort are as a rule premature. They have little reality until the following day, when they occupy the attention of the people who were not invited. A real author, devoid of the foolish self-esteem of so many literary people, if, when he reads an article by a critic who has always expressed the greatest admiration for his works, he sees the names of various inferior writers mentioned, but not his own, has no time to stop and consider what might be to him a matter for astonishment: his books are calling him. But a society woman has nothing to do and, on seeing in the *Figaro:* "Last night the Prince and Princesse de Guermantes gave a large party," etc., exclaims: "What! Only three days ago I talked to Marie-Gilbert for an hour, and she never said a word about it!" and racks her brains to discover how she can have offended the Guermantes. It must be said that, so far as the Princess's parties were concerned, the astonishment was sometimes as great among those who were invited as among those who were not. For they would burst forth at the moment when one least expected them, and summoned in people whose existence Mme. de Guermantes had forgotten for years. And almost all the people in society are so insignificant that others of their sort adopt, in judging them, only the measure of their social success, cherish them if they are invited, if they are omitted detest them. As to the latter, if it was the fact that the Princess often, even when they were her friends, did not invite them, that was often due to her fear of annoying "Palamède," who had excommunicated them. And so I might be certain that she had not spoken of me to M. de Charlus, for otherwise I should not have found myself there. He meanwhile was posted between the house and the garden, by the side of the German Ambassador, leaning upon the balustrade of the great staircase which led from the garden to the house, so that the other guests, in spite of the three or four feminine admirers who were grouped round the Baron and almost concealed him, were obliged to greet him as they passed. He responded by naming each of them in turn. And one heard an incessant: "Good evening, Monsieur du Hazay, good evening, Madame de la Tour du Pin-Verclause, good evening, Madame de la Tour du Pin-Gouvernet, good evening, Philibert, good evening, my dear Ambassadress," and so on. This created a continuous barking sound, interspersed with benevolent suggestions or inquiries (to the answers to which he paid no attention), which M. de Charlus addressed to them in a tone softened, artificial to shew his indifference, and benign: "Take care the child doesn't catch cold, it is always rather damp in the gardens. Good evening, Madame de Brantes. Good evening, Madame de Mecklembourg. Have you brought your daughter? Is she wearing that delicious pink frock? Good evening, Saint-Geran." Certainly there was an element of pride in this attitude, for M. de Charlus was aware that he was a Guermantes, and that he occupied a supreme place at this party. But there was more in it than pride, and the very word *fête* suggested, to the man with aesthetic gifts, the luxurious, curious sense that it might bear if this party were being given not by people in contemporary society but in a painting by Carpaccio or Veronese. It is indeed highly probable that the German Prince that M. de Charlus was must rather have been picturing to himself the reception that occurs in *Tannhäuser,* and himself as the Margrave, standing at the entrance to the Warburg with a kind word of condescension for each of his guests, while their procession into the castle or the park is greeted by the long phrase, a hundred times renewed, of the famous March.

I must, however, make up my mind. I could distinguish beneath the trees various women with whom I was more or less closely acquainted, but they seemed transformed because they were at the Princess's and not at her cousin's, and because I saw them seated not in front of Dresden china plates but beneath the boughs of a chestnut. The refinement of their setting mattered nothing. Had it been infinitely less refined than at Oriane's, I should have felt the same uneasiness. When the electric light in our drawing-room fails, and we are obliged to replace it with oil lamps, everything seems altered. I was recalled from my uncertainty by Mme. de Souvré. "Good evening," she said as she approached me. "Have you seen the Duchesse de Guermantes lately?" She excelled in giving to speeches of this sort an intonation which proved that she was not uttering them from sheer silliness, like people who, not knowing what to talk about, come up to you a thousand times over to mention some bond of common acquaintance, often extremely slight. She had on the contrary a fine conducting wire in her glance which signified: "Don't suppose for a moment that I haven't recognised you. You are the young man I met at the Duchesse de Guermantes. I remember quite well." Unfortunately, this protection, extended over me by this phrase, stupid in appearance but delicate in intention, was extremely fragile, and vanished as soon as I tried to make use of it. Madame de Souvré had the art, if called upon to convey a request to some influential person, of appearing at the same time, in the petitioner's eyes, to be recommending him, and in those of the influential person not to be recommending the petitioner, so that her ambiguous gesture opened a credit balance of gratitude to her with the latter without placing her in any way in debt to the former. Encouraged by this lady's civilities to ask her to introduce me to M. de Guermantes, I found that she took advantage of a moment when our host was not looking in our direction, laid a motherly hand on my shoulder, and, smiling at the averted face of the Prince who was unable to see her, thrust me towards him with a gesture of feigned protection, but deliberately ineffective, which left me stranded almost at my starting point. Such is the cowardice of people in society.

That of a lady who came to greet me, addressing me by my name, was greater still. I tried to recall her own name as I talked to her; I remembered quite well having met her at dinner, I could remember things that she had said. But my attention, concentrated upon the inward region in which these memories of her lingered, was unable to discover her name there. It was there, nevertheless. My thoughts began playing a sort of game with it to grasp its outlines, its initial letter, and so finally to bring the whole name to light. It was labour in vain, I could more or less estimate its mass, its weight, but as for its forms, confronting them with the shadowy captive lurking in the inward night, I said to myself: "It is not that." Certainly my mind would have been capable of creating the most difficult names. Unfortunately, it had not to create but to reproduce. All action by the mind is easy, if it is not subjected to the test of reality. Here, I was forced to own myself beaten. Finally, in a flash, the name came back to me as a whole: "Madame d'Arpajon." I am wrong in saying that it came, for it did not, I think, appear to me by a spontaneous propulsion. I do not think either that the many slight memories which associated me with the lady, and to which I did not cease to appeal for help (by such exhortations as: "Come now, it is the lady who is a friend of Mme. de Souvré, who feels for Victor Hugo so artless an admiration, mingled with so much alarm and horror,")—I do not believe that all these memories, hovering between me and her name, served in any way to bring it to light. In that great game of hide and seek which is played in our memory when we seek to recapture a name, there is not any series of gradual approximations. We see nothing, then suddenly the name appears in its exact form and very different from what we thought we could make out. It is not the name that has come to us. No, I believe rather that, as we go on living, we pass our time in keeping away from the zone in which a name is distinct, and it was by an exercise of my will and attention which increased the acuteness of my inward vision that all of a sudden I had pierced the semi-darkness and seen daylight. In any case, if there are transitions between oblivion and memory, then, these transitions are unconscious. For the intermediate names through which we pass, before finding the real name, are themselves false, and bring us nowhere nearer to it. They are not even, properly speaking, names at all, but often mere consonants which are not to be found in the recaptured name. And yet, this operation of the mind passing from a blank to reality is so mysterious, that it is possible after all that these false consonants are really handles, awkwardly held out to enable us to seize hold of the correct name. "All this," the reader will remark, "tells us nothing as to the lady's failure to oblige; but since you have made so long a digression, allow me, gentle author, to waste another moment of your time in telling you that it is a pity that, young as you were (or as your hero was, if he be not yourself), you had already so feeble a memory that you could not recall the name of a lady whom you knew quite well." It is indeed a pity, gentle reader. And sadder than you think when one feels the time approaching when names and words will vanish from the clear zone of consciousness, and when one must for ever cease to name to oneself the people whom one has known most intimately. It is indeed a pity that one should require this effort, when one is still young, to recapture names which one knows quite well. But if this infirmity occurred only in the case of names barely known, quite naturally forgotten, names which one would not take the trouble to remember, the infirmity would not be without its advantages. "And what are they, may I ask?" Well, Sir, that the malady alone makes us remark and apprehend, and allows us to dissect the mechanism of which otherwise we should know nothing. A man who, night after night, falls like a lump of lead upon his bed, and ceases to live until the moment when he wakes and rises, will such a man ever dream of making, I do not say great discoveries, but even minute observations upon sleep? He barely knows that he does sleep. A little insomnia is not without its value in making us appreciate sleep, in throwing a ray of light upon that darkness. A memory without fault is not a very powerful incentive to studying the phenomena of memory. "In a word, did Mme. d'Arpajon introduce you to the Prince?" No, but be quiet and let me go on with my story.

Mme. d'Arpajon was even more cowardly than Mme.

de Souvré, but there was more excuse for her cowardice. She knew that she had always had very little influence in society. This influence, such as it was, had been reduced still farther by her connexion with the Duc de Guermantes; his desertion of her dealt it the final blow. The resentment which she felt at my request that she should introduce me to the Prince produced a silence which, she was artless enough to suppose, conveyed the impression that she had not heard what I said. She was not even aware that she was knitting her brows with anger. Perhaps, on the other hand, she was aware of it, did not bother about the inconsistency, and made use of it for the lesson which she was thus able to teach me without undue rudeness; I mean a silent lesson, but none the less eloquent for that.

Apart from this, Mme. d'Arpajon was extremely annoyed; many eyes were raised in the direction of a renaissance balcony at the corner of which, instead of one of those monumental statues which were so often used as ornaments at that period, there leaned, no less sculptural than they, the magnificent Marquise de Surgis-le-Duc, who had recently succeeded Mme. d'Arpajon in the heart of Basin de Guermantes. Beneath the flimsy white tulle which protected her from the cool night air, one saw the supple form of a winged victory. I had no recourse left save to M. de Charlus, who had withdrawn to a room downstairs which opened on the garden. I had plenty of time (as he was pretending to be absorbed in a fictitious game of whist which enabled him to appear not to notice people) to admire the deliberate, artistic simplicity of his evening coat which, by the merest trifles which only a tailor's eye could have picked out, had the air of a "Harmony in Black and White" by Whistler; black, white and red, rather, for M. de Charlus was wearing, hanging from a broad ribbon pinned to the lapel of his coat, the Cross, in white, black and red enamel, of a Knight of the religious Order of Malta. At that moment the Baron's game was interrupted by Mme. de Gallardon, leading her nephew, the Vicomte de Courvoisier, a young man with an attractive face and an impertinent air. "Cousin," said Mme. de Gallardon, "allow me to introduce my nephew Adalbert. Adalbert, you remember the famous Palamède of whom you have heard so much." "Good evening, Madame de Gallardon," M. de Charlus replied. And he added, without so much as a glance at the young man: "Good evening, Sir," with a truculent air and in a tone so violently discourteous that everyone in the room was stupefied. Perhaps M. de Charlus, knowing that Mme. de Gallardon had her doubts as to his morals and guessing that she had not been able to resist, for once in a way, the temptation to allude to them, was determined to nip in the bud any scandal that she might have embroidered upon a friendly reception of her nephew, making at the same time a resounding profession of indifference with regard to young men in general; perhaps he had not considered that the said Adalbert had responded to his aunt's speech with a sufficiently respectful air; perhaps, desirous of making headway in time to come with so attractive a cousin, he chose to give himself the advantage of a preliminary assault, like those sovereigns who, before engaging upon diplomatic action, strengthen it by an act of war.

It was not so difficult as I supposed to secure M. de Charlus's consent to my request that he should introduce me to the Prince de Guermantes. For one thing, in the course of the last twenty years, this Don Quixote had tilted against so many windmills (often relatives who, he imagined, had behaved badly to him), he had so frequently banned people as being "impossible to have in the house" from being invited by various male or female Guermantes, that these were beginning to be afraid of quarrelling with all the people they knew and liked, of condemning themselves to a lifelong deprivation of the society of certain newcomers whom they were curious to meet, by espousing the thunderous but unexplained rancours of a brother-in-law or cousin who expected them to abandon for his sake, wife, brother, children. More intelligent than the other Guermantes, M. de Charlus realised that people were ceasing to pay any attention, save once in a while, to his veto, and, looking to the future, fearing lest one day it might be with his society that they would dispense, he had begun to make allowances, to reduce, as the saying is, his terms. Furthermore, if he had the faculty of ascribing for months, for years on end, an identical life to a detested person—to such an one he would not have tolerated their sending an invitation, and would have fought, rather, like a trooper, against a queen, the status of the person who stood in his way ceasing to count for anything in his eyes; on the other hand, his explosions of wrath were too frequent not to be somewhat fragmentary. "The imbecile, the rascal! We shall have to put him in his place, sweep him into the gutter, where unfortunately he will not be innocuous to the health of the town," he would scream, even when he was alone in his own room, while reading a letter that he considered irreverent, or upon recalling some remark that had been repeated to him. But a fresh outburst against a second imbecile cancelled the first, and the former victim had only to shew due deference for the crisis that he had occasioned to be forgotten, it not having lasted long enough to establish a foundation of hatred upon which to build. And so, I might perhaps—despite his ill-humour towards me—have been successful when I asked him to introduce me to the Prince, had I not been so ill-inspired as to add, from a scruple of conscience, and so that he might not suppose me guilty of the indelicacy of entering the house at a venture, counting upon him to enable me to remain there: "You are aware that I know them quite well, the Princess has been very kind to me." "Very well, if you know them, why do you need me to introduce you?" he replied in a sharp tone, and, turning his back, resumed his make-believe game with the Nuncio, the German Ambassador and another personage whom I did not know by sight.

Then, from the depths of those gardens where in days past the Duc d'Aiguillon used to breed rare animals, there came to my ears, through the great, open doors, the sound of a sniffing nose that was savouring all those refinements and determined to miss none of them. The sound approached, I moved at a venture in its direction, with the result that the words *good evening* were murmured in my ear by M. de Bréauté, not like the rusty metallic sound of a knife being sharpened on a grindstone, even less like the cry of the wild boar, devastator of tilled fields, but like the voice of a possible saviour.

Less influential than Mme. de Souvré, but less deeply ingrained than she with the incapacity to oblige, far more at his ease with the Prince than was Mme. d'Arpajon, entertaining some illusion perhaps as to my position in the Guermantes set, or perhaps knowing more about it than myself, I had nevertheless for the first few moments some difficulty in arresting his attention, for, with fluttering, distended nostrils, he was turning in every direction, inquisitively protruding his monocle, as though he found himself face to face with five hundred matchless works of art. But, having heard my request, he received it with satisfaction, led me towards the Prince and presented me to him with a relishing, ceremonious, vulgar air, as though he had been handing him, with a word of commendation, a plate of cakes. Just as the greeting of the Duc de Guermantes was, when he chose, friendly, instinct with good fellowship, cordial and familiar, so I found that of the Prince stiff, solemn, haughty. He barely smiled at me, addressed me gravely as "Sir." I had often heard the Duke make fun of his cousin's stiffness. But from the first words that he addressed to me, which by their cold and serious tone formed the most entire contrast with the language of Basin, I realised at once that the fundamentally disdainful man was the Duke, who spoke to you at your first meeting with him as "man to man," and that, of the two cousins, the one who was really simple was the Prince. I found in his reserve a stronger feeling, I do not say of equality, for that would have been inconceivable to him, but at least of the consideration which one may shew for an inferior, such as may be found in all strongly hierarchical societies, in the Law Courts, for instance; in a Faculty, where a public prosecutor or dean, conscious of their high charge, conceal perhaps more genuine simplicity, and, when you come to know them better, more kindness, true simplicity, cordiality, beneath their traditional aloofness than the more modern brethren beneath their jocular affectation of comradeship. "Do you intend to follow the career of Monsieur, your father?" he said to me with a distant but interested air. I answered his question briefly, realising that he had asked it only out of politeness, and moved away to allow him to greet the fresh arrivals.

I caught sight of Swann, and meant to speak to him, but at that moment I saw that the Prince de Guermantes, instead of waiting where he was to receive the greeting of Odette's husband, had immediately, with the force of a suction pump, carried him off to the farther end of the garden, in order, as some said, "to shew him the door."

So entirely absorbed in the company that I did not learn until two days later, from the newspapers, that a Czech orchestra had been playing throughout the evening, and that Bengal lights had been burning in constant succession, I recovered some power of attention with the idea of going to look at the celebrated fountain of Hubert Robert.

In a clearing surrounded by fine trees several of which were as old as itself, set in a place apart, one could see it in the distance, slender, immobile, stiffened, allowing the breeze to stir only the lighter fall of its pale and quivering plume. The eighteenth century had refined the elegance of its lines, but, by fixing the style of the jet, seemed to have arrested its life; at this distance one had the impression of a work of art rather than the sensation of water. The moist cloud itself that was perpetually gathering at its crest preserved the character of the period like those that in the sky assemble round the palaces of Versailles. But from a closer view one realised that, while it respected, like the stones of an ancient palace, the design traced for it beforehand, it was a constantly changing stream of water that, springing upwards and seeking to obey the architect's traditional orders, performed them to the letter only by seeming to infringe them, its thousand separate bursts succeeding only at a distance in giving the impression of a single flow. This was in reality as often interrupted as the scattering of the fall, whereas from a distance it had appeared to me unyielding, solid, unbroken in its continuity. From a little nearer, one saw that this continuity, apparently complete, was assured, at every point in the ascent of the jet, wherever it must otherwise have been broken, by the entering into line, by the lateral incorporation of a parallel jet which mounted higher than the first and was itself, at an altitude greater but already a strain upon its endurance, relieved by a third. Seen close at hand, drops without strength fell back from the column of water crossing on their way their climbing sisters and, at times, torn, caught in an eddy of the night air, disturbed by this ceaseless flow, floated awhile before being drowned in the basin. They teased with their hesitations, with their passage in the opposite direction, and blurred with their soft vapour the vertical tension of that stem, bearing aloft an oblong cloud composed of a thousand tiny drops, but apparently painted in an unchanging, golden brown which rose, unbreakable, constant, urgent, swift, to mingle with the clouds in the sky. Unfortunately, a gust of wind was enough to scatter it obliquely on the ground; at times indeed a single jet, disobeying its orders, swerved and, had they not kept a respectful distance, would have drenched to their skins the incautious crowd of gazers.

One of these little accidents, which could scarcely occur

save when the breeze freshened for a moment, was distinctly unpleasant. Somebody had told Mme. d'Arpajon that the Duc de Guermantes, who as a matter of fact had not yet arrived, was with Mme. de Surgis in one of the galleries of pink marble to which one ascended by the double colonnade, hollowed out of the wall, which rose from the brink of the fountain. Now, just as Mme. d'Arpajon was making for one of these staircases, a strong gust of warm air made the jet of water swerve and inundated the fair lady so completely that, the water streaming down from her open bosom inside her dress, she was soaked as if she had been plunged into a bath. Whereupon, a few feet away, a rhythmical roar resounded, loud enough to be heard by a whole army, and at the same time protracted in periods as though it were being addressed not to the army as a whole but to each unit in turn; it was the Grand Duke Vladimir, who was laughing whole-heartedly upon seeing the immersion of Mme. d'Arpajon, one of the funniest sights, as he was never tired of repeating afterwards, that he had ever seen in his life. Some charitable persons having suggested to the Muscovite that a word of sympathy from himself was perhaps deserved and would give pleasure to the lady who, notwithstanding her tale of forty winters fully told, wiping herself with her scarf, without appealing to anyone for help, was stepping clear in spite of the water that was maliciously spilling over the edge of the basin, the Grand Duke, who had a kind heart, felt that he must say a word in season, and, before the last military tattoo of his laughter had altogether subsided, one heard a fresh roar, more vociferous even than the last. "Bravo, old girl!" he cried, clapping his hands as though at the theatre.

Mme. d'Arpajon was not at all pleased that her dexterity should be commended at the expense of her youth. And when some one remarked to her, in a voice drowned by the roar of the water, over which nevertheless rose the princely thunder: "I think His Imperial Highness said something to you." "No! It was to Mme. de Souvré," was her reply.

I passed through the gardens and returned by the stair, upon which the absence of the Prince, who had vanished with Swann, enlarged the crowd of guests round M. de Charlus, just as, when Louis XIV was not at Versailles, there was a more numerous attendance upon Monsieur, his brother. I was stopped on my way by the Baron, while behind me two ladies and a young man came up to greet him.

"It is nice to see you here," he said to me, as he held out his hand. "Good evening, Madame de la Trémoïlle, good evening, my dear Herminie." But doubtless the memory of what he had said to me as to his own supreme position in the Hôtel Guermantes made him wish to appear to be feeling, with regard to a matter which annoyed him but which he had been unable to prevent, a satisfaction which his high-and-mighty impertinence and his hysterical excitement immediately invested in a cloak of exaggerated irony. "It is nice," he repeated, "but it is, really, very odd." And he broke into peals of laughter which appeared to be indicative at once of his joy and of the inadequacy of human speech to express it. Certain persons, meanwhile, who knew both how difficult he was of access and how prone to insolent retorts, had been drawn towards us by curiosity, and, with an almost indecent haste, took to their heels. "Come, now, don't be cross," he said to me, patting me gently on the shoulder, "you know that I am your friend. Good evening, Antioche, good evening, Louis-René. Have you been to look at the fountain?" he asked me in a tone that was affirmative rather than questioning. "It is quite pretty, ain't it? It is marvellous. It might be made better still, naturally, if certain things were removed, and then there would be nothing like it in France. But even as it stands, it is quite one of the best things. Bréauté will tell you that it was a mistake to put lamps round it, to try and make people forget that it was he who was responsible for that absurd idea. But after all he has only managed to spoil it a very little. It is far more difficult to deface a great work of art than to create one. Not that we had not a vague suspicion all the time that Bréauté was not quite a match for Hubert Robert."

I drifted back into the stream of quests who were entering the house. "Have you seen my delicious cousin Oriane lately?" I was asked by the Princess who had now deserted her post by the door and with whom I was making my way back to the rooms. "She's sure to be here to-night, I saw her this afternoon," my hostess added. "She promised me to come. I believe too that you will be dining with us both to meet the Queen of Italy, at the Embassy, on Thursday. There are to be all the Royalties imaginable, it will be most alarming." They could not in any way alarm the Princesse de Guermantes, whose rooms swarmed with them, and who would say: "My little Coburgs" as she might have said "my little dogs." And so Mme. de Guermantes said: "It will be most alarming," out of sheer silliness, which, among people in society, overrides even their vanity. With regard to her own pedigree, she knew less than a passman in history. As for the people of her circle, she liked to shew that she knew the nicknames with which they had been labelled. Having asked me whether I was dining, the week after, with the Marquise de la Pommelière, who was often called "la Pomme," the Princess, having elicited a reply in the negative, remained silent for some moments. Then, without any other motive than a deliberate display of instinctive erudition, banality, and conformity to the prevailing spirit, she added: "She's not a bad sort, the Pomme!"

While the Princess was talking to me, it so happened that the Duc and Duchesse de Guermantes made their entrance. But I could not go at once to greet them, for I was waylaid by the Turkish Ambassadress, who, pointing to our hostess whom I had just left, exclaimed as she seized me by the arm: "Ah! What a delicious woman the Princess is! What a superior being! I feel sure that, if I were a man," she went on, with a trace of Oriental servility and sensuality, "I would give my life for that heavenly creature." I replied that I did indeed find her charming, but that I knew her cousin, the Duchess, better. "But there is no comparison," said the Ambassadress. "Oriane is a charming society woman who gets her wit from Mémé and Babal, whereas Marie-Gilbert is *somebody.*"

I never much like to be told like this, without a chance to reply, what I ought to think about people whom I know. And there was no reason why the Turkish Ambassadress should be in any way better qualified than myself to judge of the worth of the Duchesse de Guermantes.

On the other hand (and this explained also my annoyance with the Ambassadress), the defects of a mere acquaintance, and even of a friend, are to us real poisons, against which we are fortunately " mithridated."

But, without applying any standard of scientific comparison and talking of anaphylaxis, let us say that, at the heart of our friendly or purely social relations, there lurks a hostility momentarily cured but recurring by fits and starts. As a rule, we suffer little from these poisons, so long as people are "natural." By saying " Babal " and " Mémé " to indicate people with whom she was not acquainted, the Turkish Ambassadress suspended the effects of the " mithridatism " which, as a rule, made me find her tolerable. She annoyed me, which was all the more unfair, inasmuch as she did not speak like this to make me think that she was an intimate friend of " Mémé," but owing to a too rapid education which made her name these noble lords according to what she believed to be the custom of the country. She had crowded her course into a few months, and had not picked up the rules. But, on thinking it over, I found another reason for my disinclination to remain in the Ambassadress's company. It was not so very long since, at Oriane's, this same diplomatic personage had said to me, with a purposeful and serious air, that she found the Princesse de Guermantes frankly antipathetic. I felt that I need not stop to consider this change of front: the invitation to the party this evening had brought it about. The Ambassadress was perfectly sincere when she told me that the Princesse de Guermantes was a sublime creature. She had always thought so. But, having never before been invited to the Princess's house, she had felt herself bound to give this non-invitation the appearance of a deliberate abstention on principle. Now that she had been asked, and would presumably continue to be asked in the future, she could give free expression to her feelings. There is no need, in accounting for three out of four of the opinions that we hold about other people, to go so far as crossed love or exclusion from public office. Our judgment remains uncertain: the withholding or bestowal of an invitation determines it. Anyhow, the Turkish Ambassadress, as the Baronne de Guermantes remarked while making a tour of inspection through the rooms with me, "was all right." She was, above all, extremely useful. The real stars of society are tired of appearing there. He who is curious to gaze at them must often migrate to another hemisphere, where they are more or less alone. But women like the Ottoman Ambassadress, of quite recent admission to society, are never weary of shining there, and, so to speak, everywhere at once. They are of value at entertainments of the sort known as *soirée* or *rout*, to which they would let themselves be dragged from their deathbeds rather than miss one. They are the supers upon whom a hostess can always count, determined never to miss a party. And so, the foolish young men, unaware that they are false stars, take them for the queens of fashion, whereas it would require a formal lecture to explain to them by virtue of what reasons Mme. Standish, who, her existence unknown to them, lives remote from the world, painting cushions, is at least as great a lady as the Duchesse de Doudeauville.

In the ordinary course of life, the eyes of the Duchesse de Guermantes were absent and slightly melancholy, she made them sparkle with a flame of wit only when she had to say how-d'ye-do to a friend; precisely as though the said friend had been some witty remark, some charming touch, some titbit for delicate palates, the savour of which has set on the face of the connoisseur an expression of refined joy. But upon big evenings, as she had too many greetings to bestow, she decided that it would be tiring to have to switch off the light after each. Just as an ardent reader, when he goes to the theatre to see a new piece by one of the masters of the stage, testifies to his certainty that he is not going to spend a dull evening by having, while he hands his hat and coat to the attendant, his lip adjusted in readiness for a sapient smile, his eye kindled for a sardonic approval; similarly it was at the moment of her arrival that the Duchess lighted up for the whole evening. And while she was handing over her evening cloak, of a magnificent Tiepolo red, exposing a huge collar of rubies round her neck, having cast over her gown that final rapid, minute and exhaustive dressmaker's glance which is also that of a woman of the world, Oriane made sure that her eyes, just as much as her other jewels, were sparkling. In vain might sundry "kind friends" such as M. de Janville fling themselves upon the Duke to keep him from entering: "But don't you know that poor Mama is at his last gasp? He had had the Sacraments." "I know, I know," answered M. de Guermantes, thrusting the tiresome fellow aside in order to enter the room. "The viaticum has acted splendidly," he added, with a smile of pleasure at the thought of the ball which he was determined not to miss after the Prince's party. "We did not want people to know that we had come back," the Duchess said to me. She never suspected that the Princess had already disproved this statement by telling me that she had seen her cousin for a moment, who had promised to come. The Duke, after a protracted stare with which he proceeded to crush his wife for the space of five minutes, observed: "I told Oriane about your misgivings." Now that she saw that they were unfounded, and that she herself need take no action in the attempt to dispel them, she pronounced them absurd, and continued to chaff me about them. "The idea of supposing that you were not invited! Besides, wasn't I there? Do you suppose that I should be unable to get you an invitation to my cousin's house?" I must admit that frequently, after this, she did things for me that were far more difficult; nevertheless, I took care not to interpret her words in the sense that I had been too modest. I was beginning to learn the exact value of the language, spoken or mute, of aristocratic affability, an affability that is happy to shed balm upon the sense of inferiority in those persons towards whom it is directed, though not to the point of dispelling that sense, for in that case it would no longer have any reason to exist. "But you are our equal, if not our superior," the Guermantes seemed, in all their actions, to be saying; and they said it in the most courteous fashion imaginable, to be loved, admired, but not to be believed; that one should discern the fictitious character of this affability was what they called being well-bred; to suppose it to be genuine, a sign of ill-breeding. I was to receive, as it happened, shortly after this, a lesson which gave me a full and perfect understanding of the extent and limitations of certain forms of aristocratic affability. It was at an afternoon party given by the Duchesse de Montmorency to meet the Queen of England; there was a sort of royal procession to the buffet, at the head of which walked Her Majesty on the arm of the Duc de Guermantes. I happened to arrive at that moment. With his disengaged hand the Duke conveyed to me, from a distance of nearly fifty yards, a thousand signs of friendly invitation, which appeared to mean that I need not be afraid to approach, that I should not be devoured alive instead of the sandwiches. But I, who was becoming word-perfect in the language of the court, instead of going even one step nearer, keeping my fifty yards' interval, made a deep bow, but without smiling, the sort of bow that I should have made to some one whom I scarcely knew, then proceeded in the opposite direction. Had I written a masterpiece, the Guermantes would have given me less credit for it than I earned by that bow. Not only did it not pass unperceived by the Duke, albeit he had that day to acknowledge the greetings of more than five hundred people, it caught the eye of the Duchess, who, happening to meet my mother, told her of it, and, so far from suggesting that I had done wrong, that I ought to have gone up to him, said that her husband had been lost in admiration of my bow, that it would have been impossible for anyone to put more into it. They never ceased to find in that bow every possible merit, without however mentioning that which had seemed the most priceless of all, to wit that it had been discreet, nor did they cease either to pay me compliments which I understood to be even less a reward for the past than a hint for the future, after the fashion of the hint delicately conveyed to his pupils by the headmaster of a school: "Do not forget, my boys, that these prizes are intended not so much for you as for your parents, so that they may send you back next term." So it was that

Mme. de Marsantes, when some one from a different world entered her circle, would praise in his hearing the discreet people whom "you find at home when you go to see them, and who at other times let you forget their existence," as one warns by an indirect allusion a servant who has an unpleasant smell, that the practice of taking a bath is beneficial to the health.

While, before she had even left the entrance hall, I was talking to Mme. de Guermantes, I could hear a voice of a sort which, for the future, I was to be able to classify without the possibility of error. It was, in this particular instance, the voice of M. de Vaugoubert talking to M. de Charlus. A skilled physician need not even make his patient unbutton his shirt, nor listen to his breathing, the sound of his voice is enough. How often, in time to come, was my ear to be caught in a drawing-room by the intonation or laughter of some man, who, for all that, was copying exactly the language of his profession or the manners of his class, affecting a stern aloofness or a coarse familiarity, but whose artificial voice was enough to indicate: "He is a Charlus" to my trained ear, like the note of a tuning fork. At that moment the entire staff of one of the Embassies went past, pausing to greet M. de Charlus. For all that my discovery of the sort of malady in question dated only from that afternoon (when I had surprised M. de Charlus with Jupien) I should have had no need, before giving a diagnosis, to put questions, to auscultate. But M. de Vaugoubert, when talking to M. de Charlus, appeared uncertain. And yet he must have known what was in the air after the doubts of his adolescence. The invert believes himself to be the only one of his kind in the universe; it is only in later years that he imagines—another exaggeration—that the unique exception is the normal man. But, ambitious and timorous, M. de Vaugoubert had not for many years past surrendered himself to what would to him have meant pleasure. The career of diplomacy had had the same effect upon his life as a monastic profession. Combined with his assiduous frequentation of the School of Political Sciences, it had vowed him from his twentieth year to the chastity of a professing Christian. And so, as each of our senses loses its strength and vivacity, becomes atrophied when it is no longer exercised, M. de Vaugoubert, just as the civilised man is no longer capable of the feats of strength, of the acuteness of hearing of the cave-dweller, had lost that special perspicacity which was rarely at fault in M. de Charlus; and at official banquets, whether in Paris or abroad, the Minister Plenipotentiary was no longer capable of identifying those who, beneath the disguise of their uniform, were at heart his congeners. Certain names mentioned by M. de Charlus, indignant if he himself was cited for his peculiarities, but always delighted to give away those of other people, caused M. de Vaugoubert an exquisite surprise. Not that, after all these years, he dreamed of profiting by any windfall. But these rapid revelations, similar to those which in Racine's tragedies inform Athalie and Abner that Joas is of the House of David, that Esther, enthroned in the purple, comes of a Yiddish stock, changing the aspect of the X—— Legation, or of one or another department of the Ministry of Foreign Affairs, rendered those palaces as mysterious, in retrospect, as the Temple of Jerusalem or the Throne-room at Susa. At the sight of the youthful staff of this Embassy advancing in a body to shake hands with M. de Charlus, M. de Vaugoubert assumed the astonished air of Elise exclaiming, in *Esther:* "Great heavens! What a swarm of innocent beauties issuing from all sides presents itself to my gaze! How charming a modesty is depicted on their faces!" Then, athirst for more definite information, he cast at M. de Charlus a smiling glance fatuously interrogative and concupiscent: "Why, of course they are," said M. de Charlus with the knowing air of a learned man speaking to an ignoramus. From that instant M. de Vaugoubert (greatly to the annoyance of M. de Charlus) could not tear his eyes from these young secretaries whom the X—— Ambassador to France, an old stager, had not chosen blindfold. M. de Vaugoubert remained silent, I could only watch his eyes. But, being accustomed from my childhood to apply, even to what is voiceless, the language of the classics, I made M. de Vaugoubert's eyes repeat the lines in which Esther explains to Elise that Mardochée, in his zeal for his religion, has made it a rule that only those maidens who profess it shall be employed about the Queen's person. "And now his love for our nation has peopled this palace with daughters of Sion, young and tender flowers wafted by fate, transplanted like myself beneath a foreign sky. In a place set apart from profane eyes, he" (the worthy Ambassador) "devotes his skill and labour to shaping them."

At length M. de Vaugoubert spoke, otherwise than with his eyes. "Who knows," he said sadly, "that in the country where I live the same thing does not exist also?" "It is probable," replied M. de Charlus, "starting with King Theodosius, not that I know anything definite about him." "Oh, dear, no! Nothing of that sort!" "Then he has no right to look it so completely. Besides, he has all the little tricks. He had that 'my dear' manner, which I detest more than anything in the world. I should never dare to be seen walking in the street with him. Anyhow, you must know what he is, they all call him the White Wolf." "You are entirely mistaken about him. He is quite charming, all the same. The day on which the agreement with France was signed, the King kissed me. I have never been so moved." "That was the moment to tell him what you wanted." "Oh, good heavens! What an idea! If he were even to suspect such a thing! But I have no fear in that direction." A conversation which I could hear, for I was standing close by, and which made me repeat to myself: "The King unto this day knows not who I am, and this secret keeps my tongue still enchained."

This dialogue, half mute, half spoken, had lasted but a few moments, and I had barely entered the first of the drawing-rooms with the Duchesse de Guermantes when a little dark lady, extremely pretty, stopped her:

"I've been looking for you everywhere. D'Annunzio saw you from a box in the theatre, he has written the Princesse de T—— a letter in which he says that he never saw anything so lovely. He would give his life for ten minutes' conversation with you. In any case, even if you can't or won't, the letter is in my possession. You must fix a day to come and see me. There are some secrets which I cannot tell you here. I see you don't remember me," she added, turning to myself; "I met you at the Princesse de Parme's" (where I had never been). "The Emperor of Russia is anxious for your father to be sent to Petersburg. If you could come in on Monday,

Isvolski himself will be there, he will talk to you about it. I have a present for you, my dear," she went on, returning to the Duchess, "which I should not dream of giving to anyone but you. The manuscripts of three of Ibsen's plays, which he sent to me by his old attendant. I shall keep one and give you the other two."

The Duc de Guermantes was not overpleased by these offers. Uncertain whether Ibsen and D'Annunzio were dead or alive, he could see in his mind's eye a tribe of authors, playwrights, coming to call upon his wife and putting her in their works. People in society are too apt to think of a book as a sort of cube one side of which has been removed, so that the author can at once "put in" the people he meets. This is obviously disloyal, and authors are a pretty low class. Certainly, it would not be a bad thing to meet them once in a way, for thanks to them, when one reads a book or an article, one can "read between the lines," "unmask" the characters. After all, though, the wisest thing is to stick to dead authors. M. de Guermantes considered "quite all right" only the gentleman who did the funeral notices in the *Gaulois*. He, at any rate, confined himself to including M. de Guermantes among the people "conspicuous by their presence" at funerals at which the Duke had given his name. When he preferred that his name should not appear, instead of giving it, he sent a letter of condolence to the relatives of the deceased, assuring them of his deep and heartfelt sympathy. If, then, the family sent to the paper "among the letters received, we may mention one from the Duc de Guermantes," etc., this was the fault not of the ink-slinger but of the son, brother, father of the deceased whom the Duke thereupon described as upstarts, and with whom he decided for the future to have no further dealings (what he called, not being very well up in the meaning of such expressions, "having a crow to pick"). In any event, the names of Ibsen and D'Annunzio, and his uncertainty as to their survival, brought a frown to the brows of the Duke, who was not far enough away from us to escape hearing the various blandishments of Mme. Timoléon d'Amoncourt. This was a charming woman, her wit, like her beauty, so entrancing that either of them by itself would have made her shine. But, born outside the world in which she now lived, having aspired at first merely to a literary salon, the friend successively—and nothing more than a friend, for her morals were above reproach—and exclusively of every great writer, who gave her all his manuscripts, wrote books for her, chance having once introduced her into the Faubourg Saint-Germain, these literary privileges were of service to her there. She had now an established position, and no longer needed to dispense other graces than those that were shed by her presence. But, accustomed in times past to act as go-between, to render services, she persevered in them even when they were no longer necessary. She had always a state secret to reveal to you, a potentate whom you must meet, a watercolour by a master to present to you. There was indeed in all these superfluous attractions a trace of falsehood, but they made her life a comedy that scintillated with complications, and it was no exaggeration to say that she appointed prefects and generals.

As she strolled by my side, the Duchesse de Guermantes allowed the azure light of her eyes to float in front of her, but vaguely, so as to avoid the people with wnom she did not wish to enter into relations, whose presence she discerned at times, like a menacing reef in the distance. We advanced between a double hedge of guests, who, conscious that they would never come to know "Oriane," were anxious at least to point her out, as a curiosity, to their wives: "Quick, Ursule, come and look at Madame de Guermantes talking to that young man." And one felt that in another moment they would be clambering upon the chairs, for a better view, as at the Military Review on the 14th of July, or the Grand Prix. Not that the Duchesse de Guermantes had a more aristocratic salon than her cousin. The former's was frequented by people whom the latter would never have been willing to invite, principally on account of her husband. She would never have been at home to Mme. Alphonse de Rothschild, who, an intimate friend of Mme. de la Trémoïlle and of Mme. de Sagan, as was Oriane herself, was constantly to be seen in the house of the last-named. It was the same with Baron Hirsch, whom the Prince of Wales had brought to see her, but not to the Princess, who would not have approved of him, and also with certain outstandingly notorious Bonapartists or even Republicans, whom the Duchess found interesting but whom the Prince, a convinced Royalist, would not have allowed inside his house. His antisemitism also being founded on principle did not yield before any social distinction, however strongly accredited, and if he was at home to Swann, whose friend he had been since their boyhood, being, however, the only one of the Guermantes who addressed him as Swann and not as Charles, this was because, knowing that Swann's grandmother, a Protestant married to a Jew, had been the Duc de Berri's mistress, he endeavoured, from time to time, to believe in the legend which made out Swann's father to be a natural son of that Prince. By this hypothesis, which incidentally was false, Swann, the son of a Catholic father, himself the son of a Bourbon by a Catholic mother, was a Christian to his finger-tips.

"What, you don't know these glories?" said the Duchess, referring to the rooms through which we were moving. But, having given its due meed of praise to her cousin's "palace," she hastened to add that she a thousand times preferred her own "humble den." "This is an admirable house to *visit*. But I should die of misery if I had to stay behind and sleep in rooms that have witnessed so many historic events. It would give me the feeling of having been left after closing-time, forgotten, in the Chateau of Blois, or Fontainebleau, or even the Louvre, with no antidote to my depression except to tell myself that I was in the room in which Monaldeschi was murdered. As a sedative, that is not good enough. Why, here comes Mme. de Saint-Euverte. We've just been dining with her. As she is giving her great annual beanfeast to-morrow, I supposed she would be going straight to bed. But she can never miss a party. If this one had been in the country, she would have jumped on a lorry rather than not go to it."

As a matter of fact, Mme. de Saint-Euverte had come this evening, less for the pleasure of not missing another person's party than in order to ensure the success of her own, recruit the latest additions to her list, and, so to speak, hold an eleventh hour review of the troops who were on the morrow to perform such brilliant evolutions at her garden party. For, in the long course of years, the guests at the Saint-Euverte parties had almost entirely changed. The female celebrities of the Guermantes world, formerly so sparsely scattered, had—loaded with attentions by their hostess—begun gradually to bring their friends. At the same time, by an enterprise equally progressive, but in the opposite direction, Mme. de Saint-Euverte had, year by year, reduced the number of persons unknown to the world of fashion. You had ceased to see first one of them, then another. For some time the "batch" system was in operation, which enabled her, thanks to parties over which a veil of silence was drawn, to summon the ineligibles separately to entertain one another, which dispensed her from having to invite them with the nice people. What cause had they for complaint? Were they not given (*panem et circenses*) light refreshments and a select musical programme? And so, in a kind of symmetry with the two exiled duchesses whom, in years past, when the Saint-Euverte salon was only starting, one used to see holding up, like a pair of Caryatides, its unstable crest, in these later years one could distinguish, mingling with the fashionable throng, only two heterogeneous persons, old Mme. de Cambremer and the architect's wife with a fine voice who was always having to be asked to sing. But, no longer knowing anybody at Mme. de Saint-Euverte's, bewailing their lost comrades, feeling that they were in the way, they stood about with a frozen-to-death air, like two swallows that have not migrated in time. And so, the following year, they were not invited; Mme. de Franquetot made an attempt on behalf of her cousin, who was so fond of music. But as she could obtain for her no more explicit reply than the words: "Why, people can always come in and listen to music, if they like; there is nothing criminal about that!" Mme. de Cambremer did not find the invitation sufficiently pressing, and abstained.

Such a transformation having been effected by Mme. de Saint-Euverte, from a leper hospice to a gathering of great ladies (the latest form, apparently in the height of fashion, that it had assumed), it might seem odd that the person who on the following day was to give the most brilliant party of the season should need to appear overnight to address a last word of command to her troops. But the fact was that the pre-eminence of Mme. de Saint-Euverte's drawing-room existed only for those whose social life consists entirely in reading the accounts of afternoon and evening parties in the *Gaulois* or *Figaro,* without ever having been present at one. To these worldlings who see the world only as reflected in the newspapers, the enumeration of the British, Austrian, etc., Ambassadresses, of the Duchesses d'Uzès, de la Trémoïlle, etc., etc., was sufficient to make them instinctively imagine the Saint-Euverte drawing-room to be the first in Paris, whereas it was among the last. Not that the reports were mendacious. The majority of the persons mentioned had indeed been present. But each of them had come in response to entreaties, civilities, services, and with the sense of doing infinite honour to Mme. de Saint-Euverte. Such drawing-rooms, shunned rather than sought after, to which people are so to speak roped in, deceive no one but the fair readers of the "Society" column. They pass over a really fashionable party, the sort at which the hostess, who could have had all the duchesses in existence, they being athirst to be "numbered among the elect," invites only two or three and does not send any list of her guests to the papers. And so these hostesses, ignorant or contemptuous of the power that publicity has acquired to-day, are considered fashionable by the Queen of Spain but are overlooked by the crowd, because the former knows and the latter does not know who they are.

Mme. de Saint-Euverte was not one of these women, and, with an eye to the main chance, had come to gather up for the morrow everyone who had been invited. M. de Charlus was not among these, he had always refused to go to her house. But he had quarrelled with so many people that Mme. de Saint-Euverte might put this down to his peculiar nature.

Assuredly, if it had been only Oriane, Mme. de Saint-Euverte need not have put herself to the trouble, for the invitation had been given by word of mouth, and, what was more, accepted with that charming, deceiving grace in the exercise of which those Academicians are unsurpassed from whose door the candidate emerges with a melting heart, never doubting that he can count upon their support. But there were others as well. The Prince d'Agrigente, would he come? And Mme. de Durfort? And so, with an eye to business, Mme. de Saint-Euverte had thought it expedient to appear on the scene in person. Insinuating with some, imperative with others, to all alike she hinted in veiled words at inconceivable attractions which could never be seen anywhere again, and promised each that he should find at her party the person he most wished, or the personage he most wanted to meet. And this sort of function with which she was invested on one day in the year—like certain public offices in the ancient world—of the person who is to give on the morrow the biggest garden-party of the season conferred upon her a momentary authority. Her lists were made up and closed, so that while she wandered slowly through the Princess's rooms to drop into one ear after another: "You won't forget about me to-morrow," she had the ephemeral glory of turning away her eyes, while continuing to smile, if she caught sight of some horrid creature who was to be avoided or some country squire for whom the bond of a schoolboy friendship had secured admission to Gilbert's, and whose presence at her garden-party would be no gain. She preferred not to speak to him, so as to be able to say later on: "I issued my invitations verbally, and unfortunately I didn't see you anywhere." And so she, a mere Saint-Euverte, set to work with her gimlet eyes to pick and choose among the guests at the Princess's party. And she imagined herself, in so doing, to be every inch a Duchesse de Guermantes.

It must be admitted that the latter lady had not, either, whatever one might suppose, the unrestricted use of her greetings and smiles. To some extent, no doubt, when she withheld them, it was deliberately: "But the woman bores me to tears," she would say, "am I expected to talk to her about her party for the next hour?"

A duchess of swarthy complexion went past, whom her ugliness and stupidity, and certain irregularities of behaviour had exiled not from society as a whole but from certain small and fashionable circles. "Ah!" murmured Mme. de Guermantes, with the sharp, unerring glance of the connoisseur who is shewn a false jewel, "So they have that sort here?" By the mere sight of this semi-tarnished lady, whose face was burdened with a surfeit of moles from which black hairs sprouted, Mme. de Guermantes gauged the mediocre importance of this party. They had been brought up together, but she had severed all relations with the lady; and responded to her greeting only with the curtest little nod. " I cannot understand," she said to me, " how Marie-Gilbert can invite us with all that scum. You might say there was a deputation of paupers from every parish. Mélanie Pourtalès arranged things far better. She could have the Holy Synod and the Oratoire Chapel in her house if she liked, but at least she didn't invite us on the same day." But, in many cases, it was from timidity, fear of a scene with her husband, who did not like her to entertain artists and such like (Marie-Gilbert took a kindly interest in dozens of them, you had to take care not to be accosted by some illustrious German diva), from some misgivings, too, with regard to Nationalist feeling, which, inasmuch as she was endowed, like M. de Charlus, with the wit of the Guermantes, she despised from the social point of view (people were now, for the greater glory of the General Staff, sending a plebeian general in to dinner before certain dukes), but to which, nevertheless, as she knew that she was considered unsound in her views, she made liberal concessions, even dreading the prospect of having to offer her hand to Swann in these anti-semitic surroundings. With regard to this, her mind was soon set at rest, for she learned that the Prince had refused to have Swann in the house, and had had " a sort of an altercation " with him. There was no risk of her having to converse in public with " poor Charles," whom she preferred to cherish in private.

" And who in the world is that? " Mme. de Guermantes

exclaimed, upon seeing a little lady with a slightly lost air, in a black gown so simple that you would have taken her for a pauper, greet her, as did also the lady's husband, with a sweeping bow. She did not recognise the lady and, in her insolent way, drew herself up as though offended and stared at her without responding. "Who is that person, Basin?" she asked with an air of astonishment, while M. de Guermantes, to atone for Oriane's impoliteness, was bowing to the lady and shaking hands with her husband. "Why, it is Mme. de Chaussepierre, you were most impolite." "I have never heard of anybody called Chaussepierre." "Old mother Chanlivault's nephew." "I haven't the faintest idea what you're talking about. Who is the woman, and why does she bow to me?" "But you know her perfectly, she's Mme. de Charleval's daughter, Henriette Montmorency." "Oh, but I knew her mother quite well, she was charming, extremely intelligent. What made her go and marry all these people I never heard of? You say that she calls herself Mme. de Chaussepierre?" she said, isolating each syllable of the name with a questioning air, and as though she were afraid of making a mistake. "It is not so ridiculous as you appear to think, to call oneself Chaussepierre! Old Chaussepierre was the brother of the aforesaid Chanlivault, of Mme. de Sennecour and of the Vicomtesse de Merlerault. They're a good family." "Oh, do stop," cried the Duchess, who, like a lion-tamer, never cared to appear to be allowing herself to be intimidated by the devouring glare of the animal. "Basin, you are the joy of my life. I can't imagine where you picked up those names, but I congratulate you on them. If I did not know Chaussepierre, I have at least read

Balzac, you are not the only one, and I have even read Labiche. I can appreciate Chanlivault, I do not object to Charleval, but I must confess that Merlerault is a masterpiece. However, let us admit that Chaussepierre is not bad either. You must have gone about collecting them, it's not possible. You mean to write a book," she turned to myself, "you ought to make a note of Charleval and Merlerault. You will find nothing better." "He will find himself in the dock, and will go to prison; you are giving him very bad advice, Oriane." "I hope, for his own sake, that he has younger people than me at his disposal if he wishes to ask for bad advice; especially if he means to follow it. But if he means to do nothing worse than write a book!" At some distance from us, a wonderful, proud young woman stood out delicately from the throng in a white dress, all diamonds and tulle. Madame de Guermantes watched her talking to a whole group of people fascinated by her grace. "Your sister is the belle of the ball, as usual; she is charming to-night," she said, as she took a chair, to the Prince de Chimay who went past. Colonel de Froberville (the General of that name was his uncle) came and sat down beside us, as did M. de Bréauté, while M. de Vaugoubert, after hovering about us (by an excess of politeness which he maintained even when playing tennis when, by dint of asking leave of the eminent personages present before hitting the ball, he invariably lost the game for his partner) returned to M. de Charlus (until that moment almost concealed by the huge skirt of the Comtesse Molé, whom he professed to admire above all other women), and, as it happened, at the moment when several members of the latest diplomatic mission to Paris were greeting the Baron. At the sight of a young secretary with a particularly intelligent air, M. de Vaugoubert fastened on M. de Charlus a smile upon which there bloomed visibly one question only. M. de Charlus would, no doubt, readily have compromised some one else, but to feel himself compromised by this smile formed on another person's lips, which, moreover, could have but one meaning, exasperated him. "I know absolutely nothing about the matter, I beg you to keep your curiosity to yourself. It leaves me more than cold. Besides, in this instance, you are making a mistage of the first order. I believe this young man to be absolutely the opposite." Here M. de Charlus, irritated at being thus given away by a fool, was not speaking the truth. The secretary would, had the Baron been correct, have formed an exception to the rule of his Embassy. It was, as a matter of fact, composed of widely different personalities, many of them extremely second-rate, so that, if one sought to discover what could have been the motive of the selection that had brought them together, the only one possible seemed to be inversion. By setting at the head of this little diplomatic Sodom an Ambassador who on the contrary ran after women with the comic exaggeration of an old buffer in a revue, who made his battalion of male impersonators toe the line, the authorities seemed to have been obeying the law of contrasts. In spite of what he had beneath his nose, he did not believe in inversion. He gave an immediate proof of this by marrying his sister to a Chargé d'Affaires whom he believed, quite mistakenly, to be a womaniser. After this he became rather a nuisance and was soon replaced by a fresh Excellency who ensured the homogeneity of the party. Other Embassies sought to rival this one, but could never dispute the prize (as in the matriculation examinations, where a certain school always heads the list), and more than ten years had to pass before, heterogeneous attachés having been introduced into this too perfect whole, another might at last wrest the grim trophy from it and march at the head.

Reassured as to her fear of having to talk to Swann, Mme. de Guermantes felt now merely curious as to the subject of the conversation he had had with their host. "Do you know what it was about?" the Duke asked M. de Bréauté. "I did hear," the other replied, "that it was about a little play which the writer Bergotte produced at their house. It was a delightful show, as it happens. But it seems the actor made up as Gilbert, whom, as it happens, Master Bergotte had intended to take off." "Oh, I should have loved to see Gilbert taken off," said the Duchess, with a dreamy smile. "It was about this little performance," M. de Bréauté went on, thrusting forward his rodent jaw, "that Gilbert demanded an explanation from Swann, who merely replied what everyone thought very witty: 'Why, not at all, it wasn't the least bit like you, you are far funnier!' It appears, though," M. de Bréauté continued, "that the little play was quite delightful. Mme. Molé was there, she was immensely amused." "What, does Mme. Molé go there?" said the Duchess in astonishment. "Ah! That must be Mémé's doing. That is what always happens, in the end, to that sort of house. One fine day everybody begins to flock to it, and I, who have deliberately remained aloof, upon principle, find myself left to mope alone in my corner." Already, since M. de Bréauté's speech, the Duchesse de Guermantes (with regard if not to Swann's house, at least to the hypothesis of encountering him at any moment) had, as we see, adopted a fresh point of view. "The explanation that you have given us," said Colonel de Froberville to M. de Bréauté, "is entirely unfounded. I have good reason to know. The Prince purely and simply gave Swann a dressing down and would have him to know, as our forebears used to say, that he was not to shew his face in the house again, seeing the opinions he flaunts. And, to my mind, my uncle Gilbert was right a thousand times over, not only in giving Swann a piece of his mind, he ought to have finished six months ago with an out and out Dreyfusard."

Poor M. de Vaugoubert, changed now from a too cautious tennis-player to a mere inert tennis ball which is tossed to and fro without compunction, found himself projected towards the Duchesse de Guermantes to whom he made obeisance. He was none too well received, Oriane living in the belief that all the diplomats—or politicians—of her world were nincompoops.

M. de Froberville had greatly benefited by the social privileges that had of late been accorded to military men. Unfortunately, if the wife of his bosom was a quite authentic relative of the Guermantes, she was also an extremely poor one, and, as he himself had lost his fortune, they went scarcely anywhere, and were the sort of people who were apt to be overlooked except on great occasions, when they had the good fortune to bury or marry a relative. Then, they did really enter into communion with the world of fashion, like those nominal Catholics who approach the holy table but once in the year. Their material situation would indeed have been deplorable had not Mme. de Saint-Euverte, faithful to her affection for the late General de Froberville, done everything to help the household, providing frocks and entertainments for the two girls. But the Colonel, though generally considered a good fellow, had not the spirit of gratitude. He was envious of the splendours of a benefactress who extolled them herself without pause or measure. The annual garden party was for him, his wife and children, a marvellous pleasure which they would not have missed for all the gold in the world, but a pleasure poisoned by the thought of the joys of satisfied pride that Mme. de Saint-Euverte derived from it. The accounts of this garden party in the newspapers, which, after giving detailed reports, would add with Machiavellian guile: "We shall refer again to this brilliant gathering," the complementary details of the women's costume, appearing for several days in succession, all this was so obnoxious to the Frobervilles, that they, cut off from most pleasures and knowing that they could count upon the pleasure of this one afternoon, were moved every year to hope that bad weather would spoil the success of the party, to consult the barometer and to anticipate with ecstasy the threatenings of a storm that might ruin everything.

"I shall not discuss politics with you, Froberville," said M. de Guermantes, "but, so far as Swann is concerned, I can tell you frankly that his conduct towards ourselves has been beyond words. Introduced into society, in the past, by ourselves, by the Duc de Chartres, they tell me now that he is openly a Dreyfusard. I should never have believed it of him, an epicure, a man of practical judgment, a collector, who goes in for old books, a member of the Jockey, a man who enjoys the respect of all that know him, who knows all the good addresses, and used to send us the best port wine you could wish to drink, a dilettante, the father of a family. Oh! I have been greatly deceived. I do not complain for myself, it is understood that I am only an old fool, whose opinion counts for nothing, mere rag tag and bobtail, but if only for Oriane's sake, he ought to have openly disavowed the Jews and the partisans of the man Dreyfus.

"Yes, after the friendship my wife has always shewn him," went on the Duke, who evidently considered that to denounce Dreyfus as guilty of high treason, whatever opinion one might hold in one's own conscience as to his guilt, constituted a sort of thank-offering for the manner in which one had been received in the Faubourg Saint-Germain, "he ought to have disassociated himself. For, you can ask Oriane, she had a real friendship for him." The Duchess, thinking that an ingenuous, calm tone would give a more dramatic and sincere value to her words, said in a schoolgirl voice, as though she were simply letting the truth fall from her lips, merely giving a slightly melancholy expression to her eyes: "It is quite true, I have no reason to conceal the fact that I did feel a sincere affection for Charles!" "There, you see, I don't have to make her say it. And after that, he carries his ingratitude to the point of being a Dreyfusard!"

"Talking of Dreyfusards," I said, "it appears, Prince Von is one." "Ah, I am glad you reminded me of him," exclaimed M. de Guermantes, "I was forgetting that he had asked me to dine with him on Monday. But whether he is a Dreyfusard or not is entirely immaterial, since he is a foreigner. I don't give two straws for his opinion. With a Frenchman, it is another matter. It is true that Swann is a Jew. But, until to-day—forgive me, Froberville—I have always been foolish enough to believe that a Jew can be a Frenchman, that is to say, an honourable Jew, a man of the world. Now, Swann was that in every sense of the word. Ah, well! He forces me to admit that I have been mistaken, since he has taken the side of this Dreyfus (who, guilty or not, never moved in his world, he cannot ever have met him) against a society that had adopted him, had treated him as one of ourselves. It goes without saying, we were all of us prepared to vouch for Swann, I would have answered for his patriotism as for my own. Ah! He is rewarding us very badly: I must confess that I should never have expected such a thing from him. I thought better of him. He was a man of intelligence (in his own line, of course). I know that he had already made that insane, disgraceful marriage. By which token, shall I tell you some one who was really hurt by Swann's marriage: my wife. Oriane often has what I might call an affectation of insensibility. But at heart she feels things with extraordinary keenness." Mme. de Guermantes, delighted by this analysis of her character, listened to it with a modest air but did not utter a word, from a scrupulous reluctance to acquiesce in it, but principally from fear of cutting it short. M. de Guermantes might have gone on talking for an hour on this subject, she would have sat as still, or even stiller than if she had been listening to music. "Very well! I remember, when she heard of Swann's marriage, she felt hurt; she considered that it was wrong in a person to whom we had given so much friendship. She was very fond of Swann; she was deeply grieved. Am I not right, Oriane?" Mme. de Guermantes felt that she ought to reply to so direct a challenge, upon a point of fact, which would allow her, unobtrusively, to confirm the tribute which, she felt, had come to an end. In a shy and simple tone, and with an air all the more studied in that it sought to shew genuine "feeling," she said with a meek reserve, "It is true, Basin is quite right." "Still, that was not quite the same. After all, love is love, although, in my opinion, it ought to confine itself within certain limits. I might excuse a young fellow, a mere boy, for letting himself be caught by an infatuation. But Swann, a man of intelligence, of proved refinement, a good judge of pictures, an intimate friend of the Duc de Chartres, of Gilbert himself!" The tone in which M. de Guermantes said this was, for that matter, quite inoffensive, without a trace of the vulgarity which he too often shewed. He spoke with a slightly indignant melancholy, but everything about him was steeped in that gentle gravity which constitutes the broad and unctuous charm of certain portraits by Rembrandt, that of the Burgomaster Six, for example. One felt that the question of the immorality of Swann's conduct with regard to "the Case" never even presented itself to the Duke, so confident was he of the answer; it caused him the grief of a father who sees one of his sons, for whose education he has made the utmost sacrifices, deliberately ruin the magnificent position he has created for him and dishonour, by pranks which the principles or prejudices of his family cannot allow, a respected name. It is true that M. de Guermantes had not displayed so profound and pained an astonishment when he learned that Saint-Loup was a Dreyfusard. But, for one thing, he regarded his nephew as a young man gone astray, as to whom nothing, until he began to mend his ways, could be surprising, whereas Swann was what M. de Guermantes called "a man of weight, a man occupying a position in the front rank." Moreover and above all, a considerable interval of time had elapsed during which, if, from the historical point of view, events had, to some extent, seemed to justify the Dreyfusard argument, the anti-Dreyfusard opposition had doubled its violence, and, from being purely political, had become social. It was now a question of militarism, of patriotism, and the waves of anger that had been stirred up in society had had time to gather the force which they never have at the beginning of a storm. "Don't you see," M. de Guermantes went on, "even from the point of view of his beloved Jews, since he is absolutely determined to stand by them, Swann has made a blunder of an incalculable magnitude. He has shewn that they are to some extent forced to give their support to anyone of their own race, even if they do not know him personally. It is a public danger. We have evidently been too easy going, and the mistake Swann is making will create all the more stir since he was respected, not to say received, and was almost the only Jew that anyone knew. People will say: *Ab uno disce omnes.*" (His satisfaction at having hit, at the right moment, in his memory, upon so apt a quotation, alone brightened with a proud smile the melancholy of the great nobleman conscious of betrayal.)

I was longing to know what exactly had happened between the Prince and Swann, and to catch the latter, if he had not already gone home. "I don't mind telling you," the Duchess answered me when I spoke to her of this desire, "that I for my part am not over anxious to see him, because it appears, by what I was told just now at Mme. de Saint-Euverte's, that he would like me before he dies to make the acquaintance of his wife and daughter. Good heavens, it distresses me terribly that he should be ill, but, I must say, I hope it is not so serious as all that. And besides, it is not really a reason at all, because if it were it would be so childishly simple. A writer with no talent would have only to say: 'Vote for me at the Academy because my wife is dying and I wish to give her this last happiness.' There would be no more entertaining if one was obliged to make friends with all the dying people. My coachman might come to me with: 'My daughter is seriously ill, get me an invitation to the Princesse de Parme's.' I adore Charles, and I should hate having to refuse him, and so that is why I prefer to avoid the risk of his asking me. I hope with all my heart that he is not dying, as he says, but really, if it has to happen, it would not be the moment for me to make the acquaintance of those two creatures who have deprived me of the most amusing of my friends for the last fifteen years, with the additional disadvantage that I should not even be able to make use of their society to see him, since he would be dead!"

Meanwhile M. de Bréauté had not ceased to ruminate the contradiction of his story by Colonel de Froberville. "I do not question the accuracy of your version, my dear fellow," he said, "but I had mine from a good source. It was the Prince de la Tour d'Auvergne who told me."

"I am surprised that an educated man like yourself should still say 'Prince de la Tour d'Auvergne,'" the Duc de Guermantes broke in, "you know that he is nothing of the kind. There is only one member of that family left. Oriane's uncle, the Duc de Boullon."

"The brother of Mme. de Villeparisis?" I asked, remembering that she had been Mlle. de Bouillon. "Precisely. Oriane, Mme. de Lambresac is bowing to you." And indeed, one saw at certain moments form and fade like a shooting star a faint smile directed by the Duchesse de Lambresac at somebody whom she had recognised. But this smile, instead of taking definite shape in an active affirmation, in a language mute but clear, was drowned almost immediately in a sort of ideal ecstasy which expressed nothing, while her head drooped in a gesture of blissful benediction, recalling the inclination towards the crowd of communicants of the head of a somewhat senile prelate. There was not the least trace of senility about Mme. de Lambresac. But I was acquainted already with this special type of old-fashioned distinction. At Combray and in Paris, all my grandmother's friends were in the habit of greeting one another at a social gathering with as seraphic an air as if they had caught sight of some one of their acquaintance in church, at the moment of the Elevation or during a funeral, and were casting him a gentle "Good morning" which ended in prayer. At this point a remark made by M. de Guermantes was to complete the likeness that I was tracing. "But you have seen the Duc de Bouillon," he said to me. "He was just going out of my library this afternoon as you came in, a short person with white hair." It was the person whom I had taken for a man of business from Combray, and yet, now that I came to think it over, I could see the resemblance to Mme. de Villeparisis. The similarity between the evanescent greetings of the Duchesse de Lambresac and those of my grandmother's friends had first aroused my interest, by shewing me how in all narrow and exclusive societies, be they those of the minor gentry or of the great nobility, the old manners persist, allowing us to recapture, like an archaeologist, what might have been the standard of upbringing, and the side of life which it reflects, in the days of the Vicomte d'Arlincourt and Loïsa Puget. Better still now, the perfect conformity in appearance between a man of business from Combray of his generation and the Duc de Bouillon reminded me of what had already struck me so forcibly when I had seen Saint-Loup's maternal grandfather, the Duc de La Rochefoucauld, in a daguerreotype in which he was exactly similar, in dress, air and manner, to my great-uncle, that social, and even individual differences are merged when seen from a distance in the uniformity of an epoch. The truth is that the similarity of dress, and also the reflexion, from a person's face, of the spirit of his age occupy so much more space than his caste, which bulks largely only in his own self-esteem and the imagination of other people, that in order to discover that a great nobleman of the time of Louis Philippe differs less from a citizen of the time of Louis Philippe than from a great nobleman of the time of Louis XV, it is not necessary to visit the galleries of the Louvre.

At that moment, a Bavarian musician with long hair, whom the Princesse de Guermantes had taken under her wing, bowed to Oriane. She responded with an inclination of her head, but the Duke, furious at seeing his wife bow to a person whom he did not know, who had a curious style, and, so far as M. de Guermantes understood, an extremely bad reputation, turned upon his wife with a terrible inquisitorial air, as much as to say: "Who in the world is that Ostrogoth?" Poor Mme. de Guermantes's position was already distinctly complicated, and if the musician had felt a little pity for this martyred wife, he would have made off as quickly as possible. But, whether from a desire not to remain under the humiliation that had just been inflicted on him in public, before the eyes of the Duke's oldest and most intimate friends, whose presence there had perhaps been responsible to some extent for his silent bow, and to shew that it was on the best of grounds and not without knowing her already that he had greeted the Duchesse de Guermantes, or else in obedience to the obscure but irresistible impulse to commit a blunder which drove him—at a moment when he ought to have trusted to the spirit—to apply the whole letter of the law, the musician came closer to Mme. de Guermantes and said to her: "Madame la Duchesse, I should like to request the honour of being presented to the Duke." Mme. de Guermantes was indeed in a quandary. But after all, she might well be a forsaken wife, she was still Duchesse de Guermantes and could not let herself appear to have forfeited the right to introduce to her husband the people whom she knew. "Basin," she said, "allow me to present to you M. d'Herweck."

"I need not ask whether you are going to Madame de Saint-Euverte's to-morrow," Colonel de Froberville said to Mme. de Guermantes, to dispel the painful impression produced by M. d'Herweck's ill-timed request. "The whole of Paris will be there." Meanwhile, turning with a single movement and as though he were carved out of a solid block towards the indiscreet musician, the Duc de Guermantes, fronting his suppliant, monumental, mute, wroth, like Jupiter Tonans, remained motionless like this for some seconds, his eyes ablaze with anger and astonishment, his waving locks seeming to issue from a crater. Then, as though carried away by an impulse which alone enabled him to perform the act of politeness that was demanded of him, and after appearing by his attitude of defiance to be calling the entire company to witness that he did not know the Bavarian musician, clasping his white-gloved hands behind his back, he jerked his body forward and bestowed upon the musician a bow so profound, instinct with such stupefaction and rage, so abrupt, so violent, that the trembling artist recoiled, stooping as he went, so as not to receive a formidable butt in the stomach. "Well, the fact is, I shall not be in Paris," the Duchess answered Colonel de Froberville. "I may as well tell you (though I ought to be ashamed to confess such a thing) that I have lived all these years without seeing the windows at Montfort-l'Amaury. It is shocking, but there it is. And so, to make amends for my shameful ignorance, I decided that I would go and see them to-morrow." M. de Bréauté smiled a subtle smile. He quite understood that, if the Duchess had been able to live all these years without seeing the windows at Montfort-l'Amaury, this artistic excursion did not all of a sudden take on the urgent character of an expedition "hot-foot" and might without danger, after having been put off for more than twenty-five years, be retarded for twenty-four hours. The plan that the Duchess had formed was simply the Guermantes way of issuing the decree that the Saint-Euverte establishment was definitely not a "really nice" house, but a house to which you were invited that you might be utilised afterwards in the account in the *Gaulois,* a house that would set the seal of supreme smartness upon those, or at any rate upon her (should there be but one) who did not go to it. The delicate amusement of M. de Bréauté, enhanced by that poetical pleasure which people in society felt when they saw Mme. de Guermantes do things which their own inferior position did not allow them to imitate, but the mere sight of which brought to their lips the smile of the peasant thirled to the soil when he sees freer and more fortunate men pass by above his head, this delicate pleasure could in no way be compared with the concealed but frantic ecstasy that was at once felt by M. de Froberville.

The efforts that this gentleman was making so that people should not hear his laughter had made him turn as red as a turkey-cock, in spite of which it was only with a running interruption of hiccoughs of joy that he exclaimed in a pitying tone: "Oh! Poor Aunt Saint-Euverte, she will take to her bed! No! The unhappy woman is not to have her Duchess, what a blow, why, it is enough to kill her!" he went on, convulsed with laughter. And in his exhilaration he could not help stamping his feet and rubbing his hands. Smiling out of one eye and with the corner of her lips at M. de Froberville, whose amiable intention she appreciated, but found the deadly boredom of his society quite intolerable, Mme. de Guermantes decided finally to leave him.

"Listen, I shall be obliged to bid you good night," she said to him as she rose with an air of melancholy resignation, and as though it had been a bitter grief to her. Beneath the magic spell of her blue eyes her gently musical voice made one think of the poetical lament of a fairy. "Basin wants me to go and talk to Marie for a little." In reality, she was tired of listening to Froberville, who did not cease to envy her her going to Montfort-l'Amaury, when she knew quite well that he had never heard of the windows before in his life, nor for that matter would he for anything in the world have missed going to the Saint-Euverte party. "Good-bye, I've barely said a word to you, it is always like that at parties, we never see the people, we never say the things we should like to say, but it is the same everywhere in this life. Let us hope that when we are dead things will be better arranged. At any rate we shall not always be having to put on low dresses. And yet, one never knows. We may perhaps have to display our bones and worms on great occasions. Why not? Look, there goes old Rampillon, do you see any great difference between her and a skeleton in an open dress? It is true that she has every right to look like that, for she must be at least a hundred. She was already one of those sacred monsters before whom I refused to bow the knee when I made my first appearance in society. I thought she had been dead for years; which for that matter would be the only possible explanation of the spectacle she presents. It is impressive and liturgical; quite *Camposanto!*" The Duchess had moved away from Froberville; he came after her: "Just one word in your ear." Slightly annoyed: "Well, what is it now?" she said to him sitffly. And he, having been afraid lest, at the last moment, she might change her mind about Montfort-l'Amaury: "I did not like to mention it for Mme. de Saint-Euverte's sake, so as not to get her into trouble, but since you don't intend to be there, I may tell you that I am glad for your sake, for she has measles in the house!" "Oh, good gracious!" said Oriane, who had a horror of illnesses. "But that wouldn't matter to me, I've had them already. You can't get them twice." "So the doctors say; I know people who've had them four times. Anyhow, you are warned." As for himself, these fictitious measles would have needed to attack him in reality and to chain him to his bed before he would have resigned himself to missing the Saint-Euverte party to which he had looked forward for so many months. He would have the pleasure of seeing so many smart people there! The still greater pleasure of remarking that certain things had gone wrong, and the supreme pleasures of being able for long afterwards to boast that he had mingled with the former and, while exaggerating or inventing them, of deploring the latter.

I took advantage of the Duchess's moving to rise also in order to make my way to the smoking-room and find out the truth about Swann. "Do not believe a word of what Babal told us," she said to me. "Little Molé would never poke her nose into a place like that. They tell us that to draw us. Nobody ever goes to them and they are never asked anywhere either. He admits it himself: 'We spend the evenings alone by our own fire-side.' As he always says *we*, not like royalty, but to include his wife, I do not press him. But I know all about it," the Duchess added. We passed two young men whose great and dissimilar beauty took its origin from one and the same woman. They were the two sons of Mme. de Surgis, the latest mistress of the Duc de Guermantes. Both were resplendent with their mother's perfections, but each in his own way. To one had passed, rippling through a virile body, the royal presence of Mme. de Surgis and the same pallor, ardent, flushed and sacred, flooded the marble cheeks of mother and son; but his brother had received the Grecian brow, the perfect nose, the statuesque throat, the eyes of infinite depth; composed thus of separate gifts, which the goddess had shared between them, their twofold beauty offered one the abstract pleasure of thinking that the cause of that beauty was something outside themselves; one would have said that the principal attributes of their mother were incarnate in two different bodies; that one of the young men was his mother's stature and her complexion, the other her gaze, like those divine beings who were no more than the strength and beauty of Jupiter or Minerva. Full of respect for M. de Guermantes, of whom they said: "He is a great friend of our parents," the elder nevertheless thought that it would be wiser not to come up and greet the Duchess, of whose hostility towards his mother he was aware, though without perhaps understanding the reason for it, and at the sight of us he slightly averted his head. The younger, who copied his brother in everything, because, being stupid and short-sighted to boot, he did not venture to own a personal opinion, inclined his head at the same angle, and the pair slipped past us towards the card-room, one behind the other, like a pair of allegorical figures.

Just as I reached this room, I was stopped by the Marquise de Citri, still beautiful but almost foaming at the mouth. Of decently noble birth, she had sought and made a brilliant match in marrying M. de Citri, whose great-grandmother had been an Aumale-Lorraine. But no sooner had she tasted this satisfaction than her natural cantankerousness gave her a horror of people in society which did not cut her off absolutely from social life. Not only, at a party, did she deride everyone present, her derision of them was so violent that mere laughter was not sufficiently bitter, and changed into a guttural hiss. "Ah!" she said to me, pointing to the Duchesse de Guermantes who had now left my side and was already some way off, "what defeats me is that she can lead this sort of existence." Was this the speech of a righteously indignant Saint, astonished that the Gentiles did not come of their own accord to perceive the Truth, or that of an anarchist athirst for carnage? In any case there could be no possible justification for this apostrophe. In the first place, the "existence led" by Mme. de Guermantes differed hardly perceptibly (except in indignation) from that led by Mme. de Citri. Mme. de Citri was stupefied when she saw the Duchess capable of that mortal sacrifice: attendance at one of Marie-Gilbert's parties. It must be said in this particular instance that Mme. de Citri was genuinely fond of the Princess, who was indeed the kindest of women, and knew that, by attending her party, she was giving her great pleasure. And so she had put off, in order to come to the party, a dancer whom she regarded as a genius, and who was to have initiated her into the mysteries of Russian choreography. Another reason which to some extent stultified the concentrated rage which Mme. de Citri felt on seeing Oriane greet one or other of the guests was that Mme. de Guermantes, albeit at a far less advanced stage, shewed the symptoms of the malady that was devouring Mme. de Citri. We have seen, moreover, that she had carried the germs of it from her birth. In fact, being more intelligent than Mme. de Citri, Mme. de Guermantes would have had better right than she to this nihilism (which was more than merely social), but it is true that certain good qualities help us rather to endure the defects of our neighbour than they make us suffer from them; and a man of great talent will normally pay less attention to other people's folly than would a fool. We have already described at sufficient length the nature of the Duchess's wit to convince the reader that, if it had nothing in common with great intellect, it was at least wit, a wit adroit in making use (like a translator) of different grammatical forms. Now nothing of this sort seemed to entitle Mme. de Citri to look down upon qualities so closely akin to her own. She found everyone idiotic, but in her conversation, in her letters, shewed herself distinctly inferior to the people whom she treated with such disdain. She had moreover such a thirst for destruction that, when she had almost given up society, the pleasures that she then sought were subjected, each in turn, to her terrible disintegrating force. After she had given up parties for musical evenings, she used to say: "You like listening to that sort of thing, to music? Good gracious, it all depends on what it is. It can be simply deadly! Oh! Beethoven! What a bore!" With Wagner, then with Franck, Debussy, she did not even take the trouble to say the word *barbe,* but merely passed her hand over her face with a tonsorial gesture.

Presently, everything became boring. "Beautiful things are such a bore. Oh! Pictures! They're enough to drive one mad. How right you are, it is such a bore having to write letters!" Finally it was life itself that she declared to be *rasante,* leaving her hearers to wonder where she applied the term.

I do not know whether it was the effect of what the Duchesse de Guermantes, on the evening when I first dined at her house, had said of this interior, but the card, or smoking-room, with its pictorial floor, its tripods, its figures of gods and animals that gazed at you, the sphinxes stretched out along the arms of the chairs, and most of all the huge table, of marble or enamelled mosaic, covered with symbolical signs more or less imitated from Etruscan and Egyptian art, gave me the impression of a magician's cell. And, on a chair drawn up to the glittering, augural table, M. de Charlus, in person, never touching a card, unconscious of what was going on round about him, incapable of observing that I had entered the room, seemed precisely a magician applying all the force of his will and reason to drawing a horoscope. Not only that, but, like the eyes of a Pythian on her tripod, his eyes were starting from his head, and that nothing might distract him from labours which required the cessation of the most simple movements, he had (like a calculator who will do nothing else until he has solved his problem) laid down beside him the cigar which he had previously been holding between his lips, but had no longer the necessary detachment of mind to think of smoking. Seeing the two crouching deities borne upon the arms of the chair that stood facing him, one might have thought that the Baron was endeavouring the solve the enigma of the Sphinx, had it not been that, rather, of a young and living Oedipus, seated in that very armchair, where he had come to join in the game. Now, the figure to which M. de Charlus was applying with such concentration all his mental powers, and which was not, to tell the truth, one of the sort that are commonly studied *more geometrico*, was that of the proposition set him by the lineaments of the young Comte de Surgis; it appeared, so profound was M. de Charlus's absorption in front of it, to be some rebus, some riddle, some algebraical problem, of which he must try to penetrate the mystery or to work out the formula. In front of him the sibylline signs and the figures inscribed upon that Table of the Law seemed the gramarye which would enable the old sorcerer to tell in what direction the young man's destiny was shaping. Suddenly he became aware that I was watching him, raised his head as though he were waking from a dream, smiled at me and blushed. At that moment Mme. de Surgis's other son came up behind the one who was playing, to look at his cards. When M. de Charlus had learned from me that they were brothers, his features could not conceal the admiration that he felt for a family which could create masterpieces so splendid and so diverse. And what added to the Baron's enthusiasm was the discovery that the two sons of Mme. de Surgis-le-Duc were sons not only of the same mother but of the same father. The children of Jupiter are dissimilar, but that is because he married first Metis, whose destiny it was to bring into the world wise children, then Themis, and after her Eurynome, and Mnemosyne, and Leto, and only as a last resort Juno. But to a single father Mme. de Surgis had borne these two sons who had each received beauty from her, but a different beauty.

I had at length the pleasure of seeing Swann come into this room, which was very big, so big that he did not at first catch sight of me. A pleasure mingled with sorrow, with a sorrow which the other guests did not, perhaps, feel, their feeling consisting rather in that sort of fascination which is exercised by the strange and unexpected forms of an approaching death, a death that a man already has, in the popular saying, written on his face. And it was with a stupefaction that was almost offensive, into which entered indiscreet curiosity, cruelty, a scrutiny at once quiet and anxious (a blend of *suave mari magno* and *memento quia pulvis*, Robert would have said), that all eyes were fastened upon that face the cheeks of which had been so eaten away by disease, like a waning moon, that, except at a certain angle, the angle doubtless at which Swann looked at himself, they stopped short like a flimsy piece of scenery to which only an optical illusion can add the appearance of solidity. Whether because of the absence of those cheeks, no longer there to modify it, or because arterio-sclerosis, which also is a form of intoxication, had reddened it, as would drunkenness, or deformed it, as would morphine, Swann's punchinello nose, absorbed for long years in an attractive face, seemed now enormous, tumid, crimson, the nose of an old Hebrew rather than of a dilettante Valois. Perhaps too in him, in these last days, the race was making appear more pronounced the physical type that characterises it, at the same time as the sentiment of a moral solidarity with the rest of the Jews, a solidarity which Swann seemed to have forgotten throughout his life, and which, one after another, his mortal illness, the Dreyfus case and the anti-semitic propaganda had revived. There are certain Israelites, superior people for all that and refined men of the world, in whom there remain in reserve and in the wings, ready to enter at a given moment in their lives, as in a play, a bounder and a prophet. Swann had arrived at the age of the prophet. Certainly, with his face from which, by the action of his disease, whole segments had vanished, as when a block of ice melts and slabs of it fall off bodily, he had greatly altered. But I could not help being struck by the discovery how far more he had altered in relation to myself. This man, excellent, cultivated, whom I was far from annoyed at meeting, I could not bring myself to understand how I had been able to invest him long ago in a mystery so great that his appearance in the Champs-Elysées used to make my heart beat so violently that I was too bashful to approach his silk-lined cape, that at the door of the flat in which such a being dwelt I could not ring the bell without being overcome by boundless emotion and dismay; all this had vanished not only from his home, but from his person, and the idea of talking to him might or might not be agreeable to me, but had no effect whatever upon my nervous system.

And besides, how he had altered since that very afternoon, when I had met him—after all, only a few hours earlier—in the Duc de Guermantes's study. Had he really had a scene with the Prince, and had it left him crushed? The supposition was not necessary. The slightest efforts that are demanded of a person who is very ill quickly become for him an excessive strain. He has only to be exposed, when already tired, to the heat of a crowded drawing-room, for his countenance to decompose and turn blue, as happens in a few hours with an overripe pear or milk that is ready to turn. Besides, Swann's hair was worn thin in patches, and, as Mme. de Guermantes remarked, needed attention from the furrier, looked as if it had been camphored, and camphored badly. I was just crossing the room to speak to Swann when unfortunately a hand fell upon my shoulder:

"Hallo, old boy, I am in Paris for forty-eight hours. I called at your house, they told me you were here, so that it is to you that my aunt is indebted for the honour of my company at her party." It was Saint-Loup. I told him how greatly I admired the house. "Yes, it makes quite a historic edifice. Personally, I think it appalling. We mustn't go near my uncle Palamède, or we shall be caught. Now that Mme. Molé has gone (for it is she that is ruling the roast just now), he is quite at a loose end. It seems it was as good as a play, he never let her out of his sight for a moment, and only left her when he had put her safely into her carriage. I bear my uncle no ill will, only I do think it odd that my family council, which has always been so hard on me, should be composed of the very ones who have led giddy lives themselves, beginning with the giddiest of the lot, my uncle Charlus, who is my official guardian, has had more women than Don Juan, and is still carrying on in spite of his age. There was a talk at one time of having me made a ward of court. I bet, when all those gay old dogs met to consider the question, and had me up to preach to me and tell me that I was breaking my mother's heart, they dared not look one another in the face for fear of laughing. Just think of the fellows who formed the council, you would think they had deliberately chosen the biggest womanisers." Leaving out of account M. de Charlus, with regard to whom my friend's astonishment no longer seemed to me to be justified, but for different reasons, and reasons which, moreover, were afterwards to undergo modification in my mind, Robert was quite wrong in finding it extraordinary that lessons in worldly wisdom should be given to a young man by people who had done foolish things, or were still doing them.

Even if we take into account only atavism, family likenesses, it is inevitable that the uncle who delivers the lecture should have more or less the same faults as the nephew whom he has been deputed to scold. Nor is the uncle in the least hypocritical in so doing, taken in as he is by the faculty that people have of believing, in every fresh experience, that "this is quite different," a faculty which allows them to adopt artistic, political and other errors without perceiving that they are the same errors which they exposed, ten years ago, in another school of painters, whom they condemned, another political affair which, they considered, merited a loathing that they no longer feel, and espouse those errors without recognising them in a fresh disguise. Besides, even if the faults of the uncle are different from those of the nephew, heredity may none the less be responsible, for the effect does not always resemble the cause, as a copy resembles its original, and even if the uncle's faults are worse, he may easily believe them to be less serious.

When M. de Charlus made indignant remonstrances to Robert, who moreover was unaware of his uncle's true inclinations, at that time, and indeed if it had still been the time when the Baron used to scarify his own inclinations, he might perfectly well have been sincere in considering, from the point of view of a man of the world, that Robert was infinitely more to blame than himself. Had not Robert, at the very moment when his uncle had been deputed to make him listen to reason, come within an inch of getting himself ostracised by society, had he not very nearly been blackballed at the Jockey, had he not made himself a public laughing stock by the vast sums that he threw away upon a woman of the lowest order, by his friendships with people—authors, actors, Jews—not one of whom moved in society, by his opinions, which were indistinguishable from those held by traitors, by the grief he was causing to all his relatives? In what respect could it be compared, this scandalous existence, with that of M. de Charlus who had managed, so far, not only to retain but to enhance still further his position as a Guermantes, being in society an absolutely privileged person, sought after, adulated in the most exclusive circles, and a man who, married to a Bourbon Princess, a woman of eminence, had been able to ensure her happiness, had shewn a devotion to her memory more fervent, more scrupulous than is customary in society, and had thus been as good a husband as a son!

"But are you sure that M. de Charlus has had all those mistresses?" I asked, not, of course, with any diabolical intent of revealing to Robert the secret that I had surprised, but irritated, nevertheless, at hearing him maintain an erroneous theory with so much certainty and assurance. He merely shrugged his shoulders in response to what he took for ingenuousness on my part. "Not that I blame him in the least, I consider that he is perfectly right." And he began to sketch in outline a theory of conduct that would have horrified him at Balbec (where he was not content with denouncing seducers, death seeming to him then the only punishment adequate to their crime). Then, however, he had still been in love and jealous. He went so far as to sing me the praises of houses of assignation. "They're the only places where you can find a shoe to fit you, sheath your weapon, as we say in the regiment." He no longer felt for places of that sort the disgust that had inflamed him at Balbec when I made an allusion to them, and, hearing what he now said, I told him that Bloch had introduced me to one, but Robert replied that the one which Bloch frequented must be "extremely mixed, the poor man's paradise!—It all depends, though: where is it?" I remained vague, for I had just remembered that it was the same house at which one used to have for a louis that Rachel whom Robert had so passionately loved. "Anyhow, I can take you to some far better ones, full of stunning women." Hearing me express the desire that he would take me as soon as possible to the ones he knew, which must indeed be far superior to the house to which Bloch had taken me, he expressed a sincere regret that he could not, on this occasion, as he would have to leave Paris next day. "It will have to be my next leave," he said. "You'll see, there are young girls there, even," he added with an air of mystery. "There is a little Mademoiselle de . . . I think it's d'Orgeville, I can let you have the exact name, who is the daughter of quite tip-top people; her mother was by way of being a La Croix-l'Evêque, and they're a really decent family, in fact they're more or less related, if I'm not mistaken, to my aunt Oriane. Anyhow, you have only to see the child, you can tell at once that she comes of decent people" (I could detect, hovering for a moment over Robert's voice, the shadow of the genius of the Guermantes, which passed like a cloud, but at a great height and without stopping). "It seems to me to promise marvellous developments. The parents are always ill and can't look after her. Gad, the child must have some amusement, and I count upon you to provide it!" "Oh! When are you coming back?" "I don't know, if you don't absolutely insist upon Duchesses" (Duchess being in aristocracy the only title that denotes a particularly brilliant rank, as the lower orders talk of "Princesses"), "in a different class of goods, there is Mme. Putbus's maid."

At this moment, Mme. de Surgis entered the room in search of her sons. As soon as he saw her M. de Charlus went up to her with a friendliness by which the Marquise was all the more agreeably surprised, in that an icy frigidity was what she had expected from the Baron, who had always posed as Oriane's protector and alone of the family—the rest being too often inclined to forgive the Duke his irregularities by the glamour of his position and their own jealousy of the Duchess—kept his brother's mistresses pitilessly at a distance. And so Mme. de Surgis had fully understood the motives of the attitude that she dreaded to find in the Baron, but never for a moment suspected those of the wholly different welcome that she did receive from him. He spoke to her with admiration of the portrait that Jacquet had painted of her years before. This admiration waxed indeed to an enthusiasm which, if it was partly deliberate, with the object of preventing the Marquise from going away, of "hooking" her, as Robert used to say of enemy armies when you seek to keep their effective strength engaged at one point, might also be sincere. For, if everyone was delighted to admire in her sons the regal bearing and eyes of Mme. de Surgis, the Baron could taste an inverse but no less keen pleasure in finding those charms combined in the mother, as in a portrait which does not by itself excite desire, but feeds with the aesthetic admiration that it does excite the desires that it revives. These came now to give, in retrospect, a voluptuous charm to Jacquet's portrait itself, and at that moment the Baron would gladly have purchased it to study upon its surface the physiognomic pedigree of the two young Surgis.

"You see, I wasn't exaggerating," Robert said in my ear. "Just look at the way my uncle is running after Mme. de Surgis. Though I must say, that does surprise me. If Oriane knew, she would be furious. Really, there are enough women in the world without his having to go and sprawl over that one," he went on; like everybody who is not in love, he imagined that one chose the person whom one loved after endless deliberations and on the strength of various qualities and advantages. Besides, while completely mistaken about his uncle, whom he supposed to be devoted to women, Robert, in his rancour, spoke too lightly of M. de Charlus. We are not always somebody's nephew with impunity. It is often through him that a hereditary habit is transmitted to us sooner or later. We might indeed arrange a whole gallery of portraits, named like the German comedy: *Uncle and Nephew,* in which we should see the uncle watching jealously, albeit unconsciously, for his nephew to end by becoming like himself.

I go so far as to say that this gallery would be incomplete were we not to include in it the uncles who are not really related by blood, being the uncles only of their nephews' wives. The Messieurs de Charlus are indeed so convinced that they themselves are the only good husbands, what is more the only husbands of whom their wives are not jealous, that generally, out of affection for their niece, they make her marry another Charlus. Which tangles the skein of family likenesses. And, to affection for the neice, is added at times affection for her betrothed as well. Such marriages are not uncommon, and are often what are called happy.

"What were we talking about? Oh yes, that big, fair girl, Mme. Putbus's maid. She goes with women too, but I don't suppose you mind that, I can tell you frankly, I have never seen such a gorgeous creature." "I imagine her rather Giorgione?" "Wildly Giorgione! Oh, if I only had a little time in Paris, what wonderful things there are to be done! And then, one goes on to the next. For love is all rot, mind you, I've finished with all that." I soon discovered, to my surprise, that he had equally finished with literature, whereas it was merely with regard to literary men that he had struck me as being disillusioned at our last meeting. ("They're practically all a pack of scoundrels," he had said to me, a saying that might be explained by his justified resentment towards certain of Rachel's friends. They had indeed persuaded her that she would never have any talent if she allowed "Robert, scion of an alien race" to acquire an influence over her, and with her used to make fun of him, to his face, at the dinners to which he entertained them.) But in reality Robert's love of Letters was in no sense profound, did not spring from his true nature, was only a by-product of his love of Rachel, and he had got rid of it, at the same time as of his horror of voluptuaries and his religious respect for the virtue of women.

"There is something very strange about those two young men. Look at that curious passion for gambling, Marquise," said M. de Charlus, drawing Mme. de Surgis's attention to her own sons, as though he were completely unaware of their identity. "They must be a pair of Orientals, they have certain characteristic features, they are perhaps Turks," he went on, so as both to give further support to his feint of innocence and to exhibit a vague antipathy, which, when in due course it gave place to affability, would prove that the latter was addressed to the young men solely in their capacity as sons of Mme. de Surgis, having begun only when the Baron discovered who they were. Perhaps too M. de Charlus, whose insolence was a natural gift which he delighted in exercising, took advantage of the few moments in which he was supposed not to know the name of these two young men to have a little fun at Mme. de Surgis's expense, and to indulge in his habitual sarcasm, as Scapin takes advantage of his master's disguise to give him a sound drubbing.

"They are my sons," said Mme. de Surgis, with a blush which would not have coloured her cheeks had she been more discerning, without necessarily being more virtuous. She would then have understood that the air of absolute indifference or of sarcasm which M. de Charlus displayed towards a young man was no more sincere than the wholly superficial admiration which he shewed for a woman, did not express his true nature. The woman to whom he could go on indefinitely paying the prettiest compliments might well be jealous of the look which, while talking to her, he shot at a man whom he would pretend afterwards not to have noticed. For that look was not of the sort which M. de Charlus kept for women; a special look, springing from the depths, which even at a party could not help straying innocently in the direction of the young men, like the look in a tailor's eye which betrays his profession by immediately fastening upon your attire.

"Oh, how very strange!" replied M. de Charlus, not without insolence, as though his mind had to make a long journey to arrive at a reality so different from what he had pretended to suppose. "But I don't know them!" he added, fearing lest he might have gone a little too far in the expression of his antipathy, and have thus paralysed the Marquise's intention to let him make their acquaintance. "Would you allow me to introduce them to you?" Mme. de Surgis inquired timidly. "Why, good gracious, just as you please, I shall be delighted, I am perhaps not very entertaining company for such young people," M. de Charlus intoned with the air of hesitation and coldness of a person who is letting himself be forced into an act of politeness.

"Arnulphe, Victurnien, come here at once," said Mme. de Surgis. Victurnien rose with decision. Arnulphe, though he could not see where his brother was going, followed him meekly.

"It's the sons' turn, now," muttered Saint-Loup. "It's enough to make one die with laughing. He tries to curry favour with every one, down to the dog in the yard. It is all the funnier, as my uncle detests pretty boys. And just look how seriously he is listening to them. If it had been I who tried to introduce them to him, he would have given me what for. Listen, I shall have to go and say how d'ye do to Oriane. I have so little time in Paris that I want to try and see all the people here that I ought to leave cards on."

"What a well-bred air they have, what charming manners," M. de Charlus was saying. "You think so?" Mme. de Surgis replied, highly delighted.

Swann having caught sight of me came over to Saint-Loup and myself. His Jewish gaiety was less refined than his witticisms as a man of the world. "Good evening," he said to us. "Heavens! All three of us together, people will think it is a meeting of the Syndicate. In another minute they'll be looking for the safe!" He had not observed that M. de Beaucerfeuil was just behind his back and could hear what he said. The General could not help wincing. We heard the voice of M. de Charlus close beside us: "What, you are called Victurnien, after the *Cabinet des Antiques*," the Baron was saying, to prolong his conversation with the two young men. "By Balzac, yes," replied the elder Surgis, who had never read a line of that novelist's work, but to whom his tutor had remarked, a few days earlier, upon the similarity of his Christian name and d'Esgrignon's. Mme. de Surgis was delighted to see her son shine, and at M. de Charlus's ecstasy before such a display of learning.

"It appears that Loubet is entirely on our side, I have it from an absolutely trustworthy source," Swann informed Saint-Loup, but this time in a lower tone so as not to be overheard by the General. Swann had begun to find his wife's Republican connexions more interesting now that the Dreyfus case had become his chief preoccupation. "I tell you this because I know that your heart is with us."

"Not quite to that extent; you are entirely mistaken," was Robert's answer. "It's a bad business, and I'm sorry I ever had a finger in it. It was no affair of mine.

If it were to begin over again, I should keep well clear of it. I am a soldier, and my first duty is to support the Army. If you will stay with M. Swann for a moment, I shall be back presently, I must go and talk to my aunt." But I saw that it was with Mlle. d'Ambresac that he went to talk, and was distressed by the thought that he had lied to me about the possibility of their engagement. My mind was set at rest when I learned that he had been introduced to her half an hour earlier by Mme. de Marsantes, who was anxious for the marriage, the Ambresacs being extremely rich.

"At last," said M. de Charlus to Mme. de Surgis, "I find a young man with some education, who has read, who knows what is meant by Balzac. And it gives me all the more pleasure to meet him where that sort of thing has become most rare, in the house of one of my peers, one of ourselves," he added, laying stress upon the words. It was all very well for the Guermantes to profess to regard all men as equal; on the great occasions when they found themselves among people who were "born," especially if they were not quite so well born as themselves, whom they were anxious and able to flatter, they did not hesitate to trot out old family memories. "At one time," the Baron went on, "the word aristocrat meant the best people, in intellect, in heart. Now, here is the first person I find among ourselves who has ever heard of Victurnien d'Esgrignon. I am wrong in saying the first. There are also a Polignac and a Montesquiou," added M. de Charlus, who knew that this twofold association must inevitably thrill the Marquise. "However, your sons have every reason to be learned, their maternal grandfather had a famous collection of eighteenth century stuff. I will shew you mine if you will do me the pleasure of coming to luncheon with me one day," he said to the young Victurnien. "I can shew you an interesting edition of the *Cabinet des Antiques* with corrections in Balzac's own hand. I shall be charmed to bring the two Victurniens face to face."

I could not bring myself to leave Swann. He had arrived at that stage of exhaustion in which a sick man's body becomes a mere retort in which we study chemical reactions. His face was mottled with tiny spots of Prussian blue, which seemed not to belong to the world of living things, and emitted the sort of odour which, at school, after the "experiments," makes it so unpleasant to have to remain in a "science" classroom. I asked him whether he had not had a long conversation with the Prince de Guermantes and if he would tell me what it had been about. "Yes," he said, "but go for a moment first with M. de Charlus and Mme. de Surgis, I shall wait for you here."

Indeed, M. de Charlus, having suggested to Mme. de Surgis that they should leave this room which was too hot, and go and sit for a little in another, had invited not the two sons to accompany their mother, but myself. In this way he made himself appear, after he had successfully hooked them, to have lost all interest in the two young men. He was moreover paying me an inexpensive compliment, Mme. de Surgis being in distinctly bad odour.

Unfortunately, no sooner had we sat down in an alcove from which there was no way of escape than Mme. de Saint-Euverte, a butt for the Baron's jibes, came past. She, perhaps to mask or else openly to shew her contempt for the ill will which she inspired in M. de Charlus, and above all to shew that she was on intimate terms with a woman who was talking so familiarly to him, gave a disdainfully friendly greeting to the famous beauty, who acknowledged it, peeping out of the corner of her eye at M. de Charlus with a mocking smile. But the alcove was so narrow that Mme. de Saint-Euverte, when she tried to continue, behind our backs, her canvass of her guests for the morrow, found herself a prisoner, and had some difficulty in escaping, a precious moment which M. de Charlus, anxious that his insolent wit should shine before the mother of the two young men, took good care not to let slip. A silly question which I had put to him, without malice aforethought, gave him the opportunity for a hymn of triumph of which the poor Saint-Euverte, almost immobilised behind us, could not have lost a word. "Would you believe it, this impertinent young man," he said, indicating me to Mme. de Surgis, "asked me just now, without any sign of that modesty which makes us keep such expeditions private, if I was going to Mme. de Saint-Euverte's, which is to say, I suppose, if I was suffering from the colic. I should endeavour, in any case, to relieve myself in some more comfortable place than the house of a person who, if my memory serves me, was celebrating her centenary when I first began to go about town, though not, of course, to her house. And yet who could be more interesting to listen to? What a host of historic memories, seen and lived through in the days of the First Empire and the Restoration, and secret history too, which could certainly have nothing of the "saint" about it, but must be decidedly "verdant" if we are to judge by the amount of kick still left in the old trot's shanks. What would prevent me from questioning her about those passionate times is the acuteness of my olfactory organ. The proximity of the lady is enough. I say to myself all at once: oh, good lord, some one has broken the lid of my cesspool, when it is simply the Marquise opening her mouth to emit some invitation. And you can understand that if I had the misfortune to go to her house, the cesspool would be magnified into a formidable sewage-cart. She bears a mystic name, though, which has always made me think with jubilation, although she has long since passed the date of her jubilee, of that stupid line of poetry called deliquescent: 'Ah, green, how green my soul was on that day. . . .' But I require a cleaner sort of verdure. They tell me that the indefatigable old street-walker gives 'garden-parties,' I should describe them as 'invitations to explore the sewers.' Are you going to wallow there?" he asked Mme. de Surgis, who this time was annoyed. Wishing to pretend for the Baron's benefit that she was not going, and knowing that she would give days of her life rather than miss the Saint-Euverte party, she got out of it by taking a middle course, that is to say uncertainty. This uncertainty took so clumsily amateurish, so sordidly material a form, that M. de Charlus, with no fear of offending Mme. de Surgis, whom nevertheless he was anxious to please, began to laugh to shew her that "it cut no ice with him."

"I always admire people who make plans," she said; "I often change mine at the last moment. There is a question of a summer frock which may alter everything. I shall act upon the inspiration of the moment."

For my part, I was furious at the abominable little speech that M. de Charlus had just made. I would have liked to shower blessings upon the giver of garden-parties. Unfortunately, in the social as in the political world, the victims are such cowards that one cannot for long remain indignant with their tormentors. Mme. de Saint-Euverte, who had succeeded in escaping from the alcove to which we were barring the entry, brushed against the Baron inadvertently as she passed him, and, by a reflex action of snobbishness which wiped out all her anger, perhaps even in the hope of securing an opening, at which this could not be the first attempt, exclaimed: "Oh! I beg your pardon, Monsieur de Charlus, I hope I did not hurt you," as though she were kneeling before her lord and master. The latter did not deign to reply save by a broad ironical smile, and conceded only a "Good evening," which, uttered as though he were only now made aware of the Marquise's presence after she had greeted him, was an insult the more. Lastly, with a supreme want of spirit which pained me for her sake, Mme. de Saint-Euverte came up to me and, drawing me aside, said in my ear: "Tell me, what have I done to offend M. de Charlus? They say that he doesn't consider me smart enough for him," she said, laughing from ear to ear. I remained serious. For one thing, I thought it stupid of her to appear to believe or to wish other people to believe that nobody, really, was as smart as herself. For another thing, people who laugh so heartily at what they themselves have said, when it is not funny, dispense us accordingly, by taking upon themselves the responsibility for the mirth, from joining in it.

"Other people assure me that he is cross because I do not invite him. But he does not give me much encouragement. He seems to avoid me." (This expression struck me as inadequate.) "Try to find out, and come and tell me to-morrow. And if he feels remorseful and wishes to come too, bring him. I shall forgive and forget. Indeed, I shall be quite glad to see him, because it will annoy Mme. de Surgis. I give you a free hand. You have the most perfect judgment in these matters and I do not wish to appear to be begging my guests to come. In any case, I count upon you absolutely."

It occurred to me that Swann must be getting tired of waiting for me. I did not wish, moreover, to be too late in returning home, because of Albertine, and, taking leave of Mme. de Surgis and M. de Charlus, I went in search of my sick man in the card-room. I asked him whether what he had said to the Prince in their conversation in the garden was really what M. de Bréauté (whom I did not name) had reported to us, about a little play by Bergotte. He burst out laughing: "There is not a word of truth in it, not one, it is entirely made up and would have been an utterly stupid thing to say. Really, it is unheard of, this spontaneous generation of falsehood. I do not ask who it was that told you, but it would be really interesting, in a field as limited as this, to work back from one person to another and find out how the story arose. Anyhow, what concern can it be of other people, what the Prince said to me? People are very inquisitive. I have never been inquisitive, except when I was in love, and when I was jealous. And a lot I ever learned! Are you jealous?" I told Swann that I had never experienced jealousy, that I did not even know what it was. "Indeed! I congratulate you. A little jealousy is not at all a bad thing, from two points of view. For one think, because it enables people who are not inquisitive to take an interest in the lives of others, or of one other at any rate. And besides, it makes one feel the pleasure of possession, of getting into a carriage with a woman, of not allowing her to go about by herself. But that occurs only in the very first stages of the disease, or when the cure is almost complete. In the interval, it is the most agonising torment. However, even the two pleasures I have mentioned, I must own to you that I have tasted very little of them: the first, by the fault of my own nature, which is incapable of sustained reflexion; the second, by force of circumstances, by the fault of the woman, I should say the women, of whom I have been jealous. But that makes no difference. Even when one is no longer interested in things, it is still something to have been interested in them; because it was always for reasons which other people did not grasp. The memory of those sentiments is, we feel, to be found only in ourselves; we must go back into ourselves to study it. You mustn't laugh at this idealistic jargon, what I mean to say is that I have been very fond of life and very fond of art. Very well! Now that I am a little too weary to live with other people, those old sentiments, so personal and individual, that I felt in the past, seem to me—it is the mania of all collectors—very precious. I open my heart to myself like a sort of showcase, and examine one by one ever so many love affairs of which the rest of the world can have known nothing. And of this collection, to which I am now even more attached than to my others, I say to myself, rather as Mazarin said of his library, but still without any keen regret, that it will be very tiresome to have to leave it all. But, to come back to my conversation with the Prince, I shall repeat it to one person only, and that person is going to be yourself." My attention was distracted by the conversation that M. de Charlus, who had returned to the card-room, was prolonging indefinitely close beside us. "And are you a reader too? What do you do?" he asked Comte Arnulphe, who had never heard even the name of Balzac. But his short-sightedness, as he saw everything very small, gave him the appearance of seeing to great distances, so that, rare poetry in a sculptural Greek god, there seemed to be engraved upon his pupils remote, mysterious stars.

"Suppose we took a turn in the garden, Sir," I said to Swann, while Comte Arnulphe, in a lisping voice which seemed to indicate that mentally at least his development was incomplete, replied to M. de Charlus with an artlessly obliging precision: "I, oh, golf chiefly, tennis, football, running, polo I'm really keen on." So Minerva, being subdivided, ceased in certain cities to be the goddess of wisdom, and incarnated part of herself in a purely sporting, horse-loving deity, Athene Hippia. And he went to Saint Moritz also to ski, for Pallas Trilogeneia frequents the high peaks and outruns swift horsemen. "Ah!" replied M. de Charlus with the transcendent smile of the intellectual who does not even take the trouble to conceal his derision, but, on the other hand, feels himself so superior to other people and so far despises the intelligence of those who are the least stupid, that he barely differentiates between them and the most stupid, the moment they can be attractive to him in some other way. While talking to Arnulphe, M. de Charlus felt that by the mere act of addressing him he was conferring upon him a superiority which everyone else must recognise and envy. "No," Swann replied, "I am too tired to walk about, let us sit down somewhere in a corner, I cannot remain on my feet any longer." This was true, and yet the act of beginning to talk had already given him back a certain vivacity. This was because, in the most genuine exhaustion, there is, especially in neurotic people, an element that depends upon attracting their attention and is kept going only by an act of memory. We at once feel tired as soon as we are afraid of feeling tired, and, to throw off our fatigue, it suffices us to forget about it. To be sure, Swann was far from being one of those indefatigable invalids who, entering a room worn out and ready to drop, revive in conversation like a flower in water and are able for hours on end to draw from their own words a reserve of strength which they do not, alas, communicate to their hearers, who appear more and more exhausted the more the talker comes back to life. But Swann belonged to that stout Jewish race, in whose vital energy, its resistance to death, its individual members seem to share. Stricken severally by their own diseases, as it is stricken itself by persecution, they continue indefinitely to struggle against terrible suffering which may be prolonged beyond every apparently possible limit, when already one sees nothing more than a prophet's beard surmounted by a huge nose which dilates to inhale its last breath, before the hour strikes for the ritual prayers and the punctual procession begins of distant relatives advancing with mechanical movements, as upon an Assyrian frieze.

We went to sit down, but, before moving away from the group formed by M. de Charlus with the two young Surgis and their mother, Swann could not resist fastening upon the lady's bosom the slow expansive concupiscent gaze of a connoisseur. He put up his monocle, for a better view, and, while he talked to me, kept glancing in the direction of the lady. "This is, word for word," he said to me when we were seated, "my conversation with the Prince, and if you remember what I said to you just now, you will see why I choose you as my confidant. There is another reason as well, which you shall one day learn.—'My dear Swann,' the Prince de Guermantes said to me, 'you must forgive me if I have appeared to be avoiding you for some time past.' (I had never even noticed it, having been ill and avoiding society myself.) 'In the first place, I had heard it said that, as I fully expected, in the unhappy affair which is splitting the country in two your views were diametrically opposed to mine. Now, it would have been extremely painful to me to have to hear you express them. So sensitive were my nerves that when the Princess, two years ago, heard her brother-in-law, the Grand Duke of Hesse, say that Dreyfus was innocent, she was not content with promptly denying the assertion but refrained from repeating it to me in order not to upset me. About the same time, the Crown Prince of Sweden came to Paris and, having probably heard some one say that the Empress Eugénie was a Dreyfusist, confused her with the Princess (a strange confusion, you will admit, between a woman of the rank of my wife and a Spaniard, a great deal less well born than people make out, and married to a mere Bonaparte), and said to her: Princess, I am doubly glad to meet you, for I know that you hold the same view as myself of the Dreyfus case, which does not surprise me since Your Highness is Bavarian. Which drew down upon the Prince the answer: Sir, I am nothing now but a French Princess, and I share the views of all my fellow-countrymen. Now, my dear Swann, about eighteen months ago, a conversation I had with General de Beaucerfeuil made me suspect that not an error, but grave illegalities had been committed in the procedure of the trial.' "

We were interrupted (Swann did not wish people to overhear his story) by the voice of M. de Charlus who (without, as it happened, paying us the slightest attention) came past escorting Mme. de Surgis, and stopped in the hope of detaining her for a moment longer, whether on account of her sons or from that reluctance common to all the Guermantes to bring anything to an end, which kept them plunged in a sort of anxious inertia. Swann informed me, in this connexion, a little later, of something that stripped the name Surgis-le-Duc, for me, of all the poetry that I had found in it. The Marquise de Surgis-le-Duc boasted a far higher social position, far finer connexions by marriage than her cousin the Comte de Surgis, who had no money and lived on his estate in the country. But the words that ended her title "le Duc" had not at all the origin which I ascribed to them, and which had made me associate it in my imagination with Bourg-l'Abbé, Bois-le-Roi, etc. All that had happened was that a Comte de Surgis had married, during the Restoration, the daughter of an immensely rich industrial magnate, M. Leduc, or Le Duc, himself the son of a chemical manufacturer, the richest man of his day, and a Peer of France. King Charles X had created for the son born of this marriage the Marquisate of Surgis-le-Duc, a Marquisate of Surgis existing already in the family.

The addition of the plebian surname had not prevented this branch from allying itself, on the strength of its enormous fortune, with the first families of the realm. And the present Marquise de Surgis-le-Duc, herself of exalted birth, might have moved in the very highest circles. A demon of perversity had driven her, scorning the position ready made for her, to flee from the conjugal roof, to live a life of open scandal. Whereupon the world which she had scorned at twenty, when it was at her feet, had cruelly failed her at thirty, when, after ten years, everybody, except a few faithful friends, had ceased to bow to her, and she set to work to reconquer laboriously, inch by inch, what she had possessed as a birthright. (An outward and return journey which are not uncommon.)

As for the great nobles, her kinsmen, whom she had disowned in the past, and who in their turn had now disowned her, she found an excuse for the joy that she would feel in gathering them again to her bosom in the memories of childhood that they would be able to recall. And in so saying, to cloak her snobbishness, she was perhaps less untruthful than she supposed. "Basin is all my girlhood!" she said on the day on which he came back to her. And as a matter of fact there was a grain of truth in the statement. But she had miscalculated when she chose him for her lover. For all the women friends of the Duchesse de Guermantes were to rally round her, and so Mme. de Surgis must descend for the second time that slope up which she had so laboriously toiled. "Well!" M. de Charlus was saying to her, in his attempt to prolong the conversation. "You will lay my tribute at the feet of the beautiful portrait. How is it? What has become of it?" "Why," replied Mme. de Surgis, "you know I haven't got it now; my husband wasn't pleased with it." "Not pleased! With one of the greatest works of art of our time, equal to Nattier's Duchesse de Châteauroux, and, moreover, perpetuating no less majestic and heart-shattering a goddess. Oh! That little blue collar! I swear, Vermeer himself never painted a fabric more consummately, but we must not say it too loud or Swann will fall upon us to avenge his favourite painter, the Master of Delft." The Marquise, turning round, addressed a smile and held out her hand to Swann, who had risen to greet her. But almost without concealment, whether in his declining days he had lost all wish for concealment, by indifference to opinion, or the physical power, by the excitement of his desire and the weakening of the control that helps us to conceal it, as soon as Swann, on taking the Marquise's hand, saw her bosom at close range and from above, he plunged an attentive, serious, absorbed, almost anxious gaze into the cavity of her bodice, and his nostrils, drugged by the lady's perfume, quivered like the wings of a butterfly about to alight upon a half-hidden flower. He checked himself abruptly on the edge of the precipice, and Mme. de Surgis herself, albeit annoyed, stifled a deep sigh, so contagious can desire prove at times. "The painter was cross," she said to M. de Charlus, "and took it back. I have heard that it is now at Diane de Saint-Euverte's." "I decline to believe," said the Baron, "that a great picture can have such bad taste."

"He is talking to her about her portrait. I could talk to her about that portrait just as well as Charlus," said Swann, affecting a drawling, slangy tone as he followed the retreating couple with his gaze. "And I should certainly enjoy talking about it more than Charlus," he added. I asked him whether the things that were said about M. de Charlus were true, in doing which I was lying twice over, for, if I had no proof that anybody ever had said anything, I had on the other hand been perfectly aware for some hours past that what I was hinting at was true. Swann shrugged his shoulders, as though I had suggested something quite absurd. "It's quite true that he's a charming friend. But, need I add, his friendship is purely platonic. He is more sentimental than other men, that is all; on the other hand, as he never goes very far with women, that has given a sort of plausibility to the idiotic rumours to which you refer. Charlus is perhaps greatly attached to his men friends, but you may be quite certain that the attachment is only in his head and in his heart. At last, we may perhaps be left in peace for a moment. Well, the Prince de Guermantes went on to say: 'I don't mind telling you that this idea of a possible illegality in the procedure of the trial was extremely painful to me, because I have always, as you know, worshipped the army; I discussed the matter again with the General, and, alas, there could be no two ways of looking at it. I don't mind telling you frankly that, all this time, the idea that an innocent man might be undergoing the most degrading punishment had never even entered my mind. But, starting from this idea of illegality, I began to study what I had always declined to read, and then the possibility not, this time, of illegal procedure but of the prisoner's innocence began to haunt me. I did not feel that I could talk about it to the Princess. Heaven knows that she has become just as French as myself. You may say what you like, from the day of our marriage, I took such pride in shewing her our country in all its beauty, and what to me is the most splendid thing in it, our Army, that it would have been too painful to me to tell her of my suspicions, which involved, it is true, a few officers only. But I come of a family of soldiers, I did not like to think that officers could be mistaken. I discussed the case again with Beaucerfeuil, he admitted that there had been culpable intrigues, that the *bordereau* was possibly not in Dreyfus's writing, but that an overwhelming proof of his guilt did exist. This was the Henry document. And, a few days later, we learned that it was a forgery. After that, without letting the Princess see me, I began to read the *Siècle* and the *Aurore* every day; soon I had no doubt left, it kept me awake all night. I confided my distress to our friend, the abbé Poiré, who, I was astonished to find, held the same conviction, and I got him to say masses for the intention of Dreyfus, his unfortunate wife and their children. Meanwhile, one morning as I was going to the Princess's room, I saw her maid trying to hide something from me that she had in her hand. I asked her, chaffingly, what it was, she blushed and refused to tell me. I had the fullest confidence in my wife, but this incident disturbed me considerably (and the Princess too, no doubt, who must have heard of it from her woman), for my dear Marie barely uttered a word to me that day at luncheon. I asked the abbé Poiré whether he could say my mass for Dreyfus on the following morning. . . .' And so much for that!" exclaimed Swann, breaking off his narrative. I looked up, and saw the Duc de Guermantes bearing down upon us. "Forgive me for interrupting you, boys. My lad," he went on, addressing myself, "I am instructed to give you a message from Oriane. Marie and Gilbert have asked her to stay and have supper at their table with only five or six other people: the Princess of Hesse, Mme. de Ligné, Mme. de Tarente, Mme. de Chevreuse, the Duchesse d'Arenberg. Unfortunately, we can't wait, we are going on to a little ball of sorts." I was listening, but whenever we have something definite to do at a given moment, we depute a certain person who is accustomed to that sort of duty to keep an eye on the clock and warn us in time. This indwelling servant reminded me, as I had asked him to remind me a few hours before, that Albertine, who at the moment was far from my thoughts, was to come and see me immediately after the theatre. And so I declined the invitation to supper. This does not mean that I was not enjoying myself at the Princesse de Guermantes's. The truth is that men can have several sorts of pleasure. The true pleasure is that for which they abandon the other. But the latter, if it is apparent, or rather if it alone is apparent, may put people off the scent of the other, reassure or mislead the jealous, create a false impression. And yet, all that is needed to make us sacrifice it to the other is a little happiness or a little suffering. Sometimes a third order of pleasures, more serious but more essential, does not yet exist for us, in whom its potential existence is indicated only by its arousing regrets, discouragement. And yet it is to these pleasures that we shall devote ourselves in time to come. To give an example of quite secondary importance, a soldier in time of peace will sacrifice a social existence to love, but, once war is declared (and without there being any need to introduce the idea of a patriotic duty), will sacrifice love to the passion, stronger than love, for fighting. It was all very well Swann's saying that he enjoyed telling me his story, I could feel that his conversation with me, because of the lateness of the hour, and because he himself was too ill, was one of those fatigues at which those who know that they are killing themselves by sitting up late, by overexerting themselves, feel when they return home an angry regret, similar to that felt at the wild extravagance of which they have again been guilty by the spendthrifts who will not, for all that, be able to restrain themselves to-morrow from throwing money out of the windows. After we have passed a certain degree of enfeeblement, whether it be caused by age or by ill health, all pleasure taken at the expense of sleep, in departure from our habits, every breach of the rules becomes a nuisance. The talker continues to talk, out of politeness, from excitement, but he knows that the hour at which he might still have been able to go to sleep has already passed, and he knows also the reproaches that he will heap upon himself during the insomnia and fatigue that must ensue. Already, moreover, even the momentary pleasure has come to an end, body and brain are too far drained of their strength to welcome with any readiness what seems to the other person entertaining. They are like a house on the morning before a journey or removal, where visitors become a perfect plague, to be received sitting upon locked trunks, with our eyes on the clock. "At last we are alone," he said; "I quite forget where I was. Oh yes, I had just told you, hadn't I, that the Prince asked the abbé Poiré if he could say his mass next day for Dreyfus. 'No, the abbé informed me' (I say *me* to you," Swann explained to me, "because it is the Prince who is speaking, you understand?), 'for I have another mass that I have been asked to say for him to-morrow as well.—What, I said to him, is there another Catholic as well as myself who is convinced of his innocence?—It appears so.—But this other supporter's conviction must be of more recent growth than mine.—Maybe, but this other was making me say masses when you still believed Dreyfus guilty.—Ah, I can see that it is not anyone in our world.—On the contrary!—Indeed! There are Dreyfusists among us, are there? You intrigue me; I should like to unbosom myself to this rare bird, if I know him.—You do know him. —His name?—The Princesse de Guermantes. While I was afraid of shocking the Nationalist opinions, the French faith of my dear wife, she had been afraid of alarming my religious opinions, my patriotic sentiments. But privately she had been thinking as I did, though for longer than I had. And what her maid had been hiding as she went into her room, what she went out to buy for her every morning, was the *Aurore*. My dear Swann, from that moment I thought of the pleasure that I should give you when I told you how closely akin my views upon this matter were to yours; forgive me for not having done so sooner. If you bear in mind that I had never said a word to the Princess, it will not surprise you to be told that thinking the same as yourself must at that time have kept me farther apart from you than thinking differently. For it was an extremely painful topic for me to approach. The more I believe that an error, that crimes even have been committed, the more my heart bleeds for the Army. It had never occurred to me that opinions like mine could possibly cause you similar pain, until I was told the other day that you were emphatically protesting against the insults to the Army and against the Dreyfusists for consenting to ally themselves with those who insulted it. That settled it, I admit that it has been most painful for me to confess to you what I think of certain officers, few in number fortunately, but it is a relief to me not to have to keep at armslength from you any longer, and especially that you should quite understand that if I was able to entertain other sentiments, it was because I had not a shadow of doubt as to the soundness of the verdict. As soon as my doubts began, I could wish for only one thing, that the mistake should be rectified.' I must tell you that this speech of the Prince de Guermantes moved me profoundly. If you knew him as I do, if you could realise the distance he has had to traverse in order to reach his present position, you would admire him as he deserves. Not that his opinion surprises me, his is such a straightforward nature!" Swann was forgetting that in the afternoon he had on the contrary told me that people's opinions as to the Dreyfus case were dictated by atavism. At the most he had made an exception in favour of intelligence, because in Saint-Loup it had managed to overcome atavism and had made a Dreyfusard of him. Now he had just seen that this victory had been of short duration and that Saint-Loup had passed into the opposite camp. And so it was to straightforwardness now that he assigned the part which had previously devolved upon intelligence. In reality we always discover afterwards that our adversaries had a reason for being on the side they espoused, which has nothing to do with any element of right that there may be on that side, and that those who think as we do do so because their intelligence, if their moral nature is too base to be invoked, or their straightforwardness, if their penetration is feeble, has compelled them.

Swann now found equally intelligent anybody who was of his opinion, his old friend the Prince de Guermantes and my schoolfellow Bloch, whom previously he had avoided and whom he now invited to luncheon. Swann interested Bloch greatly by telling him that the Prince de Guermantes was a Dreyfusard. "We must ask him to sign our appeal for Picquart; a name like his would have a tremendous effect." But Swann, blending with his ardent conviction as an Israelite the diplomatic moderation of a man of the world, whose habits he had too thoroughly acquired to be able to shed them at this late hour, refused to allow Bloch to send the Prince a circular to sign, even on his own initiative. "He cannot do such a thing, we must not expect the impossible," Swann repeated. "There you have a charming man who has travelled thousands of miles to come over to our side. He can be very useful to us. If he were to sign your list, he would simply be compromising himself with his own people, would be made to suffer on our account, might even repent of his confidences and not confide in us again." Nor was this all, Swann refused his own signature. He felt that his name was too Hebraic not to create a bad effect. Besides, even if he approved of all the attempts to secure a fresh trial, he did not wish to be mixed up in any way in the antimilitarist campaign. He wore, a thing he had never done previously, the decoration he had won as a young militiaman, in '70, and added a codicil to his will asking that, contrary to his previous dispositions, he might be buried with the military honours due to his rank as Chevalier of the Legion of Honour. A request which assembled round the church of Combray a whole squadron of those troopers over whose fate Françoise used to weep in days gone by, when she envisaged the prospect of a war. In short, Swann refused to sign Bloch's circular, with the result that, if he passed in the eyes of many people as a fanatical Dreyfusard, my friend found him lukewarm, infected with Nationalism, and a militarist.

Swann left me without shaking hands so as not to be forced into a general leave-taking in this room which swarmed with his friends, but said to me: "You ought to come and see your friend Gilberte. She has really grown up now and altered, you would not know her. She would be so pleased!" I was no longer in love with Gilberte. She was for me like a dead person for whom one has long mourned, then forgetfulness has come, and if she were to be resuscitated, she could no longer find any place in a life which has ceased to be fashioned for her. I had no desire now to see her, not even that desire to shew her that I did not wish to see her which, every day, when I was in love with her, I vowed to myself that I would flaunt before her, when I should be in love with her no longer.

And so, seeking now only to give myself, in Gilberte's eyes, the air of having longed with all my heart to meet her again and of having been prevented by circumstances of the kind called "beyond our control" albeit they only occur, with any certainty at least, when we have done nothing to prevent them, so far from accepting Swann's invitation with reserve, I would not let him go until he had promised to explain in detail to his daughter the mischances that had prevented and would continue to prevent me from going to see her. "Anyhow, I am going to write to her as soon as I go home," I added. "But be sure you tell her it will be a threatening letter, for in a month or two I shall be quite free, and then let her tremble, for I shall be coming to your house as regularly as in the old days."

Before parting from Swann, I said a word to him about his health. "No, it is not as bad as all that," he told me. "Still, as I was saying, I am quite worn out, and I accept with resignation whatever may be in store for me. Only, I must say that it would be most annoying to die before the end of the Dreyfus case. Those scoundrels have more than one card up their sleeves. I have no doubt of their being defeated in the end, but still they are very powerful, they have supporters everywhere. Just as everything is going on splendidly, it all collapses. I should like to live long enough to see Dreyfus rehabilitated and Picquart a colonel."

When Swann had left, I returned to the great drawing-room in which was to be found that Princesse de Guermantes with whom I did not then know that I was one day to be so intimate. Her passion for M. de Charlus did not reveal itself to me at first. I noticed only that the Baron, after a certain date, and without having taken one of those sudden dislikes, which were not surprising in him, to the Princesse de Guermantes, while continuing to feel for her just as strong an affection, a stronger affection perhaps than ever, appeared worried and annoyed whenever anyone mentioned her name to him. He never included it now in his list of the people whom he wished to meet at dinner.

It is true that before this time I had heard an extremely malicious man about town say that the Princess had completely changed, that she was in love with M. de Charlus, but this slander had appeared to me absurd and had made me angry. I had indeed remarked with astonishment that, when I was telling her something that concerned myself, if M. de Charlus's name cropped up in the middle, the Princess immediately screwed up her attention to the narrower focus of a sick man who, hearing us talk about ourselves, and listening, in consequence, in a careless and distracted fashion, suddenly realises that a name we have mentioned is that of the disease from which he is suffering, which at once interests and delights him. So, if I said to her: "Why, M. de Charlus told me . . ." the Princess at once gathered up the slackened reins of her attention. And having on one occasion said in her hearing that M. de Charlus had at that moment a warm regard for a certain person, I was astonished to see appear in the Princess's eyes that momentary change of colour, like the line of a fissure in the pupil, which is due to a thought which our words have unconsciously aroused in the mind of the person to whom we are talking, a secret thought that will not find expression in words, but will rise from the depths which we have stirred to the surface—altered for an instant—of his gaze. But if my remark had moved the Princess, I did not then suspect in what fashion.

Anyhow, shortly after this, she began to talk to me about M. de Charlus, and almost without ambiguity. If she made any allusion to the rumours which a few people here and there were spreading about the Baron, it was merely as though to absurd and scandalous inventions. But, on the other hand, she said: "I feel that any woman who fell in love with a man of such priceless worth as Palamède ought to have sufficient breadth of mind, enough devotion, to accept him and understand him as a whole, for what he is, to respect his freedom, humour his fancies, seek only to smooth out his difficulties and console him in his griefs." Now, by such a speech, vague as it was, the Princesse de Guermantes revealed the weakness of the character she was seeking to extol, just as M. de Charlus himself did at times. Have I not heard him, over and again, say to people who until then had been uncertain whether or not he was being slandered: "I, who have climbed many hills and crossed many valleys in my life, who have known all manner of people, burglars as well as kings, and indeed, I must confess, with a slight preference for the burglars, who have pursued beauty in all its forms," and so forth; and by these words which he thought adroit, and in contradicting rumours the currency of which no one suspected (or to introduce, from inclination, moderation, love of accuracy, an element of truth which he was alone in regarding as insignificant), he removed the last doubts of some of his hearers, inspired others, who had not yet begun to doubt him, with their first. For the most dangerous of all forms of concealment is that of the crime itself in the mind of the guilty party. His permanent consciousness of it prevents him from imagining how generally it is unknown, how readily a complete lie would be accepted, and on the other hand from realising at what degree of truth other people will detect, in words which he believes to be innocent, a confession. Not that he would not be entirely wrong in seeking to hush it up, for there is no vice that does not find ready support in the best society, and one has seen a country house turned upside down in order that two sisters might sleep in adjoining rooms as soon as their hostess learned that theirs was a more than sisterly affection. But what revealed to me all of a sudden the Princess's love was a trifling incident upon which I shall not dwell here, for it forms part of quite another story, in which M. de Charlus allowed a Queen to die rather than miss an appointment with the hairdresser who was to singe his hair for the benefit of an omnibus conductor who filled him with alarm. However, to be done with the Princess's love, let us say what the trifle was that opened my eyes. I was, on the day in question, alone with her in her carriage. As we were passing a post office she stopped the coachman. She had come out without a footman. She half drew a letter from her muff and was preparing to step down from the carriage to put it into the box. I tried to stop her, she made a show of resistance, and we both realised that our instinctive movements had been, hers compromising, in appearing to be guarding a secret, mine indiscreet, in attempting to pass that guard. She was the first to recover. Suddenly turning very red, she gave me the letter. I no longer dared not to take it, but, as I slipped it into the box, I could not help seeing that it was addressed to M. de Charlus.

To return to this first evening at the Princesse de Guermantes's, I went to bid her good-night, for her cousins, who had promised to take me home, were in a hurry to be gone. M. de Guermantes wished, however, to say good-bye to his brother, Mme. de Surgis having found time to mention to the Duke as she left that M. de Charlus had been charming to her and to her sons. This great courtesy on his brother's part, the first moreover that he had ever shewn in that line, touched Basin deeply and aroused in him old family sentiments which were never asleep for long. At the moment when we were saying good-bye to the Princess he was attempting, without actually thanking M. de Charlus, to give expression to his fondness for him, whether because he really found a difficulty in controlling it or in order that the Baron might remember that actions of the sort that he had performed this evening did not escape the eyes of a brother, just as, with the object of creating a chain of pleasant associations in the future, we give sugar to a dog that has done its trick. "Well, little brother!" said the Duke, stopping M. de Charlus and taking him lovingly by the arm, "so this is how one walks past one's elders and betters without so much as a word. I never see you now, Mémé, and you can't think how I miss you. I was turning over some old letters just now and came upon some from poor Mamma, which are all so full of love for you." "Thank you, Basin," replied M. de Charlus in a broken voice, for he could never speak without emotion of their mother. "You must make up your mind to let me fix up bachelor quarters for you at Guermantes," the Duke went on. "It is nice to see the two brothers so affectionate towards each other," the Princess said to Oriane. "Yes, indeed! I don't suppose you could find many brothers like that. I shall invite you to meet him," she promised me. "You've not quarrelled with him? . . . But what can they be talking about?" she added in an anxious tone, for she could catch only an occasional word of what they were saying. She had always felt a certain jealousy of the pleasure that M. de Guermantes found in talking to his brother of a past from which he was inclined to keep his wife shut out. She felt that, when they were happy at being together like this, and she, unable to restrain her impatient curiosity, came and joined them, her coming did not add to their pleasure. But this evening, this habitual jealousy was reinforced by another. For if Mme. de Surgis had told M. de Guermantes how kind his brother had been to her so that the Duke might thank his brother, at the same time certain devoted female friends of the Guermantes couple had felt it their duty to warn the Duchess that her husband's mistress had been seen in close conversation with his brother. And this information was torture to Mme. de Guermantes. "Think of the fun we used to have at Guermantes long ago," the Duke went on. "If you came down sometimes in summer we could take up our old life again. Do you remember old Father Courveau: 'Why is Pascal vexing? Because he is vec . . . vec . . .'" "*Said!*" put in M. de Charlus as though he were still answering his tutor's question. "And why is Pascal vexèd; because he is vec . . . because he is vec . . . *Sing!* Very good, you will pass, you are certain to be mentioned, and Madame la Duchesse will give you a Chinese dictionary." "How it all comes back to me, young Mémé, and the old china vase Hervey brought you from Saint-Denis, I can see it now. You used to threaten us that you would go and spend your life in China, you were so fond of the country; even then you used to love wandering about all night. Ah! You were a peculiar type, for I can honestly say that never in anything did you have the same tastes as other people. . . ." But no sooner had he uttered these words than the Duke flamed up, as the saying is, for he was aware of his brother's reputation, if not of his actual habits. As he never made any allusion to them before his brother, he was all the more annoyed at having said something which might be taken to refer to them, and more still at having shewn his annoyance. After a moment's silence: "Who knows," he said, to cancel the effect of his previous speech, "you were perhaps in love with a Chinese girl, before loving so many white ones and finding favour with them, if I am to judge by a certain lady to whom you have given great pleasure this evening by talking to her. She was delighted with you." The Duke had vowed that he would not mention Mme. de Surgis, but, in the confusion that the blunder he had just made had wrought in his ideas, he had fallen upon the first that occurred to him, which happened to be precisely the one that ought not to have appeared in the conversation, although it had started it. But M. de Charlus had observed his brother's blush. And, like guilty persons who do not wish to appear embarrassed that you should talk in their presence of the crime which they are supposed not to have committed, and feel that they ought to prolong a dangerous conversation: "I am charmed to hear it," he replied, "but I should like to go back to what you were saying before, which struck me as being profoundly true. You were saying that I never had the same ideas as other people, how right you are, you said that I had peculiar tastes." "No," protested M. de Guermantes who, as a matter of fact, had not used those words, and may not have believed that their meaning was applicable to his brother. Besides, what right had he to bully him about eccentricities which in any case were vague enough or secret enough to have in no way impaired the Baron's tremendous position in society? What was more, feeling that the resources of his brother's position were about to be placed at the service of his mistresses, the Duke told himself that this was well worth a little tolerance in exchange; had he at that moment known of some "peculiar" intimacy of his brother, M. de Guermantes would, in the hope of the support that the other was going to give him, have passed it over, shutting his eyes to it, and if need be lending a hand. "Come along, Basin; good night, Palamède," said the Duchess, who, devoured by rage and curiosity, could endure no more, "if you have made up your minds to spend the night here, we might just as well have stayed to supper. You have been keeping Marie and me standing for the last half-hour." The Duke parted from his brother after a significant pressure of his hand, and the three of us began to descend the immense staircase of the Princess's house.

On either side of us, on the topmost steps, were scattered couples who were waiting for their carriages to come to the door. Erect, isolated, flanked by her husband and myself, the Duchess kept to the left of the staircase, already wrapped in her Tiepolo cloak, her throat clasped in its band of rubies, devoured by the eyes of women and men alike, who sought to divine the secret of her beauty and distinction. Waiting for her carriage upon the same step of the stair as Mme. de Guermantes, but at the opposite side of it, Mme. de Gallardon, who had long abandoned all hope of ever receiving a visit from her cousin, turned her back so as not to appear to have seen her, and, what was more important, so as not furnish a proof of the fact that the other did not greet her. Mme. de Gallardon was in an extremely bad temper because some gentlemen in her company had taken it upon themselves to speak to her of Oriane: "I have not the slightest desire to see her," she had replied to them, "I did see her, as a matter of fact, just now, she is beginning to shew her age; it seems she can't get over it. Basin says so himself. And, good lord, I can understand that, for, as she has no brains, is as michievous as a weevil, and has shocking manners, she must know very well that, once her looks go, she will have nothing left to fall back upon."

I had put on my greatcoat, for which M. de Guermantes, who dreaded chills, reproached me, as we went down together, because of the heated atmosphere indoors. And the generation of noblemen which more or less passed through the hands of Mgr. Dupanloup speaks such bad French (except the Castellane brothers) that the Duke expressed what was in his mind thus: "It is better not to put on your coat before going out of doors, at least *as a general rule*." I can see all that departing crowd now, I can see, if I be not mistaken in placing him upon that staircase, a portrait detached from its frame, the Prince de Sagan, whose last appearance in society this must have been, baring his head to offer his homage to the Duchess, with so sweeping a revolution of his tall hat in his white-gloved hand (harmonising with the gardenia in his buttonhole), that one felt surprised that it was not a plumed felt hat of the old regime, several ancestral faces from which were exactly reproduced in the face of this great gentleman. He stopped for but a short time in front of her, but even his momentary attitudes were sufficient to compose a complete tableau vivant, and, as it were, an historical scene. Moreover, as he has since then died, and as I never had more than a glimpse of him in his lifetime, he has so far become for me a character in history, social history at least, that I am quite astonished when I think that a woman and a man whom I know are his sister and nephew.

While we were going downstairs, there came up, with an air of weariness that became her, a woman who appeared to be about forty, but was really older. This was the Princesse d'Orvillers, a natural daughter, it was said, of the Duke of Parma, whose pleasant voice rang with a vaguely Austrian accent. She advanced, tall, stooping, in a gown of white flowered silk, her exquisite, throbbing, cankered bosom heaving beneath a harness of diamonds and sapphires. Tossing her head like a royal palfrey embarrassed by its halter of pearls, of an incalculable value but an inconvenient weight, she let fall here and there a gentle, charming gaze, of an azure which, as time began to fade it, became more caressing than ever, and greeted most of the departing guests with a friendly nod "You choose a nice time to arrive, Paulette!" said the Duchess. "Yes, I am so sorry! But really it was a physical impossibility," replied the Princesse d'Orvillers, who had acquired this sort of expression from the Duchesse de Guermantes, but added to it her own natural sweetness and the air of sincerity conveyed by the force of a remotely Teutonic accent in so tender a voice. She appeared to be alluding to complications of life too elaborate to be related, and not merely to evening parties, although she had just come on from a succession of these. But it was not they that obliged her to come so late. As the Prince de Guermantes had for many years forbidden his wife to receive Mme. d'Orvillers, that lady, when the ban was withdrawn, contented herself with replying to the other's invitations, so as not to appear to be thirsting after them, by simply leaving cards. After two or three years of this method, she came in person, but very late, as though after the theatre. In this way she gave herself the appearance of attaching no importance to the party, nor to being seen at it, but simply of having come to pay the Prince and Princess a visit, for their own sakes, because she liked them, at an hour when, the great majority of their guests having already gone, she would "have them more to herself."

"Oriane has really sunk very low," muttered Mme. de Gallardon. "I cannot understand Basin's allowing her to speak to Mme. d'Orvillers. I am sure M. de Gallardon would never have allowed me." For my part, I had recognised in Mme. d'Orvillers the woman who, outside the Hôtel Guermantes, used to cast languishing glances at me, turn round, stop and gaze into shop windows. Mme. de Guermantes introduced me, Mme. d'Orvillers was charming, neither too friendly nor annoyed. She gazed at me as at everyone else out of her gentle eyes. . . . But I was never again, when I met her, to receive from her one of those overtures with which she had seemed to be offering herself. There is a special kind of glance, apparently of recognition, which a young man never receives from certain women—nor from certain men—after the day on which they have made his acquaintance and have learned that he is the friend of people with whom they too are intimate.

We were told that the carriage was at the door. Mme. de Guermantes gathered up her red skirt as though to go downstairs and get into the carriage, but, seized perhaps by remorse, or by the desire to give pleasure, and above all to profit by the brevity which the material obstacle to prolonging it imposed upon so boring an action, looked at Mme. de Gallardon; then, as though she had only just caught sight of her, acting upon a sudden inspiration, before going down tripped across the whole width of the step and, upon reaching her delighted cousin, held out her hand. "Such a long time," said the Duchess who then, so as not to have to develop all the regrets and legitimate excuses that this formula might be supposed to contain, turned with a look of alarm towards the Duke, who as a matter of fact, having gone down with me to the carriage, was storming with rage when he saw that his wife had gone over to Mme. de Gallardon and was holding up the stream of carriages behind. "Oriane is still very good looking, after all!" said Mme. de Gallardon. "People amuse me when they say that we have quarrelled; we may (for reasons which we have no need to tell other people) go for years without seeing one another, we have too many memories in common ever to be separated, and in her heart she must know that she cares far more for me than for all sorts of people whom she sees every day and who are not of her rank." Mme. de Gallardon was in fact like those scorned lovers who try desperately to make people believe that they are better loved than those whom their fair one cherishes. And (by the praises which, without heeding their contradiction of what she had been saying a moment earlier, she now lavished in speaking of the Duchesse de Guermantes) she proved indirectly that the other was thoroughly conversant with the maxims that ought to guide in her career a great lady of fashion who, at the selfsame moment when her most marvellous gown is exciting an admiration not unmixed with envy, must be able to cross the whole width of a staircase to disarm it. "Do at least take care not to wet your shoes" (a brief but heavy shower of rain had fallen), said the Duke, who was still furious at having been kept waiting.

On our homeward drive, in the confined space of the coupé, the red shoes were of necessity very close to mine, and Mme. de Guermantes, fearing that she might actually have touched me, said to the Duke: "This young man will have to say to me, like the person in the caricature: 'Madame, tell me at once that you love me, but don't tread on my feet like that.'" My thoughts, however, were far from Mme. de Guermantes. Ever since Saint-Loup had spoken to me of a young girl of good family who frequented a house of ill-fame, and of the Baroness Putbus's maid, it was in these two persons that were coalesced and embodied the desires inspired in me day by day by countless beauties of two classes, on the one hand the plebeian and magnificent, the majestic lady's maids of great houses, swollen with pride and saying "we" when they spoke of Duchesses, on the other hand those girls of whom it was enough for me sometimes, without even having seen them go past in carriages or on foot, to have read the names in the account of a ball for me to fall in love with them and, having conscientiously searched the year-book for the country houses in which they spent the summer (as often as not letting myself be led astray by a similarity of names), to dream alternately of going to live amid the plains of the West, the sandhills of the North, the pine-forests of the South. But in vain might I fuse together all the most exquisite fleshly matter to compose, after the ideal outline traced for me by Saint-Loup, the young girl of easy virtue and Mme. Putbus's maid, my two possessible beauties still lacked what I should never know until I had seen them: individual character. I was to wear myself out in seeking to form a mental picture, during the months in which I would have preferred a lady's maid, of the maid of Mme. Putbus. But what peace of mind after having been perpetually troubled by my restless desires, for so many fugitive creatures whose very names I often did not know, who were in any case so hard to find again, harder still to become acquainted with, impossible perhaps to captivate, to have subtracted from all that scattered, fugitive, anonymous beauty, two choice specimens duly labelled, whom I was at least certain of being able to procure when I chose. I kept putting off the hour for devoting myself to this twofold pleasure, as I put off that for beginning to work, but the certainty of having it whenever I chose dispensed me almost from the necessity of taking it, like those soporific tablets which one has only to have within reach of one's hand not to need them and to fall asleep. In the whole universe I desired only two women, of whose faces I could not, it is true, form any picture, but whose names Saint-Loup had told me and had guaranteed their consent. So that, if he had, by what he had said this evening, set my imagination a heavy task, he had at the same time procured an appreciable relaxation, a prolonged rest for my will.

"Well!" said the Duchess to me, "apart from your balls, can't I be of any use to you? Have you found a house where you would like me to introduce you?" I replied that I was afraid the only one that tempted me was hardly fashionable enough for her. "Whose is that?" she asked in a hoarse and menacing voice, scarcely opening her lips. "Baroness Putbus." This time she pretended to be really angry. "No, not that! I believe you're trying to make a fool of me. I don't even know how I come to have heard the creature's name. But she is the dregs of society. It's just as though you were to ask me for an introduction to my milliner. And worse than that, for my milliner is charming. You are a little bit cracked, my poor boy. In any case, I beg that you will be polite to the people to whom I have introduced you, leave cards on them, and go and see them, and not talk to them about Baroness Putbus of whom they have never heard." I asked whether Mme. d'Orvillers was not inclined to be flighty. "Oh, not in the least, you are thinking of some one else, why, she's rather a prude, if anything. Ain't she, Basin?" "Yes, in any case I don't thing there has ever been anything to be said about her," said the Duke.

"You won't come with us to the ball?" he asked me. "I can lend you a Venetian cloak and I know some one who will be damned glad to see you there—Oriane for one, that I needn't say—but the Princesse de Parme. She's never tired of singing your praises, and swears by you alone. It's fortunate for you—since she is a trifle mature—that she is the model of virtue. Otherwise she would certainly have chosen you as a sigisbee, as it was called in my young days, a sort of cavaliere servente.

I was interested not in the ball but in my appointment with Albertine. And so I refused. The carriage had stopped, the footman was shouting for the gate to be opened, the horses pawing the ground until it was flung apart and the carriage passed into the courtyard. "Till we meet again," said the Duke. "I have sometimes regretted living so close to Marie," the Duchess said to me, "because I may be very fond of her, but I am not quite so fond of her company. But have never regretted it so much as to-night, since it has allowed me so little of yours." "Come, Oriane, no speechmaking." The Duchess would have liked me to come inside for a minute. She laughed heartily, as did the Duke, when I said that I could not because I was expecting a girl to call at any moment. "You choose a funny time to receive visitors," she said to me.

"Come along, my child, there is no time to waste," said M. de Guermantes to his wife. "It is a quarter to twelve, and time we were dressed. . . ." He came in collision, outside his front door which they were grimly guarding, with the two ladies of the walking-sticks, who had not been afraid to descend at dead of night from their mountain-top to prevent a scandal. "Basin, we felt we must warn you, in case you were seen at that ball: poor Amanien has just passed away, an hour ago." The Duke felt a momentary alarm. He saw the delights of the famous ball snatched from him as soon as these accursed mountaineers had informed him of the death of M. d'Osmond. But he quickly recovered himself and flung at his cousins a retort into which he introduced, with his determination not to forego a pleasure, his incapacity to assimilate exactly the niceties of the French language: "He is dead! No, no, they exaggerate, they exaggerate!" And without giving a further thought to his two relatives who, armed with their alpenstocks, were preparing to make their nocturnal ascent, he fired off a string of questions at his valet:

"Are you sure my helmet has come?" "Yes, Monsieur le Duc." "You're sure there's a hole in it I can breathe through? I don't want to be suffocated, damn it!" "Yes, Monsieur le Duc." "Oh, thunder of heaven, this is an unlucky evening. Oriane, I forgot to ask Babal whether the shoes with pointed toes were for you!" "But, my dear, the dresser from the Opéra-Comique is here, he will tell us. I don't see how they could go with your spurs." "Let us go and find the dresser," said the Duke. "Good-bye, my boy, I should ask you to come in while we are trying on, it would amuse you. But we should only waste time talking, it is nearly midnight and we must not be late in getting there or we shall spoil the set."

I too was in a hurry to get away from M. and Mme. de Guermantes as quickly as possible. *Phèdre* finished at about half past eleven. Albertine must have arrived by now. I went straight to Françoise: "Is Mlle. Albertine in the house?" "No one has called."

Good God, that meant that no one would call! I was in torment, Albertine's visit seeming to me now all the more desirable, the less certain it had become.

Françoise was cross too, but for quite a different reason. She had just installed her daughter at the table for a succulent repast. But, on hearing me come in, and seeing that there was not time to whip away the dishes and put out needles and thread as though it were a work party and not a supper party: "She has just been taking a spoonful of soup," Françoise explained to me, "I forced her to gnaw a bit of bone," to reduce thus to nothing her daughter's supper, as though the crime lay in its abundance. Even at luncheon or dinner, if I committed the error of entering the kitchen, Françoise would pretend that they had finished, and would even excuse herself with: "I just felt I could eat a *scrap*," or "a *mouthful*." But I was speedily reassured on seeing the multitude of the plates that covered the table, which Françoise, surprised by my sudden entry, like a thief in the night which she was not, had not had time to conjure out of sight. Then she added: "Go along to your bed now, you have done enough work to-day" (for she wished to make it appear that her daughter not only cost us nothing, lived by privations, but was actually working herself to death in our service). "You are only crowding up the kitchen, and disturbing Master, who is expecting a visitor. Go on, upstairs," she repeated, as though she were obliged to use her authority to send her daughter to bed, who, the moment supper was out of the question, remained in the kitchen only for appearance's sake, and if I had stayed five minutes longer would have withdrawn of her own accord. And turning to me, in that charming popular and yet, somehow, personal French which was her spoken language: "Master doesn't see that her face is just cut in two with want of sleep." I remained, delighted at not having to talk to Françoise's daughter.

I have said that she came from a small village which was quite close to her mother's, and yet differed from it in the nature of the soil, its cultivation, in dialect; above all in certain characteristics of the inhabitants. Thus the "butcheress" and Françoise's niece did not get on at all well together, but had this point in common, that, when they went out on an errand, they would linger for hours at "the sister's" or "the cousin's," being themselves incapable of finishing a conversation, in the course of which the purpose with which they had set out faded so completely from their minds that, if we said to them on their return:

"Well! Will M. le Marquis de Norpois be at home at a quarter past six?" they did not even beat their brows and say: "Oh, I forgot all about it," but "Oh! I didn't understand that Master wanted to know that, I thought I had just to go and bid him good day." If they "lost their heads" in this manner about a thing that had been said to them an hour earlier, it was on the other hand impossible to get out of their heads what they had once heard said, by "the" sister or cousin. Thus, if the butcheress had heard it said that the English made war upon us in '70 at the same time as the Prussians, and I had explained to her until I was tired that this was not the case, every three weeks the butcheress would repeat to me in the course of conversation: "It's all because of that war the English made on us in '70, with the Prussians." "But I've told you a hundred times that you are wrong."—She would then answer, implying that her conviction was in no way shaken: "In any case, that's no reason for wishing them any harm. Plenty of water has run under the bridges since '70," and so forth. On another occasion, advocating a war with England which I opposed, she said: "To be sure, it's always better not to go to war; but when you must, it's best to do it at once. As the sister was explaining just now, ever since that war the English made on us in '70, the commercial treaties have ruined us. After we've beaten them, we won't allow one Englishman into France, unless he pays three hundred francs to come in, as we have to pay now to land in England."

Such was, in addition to great honesty and, when they were speaking, an obstinate refusal to allow any interruption, going back twenty times over to the point at which they had been interrupted, which ended by giving to their talk the unshakable solidity of a Bach fugue, the character of the inhabitants of this tiny village which did not boast five hundred, set among its chestnuts, its willows, and its fields of potatoes and beetroot.

Françoise's daughter, on the other hand, spoke (regarding herself as an up-to-date woman who had got out of the old ruts) Parisian slang and was well versed in all the jokes of the day. Françoise having told her that I had come from the house of a Princess: "Oh, indeed! The Princess of Brazil, I suppose, where the nuts come from." Seeing that I was expecting a visitor, she pretended to suppose that my name was Charles. I replied innocently that it was not, which enabled her to get in: "Oh, I thought it was! And I was just saying to myself, *Charles attend* (charlatan)." This was not in the best of taste. But I was less unmoved when, to console me for Albertine's delay, she said to me: "I expect you'll go on waiting till doomsday. She's never coming. Oh! Those modern flappers!"

And so her speech differed from her mother's; but, what is more curious, her mother's speech was not the same as that of her grandmother, a native of Bailleau-le-Pin, which was so close to Françoise's village. And yet the dialects differed slightly, like the scenery. Françoise's mother's village, scrambling down a steep bank into a ravine, was overgrown with willows. And, miles away from either of them, there was, on the contrary, a small district of France where the people spoke almost precisely the same dialect as at Méséglise. I made this discovery only to feel its drawbacks. In fact, I once came upon Françoise eagerly conversing with a neighbour's housemaid, who came from this village and spoke its dialect. They could more or less understand one another, I did not understand a word, they knew this but did not however cease (excused, they felt, by the joy of being fellow-countrywomen although born so far apart) to converse in this strange tongue in front of me, like people who do not wish to be understood. These picturesque studies in linguistic geography and comradeship belowstairs were continued weekly in the kitchen, without my deriving any pleasure from them.

Since, whenever the outer gate opened, the doorkeeper pressed an electric button which lighted the stairs, and since all the occupants of the building had already come in, I left the kitchen immediately and went to sit down in the hall, keeping watch, at a point where the curtains did not quite meet over the glass panel of the outer door, leaving visible a vertical strip of semi-darkness on the stair. If, all of a sudden, this strip turned to a golden yellow, that would mean that Albertine had just entered the building and would be with me in a minute; nobody else could be coming at that time of night. And I sat there, unable to take my eyes from the strip which persisted in remaining dark; I bent my whole body forward to make certain of noticing any change; but, gaze as I might, the vertical black band, despite my impassioned longing, did not give me the intoxicating delight that I should have felt had I seen it changed by a sudden and significant magic to a luminous bar of gold. This was a great to do to make about that Albertine to whom I had not given three minutes' thought during the Guermantes party! But, reviving my feelings when in the past I had been kept waiting by other girls, Gilberte especially, when she delayed her coming, the prospect of having to forego a simple bodily pleasure caused me an intense mental suffering.

I was obliged to retire to my room. Françoise followed me. She felt that, as I had come away from my party, there was no point in my keeping the rose that I had in my buttonhole, and approached to take it from me. Her action, by reminding me that Albertine was perhaps not coming, and by obliging me also to confess that I wished to look smart for her benefit, caused an irritation that was increased by the fact that, in tugging myself free, I crushed the flower and Françoise said to me: "It would have been better to let me take it than to go and spoil it like that." But anything that she might say exasperated me. When we are kept waiting, we suffer so keenly from the absence of the person for whom we are longing that we cannot endure the presence of anyone else.

When Françoise had left my room, it occurred to me that, if it only meant that now I wanted to look my best before Albertine, it was a pity that I had so many times let her see me unshaved, with several days' growth of beard, on the evenings when I let her come in to renew our caresses. I felt that she took no interest in me and was giving me the cold shoulder. To make my room look a little brighter, in case Albertine should still come, and because it was one of the prettiest things that I possessed, I set out, for the first time for years, on the table by my bed, the turquoise-studded cover which Gilberte had had made for me to hold Bergotte's pamphlet, and which, for so long a time, I had insisted on keeping by me while I slept, with the agate marble. Besides, as much perhaps as Albertine herself, who still did not come, her presence at that moment in an "alibi" which she had evidently found more attractive, and of which I knew nothing, gave me a painful feeling which, in spite of what I had said, barely an hour before, to Swann, as to my incapacity for being jealous, might, if I had seen my friend at less protracted intervals, have changed into an anxious need to know where, with whom, she was spending her time. I dared not send round to Albertine's house, it was too late, but in the hope that, having supper perhaps with some other girls, in a café, she might take it into her head to telephone to me, I turned the switch and, restoring the connexion to my own room, cut it off between the post office and the porter's lodge to which it was generally switched at that hour. A receiver in the little passage on which Françoise's room opened would have been simpler, less inconvenient, but useless. The advance of civilisation enables each of us to display unsuspected merits or fresh defects which make him dearer or more insupportable to his friends. Thus Dr. Bell's invention had enabled Françoise to acquire an additional defect, which was that of refusing, however important, however urgent the occasion might be, to make use of the telephone. She would manage to disappear whenever anybody was going to teach her how to use it, as people disappear when it is time for them to be vaccinated. And so the telephone was installed in my bedroom, and, that it might not disturb my parents, a rattle had been substituted for the bell. I did not move, for fear of not hearing it sound. So motionless did I remain that, for the first time for months, I noticed the tick of the clock. Françoise came in to make the room tidy. She began talking to me, but I hated her conversation, beneath the uniformly trivial continuity of which my feelings were changing from one minute to another, passing from fear to anxiety; from anxiety to complete disappointment. Belying the words of vague satisfaction which I thought myself obliged to address to her, I could feel that my face was so wretched that I pretended to be suffering from rheumatism, to account for the discrepancy between my feigned indifference and my woebegone expression; besides, I was afraid that her talk, which, for that matter, Françoise carried on in an undertone (not on account of Albertine, for she considered that all possibility of her coming was long past), might prevent me from hearing the saving call which now would not sound. At length Françoise went off to bed; I dismissed her with an abrupt civility, so that the noise she made in leaving the room should not drown that of the telephone. And I settled down again to listen, to suffer; when we are kept waiting, from the ear which takes in sounds to the mind which dissects and analyses them, and from the mind to the heart, to which it transmits its results, the double journey is so rapid that we cannot even detect its course, and imagine that we have been listening directly with our heart.

I was tortured by the incessant recurrence of my longing, ever more anxious and never to be gratified, for the sound of a call; arrived at the culminating point of a tortuous ascent through the coils of my lonely anguish, from the heart of the populous, nocturnal Paris that had suddenly come close to me, there beside my bookcase, I heard all at once, mechanical and sublime, like, in *Tristan*, the fluttering veil or the shepherd's pipe, the purr of the telephone. I sprang to the instrument, it was Albertine. "I'm not disturbing you, ringing you up at this hour?" "Not at all . . ." I said, restraining my joy, for her remark about the lateness of the hour was doubtless meant as an apology for coming, in a moment, so late, and did not mean that she was not coming. "Are you coming round?" I asked in a tone of indifference. "Why . . . no, unless you absolutely must see me."

Part of me which the other part sought to join was in Albertine. It was essential that she came, but I did not tell her so at first; now that we were in communication, I said to myself that I could always oblige her at the last moment either to come to me or to let me hasten to her. "Yes, I am near home," she said, "and miles away from you; I hadn't read your note properly. I have just found it again and was afraid you might be waiting up for me." I felt sure that she was lying, and it was now, in my fury, from a desire not so much to see her as to upset her plans that I determined to make her come. But I felt it better to refuse at first what in a few moments I should try to obtain from her. But where was she? With the sound of her voice were blended other sounds: the braying of a bicyclist's horn, a woman's voice singing, a brass band in the distance rang out as distinctly as the beloved voice, as though to shew me that it was indeed Albertine in her actual surroundings who was beside me at that moment, like a clod of earth with which we have carried away all the grass that was growing from it. The same sounds that I heard were striking her ear also, and were distracting her attention: details of truth, extraneous to the subject under discussion, valueless in themselves, all the more necessary to our perception of the miracle for what it was; elements sober and charming, descriptive of some street in Paris, elements heart-rending also and cruel of some unknown festivity which, after she came away from *Phèdre,* had prevented Albertine from coming to me. "I must warn you first of all that I don't in the least want you to come, because, at this time of night, it will be a frightful nuisance . . ." I said to her, "I'm dropping with sleep. Besides, oh, well, there are endless complications. I am bound to say that there was no possibility of your misunderstanding my letter. You answered that it was all right. Very well, if you hadn't understood, what did you mean by that?" "I said it was all right, only I couldn't quite remember what we had arranged. But I see you're cross with me, I'm sorry. I wish now I'd never gone to *Phèdre.* If I'd known there was going to be all this fuss about it . . ." she went on, as people invariably do when, being in the wrong over one thing, they pretend to suppose that they are being blamed for another. "I am not in the least annoyed about *Phèdre,* seeing it was I that asked you to go to it." "Then you are angry with me;

it's a nuisance it's so late now, otherwise I should have come to you, but I shall call to-morrow or the day after and make it up." "Oh, please, Albertine, I beg of you not to, after making me waste an entire evening, the least you can do is to leave me in peace for the next few days. I shan't be free for a fortnight or three weeks. Listen, if it worries you to think that we seem to be parting in anger, and perhaps you are right, after all, then I greatly prefer, all things considered, since I have been waiting for you all this time and you have not gone home yet, that you should come at once. I shall take a cup of coffee to keep myself awake." "Couldn't you possibly put it off till to-morrow? Because the trouble is. . . ." As I listened to these words of deprecation, uttered as though she did not intend to come, I felt that, with the longing to see again the velvet-blooming face which in the past, at Balbec, used to point all my days to the moment when, by the mauve September sea, I should be walking by the side of that roseate flower, a very different element was painfully endeavouring to combine. This terrible need of a person, at Combray I had learned to know it in the case of my mother, and to the pitch of wanting to die if she sent word to me by Françoise that she could not come upstairs. This effort on the part of the old sentiment, to combine and form but a single element with the other, more recent, which had for its voluptuous object only the coloured surface, the rosy complexion of a flower of the beach, this effort results often only in creating (in the chemical sense) a new body, which can last for but a few moments. This evening, at any rate, and for long afterwards, the two elements remained apart. But already, from the last words that had reached me over the telephone, I was beginning to understand that Albertine's life was situated (not in a material sense, of course) at so great a distance from mine that I should always have to make a strenuous exploration before I could lay my hand on her, and, what was more, organised like a system of earthworks, and, for greater security, after the fashion which, at a later period, we learned to call camouflaged. Albertine, in fact, belonged, although at a slightly higher social level, to that class of persons to whom their door-keeper promises your messenger that she will deliver your letter when she comes in (until the day when you realise that it is precisely she, the person whom you met out of doors, and to whom you have allowed yourself to write, who is the door-keeper. So that she does indeed live (but in the lodge, only) at the address she has given you, which for that matter is that of a private brothel, in which the door-keeper acts as pander), or who gives as her address a house where she is known to accomplices who will not betray her secret to you, from which your letters will be forwarded to her, but in which she does not live, keeps at the most a few articles of toilet. Lives entrenched behind five or six lines of defence, so that when you try to see the woman, or to find out about her, you invariably arrive too far to the right, or to the left, or too early, or too late, and may remain for months on end, for years even, knowing nothing. About Albertine, I felt that I should never find out anything, that, out of that tangled mass of details of fact and falsehood, I should never unravel the truth: and that it would always be so, unless I were to shut her up in prison (but prisoners escape) until the end. This evening, this conviction gave me only a vague uneasiness, in which however I could detect a shuddering anticipation of long periods of suffering to come.

"No," I replied, "I told you a moment ago that I should not be free for the next three weeks—no more tomorrow than any other day." "Very well, in that case . . . I shall come this very instant . . . it's a nuisance, because I am at a friend's house, and she. . . ." I saw that she had not believed that I would accept her offer to come, which therefore was not sincere, and I decided to force her hand. "What do you suppose I care about your friend, either come or don't, it's for you to decide, it wasn't I that asked you to come, it was you who suggested it to me." "Don't be angry with me, I am going to jump into a cab now and shall be with you in ten minutes." And so from that Paris out of whose murky depths there had already emanated as far as my room, delimiting the sphere of action of an absent person, a voice which was now about to emerge and appear, after this preliminary announcement, it was that Albertine whom I had known long ago beneath the sky of Balbec, when the waiters of the Grand Hotel, as they laid the tables, were blinded by the glow of the setting sun, when, the glass having been removed from all the windows, every faintest murmur of the evening passed freely from the beach where the last strolling couples still lingered, into the vast dining-room in which the first diners had not yet taken their places, and, across the mirror placed behind the cashier's desk, there passed the red reflexion of the hull, and lingered long after it the grey reflexion of the smoke of the last steamer for Rivebelle. I no longer asked myself what could have made Albertine late, and, when Françoise came into my room to inform me: "Mademoiselle Albertine is here," if I answered without even turning my head, that was only to conceal my emotion: "What in the world makes Mademoiselle Albertine come at this time of night!" But then, raising my eyes to look at Françoise, as though curious to hear her answer which must corroborate the apparent sincerity of my question, I perceived, with admiration and wrath, that, capable of rivalling Berma herself in the art of endowing with speech inanimate garments and the lines of her face, Françoise had taught their part to her bodice, her hair—the whitest threads of which had been brought to the surface, were displayed there like a birth-certificate—her neck bowed by weariness and obedience. They commiserated her for having been dragged from her sleep and from her warm bed, in the middle of the night, at her age, obliged to bundle into her clothes in haste, at the risk of catching pneumonia. And so, afraid that I might have seemed to be apologising for Albertine's late arrival: "Anyhow, I'm very glad she has come, it's just what I wanted," and I gave free vent to my profound joy. It did not long remain unclouded, when I had heard Françoise's reply. Without uttering a word of complaint, seeming indeed to be doing her best to stifle an irrepressible cough, and simply folding her shawl over her bosom as though she were feeling cold, she began by telling me everything that she had said to Albertine, whom she had not forgotten to ask after her aunt's health. "I was just saying, Monsieur must have been afraid that Mademoiselle was not coming, because this is no time to pay visits, it's nearly morning. But she must have been in some place where she was enjoying herself, because she never even said as much as that she was sorry she had kept Monsieur waiting, she answered me with a devil-may-care look, 'Better late than never!'" And Françoise added, in words that pierced my heart: "When she spoke like that she gave herself away. She would have liked to hide what she was thinking, perhaps, but. . . ."

I had no cause for astonishment. I said, a few pages back, that Françoise rarely paid attention, when she was sent with a message, if not to what she herself had said, which she would willingly relate in detail, at any rate to the answer that we were awaiting. But if, making an exception, she repeated to us the things that our friends had said, however short they might be, she generally arranged, appealing if need be to the expression, the tone that, she assured us, had accompanied them, to make them in some way or other wounding. At a pinch, she would bow her head beneath an insult (probably quite imaginary) which she had received from a tradesman to whom we had sent her, provided that, being addressed to her as our representative, who was speaking in our name, the insult might indirectly injure us. The only thing would have been to tell her that she had misunderstood the man, that she was suffering from persecution mania and that the shopkeepers were not at all in league against her. However, their sentiments affected me little. It was a very different matter, what Albertine's sentiments were. And, as she repeated the ironical words: "Better late than never!" Françoise at once made me see the friends in whose company Albertine had finished the evening, preferring their company, therefore, to mine. "She's a comical sight, she has a little flat hat on, with those big eyes of hers, it does make her look funny, especially with her cloak which she did ought to have sent to the amender's, for it's all in holes. She amuses me," added, as though laughing at Albertine, Françoise who rarely shared my impressions, but felt a need to communicate her own. I refused even to appear to understand that this laugh was indicative of scorn, but, to give tit for tat, replied, although I had never seen the little hat to which she referred: "What you call a 'little flat hat' is a simply charming. . . ." "That is to say, it's just nothing at all," said Françoise, giving expression, frankly this time, to her genuine contempt. Then (in a mild and leisurely tone so that my mendacious answer might appear to be the expression not of my anger but of the truth), wasting no time, however, so as not to keep Albertine waiting, I heaped upon Françoise these cruel words: "You are excellent," I said to her in a honeyed voice, "you are kind, you have a thousand merits, but you have never learned a single thing since the day when you first came to Paris, either about ladies' clothes or about how to pronounce words without making silly blunders." And this reproach was particularly stupid, for those French words which we are so proud of pronouncing accurately are themselves only blunders made by the Gallic lips which mispronounced Latin or Saxon, our language being merely a defective pronunciation of several others.

The genius of language in a living state, the future and past of French, that is what ought to have interested me in Françoise's mistakes. Her "amender" for "mender" was not so curious as those animals that survive from remote ages, such as the whale or the giraffe, and shew us the states through which animal life has passed. "And," I went on, "since you haven't managed to learn in all these years, you never will. But don't let that distress you, it doesn't prevent you from being a very good soul, and making spiced beef with jelly to perfection, and lots of other things as well. The hat that you think so simple is copied from a hat belonging to the Princesse de Guermantes which cost five hundred francs. However, I mean to give Mlle. Albertine an even finer one very soon." I knew that what would annoy Françoise more than anything was the thought of my spending money upon people whom she disliked. She answered me in a few words which were made almost unintelligible by a sudden attack of breathlessness. When I discovered afterwards that she had a weak heart, how remorseful I felt that I had never denied myself the fierce and sterile pleasure of making these retorts to her speeches. Françoise detested Albertine, moreover, because, being poor, Albertine could not enhance what Françoise regarded as my superior position. She smiled benevolently whenever I was invited by Mme. de Villeparisis. On the other hand, she was indignant that Albertine did not practise reciprocity. It came to my being obliged to invent fictitious presents which she was supposed to have given me, in the existence of which Françoise never for an instant believed. This want of reciprocity shocked her most of all in the matter of food. That Albertine should accept dinners from Mamma, when we were not invited to Mme. Bontemps's (who for that matter spent half her time out of Paris, her husband accepting "posts" as in the old days when he had had enough of the Ministry), seemed to her an indelicacy on the part of my friend which she rebuked indirectly by repeating a saying current at Combray:

"Let's eat my bread."
"Ay, that's the stuff."
"Let's eat thy bread."
"I've had enough."

I pretended that I was obliged to write a letter. "To whom were you writing?" Albertine asked me as she entered the room. "To a pretty little friend of mine, Gilberte Swann. Don't you know her?" "No." I decided not to question Albertine as to how she had spent the evening, I felt that I should only find fault with her and that we should not have any time left, seeing how late it was already, to be reconciled sufficiently to pass to kisses and caresses. And so it was with these that I chose to begin from the first moment. Besides, if I was a little calmer, I was not feeling happy. The loss of all orientation, of all sense of direction that we feel when we are kept waiting, still continues, after the coming of the person awaited, and, taking the place, inside us, of the calm spirit in which we were picturing her coming as so great a pleasure, prevents us from deriving any from it. Albertine was in the room: my unstrung nerves, continuing to flutter, were still expecting her. "I want a nice kiss, Albertine." "As many as you like," she said to me in her kindest manner. I had never seen her looking so pretty. "Another?" "Why, you know it's a great, great pleasure to me." "And a thousand times greater to me," she replied. "Oh! What a pretty book-cover you have there!" "Take it, I give it to you as a keepsake." "You are too kind. . . ." People would be cured for ever of romanticism if they could make up their minds, in thinking of the girl they love, to try to be the man they will be when they are no longer in love with her. Gilberte's book-cover, her agate marble, must have derived their importance in the past from some purely inward distinction, since now they were to me a book-cover, a marble like any others.

I asked Albertine if she would like something to drink. "I seem to see oranges over there and water," she said. "That will be perfect." I was thus able to taste with her kisses that refreshing coolness which had seemed to me to be better than they, at the Princesse de Guermantes's. And the orange squeezed into the water seemed to yield to me, as I drank, the secret life of its ripening growth, its beneficent action upon certain states of that human body which belongs to so different a kingdom, its powerlessness to make that body live, but on the other hand the process of irrigation by which it was able to benefit it, a hundred mysteries concealed by the fruit from my senses, but not from my intellect.

When Albertine had gone, I remembered that I had promised Swann that I would write to Gilberte, and courtesy, I felt, demanded that I should do so at once. It was without emotion and as though drawing a line at the foot of a boring school essay, that I traced upon the envelope the name *Gilberte Swann,* with which at one time I used to cover my exercise-books to give myself the illusion that I was corresponding with her. For if, in the past, it had been I who wrote that name, now the task had been deputed by Habit to one of the many secretaries whom she employs. He could write down Gilberte's name with all the more calm, in that, placed with me only recently by Habit, having but recently entered my service, he had never known Gilberte, and knew only, without attaching any reality to the words, because he had heard me speak of her, that she was a girl with whom I had once been in love.

I could not accuse her of hardness. The person that I now was in relation to her was the clearest possible proof of what she herself had been: the book-cover, the agate marble had simply become for me in relation to Albertine what they had been for Gilberte, what they would have been to anybody who had not suffused them with the glow of an internal flame. But now I felt a fresh disturbance which in its turn destroyed the very real power of things and words. And when Albertine said to me, in a further outburst of gratitude: "I do love turquoises!" I answered her: "Do not let them die," entrusting to them as to some precious jewel the future of our friendship which however was no more capable of inspiring a sentiment in Albertine than it had been of preserving the sentiment that had bound me in the past to Gilberte.

There appeared about this time a phenomenon which deserves mention only because it recurs in every important period of history. At the same moment when I was writing to Gilberte, M. de Guermantes, just home from his ball, still wearing his helmet, was thinking that next day he would be compelled to go into formal mourning, and decided to proceed a week earlier to the cure that he had been ordered to take. When he returned from it three weeks later (to anticipate for a moment, since I am still finishing my letter to Gilberte), those friends of the Duke who had seen him, so indifferent at the start, turn into a raving anti-Dreyfusard, were left speechless with amazement when they heard him (as though the action of the cure had not been confined to his bladder) answer:

"Oh, well, there'll be a fresh trial and he'll be acquitted; you can't sentence a fellow without any evidence against him. Did you ever see anyone so gaga as Forcheville? An officer, leading the French people to the shambles, heading straight for war. Strange times we live in." The fact was that, in the interval, the Duke had met, at the spa, three charming ladies (an Italian princess and her two sisters-in-law). After hearing them make a few remarks about the books they were reading, a play that was being given at the Casino, the Duke had at once understood that he was dealing with women of superior intellect, by whom, as he expressed it, he would be knocked out in the first round. He was all the more delighted to be asked to play bridge by the Princess. But, the moment he entered her sitting room, as he began, in the fervour of his double-dyed anti-Dreyfusism: "Well, we don't hear very much more of the famous Dreyfus and his appeal," his stupefaction had been great when he heard the Princess and her sisters-in-law say: "It's becoming more certain every day. They can't keep a man in prison who has done nothing." "Eh? Eh?" the Duke had gasped at first, as at the discovery of a fantastic nickname employed in this household to turn to ridicule a person whom he had always regarded as intelligent. But, after a few days, as, from cowardice and the spirit of imitation, we shout "Hallo, Jojotte," without knowing why at a great artist whom we hear so addressed by the rest of the household, the Duke, still greatly embarrassed by the novelty of this attitude, began nevertheless to say: "After all, if there is no evidence against him." The three charming ladies decided that he was not progressing rapidly enough and began to bully him: "But really, nobody with a grain of intelligence can ever have believed for a moment that there was anything." Whenever any revelation came out that was "damning" to Dreyfus, and the Duke, supposing that now he was going to convert the three charming ladies, came to inform them of it, they burst out laughing and had no difficulty in proving to him, with great dialectic subtlety, that his argument was worthless and quite absurd. The Duke had returned to Paris a frantic Dreyfusard. And certainly we do not suggest that the three charming ladies were not, in this instance, messengers of truth. But it is to be observed that, every ten years or so, when we have left a man filled with a genuine conviction, it so happens that an intelligent couple, or simply a charming lady, come in touch with him and after a few months he is won over to the opposite camp. And in this respect there are plenty of countries that behave like the sincere man, plenty of countries which we have left full of hatred for another race, and which, six months later, have changed their attitude and broken off all their alliances.

I ceased for some time to see Albertine, but continued, failing Mme. de Guermantes who no longer spoke to my imagination, to visit other fairies and their dwellings, as inseparable from themselves as is from the mollusc that fashioned it and takes shelter within it the pearly or enamelled valve or crenellated turret of its shell. I should not have been able to classify these ladies, the difficulty being that the problem was so vague in its terms and impossible not merely to solve but to set. Before coming to the lady, one had first to approach the faery mansion. Now as one of them was always at home after luncheon in the summer months, before I reached her house I was obliged to close the hood of my cab, so scorching were the sun's rays, the memory of which was, without my realising it, to enter into my general impression. I supposed that I was merely being driven to the Cours-la-Reine; in reality, before arriving at the gathering which a man of wider experience would perhaps have despised, I received, as though on a journey through Italy, a delicious, dazzled sensation from which the house was never afterwards to be separated in my memory. What was more, in view of the heat of the season and the hour, the lady had hermetically closed the shutters of the vast rectangular saloons on the ground floor in which she entertained her friends. I had difficulty at first in recognising my hostess and her guests, even the Duchesse de Guermantes, who in her hoarse voice bade me come and sit down next to her, in a Beauvais armchair illustrating the Rape of Europa. Then I began to make out on the walls the huge eighteenth century tapestries representing vessels whose masts were hollyhocks in blossom, beneath which I sat as though in the palace not of the Seine but of Neptune, by the brink of the river Oceanus, where the Duchesse de Guermantes became a sort of goddess of the waters. I should never stop if I began to describe all the different types of drawing-room. This example is sufficient to shew that I introduced into my social judgments poetical impressions which I never included among the items when I came to add up the sum, so that, when I was calculating the importance of a drawing-room, my total was never correct.

Certainly, these were by no means the only sources of error, but I have no time left now, before my departure for Balbec (where to my sorrow I am going to make a second stay which will also be my last), to start upon a series of pictures of society which will find their place in due course. I need here say only that to this first erroneous reason (my relatively frivolous existence which made people suppose that I was fond of society) for my letter to Gilberte, and for that reconciliation with the Swann family to which it seemed to point, Odette might very well, and with equal inaccuracy, have added a second. I have suggested hitherto the different aspects that the social world assumes in the eyes of a single person only by supposing that, if a woman who, the other day, knew nobody now goes everywhere, and another who occupied a commanding position is ostracised, one is inclined to regard these changes merely as those purely personal ups and downs of fortune which from time to time bring about in a given section of society, in consequence of speculations on the stock exchange, a crashing downfall or enrichment beyond the dreams of avarice. But there is more in it than that. To a certain extent social manifestations (vastly less important than artistic movements, political crises, the evolution that sweeps the public taste in the direction of the theatre of ideas, then of impressionist painting, then of music that is German and complicated, then of music that is Russian and simple, or of ideas of social service, justice, religious reaction, patriotic outbursts) are nevertheless an echo of them, remote, broken, uncertain, disturbed, changing. So that even drawing-rooms cannot be portrayed in a static immobility which has been conventionally employed up to this point for the study of characters, though these too must be carried along in an almost historical flow. The thirst for novelty that leads men of the world who are more or less sincere in their eagerness for information as to intellectual evolution to frequent the circles in which they can trace its development makes them prefer as a rule some hostess as yet undiscovered, who represents still in their first freshness the hopes of a superior culture so faded and tarnished in the women who for long years have wielded the social sceptre and who, having no secrets from these men, no longer appeal to their imagination. And every age finds itself personified thus in fresh women, in a fresh group of women, who, closely adhering to whatever may at that moment be the latest object of interest, seem, in their attire, to be at that moment making their first public appearance, like an unknown species, born of the last deluge, irresistible beauties of each new Consulate, each new Directory. But very often the new hostess is simply like certain statesmen who may be in office for the first time but have for the last forty years been knocking at every door without seeing any open, women who were not known in society but who nevertheless had been receiving, for years past, and failing anything better, a few "chosen friends" from its ranks. To be sure, this is not always the case, and when, with the prodigious flowering of the Russian Ballet, revealing one after another Bakst, Nijinski, Benoist, the genius of Stravinski, Princess Yourbeletieff, the youthful sponsor of all these new great men, appeared bearing on her head an immense, quivering egret, unknown to the women of Paris, which they all sought to copy, one might have supposed that this marvellous creature had been imported in their innumerable baggage, and as their most priceless treasure, by the Russian dancers; but when presently, by her side, in her stage box, we see, at every performance of the "Russians," seated like a true fairy godmother, unknown until that moment to the aristocracy, Mme. Verdurin, we shall be able to tell the society people who naturally supposed that Mme. Verdurin had recently entered the country with Diaghileff's troop, that this lady had already existed in different periods, and had passed through various avatars of which this is remarkable only in being the first that is bringing to pass at last, assured henceforth, and at an increasingly rapid pace, the success so long awaited by the Mistress. In Mme. Swann's case, it is true, the novelty she represented had not the same collective character. Her drawing-room was crystallised round a man, a dying man, who had almost in an instant passed, at the moment when his talent was exhausted, from obscurity to a blaze of glory. The passion for Bergotte's works was unbounded. He spent the whole day, on show, at Mme. Swann's, who would whisper to some influential man: "I shall say a word to him, he will write an article for you." He was, for that matter, quite capable of doing so and even of writing a little play for Mme. Swann. A stage nearer to death, he was not quite so feeble as at the time when he used to come and inquire after my grandmother. This was because intense physical suffering had enforced a regime on him. Illness is the doctor to whom we pay most heed: to kindness, to knowledge we make promises only; pain we obey.

It is true that the Verdurins and their little clan had at this time a far more vital interest than the drawing-room faintly nationalist, more markedly literary, and preeminently Bergottic of Mme. Swann. The little clan was in fact the active centre of a long political crisis which had reached its maximum of intensity: Dreyfusism. But society people were for the most part so violently opposed to the appeal that a Dreyfusian house seemed to them as inconceivable a thing as, at an earlier period, a Communard house. The Principessa di Caprarola, who had made Mme. Verdurin's acquaintance over a big exhibition which she had organised, had indeed been to pay her a long call, in the hope of seducing a few interesting specimens of the little clan and incorporating them in her own drawing-room, a call in the course of which the Princess (playing the Duchesse de Guermantes in miniature) had made a stand against current ideas, declared that the people in her world were idiots, all of which, thought Mme. Verdurin, shewed great courage. But this courage was not, in the sequel, to go the length of venturing, under fire of the gaze of nationalist ladies, to bow to Mme. Verdurin at the Balbec races. With Mme. Swann, on the contrary, the anti-Dreyfusards gave her credit for being "sound," which, in a woman married to a Jew, was doubly meritorious. Nevertheless, the people who had never been to her house imagined her as visited only by a few obscure Israelites and disciples of Bergotte. In this way we place women far more outstanding than Mme. Swann on the lowest rung of the social ladder, whether on account of their origin, or because they do not care about dinner parties and receptions at which we never see them, and suppose this, erroneously, to be due to their not having been invited, or because they never speak of their social connexions, but only of literature and art, or because people conceal the fact that they go to their houses, or they, to avoid impoliteness to yet other people, conceal the fact that they open their doors to these, in short for a thousand reasons which, added together, make of one or other of them in certain people's eyes, the sort of woman whom one does not know. So it was with Odette. Mme. d'Epinoy, when busy collecting some subscription for the "Patrie Française," having been obliged to go and see her, as she would have gone to her dressmaker, convinced moreover that she would find only a lot of faces that were not so much impossible as completely unknown, stood rooted to the ground when the door opened not upon the drawing-room she imagined but upon a magic hall in which, as in the transformation scene of a pantomime, she recognised in the dazzling chorus, half reclining upon divans, seated in armchairs, addressing their hostess by her Christian name, the royalties, the duchesses, whom she, the Princesse d'Epinoy, had the greatest difficulty in enticing into her own drawing-room, and to whom at that moment, beneath the benevolent eyes of Odette, the Marquis du Lau, Comte Louis de Turenne, Prince Borghese, the Duc d'Estrées, carrying orangeade and cakes, were acting as cupbearers and henchmen. The Princesse d'Epinoy, as she instinctively made people's social value inherent in themselves, was obliged to disincarnate Mme. Swann and reincarnate her in a fashionable woman. Our ignorance of the real existence led by the women who do not advertise it in the newspapers draws thus over certain situations (thereby helping to differentiate one house from another) a veil of mystery. In Odette's case, at the start, a few men of the highest society, anxious to meet Bergotte, had gone to dine, quite quietly, at her house. She had had the tact, recently acquired, not to advertise their presence, they found when they went there, a memory perhaps of the little nucleus, whose traditions Odette had preserved in spite of the schism, a place laid for them at table, and so forth. Odette took them with Bergotte (whom these excursions, incidentally, finished off) to interesting first nights. They spoke of her to various women of their own world who were capable of taking an interest in such a novelty. These women were convinced that Odette, an intimate friend of Bergotte, had more or less collaborated in his works, and believed her to be a thousand times more intelligent than the most outstanding women of the Faubourg, for the same reason that made them pin all their political faith to certain Republicans of the right shade such as M. Doumer and M. Deschanel, whereas they saw France doomed to destruction were her destinies entrusted to the Monarchy men who were in the habit of dining with them, men like Charette or Doudeauville. This change in Odette's status was carried out, so far as she was concerned, with a discretion that made it more secure and more rapid but allowed no suspicion to filter through to the public that is prone to refer to the social columns of the *Gaulois* for evidence as to the advance or decline of a house, with the result that one day, at the dress rehearsal of a play by Bergotte, given in one of the most fashionable theatres in aid of a charity, the really dramatic moment was when people saw enter the box opposite, which was that reserved for the author, and sit down by the side of Mme. Swann, Mme. de Marsantes and her who, by the gradual self-effacement of the Duchesse de Guermantes (glutted with fame, and retiring to save the trouble of going on), was on the way to becoming the lion, the queen of the age, Comtesse Molé. "We never even supposed that she had begun to climb," people said of Odette as they saw Comtesse Molé enter her box, "and look, she has reached the top of the ladder."

So that Mme. Swann might suppose that it was from snobbishness that I was taking up again with her daughter.

Odette, notwithstanding her brilliant escort, listened with close attention to the play, as though she had come there solely to see it performed, just as in the past she used to walk across the Bois for her health, as a form of exercise. Men who in the past had shewn less interest in her came to the edge of the box, disturbing the whole audience, to reach up to her hand and so approach the imposing circle that surrounded her. She, with a smile that was still more friendly than ironical, replied patiently to their questions, affecting greater calm than might have been expected, a calm which was, perhaps, sincere, this exhibition being only the belated revelation of a habitual and discreetly hidden intimacy. Behind these three ladies to whom every eye was drawn was Bergotte flanked by the Prince d'Agrigente, Comte Louis de Turenne, and the Marquis de Bréauté. And it is easy to understand that, to men who were received everywhere and could not expect any further advancement save as a reward for original research, this demonstration of their merit which they considered that they were making in letting themselves succumb to a hostess with a reputation for profound intellectuality, in whose house they expected to meet all the dramatists and novelists of the day, was more exciting, more lively than those evenings at the Princesse de Guermantes's, which, without any change of programme or fresh attraction, had been going on year after year, all more or less like the one we have described in such detail. In that exalted sphere, the sphere of the Guermantes, in which people were beginning to lose interest, the latest intellectual fashions were not incarnate in entertainments fashioned in their image, as in those sketches that Bergotte used to write for Mme. Swann, or those positive committees of public safety (had society been capable of taking an interest in the Dreyfus case) at which, in Mme. Verdurin's drawing-room, used to assemble Picquart, Clémenceau, Zola, Reinach and Labori.

Gilberte, too, helped to strengthen her mother's position, for an uncle of Swann had just left nearly twenty-four million francs to the girl, which meant that the Faubourg Saint-Germain was beginning to take notice of her. The reverse of the medal was that Swann (who, however, was dying) held Dreyfusard opinions, though this as a matter of fact did not injure his wife, but was actually of service to her. It did not injure her because people said: "He is dotty, his mind has quite gone, nobody pays any attention to him, his wife is the only person who counts and she is charming." But even Swann's Dreyfusism was useful to Odette. Left to herself, she would quite possibly have allowed herself to make advances to fashionable women which would have been her undoing. Whereas on the evenings when she dragged her husband out of dine in the Faubourg Saint-Germain, Swann, sitting sullenly in his corner, would not hesitate, if he saw Odette seeking an introduction to some Nationalist lady, to exclaim aloud: "Really, Odette, you are mad. Why can't you keep yourself to yourself. It is idiotic of you to get yourself introduced to anti-semites. I forbid you." People in society whom everyone else runs after are not accustomed either to such pride or to such ill-breeding. For the first time they beheld some one who though himself "superior" to them. The fame of Swann's mutterings was spread abroad, and cards with turned-down corners rained upon Odette. When she came to call upon Mme. d'Arpajon there was a brisk movement of friendly curiosity. "You didn't mind my introducing her to you," said Mme. d'Arpajon. "She is so nice. It was Marie de Marsantes that told me about her." "No, not at all, I hear she's so wonderfully clever, and she is charming. I had been longing to meet her; do tell me where she lives." Mme. d'Arpajon told Mme. Swann that she had enjoyed herself hugely at the latter's house the other evening, and had joyfully forsaken Mme. de Saint-Euverte for her. And it was true, for to prefer Mme. Swann was to shew that one was intelligent, like going to concerts instead of to tea-parties. But when Mme. de Saint-Euverte called on Mme. d'Arpajon at the same time as Odette, as Mme. de Saint-Euverte was a great snob and Mme. d'Arpajon, albeit she treated her without ceremony, valued her invitations, she did not introduce Odette, so that Mme. de Saint-Euverte should not know who it was. The Marquise imagined that it must be some Princess who never went anywhere, since she had never seen her before, prolonged her call, replied indirectly to what Odette was saying, but Mme. d'Arpajon remained adamant. And when Mme. de Saint-Euverte owned herself defeated and took her leave: "I did not introduce you," her hostess told Odette, "because people don't much care about going to her parties and she is always inviting one; you would never hear the last of her." "Oh, that is all right," said Odette with a pang of regret. But she retained the idea that people did not care about going to Mme. de Saint-Euverte's, which was to a certain extent true, and concluded that she herself held a position in society vastly superior to Mme. de Saint-Euverte's, albeit that lady held a very high position, and Odette, so far, had none at all.

That made no difference to her, and, albeit all Mme. de Guermantes's friends were friends also of Mme. d'Arpajon, whenever the latter invited Mme. Swann, Odette would say with an air of compunction: "I am going to Mme. d'Arpajon's; you will think me dreadfully old-fashioned, I know, but I hate going, for Mme. de Guermantes's sake" (whom, as it happened, she had never met). The distinguished men thought that the fact that Mme. Swann knew hardly anyone in good society meant that she must be a superior woman, probably a great musician, and that it would be a sort of extra distinction, as for a Duke to be a Doctor of Science, to go to her house. The completely unintelligent women were attracted by Odette for a diametrically opposite reason; hearing that she attended the Colonne concerts and professed herself a Wagnerian, they concluded from this that she must be "rather a lark," and were greatly excited by the idea of getting to know her. But, being themselves none too firmly established, they were afraid of compromising themselves in public if they appeared to be on friendly terms with Odette, and if, at a charity concert, they caught sight of Mme. Swann, would turn away their heads, deeming it impossible to bow, beneath the very nose of Mme. de Rochechouart, to a woman who was perfectly capable of having been to Bayreauth, which was as good as saying that she would stick at nothing.

Everybody becomes different upon entering another person's house. Not to speak of the marvellous metamorphoses that were accomplished thus in the faery palaces, in Mme. Swann's drawing-room, M. de Bréauté, acquiring a sudden importance from the absence of the people by whom he was normally surrounded, by his air of satisfaction at finding himself there, just as if instead of going out to a party he had slipped on his spectacles to shut himself up in his study and read the *Revue des Deux Mondes*, the mystic rite that he appeared to be performing in coming to see Odette, M. de Bréauté himself seemed another man. I would have given anything to see what alterations the Duchesse de Montmorency-Luxembourg would undergo in this new environment. But she was one of the people who could never be induced to meet Odette. Mme. de Montmorency, a great deal kinder to Oriane than Oriane was to her, surprised me greatly by saying, with regard to Mme. de Guermantes: "She knows some quite clever people, everybody likes her, I believe that if she had just had a slightly more coherent mind, she would have succeeded in forming a salon. The fact is, she never bothered about it, she is quite right, she is very well off as she is, with everybody running after her." If Mme. de Guermantes had not a "salon," what in the world could a "salon" be? The stupefaction in which this speech plunged me was no greater than that which I caused Mme. de Guermantes when I told her that I should like to be invited to Mme. de Montmorency's. Oriane thought her an old idiot. "I go there," she said, "because I'm forced to, she's my aunt, but you! She don't even know how to get nice people to come to her house." Mme. de Guermantes did not realise that nice people left me cold, that when she spoke to me of the Arpajon drawing-room I saw a yellow butterfly, and the Swann drawing-room (Mme. Swann was at home in the winter months between 6 and 7) a black butterfly, its wings powdered with snow. Even this last drawing-room, which was not a "salon" at all, she considered, albeit out of bounds for herself, permissible to me, on account of the "clever people" to be found there. But Mme. de Luxembourg! Had I already produced something that had attracted attention, she would have concluded that an element of snobbishness may be combined with talent. But I put the finishing touch to her disillusionment; I confessed to her that I did not go to Mme. de Montmorency's (as she supposed) to "take notes" and "make a study." Mme. de Guermantes was in this respect no more in error than the social novelists who analyse mercilessly from outside the actions of a snob or supposed snob, but never place themselves in his position, at the moment when a whole social springtime is bursting into blossom in his imagination. I myself, when I sought to discover what was the great pleasure that I found in going to Mme. de Montmorency's, was somewhat taken aback. She occupied, in the Faubourg Saint-Germain, an old mansion ramifying into pavilions which were separated by small gardens. In the outer hall a statuette, said to be by Falconnet, represented a spring which did, as it happened, exude a perpetual moisture. A little farther on the doorkeeper, her eyes always red, whether from grief or neurasthenia, a headache or a cold in the head, never answered your inquiry, waved her arm vaguely to indicate that the Duchess was at home, and let a drop or two trickle from her eyelids into a bowl filled with forget-me-nots. The pleasure that I felt on seeing the statuette, because it reminded me of a "little gardener" in plaster that stood in one of the Combray gardens, was nothing to that which was given me by the great staircase, damp and resonant, full of echoes, like the stairs in certain old-fashioned bathing establishments, with the vases filled with cinerarias—blue against blue—in the entrance hall and most of all the tinkle of the bell, which was exactly that of the bell in Eulalie's room. This tinkle raised my enthusiasm to a climax, but seemed to me too humble a matter for me to be able to explain it to Mme. de Montmorency, with the result that she invariably saw me in a state of rapture of which she might never guess the cause.

THE HEART'S INTERMISSIONS

MY second arrival at Balbec was very different from the other. The manager had come in person to meet me at Pont-à-Couleuvre, reiterating how greatly he valued his titled patrons, which made me afraid that he had ennobled me, until I realised that, in the obscurity of his grammatical memory, *titré* meant simply *attitré*, or accredited. In fact, the more new languages he learned the worse he spoke the others. He informed he that he had placed me at the very top of the hotel. "I hope," he said, "that you will not interpolate this as a want of discourtesy, I was sorry to give you a room of which you are unworthy, but I did it in connexion with the noise, because in that room you will not have anyone above your head to disturb your trepanum" (tympanum). "Don't be alarmed, I shall have the windows closed, so that they shan't bang. Upon that point, I am intolerable" (the last word expressing not his own thought, which was that he would always be found inexorable in that respect, but, quite possibly, the thoughts of his underlings). The rooms were, as it proved, those we had had before. They were no humbler, but I had risen in the manager's esteem. I could light a fire if I liked (for, by the doctors' orders, I had left Paris at Easter), but he was afraid there might be "fixtures" in the ceiling. "See that you always wait before alighting a fire until the preceding one is extenuated" (extinct). "The important thing is to take care not to avoid setting fire to the chimney, especially as, to cheer things up a bit, I have put an old china pottage on the mantelpiece which might become insured."

He informed me with great sorrow of the death of the leader of the Cherbourg bar: "He was an old retainer," he said (meaning probably "campaigner") and gave me to understand that his end had been hastened by the quickness, otherwise the fastness, of his life. "For some time past I noticed that after dinner he would take a doss in the reading-room" (take a doze, presumably). "The last times, he was so changed that if you hadn't known who it was, to look at him, he was barely recognisant" (presumably, recognisable).

A happy compensation: the chief magistrate of Caen had just received his "bags" (badge) as Commander of the Legion of Honour. "Surely to goodness, he has capacities, but seems they gave him it principally because of his general 'impotence.'" There was a mention of this decoration, as it happened, in the previous day's *Echo de Paris,* of which the manager had as yet read only "the first paradox" (meaning paragraph). The paper dealt admirably with M. Caillaux's policy. "I consider, they're quite right," he said. "He is putting us too much under the thimble of Germany" (under the thumb). As the discussion of a subject of this sort with a hotel-keeper seemed to me boring, I ceased to listen. I thought of the visual images that had made me decide to return to Balbec. They were very different from those of the earlier time, the vision in quest of which I came was as dazzlingly clear as the former had been clouded; they were to prove deceitful nevertheless. The images selected by memory are as arbitrary, as narrow, as intangible as those which imagination had formed and reality has destroyed. There is no reason why, existing outside ourself, a real place should conform to the pictures in our memory rather than to those in our dreams. And besides, a fresh reality will perhaps make us forget, detest even, the desires that led us forth upon our journey.

Those that had led me forth to Balbec sprang to some extent from my discovery that the Verdurins (whose invitations I had invariably declined, and who would certainly be delighted to see me, if I went to call upon them in the country with apologies for never having been able to call upon them in Paris), knowing that several of the faithful would be spending the holidays upon that part of the coast, and having, for that reason, taken for the whole season one of M. de Cambremer's houses (La Raspelière), had invited Mme. Putbus to stay with them. The evening on which I learned this (in Paris) I lost my head completely and sent our young footman to find out whether the lady would be taking her Abigail to Balbec with her. It was eleven o'clock. Her porter was a long time in opening the front door, and, for a wonder, did not send my messenger packing, did not call the police, merely gave him a dressing down, but with it the information that I desired. He said that the head lady's maid would indeed be accompanying her mistress, first of all to the waters in Germany, then to Biarritz, and at the end of the season to Mme. Verdurin's. From that moment my mind had been at rest, and glad to have this iron in the fire. I had been able to dispense with those pursuits in the streets, in which I had not that letter of introduction to the beauties I encountered which I should have to the "Giorgione" in the fact of my having dined that very evening, at the Verdurins', with her mistress. Besides, she might form a still better opinion of me perhaps when she learned that I knew not merely the middle class tenants of La Raspelière but its owners, and above all Saint-Loup who, prevented from commending me personally to the maid (who did not know him by name), had written an enthusiastic letter about me to the Cambremers. He believed that, quite apart from any service that they might be able to render me, Mme. de Cambremer, the Legrandin daughter-in-law, would interest me by her conversation. " She is an intelligent woman," he had assured me. " She won't say anything final " (*final* having taken the place of *sublime* things with Robert, who, every five or six years, would modify a few of his favourite expressions, while preserving the more important intact), " but it is an interesting nature, she has a personality, intuition; she has the right word for everything. Every now and then she is maddening, she says stupid things on purpose, to seem smart, which is all the more ridiculous as nobody could be less smart than the Cambremers, she is not always in the picture, but, taking her all round, she is one of the people it is more or less possible to talk to."

No sooner had Robert's letter of introduction reached them than the Cambremers, whether from a snobbishness that made them anxious to oblige Saint-Loup, even indirectly, or from gratitude for what he had done for one of their nephews at Doncières, or (what was most likely) from kindness of heart and traditions of hospitality, had written long letters insisting that I should stay with them, or, if I preferred to be more independent, offering to find me lodgings. When Saint-Loup had pointed out that I should be staying at the Grand Hotel, Balbec, they replied that at least they would expect a call from me as soon as I arrived and, if I did not appear, would come without fail to hunt me out and invite me to their garden parties.

No doubt there was no essential connexion between Mme. Putbus's maid and the country round Balbec; she would not be for me like the peasant girl whom, as I strayed alone along the Méséglise way, I had so often sought in vain to evoke, with all the force of my desire.

But I had long since given up trying to extract from a woman as it might be the square root of her unknown quantity, the mystery of which a mere introduction was generally enough to dispel. Anyhow at Balbec, where I had not been for so long, I should have this advantage, failing the necessary connexion which did not exist between the place and this particular woman, that my sense of reality would not be destroyed by familiarity, as in Paris, where, whether in my own home or in a bedroom that I already knew, pleasure indulged in with a woman could not give me for one instant, amid everyday surroundings, the illusion that it was opening the door for me to a new life. (For if habit is a second nature, it prevents us from knowing our original nature, whose cruelties it lacks and also its enchantments.) Now this illusion I might perhaps feel in a strange place, where one's sensibility is revived by a ray of sunshine, and where my ardour would be raised to a climax by the lady's maid whom I desired: we shall see, in the course of events, not only that this woman did not come to Balbec, but that I dreaded nothing so much as the possibility of her coming, so that the principal object of my expedition was neither attained, nor indeed pursued. It was true that Mme. Putbus was not to be at the Verdurins' so early in the season; but these pleasures which we have chosen beforehand may be remote, if their coming is assured, and if, in the interval of waiting, we can devote ourselves to the pastime of seeking to attract, while powerless to love. Moreover, I was not going to Balbec in the same practical frame of mind as before; there is always less egoism in pure imagination than in recollection; and I knew that I was going to find myself in one of those very places where fair strangers most abound; a beach presents them as numerously as a ball-room, and I looked forward to strolling up and down outside the hotel, on the front, with the same sort of pleasure that Mme. de Guermantes would have procured me if, instead of making other hostesses invite me to brilliant dinner-parties, she had given my name more frequently for their lists of partners to those of them who gave dances. To make female acquaintances at Balbec would be as easy for me now as it had been difficult before, for I was now as well supplied with friends and resources there as I had been destitute of them on my former visit.

I was roused from my meditations by the voice of the manager, to whose political dissertations I had not been listening. Changing the subject, he told me of the chief magistrate's joy on hearing of my arrival, and that he was coming to pay me a visit in my room, that very evening. The thought of this visit so alarmed me (for I was beginning to feel tired) that I begged him to prevent it (which he promised to do, and, as a further precaution, to post members of his staff on guard, for the first night, on my landing). He did not seem overfond of his staff. "I am obliged to keep running after them all the time because they are lacking in inertia. If I was not there they would never stir. I shall post the lift-boy on sentry outside your door." I asked him if the boy had yet become "head page." "He is not old enough yet in the house," was the answer. "He has comrades more aged than he is. It would cause an outcry. We must act with granulation in everything. I quite admit that he strikes a good aptitude" (meaning attitude) "at the door of his lift. But he is still a trifle young for such positions. With others in the place of longer standing, it would make a contrast. He is a little wanting in seriousness, which is the primitive quality" (doubtless, the primordial, the most important quality). "He needs his leg screwed on a bit tighter" (my informant meant to say his head). "Anyhow, he can leave it all to me. I know what I'm about. Before I won my stripes as manager of the Grand Hotel, I smelt powder under M. Paillard." I was impressed by this simile, and thanked the manager for having come in person as far as Pont-à-Couleuvre. "Oh, that's nothing! The loss of time has been quite infinite" (for infinitesimal). Meanwhile, we had arrived.

Complete physical collapse. On the first night, as I was suffering from cardiac exhaustion, trying to master my pain, I bent down slowly and cautiously to take off my boots. But no sooner had I touched the topmost button than my bosom swelled, filled with an unknown, a divine presence, I shook with sobs, tears streamed from my eyes. The person who came to my rescue, who saved me from barrenness of spirit, was the same who, years before, in a moment of identical distress and loneliness, in a moment when I was no longer in any way myself, had come in, and had restored me to myself, for that person was myself and more than myself (the container that is greater than the contents, which it was bringing to me). I had just perceived, in my memory, bending over my weariness, the tender, preoccupied, dejected face of my grandmother, as she had been on that first evening of our arrival, the face not of that grandmother whom I was astonished—and reproached myself—to find that I regretted so little and who was no more of her than just her name, but of my own true grandmother, of whom, for the first time since that afternoon in the Champs-Elysées on which she had had her stroke, I now recaptured, by an instinctive and complete act of recollection, the living reality. That reality has no existence for us, so long as it has not been created anew by our mind (otherwise the men who have been engaged in a Titanic conflict would all of them be great epic poets); and so, in my insane desire to fling myself into her arms, it was not until this moment, more than a year after her burial, because of that anachronism which so often prevents the calendar of facts from corresponding to that of our feelings, that I became conscious that she was dead. I had often spoken about her in the interval, and thought of her also, but behind my words and thoughts, those of an ungrateful, selfish, cruel youngster, there had never been anything that resembled my grandmother, because, in my frivolity, my love of pleasure, my familiarity with the spectacle of her ill health, I retained only in a potential state the memory of what she had been. At whatever moment we estimate it, the total value of our spiritual nature is more or less fictitious, notwithstanding the long inventory of its treasures, for now one, now another of these is unrealisable, whether we are considering actual treasures or those of the imagination, and, in my own case, fully as much as the ancient name of Guermantes, this other, how far more important item, my real memory of my grandmother. For with the troubles of memory are closely linked the heart's intermissions. It is, no doubt, the existence of our body, which we may compare to a jar containing our spiritual nature, that leads us to suppose that all our inward wealth, our past joys, all our sorrows, are perpetually in our possession. Perhaps it is equally inexact to suppose that they escape or return. In any case, if they remain within us, it is, for most of the time, in an unknown region where they are of no service to us, and where even the most ordinary are crowded out by memories of a different kind, which preclude any simultaneous occurrence of them in our consciousness. But if the setting of sensations in which they are preserved be recaptured, they acquire in turn the same power of expelling everything that is incompatible with them, of installing alone in us the self that originally lived them. Now, inasmuch as the self that I had just suddenly become once again had not existed since that evening long ago when my grandmother undressed me after my arrival at Balbec, it was quite naturally, not at the end of the day that had just passed, of which that self knew nothing, but—as though there were in time different and parallel series—without loss of continuity, immediately after the first evening at Balbec long ago, that I clung to the minute in which my grandmother had leaned over me. The self that I then was, that had so long disappeared, was once again so close to me that I seemed still to hear the words that had just been spoken, albeit they were nothing more now than illusion, as a man who is half awake thinks he can still make out close at hand the sounds of his receding dream. I was nothing now but the person who sought a refuge in his grandmother's arms, sought to wipe away the traces of his suffering by giving her kisses, that person whom I should have had as great difficulty in imagining when I was one or other of those persons which, for some time past, I had successively been, as the efforts, doomed in any event to sterility, that I should now have had to make to feel the desires and joys of any of those which, for a time at least, I no longer was. I reminded myself how, an hour before the moment at which my grandmother had stooped down like that, in her dressing gown, to unfasten my boots, as I wandered along the stiflingly hot street, past the pastry-cook's, I had felt that I could never, in my need to feel her arms round me, live through the hour that I had still to spend without her. And now that this same need was reviving in me, I knew that I might wait hour after hour, that she would never again be by my side, I had only just discovered this because I had only just, on feeling her for the first time, alive, authentic, making my heart swell to breaking-point, on finding her at last, learned that I had lost her for ever. Lost for ever; I could not understand and was struggling to bear the anguish of this contradiction: on the one hand an existence, an affection, surviving in me as I had known them, that is to say created for me, a love in whose eyes everything found in me so entirely its complement, its goal, its constant lodestar, that the genius of great men, all the genius that might have existed from the beginning of the world would have been less precious to my grandmother than a single one of my defects; and on the other hand, as soon as I had lived over again that bliss, as though it were present, feeling it shot through by the certainty, throbbing like a physical anguish, of an annihilation that had effaced my image of that affection, had destroyed that existence, abolished in retrospect our interwoven destiny, made of my grandmother at the moment when I found her again as in a mirror, a mere stranger whom chance had allowed to spend a few years in my company, as it might have been in anyone's else, but to whom, before and after those years, I was, I could be nothing.

Instead of the pleasures that I had been experiencing of late, the only pleasure that it would have been possible for me to enjoy at that moment would have been, by modifying the past, to diminish the sorrows and sufferings of my grandmother's life. Now, I did not recall her only in that dressing-gown, a garment so appropriate as to have become almost their symbol to the labours, foolish no doubt but so lovable also, that she performed for me, gradually I began to remember all the opportunities that I had seized, by letting her perceive, by exaggerating if necessary my sufferings, to cause her a grief which I imagined as being obliterated immediately by my kisses, as though my affection had been as capable as my happiness of creating hers; and, what was worse, I, who could conceive no other happiness now than in finding happiness shed in my memory over the contours of that face, moulded and bowed by love, had set to work with frantic efforts, in the past, to destroy even its most modest pleasures, as on the day when Saint-Loup had taken my grandmother's photograph and I, unable to conceal from her what I thought of the ridiculous childishness of the coquetry with which she posed for him, with her wide-brimmed hat, in a flattering half light, had allowed myself to mutter a few impatient, wounding words, which, I had perceived from a contraction of her features, had carried, had pierced her; it was I whose heart they were rending now that there was no longer possible, ever again, the consolation of a thousand kisses.

But never should I be able to wipe out of my memory that contraction of her face, that anguish of her heart, or rather of my own: for as the dead exist only in us, it is ourselves that we strike without ceasing when we persist in recalling the blows that we have dealt them. To these griefs, cruel as they were, I clung with all my might and main, for I realised that they were the effect of my memory of my grandmother, the proof that this memory which I had of her was really present within me. I felt that I did not really recall her save by grief and should have liked to feel driven yet deeper into me these nails which fastened the memory of her to my consciousness. I did not seek to mitigate my suffering, to set it off, to pretend that my grandmother was only somewhere else and momentarily invisible, by addressing to her photograph (the one taken by Saint-Loup, which I had beside me) words and prayers as to a person who is separated from us but, retaining his personality, knows us and remains bound to us by an indissoluble harmony. Never did I do this, for I was determined not merely to suffer, but to respect the original form of my suffering, as it had suddenly come upon me unawares, and I wished to continue to feel it, according to its own laws, whenever those strange contradictory impressions of survival and obliteration crossed one another again in my mind. This painful and, at the moment, incomprehensible impression,

I knew—not, forsooth, whether I should one day distil a grain of truth from it—but that if I ever should succeed in extracting that grain of truth, it could only be from it, from so singular, so spontaneous an impression, which had been neither traced by my intellect nor attenuated by my pusillanimity, but which death itself, the sudden revelation of death, had, like a stroke of lightning, carved upon me, along a supernatural, inhuman channel, a twofold and mysterious furrow. (As for the state of forgetfulness of my grandmother in which I had been living until that moment, I could not even think of turning to it to extract truth from it; since in itself it was nothing but a negation, a weakening of the mind incapable of recreating a real moment of life and obliged to substitute for it conventional and neutral images.) Perhaps, however, as the instinct of preservation, the ingenuity of the mind in safeguarding us from grief, had begun already to build upon still smouldering ruins, to lay the first courses of its serviceable and ill-omened structure, I relished too keenly the delight of recalling this or that opinion held by my dear one, recalling them as though she had been able to hold them still, as though she existed, as though I continued to exist for her. But as soon as I had succeeded in falling asleep, at that more truthful hour when my eyes closed to the things of the outer world, the world of sleep (on whose frontier intellect and will, momentarily paralysed, could no longer strive to rescue me from the cruelty of my real impressions) reflected, refracted the agonising synthesis of survival and annihilation, in the mysteriously lightened darkness of my organs. World of sleep in which our inner consciousness, placed in bondage to the disturbances of our organs, quickens the rhythm of heart or breath because a similar dose of terror, sorrow, remorse acts with a strength magnified an hundredfold if it is thus injected into our veins; as soon as, to traverse the arteries of the subterranean city, we have embarked upon the dark current of our own blood as upon an inward Lethe meandering sixfold, huge solemn forms appear to us, approach and glide away, leaving us in tears. I sought in vain foı my grandmother's form when I had stepped ashore beneath the sombre portals; I knew, indeed, that she did still exist, but with a diminished vitality, as pale as that of memory; the darkness was increasing, and the wind; my father, who was to take me where she was, did not appear. Suddenly my breath failed me, I felt my heart turn to stone; I had just remembered that for week after week I had forgotten to write to my grandmother. What must she be thinking of me? "Great God!" I said to myself, "how wretched she must be in that little room which they have taken for her, no bigger than what one would take for an old servant, where she is all alone with the nurse they have put there to look after her, from which she cannot stir, for she is still slightly paralysed and has always refused to rise from her bed. She must be thinking that I have forgotten her now that she is dead; how lonely she must be feeling, how deserted! Oh, I must run to see her, I mustn't lose a minute, I mustn't wait for my father to come, even—but where is it, how can I have forgotten the address, will she know me again, I wonder? How can I have forgotten her all these months?" It is so dark, I shall not find her; the wind is keeping me back; but look! there is my father walking ahead of me; I call out to him: "Where is grandmother? Tell me her address. Is she all right? Are you quite sure she has everything she wants?" "Why," says my father, "you need not alarm yourself. Her nurse is well trained. We send her a trifle, from time to time, so that she can get your grandmother anything she may need. She asks, sometimes, how you are getting on. She was told that you were going to write a book. She seemed pleased. She wiped away a tear." And then I fancied I could remember that, a little time after her death, my grandmother had said to me, crying, with a humble expression, like an old servant who has been given notice to leave, like a stranger, in fact: "You will let me see something of you occasionally, won't you; don't let too many years go by without visiting me. Remember that you were my grandson, once, and that grandmothers never forget." And seeing again that face, so submissive, so sad, so tender, which was hers, I wanted to run to her at once and say to her, as I ought to have said to her then: "Why, grandmother, you can see me as often as you like, I have only you in the world, I shall never leave you any more." What tears my silence must have made her shed through all those months in which I have never been to the place where she lies, what can she have been saying to herself about me? And it is in a voice choked with tears that I too shout to my father: "Quick, quick, her address, take me to her." But he says: "Well . . . I don't know whether you will be able to see her. Besides, you know, she is very frail now, very frail, she is not at all herself, I am afraid you would find it rather painful. And I can't be quite certain of the number of the avenue." "But tell me, you who know, it is not true that the dead have ceased to exist. It can't possibly be true, in spite of what they say, because grandmother does exist still." My father smiled a mournful smile: "Oh, hardly at all, you know, hardly at all. I think that it would be better if you did not go. She has everything that she wants. They come and keep the place tidy for her." "But she is often left alone?" "Yes, but that is better for her. It is better for her not to think, which could only be bad for her. It often hurts her, when she tries to think. Besides, you know, she is quite lifeless now. I shall leave a note of the exact address, so that you can go to her; but I don't see what good you can do there, and I don't suppose the nurse will allow you to see her." "You know quite well I shall always stay beside her, dear, deer, deer, Francis Jammes, fork." But already I had retraced the dark meanderings of the stream, had ascended to the surface where the world of living people opens, so that if I still repeated: "Francis Jammes, deer, deer," the sequence of these words no longer offered me the limpid meaning and logic which they had expressed to me so naturally an instant earlier and which I could not now recall. I could not even understand why the word "Aias" which my father had just said to me, had immediately signified: "Take care you don't catch cold," without any possible doubt. I had forgotten to close the shutters, and so probably the daylight had awakened me. But I could not bear to have before my eyes those waves of the sea which my grandmother could formerly contemplate for hours on end; the fresh image of their heedless beauty was at once supplemented by the thought that she did not see them; I should have liked to stop my ears against their sound, for now the luminous plenitude of the beach carved out an emptiness in my heart; everything seemed to be saying to me, like those paths and lawns of a public garden in which I had once lost her, long ago, when I was still a child: "We have not seen her," and beneath the hemisphere of the pale vault of heaven I felt myself crushed as though beneath a huge bell of bluish glass, enclosing an horizon within which my grandmother was not. To escape from the sight of it, I turned to the wall, but alas what was now facing me was that partition which used to serve us as a morning messenger, that partition which, as responsive as a violin in rendering every fine shade of sentiment, reported so exactly to my grandmother my fear at once of waking her and, if she were already awake, of not being heard by her and so of her not coming, then immediately, like a second instrument taking up the melody, informed me that she was coming and bade me be calm. I dared not put out my hand to that wall, any more than to a piano on which my grandmother had played and which still throbbed from her touch. I knew that I might knock now, even louder, that I should hear no response, that my grandmother would never come again. And I asked nothing better of God, if a Paradise exists, than to be able, there, to knock upon that wall the three little raps which my grandmother would know among a thousand, and to which she would reply with those other raps which said: "Don't be alarmed, little mouse, I know you are impatient, but I am just coming," and that He would let me remain with her throughout eternity which would not be too long for us.

The manager came in to ask whether I would not like to come down. He had most carefully supervised my "placement" in the dining-room. As he had seen no sign of me, he had been afraid that I might have had another of my choking fits. He hoped that it might be only a little "sore throats" and assured me that he had heard it said that they could be soothed with what he called "calyptus."

He brought me a message from Albertine. She was not supposed to be coming to Balbec that year but, having changed her plans, had been for the last three days not in Balbec itself but ten minutes away by the tram at a neighbouring watering-place. Fearing that I might be tired after the journey, she had stayed away the first evening, but sent word now to ask when I could see her. I inquired whether she had called in person, not that I wished to see her, but so that I might arrange not to see her. "Yes," replied the manager. "But she would like it to be as soon as possible, unless you have not some quite necessitous reasons. You see," he concluded, "that everybody here desires you, definitively." But for my part, I wished to see nobody.

And yet the day before, on my arrival, I had felt myself recaptured by the indolent charm of a seaside existence. The same taciturn lift-boy, silent this time from respect and not from scorn, and glowing with pleasure, had set the lift in motion. As I rose upon the ascending column, I had passed once again through what had formerly been for me the mystery of a strange hotel, in which when you arrive, a tourist without protection or position, each old resident returning to his room, each chambermaid passing along the eery perspective of a corridor, not to mention the young lady from America with her companion, on their way down to dinner, give you a look in which you can read nothing that you would have liked to see. This time on the contrary I had fel the entirely soothing pleasure of passing up through an hotel that I knew, where I felt myself at home, where I had performed once again that operation which we must always start afresh, longer, more difficult than the turning outside in of an eyelid, which consists in investing things with the spirit that is familiar to us instead of their own which we found alarming. Must I always, I had asked myself, little thinking of the sudden change of mood that was in store for me, be going to strange hotels where I should be dining for the first time, where Habit would not yet have killed upon each landing, outside every door, the terrible dragon that seemed to be watching over an enchanted life, where I should have to approach those strange women whom fashionable hotels, casinos, watering-places, seem to draw together and endow with a common existence.

I had found pleasure even in the thought that the boring chief magistrate was so eager to see me, I could see, on that first evening, the waves, the azure mountain ranges of the sea, its glaciers and its cataracts, its elevation and its careless majesty—merely upon smelling for the first time after so long an interval, as I washed my hands, that peculiar odour of the over-scented soaps of the Grand Hotel—which, seeming to belong at once to the present moment and to my past visit, floated between them like the real charm of a particular form of existence to which one returns only to change one's necktie. The sheets on my bed, too fine, too light, too large, impossible to tuck in, to keep in position, which billowed out from beneath the blankets in moving whorls had distressed me before. Now they merely cradled upon the awkward, swelling fulness of their sails the glorious sunrise, big with hopes, of my first morning. But that sun had not time to appear. In the dead of night, the awful, godlike presence had returned to life. I asked the manager to leave me, and to give orders that no one was to enter my room. I told him that I should remain in bed and rejected his offer to send to the chemist's for the excellent drug. He was delighted by my refusal for he was afraid that other visitors might be annoyed by the smell of the "calyptus." It earned me the compliment: "You are in the movement" (he meant: "in the right"), and the warning: "take care you don't defile yourself at the door, I've had the lock 'elucidated' with oil; if any of the servants dares to knock at your door, he'll be beaten 'black and white.' And they can mark my words, for I'm not a repeater" (this evidently meant that he did not say a thing twice). "But wouldn't you care for a drop of old wine, just to set you up; I have a pig's head of it downstairs" (presumably hogshead). "I shan't bring it to you on a silver dish like the head of Jonathan, and I warn you that it is not Château-Laffite, but it is virtuously equivocal" (virtually equivalent). "And as it's quite light, they might fry you a little sole." I declined everything, but was suprised to hear the name of the fish (sole) pronounced like that of the King of Israel, Saul, by a man who must have ordered so many in his life.

Despite the manager's promises, they brought me in a little later the turned down card of the Marquise de Cambremer. Having come over to see me, the old lady had sent to inquire whether I was there and when she heard that I had arrived only the day before, and was unwell, had not insisted, but (not without stopping, doubtless, at the chemist's or the haberdasher's, while the footman jumped down from the box and went in to pay a bill or to give an order) had driven back to Féterne, in her old barouche upon eight springs, drawn by a pair of horses. Not infrequently did one hear the rumble and admire the pomp of this carriage in the streets of Balbec and of various other little places along the coast, between Balbec and Féterne. Not that these halts outside shops were the object of these excursions. It was on the contrary some tea-party or garden-party at the house of some squire or functionary, socially quite unworthy of the Marquise. But she, although completely overshadowing, by her birth and wealth, the petty nobility of the district, was in her perfect goodness and simplicity of heart so afraid of disappointing anyone who had sent her an invitation that she would attend all the most insignificant social gatherings in the neighbourhood. Certainly, rather than travel such a distance to listen, in the stifling heat of a tiny drawing-room, to a singer who generally had no voice and whom in her capacity as the lady bountiful of the countryside and as a famous musician she would afterwards be compelled to congratulate with exaggerated warmth, Mme. de Cambremer would have preferred to go for a drive or to remain in her marvellous gardens at Féterne, at the foot of which the drowsy waters of a little bay float in to die amid the flowers. But she knew that the probability of her coming had been announced by the host, whether he was a noble or a free burgess of Maineville-la Teinturière or of Chattoncourt-l'Orgueilleux. And if Mme. de Cambremer had driven out that afternoon without making a formal appearance at the party, any of the guests who had come from one or other of the little places that lined the coast might have seen and heard the Marquise's barouche, which would deprive her of the excuse that she had not been able to get away from Féterne. On the other hand, these hosts might have seen Mme. de Cambremer, time and again, appear at concerts given in houses which, they considered, were no place for her; the slight depreciation caused thereby, in their eyes, to the position of the too obliging Marquise vanished as soon as it was they who were entertaining her, and it was with feverish anxiety that they kept asking themselves whether or not they were going to have her at their "small party." What an allaying of the doubts and fears of days if, after the first song had been sung by the daughter of the house or by some amateur on holiday in the neighbourhood, one of the guests announced (an infallible sign that the Marquise was coming to the party) that he had seen the famous barouche and pair drawn up outside the watchmaker's or the chemist's! Thereupon Mme. de Cambremer (who indeed was to enter before long followed by her daughter-in-law, the guests who were staying with her at the moment and whom she had asked permission, granted with such joy, to bring) shone once more with undiminished lustre in the eyes of her host and hostess, to whom the hoped-for reward of her coming had perhaps been the determining if unavowed cause of the decision they had made a month earlier: to burden themselves with the trouble and expense of an afternoon party. Seeing the Marquise present at their gathering, they remembered no longer her readiness to attend those given by their less deserving neighbours, but the antiquity of her family, the splendour of her house, the rudeness of her daughter-in-law, born Legrandin, who by her arrogance emphasised the slightly insipid good-nature of the dowager. Already they could see in their mind's eye, in the social column of the *Gaulois*, the paragraph which they would draft themselves in the family circle, with all the doors shut and barred, upon "the little corner of Brittany which is at present a whirl of gaiety, the select party from which the guests could hardly tear themselves away, promising their charming host and hostess that they would soon pay them another visit." Day after day they watched for the newspaper to arrive, worried that they had not yet seen any notice in it of their party, and afraid lest they should have had Mme. de Cambremer for their other guests alone and not for the whole reading public. At length the blessed day arrived: "The season is exceptionally brilliant this year at Balbec. Small afternoon concerts are the fashion. . . ." Heaven be praised, Mme. de Cambremer's name was spelt correctly, and included "among others we may mention" but at the head of the list. All that remained was to appear annoyed at this journalistic indiscretion which might get them into difficulties with people whom they had not been able to invite, and to ask hypocritically in Mme. de Cambremer's hearing who could have been so treacherous as to send the notice, upon which the Marquise, every inch the lady bountiful, said: "I can understand your being annoyed, but I must say I am only too delighted that people should know I was at your party."

On the card that was brought me, Mme. de Cambremer had scribbled the message that she was giving an afternoon party "the day after to-morrow." To be sure, as recently as the day before yesterday, tired as I was of the social round, it would have been a real pleasure to me to taste it, transplanted amid those gardens in which there grew in the open air, thanks to the exposure of Féterne, fig trees, palms, rose bushes extending down to a sea as blue and calm often as the Mediterranean, upon which the host's little yacht sped across, before the party began, to fetch from the places on the other side of the bay the most important guests, served, with its awnings spread to shut out the sun, after the party had assembled, as an open air refreshment room, and set sail again in the evening to take back those whom it had brought. A charming luxury, but so costly that it was partly to meet the expenditure that it entailed that Mme. de Cambremer had sought to increase her income in various ways, and notably by letting, for the first time, one of her properties, very different from Féterne: la Raspelière. Yes, two days earlier, how welcome such a party, peopled with minor nobles all unknown to me, would have been to me as a change from the "high life" of Paris. But now pleasures had no longer any meaning for me. And so I wrote to Mme. de Cambremer to decline, just as, an hour ago, I had put off Albertine: grief had destroyed in me the possibility of desire as completely as a high fever takes away one's appetite. . . . My mother was to arrive on the morrow. I felt that I was less unworthy to live in her company, that I should understand her better, now that an alien and degrading existence had wholly given place to the resurging, heartrending memories that wreathed and ennobled my soul, like her own, with their crown of thorns. I thought so: in reality there is a world of difference between real griefs, like my mother's, which literally crush out our life for years if not for ever, when we have lost the person we love—and those other griefs, transitory when all is said, as mine was to be, which pass as quickly as they have been slow in coming, which we do not realise until long after the event, because, in order to feel them, we need first to understand them; griefs such as so many people feel, from which the grief that was torturing me at this moment differed only in assuming the form of unconscious memory.

That I was one day to experience a grief as profound as that of my mother, we shall find in the course of this narrative, but it was neither then nor thus that I imagined it. Nevertheless, like a principal actor who ought to have learned his part and to have been in his place long beforehand but has arrived only at the last moment and, having read over once only what he has to say, manages to "gag" so skilfully when his cue comes that nobody notices his unpunctuality, my new found grief enabled me, when my mother came, to talk to her as though it had existed always. She supposed merely that the sight of these places which I had visited with my grandmother (which was not at all the case) had revived it. For the first time then, and because I felt a sorrow which was nothing compared with hers, but which opened my eyes, I realised and was appalled to think what she must be suffering. For the first time I understood that the fixed and tearless gaze (which made Françoise withhold her sympathy) that she had worn since my grandmother's death had been arrested by that incomprehensible contradiction of memory and nonexistence. Besides, since she was, although still in deep mourning, more fashionably dressed in this strange place, I was more struck by the transformation that had occurred in her. It is not enough to say that she had lost all her gaiety; melted, congealed into a sort of imploring image, she seemed to be afraid of shocking by too sudden a movement, by too loud a tone, the sorrowful presence that never parted from her. But, what struck me most of all, when I saw her cloak of crape, was—what had never occurred to me in Paris—that it was no longer my mother that I saw before me, but my grandmother. As, in royal and princely families, upon the death of the head of the house his son takes his title and, from being Duc d'Orléans, Prince de Tarente or Prince des Laumes, becomes King of France, Duc de la Trémoïlle, Duc de Guermantes, so by an accession of a different order and more remote origin, the dead man takes possession of the living who becomes his image and successor, carries on his interrupted life. Perhaps the great sorrow that follows, in a daughter such as Mamma, the death of her mother only makes the chrysalis break open a little sooner, hastens the metamorphosis and the appearance of a person whom we carry within us and who, but for this crisis which annihilates time and space, would have come more gradually to the surface. Perhaps, in our regret for her who is no more, there is a sort of auto-suggestion which ends by bringing out on our features resemblances which potentially we already bore, and above all a cessation of our most characteristically personal activity (in my mother, her common sense, the sarcastic gaiety that she inherited from her father) which we did not shrink, so long as the beloved was alive, from exercising, even at her expense, and which counterbalanced the traits that we derived exclusively from her. Once she is dead, we should hesitate to be different, we begin to admire only what she was, what we ourselves already were only blended with something else, and what in future we are to be exclusively. It is in this sense (and not in that other, so vague, so false, in which the phrase is generally used) that we may say that death is not in vain, that the dead man continues to react upon us. He reacts even more than a living man because, true reality being discoverable only by the mind, being the object of a spiritual operation, we acquire a true knowledge only of things that we are obliged to create anew by thought, things that are hidden from us in everyday life. . . . Lastly, in our mourning for our dead we pay an idolatrous worship to the things that they liked. Not only could not my mother bear to be parted from my grandmother's bag, become more precious than if it had been studded with sapphires and diamonds, from her muff, from all those garments which served to enhance their personal resemblance, but even from the volumes of Mme. de Sévigné which my grandmother took with her everywhere, copies which my mother would not have exchanged for the original manuscript of the letters. She had often teased my grandmother who could never write to her without quoting some phrase of Mme. de Sévigné or Mme. de Beausergent. In each of the three letters that I received from Mamma before her arrival at Balbec, she quoted Mme. de Sévigné to me, as though those three letters had been written not by her to me but by my grandmother and to her. She must at once go out upon the front to see that beach of which my grandmother had spoken to her every day in her letters. Carrying her mother's sunshade, I saw her from my window advance, a sable figure, with timid, pious steps, over the sands that beloved feet had trodden before her, and she looked as though she were going down to find a corpse which the waves would cast up at her feet. So that she should not have to dine by herself, I was to join her downstairs. The chief magistrate and the barrister's widow asked to be introduced to her. And everything that was in any way connected with my grandmother was so precious to her that she was deeply touched, remembered ever afterwards with gratitude what the chief magistrate had said to her, just as she was hurt and indignant that the barrister's wife had not a word to say in memory of the dead. In reality, the chief magistrate was no more concerned about my grandmother than the barrister's wife. The heartfelt words of the one and the other's silence, for all that my mother imagined so vast a difference between them, were but alternative ways of expressing that indifference which we feel towards the dead. But I think that my mother found most comfort in the words in which, quite involuntarily, I conveyed to her a little of my own anguish. It could not but make Mamma happy (notwithstanding all her affection for myself), like everything else that guaranteed my grandmother survival in our hearts. Daily after this my mother went down and sat upon the beach, so as to do exactly what her mother had done, and read her mother's two favourite books, the *Memoirs* of Madame de Beausergent and the *Letters* of Madame de Sévigné. She, like all the rest of us, could not bear to hear the latter lady called the " spirituelle Marquise " any more than to hear La Fontaine called " le Bonhomme." But when, in reading the *Letters,* she came upon the words: " My daughter," she seemed to be listening to her mother's voice.

She had the misfortune, upon one of these pilgrimages during which she did not like to be disturbed, to meet upon the beach a lady from Combray, accompanied by her daughters. Her name was, I think, Madame Poussin. But among ourselves we always referred to her as the "Pretty Kettle of Fish," for it was by the perpetual repetition of this phrase that she warned her daughters of the evils that they were laying up for themselves, saying for instance if one of them was rubbing her eyes: "When you go and get ophthalmia, that will be a pretty kettle of fish." She greeted my mother from afar with slow and melancholy bows, a sign not of condolence but of the nature of her social training. We might never have lost my grandmother, or had any reason to be anything but happy. Living in comparative retirement at Combray within the walls of her large garden, she could never find anything soft enough to her liking, and subjected to a softening process the words and even the proper names of the French language. She felt "spoon" to be too hard a word to apply to the piece of silver which measured out her syrups, and said, in consequence, "spune"; she would have been afraid of hurting the feelings of the sweet singer of Télémaque by calling him bluntly Fénelon—as I myself said with a clear conscience, having had as a friend the dearest and cleverest of men, good and gallant, never to be forgotten by any that knew him, Bertrand de Fénelon—and never said anything but "Fénélon," feeling that the acute accent added a certain softness. The far from soft son-in-law of this Madame Poussin, whose name I have forgotten, having been a lawyer at Combray, ran off with the contents of the safe, and relieved my uncle among others of a considerable sum of money. But most of the people of Combray were on such friendly terms with the rest of the family that no coolness ensued and her neighbours said merely that they were sorry for Madame Poussin. She never entertained, but whenever people passed by her railings they would stop to admire the delicious shade of her trees, which was the only thing that could be made out. She gave us no trouble at Balbec, where I encountered her only once, at a moment when she was saying to a daughter who was biting her nails: "When they begin to fester, that will be a pretty kettle of fish."

While Mamma sat reading on the beach I remained in my room by myself. I recalled the last weeks of my grandmother's life, and everything connected with them, the outer door of the flat which had been propped open when I went out with her for the last time. In contrast to all this the rest of the world seemed scarcely real and my anguish poisoned everything in it. Finally my mother insisted upon my going out. But at every step, some forgotten view of the casino, of the street along which, as I waited until she was ready, that first evening, I had walked as far as the monument to Duguay-Trouin, prevented me, like a wind against which it is hopeless to struggle, from going farther; I lowered my eyes in order not to see. And after I had recovered my strength a little I turned back towards the hotel, the hotel in which I knew that it was henceforth impossible that, however long I might wait, I should find my grandmother, whom I had found there before, on the evening of our arrival. As it was the first time that I had gone out of doors, a number of servants whom I had not yet seen were gazing at me curiously. Upon the very threshold of the hotel a young page took off his cap to greet me and at once put it on again. I supposed that Aimé had, to borrow his own expression, "given him the office" to treat me with respect. But I saw a moment later that, as some one else entered the hotel, he doffed it again. The fact of the matter was that this young man had no other occupation in life than to take off and put on his cap, and did it to perfection. Having realised that he was incapable of doing anything else and that in this art he excelled, he practised it as often as was possible daily, which won him a discreet but widespread regard from the visitors, coupled with great regard from the hall porter upon whom devolved the duty of engaging the boys and who, until this rare bird alighted, had never succeeded in finding one who did not receive notice within a week, greatly to the astonishment of Aimé who used to say: "After all, in that job they've only got to be polite, which can't be sc very difficult." The manager required in addition that they should have what he called a good "presence," meaning thereby that they should not be absent from their posts, or perhaps having heard the word "presence" used of personal appearance. The appearance of the lawn behind the hotel had been altered by the creation of several flower-beds and by the removal not only of an exotic shrub but of the page who, at the time of my former visit, used to provide an external decoration with the supple stem of his figure crowned by the curious colouring of his hair. He had gone with a Polish countess who had taken him as her secretary, following the example of his two elder brothers and their typist sister, torn from the hotel by persons of different race and sex who had been attracted by their charm. The only one remaining was the youngest, whom nobody wanted, because he squinted. He was highly delighted when the Polish countess or the protectors of the other two brothers came on a visit to the hotel at Balbec. For, albeit he was jealous of his brothers, he was fond of them and could in this way cultivate his family affections for a few weeks in the year. Was not the Abbess of Fontevrault accustomed, deserting her nuns for the occasion, to come and partake of the hospitality which Louis XIV offered to that other Mortemart, his mistress, Madame de Montespan? The boy was still in his first year at Balbec; he did not as yet know me, but having heard his comrades of longer standing supplement the word "Monsieur," when they addressed me, with my surname, he copied them from the first with an air of satisfaction, whether at shewing his familiarity with a person whom he supposed to be well-known, or at conforming with a custom of which five minutes earlier he had never heard but which he felt it to be indispensable that he should not fail to observe. I could quite well appreciate the charm that this great "Palace" might have for certain persons. It was arranged like a theatre, and a numerous cast filled it to the doors with animation. For all that the visitor was only a sort of spectator, he was perpetually taking part in the performance, and that not as in one of those theatres where the actors perform a play among the audience, but as though the life of the spectator were going on amid the sumptuous fittings of the stage. The lawn-tennis player might come in wearing a white flannel blazer, the porter would have put on a blue frock coat with silver braid before handing him his letters. If this lawn-tennis player did not choose to walk upstairs, he was equally involved with the actors in having by his side, to propel the lift, its attendant no less richly attired. The corridors on each landing engulfed a flying band of nymphlike chambermaids, fair visions against the sea, at whose modest chambers the admirers of feminine beauty arrived by cunning detours. Downstairs, it was the masculine element that predominated and made this hotel, in view of the extreme and effortless youth of the servants, a sort of Judaeo-Christian tragedy given bodily form and perpetually in performance. And so I could not help repeating to myself, when I saw them, not indeed the lines of Racine that had come into my head at the Princesse de Guermantes's while M. de Vaugoubert stood watching young secretaries of embassy greet M. de Charlus, but other lines of Racine, taken this time not from *Esther* but from *Athalie:* for in the doorway of the hall, what in the seventeenth century was called the portico, "a flourishing race" of young pages clustered, especially at teatime, like the young Israelites of Racine's choruses. But I do not believe that one of them could have given even the vague answer that Joas finds to satisfy Athalie when she inquires of the infant Prince: "What is your office, then?" for they had none. At the most, if one had asked of any of them, like the new Queen: "But all this race, what do they then, imprisoned in this place?" he might have said: "I watch the solemn pomp and bear my part." Now and then one of the young supers would approach some more important personage, then this young beauty would rejoin the chorus, and, unless it were the moment for a spell of contemplative relaxation, they would proceed with their useless, reverent, decorative, daily evolutions. For, except on their "day off," "reared in seclusion from the world" and never crossing the threshold, they led the same ecclesiastical existence as the Levites in *Athalie,* and as I gazed at that "young and faithful troop" playing at the foot of the steps draped with sumptuous carpets, I felt inclined to ask myself whether I were entering the Grand Hotel at Balbec or the Temple of Solomon.

I went straight up to my room. My thoughts kept constantly turning to the last days of my grandmother's illness, to her sufferings which I lived over again, intensifying them with that element which is even harder to endure than the sufferings of other people, and is added to them by our merciless pity; when we think that we are merely reviving the pains of a beloved friend, our pity exaggerates them; but perhaps it is our pity that is in the right, more than the sufferers' own consciousness of their pains, they being blind to that tragedy of their own existence which pity sees and deplores. Certainly my pity would have taken fresh strength and far exceeded my grandmother's sufferings had I known then what I did not know until long afterwards, that my grandmother, on the eve of her death, in a moment of consciousness and after making sure that I was not in the room, had taken Mamma's hand, and, after pressing her fevered lips to it, had said: "Farewell, my child, farewell for ever." And this may perhaps have been the memory upon which my mother never ceased to gaze so fixedly. Then more pleasant memories returned to me. She was my grandmother and I was her grandson. Her facial expressions seemed written in a language intended for me alone; she was everything in my life, other people existed merely in relation to her, to the judgment that she would pass upon them; but no, our relations were too fleeting to have been anything but accidental. She no longer knew me, I should never see her again. We had not been created solely for one another, she was a stranger to me. This stranger was before my eyes at the moment in the photograph taken of her by Saint-Loup. Mamma, who had met Albertine, insisted upon my seeing her, because of the nice things that she had said about my grandmother and myself. I had accordingly made an appointment with her. I told the manager that she was coming, and asked him to let her wait for me in the drawing-room. He informed me that he had known her for years, her and her friends, long before they had attained "the age of purity" but that he was annoyed with them because of certain things that they had said about the hotel. "They can't be very 'gentlemanly' if they talk like that. Unless people have been slandering them." I had no difficulty in guessing that "purity" here meant "puberty." As I waited until it should be time to go down and meet Albertine, I was keeping my eyes fixed, as upon a picture which one ceases to see by dint of staring at it, upon the photograph that Saint-Loup had taken, when all of a sudden I thought once again: "It's grandmother, I am her grandson" as a man who has lost his memory remembers his name, as a sick man changes his personality. Françoise came in to tell me that Albertine was there, and, catching sight of the photograph: "Poor Madame, it's the very image of her, even the beauty spot on her cheek; that day the Marquis took her picture, she was very poorly, she had been taken bad twice. 'Whatever happens, Françoise,' she said, 'you must never let my grandson know.' And she kept it to herself, she was always bright with other people. When she was by herself, though, I used to find that she seemed to be in rather monotonous spirits now and then. But that soon passed away. And then she said to me, she said: 'If anything were to happen to me, he ought to have a picture of me to keep. And I have never had one done in my life.' So then she sent me along with a message to the Marquis, and he was never to let you know that it was she who had asked him, but could he take her photograph. But when I came back and told her that he would, she had changed her mind again, because she was looking so poorly. 'It would be even worse,' she said to me, 'than no picture at all.' But she was a clever one, she was, and in the end she got herself up so well in that big shady hat that it didn't shew at all when she was out of the sun. She was very glad to have that photograph, because at that time she didn't think she would ever leave Balbec alive.' It was no use my saying to her: 'Madame, it's wrong to talk like that, I don't like to hear Madame talk like that,' she had got it into her head. And, lord, there were plenty days when she couldn't eat a thing. That was why she used to make Monsieur go and dine away out in the country with M. le Marquis. Then, instead of going in to dinner, she would pretend to be reading a book, and as soon as the Marquis's carriage had started, up she would go to bed. Some days she wanted to send word to Madame, to come down and see her in time. And then she was afraid of alarming her, as she had said nothing to her about it. 'It will be better for her to stay with her husband, don't you see, Françoise.'" Looking me in the face, Françoise asked me all of a sudden if I was "feeling indisposed." I said that I was not; whereupon she: "And you make me waste my time talking to you. Your visitor has been here all this time. I must go down and tell her. She is not the sort of person to have here. Why, a fast one like that, she may be gone again by now. She doesn't like to be kept waiting. Oh, nowadays, Mademoiselle Albertine, she's somebody!" "You are quite wrong, she is a very respectable person, too respectable for this place. But go and tell her that I shan't be able to see her to-day."

What compassionate declamations I should have provoked from Françoise if she had seen me cry. I carefully hid myself from her. Otherwise I should have had her sympathy. But I gave her mine. We do not put ourselves sufficiently in the place of these poor maidservants who cannot bear to see us cry, as though crying were bad for us; or bad, perhaps, for them, for Françoise used to say to me when I was a child: "Don't cry like that, I don't like to see you crying like that." We dislike highfalutin language, asseverations, we are wrong, we close our hearts to the pathos of the countryside, to the legend which the poor servant girl, dismissed, unjustly perhaps, for theft, pale as death, grown suddenly more humble than if it were a crime merely to be accused, unfolds, invoking her father's honesty, her mother's principles, her grandam's counsels. It is true that those same servants who cannot bear our tears will have no hesitation in letting us catch pneumonia, because the maid downstairs like draughts and it would not be polite to her to shut the windows. For it is necessary that even those who are right, like Françoise, should be wrong also, so that Justice may be made an impossible thing. Even the humble pleasures of servants provoke either the refusal or the ridicule of their masters. For it is always a mere nothing, but foolishly sentimental, unhygienic. And so, they are in a position to say: "How is it that I ask for only this one thing in the whole year, and am not allowed it." And yet the masters will allow them something far more difficult, which was not stupid and dangerous for the servants—or for themselves. To be sure, the humility of the wretched maid, trembling, ready to confess the crime that she has not committed, saying "I shall leave to-night if you wish it," is a thing that nobody can resist. But we must learn also not to remain unmoved, despite the solemn, menacing fatuity of the things that she says, her maternal heritage and the dignity of the family "kailyard," before an old cook draped in the honour of her life and of her ancestry, wielding her broom like a sceptre, donning the tragic buskin, stifling her speech with sobs, drawing herself up with majesty. That afternoon, I remembered or imagined scenes of this sort which I associated with our old servant, and from then onwards, in spite of all the harm that she might do to Albertine, I loved Françoise with an affection, intermittent it is true, but of the strongest kind, the kind that is founded upon pity.

To be sure, I suffered agonies all that day, as I sat gazing at my grandmother's photograph. It tortured me. Not so acutely, though, as the visit I received that evening from the manager. After I had spoken to him about my grandmother, and he had reiterated his condolences, I heard him say (for he enjoyed using the words that he pronounced wrongly): "Like the day when Madame your grandmother had that sincup, I wanted to tell you about it, because of the other visitors, don't you know, it might have given the place a bad name. She ought really to have left that evening. But she begged me to say nothing about it and promised me that she wouldn't have another sincup, or the first time she had one, she would go. The floor waiter reported to me that she had had another. But, lord, you were old friends that we try to please, and so long as nobody made any complaint." And so my grandmother had had syncopes which she had never mentioned to me. Perhaps at the very moment when I was being most beastly to her, when she was obliged, amid her pain, to see that she kept her temper, so as not to anger me, and her looks, so as not to be turned out of the hotel. " Sincup " was a word which, so pronounced, I should never have imagined, which might perhaps, applied to other people, have struck me as ridiculous, but which in its strange sonorous novelty, like that of an original discord, long retained the faculty of arousing in me the most painful sensations.

Next day I went, at Mamma's request, to lie down for a little on the sands, or rather among the dunes, where one is hidden by their folds, and I knew that Albertine and her friends would not be able to find me. My drooping eyelids allowed but one kind of light to pass, all rosy, the light of the inner walls of the eyes. Then they shut altogether. Whereupon my grandmother appeared to me, seated in an armchair. So feeble she was, she seemed to be less alive than other people. And yet I could hear her breathe; now and again she made a sign to shew that she had understood what we were saying, my father and I. But in vain might I take her in my arms, I failed utterly to kindle a spark of affection in her eyes, a flush of colour in her cheeks. Absent from herself, she appeared somehow not to love me, not to know me, perhaps not to see me. I could not interpret the secret of her indifference, of her dejection, of her silent resentment. I drew my father aside. "You can see, all the same," I said to him, "there's no doubt about it, she understands everything perfectly. It is a perfect imitation of life. If we could have your cousin here, who maintains that the dead don't live. Why, she's been dead for more than a year now, and she's still alive. But why won't she give me a kiss?" "Look, her poor head is drooping again." "But she wants to go, now, to the Champs-Elysées." "It's madness!" "You really think it can do her any harm, that she can die any further? It isn't possible that she no longer loves me. I keep on hugging her, won't she ever smile at me again?" "What can you expect, when people are dead they are dead."

A few days later I was able to look with pleasure at the photograph that Saint-Loup had taken of her; it did not revive the memory of what Françoise had told me, because that memory had never left me and I was growing used to it. But with regard to the idea that I had received of the state of her health—so grave, so painful—on that day, the photograph, still profiting by the ruses that my grandmother had adopted, which succeeded in taking me in even after they had been disclosed to me, shewed me her so smart, so care-free, beneath the hat which partly hid her face, that I saw her looking less unhappy and in better health than I had imagined. And yet, her cheeks having unconsciously assumed an expression of their own, livid, haggard, like the expression of an animal that feels that it has been marked down for slaughter, my grandmother had an air of being under sentence of death, an air involuntarily sombre, unconsciously tragic, which passed unperceived by me but prevented Mamma from ever looking at that photograph, that photograph which seemed to her a photograph not so much of her mother as of her mother's disease, of an insult that the disease was offering to the brutally buffeted face of my grandmother.

Then one day I decided to send word to Albertine that I would see her presently. This was because, on a morning of intense and premature heat, the myriad cries of children at play, of bathers disporting themselves, of newsvendors, had traced for me in lines of fire, in wheeling, interlacing flashes, the scorching beach which the little waves came up one after another to sprinkle with their coolness; then had begun the symphonic concert mingled with the splashing of the water, through which the violins hummed like a swarm of bees that had strayed out over the sea. At once I had longed to hear again Albertine's laughter, to see her friends, those girls outlined against the waves who had remained in my memory the inseparable charm, the typical flora of Balbec; and I had determined to send a line by Françoise to Albertine, making an appointment for the following week, while, gently rising, the sea as each wave uncurled completely buried in layers of crystal the melody whose phrases appeared to be separated from one another like those angel lutanists which on the roof of the Italian cathedral rise between the peaks of blue porphyry and foaming jasper. But on the day on which Albertine came, the weather had turned dull and cold again, and moreover I had no opportunity of hearing her laugh; she was in a very bad temper. "Balbec is deadly dull this year," she said to me. "I don't mean to stay any longer than I can help. You know I've been here since Easter, that's more than a month. There's not a soul here. You can imagine what fun it is." Notwithstanding the recent rain and a sky that changed every moment, after escorting Albertine as far as Epreville, for she was, to borrow her expression, "on the run" between that little watering-place, where Mme. Bontemps had her villa, and Incarville, where she had been taken "en pension" by Rosemonde's family, I went off by myself in the direction of the highroad that Mme. de Villeparisis's carriage had taken when we went for a drive with my grandmother; pools of water which the sun, now bright again, had not dried made a regular quagmire of the ground, and I thought of my grandmother who, in the old days, could not walk a yard without covering herself in mud. But on reaching the road I found a dazzling spectacle. Where I had seen with my grandmother in the month of August only the green leaves and, so to speak, the disposition of the apple-trees, as far as the eye could reach they were in full bloom, marvellous in their splendour, their feet in the mire beneath their ball-dresses, taking no precaution not to spoil the most marvellous pink satin that was ever seen, which glittered in the sunlight; the distant horizon of the sea gave the trees the background of a Japanese print; if I raised my head to gaze at the sky through the blossom, which made its serene blue appear almost violent, the trees seemed to be drawing apart to reveal the immensity of their paradise. Beneath that azure a faint but cold breeze set the blushing bouquets gently trembling. Blue tits came and perched upon the branches and fluttered among the flowers, indulgent, as though it had been an amateur of exotic art and colours who had artificially created this living beauty. But it moved one to tears because, to whatever lengths the artist went in the refinement of his creation, one felt that it was natural, that these apple-trees were there in the heart of the country, like peasants, upon one of the highroads of France. Then the rays of the sun gave place suddenly to those of the rain; they streaked the whole horizon, caught the line of apple-trees in their grey net. But they continued to hold aloft their beauty, pink and blooming, in the wind that had turned icy beneath the drenching rain: it was a day in spring.

CHAPTER II

The mysteries of Albertine—The girls whom she sees reflected in the glass—The other woman—The lift-boy—Madame de Cambremer—The pleasures of M. Nissim Bernard—Outline of the strange character of Morel—M. de Charlus dines with the Verdurins.

IN my fear lest the pleasure I found in this solitary excursion might weaken my memory of my grandmother, I sought to revive this by thinking of some great mental suffering that she had undergone; in response to my appeal that suffering tried to build itself in my heart, threw up vast pillars there; but my heart was doubtless too small for it, I had not the strength to bear so great a grief, my attention was distracted at the moment when it was approaching completion, and its arches collapsed before joining as, before they have perfected their curve, the waves of the sea totter and break.

And yet, if only from my dreams when I was asleep, I might have learned that my grief for my grandmother's death was diminishing, for she appeared in them less crushed by the idea that I had formed of her non-existence. I saw her an invalid still, but on the road to recovery, I found her in better health. And if she made any allusion to what she had suffered, I stopped her mouth with my kisses and assured her that she was now permanently cured. I should have liked to call the sceptics to witness that death is indeed a malady from which one recovers. Only, I no longer found in my grandmother the rich spontaneity of old times. Her words were no more than a feeble, docile response, almost a mere echo of mine; she was nothing more than the reflexion of my own thoughts.

Incapable as I still was of feeling any fresh physical desire, Albertine was beginning nevertheless to inspire in me a desire for happiness. Certain dreams of shared affection, always floating on the surface of our minds, ally themselves readily by a sort of affinity with the memory (provided that this has already become slightly vague) of a woman with whom we have taken our pleasure. This sentiment recalled to me aspects of Albertine's face, more gentle, less gay, quite different from those that would have been evoked by physical desire; and as it was also less pressing than that desire I would gladly have postponed its realisation until the following winter, without seeking to see Albertine again at Balbec, before her departure. But even in the midst of a grief that is still keen physical desire will revive. From my bed, where I was made to spend hours every day resting, I longed for Albertine to come and resume our former amusements. Do we not see, in the very room in which they have lost a child, its parents soon come together again to give the little angel a baby brother? I tried to distract my mind from this desire by going to the window to look at that day's sea. As in the former year, the seas, from one day to another, were rarely the same. Nor, however, did they at all resemble those of that first year, whether because we were now in spring with its storms, or because even if I had come down at the same time as before, the different, more changeable weather might have discouraged from visiting this coast certain seas, indolent, vaporous and fragile, which I had seen throughout long, scorching days, asleep upon the beach, their bluish bosoms, only, faintly stirring, with a soft palpitation, or, as was most probable, because my eyes, taught by Elstir to retain precisely those elements that before I had deliberately rejected, would now gaze for hours at what in the former year they had been incapable of seeing. The contrast that used then to strike me so forcibly between the country drives that I took with Mme. de Villeparisis and this proximity, fluid, inaccessible, mythological, of the eternal Ocean, no longer existed for me. And there were days now when, on the contrary, the sea itself seemed almost rural. On the days, few and far between, of really fine weather, the heat had traced upon the waters, as it might be across country, a dusty white track, at the end of which the pointed mast of a fishing-boat stood up like a village steeple. A tug, of which one could see only the funnel, was smoking in the distance like a factory amid the fields, while alone against the horizon a convex patch of white, sketched there doubtless by a sail but apparently a solid plastered surface, made one think of the sunlit wall of some isolated building, an hospital or a school. And the clouds and the wind, on days when these were added to the sun, completed if not the error of judgment, at any rate the illusion of the first glance, the suggestion that it aroused in the imagination. For the alternation of sharply defined patches of colour like those produced in the country by the proximity of different crops, the rough, yellow, almost muddy irregularities of the marine surface, the banks, the slopes that hid from sight a vessel upon which a crew of nimble sailors seemed to be reaping a harvest, all this upon stormy days made the ocean a thing as varied, as solid, as broken, as populous, as civilised as the earth with its carriage roads over which I used to travel, and was soon to be travelling again. And once, unable any longer to hold out against my desire, instead of going back to bed I put on my clothes and started off to Incarville, to find Albertine. I would ask her to come with me to Douville, where I would pay calls at Féterne upon Mme. de Cambremer and at la Raspelière upon Mme. Verdurin. Albertine would wait for me meanwhile upon the beach and we would return together after dark. I went to take the train on the local light railway, of which I had picked up, the time before, from Albertine and her friends all the nicknames current in the district, where it was known as the *Twister* because of its numberless windings, the *Crawler* because the train never seemed to move, the *Transatlantic* because of a horrible siren which it sounded to clear people off the line, the *Decauville* and the *Funi,* albeit there was nothing funicular about it but because it climbed the cliff, and, although not, strictly speaking, a Decauville, had a 60 centimetre gauge, the *B. A. G.* because it ran between Balbec and Grattevast *via* Angerville, the *Tram* and the *T. S. N.* because it was a branch of the Tramways of Southern Normandy. I took my seat in a compartment in which I was alone; it was a day of glorious sunshine, and stiflingly hot; I drew down the blue blind which shut off all but a single ray of sunlight. But immediately I beheld my grandmother, as she had appeared sitting in the train, on our leaving Paris for Balbec, when, in her sorrow at seeing me drink beer, she had preferred not to look, to shut her eyes and pretend to be asleep. I, who in my childhood had been unable to endure her anguish when my grandfather tasted brandy, I had inflicted this anguish upon her, not merely of seeing me accept, at the invitation of another, a drink which she regarded as bad for me, I had forced her to leave me free to swill it down to my heart's content, worse still, by my bursts of passion, my choking fits, I had forced her to help, to advise me to do so, with a supreme resignation of which I saw now in my memory the mute, despairing image, her eyes closed to shut out the sight. So vivid a memory had, like the stroke of a magic wand, restored the mood that I had been gradually outgrowing for some time past; what had I to do with Rosemonde when my lips were wholly possessed by the desperate longing to kiss a dead woman, what had I to say to the Cambremers and Verdurins when my heart was beating so violently because at every moment there was being renewed in it the pain that my grandmother had suffered. I could not remain in the compartment. As soon as the train stopped at Maineville-la-Teinturière, abandoning all my plans, I alighted. Maineville had of late acquired considerable importance and a reputation all its own, because a director of various casinos, a caterer in pleasure, had set up, just outside it, with a luxurious display of bad taste that could vie with that of any smart hotel, an establishment to which we shall return anon, and which was, to put it briefly, the first brothel for "exclusive" people that it had occurred to anyone to build upon the coast of France. It was the only one. True, every port has its own, but intended for sailors only, and for lovers of the picturesque whom it amuses to see, next door to the primeval parish church, the bawd, hardly less ancient, venerable and moss-grown, standing outside her ill-famed door, waiting for the return of the fishing fleet.

Hurrying past the glittering house of "pleasure," insolently erected there despite the protests which the heads of families had addressed in vain to the mayor, I reached the cliff and followed its winding paths in the direction of

Balbec. I heard, without responding to it, the appeal of the hawthorns. Neighbours, in humbler circumstances, of the blossoming apple trees, they found them very coarse, without denying the fresh complexion of the rosy-petalled daughters of those wealthy brewers of cider. They know that, with a lesser dowry, they were more sought after, and were attractive enough by themselves in their tattered whiteness.

On my return, the hotel porter handed me a black-bordered letter in which the Marquis and the Marquise de Gonneville, the Vicomte and the Vicomtesse d'Amfreville, the Comte and the Comtesse de Berneville, the Marquis and the Marquise de Graincourt, the Comte d'Amenoncourt, the Comtesse de Maineville, the Comte and the Comtesse de Franquetot, the Comtesse de Chaverny *née* d'Aigleville, begged to announce, and from which I understood at length why it had been sent to me when I caught sight of the names of the Marquise de Cambremer *née* du Mesnil la Guichard, the Marquis and the Marquise de Cambremer, and saw that the deceased, a cousin of the Cambremers, was named Éléonore-Euphrasie-Humbertine de Cambremer, Comtesse de Criquetot. In the whole extent of this provincial family, the enumeration of which filled the closely printed lines, not a single commoner, and on the other hand not a single title that one knew, but the entire muster-roll of the nobles of the region who made their names—those of all the interesting spots in the neighbourhood—ring out their joyous endings in *ville,* in *court,* sometimes on a duller note (in *tot*). Garbed in the roof-tiles of their castle or in the roughcast of their parish church, their nodding heads barely reaching above the vault of the nave or banqueting hall, and then only to cap themselves with the Norman lantern or the dovecot of the pepperpot turret, they gave the impression of having sounded the rallying call to all the charming villages straggling or scattered over a radius of fifty leagues, and to have paraded them in massed formation, without one absentee, one intruder, on the compact, rectangular draught-board of the aristocratic letter edged with black.

My mother had gone upstairs to her room, meditating the phrase of Madame de Sévigné: "I see nothing of the people who seek to distract me from you; the truth of the matter is that they are seeking to prevent me from thinking of you, and that annoys me."—because the chief magistrate had told her that she ought to find some distraction. To me he whispered: "That's the Princesse de Parme!" My fears were dispelled when I saw that the woman whom the magistrate pointed out to me bore not the slightest resemblance to Her Royal Highness. But as she had engaged a room in which to spend the night after paying a visit to Mme. de Luxembourg, the report of her coming had the effect upon many people of making them take each newcomer for the Princesse de Parme—and upon me of making me go and shut myself up in my attic.

I had no wish to remain there by myself. It was barely four o'clock. I asked Françoise to go and find Albertine, so that she might spend the rest of the afternoon with me.

It would be untrue, I think, to say that there were already symptoms of that painful and perpetual mistrust which Albertine was to inspire in me, not to mention the special character, emphatically Gomorrhan, which that mistrust was to assume. Certainly, even that afternoon

—but this was not the first time—I grew anxious as I was kept waiting. Françoise, once she had started, stayed away so long that I began to despair. I had not lighted the lamp. The daylight had almost gone. The wind was making the flag over the Casino flap. And, fainter still in the silence of the beach over which the tide was rising, and like a voice rendering and enhancing the troubling emptiness of this restless, unnatural hour, a little barrel organ that had stopped outside the hotel was playing Viennese waltzes. At length Françoise arrived, but unaccompanied. "I have been as quick as I could but she wouldn't come because she didn't think she was looking smart enough. If she was five minutes painting herself and powdering herself, she was an hour by the clock. You'll be having a regular scentshop in here. She's coming, she stayed behind to tidy herself at the glass. I thought I should find her here." There was still a long time to wait before Albertine appeared. But the gaiety, the charm that she shewed on this occasion dispelled my sorrow. She informed me (in contradiction of what she had said the other day) that she would be staying for the whole season and asked me whether we could not arrange, as in the former year, to meet daily. I told her that at the moment I was too melancholy and that I would rather send for her from time to time at the last moment, as I did in Paris. "If ever you're feeling worried, or feel that you want me, do not hesitate," she told me, "to send for me, I shall came immediately, and if you are not afraid of its creating a scandal in the hotel, I shall stay as long as you like." Françoise, in bringing her to me, had assumed the joyous air she wore whenever she had gone out of her way to please me and had been successful. But Albertine herself contributed nothing to her joy, and the very next day Françoise was to greet me with the profound observation: "Monsieur ought not to see that young lady. I know quite well the sort she is, she'll land you in trouble." As I escorted Albertine to the door I saw in the lighted dining-room the Princesse de Parme. I merely gave her a glance, taking care not to be seen. But I must say that I found a certain grandeur in the royal politeness which had made me smile at the Guermantes'. It is a fundamental rule that sovereign princes are at home wherever they are, and this rule is conventionally expressed in obsolete and useless customs such as that which requires the host to carry his hat in his hand, in his own house, to shew that he is not in his own home but in the Prince's. Now the Princesse de Parme may not have formulated this idea to herself, but she was so imbued with it that all her actions, spontaneously invented to suit the circumstances, pointed to it. When she rose from table she handed a lavish tip to Aimé, as though he had been there solely for her and she were rewarding, before leaving a country house, a footman who had been detailed to wait upon her. Nor did she stop at the tip, but with a gracious smile bestowed on him a few friendly, flattering words, with a store of which her mother had provided her. Another moment, and she would have told him that, just as the hotel was perfectly managed, so Normandy was a garden of roses and that she preferred France to any other country in the world. Another coin slipped from the Princess's fingers, for the wine waiter, for whom she had sent and to whom she made a point of expressing her satisfaction like a general after an inspection. The lift-boy had come up at that moment with a message for her; he too received a little speech, a smile and a tip, all this interspersed with encouraging and humble words intended to prove to them that she was only one of themselves. As Aimé, the wine waiter, the lift-boy and the rest felt that it would be impolite not to grin from ear to ear at a person who smiled at them, she was presently surrounded by a cluster of servants with whom she chatted kindly; such ways being unfamiliar in smart hotels, the people who passed by, not knowing who she was, thought they beheld a permanent resident at Balbec, who, because of her humble origin, or for professional reasons (she was perhaps the wife of an agent for champagne) was less different from the domestics than the really smart visitors. As for me, I thought of the palace at Parma, of the counsels, partly religious, partly political, given to this Princess, who behaved towards the lower orders as though she had been obliged to conciliate them in order to reign over them one day. All the more, as if she were already reigning.

I went upstairs again to my room, but I was not alone there. I could hear some one softly playing Schumann. No doubt it happens at times that people, even those whom we love best, become saturated with the melancholy or irritation that emanates from us. There is nevertheless an inanimate object which is capable of a power of exasperation to which no human being will ever attain: to wit, a piano.

Albertine had made me take a note of the dates on which she would be going away for a few days to visit various girl friends, and had made me write down their addresses as well, in case I should want her on one of those evenings, for none of them lived very far away.

This meant that when I tried to find her, going from one girl to another, she became more and more entwined in ropes of flowers. I must confess that many of her friends —I was not yet in love with her—gave me, at one watering-place or another, moments of pleasure. These obliging young comrades did not seem to me to be very many. But recently I have thought it over, their names have recurred to me. I counted that, in that one season, a dozen conferred on me their ephemeral favours. A name came back to me later, which made thirteen. I then, with almost a child's delight in cruelty, dwelt upon that number. Alas, I realised that I had forgotten the first of them all, Albertine who no longer existed and who made the fourteenth.

I had, to resume the thread of my narrative, written down the names and addresses of the girls with whom I should find her upon the days when she was not to be at Incarville, but privately had decided that I would devote those days rather to calling upon Mme. Verdurin. In any case, our desire for different women varies in intensity. One evening we cannot bear to let one out of our sight who, after that, for the next month or two, will never enter our mind. Then there is the law of change, for a study of which this is not the place, under which, after an over-exertion of the flesh, the woman whose image haunts our momentary senility is one to whom we would barely give more than a kiss on the brow. As for Albertine, I saw her seldom, and only upon the very infrequent evenings when I felt that I could not live without her. If this desire seized me when she was too far from Balbec for Françoise to be able to go and fetch her, I used to send the lift-boy to Egreville, to La Sogne, to

Saint-Frichoux, asking him to finish his work a little earlier than usual. He would come into my room, but would leave the door open for, albeit he was conscientious at his " job " which was pretty hard, consisting in endless cleanings from five o'clock in the morning, he could never bring himself to make the effort to shut a door, and, if one were to remark to him that it was open, would turn back and, summoning up all his strength, give it a gentle push. With the democratic pride that marked him, a pride to which, in more liberal careers, the members of a profession that is at all numerous never attain, barristers, doctors and men of letters speaking simply of a " brother " barrister, doctor or man of letters, he, employing, and rightly, a term that is confined to close corporations like the Academy, would say to me in speaking of a page who was in charge of the lift upon alternate days: " I shall get my *colleague* to take my place." This pride did not prevent him from accepting, with a view to increasing what he called his " salary," remuneration for his errands, a fact which had made Françoise take a dislike to him: " Yes, the first time you see him you would give him the sacrament without confession, but there are days when his tongue is as smooth as a prison door. It's your money he's after." This was the category in which she had so often included Eulalie, and in which, alas (when I think of all the trouble that was one day to come of it), she already placed Albertine, because she saw me often asking Mamma, on behalf of my impecunious friend, for trinkets and other little presents, which Françoise held to be inexcusable because Mme. Bontemps had only a general servant. A moment later the lift-boy, having removed what I should have called his livery and he called his tunic, appeared wearing a straw hat, carrying a cane, holding himself stiffly erect, for his mother had warned him never to adopt the "working-class" or "pageboy" style. Just as, thanks to books, all knowledge is open to a working man, who ceases to be such when he has finished his work, so, thanks to a "boater" hat and a pair of gloves, elegance became accessible to the lift-boy who, having ceased for the evening to take the visitors upstairs, imagined himself, like a young surgeon who has taken off his overall, or Serjeant Saint-Loup out of uniform, a typical young man about town. He was not for that matter lacking in ambition, or in talent either in manipulating his machine and not bringing you to a standstill between two floors. But his vocabulary was defective. I credited him with ambition because he said in speaking of the porter, under whom he served: "My porter," in the same tone in which a man who owned what the page would have called a "private mansion" in Paris would have referred to his footman. As for the lift-boy's vocabulary, it is curious that anybody who heard people, fifty times a day, calling for the "lift," should never himself call it anything but a "left." There were certain things about this boy that were extremely annoying: whatever I might be saying to him he would interrupt with a phrase: "I should say so!" or "I say!" which seemed either to imply that my remark was so obvious that anybody would have thought of it, or else to take all the credit for it to himself, as though it were he that was drawing my attention to the subject. "I should say so!" or "I say!" exclaimed with the utmost emphasis, issued from his lips every other minute, over matters to which he had never given a thought, a trick which irritated me so much that I immediately began to say the opposite to shew him that he knew nothing about it. But to my second assertion, albeit it was incompatible with the first, he replied none the less stoutly: "I should say so!" "I say!" as though these words were inevitable. I found it difficult, also, to forgive him the trick of employing certain terms proper to his calling, which would therefore have sounded perfectly correct in their literal sense, in a figurative sense only, which gave them an air of feeble witticism, for instance the verb to pedal. He never used it when he had gone anywhere on his bicycle. But if, on foot, he had hurried to arrive somewhere in time, then, to indicate that he had walked fast, he would exclaim: "I should say I didn't half pedal!" The lift-boy was on the small side, clumsily built and by no means good looking. This did not prevent him, whenever one spoke to him of some tall, slim, handsome young man, from saying: "Oh, yes, I know, a fellow who is just my height." And one day when I was expecting him to bring me the answer to a message, hearing somebody come upstairs, I had in my impatience opened the door of my room and caught sight of a page as beautiful as Endymion, with incredibly perfect features, who was bringing a message to a lady whom I did not know. When the lift-boy returned, in telling him how impatiently I had waited for the answer, I mentioned to him that I had thought I heard him come upstairs but that it had turned out to be a page from the Hôtel de Normandie. "Oh, yes, I know," he said, "they have only the one, a boy about my build. He's so like me in face, too, that we're always being mistaken; anybody would think he was my brother." Lastly, he always wanted to appear to have understood you perfectly from the first second, which meant that as soon as you asked him to do anything he would say: "Yes, yes, yes, yes, I understand all that," with a precision and a tone of intelligence which for some time deceived me; but other people, as we get to know them, are like a metal dipped in an acid bath, and we see them gradually lose their good qualities (and their bad qualities too, at times). Before giving him my instructions, I saw that he had left the door open; I pointed this out to him, I was afraid that people might hear us; he acceded to my request and returned, having reduced the gap. "Anything to oblige. But there's nobody on this floor except us two." Immediately I heard one, then a second, then a third person go by. This annoyed me partly because of the risk of my being overheard, but more still because I could see that it did not in the least surprise him and was a perfectly normal occurrence. "Yes, that'll be the maid next door going for her things. Oh, that's of no importance, it's the bottler putting away his keys. No, no, it's nothing, you can say what you want, it's my colleague just going on duty." Then, as the reasons that all these people had for passing did not diminish my dislike of the thought that they might overhear me, at a formal order from me he went, not to shut the door, which was beyond the strength of this bicyclist who longed for a "motor," but to push it a little closer to. "Now we shall be quite quiet." So quiet were we that an American lady burst in and withdrew with apologies for having mistaken the number of her room. "You are going to bring this young lady back with you," I told him, after first going and banging the door with all my might (which brought in another page to see whether a window had been left open). "You remember the name: Mlle. Albertine Simonet. Anyhow, it's on the envelope. You need only say to her that it's from me. She will be delighted to come," I added, to encourage him and preserve a scrap of my own self-esteem. "I should say so!" "Not at all, there is not the slightest reason to suppose that she will be glad to come. It's a great nuisance getting here from Berneville." "I understand!" "You will tell her to come with you." "Yes, yes, yes, yes, I understand perfectly," he replied, in that sharp, precise tone which had long ceased to make a "good impression" upon me because I knew that it was almost mechanical and covered with its apparent clearness plenty of uncertainty and stupidity. "When will you be back?" "Haven't any too much time," said the lift-boy, who, carrying to extremes the grammatical rule that forbids the repetition of personal pronouns before coordinate verbs, omitted the pronoun altogether. "Can go there all right. Leave was stopped this afternoon, because there was a dinner for twenty at luncheon. And it was my turn off duty to-day. So it's all right if I go out a bit this evening. Take my bike with me. Get there in no time." And an hour later he reappeared and said: "Monsieur's had to wait, but the young lady's come with me. She's down below." "Oh, thanks very much; the porter won't be cross with me?" "Monsieur Paul? Doesn't even know where I've been. The head of the door himself can't say a word." But once, after I had told him: "You absolutely must bring her back with you," he reported to me with a smile: "You know, I couldn't find her. She's not there. Couldn't wait any longer; was afraid of getting it like my colleague who was 'missed from the hotel" (for the lift-boy, who used the word "rejoin" of a profession which one joined for the first time, "I should like to rejoin the post-office," to make up for this, or to mitigate the calamity, were his own career at stake, or to insinuate it more delicately and treacherously were the victim some one else, elided the prefix and said: "I know he's been 'missed"). It was not with any evil intent that he smiled, but from sheer timidity. He thought that he was diminishing the magnitude of his crime by making a joke of it. In the same way, if he had said to me: "*You know,* I couldn't find her," this did not mean that he really thought that I knew it already. On the contrary, he was all too certain that I did not know it, and, what was more, was afraid to tell me. And so he said "you know" to ward off the terror which menaced him as he uttered the words that were to bring me the knowledge. We ought never to lose our tempers with people who, when we find fault with them, begin to titter. They do so not because they are laughing at us, but because they are trembling lest we should be angry. Let us shew all pity and tenderness to those who laugh. For all the world like a stroke, the lift-boy's anxiety had wrought in him not merely an apoplectic flush but an alteration in his speech which had suddenly become familiar. He wound up by telling me that Albertine was not at Egreville, that she would not be coming back there before nine o'clock, and that if betimes (which meant, by chance) she came back earlier, my message would be given her, and in any case she would be with me before one o'clock in the morning.[1]

[1] In the French text of *Sodome et Gomorrhe*, Volume I ends at this point.

It was not this evening, however, that my cruel mistrust began to take solid form. No, to make no mystery about it, although the incident did not occur until some weeks later, it arose out of a remark made by Cottard. Albertine and her friends had insisted that day upon dragging me to the casino at Incarville where, as luck would have it, I should not have joined them (having intended to go and see Mme. Verdurin who had invited me again and again), had I not been held up at Incarville itself by a breakdown of the tram which it would take a considerable time to repair. As I strolled up and down waiting for the men to finish working at it, I found myself all of a sudden face to face with Doctor Cottard, who had come to Incarville to see a patient. I almost hesitated to greet him as he had not answered any of my letters. But friendship does not express itself in the same way in different people. Not having been brought up to observe the same fixed rules of behaviour as well-bred people, Cottard was full of good intentions of which one knew nothing, even denying their existence, until the day when he had an opportunity of displaying them. He apologised, had indeed received my letters, had reported my whereabouts to the Verdurins who were most anxious to see me and whom he urged me to go and see. He even proposed to take me to them there and then, for he was waiting for the little local train to take him back there for dinner. As I hesitated and as he had still some time before his train, (for there was bound to be still a considerable delay) I made him come with me to the little casino, one of those that had struck me as being so gloomy on the evening of my first arrival, now filled with the tumult of the girls, who, in the absence of male partners, were dancing together. Andrée came sliding along the floor towards me; I was meaning to go off with Cottard in a moment to the Verdurins', when I definitely declined his offer, seized by an irresistable desire to stay with Albertine. The fact was, I had just heard her laugh. And her laugh at once suggested the rosy flesh, the fragrant portals between which it had just made its way, seeming also, as strong, sensual and revealing as the scent of geraniums, to carry with it some microscopic particles of their substance, irritant and secret.

One of the girls, a stranger to me, sat down at the piano, and Andrée invited Albertine to waltz with her. Happy in the thought that I was going to remain in this little casino with these girls, I remarked to Cottard how well they danced together. But he, taking the professional point of view of a doctor and with an ill-breeding which overlooked the fact that they were my friends, although he must have seen me shaking hands with them, replied: "Yes, but parents are very rash to allow their daughters to form such habits. I should certainly never let mine come here. Are they nice-looking, though? I can't see their faces. There now, look," he went on, pointing to Albertine and Andrée who were waltzing slowly, tightly clasped together, "I have left my glasses behind and I don't see very well, but they are certainly keenly roused. It is not sufficiently known that women derive most excitement from their breasts. And theirs' as you see, are completely touching." And indeed the contact had been unbroken between the breasts of Andrée and of Albertine. I do not know whether they heard or guessed Cottard's observation, but they gently broke the contact while continuing to waltz. At that moment Andrée said something to Albertine, who laughed, the same deep and penetrating laugh that I had heard before. But all that it wafted to me this time was a feeling of pain; Albertine appeared to be revealing by it, to be making Andrée share some exquisite, secret thrill. It rang out like the first or the last strains of a ball to which one has not been invited. I left the place with Cottard, distracted by his conversation, thinking only at odd moments of the scene I had just witnessed. This does not mean that Cottard's conversation was interesting. It had indeed, at that moment, become bitter, for we had just seen Doctor du Boulbon go past without noticing us. He had come down to spend some time on the other side of Balbec bay, where he was greatly in demand. Now, albeit Cottard was in the habit of declaring that he did no professional work during the holidays, he had hoped to build up a select practice along the coast, a hope which du Boulbon's presence there doomed to disappointment. Certainly, the Balbec doctor could not stand in Cottard's way. He was merely a thoroughly conscientious doctor who knew everything, and to whom you could not mention the slightest irritation of the skin without his immediately prescribing, in a complicated formula, the ointment, lotion or liniment that would put you right. As Marie Gineste used to say, in her charming speech, he knew how to "charm" cuts and sores. But he was in no way eminent. He had indeed caused Cottard some slight annoyance. The latter, now that he was anxious to exchange his Chair for that of Therapeutics, had begun to specialise in toxic actions. These, a perilous innovation in medicine, give an excuse for changing the labels in the chemists' shops, where every preparation is declared to be in no way toxic, unlike its substitutes, and indeed to be disintoxicant. It is the fashionable cry; at the most there may survive below in illegible lettering, like the faint trace of an older fashion, the assurance that the preparation has been carefully disinfected. Toxic actions serve also to reassure the patient, who learns with joy that his paralysis is merely a toxic disturbance. Now, a Grand Duke who had come for a few days to Balbec and whose eye was extremely swollen had sent for Cottard who, in return for a wad of hundred-franc notes (the Professor refused to see anyone for less), had put down the inflammation to a toxic condition and prescribed a disintoxicant treatment. As the swelling did not go down, the Grand Duke fell back upon the general practitioner of Balbec, who in five minutes had removed a speck of dust. The following day the swelling had gone. A celebrated specialist in nervous diseases was, however, a more dangerous rival. He was a rubicund, jovial person, since, for one thing, the constant society of nervous wrecks did not prevent him from enjoying excellent health, but also so as to reassure his patients by the hearty merriment of his "Good morning" and "Good-bye," while quite ready to lend the strength of his muscular arms to fastening them in strait-waistcoats later on. Nevertheless, whenever you spoke to him at a party, whether of politics or of literature, he would listen to you with a kindly attention, as though he were saying: "What is it all about?" without at once giving an opinion, as though it were a matter for consultation. But anyhow he, whatever his talent might be, was a specialist. And so the whole of Cottard's rage was heaped upon du Boulbon. But I soon bade good-bye to the Verdurins' professional friend, and returned to Balbec, after promising him that I would pay them a visit before long.

The mischief that his remarks about Albertine and Andrée had done me was extreme, but its worst effects were not immediately felt by me, as happens with those forms of poisoning which begin to act only after a certain time.

Albertine, on the night after the lift-boy had gone in search of her, did not appear, notwithstanding his assurances. Certainly, personal charm is a less frequent cause of love than a speech such as: "No, this evening I shall not be free." We barely notice this speech if we are with friends; we are gay all the evening, a certain image never enters our mind; during those hours it remains dipped in the necessary solution; when we return home we find the plate developed and perfectly clear. We become aware that life is no longer the life which we would have surrendered for a trifle the day before, because, even if we continue not to fear death, we no longer dare think of a parting.

From, however, not one o'clock in the morning (the limit fixed by the lift-boy), but three o'clock, I no longer felt as in former times the anguish of seeing the chance of her coming diminish. The certainty that she would not now come brought me a complete, refreshing calm; this night was simply a night like all the rest during which I did not see her, such was the idea from which I started. After which, the thought that I should see her in the morning, or some other day, outlining itself upon the blank which I submissively accepted, became pleasant. Sometimes, during these nights of waiting, our anguish is due to a drug which we have taken. The sufferer, misinterpreting his own symptoms, thinks that he is anxious about the woman who fails to appear. Love is engendered in these cases, as are certain nervous maladies, by the inaccurate explanation of a state of discomfort. An explanation which it is useless to correct, at any rate so far as love is concerned, a sentiment which (whatever its cause) is invariably in error.

Next day, when Albertine wrote to me that she had only just got back to Epreville, and so had not received my note in time, and was coming, if she might, to see me that evening, behind the words of her letter, as behind those that she had said to me once over the telephone, I thought I could detect the presence of pleasures, of people whom she had preferred to me. Once again, I was stirred from head to foot by the painful longing to know what she could have been doing, by the latent love which we always carry within us; I almost thought for a moment that it was going to attach me to Albertine, but it confined itself to a stationary throbbing, the last echo of which died away without the machine's having been set in motion.

I had failed during my first visit to Balbec—and perhaps, for that matter, Andrée had failed equally—to understand Albertine's character. I had put it down as frivolous, but had not known whether our combined supplications might not succeed in keeping her with us and making her forego a garden-party, a donkey ride, a picnic. During my second visit to Balbec, I began to suspect that this frivolity was only for show, the garden-party a mere screen, if not an invention. She shewed herself in various colours in the following incident (by which I mean the incident as seen by me, from my side of the glass which was by no means transparent, and without my having any means of determining what reality there was on the other side). Albertine was making me the most passionate protestations of affection. She looked at the time because she had to go and call upon a lady who was at home, it appeared, every afternoon at five o'clock, at Infreville. Tormented by suspicion, and feeling at the same time far from well, I asked Albertine, I implored her to remain with me. It was impossible (and indeed she could wait only five minutes longer) because it would annoy the lady who was far from hospitable, highly susceptible and, said Albertine, a perfect nuisance. "But one can easily cut a call." "No, my aunt has always told me that the chief thing is politeness." "But I have so often seen you being impolite." "It's not the same thing, the lady would be angry with me and would say nasty things about me to my aunt. I'm pretty well in her bad books already. She expects me to go and see her." "But if she's at home every day?" Here Albertine, feeling that she was caught, changed her line of argument. "So she is at home every day. But to-day I've made arrangements to meet some other girls there. It will be less boring that way." "So then, Albertine, you prefer this lady and your friends to me, since, rather than miss paying an admittedly boring call, you prefer to leave me here alone, sick and wretched?" "I don't care if it is boring. I'm going for their sake. I shall bring them home in my trap. Otherwise they won't have any way of getting back." I pointed out to Albertine that there were trains from Infreville up to ten o'clock at night. "Quite true, but don't you see, it is possible that we may be asked to stay to dinner. She is very hospitable." "Very well then, you won't." "I should only make my aunt angry." "Besides, you can dine with her and catch the ten o'clock train." "It's cutting it rather fine." "Then I can never go and dine in town and come back by train. But listen, Albertine. We are going to do something quite simple, I feel that the fresh air will do me good; since you can't give up your lady, I am going to come with you to Infreville. Don't be alarmed, I shan't go as far as the Tour Élisabeth" (the lady's villa), "I shall see neither the lady nor your friends." Albertine started as though she had received a violent blow. For a moment, she was unable to speak. She explained that the sea bathing was not doing her any good. "If you don't want me to come with you?" "How can you say such a thing, you know that there's nothing I enjoy more than going out with you." A sudden change of tactics had occurred. "Since we are going for a drive together," she said to me, "why not go out in the other direction, we might dine together. It would be so nice. After all, that side of Balbec is much the prettier. I'm getting sick of Infreville and all those little spinach-bed places." "But your aunt's friend will be annoyed if you don't go and see her." "Very well, let her be." "No, it is wrong to annoy people." "But she won't even notice that I'm not there, she has people every day; I can go to-morrow, the next day, next week, the week after, it's exactly the same." "And what about your friends?" "Oh, they've cut me often enough. It's my turn now." "But from the side you suggest there's no train back after nine." "Well, what's the matter with that? Nine will do perfectly. Besides, one need never think about getting back. We can always find a cart, a bike, if the worse comes to the worst, we have legs." "We can always find, Albertine, how you go on! Out Infreville way, where the villages run into one another, well and good. But the other way, it's a very different matter." "That way too. I promise to bring you back safe and sound." I felt that Albertine was giving up for my sake some plan arranged beforehand of which she refused to tell me, and that there was some one else who would be as unhappy as I was. Seeing that what she had intended to do was out of the question, since I insisted upon accompanying her, she gave it up altogether. She knew that the loss was not irremediable. For, like all women who have a number of irons in the fire, she had one resource that never failed: suspicion and jealousy. Of course she did not seek to arouse them, quite the contrary. But lovers are so suspicious that they instantly scent out falsehood. With the result that Albertine, being no better than anyone else, knew by experience (without for a moment imagining that she owed her experience to jealousy) that she could always be certain of meeting people again after she had failed to keep an appointment. The stranger whom she was deserting for me would be hurt, would love her all the more for that (though Albertine did not know that this was the reason), and, so as not to prolong the agony, would return to her of his own accord, as I should have done. But I had no desire either to give pain to another, or to tire myself, or to enter upon the terrible course of investigation, of multiform, unending vigilance. "No, Albertine, I do not wish to spoil your pleasure, go to your lady at Infreville, or rather to the person you really mean to see, it is all the same to me. The real reason why I am not coming with you is that you do not wish it, the outing you would be taking with me is not the one you meant to take, which is proved by your having contradicted yourself at least five times without noticing it." Poor Albertine was afraid that her contradictions, which she had not noticed, had been more serious than they were. Not knowing exactly what fibs she had told me: "It is quite on the cards that I did contradict myself. The sea air makes me lose my head altogether. I'm always calling things by the wrong names." And (what proved to me that she would not, now, require many tender affirmations to make me believe her) I felt a stab in my heart as I listened to this admission of what I had but faintly imagined. "Very well, that's settled, I'm off," she said in a tragic tone, not without looking at the time to see whether she was making herself late for the other person, now that I had provided her with an excuse for not spending the evening with myself. "It's too bad of you. I alter all my plans to spend a nice, long evening with you, and it's you that won't have it, and you accuse me of telling lies. I've never known you be so cruel. The sea shall be my tomb. I will never see you any more." (My heart leaped at these words, albeit I was certain that she would come again next day, as she did.) "I shall drown myself, I shall throw myself into the water." "Like Sappho." "There you go, insulting me again. You suspect not only what I say but what I do." "But, my lamb, I didn't mean anything, I swear to you, you know Sappho flung herself into the sea." "Yes, yes, you have no faith in me." She saw that it was twenty minutes to the hour by the clock; she was afraid of missing her appointment, and choosing the shortest form of farewell (for which as it happened she apologised by coming to see me again next day, the other person presumably not being free then), she dashed from the room, crying: "Good-bye for ever," in a heartbroken tone. And perhaps she was heartbroken. For knowing what she was about at that moment better than I, being at the same time more strict and more indulgent towards herself than I was towards her, she may all the same have had a fear that I might refuse to see her again after the way in which she had left me. And I believe that she was attached to me, so much so that the other person was more jealous than I was.

Some days later, at Balbec, while we were in the ballroom of the casino, there entered Bloch's sister and cousin, who had both turned out quite pretty, but whom I refrained from greeting on account of my girl friends, because the younger one, the cousin, was notoriously living with the actress whose acquaintance she had made during my first visit. Andrée, at a murmured allusion to this scandal, said to me: "Oh! About that sort of thing I'm like Albertine; there's nothing we both loathe so much as that sort of thing." As for Albertine, on sitting down to talk to me upon the sofa, she had turned her back on the disreputable pair. I had noticed, however, that, before she changed her position, at the moment when Mlle. Bloch and her cousin appeared, my friend's eyes had flashed with that sudden, close attention which now and again imparted to the face of this frivolous girl a serious, indeed a grave air, and left her pensive afterwards. But Albertine had at once turned towards myself a gaze which nevertheless remained singularly fixed and meditative. Mlle. Bloch and her cousin having finally left the room after laughing and shouting in a loud and vulgar manner, I asked Albertine whether the little fair one (the one who was so intimate with the actress) was not the girl who had won the prize the day before in the procession of flowers. "I don't know," said Albertine, "is one of them fair? I must confess they don't interest me particularly, I have never looked at them. Is one of them fair?" she asked her three girl friends with a detached air of inquiry. When applied to people whom Albertine passed every day on the front, this ignorance seemed to me too profound to be genuine. "They didn't appear to be looking at us much either," I said to Albertine, perhaps (on the assumption, which I did not however consciously form, that Albertine loved her own sex), to free her from any regret by pointing out to her that she had not attracted the attention of these girls and that, generally speaking, it is not customary even for the most vicious of women to take an interest in girls whom they do not know. "They weren't looking at us," was Albertine's astonished reply. "Why, they did nothing else the whole time." "But you can't possibly tell," I said to her, "you had your back to them." "Very well, and what about that?" she replied, pointing out to me, set in the wall in front of us, a large mirror which I had not noticed and upon which I now realised that my friend, while talking to me, had never ceased to fix her troubled, preoccupied eyes.

Ever since the day when Cottard had accompanied me into the little casino at Incarville, albeit I did not share the opinion that he had expressed, Albertine had seemed to me different; the sight of her made me lose my temper. I myself had changed, quite as much as she had changed in my eyes. I had ceased to bear her any good will; to her face, behind her back when there was a chance of my words' being repeated to her, I spoke of her in the most insulting language. There were, however, intervals of calmer feeling. One day I learned that Albertine and Andrée had both accepted an invitation to Elstir's. Feeling certain that this was in order that they might, on the return journey, amuse themselves like schoolgirls on holiday by imitating the manners of fast young women, and in so doing find an unmaidently pleasure the thought of which wrung my heart, without announcing my intention, to embarrass them and to deprive Albertine of the pleasure on which she was reckoning, I paid an unexpected call at his studio. But I found only Andrée there. Albertine had chosen another day when her aunt was to go there with her. Then I said to myself that Cottard must have been mistaken; the favourable impression that I received from Andrée's presence there without her friend remained with me and made me feel more kindly disposed towards Albertine. But this feeling lasted no longer than the healthy moments of delicate people subject to passing maladies, who are prostrated again by the merest trifle. Albertine incited Andrée to actions which, without going very far, were perhaps not altogether innocent; pained by this suspicion, I managed in the end to repel it. No sooner was I healed of it than it revived under another form. I had just seen Andrée, with one of those graceful gestures that came naturally to her, lay her head coaxingly on Albertine's shoulder, kiss her on the throat, half shutting her eyes;

or else they had exchanged a glance; a remark had been made by somebody who had seen them going down together to bathe: little trifles such as habitually float in the surrounding atmosphere where the majority of people absorb them all day long without injury to their health or alteration of their mood, but which have a morbid effect and breed fresh sufferings in a nature predisposed to receive them. Sometimes even without my having seen Albertine again, without anyone's having spoken to me about her, there would flash from my memory some vision of her with Gisèle in an attitude which had seemed to me innocent at the time; it was enough now to destroy the peace of mind that I had managed to recover, I had no longer any need to go and breathe dangerous germs outside, I had, as Cottard would have said, supplied my own toxin. I thought then of all that I had been told about Swann's love for Odette, of the way in which Swann had been tricked all his life. Indeed, when I come to think of it, the hypothesis that made me gradually build up the whole of Albertine's character and give a painful interpretation to every moment of a life that I could not control in its entirety, was the memory, the rooted idea of Mme. Swann's character, as it had been described to me. These accounts helped my imagination, in after years, to take the line of supposing that Albertine might, instead of being a good girl, have had the same immorality, the same faculty of deception as a reformed prostitute, and I thought of all the sufferings that would in that case have been in store for me had I ever really been her lover.

One day, outside the Grand Hotel, where we were gathered on the front, I had just been addressing Albertine in the harshest, most humiliating language, and Rosemonde was saying: "Oh, how you have changed your mind about her; why, she used to be everything, it was she who ruled the roast, and now she isn't even fit to be thrown to the dogs." I was beginning, in order to make my attitude towards Albertine still more marked, to say all the nicest things I could think of to Andrée, who, if she was tainted with the same vice, seemed to me to have more excuse for it since she was sickly and neurasthenic, when we saw emerging at the steady trot of its pair of horses into the street at right angles to the front, at the corner of which we were standing, Mme. de Cambremer's barouche. The chief magistrate who, at that moment, was advancing towards us, sprang back upon recognising the carriage, in order not to be seen in our company; then, when he thought that the Marquise's eye might catch his, bowed to her with an immense sweep of his hat. But the carriage, instead of continuing, as might have been expected, along the Rue de la Mer, disappeared through the gate of the hotel. It was quite ten minutes later when the lift-boy, out of breath, came to announce to me: "It's the Marquise de Camembert, she's come here to see Monsieur. I've been up to the room, I looked in the reading-room, I couldn't find Monsieur anywhere. Luckily I thought of looking on the beach." He had barely ended this speech when, followed by her daughter-in-law and by an extremely ceremonious gentleman, the Marquise advanced towards me, coming on probably from some afternoon tea-party in the neighbourhood, and bowed down not so much by age as by the mass of costly trinkets with which she felt it more sociable and more befitting her rank to cover herself, in order to appear as "well dressed" as possible to the people whom she went to visit. It was in fact that "landing" of the Cambremers at the hotel which my grandmother had so greatly dreaded long ago when she wanted us not to let Legrandin know that we might perhaps be going to Balbec. Then Mamma used to laugh at these fears inspired by an event which she considered impossible. And here it was actually happening, but by different channels and without Legrandin's having had any part in it. "Do you mind my staying here, if I shan't be in your way?" asked Albertine (in whose eyes there lingered, brought there by the cruel things I had just been saying to her, a pair of tears which I observed without seeming to see them, but not without rejoicing inwardly at the sight), "there is something I want to say to you." A hat with feathers, itself surmounted by a sapphire pin, was perched haphazard upon Mme. de Cambremer's wig, like a badge the display of which was necessary but sufficient, its place immaterial, its elegance conventional and its stability superfluous. Notwithstanding the heat, the good lady had put on a jet cloak, like a dalmatic, over which hung an ermine stole the wearing of which seemed to depend not upon the temperature and season, but upon the nature of the ceremony. And on Mme. de Cambremer's bosom a baronial torse, fastened to a chain, dangled like a pectoral cross. The gentleman was an eminent lawyer from Paris, of noble family, who had come down to spend a few days with the Cambremers. He was one of those men whom their vast professional experience inclines to look down upon their profession, and who say, for instance: "I know that I am a good pleader, so it no longer amuses me to plead," or: "I'm no longer interested in operating, I know that I'm a good operator." Men of intelligence, *artists,* they see themselves in their maturity, richly endowed by success, shining with that intellect, that artistic nature which their professional brethren recognise in them and which confer upon them a kind of taste and discernment. They form a passion for the paintings not of a great artist, but of an artist who nevertheless is highly distinguished, and spend upon the purchase of his work the large sums that their career procures for them. Le Sidaner was the artist chosen by the Cambremers' friend, who incidentally was a delightful person. He talked well about books, but not about the books of the true masters, those who have mastered themselves. The only irritating habit that this amateur displayed was his constant use of certain ready made expressions, such as "for the most part," which gave an air of importance and incompleteness to the matter of which he was speaking. Madame de Cambremer had taken the opportunity, she told me, of a party which some friends of hers had been giving that afternoon in the Balbec direction to come and call upon me, as she had promised Robert de Saint-Loup. "You know he's coming down to these parts quite soon for a few days. His uncle Charlus is staying near here with his sister-in-law, the Duchesse de Luxembourg, and M. de Saint-Loup means to take the opportunity of paying his aunt a visit and going to see his old regiment, where he is very popular, highly respected. We often have visits from officers who are never tired of singing his praises. How nice it would be if you and he would give us the pleasure of coming together to Féterne." I presented Albertine and her friends. Mme. de Cambremer introduced us all to her daughter-in-law. The latter, so frigid towards the petty nobility with whom her seclusion at Féterne forced her to associate, so reserved, so afraid of compromising herself, held out her hand to me with a radiant smile, safe as she felt herself and delighted at seeing a friend of Robert de Saint-Loup, whom he, possessing a sharper social intuition than he allowed to appear, had mentioned to her as being a great friend of the Guermantes. So, unlike her mother-in-law, Mme. de Cambremer employed two vastly different forms of politeness. It was at the most the former kind, dry, insupportable, that she would have conceded me had I met her through her brother Legrandin. But for a friend of the Guermantes she had not smiles enough. The most convenient room in the hotel for entertaining visitors was the reading-room, that place once so terrible into which I now went a dozen times every day, emerging freely, my own master, like those mildly afflicted lunatics who have so long been inmates of an asylum that the superintendent trusts them with a latchkey. And so I offered to take Mme. de Cambremer there. And as this room no longer filled me with shyness and no longer held any charm for me, since the faces of things change for us like the faces of people, it was without the slightest emotion that I made this suggestion. But she declined it, preferring to remain out of doors, and we sat down in the open air, on the terrace of the hotel. I found there and rescued a volume of Madame de Sévigné which Mamma had not had time to carry off in her precipitate flight, when she heard that visitors had called for me. No less than my grandmother, she dreaded these invasions of strangers, and, in her fear of being too late to escape if she let herself be seen, would fly from the room with a rapidity which always made my father and me laugh at her. Madame de Cambremer carried in her hand, with the handle of a sunshade, a number of embroidered bags, a hold-all, a gold purse from which there dangled strings of garnets, and a lace handkerchief. I could not help thinking that it would be more convenient for her to deposit them on a chair; but I felt that it would be unbecoming and useless to ask her to lay aside the ornaments of her pastoral visitation and her social priesthood. We gazed at the calm sea upon which, here and there, a few gulls floated like white petals. Because of the "mean level" to which social conversation reduces us and also of our desire to attract not by means of those qualities of which we are ourselves unaware but of those which, we suppose, ought to be appreciated by the people who are with us, I began instinctively to talk to Mme. de Cambremer *née* Legrandin in the strain in which her brother might have talked. "They appear," I said, referring to the gulls, "as motionless and as white as water-lilies." And indeed they did appear to be offering a lifeless object to the little waves which tossed them about, so much so that the waves, by contrast, seemed in their pursuit of them to be animated by a deliberate intention, to have acquired life. The dowager Marquise could not find words enough to do justice to the superb view of the sea that we had from Balbec, or to say how she envied it, she who from la Raspelière (where for that matter she was not living that year) had only such a distant glimpse of the waves. She had two remarkable habits, due at once to her exalted passion for the arts (especially for the art of music), and to her want of teeth. Whenever she talked of aesthetic subjects her salivary glands—like those of certain animals when in rut—became so overcharged that the old lady's edentulous mouth allowed to escape from the corners of her faintly moustached lips a trickle of moisture for which that was not the proper place. Immediately she drew it in again with a deep sigh, like a person recovering his breath. Secondly, if her subject were some piece of music of surpassing beauty, in her enthusiasm she would raise her arms and utter a few decisive opinions, vigorously chewed and at a pinch issuing from her nose. Now it had never occurred to me that the vulgar beach at Balbec could indeed offer a "seascape," and Mme. de Cambremer's simple words changed my ideas in that respect. On the other hand, as I told her, I had always heard people praise the matchless view from la Raspelière, perched on the summit of the hill, where, in a great drawing-room with two fireplaces, one whole row of windows swept the gardens, and, through the branches of the trees, the sea as far as Balbec and beyond it, and the other row the valley. "How nice of you to say so, and how well you put it: the sea through the branches. It is exquisite, one would say . . . a painted fan." And I gathered from a deep breath intended to catch the falling spittle and dry the moustaches, that the compliment was sincere. But the Marquise *née* Legrandin remained cold, to shew her contempt not for my words but for those of her mother-in-law. Besides, she not only despised the other's intellect but deplored her affability, being always afraid that people might not form a sufficiently high idea of the Cambremers. "And how charming the name is," said I. "One would like to know the origin of all those names." "That one I can tell you," the old lady answered modestly. "It is a family place, it came from my grandmother Arrachepel, not an illustrious family, but a decent and very old country stock." "What! Not illustrious!" her daughter-in-law tartly interrupted her. "A whole window in Bayeux cathedral is filled with their arms, and the principal church at Avranches has their tombs. If these old names interest you," she added, "you've come a year too late. We managed to appoint to the living of Criquetot, in spite of all the difficulties about changing from one diocese to another, the parish priest of a place where I myself have same land, a long way from here, Combray, where the worthy cleric felt that he was becoming neurasthenic. Unfortunately, the sea air was no good to him at his age; his neurasthenia grew worse and he has returned to Combray. But he amused himself while he was our neighbour in going about looking up all the old charters, and he compiled quite an interesting little pamphlet on the place names of the district. It has given him a fresh interest, too, for it seems he is spending his last years in writing a great work upon Combray and its surroundings. I shall send you his pamphlet on the surroundings of Féterne. It is worthy of a Benedictine. You will find the most interesting things in it about our old Raspelière, of which my mother-in-law speaks far too modestly." "In any case, this year," replied the dowager Mme. de Cambremer, "la Raspelière is no longer ours and does not belong to me. But I can see that you have a painter's instincts; I am sure you sketch, and I should so like to shew you Féterne, which is far finer than la Raspelière." For as soon as the Cambremers had let this latter residence to the Verdurins, its commanding situation had at once ceased to appear to them as it had appeared for so many years past, that is to say to offer the advantage, without parallel in the neighbourhood, of looking out over both sea and valley, and had on the other hand, suddenly and retrospectively, presented the drawback that one had always to go up or down hill to get to or from it. In short, one might have supposed that if Mme. de Cambremer had let it, it was not so much to add to her income as to spare her horses. And she proclaimed herself delighted at being able at last to have the sea always so close at hand, at Féterne, she who for so many years (forgetting the two months that she spent there) had seen it only from up above and as though in a panorama. "I am discovering it at my age," she said, "and how I enjoy it! It does me a world of good. I would let la Raspelière for nothing so as to be obliged to live at Féterne."

"To return to more interesting topics," went on Legrandin's sister, who addressed the old Marquise as "Mother," but with the passage of years had come to treat her with insolence, "you mentioned water-lilies: I suppose you know Claude Monet's pictures of them. What a genius! They interest me particularly because near Combray, that place where I told you I had some land. . . ." But she preferred not to talk too much about Combray. "Why! That must be the series that Elstir told us about, the greatest painter of this generation," exclaimed Albertine, who had said nothing so far. "Ah! I can see that this young lady loves the arts," cried Mme. de Cambremer and, drawing a long breath, recaptured a trail of spittle. "You will allow me to put Le Sidaner before him, Mademoiselle," said the lawyer, smiling with the air of an expert. And, as he had enjoyed, or seen people enjoy, years ago, certain "daring" work by Elstir, he added: "Elstir was gifted, indeed he was one of the advanced guard, but for some reason or other he never kept up, he has wasted his life." Mme. de Cambremer disagreed with the lawyer, so far as Elstir was concerned, but, greatly to the annoyance of her guest, bracketed Monet with Le Sidaner. It would be untrue to say that she was a fool; she was overflowing with a kind of intelligence that meant nothing to me. As the sun was beginning to set, the seagulls were now yellow, like the water-lilies on another canvas of that series by Monet. I said that I knew it, and (continuing to copy the diction of her brother, whom I had not yet dared to name) added that it was a pity that she had not thought of coming a day earlier, for, at the same hour, there would have been a Poussin light for her to admire. Had some Norman squireen, unknown to the Guermantes, told her that she ought to have come a day earlier, Mme. de Cambremer-Legrandin would doubtless have drawn herself up with an offended air. But I might have been far more familiar still, and she would have been all smiles and sweetness; I might in the warmth of that fine afternoon devour my fill of that rich honey cake which Mme. de Cambremer so rarely was and which took the place of the dish of pastry that it had not occurred to me to offer my guests. But the name of Poussin, without altering the amenity of the society lady, called forth the protests of the connoisseur. On hearing that name, she produced six times in almost continuous succession that little smack of the tongue against the lips which serves to convey to a child who is misbehaving at once a reproach for having begun and a warning not to continue. "In heaven's name, after a painter like Monet, who is an absolute genius, don't go and mention an old hack without a vestige of talent, like Poussin. I don't mind telling you frankly that I find him the deadliest bore. I mean to say, you can't really call that sort of thing painting. Monet, Degas, Manet, yes, there are painters if you like! It is a curious thing," she went on, fixing a scrutinous and ecstatic gaze upon a vague point in space where she could see what was in her mind, "it is a curious thing, I used at one time to prefer Manet. Nowadays, I still admire Manet, of course, but I believe I like Monet even more. Oh! The *Cathedrals!*" She was as scrupulous as she was condescending in informing me of the evolution of her taste. And one felt that the phases through which that taste had evolved were not, in her eyes, any less important than the different manners of Monet himself. Not that I had any reason to feel flattered by her taking me into her confidence as to her preferences, for even in the presence of the narrowest of provincial ladies she could not remain for five minutes without feeling the need to confess them. When a noble dame of Avranches, who would have been incapable of distinguishing between Mozart and Wagner, said in Mme. de Cambremer's hearing: "We saw nothing of any interest while we were in Paris, we went once to the Opéra-Comique, they were doing *Pelléas et Mélisande*, it's dreadful stuff," Mme. de Cambremer not only boiled with rage but felt obliged to exclaim: "Not at all, it's a little gem," and to "argue the point." It was perhaps a Combray habit which she had picked up from my grandmother's sisters, who called it "fighting in the good cause," and loved the dinner-parties at which they knew all through the week that they would have to defend their idols against the Philistines. Similarly, Mme. de

Cambremer liked to "fly into a passion" and wrangle about art, as other people do about politics. She stood up for Debussy as she would have stood up for a woman friend whose conduct had been criticised. She must however have known very well that when she said: "Not at all, it's a little gem," she could not improvise in the other lady, whom she was putting in her place, the whole progressive development of artistic culture on the completion of which they would come naturally to an agreement without any need of discussion. "I must ask Le Sidaner what he thinks of Poussin," the lawyer remarked to me. "He's a regular recluse, never opens his mouth, but I know how to get things out of him."

"Anyhow," Mme. de Cambremer went on, "I have a horror of sunsets, they're so romantic, so operatic. That is why I can't abide my mother-in-law's house, with its tropical plants. You will see it, it's just like a public garden at Monte-Carlo. That's why I prefer your coast, here. It is more sombre, more sincere; there's a little lane from which one doesn't see the sea. On rainy days, there's nothing but mud, it's a little world apart. It's just the same at Venice, I detest the Grand Canal and I don't know anything so touching as the little alleys. But it's all a question of one's surroundings." "But," I remarked to her, feeling that the only way to rehabilitate Poussin in Mme. de Cambremer's eyes was to inform her that he was once more in fashion, "M. Degas assures us that he knows nothing more beautiful than the Poussins at Chantilly." "Indeed? I don't know the ones at Chantilly," said Mme. de Cambremer who had no wish to differ from Degas, "but I can speak about the ones in the Louvre, which are appalling." "He admires them immensely too." "I must look at them again. My impressions of them are rather distant," she replied after a moment's silence, and as though the favourable opinion which she was certain, before very long, to form of Poussin would depend, not upon the information that I had just communicated to her, but upon the supplementary and, this time, final examination that she intended to make of the Poussins in the Louvre in order to be in a position to change her mind. Contenting myself with what was a first step towards retractation since, if she did not yet admire the Poussins, she was adjourning the matter for further consideration, in order not to keep her on tenterhooks any longer, I told her mother-in-law how much I had heard of the wonderful flowers at Féterne. In modest terms she spoke of the little presbytery garden that she had behind the house, into which in the mornings, by simply pushing open a door, she went in her wrapper to feed her peacocks, hunt for newlaid eggs, and gather the zinnias or roses which, on the sideboard, framing the creamed eggs or fried fish in a border of flowers, reminded her of her garden paths. "It is true, we have a great many roses," she told me, "our rose garden is almost too near the house, there are days when it makes my head ache. It is nicer on the terrace at la Raspelière where the breeze carries the scent of the roses, but it is not so heady." I turned to her daughter-in-law: "It is just like Pelléas," I said to her, to gratify her taste for the modern, "that scent of roses wafted up to the terraces. It is so strong in the score that, as I suffer from hay-fever and rose-fever, it sets me sneezing every time I listen to that scene."

"What a marvellous thing *Pelléas* is," cried Mme. de

Cambremer, " I'm mad about it; " and, drawing closer to me with the gestures of a savage woman seeking to captivate me, using her fingers to pick out imaginary notes, she began to hum something which, I supposed, represented to her the farewells of Pelléas, and continued with a vehement persistence as though it had been important that Mme. de Cambremer should at that moment remind me of that scene or rather should prove to me that she herself remembered it. " I think it is even finer than *Parsifal*," she added, " because in *Parsifal* the most beautiful things are surrounded with a sort of halo of melodious phrases, which are bad simply because they are melodious." " I know, you are a great musician, Madame," I said to the dowager. " I should so much like to hear you play." Mme. de Cambremer-Legrandin gazed at the sea so as not to be drawn into the conversation. Being of the opinion that what her mother-in-law liked was not music at all, she regarded the talent, a sham talent according to her, though in reality of the very highest order, that the other was admitted to possess as a technical accomplishment devoid of interest. It was true that Chopin's only surviving pupil declared, and with justice, that the Master's style of playing, his " feeling " had been transmitted, through herself, to Mme. de Cambremer alone, but to play like Chopin was far from being a recommendation in the eyes of Legrandin's sister, who despised nobody so much as the Polish composer. " Oh! They are flying away," exclaimed Albertine, pointing to the gulls which, casting aside for a moment their flowery incognito, were rising in a body towards the sun. " Their giant wings from walking hinder them," quoted Mme. de Cambremer, confusing the seagull with the albatross. " I do love them; I used to see them at Amsterdam," said Albertine. "They smell of the sea, they come and breathe the salt air through the paving stones even." "Oh! So you have been in Holland, you know the Vermeers?" Mme. de Cambremer asked imperiously, in the tone in which she would have said: "You know the Guermantes?" for snobbishness in changing its subject does not change its accent. Albertine replied in the negative, thinking that they were living people. But her mistake was not apparent. "I should be delighted to play to you," Mme. de Cambremer said to me. "But you know I only play things that no longer appeal to your generation. I was brought up in the worship of Chopin," she said in a lowered tone, for she was afraid of her daughter-in-law, and knew that to the latter, who considered that Chopin was not music, playing him well or badly were meaningless terms. She admitted that her mother-in-law had technique, was a finished pianist. "Nothing will ever make me say that she is a musician," was Mme. de Cambremer-Legrandin's conclusion. Because she considered herself "advanced," because (in matters of art only) "one could never move far enough to the Left," she said, she maintained not merely that music progressed, but that it progressed along one straight line, and that Debussy was in a sense a super-Wagner, slightly more advanced again than Wagner. She did not take into account the fact that if Debussy was not as independent of Wagner as she herself was to suppose in a few years' time, because we must always make use of the weapons that we have captured to free ourselves finally from the foe whom we have for the moment overpowered, he was seeking nevertheless, after the feeling of satiety that people were beginning to derive from work that was too complete, in which everything was expressed, to satisfy an opposite demand. There were theories of course, to support this reaction for the time being, like those theories which, in politics, come to the support of the laws against religious communities, of wars in the East (unnatural teaching, the Yellow Peril, etc., etc.). People said that an age of speed required rapidity in art, precisely as they might have said that the next war could not last longer than a fortnight, or that the coming of railways would kill the little places beloved of the coaches, which the motor-car, for all that, was to restore to favour. Composers were warned not to strain the attention of their audience, as though we had not at our disposal different degrees of attention, among which it rests precisely with the artist himself to arouse the highest. For the people who yawn with boredom after ten lines of a mediocre article have journeyed year after year to Bayreuth to listen to the Ring. Besides, the day was to come when, for a season, Debussy would be pronounced as trivial as Massenet, and the trills of Mélisande degraded to the level of Manon's. For theories and schools, like microbes and corpuscles, devour one another and by their warfare ensure the continuity of existence. But that time was still to come.

As on the Stock Exchange, when a rise occurs, a whole group of securities benefit by it, so a certain number of despised composers were gaining by the reaction, either because they did not deserve such scorn, or simply—which enabled one to be original when one sang their praises—because they had incurred it. And people even went the length of seeking out, in an isolated past, men of independent talent upon whose reputation the present movement did not seem calculated to have any influence, but of whom one of the new masters was understood to have spoken favourably. Often it was because a master, whoever he may be, however exclusive his school, judges in the light of his own untutored instincts, does justice to talent wherever it be found, or rather not so much to talent as to some agreeable inspiration which he has enjoyed in the past, which reminds him of a precious moment in his adolescence. Or, it may be, because certain artists of an earlier generation have in some fragment of their work realised something that resembles what the master has gradually become aware that he himself meant at one time to create. Then he sees the old master as a sort of precursor; he values in him, under a wholly different form, an effort that is momentarily, partially fraternal. There are bits of Turner in the work of Poussin, we find a phrase of Flaubert in Montesquieu. Sometimes, again, this rumoured predilection of the Master was due to an error, starting heaven knows where and circulated through the school. But in that case the name mentioned profited by the auspices under which it was introduced in the nick of time, for if there is an element of free will, some genuine taste expressed in the master's choice, the schools themselves go only by theory. Thus it is that the mind, following its habitual course which advances by digression, inclining first in one direction, then in the other, had brought back into the light of day a number of works to which the need for justice, or for a renewal of standards, or the taste of Debussy, or his caprice, or some remark that he had perhaps never made had added the works of Chopin. Commended by the judges in whom one had entire confidence, profiting by the admiration that was aroused by *Pelléas,* they had acquired a fresh lustre, and even the people who had not heard them again were so anxious to admire them that they did so in spite of themselves, albeit preserving the illusion of free will. But Mme. de Cambremer-Legrandin spent part of the year in the country. Even in Paris, being an invalid, she was largely confined to her own room. It is true that the drawbacks of this mode of existence were noticeable chiefly in her choice of expressions which she supposed to be fashionable and which would have been more appropriate to the written language, a distinction that she did not perceive, for she derived them more from reading than from conversation. The latter is not so necessary for an exact knowledge of current opinion as of the latest expressions. Unfortunately this revival of the *Nocturnes* had not yet been announced by the critics. The news of it had been transmitted only by word of mouth among the "younger" people. It remained unknown to Mme. de Cambremer-Legrandin. I gave myself the pleasure of informing her, but by addressing my remark to her mother-in-law, as when at billiards in order to hit a ball one aims at the cushion, that Chopin, so far from being out of date, was Debussy's favourite composer. "Indeed, that's quaint," said the daughter-in-law with a subtle smile as though it had been merely a deliberate paradox on the part of the composer of *Pelléas.* Nevertheless it was now quite certain that in future she would always listen to Chopin with respect and even pleasure. Moreover my words which had sounded the hour of deliverance for the dowager produced on her face an expression of gratitude to myself and above all of joy.

Her eyes shone like the eyes of Latude in the play entitled *Latude, or Thirty-five Years in Captivity,* and her bosom inhaled the sea air with that dilatation which Beethoven has so well described in *Fidelio,* at the point where his prisoners at last breathe again "this life-giving air." As for the dowager, I thought that she was going to press her hirsute lips to my cheek. "What, you like Chopin? He likes Chopin, he likes Chopin," she cried with a nasal trumpet-tone of passion; she might have been saying: "What, you know Mme. de Franquetot too?" with this difference, that my relations with Mme. de Franquetot would have left her completely indifferent, whereas my knowledge of Chopin plunged her in a sort of artistic delirium. Her salivary super-secretion no longer sufficed. Not having attempted even to understand the part played by Debussy in the rediscovery of Chopin, she felt only that my judgment of him was favourable. Her musical enthusiasm overpowered her. "Elodie! Elodie! He likes Chopin!" her bosom rose and she beat the air with her arms. "Ah! I knew at once that you were a musician," she cried. "I can quite understand an artist such as you are liking him. He's so lovely!" And her voice was as pebbly as if, to express her ardour for Chopin, she had copied Demosthenes and filled her mouth with all the shingle on the beach. Then came the turn of the tide, reaching as far as her veil which she had not time to lift out of harm's way and which was flooded; and lastly the Marquise wiped away with her embroidered handkerchief the tidemark of foam in which the memory of Chopin had steeped her moustaches.

"Good heavens," Mme. de Cambremer-Legrandin remarked to me, "I'm afraid my mother-in-law's cutting it rather fine, she's forgotten that we've got my Uncle de Ch'nouville dining. Besides, Cancan doesn't like to be kept waiting." The word "Cancan" was beyond me, and I supposed that she might perhaps be referring to a dog. But as for the Ch'nouville relatives, the explanation was as follows. With the lapse of time the young Marquise had outgrown the pleasure that she had once found in pronouncing their name in this manner. And yet it was the prospect of enjoying that pleasure that had decided her choice of a husband. In other social circles, when one referred to the Chenouville family, the custom was (whenever, that is to say, the particle was preceded by a word ending in a vowel sound, for otherwise you were obliged to lay stress upon the *de*, the tongue refusing to utter Madam' d'Ch'nonceaux) that it was the mute *e* of the particle that was sacrificed. One said: "Monsieur d'Chenouville." The Cambremer tradition was different, but no less imperious. It was the mute *e* of Chenouville that was suppressed. Whether the name was preceded by *mon cousin* or by *ma cousine,* it was always *de Ch'nouville* and never *de Chenouville.* (Of the father of these Chenouvilles, one said "our Uncle" for they were not sufficiently "smart set" at Féterne to pronounce the word "Unk" like the Guermantes, whose deliberate jargon, suppressing consonants and naturalising foreign words, was as difficult to understand as Old French or a modern dialect). Every newcomer into the family circle at once received, in the matter of the Ch'nouvilles, a lesson which Mme. de Cambremer-Legrandin had not required. When, paying a call one day, she had heard a girl say: "My Aunt d'Uzai," "My Unk de Rouan," she had not at first recognised the illustrious names which she was in the habit of pronouncing: Uzès, and Rohan, she had felt the astonishment, embarrassment and shame of a person who sees before him on the table a recently invented implement of which he does not know the proper use and with which he dares not begin to eat. But during that night and the next day she had rapturously repeated: "My Aunt Uzai," with that suppression of the final *s*, a suppression that had stupefied her the day before, but which it now seemed to her so vulgar not to know that, one of her friends having spoken to her of a bust of the Duchesse d'Uzès, Mlle. Legrandin had answered her crossly, and in an arrogant tone: "You might at least pronounce her name properly: Mame d'Uzai." From that moment she had realised that, by virtue of the transmutation of solid bodies into more and more subtle elements, the considerable and so honourably acquired fortune that she had inherited from her father, the finished education that she had received, her regular attendance at the Sorbonne, whether at Caro's lectures or at Brunetière's, and at the Lamoureux concerts, all this was to be rendered volatile, to find its utmost sublimation in the pleasure of being able one day to say: "My Aunt d'Uzai." This did not exclude the thought that she would continue to associate, in the earlier days, at least, of her married life, not indeed with certain women friends whom she liked and had resigned herself to sacrificing, but with certain others whom she did not like and to whom she looked forward to being able to say (since that, after all was why she was marrying): "I must introduce you to my Aunt d'Uzai," and, when she saw that such an alliance was beyond her reach, "I must introduce you to my Aunt de Ch'nouville," and "I shall ask you to dine to meet the Uzai." Her marriage to M. de Cambremer had procured for Mlle. Legrandin the opportunity to use the former of these phrases but not the latter, the circle in which her parents-in-law moved not being that which she had supposed and of which she continued to dream. After saying to me of Saint-Loup (adopting for the occasion one of his expressions, for if in talking to her I used those expressions of Legrandin, she by a reverse suggestion answered me in Robert's dialect which she did not know to be borrowed from Rachel), bringing her thumb and forefinger together and half-shutting her eyes as though she were gazing at something infinitely delicate which she had succeeded in capturing: "He has a charming quality of mind;" she began to extol him with such warmth that one might have supposed that she was in love with him (it had indeed been alleged that, some time back, when he was at Doncières, Robert had been her lover), in reality simply that I might repeat her words to him, and ended up with: "You are a great friend of the Duchesse de Guermantes. I am an invalid, I never go anywhere, and I know that she sticks to a close circle of chosen friends, which I do think so wise of her, and so I know her very slightly, but I know she is a really remarkable woman." Aware that Mme. de Cambremer barely knew her, and anxious to reduce myself to her level, I avoided the subject and answered the Marquise that the person whom I did know well was her brother, M. Legrandin. At the sound of his name she assumed the same evasive air as myself over the name of Mme. de Guermantes, but combined with it an expression of annoyance, for she supposed that I had said this with the object of humiliating not myself but her. Was she gnawed by despair at having been born a Legrandin? So at least her husband's sisters and sisters-in-law asserted, ladies of the provincial nobility who knew nobody and nothing, and were jealous of Mme. de Cambremer's intelligence, her education, her fortune, the physical attractions that she had possessed before her illness. "She can think of nothing else, that is what is killing her," these slanderers would say whenever they spoke of Mme. de Cambremer to no matter whom, but preferably to a plebeian, whether, were he conceited and stupid, to enhance, by this affirmation of the shamefulness of a plebeian origin, the value of the affability that they were shewing him, of, if he were shy and clever and applied the remark to himself, to give themselves the pleasure, while receiving him hospitably, of insulting him indirectly. But if these ladies thought that they were speaking the truth about their sister-in-law, they were mistaken. She suffered not at all from having been born Legrandin, for she had forgotten the fact altogether. She was annoyed at my reminding her of it, and remained silent as though she had not understood, not thinking it necessary to enlarge upon or even to confirm my statement.

"Our cousins are not the chief reason for our cutting short our visit," said the dowager Mme. de Cambremer, who was probably more satiated than her daughter-in-law with the pleasure to be derived from saying "Ch'nouville." "But, so as not to bother you with too many people, Monsieur," she went on, indicating the lawyer, "was afraid to bring his wife and son to the hotel. They are waiting for us on the beach, and they will be growing impatient." I asked for an exact description of them and hastened in search of them. The wife had a round face like certain flowers of the ranunculus family, and a large vegetable growth at the corner of her eye. And as the generations of mankind preserve their characteristic like a family of plants, just as on the blemished face of his mother, an identical mole, which might have helped one in classifying a variety of the species, protruded below the eye of the son. The lawyer was touched by my civility to his wife and son. He shewed an interest in the subject of my stay at Balbec. "You must find yourself rather out of your element, for the people here are for the most part foreigners." And he kept his eye on me as he spoke, for, not caring for foreigners, albeit he had many foreign clients, he wished to make sure that I was not hostile to his xenophobia, in which case he would have beaten a retreat saying: "Of course, Mme. X—— may be a charming woman. It's a question of principle." As at that time I had no definite opinion about foreigners, I shewed no sign of disapproval; he felt himself to be on safe ground. He went so far as to invite me to come one day, in Paris, to see his collection of Le Sidaner, and to bring with me the Cambremers, with whom he evidently supposed me to be on intimate terms. "I shall invite you to meet Le Sidaner," he said to me, confident that from that moment I would live only in expectation of that happy day. "You shall see what a delightful man he is. And his pictures will enchant you. Of course, I can't compete with the great collectors, but I do believe that I am the one that possesses the greatest number of his favourite canvases. They will interest you all the more, coming from Balbec, since they are marine subjects, for the most part, at least." The wife and son, blessed with a vegetable nature, listened composedly.

One felt that their house in Paris was a sort of temple of Le Sidaner. Temples of this sort are not without their use. When the god has doubts as to his own merits, he can easily stop the cracks in his opinion of himself with the irrefutable testimony of people who have devoted their lives to his work.

At a signal from her daughter-in-law, Mme. de Cambremer prepared to depart, and said to me: "Since you won't come and stay at Féterne, won't you at least come to luncheon, one day this week, to-morrow for instance?" And in her bounty, to make the invitation irresistible, she added: "You will *find* the Comte de Crisenoy," whom I had never lost, for the simple reason that I did not know him. She was beginning to dazzle me with yet further temptations, but stopped short. The chief magistrate who, on returning to the hotel, had been told that she was on the premises had crept about searching for her everywhere, then waited his opportunity, and pretending to have caught sight of her by chance, came up now to greet her. I gathered that Mme. de Cambremer did not mean to extend to him the invitation to luncheon that she had just addressed to me. And yet he had known her far longer than I, having for years past been one of the regular guests at the afternoon parties at Féterne whom I used so to envy during my former visit to Balbec. But old acquaintance is not the only thing that counts in society. And hostesses are more inclined to reserve their luncheons for new acquaintances who still whet their curiosity, especially when they arrive preceded by a glowing and irresistible recommendation like Saint-Loup's of me. Mme. de Cambremer decided that the chief magistrate could not have heard what she was saying to me, but, to calm her guilty conscience, began addressing him in the kindest tone. In the sunlight that flooded, on the horizon, the golden coastline, invisible as a rule, of Rivebelle, we could just make out, barely distinguishible from the luminous azure, rising from the water, rosy, silvery, faint, the little bells that were sounding the angelus round about Féterne. "That is rather *Pelléas,* too," I suggested to Mme. de Cambremer-Legrandin. "You know the scene I mean." "Of course I do!" was what she said; but "I haven't the faintest idea" was the message proclaimed by her voice and features which did not mould themselves to the shape of any recollection and by a smile that floated without support, in the air. The dowager could not get over her astonishment that the sound of the bells should carry so far, and rose, reminded of the time: "But, as a rule," I said, "we never see that part of the coast from Balbec, nor hear it either. The weather must have changed and enlarged the horizon in more ways than one. Unless, that is to say, the bells have come to look for you, since I see that they are making you leave; to you they are a dinner bell." The chief magistrate, little interested in the bells, glanced furtively along the front, on which he was sorry to see so few people that evening. "You are a true poet," said Mme. de Cambremer to me. "One feels you are so responsive, so artistic, come, I will play you Chopin," she went on, raising her arms with an air of ecstasy and pronouncing the words in a raucous voice like the shifting of shingle on the beach. Then came the deglutition of spittle, and the old lady instinctively wiped the stubble of her moustaches with her handkerchief. The chief magistrate did me, unconsciously, a great service by offering the Marquise his arm to escort her to her carriage, a certain blend of vulgarity, boldness and love of ostentation prompting him to actions which other people would have hesitated to risk, and which are by no means unsuccessful in society. He was, moreover, and had been for years past far more in the habit of these actions than myself. While blessing him for what he did I did not venture to copy him, and walked by the side of Mme. de Cambremer-Legrandin who insisted upon seeing the book that I had in my hand. The name of Madame de Sévigné drew a grimace from her; and using a word which she had seen in certain newspapers, but which, used in speech and given a feminine form, and applied to a seventeenth century writer, had an odd effect, she asked me: "Do you think her really masterly?" The Marquise gave her footman the address of a pastrycook where she had to call before taking the road, rosy with the evening haze, through which loomed one beyond another the dusky walls of cliff. She asked her old coachman whether one of the horses which was apt to catch cold had been kept warm enough, whether the other's shoe were not hurting him. "I shall write to you and make a definite engagement," she murmured to me. "I heard you talking about literature to my daughter-in-law, she's a darling," she went on, not that she really thought so, but she had acquired the habit—and kept it up in her kindness of heart—of saying so, in order that her son might not appear to have married for money. "Besides," she added with a final enthusiastic gnashing of her teeth, "she's so harttissttick!" With this she stepped into her carriage, nodding her head, holding the crook of her sunshade aloft like a crozier, and set off through the streets of Balbec, overloaded with the ornaments of her priesthood, like an old Bishop on a confirmation tour.

"She has asked you to luncheon," the chief magistrate said to me sternly when the carriage had passed out of sight and I came indoors with the girls. "We're not on the best of terms just now. She feels that I neglect her. Gad, I'm easy enough to get on with. If anybody needs me, I'm always there to say: Adsum! But they tried to force my hand. That, now," he went on with an air of subtlety, holding up his finger as though making and arguing a distinction, "that is a thing I do not allow. It is a threat to the liberty of my holidays. I was obliged to say: Stop! You seem to be in her good books. When you reach my age you will see that society is a very trumpery thing, and you will be sorry you attached so much importance to these trifles. Well, I am going to take a turn before dinner. Good-bye, children," he shouted back at us, as though he were already fifty yards away.

When I had said good-bye to Rosemonde and Gisèle, they saw with astonishment that Albertine was staying behind instead of accompanying them. "Why, Albertine, what are you doing, don't you know what time it is?" "Go home," she replied in a tone of authority. "I want to talk to him," she added, indicating myself with a submissive air. Rosemonde and Gisèle stared at me, filled with a new and strange respect. I enjoyed the feeling that, for a moment at least, in the eyes even of Rosemonde and Gisèle, I was to Albertine something more important than the time, than her friends, and might indeed share solemn secrets with her into which it was impossible for them to be admitted. "Shan't we see you again this evening?" "I don't know, it will depend on this person. Anyhow, to-morrow." "Let us go up to my room," I said to her, when her friends had gone. We took the lift; she remained silent in the boy's presence. The habit of being obliged to resort to personal observation and deduction in order to find out the business of their masters, those strange beings who converse among themselves and do not speak to them, develops in "employees" (as the lift-boy styled servants), a stronger power of divination than the "employer" possesses. Our organs become atrophied or grow stronger or more subtle, accordingly as our need of them increases or diminishes. Since railways came into existence, the necessity of not missing the train has taught us to take account of minutes whereas among the ancient Romans, who not only had a more cursory science of astronomy but led less hurried lives, the notion not of minutes but even of fixed hours barely existed. And so the lift-boy had gathered and meant to inform his comrades that Albertine and I were preoccupied. But he talked to us without ceasing because he had no tact. And yet I could see upon his face, in place of the customary expression of friendliness and joy at taking me up in his lift, an air of extraordinary depression and uneasiness. As I knew nothing of the cause of this, in an attempt to distract his thoughts, and albeit I was more preoccupied than Albertine, I told him that the lady who had just left was called the Marquise de Cambremer and not de Camembert. On the landing at which we were pausing at the moment, I saw, carrying a pair of pails, a hideous chambermaid who greeted me with respect, hoping for a tip when I left. I should have liked to know if she were the one whom I had so ardently desired on the evening of my first arrival at Balbec, but I could never arrive at any certainty. The lift-boy swore to me with the sincerity of most false witnesses, but without shedding his expression of despair, that it was indeed by the name of Camembert that the Marquise had told him to announce her. And as a matter of fact it was quite natural that he should have heard her say a name which he already knew. Besides, having those very vague ideas of nobility, and of the names of which titles are composed, which are shared by many people who are not lift-boys, the name Camembert had seemed to him all the more probable inasmuch as, that cheese being universally known, it was not in the least surprising that people should have acquired a marquisate from so glorious a distinction, unless it were the marquisate that had bestowed its renown upon the cheese. Nevertheless as he saw that I refused to admit that I might be mistaken, and as he knew that masters like to see their most futile whims obeyed and their most obvious lies accepted, he promised me like a good servant that in future he would say Cambremer. It is true that none of the shopkeepers in the town, none of the peasants in the district, where the name and persons of the Cambremers were perfectly familiar, could ever have made the lift-boy's mistake. But the staff of the "Grand Hotel of Balbec" were none of them natives. They came direct, with the furniture and stock, from Biarritz, Nice and Monte-Carlo, one division having been transferred to Deauville, another to Dinard and the third reserved for Balbec.

But the lift-boy's pained anxiety continued to grow. That he should thus forget to shew his devotion to me by the customary smiles, some misfortune must have befallen him. Perhaps he had been "missed." I made up my mind in that case to try to secure his reinstatement, the manager having promised to ratify all my wishes with regard to his staff. "You can always do just what you like, I rectify everything in advance." Suddenly, as I stepped out of the lift, I guessed the meaning of the boy's distress, his panic-stricken air. Because Albertine was with me, I had not given him the five francs which I was in the habit of slipping into his hand when I went up. And the idiot, instead of understanding that I did not wish to make a display of generosity in front of a third person, had begun to tremble, supposing that it was all finished, that I would never give him anything again. He imagined that I was "on the rocks" (as the Duc de Guermantes would have said), and the supposition inspired him with no pity for myself but with a terrible selfish disappointment. I told myself that I was less unreasonable than my mother thought when I dared not, one day, refrain from giving the extravagant but feverishly awaited sum that I had given the day before. But at the same time the meaning that I had until then, and without a shadow of doubt, ascribed to his habitual expression of joy, in which I had no hesitation in seeing a sign of devotion, seemed to me to have become less certain. Seeing the lift-boy ready, in his despair, to fling himself down from the fifth floor of the hotel, I asked myself whether, if our respective social stations were to be altered, in consequence let us say of a revolution, instead of politely working his lift for me, the boy, grown independent, would not have flung me down the well, and whether there was not, in certain of the lower orders, more duplicity than in society, where, no doubt, people reserve their offensive remarks until we are out of earshot, but where their attitude towards us would not be insulting if we were reduced to poverty.

One cannot however say that, in the Balbec hotel, the lift-boy was the most commercially minded. From this point of view the staff might be divided into two categories; on the one hand, those who drew distinctions between the visitors, and were more grateful for the modest tip of an old nobleman (who, moreover, was in a position to relieve them from 28 days of military service by saying a word for them to General de Beautreillis) than for the thoughtless liberalities of a cad who by his very profusion revealed a want of practice which only to his face did they call generosity. On the other hand, those to whom nobility, intellect, fame, position, manners were nonexistent, concealed under a cash valuation. For these there was but a single standard, the money one has, or rather the money one bestows. Possibly Aimé himself, albeit pretending, in view of the great number of hotels in which he had served, to a great knowledge of the world, belonged to this latter category. At the most he would give a social turn, shewing that he knew who was who, to this sort of appreciation, as when he said of the Princesse de Luxembourg: "There's a pile of money among that lot?" (the question mark at the end being to ascertain the facts or to check such information as he had already ascertained, before supplying a client with a "chef" for Paris, or promising him a table on the left, by the door, with a view of the sea, at Balbec). In spite of this, and albeit not free from sordid considerations, he would not have displayed them with the fatuous despair of the lift-boy. And yet, the latter's artlessness helped perhaps to simplify things. It is the convenience of a big hotel, of a house such as Rachel used at one time to frequent, that, without any intermediary, the face, frozen stiff until that moment, of a servant or a woman, at the sight of a hundred franc note, still more of one of a thousand, even although it is being given to some one else, will melt in smiles and offers of service. Whereas in the dealings, in the relations between lover and mistress, there are too many things interposed between money and docility. So many things that the very people upon whose faces money finally evokes a smile are often incapable of following the internal process that links them together, believe themselves to be, and indeed are more refined. Besides, it rids polite conversation of such speeches as: "There's only one thing left for me to do, you will find me to-morrow in the mortuary." And so one meets in polite society few novelists, or poets, few of all those sublime creatures who speak of the things that are not to be mentioned.

As soon as we were alone and had moved along the corridor, Albertine began: "What is it, you have got against me?" Had my harsh treatment of her been painful to myself? Had it been merely an unconscious ruse on my part, with the object of bringing my mistress to that attitude of fear and supplication which would enable me to interrogate her, and perhaps to find out which of the alternative hypotheses that I had long since formed about her was correct. However that may be, when I heard her question, I suddenly felt the joy of one who attains to a long desired goal. Before answering her, I escorted her to the door of my room. Opening it, I scattered the roseate light that was flooding the room and turning the white muslin of the curtains drawn for the night to golden damask. I went across to the window; the gulls had settled again upon the waves; but this time they were pink. I drew Albertine's attention to them. "Don't change the subject," she said, "be frank with me." I lied. I declared to her that she must first listen to a confession, that of my passionate admiration, for some time past, of Andrée, and I made her this confession with a simplicity and frankness worthy of the stage, but seldom employed in real life except for a love which people do not feel. Harking back to the fiction I had employed with Gilberte before my first visit to Balbec, but adapting its terms, I went so far (in order to make her more ready to believe me when I told her now that I was not in love with her) as to let fall the admission that at one time I had been on the point of falling in love with her, but that too long an interval had elapsed, that she could be nothing more to me now than a good friend and comrade, and that even if I wished to feel once again a more ardent sentiment for her it would be quite beyond my power. As it happened, in taking my stand thus before Albertine on these protestations of coldness towards her, I was merely—because of a particular circumstance and with a particular object in view—making more perceptible, accentuating more markedly, that dual rhythm which love adopts in all those who have too little confidence in themselves to believe that a woman can ever fall in love with them, and also that they themselves can genuinely fall in love with her. They know themselves well enough to have observed that in the presence of the most divergent types of woman they felt the same hopes, the same agonies, invented the same romances, uttered the same words, to have deduced therefore that their sentiments, their actions bear no close and necessary relation to the woman they love, but pass by her, spatter her, surround her, like the waves that break round upon the rocks, and their sense of their own instability increases still further their misgivings that this woman, by whom they would so fain be loved, is not in love with them. Why should chance have brought it about, when she is simply an accident placed so as to catch the ebullience of our desire, that we should ourself be the object of the desire that is animating her? And so, while we feel the need to pour out before her all those sentiments, so different from the merely human sentiments that our neighbour inspires in us, those so highly specialised sentiments which are a lover's, after we have taken a step forward, in avowing to her whom we love our affection for her, our hopes, overcome at once by the fear of offending her, ashamed too that the speech we have addressed to her was not composed expressly for her, that it has served us already, will serve us again for others, that if she does not love us she cannot understand us and we have spoken in that case with the want of taste, of modesty shewn by the pedant who addresses an ignorant audience in subtle phrases which are not for them, this fear, this shame bring into play the counter-rhythm, the reflux, the need, even by first drawing back, hotly denying the affection we have already confessed, to resume the offensive, and to recapture her esteem, to dominate her; the double rhythm is perceptible in the various periods of a single love affair, in all the corresponding periods of similar love affairs, in all those people whose self-analysis outweighs their self-esteem. If it was however somewhat more vigorously accentuated than usual in this speech which I was now preparing to make to Albertine, that was simply to allow me to pass more speedily and more emphatically to the alternate rhythm which should sound my affection.

As though it must be painful to Albertine to believe what I was saying to her as to the impossibility of my loving her again, after so long an interval, I justified what I called an eccentricity of my nature by examples taken from people with whom I had, by their fault or my own, allowed the time for loving them to pass, and been unable, however keenly I might have desired it, to recapture it. I thus appeared at one and the same time to be apologising to her, as for a want of courtesy, for this inability to begin loving her again, and to be seeking to make her understand the psychological reasons for that incapacity as though they had been peculiar to myself. But by explaining myself in this fashion, by dwelling upon the case of Gilberte, in regard to whom the argument had indeed been strictly true which was becoming so far from true when applied to Albertine, all that I did was to render my assertions as plausible as I pretended to believe that they were not. Feeling that Albertine appreciated what she called my "frank speech" and recognising in my deductions the clarity of the evidence, I apologised for the former by telling her that I knew that the truth was always unpleasant and in this instance must seem to her incomprehensible. She, on the contrary, thanked me for my sincerity and added that so far from being puzzled she understood perfectly a state of mind so frequent and so natural.

This avowal to Albertine of an imaginary sentiment for Andrée, and, towards herself, an indifference which, that it might appear altogether sincere and without exaggeration, I assured her incidentally, as though by a scruple of politeness, must not be taken too literally, enabled me at length, without any fear of Albertine's suspecting me of loving her, to speak to her with a tenderness which I had so long denied myself and which seemed to me exquisite. I almost caressed my confidant; as I spoke to her of her friend whom I loved, tears came to my eyes. But, coming at last to the point, I said to her that she knew what love meant, its susceptibilities, its sufferings, and that perhaps, as the old friend that she now was, she might feel it in her heart to put a stop to the bitter grief that she was causing me, not directly, since it was not herself that I loved, if I might venture to repeat that without offending her, but indirectly by wounding me in my love for Andrée. I broke off to admire and point out to Albertine a great bird, solitary and hastening, which far out in front of us, lashing the air with the regular beat of its wings, was passing at full speed over the beach stained here and there with reflexions like little torn scraps of red paper, and crossing it from end to end without slackening its pace, without diverting its attention, without deviating from its path, like an envoy carrying far afield an urgent and vital message. "He at least goes straight to the point!" said Albertine in a tone of reproach. "You say that because you don't know what it is I was going to tell you. But it is so difficult that I prefer to give it up; I am certain that I should make you angry; and then all that will have happened will be this: I shall be in no way better off with the girl I really love and I shall have lost a good friend." "But when I swear to you that I will not be angry." She had so sweet, so wistfully docile an air, as though her whole happiness depended on me, that I could barely restrain myself from kissing—with almost the same kind of pleasure that I should have taken in kissing my mother—this novel face which no longer presented the startled, blushing expression of a rebellious and perverse kitten with its little pink, tip-tilted nose, but seemed, in the fulness of its crushing sorrow, moulded in broad, flattened, drooping slabs of pure goodness. Making an abstraction of my love as of a chronic mania that had no connexion with her, putting myself in her place, I let my heart be melted before this honest girl, accustomed to being treated in a friendly and loyal fashion, whom the good comrade that she might have supposed me had been pursuing for weeks past with persecutions which had at last arrived at their culminating point. It was because I placed myself at a standpoint that was purely human, external to both of us, at which my jealous love dissolved, that I felt for Albertine that profound pity, which would have been less profound if I had not loved her. However, in that rhythmical oscillation which leads from a declaration to a quarrel (the surest, the most certainly perilous way of forming by opposite and successive movements a knot which will not be loosed and attaches us firmly to a person by the strain of the movement of withdrawal which constitutes one of the two elements of the rhythm), of what use is it to analyse farther the refluences of human pity, which, the opposite of love, though springing perhaps unconsciously from the same cause, produces in every case the same effects? When we count up afterwards the total amount of all that we have done for a woman, we often discover that the actions prompted by the desire to shew that we love her, to make her love us, to win her favours, bulk little if any greater than those due to the human need to repair the wrongs that we have done to the creature whom we love, from a mere sense of moral duty, as though we were not in love with her. "But tell me, what on earth have I done?" Albertine asked me. There was a knock at the door; it was the lift-boy; Albertine's aunt, who was passing the hotel in a carriage, had stopped on the chance of finding her there, to take her home. Albertine sent word that she could not come, that they were to begin dinner without her, that she could not say at what time she would return. "But won't your aunt be angry?" "What do you suppose? She will understand all right." And so, at this moment at least, a moment such as might never occur again—a conversation with myself was proved by this incident to be in Albertine's eyes a thing of such self-evident importance that it must be given precedence over everything, a thing to which, referring no doubt instinctively to a family code, enumerating certain crises in which, when the career of M. Bontemps was at stake, a journey had been made without a thought, my friend never doubted that her aunt would think it quite natural to see her sacrifice the dinner-hour. That remote hour which she passed without my company, among her own people, Albertine, having brought it to me, bestowed it on me; I might make what use of it I chose. I ended by making bold to tell her what had been reported to me about her way of living, and that notwithstanding the profound disgust that I felt for women tainted with that vice, I had not given it a thought until I had been told the name of her accomplice, and that she could readily understand, loving Andrée as I did, the grief that the news had caused me. It would have been more tactful perhaps to say that I had been given the names of other women as well, in whom I was not interested. But the sudden and terrible revelation that Cottard had made to me had entered my heart to lacerate it, complete in itself but without accretions. And just as, before that moment, it would never have occurred to me that Albertine was in love with Andrée, or at any rate could find pleasure in caressing her, if Cottard had not drawn my attention to their attitude as they waltzed together, so I had been incapable of passing from that idea to the idea, so different for me, that Albertine might have, with other women than Andrée, relations for which affection could not be pleaded in excuse. Albertine, before even swearing to me that it was not true, shewed, like everyone upon learning that such things are being said about him, anger, concern, and, with regard to the unknown slanderer, a fierce curiosity to know who he was and a desire to be confronted with him so as to be able to confound him. But she assured me that she bore me, at least, no resentment. "If it had been true, I should have told you. But Andrée and I both loathe that sort of thing. We have not lived all these years without seeing women with cropped hair who behave like men and do the things you mean, and nothing revolts us more." Albertine gave me merely her word, a peremptory word unsupported by proof. But this was just what was best calculated to calm me, jealousy belonging to that family of sickly doubts which are better purged by the energy than by the probability of an affirmation. It is moreover the property of love to make us at once more distrustful and more credulous, to make us suspect, more readily than we should suspect anyone else, her whom we love, and be convinced more easily by her denials. We must be in love before we can care that all women are not virtuous, which is to say before we can be aware of the fact, and we must be in love too before we can hope, that is to say assure ourselves that some are. It is human to seek out what hurts us and then at once to seek to get rid of it. The statements that are capable of so relieving us seem quite naturally true, we are not inclined to cavil at a sedative that acts. Besides, however multiform may be the person with whom we are in love, she can in any case offer us two essential personalities accordingly as she appears to us as ours, or as turning her desires in another direction. The former of these personalities possesses the peculiar power which prevents us from believing in the reality of the other, the secret remedy to heal the sufferings that this latter has caused us. The beloved object is successively the malady and the remedy that suspends and aggravates it. No doubt, I had long since been prepared, by the strong impression made on my imagination and my faculty for emotion by the example of Swann, to believe in the truth of what I feared rather than of what I should have wished. And so the comfort brought me by Albertine's affirmations came near to being jeopardised for a moment, because I was reminded of the story of Odette. But I told myself that, if it was only right to allow for the worst, not only when, in order to understand Swann's sufferings, I had tried to put myself in his place, but now, when I myself was concerned, in seeking the truth as though it referred to some one else, still I must not, out of cruelty to myself, a soldier who chooses the post not where he can be of most use but where he is most exposed, end in the mistake of regarding one supposition as more true than the rest, simply because it was more painful. Was there not a vast gulf between Albertine, a girl of good, middle-class parentage, and Odette, a courtesan bartered by her mother in her childhood? There could be no comparison of their respective credibility. Besides, Albertine had in no respect the same interest in lying to me that Odette had had in lying to Swann. Moreover to him Odette had admitted what Albertine had just denied. I should therefore be guilty of an error in reasoning as serious—though in the opposite direction—as that which had inclined me towards a certain hypothesis because it had caused me less pain than the rest, were I not to take into account these material differences in their positions, but to reconstruct the real life of my mistress solely from what I had been told about the life of Odette. I had before me a new Albertine, of whom I had already, it was true, caught more than one glimpse towards the end of my previous visit to Balbec, frank and honest, an Albertine who had, out of affection for myself, forgiven me my suspicions and tried to dispel them. She made me sit down by her side upon my bed. I thanked her for what she had said to me, assured her that our reconciliation was complete, and that I would never be horrid to her again. I suggested to her that she ought, at the same time, to go home to dinner. She asked me whether I was not glad to have her with me. Drawing my head towards her for a caress which she had never before given me and which I owed perhaps to the healing of our rupture, she passed her tongue lightly over my lips which she attempted to force apart. At first I kept them tight shut. "You are a great bear!" she informed me.

I ought to have left the place that evening and never set eyes on her again. I felt even then that in a love which is not reciprocated—I might as well say, in love, for there are people for whom there is no such thing as reciprocated love—we can enjoy only that simulacrum of happiness which had been given me at one of those unique moments in which a woman's good nature, or her caprice, or mere chance, bring to our desires, in perfect coincidence, the same words, the same actions as if we were really loved. The wiser course would have been to consider with curiosity, to possess with delight that little parcel of happiness failing which I should have died without ever suspecting what it could mean to hearts less difficult to please or more highly favoured; to suppose that it formed part of a vast and enduring happiness of which this fragment only was visible to me, and—lest the next day should expose this fiction—not to attempt to ask for any fresh favour after this, which had been due only to the artifice of an exceptional moment. I ought to have left Balbec, to have shut myself up in solitude, to have remained so in harmony with the last vibrations of the voice which I had contrived to render amorous for an instant, and of which I should have asked nothing more than that it might never address another word to me; for fear lest, by an additional word which now could only be different, it might shatter with a discord the sensitive silence in which, as though by the pressure of a pedal, there might long have survived in me the throbbing chord of happiness.

Soothed by my explanation with Albertine, I began once again to live in closer intimacy with my mother. She loved to talk to me gently about the days in which my grandmother had been younger. Fearing that I might reproach myself with the sorrows with which I had perhaps darkened the close of my grandmother's life, she preferred to turn back to the years when the first signs of my dawning intelligence had given my grandmother a satisfaction which until now had always been kept from me. We talked of the old days at Combray. My mother reminded me that there at least I used to read, and that at Balbec I might well do the same, if I was not going to work. I replied that, to surround myself with memories of Combray and of the charming coloured plates, I should like to read again the *Thousand and One Nights*. As, long ago at Combray, when she gave me books for my birthday, so it was in secret, as a surprise for me, that my mother now sent for both the *Thousand and One Nights* of Galland and the *Thousand Nights and a Night* of Mardrus. But, after casting her eye over the two translations, my mother would have preferred that I should stick to Galland's, albeit hesitating to influence me because of the respect that she felt for intellectual liberty, her dread of interfering with my intellectual life and the feeling that, being a woman, on the one hand she lacked, or so she thought, the necessary literary equipment, and on the other hand ought not to condemn because she herself was shocked by it the reading of a young man. Happening upon certain of the tales, she had been revolted by the immorality of the subject and the crudity of the expression. But above all, preserving, like precious relics, not only the brooch, the sunshade, the cloak, the volume of Madame de Sévigné, but also the habits of thought and speech of her mother, seeking on every occasion the opinion that she would have expressed, my mother could have no doubt of the horror with which my grandmother would have condemned Mardrus's book. She remembered that at Combray while before setting out for a walk, Méséglise way, I was reading Augustin Thierry, my grandmother, glad that I should be reading, and taking walks, was indignant nevertheless at seeing him whose name remained enshrined in the hemistich: "Then reignèd Mérovée" called Merowig, refused to say "Carolingians" for the "Carlovingians" to which she remained loyal. And then I told her what my grandmother had thought of the Greek names which Bloch, following Lecomte de Lisle, gave to the gods of Homer, going so far, in the simplest matters, as to made it a religious duty, in which he supposed literary talent to consist, to adopt a Greek system of spelling. Having occasion, for instance, to mention in a letter that the wine which they drank at his home was real nectar, he would write "real nektar," with a *k*, which enabled him to titter at the mention of Lamartine. And if an *Odyssey* from which the names of Ulysses and Minerva were missing was no longer the *Odyssey* to her, what would she have said upon seeing corrupted even upon the cover the title of her *Thousand and One Nights*, upon no longer finding, exactly transcribed as she had all her life been in the habit of pronouncing them, the immortally familiar names of Scheherazade, of Dinarzade, in which, debaptised themselves (if one may use the expression of Musulman tales), the charming Caliph and the powerful Genies were barely recognisable, being renamed, he the "Khalifat" and they the "Gennis." Still, my mother handed over both books to me, and I told her that I would read them on the days when I felt too tired to go out.

These days were not very frequent, however. We used to go out picnicking as before in a band, Albertine, her friends and myself, on the cliff or to the farm called Marie-Antoinette. But there were times when Albertine bestowed on me this great pleasure. She would say to me: "To-day I want to be alone with you for a little, it will be nicer if we are just by ourselves." Then she would give out that she was busy, not that she need furnish any explanation, and so that the others, if they went all the same, without us, for an excursion and picnic, might not be able to find us, we would steal away like a pair of lovers, all by ourselves to Bagatelle or the Cross of Heulan, while the band, who would never think of looking for us there and never went there, waited indefinitely, in the hope of seeing us appear, at Marie-Antoinette. I recall the hot weather that we had then, when from the brow of each of the farm-labourers toiling in the sun a drop of sweat would fall, vertical, regular, intermittent, like the drop of water from a cistern, and alternate with the fall of the ripe fruit dropping from the tree in the adjoining "closes"; they have remained, to this day, with that mystery of a woman's secret, the most substantial part of every love that offers itself to me. A woman who has been mentioned to me and to whom I would not give a moment's thought—I upset all my week's engagements to make her acquaintance, if it is a week of similar weather, and I am to meet her in some isolated farmhouse. It is no good my knowing that this kind of weather, this kind of assignation are not part of her, they are still the bait, which I know all too well, by which I allow myself to be tempted and which is sufficient to hook me. I know that this woman, in cold weather, in a town, I might perhaps have desired, but without the accompaniment of a romantic sentiment, without becoming amorous; my love for her is none the less keen as soon as, by force of circumstances, it has enthralled me—it is only the more melancholy, as in the course of life our sentiments for other people become, in proportion as we become more clearly aware of the ever smaller part that they play in our life and that the new love which we would like to be so permanent, cut short in the same moment as life itself, will be the last.

There were still but a few people at Balbec, hardly any girls. Sometimes I saw some girl resting upon the beach, devoid of charm, and yet apparently identified by various features as one whom I had been in despair at not being able to approach at the moment when she emerged with her friends from the riding school or gymnasium. If it was the same (and I took care not to mention the matter to Albertine), then the girl that I had thought so exciting did not exist. But I could not arrive at any certainty, for the face of any one of these girls did not fill any space upon the beach, did not offer a permanent form, contracted, dilated, transformed as it was by my own observation, the uneasiness of my desire or a sense of comfort that was self-sufficient, by the different clothes that she was wearing, the rapidity of her movements or her immobility. All the same, two or three of them seemed to me adorable. Whenever I saw one of these, I longed to take her away along the Avenue des Tamaris, or among the sandhills, better still upon the cliff. But, albeit into desire, as opposed to indifference, there enters already that audacity which is a first stage, if only unilateral, towards realisation, all the same, between my desire and the action that my request to be allowed to kiss her would have been, there was all the indefinite blank of hesitation, of timidity. Then I went into the pastrycook's bar, I drank, one after another, seven or eight glasses of port wine. At once, instead of the impassable gulf between my desire and action, the effect of the alcohol traced a line that joined them together. No longer was there any room for hesitation or fear. It seemed to me that the girl was about to fly into my arms. I went up to her, the words came spontaneously to my lips: " I should like to go for a walk with you. You wouldn't care to go along the cliff, we shan't be disturbed behind the little wood that keeps the wind off the wooden bungalow that is empty just now? " All the difficulties of life were smoothed away, there was no longer any obstacle to the conjunction of our two bodies. No obstacle for me, at least. For they had not been volatilised for her, who had not been drinking port wine. Had she done so, had the outer world lost some of its reality in her eyes, the long cherished dream that would then have appeared to her to be suddenly realisable might perhaps have been not at all that of falling into my arms.

Not only were the girls few in number but at this season which was not yet " the season " they stayed but a short time. There is one I remember with a reddish skin, green eyes and a pair of ruddy cheeks, whose slight symmetrical face resembled the winged seeds of certain trees. I cannot say what breeze wafted her to Balbec or what other bore her away. So sudden was her removal that for some days afterwards I was haunted by a grief which I made bold to confess to Albertine when I realised that the girl had gone for ever.

I should add that several of them were either girls whom I did not know at all or whom I had not seen for years. Often, before addressing them, I wrote to them. If their answer allowed me to believe in the possibility of love, what joy! We cannot, at the outset of our friendship with a woman, even if that friendship is destined to come to nothing, bear to part from those first letters that we have received from her. We like to have them beside us all the time, like a present of rare flowers, still quite fresh, at which we cease to gaze only to draw them closer to us and smell them. The sentence that we know by heart, it is pleasant to read again, and in those that we have committed less accurately to memory we like to verify the degree of affection in some expression. Did she write: "Your dear letter"? A slight marring of our bliss, which must be ascribed either to our having read too quickly, or to the illegible handwriting of our correspondent; she did not say: "Your dear letter" but "From your letter." But the rest is so tender. Oh, that more such flowers may come to-morrow. Then that is no longer enough, we must with the written words compare the writer's eyes, her face. We make an appointment, and—without her having altered, perhaps—whereas we expected, from the description given us or our personal memory, to meet the fairy Viviane, we encounter Puss-in-Boots. We make an appointment, nevertheless, for the following day, for it is, after all, *she,* and the person we desired is she. And these desires for a woman of whom we have been dreaming do not make beauty of form and feature essential. These desires are only the desire for a certain person; vague as perfumes, as styrax was the desire of Prothyraia, saffron the ethereal desire, aromatic scents the desire of Hera, myrrh the perfume of the Magi, manna the desire of Nike, incense the perfume of the sea. But these perfumes that are sung in the Orphic hymns are far fewer in number than the deities they worship. Myrrh is the perfume of the Magi, but also of Protogonos, Neptune, Nereus, Leto; incense is the perfume of the sea, but also of the fair Dike, of Themis, of Circe, of the Nine Muses, of Eos, of Mnemosyne, of the Day, of Dikaiosyne. As for styrax, manna and aromatic scents, it would be impossible to name all the deities that inhale them, so many are they. Amphietes has all the perfumes except incense, and Gaia rejects only beans and aromatic scents. So was it with these desires for different girls that I felt. Fewer in number than the girls themselves, they changed into disappointments and regrets closely similar one to another. I never wished for myrrh. I reserved it for Jupien and for the Prince de Guermantes, for it is the desire of Protogonos "of twofold sex, who roars like a bull, of countless orgies, memorable, unspeakable, descending, joyous, to the sacrifices of the Orgiophants."

But presently the season was in full swing; every day there was some fresh arrival, and for the sudden increase in the frequency of my outings, which took the place of the charmed perusal of the *Thousand and One Nights*, there was a reason devoid of pleasure which poisoned them all. The beach was now peopled with girls, and, since the idea suggested to me by Cottard had not indeed furnished me with fresh suspicions but had rendered me sensitive and weak in that quarter and careful not to let any suspicion take shape in my mind, as soon as a young woman arrived at Balbec, I began to feel ill at ease, I proposed to Albertine the most distant excursions, in order that she might not make the newcomer's acquaintance, and indeed, if possible, might not set eyes on her. I dreaded naturally even more those women whose dubious ways were remarked or their bad reputation already known; I tried to persuade my mistress that this bad reputation had no foundation, was a slander, perhaps, without admitting it to myself, from a fear, still unconscious, that she might seek to make friends with the depraved woman or regret her inability to do so, because of me, or might conclude from the number of examples that a vice so widespread was not to be condemned. In denying the guilt of each of them, my intention was nothing less than to pretend that sapphism did not exist. Albertine adopted my incredulity as to the viciousness of this one or that. "No, I think it's just a pose, she wants to look the part." But then, I regretted almost that I had pleaded the other's innocence, for it distressed me that Albertine, formerly so severe, could believe that this "part" was a thing so flattering, so advantageous, that a woman innocent of such tastes could seek to "look it." I would have liked to be sure that no more women were coming to Balbec; I trembled when I thought that, as it was almost time for Mme. Putbus to arrive at the Verdurins', her maid, whose tastes Saint-Loup had not concealed from me, might take it into her head to come down to the beach, and, if it were a day on which I was not with Albertine, might seek to corrupt her. I went the length of asking myself whether, as Cottard had made no secret of the fact that the Verdurins thought highly of me and, while not wishing to appear, as he put it, to be running after me, would give a great deal to have me come to their house, I might not, on the strength of promises to bring all the Guermantes in existence to call on them in Paris, induce Mme. Verdurin, upon some pretext or other, to inform Mme. Putbus that it was impossible to keep her there any longer and make her leave the place at once. Notwithstanding these thoughts, and as it was chiefly the presence of Andrée that was disturbing me, the soothing effect that Albertine's words had had upon me still to some extent persisted—I knew moreover that presently I should have less need of it, as Andrée would be leaving the place with Rosemonde and Gisèle just about the time when the crowd began to arrive and would be spending only a few weeks more with Albertine. During these weeks, moreover, Albertine seemed to have planned everything that she did, everything that she said, with a view to destroying my suspicions if any remained, or to prevent them from reviving. She contrived never to be left alone with André, and insisted, when we came back from an excursion, upon my accompanying her to her door, upon my coming to fetch her when we were going anywhere. Andrée meanwhile took just as much trouble on her side, seemed to avoid meeting Albertine. And this apparent understanding between them was not the only indication that Albertine must have informed her friend of our conversation and have asked her to be so kind as to calm my absurd suspicions.

About this time there occurred at the Grand Hotel a scandal which was not calculated to modify the intensity of my torment. Bloch's cousin had for some time past been indulging, with a retired actress, in secret relations which presently ceased to satisfy them. That they should be seen seemed to them to add perversity to their pleasure, they chose to flaunt their perilous sport before the eyes of all the world. They began with caresses, which might, after all, be set down to a friendly intimacy, in the card-room, by the baccarat-table. Then they grew more bold. And finally, one evening, in a corner that was not even dark of the big ball-room, on a sofa, they made no more attempt to conceal what they were doing than if they had been in bed. Two officers who happened to be near, with their wives, complained to the manager. It was thought for a moment that their protest would be effective. But they had this against them that, having come over for the evening from Netteholme, where they were staying, they could not be of any use to the manager. Whereas, without her knowing it even, and whatever remarks the manager may have made to her, there hovered over Mlle. Bloch the protection of M. Nissim Bernard. I must explain why. M. Nissim Bernard carried to their highest pitch the family virtues. Every year he took a magnificent villa at Balbec for his nephew, and no invitation would have dissuaded him from going home to dine at his own table, which was in reality theirs. But he never took his luncheon at home. Every day at noon he was at the Grand Hotel. The fact of the matter was that he was keeping, as other men keep a chorus-girl from the opera, an embryo waiter of much the same type as the pages of whom we have spoken, and who made us think of the young Israelites in *Esther* and *Athalie*. It is true that the forty years' difference in age between M. Nissim Bernard and the young waiter ought to have preserved the latter from a contact that was scarcely pleasant. But, as Racine so wisely observes in those same choruses:

> Great God, with what uncertain tread
> A budding virtue 'mid such perils goes!
> What stumbling-blocks do lie before a soul
> That seeks Thee and would fain be innocent.

The young waiter might indeed have been brought up "remote from the world" in the Temple-Caravanserai of Balbec, he had not followed the advice of Joad:

> In riches and in gold put not thy trust.

He had perhaps justified himself by saying: "The wicked cover the earth." However that might be, and albeit M. Nissim Bernard had not expected so rapid a conquest, on the very first day,

> Were't in alarm, or anxious to caress,
> He felt those childish arms about him thrown.

And by the second day, M. Nissim Bernard having taken the young waiter out,

> The dire assault his innocence destroyed.

From that moment the boy's life was altered. He might indeed carry bread and salt, as his superior bade him, his whole face sang:

> From flowers to flowers, from joys to keener joys
> Let our desires now range.
> Uncertain is our tale of fleeting years.
> Haste we then to enjoy this life!
> Honours and fame are the reward
> Of blind and meek obedience.
> For moping innocence
> Who now would raise his voice!

Since that day, M. Nissim Bernard had never failed to come and occupy his seat at the luncheon-table (as a man would occupy his in the stalls who was keeping a dancer, a dancer in this case of a distinct and special type, which still awaits its Degas). It was M. Nissim Bernard's delight to follow over the floor of the restaurant and down the remote vista to where beneath her palm the cashier sat enthroned, the evolutions of the adolescent hurrying in service, in the service of everyone, and, less than anyone, of M. Nissim Bernard, now that the latter was keeping him, whether because the young chorister did not think it necessary to display the same friendliness to a person by whom he supposed himself to be sufficiently well loved, or because that love annoyed him or he feared lest, if discovered, it might make him lose other opportunities. But this very coldness pleased M. Nissim Bernard, because of all that it concealed; whether from Hebraic atavism or from profanation of the Christian spirit, he took a singular pleasure, were it Jewish or Catholic, in the Racinian ceremony. Had it been a real performance of *Esther* or *Athalie*, M. Bernard would have regretted that the gulf of centuries must prevent him from making the acquaintance of the author, Jean Racine, so that he might obtain for his protégé a more substantial part. But as the luncheon ceremony came from no author's pen, he contented himself with being on good terms with the manager and Aimé, so that the "young Israelite" might be promoted to the coveted post of under waiter, or even full waiter to a row of tables. The post of wine waiter had been offered him. But M. Bernard made him decline it, for he would no longer have been able to come every day to watch him race about the green dining-room and to be waited upon by him like a stranger. Now this pleasure was so keen that every year M. Bernard returned to Balbec and took his luncheon away from home, habits in which M. Bloch saw, in the former a poetical fancy for the bright sunshine, the sunsets of this coast favoured above all others, in the latter the inveterate mania of an old bachelor.

As a matter of fact, the mistake made by M. Nissim Bernard's relatives, who never suspected the true reason for his annual return to Balbec and for what the pedantic Mme. Bloch called his absentee palate, was really a more profound and secondary truth. For M. Nissim Bernard himself was unaware how much there was of love for the beach at Balbec, for the view one enjoyed from the restaurant over the sea, and of maniacal habits in the fancy that he had for keeping, like a dancing girl of another kind which still lacks a Degas, one of his servants the rest of whom were still girls. And so M. Nissim Bernard maintained, with the director of this theatre which was the hotel at Balbec, and with the stage-manager and producer Aimé—whose part in all this affair was anything but simple—excellent relations. One day they would intrigue to procure an important part, a place perhaps as head-waiter. In the meantime M. Nissim Bernard's pleasure, poetical and calmly contemplative as it might be, reminded one a little of those women-loving men who always know—Swann, for example, in the past—that if they go out to a party they will meet their mistress. No sooner had M. Nissim Bernard taken his seat than he would see the object of his affections appear on the scene, bearing in his hand fruit or cigars upon a tray. And so every morning, after kissing his niece, bothering my friend

Bloch about his work and feeding his horses with lumps of sugar from the palm of his outstretched hand, he would betray a feverish haste to arrive in time for luncheon at the Grand Hotel. Had the house been on fire, had his niece had a stroke, he would doubtless have started off just the same. So that he dreaded like the plague a cold that would confine him to his bed—for he was a hypochondriac—and would oblige him to ask Aimé to send his young friend across to visit him at home, between luncheon and tea-time.

He loved moreover all the labyrinth of corridors, private offices, reception-rooms, cloakrooms, larders, galleries which composed the hotel at Balbec. With a strain of oriental atavism he loved a seraglio, and when he went out at night might be seen furtively exploring its passages.

While, venturing down to the basement and endeavouring at the same time to escape notice and to avoid a scandal, M. Nissim Bernard, in his quest of the young Levites, put one in mind of those lines in *La Juive:*

> O God of our Fathers, come down to us again,
> Our mysteries veil from the eyes of wicked men!

I on the contrary would go up to the room of two sisters who had come to Balbec, as her maids, with an old lady, a foreigner. They were what the language of hotels called two "couriers," and that of Françoise, who imagined that a courier was a person who was there to run his course, two "coursers." The hotels have remained, more nobly, in the period when people sang: "*C'est un courrier de cabinet.*"

Difficult as it was for a visitor to penetrate to the servants' quarters, I had very soon formed a mutual bond of friendship, as strong as it was pure, with these two young persons, Mademoiselle Marie Gineste and Madame Céleste Albaret. Born at the foot of the high mountains in the centre of France, on the banks of rivulets and torrents (the water passed actually under their old home, turning a millwheel, and the house had often been damaged by floods), they seemed to embody the features of that region. Marie Gineste was more regularly rapid and abrupt, Céleste Albaret softer and more languishing, spread out like a lake, but with terrible boiling rages in which her fury suggested the peril of spates and gales that sweep everything before them. They often came in the morning to see me when I was still in bed. I have never known people so deliberately ignorant, who had learned absolutely nothing at school, and yet whose language was somehow so literary that, but for the almost savage naturalness of their tone, one would have thought their speech affected. With a familiarity which I reproduce verbatim, notwithstanding the praises (which I set down here in praise not of myself but of the strange genius of Céleste) and the criticisms, equally unfounded, in which her remarks seem to involve me, while I dipped crescent rolls in my milk, Céleste would say to me: "Oh! Little black devil with hair of jet, O profound wickedness! I don't know what your mother was thinking of when she made you, for you are just like a bird. Look, Marie, wouldn't you say he was preening his feathers, and turning his head right round, so light he looks, you would say he was just learning to fly. Ah! It's fortunate for you that those who bred you brought you into the world to rank and riches; what would ever have become of you, so wasteful as you are.

Look at him throwing away his crescent because it touched the bed. There he goes, now, look, he's spilling his milk, wait till I tie a napkin round you, for you could never do it for yourself, never in my life have I seen anyone so helpless and so clumsy as you." I would then hear the more regular sound of the torrent of Marie Gineste who was furiously reprimanding her sister: "Will you hold your tongue, now, Céleste. Are you mad, talking to Monsieur like that?" Céleste merely smiled; and as I detested having a napkin tied round my neck: "No, Marie, look at him, bang, he's shot straight up on end like a serpent. A proper serpent, I tell you." These were but a few of her zoological similes, for, according to her, it was impossible to tell when I slept, I fluttered about all night like a butterfly, and in the day time I was as swift as the squirrels. "You know, Marie, the way we see them at home, so nimble that even with your eyes you can't follow them." "But, Céleste, you know he doesn't like having a napkin when he's eating." "It isn't that he doesn't like it, it's so that he can say nobody can make him do anything against his will. He's a grand gentleman and he wants to shew that he is. They can change the sheets ten times over, if they must, but he won't give way. Yesterday's had served their time, but to-day they have only just been put on the bed and they'll have to be changed already. Oh, I was right when I said that he was never meant to be born among the poor. Look, his hair's standing on end, swelling with rage like a bird's feathers. Poor *ploumissou!*" Here it was not only Marie that protested, but myself, for I did not feel in the least like a grand gentleman. But Céleste would never believe in the sincerity of my modesty and cut me short.

"Oh! The story-teller! Oh! The flatterer! Oh! The false one! The cunning rogue! Oh! Molière!" (This was the only writer's name that she knew, but she applied it to me, meaning thereby a person who was capable both of writing plays and of acting them.) "Céleste!" came the imperious cry from Marie, who, not knowing the name of Molière, was afraid that it might be some fresh insult. Céleste continued to smile: "Then you haven't seen the photograph of him in his drawer, when he was little. He tried to make us believe that he was always dressed quite simply. And there, with his little cane, he's all furs and laces, such as no Prince ever wore. But that's nothing compared with his tremendous majesty and kindness which is even more profound." "So then," scolded the torrent Marie, "you go rummaging in his drawers now, do you?" To calm Marie's fears I asked her what she thought of M. Nissim Bernard's behaviour. . . . "Ah! Monsieur, there are things I wouldn't have believed could exist. One has to come here to learn." And, for once outrivalling Céleste by an even more profound observation: "Ah! You see, Monsieur, one can never tell what there may be in a person's life." To change the subject, I spoke to her of the life led by my father, who toiled night and day. "Ah! Monsieur, there are people who keep nothing of their life for themselves, not one minute, not one pleasure, the whole thing is a sacrifice for others, they are lives that are *given away*." "Look, Marie, he has only to put his hand on the counterpane and take his crescent, what distinction. He can do the most insignificant things, you would say that the whole nobility of France, from here to the Pyrenees, was stirring in each of his movements."

Overpowered by this portrait so far from lifelike, I remained silent; Céleste interpreted my silence as a further instance of guile: "Oh! Brow that looks so pure, and hides so many things, nice, cool cheeks like the inside of an almond, little hands of satin all velvety, nails like claws," and so forth. "There, Marie, look at him sipping his milk with a devoutness that makes me want to say my prayers. What a serious air! They ought really to take his portrait as he is just now. He's just like a child. Is it drinking milk, like them, that has kept you their bright colour? Oh! Youth! Oh! Lovely skin. You will never grow old. You are a lucky one, you will never need to raise your hand against anyone, for you have a pair of eyes that can make their will be done. Look at him now, he's angry. He shoots up, straight as a sign-post."

Françoise did not at all approve of what she called the two "tricksters" coming to talk to me like this. The manager, who made his staff keep watch over everything that went on, even gave me a serious warning that it was not proper for a visitor to talk to servants. I, who found the "tricksters" far better than any visitor in the hotel, merely laughed in his face, convinced that he would not understand my explanations. And the sisters returned. "Look, Marie, at his delicate lines. Oh, perfect miniature, finer than the most precious you could see in a glass case, for he can move, and utters words you could listen to for days and nights."

It was a miracle that a foreign lady could have brought them there, for, without knowing anything of history or geography, they heartily detested the English, the Germans, the Russians, the Italians, all foreign vermin, and cared, with certain exceptions, for French people alone. Their faces had so far preserved the moisture of the pliable clay of their native river beds, that, as soon as one mentioned a foreigner who was staying in the hotel, in order to repeat what he had said, Céleste and Marie imposed upon their faces his face, their mouths became his mouth, their eyes his eyes, one would have liked to preserve these admirable comic masks. Céleste indeed, while pretending merely to be repeating what the manager had said, or one of my friends, would insert in her little narrative fictitious remarks in which were maliciously portrayed all the defects of Bloch, the chief magistrate, etc., while apparently unconscious of doing so. It was, under the form of the delivery of a simple message which she had obligingly undertaken to convey, an inimitable portrait. They never read anything, not even a newspaper. One day, however, they found lying on my bed a book. It was a volume of the admirable but obscure poems of Saint-Léger Léger. Céleste read a few pages and said to me: "But are you quite sure that these are poetry, wouldn't they just be riddles?" Obviously, to a person who had learned in her childhood a single poem: "Down here the lilacs die," there was a gap in evolution. I fancy that their obstinate refusal to learn anything was due in part to the unhealthy climate of their early home. They had nevertheless all the gifts of a poet with more modesty than poets generally shew. For if Céleste had said something noteworthy and, unable to remember it correctly, I asked her to repeat it, she would assure me that she had forgotten. They will never read any books, but neither will they ever write any.

Françoise was considerably impressed when she learned that the two brothers of these humble women had married, one the niece of the Archbishop of Tours, the other a relative of the Bishop of Rodez. To the manager, this would have conveyed nothing. Céleste would sometimes reproach her husband with his failure to understand her, and as for me, I was astonished that he could endure her. For at certain moments, raging, furious, destroying everything, she was detestable. It is said that the salt liquid which is our blood is only an internal survival of the primitive marine element. Similarly, I believe that Céleste, not only in her bursts of fury, but also in her hours of depression preserved the rhythm of her native streams. When she was exhausted, it was after their fashion; she had literally run dry. Nothing could then have revived her. Then all of a sudden the circulation was restored in her large body, splendid and light. The water flowed in the opaline transparence of her bluish skin. She smiled at the sun and became bluer still. At such moments she was truly celestial.

Bloch's family might never have suspected the reason which made their uncle never take his luncheon at home and have accepted it from the first as the mania of an elderly bachelor, due perhaps to the demands of his intimacy with some actress; everything that concerned M. Nissim Bernard was tabu to the manager of the Balbec hotel. And that was why, without even referring to the uncle, he had finally not ventured to find fault with the niece, albeit recommending her to be a little more circumspect. And so the girl and her friend who, for some days, had pictured themselves as excluded from the casino and the Grand Hotel, seeing that everything was settled, were delighted to shew those fathers of families who held aloof from them that they might with impunity take the utmost liberties. No doubt they did not go so far as to repeat the public exhibition which had revolted everybody. But gradually they returned to their old ways. And one evening as I came out of the casino which was half in darkness with Albertine and Bloch whom we had met there, they came towards us, linked together, kissing each other incessantly, and, as they passed us, crowed and laughed, uttering indecent cries. Bloch lowered his eyes, so as to seem not to have recognized his cousin, and as for myself I was tortured by the thought that this occult, appalling language was addressed perhaps to Albertine.

Another incident turned my thoughts even more in the direction of Gomorrah. I had noticed upon the beach a handsome young woman, erect and pale, whose eyes, round their centre, scattered rays so geometrically luminous that one was reminded, on meeting her gaze, of some constellation. I thought how much more beautiful this girl was than Albertine, and that it would be wiser to give up the other. Only, the face of this beautiful young woman had been smoothed by the invisible plane of an utterly low life, of the constant acceptance of vulgar expedients, so much so that her eyes, more noble however than the rest of her face, could radiate nothing but appetites and desires. Well, on the following day, this young woman being seated a long way away from us in the casino, I saw that she never ceased to fasten upon Albertine the alternate, circling fires of her gaze. One would have said that she was making signals to her from a lighthouse. I dreaded my friend's seeing that she was being so closely observed, I was afraid that these incessantly rekindled glances might have the conventional meaning of an amorous assignation for the morrow. For all I knew, this assignation might not be the first. The young woman with the radiant eyes might have come another year to Balbec? It was perhaps because Albertine had already yielded to her desires, or to those of a friend, that this woman allowed herself to address to her those flashing signals. If so, they did more than demand something for the present, they found a justification in pleasant hours in the past.

This assignation, in that case, must be not the first, but the sequel to adventures shared in past years. And indeed her glance did not say: "Will you?" As soon as the young woman had caught sight of Albertine, she had turned her head and beamed upon her glances charged with recollection, as though she were terribly afraid that my friend might not remember. Albertine, who could see her plainly, remained phlegmatically motionless, with the result that the other, with the same sort of discretion as a man who sees his old mistress with a new lover, ceased to look at her and paid no more attention to her than if she had not existed.

But, a day or two later, I received a proof of this young woman's tendencies, and also of the probability of her having known Albertine in the past. Often, in the hall of the casino, when two girls were smitten with mutual desire, a luminous phenomenon occurred, a sort of phosphorescent train passing from one to the other. Let us note in passing that it is by the aid of such materialisations, even if they be imponderable, by these astral signs that set fire to a whole section of the atmosphere, that the scattered Gomorrah tends, in every town, in every village, to reunite its separated members, to reform the biblical city while everywhere the same efforts are being made, be it in view of but a momentary reconstruction, by the nostalgic, the hypocritical, sometimes by the courageous exiles from Sodom.

Once I saw the stranger whom Albertine had appeared not to recognise, just at the moment when Bloch's cousin was approaching her. The young woman's eyes flashed, but it was quite evident that she did not know the Israelite maiden. She beheld her for the first time, felt a desire, a shadow of doubt, by no means the same certainty as in the case of Albertine, Albertine upon whose comradeship she must so far have reckoned that, in the face of her coldness, she had felt the surprise of a foreigner familiar with Paris but not resident there, who, having returned to spend a few weeks there, on the site of the little theatre where he was in the habit of spending pleasant evenings, sees that they have now built a bank.

Bloch's cousin went and sat down at a table where she turned the pages of a magazine. Presently the young woman came and sat down, with an abstracted air, by her side. But under the table one could presently see their feet wriggling, then their legs and hands, in a confused heap. Words followed, a conversation began, and the young woman's innocent husband, who had been looking everywhere for her, was astonished to find her making plans for that very evening with a girl whom he did not know. His wife introduced Bloch's cousin to him as a friend of her childhood, by an inaudible name, for she had forgotten to ask her what her name was. But the husband's presence made their intimacy advance a stage farther, for they addressed each other as *tu*, having known each other at their convent, an incident at which they laughed heartily later on, as well as at the hoodwinked husband, with a gaiety which afforded them an excuse for more caresses.

As for Albertine, I cannot say that anywhere in the casino or on the beach was her behaviour with any girl unduly free. I found in it indeed an excess of coldness and indifference which seemed to be more than good breeding, to be a ruse planned to avert suspicion. When questioned by some girl, she had a quick, icy, decent way of replying in a very loud voice: "Yes, I shall be going to the tennis court about five. I shall bathe to-morrow morning about eight," and of at once turning away from the person to whom she had said this—all of which had a horrible appearance of being meant to put people off the scent, and either to make an assignation, or, the assignation already made in a whisper, to utter this speech, harmless enough in itself, aloud, so as not to attract attention. And when later on I saw her mount her bicycle and scorch away into the distance, I could not help thinking that she was hurrying to overtake the girl to whom she had barely spoken.

Only, when some handsome young woman stepped out of a motor-car at the end of the beach, Albertine could not help turning round. And she at once explained: "I was looking at the new flag they've put up over the bathing place. The old one was pretty moth-eaten. But I really think this one is mouldier still."

On one occasion Albertine was not content with cold indifference, and this made me all the more wretched. She knew that I was annoyed by the possibility of her sometimes meeting a friend of her aunt, who had a "bad style" and came now and again to spend a few days with Mme. Bontemps. Albertine had pleased me by telling me that she would not speak to her again. And when this woman came to Incarville, Albertine said: "By the way, you know she's here. Have they told you?" as though to shew me that she was not seeing her in secret. One day, when she told me this, she added: "Yes, I ran into her on the beach, and knocked against her as I passed, on purpose, to be rude to her." When Albertine told me this, there came back to my mind a remark made by Mme. Bontemps, to which I had never given a second thought, when she had said to Mme. Swann in my presence how brazen her niece Albertine was, as though that were a merit, and told her how Albertine had reminded some official's wife that her father had been employed in a kitchen. But a thing said by her whom we love does not long retain its purity; it withers, it decays. An evening or two later, I thought again of Albertine's remark, and it was no longer the ill breeding of which she was so proud—and which could only make me smile—that it seemed to me to signify, it was something else, to wit that Albertine, perhaps even without any definite object, to irritate this woman's senses, or wantonly to remind her of former proposals, accepted perhaps in the past, had swiftly brushed against her, thought that I had perhaps heard of this as it had been done in public, and had wished to forestall an unfavourable interpretation.

However, the jealousy that was caused me by the women whom Albertine perhaps loved was abruptly to cease.

PART II

CHAPTER II (*continued*)

The pleasures of M. Nissim Bernard (*continued*)—Outline of the strange character of Morel—M. de Charlus dines with the Verdurins.

WE were waiting, Albertine and I, at the Balbec station of the little local railway. We had driven there in the hotel omnibus, because it was raining. Not far away from us was M. Nissim Bernard, with a black eye. He had recently forsaken the chorister from *Athalie* for the waiter at a much frequented farmhouse in the neighbourhood, known as the "Cherry Orchard." This rubicund youth, with his blunt features, appeared for all the world to have a tomato instead of a head. A tomato exactly similar served as head to his twin brother. To the detached observer there is this attraction about these perfect resemblances between pairs of twins, that nature, becoming for the moment industrialised, seems to be offering a pattern for sale. Unfortunately M. Nissim Bernard looked at it from another point of view, and this resemblance was only external. Tomato II shewed a frenzied zeal in furnishing the pleasures exclusively of ladies, Tomato I did not mind condescending to meet the wishes of certain gentlemen. Now on each occasion when, stirred, as though by a reflex action, by the memory of pleasant hours spent with Tomato I, M. Bernard presented himself at the Cherry Orchard, being short-sighted (not that one need be short-sighted to mistake them), the old Israelite, unconsciously playing Amphitryon, would accost the twin brother with: "Will you meet me somewhere this evening?" He at once received a resounding smack in the face. It might even be repeated in the course of a single meal, when he continued with the second brother the conversation he had begun with the first. In the end this treatment so disgusted him, by association of ideas, with tomatoes, even of the edible variety, that whenever he heard a newcomer order that vegetable, at the next table to his own, in the Grand Hotel, he would murmur to him: "You must excuse me, Sir, for addressing you, without an introduction. But I heard you order tomatoes. They are stale to-day. I tell you in your own interest, for it makes no difference to me, I never touch them myself." The stranger would reply with effusive thanks to this philanthropic and disinterested neighbour, call back the waiter, pretend to have changed his mind: "No, on second thoughts, certainly not, no tomatoes." Aimé, who had seen it all before, would laugh to himself, and think: "He's an old rascal, that Monsieur Bernard, he's gone and made another of them change his order." M. Bernard, as he waited for the already overdue tram, shewed no eagerness to speak to Albertine and myself, because of his black eye. We were even less eager to speak to him. It would however have been almost inevitable if, at that moment, a bicycle had not come dashing towards us; the lift-boy sprang from its saddle, breathless. Madame Verdurin had telephoned shortly after we left the hotel, to know whether I would dine with her two days later; we shall see presently why. Then, having given me the message in detail, the lift-boy left us, and, being one of these democratic "employees" who affect independence with regard to the middle classes, and among themselves restore the principle of authority, explained: "I must be off, because of my chiefs."

Albertine's girl friends had gone, and would be away for some time. I was anxious to provide her with distractions. Even supposing that she might have found some happiness in spending the afternoons with no company but my own, at Balbec, I knew that such happiness is never complete, and that Albertine, being still at the age (which some of us never outgrow) when we have not yet discovered that this imperfection resides in the person who receives the happiness and not in the person who gives it, might have been tempted to put her disappointment down to myself. I preferred that she should impute it to circumstances which, arranged by myself, would not give us an opportunity of being alone together, while at the same time preventing her from remaining in the casino and on the beach without me. And so I had asked her that day to come with me to Doncières, where I was going to meet Saint-Loup. With a similar hope of occupying her mind, I advised her to take up painting, in which she had had lessons in the past. While working she would not ask herself whether she was happy or unhappy. I would gladly have taken her also to dine now and again with the Verdurins and the Cambremers, who certainly would have been delighted to see any friend introduced by myself, but I must first make certain that Mme. Putbus was not yet at la Raspelière. It was only by going there in person that I could make sure of this, and, as I knew beforehand that on the next day but one Albertine would be going on a visit with her aunt, I had seized this opportunity to send Mme. Verdurin a telegram asking her whether she would be at home upon Wednesday. If Mme. Putbus was there, I would manage to see her maid, ascertain whether there was any danger of her coming to Balbec, and if so find out when, so as to take Albertine out of reach on the day. The little local railway, making a loop which did not exist at the time when I had taken it with my grandmother, now extended to Doncières-la-Goupil, a big station at which important trains stopped, among them the express by which I had come down to visit Saint-Loup, from Paris, and the corresponding express by which I had returned. And, because of the bad weather, the omnibus from the Grand Hotel took Albertine and myself to the station of the little tram, Balbec-Plage.

The little train had not yet arrived, but one could see, lazy and slow, the plume of smoke that it had left in its wake, which, confined now to its own power of locomotion as an almost stationary cloud, was slowly mounting the green slope of the cliff of Criquetot. Finally the little tram, which it had preceded by taking a vertical course, arrived in its turn, at a leisurely crawl. The passengers who were waiting to board it stepped back to make way for it, but without hurrying, knowing that they were dealing with a good-natured, almost human traveller, who, guided like the bicycle of a beginner, by the obliging signals of the station-master, in the strong hands of the engine-driver, was in no danger of running over anybody, and would come to a halt at the proper place.

My telegram explained the Verdurins' telephone message and had been all the more opportune since Wednesday (the day I had fixed happened to be a Wednesday) was the day set apart for dinner-parties by Mme. Verdurin, at la Raspelière, as in Paris, a fact of which I was unaware. Mme. Verdurin did not give "dinners," but she had "Wednesdays." These Wednesdays were works of art. While fully conscious that they had not their match anywhere, Mme. Verdurin introduced shades of distinction between them. "Last Wednesday was not as good as the one before," she would say. "But I believe the next will be one of the best I have ever given." Sometimes she went so far as to admit: "This Wednesday was not worthy of the others. But I have a big surprise for you next week." In the closing weeks of the Paris season, before leaving for the country, the Mistress would announce the end of the Wednesdays. It gave her an opportunity to stimulate the faithful. "There are only three more Wednesdays left, there are only two more," she would say, in the same tone as though the world were coming to an end. "You aren't going to miss next Wednesday, for the finale." But this finale was a sham, for she would announce: "Officially, there will be no more Wednesdays. To-day was the last for this year. But I shall be at home all the same on Wednesday. We shall have a little Wednesday to ourselves; I dare say these little private Wednesdays will be the nicest of all." At la Raspelière, the Wednesdays were of necessity restricted, and since, if they had discovered a friend who was passing that way, they would invite him for one or another evening, almost every day of the week became a Wednesday. "I don't remember all the guests, but I know there's Madame la Marquise de Camembert," the lift-boy had told me; his memory of our discussion of the name Cambremer had not succeeded in definitely supplanting that of the old word, whose syllables, familiar and full of meaning, came to the young employee's rescue when he was embarrassed by this difficult name, and were immediately preferred and readopted by him, not by any means from laziness or as an old and ineradicable usage, but because of the need for logic and clarity which they satisfied.

We hastened in search of an empty carriage in which I could hold Albertine in my arms throughout the journey. Having failed to find one, we got into a compartment in which there was already installed a lady with a massive face, old and ugly, with a masculine expression, very much in her Sunday best, who was reading the *Revue des Deux Mondes*. Notwithstanding her commonness, she was eclectic in her tastes, and I found amusement in asking myself to what social category she could belong; I at once concluded that she must be the manager of some large brothel, a procuress on holiday. Her face, her manner, proclaimed the fact aloud. Only, I had never yet supposed that such ladies read the *Revue des Deux Mondes*. Albertine drew my attention to her with a wink and a smile. The lady wore an air of extreme dignity; and as I, for my part, bore within me the consciousness that I was invited, two days later, to the terminal point of the little railway, by the famous Mme. Verdurin, that at an intermediate station I was awaited by Robert de Saint-Loup, and that a little farther on I had it in my power to give great pleasure to Mme. de Cambremer, by going to stay at Féterne, my eyes sparkled with irony as I studied this self-important lady who seemed to think that, because of her elaborate attire, the feathers in her hat, her *Revue des Deux Mondes*, she was a more considerable personage than myself. I hoped that the lady would not remain in the train much longer than M. Nissim Bernard, and that she would alight at least at Toutainville, but no. The train stopped at Evreville, she remained seated. Similarly at Montmartin-sur-Mer, at Parville-la-Bingard, at Incarville, so that in despair, when the train had left Saint-Frichoux, which was the last station before Doncières, I began to embrace Albertine without bothering about the lady. At Doncières, Saint-Loup had come to meet me at the station, with the greatest difficulty, he told me, for, as he was staying with his aunt, my telegram had only just reached him and he could not, having been unable to make any arrangements beforehand, spare me more than an hour of his time. This hour seemed to me, alas, far too long, for as soon as we had left the train Albertine devoted her whole attention to Saint-Loup. She never talked to me, barely answered me if I addressed her, repulsed me when I approached her. With Robert, on the other hand, she laughed her provoking laugh, talked to him volubly, played with the dog he had brought with him, and, as she excited the animal, deliberately rubbed against its master. I remembered that, on the day when Albertine had allowed me to kiss her for the first time, I had had a smile of gratitude for the unknown seducer who had wrought so profound a change in her and had so far simplified my task. I thought of him now with horror. Robert must have noticed that I was not unconcerned about Albertine, for he offered no response to her provocations, which made her extremely annoyed with myself; then he spoke to me as though I had been alone, which, when she realised it, raised me again in her esteem. Robert asked me if I would not like to meet those of his friends with whom he used to make me dine every evening at Doncières, when I was staying there, who were still in the garrison. And as he himself adopted that irritating manner which he rebuked in others: "What is the good of your having worked so hard to *charm* them if you don't want to see them again?" I declined his offer, for I did not wish to run any risk of being parted from Albertine, but also because now I was detached from them. From them, which is to say from myself. We passionately long that there may be another life in which we shall be similar to what we are here below. But we do not pause to reflect that, even without waiting for that other life, in this life, after a few years we are unfaithful to what we have been, to what we wished to remain immortally. Even without supposing that death is to alter us more completely than the changes that occur in the course of a lifetime, if in that other life we were to encounter the self that we have been, we should turn away from ourself as from those people with whom we were once on friendly terms but whom we have not seen for years—such as Saint-Loup's friends whom I used so much to enjoy meeting again every evening at the Faisan Doré, and whose conversation would now have seemed to me merely a boring importunity. In this respect, and because I preferred not to go there in search of what had pleased me there in the past, a stroll through Doncières might have seemed to me a prefiguration of an arrival in Paradise. We dream much of Paradise, or rather of a number of successive Paradises, but each of them is, long before we die, a Paradise lost, in which we should feel ourself lost also.

He left us at the station. "But you may have about

an hour to wait," he told me. "If you spend it here, you will probably see my uncle Charlus, who is going by the train to Paris, ten minutes before yours. I have said good-bye to him already, because I have to go back before his train starts. I didn't tell him about you, because I hadn't got your telegram." To the reproaches which I heaped upon Albertine when Saint-Loup had left us, she replied that she had intended, by her coldness towards me, to destroy any idea that he might have formed if, at the moment when the train stopped, he had seen me leaning against her with my arm round her waist. He had indeed noticed this attitude (I had not caught sight of him, otherwise I should have adopted one that was more correct), and had had time to murmur in my ear: "So that's how it is, one of those priggish little girls you told me about, who wouldn't go near Mlle. de Stermaria because they thought her fast?" I had indeed mentioned to Robert, and in all sincerity, when I went down from Paris to visit him at Doncières, and when we were talking about our time at Balbec, that there was nothing to be had from Albertine, that she was the embodiment of virtue. And now that I had long since discovered for myself that this was false, I was even more anxious that Robert should believe it to be true. It would have been sufficient for me to tell Robert that I was in love with Albertine. He was one of those people who are capable of denying themselves a pleasure to spare their friend sufferings which they would feel even more keenly if they themselves were the victims. "Yes, she is still rather childish. But you don't know anything against her?" I added anxiously. "Nothing, except that I saw you clinging together like a pair of lovers."

"Your attitude destroyed absolutely nothing," I told Albertine when Saint-Loup had left us. "Quite true," she said to me, "it was stupid of me, I hurt your feelings, I'm far more unhappy about it than you are. You'll see, I shall never be like that again; forgive me," she pleaded, holding out her hand with a sorrowful air. At that moment, from the entrance to the waiting-room in which we were sitting, I saw advance slowly, followed at a respectful distance by a porter loaded with his baggage, M. de Charlus.

In Paris, where I encountered him only in evening dress, immobile, straitlaced in a black coat, maintained in a vertical posture by his proud aloofness, his thirst for admiration, the soar of his conversation, I had never realised how far he had aged. Now, in a light travelling suit which made him appear stouter, as he swaggered through the room, balancing a pursy stomach and an almost symbolical behind, the cruel light of day broke up into paint, upon his lips, rice-powder fixed by cold cream, on the tip of his nose, black upon his dyed moustaches whose ebon tint formed a contrast to his grizzled hair, all that by artificial light had seemed the animated colouring of a man who was still young.

While I stood talking to him, though briefly, because of his train, I kept my eye on Albertine's carriage to shew her that I was coming. When I turned my head towards M. de Charlus, he asked me to be so kind as to summon a soldier, a relative of his, who was standing on the other side of the platform, as though he were waiting to take our train, but in the opposite direction, away from Balbec. "He is in his regimental band," said M. de Charlus. "As you are so fortunate as to be still young enough, and I unfortunately am old enough for you to save me the trouble of going across to him." I took it upon myself to go across to the soldier he pointed out to me, and saw from the lyres embroidered on his collar that he was a bandsman. But, just as I was preparing to execute my commission, what was my surprise, and, I may say, my pleasure, on recognising Morel, the son of my uncle's valet, who recalled to me so many memories. They made me forget to convey M. de Charlus's message. "What, you are at Doncières?" "Yes, and they've put me in the band attached to the batteries." But he made this answer in a dry and haughty tone. He had become an intense "poseur," and evidently the sight of myself, reminding him of his father's profession, was not pleasing to him. Suddenly I saw M. de Charlus descending upon us. My delay had evidently taxed his patience. "I should like to listen to a little music this evening," he said to Morel without any preliminaries, "I pay five hundred francs for the evening, which may perhaps be of interest to one of your friends, if you have any in the band." Knowing as I did the insolence of M. de Charlus, I was astonished at his not even saying how d'ye do to his young friend. The Baron did not however give me time to think. Holding out his hand in the friendliest manner: "Good-bye, my dear fellow," he said, as a hint that I might now leave them. I had, as it happened, left my dear Albertine too long alone. "D'you know," I said to her as I climbed into the carriage, "life by the sea-side, and travelling make me realise that the theatre of the world is stocked with fewer settings than actors, and with fewer actors than situations." "What makes you say that?" "Because M. de Charlus asked me just now to fetch one of his friends, whom, this instant, on the platform of this station, I have just discovered to be one of my own." But as I uttered these words, I began to wonder how the Baron could have bridged the social gulf to which I had not given a thought. It occurred to me first of all that it might be through Jupien, whose niece, as the reader may remember, had seemed to shew a preference for the violinist. What did baffle me completely was that, when due to leave for Paris in five minutes, the Baron should have asked for a musical evening. But, visualising Jupien's niece again in my memory, I was beginning to find that " recognitions " did indeed play an important part in life, when all of a sudden the truth flashed across my mind and I realised that I had been absurdly innocent. M. de Charlus had never in his life set eyes upon Morel, nor Morel upon M. de Charlus, who, dazzled but also terrified by a warrior, albeit he bore no weapon but a lyre, had called upon me in his emotion to bring him the person whom he never suspected that I already knew. In any case, the offer of five hundred francs must have made up to Morel for the absence of any previous relations, for I saw that they continued to talk, without reflecting that they were standing close beside our tram. As I recalled the manner in which M. de Charlus had come up to Morel and myself, I saw at once the resemblance to certain of his relatives, when they picked up a woman in the street. Only the desired object had changed its sex. After a certain age, and even if different evolutions are occurring in us, the more we become ourself, the more our characteristic features are accentuated. For Nature, while harmoniously contributing the design of her tapestry, breaks the monotony of the composition thanks to the variety of the intercepted forms. Besides, the arrogance with which M. de Charlus had accosted the violinist is relative, and depends upon the point of view one adopts. It would have been recognised by three out of four of the men in society who nodded their heads to him, not by the prefect of police who, a few years later, was to keep him under observation.

"The Paris train is signalled, Sir," said the porter who was carrying his luggage. "But I am not going by the train, put it in the cloakroom, damn you!" said M. de Charlus, as he gave twenty francs to the porter, astonished by the change of plan and charmed by the tip. This generosity at once attracted a flower-seller. "Buy these carnations, look, this lovely rose, kind gentlemen, it will bring you luck." M. de Charlus, out of patience, handed her a couple of francs, in exchange for which the woman gave him her blessing, and her flowers as well. "Good God, why can't she leave us alone," said M. de Charlus, addressing himself in an ironical and complaining tone, as of a man distraught, to Morel, to whom he found a certain comfort in appealing. "We've quite enough to talk about as it is." Perhaps the porter was not yet out of earshot, perhaps M. de Charlus did not care to have too numerous an audience, perhaps these incidental remarks enabled his lofty timidity not to approach too directly the request for an assignation. The musician, turning with a frank, imperative and decided air to the flower-seller, raised a hand which repulsed her and indicated to her that they did not want her flowers and that she was to get out of their way as quickly as possible. M. de Charlus observed with ecstasy this authoritative, virile gesture, made by the graceful hand for which it ought still to have been too weighty, too massively brutal, with a precocious firmness and suppleness which gave to this still beardness adolescent the air of a young David capable of waging war against Goliath. The Baron's admiration was unconsciously blended with the smile with which we observe in a child an expression of gravity beyond his years. "This is a person whom I should like to accompany me on my travels and help me in my business. How he would simplify my life," M. de Charlus said to himself.

The train for Paris (which M. de Charlus did not take) started. Then we took our seats in our own train, Albertine and I, without my knowing what had become of M. de Charlus and Morel. "We must never quarrel any more, I beg your pardon again," Albertine repeated, alluding to the Saint-Loup incident. "We must always be nice to each other," she said tenderly. "As for your friend Saint-Loup, if you think that I am the least bit interested in him, you are quite mistaken. All that I like about him is that he seems so very fond of you." "He's a very good fellow," I said, taking care not to supply Robert with those imaginary excellences which I should not have failed to intent, out of friendship for himself, had I been with anybody but Albertine. "He's an excellent creature, frank, devoted, loyal, a person you can rely on to do anything." In saying this I confined myself, held in check by my jealousy, to telling the truth about Saint-Loup, but what I said was literally true. It found expression in precisely the same terms that Mme. de Villeparisis had employed in speaking to me of him, when I did not yet know him, imagined him to be so different, so proud, and said to myself: "People think him good because he is a great gentleman." Just as when she had said to me: "He would be so pleased," I imagined, after seeing him outside the hotel, preparing to drive away, that his aunt's speech had been a mere social banality, intended to flatter me. And I had realised afterwards that she had said what she did sincerely, thinking of the things that interested me, of my reading, and because she knew that that was what Saint-Loup liked, as it was to be my turn to say sincerely to somebody who was writing a history of his ancestor La Rochefoucauld, the author of the *Maximes*, who wished to consult Robert about him: "He will be so pleased." It was simply that I had learned to know him. But, when I set eyes on him for the first time, I had not supposed that an intelligence akin to my own could be enveloped in so much outward elegance of dress and attitude. By his feathers I had judged him to be a bird of another species. It was Albertine now who, perhaps a little because Saint-Loup, in his kindness to myself, had been so cold to her, said to me what I had already thought: "Ah! He is as devoted as all that! I notice that people always find all the virtues in other people, when they belong to the Faubourg Saint-Germain." Now that Saint-Loup belonged to the Faubourg Saint-Germain was a thing of which I had never once thought in the course of all these years in which, stripping himself of his prestige, he had displayed to me his virtues. A change in our perspective in looking at other people, more striking already in friendship than in merely social relations, but how much more striking still in love, where desire on so vast a scale increases to such proportions the slightest signs of coolness, that far less than the coolness Saint-Loup had shewn me in the beginning had been enough to make me suppose at first that Albertine scorned me, imagine her friends to be creatures marvellously inhuman, and ascribe merely to the indulgence that people feel for beauty and for a certain elegance, Elstir's judgment when he said to me of the little band, with just the same sentiment as Mme. de Villeparisis speaking of Saint-Loup: "They are good girls." But this was not the opinion that I would instinctively have formed when I heard Albertine say: "In any case, whether he's devoted or not, I sincerely hope I shall never see him again, since he's made us quarrel. We must never quarrel again. It isn't nice." I felt, since she had seemed to desire Saint-Loup, almost cured for the time being of the idea that she cared for women, which I had supposed to be incurable. And, faced by Albertine's mackintosh in which she seemed to have become another person, the tireless vagrant of rainy days, and which, close-fitting, malleable and grey, seemed at that moment not so much intended to protect her garments from the rain as to have been soaked by her and to be clinging to my mistress's body as though to take the imprint of her form for a sculptor, I tore apart that tunic which jealously espoused a longed-for bosom and, drawing Albertine towards me: "But won't you, indolent traveller, dream upon my shoulder, resting your brow upon it?" I said, taking her head in my hands, and shewing her the wide meadows, flooded and silent, which extended in the gathering dusk to the horizon closed by the parallel openings of valleys far and blue.

Two days later, on the famous Wednesday, in that same little train, which I had again taken, at Balbec, to go and dine at la Raspelière, I was taking care not to miss Cottard at Graincourt-Saint-Vast, where a second telephone message from Mme. Verdurin had told me that I should find him. He was to join my train and would tell me where we had to get out to pick up the carriages that would be sent from la Raspelière to the station. And so, as the little train barely stopped for a moment at Graincourt, the first station after Doncières, I was standing in readiness at the open window, so afraid was I of not seeing Cottard or of his not seeing me. Vain fears! I had not realised to what an extent the little clan had moulded all its regular members after the same type, so that they, being moreover in full evening dress, as they stood waiting upon the platform, let themselves be recognised immediately by a certain air of assurance, fashion and familiarity, by a look in their eyes which seemed to sweep, like an empty space in which there was nothing to arrest their attention, the serried ranks of the common herd, watched for the arrival of some fellow-member who had taken the train at an earlier station, and sparkled in anticipation of the talk that was to come. This sign of election, with which the habit of dining together had marked the members of the little group, was not all that distinguished them; when numerous, in full strength, they were massed together, forming a more brilliant patch in the midst of the troop of passengers—what Brichot called the *pecus*—upon whose dull countenances could be read no conception of what was meant by the name Verdurin, no hope of ever dining at la Raspelière. To be sure, these common travellers would have been less interested than myself had anyone quoted in their hearing—notwithstanding the notoriety that several of them had achieved

—the names of those of the faithful whom I was astonished to see continuing to dine out, when many of them had already been doing so, according to the stories that I had heard, before my birth, at a period at once so distant and so vague that I was inclined to exaggerate its remoteness. The contrast between the continuance not only of their existence, but of the fulness of their powers, and the annihilation of so many friends whom I had already seen, in one place or another, pass away, gave me the same sentiment that we feel when in the stop-press column of the newspapers we read the very announcement that we least expected, for instance that of an untimely death, which seems to us fortuitous because the causes that have led up to it have remained outside our knowledge. This is the feeling that death does not descend upon all men alike, but that a more oncoming wave of its tragic tide carries off a life placed at the same level as others which the waves that follow will long continue to spare. We shall see later on that the diversity of the forms of death that circulate invisibly is the cause of the peculiar unexpectedness presented, in the newspapers, by their obituary notices. Then I saw that, with the passage of time, not only do the real talents that may coexist with the most commonplace conversation reveal and impose themselves, but furthermore that mediocre persons arrive at those exalted positions, attached in the imagination of our childhood to certain famous elders, when it never occurred to us that, after a certain number of years, their disciples, become masters, would be famous also, and would inspire the respect and awe that once they felt. But if the names of the faithful were unknown to the *pecus,* their aspect still singled them out in its eyes.

Indeed in the train (when the coincidence of what one or another of them might have been doing during the day, assembled them all together), having to collect at a subsequent station only an isolated member, the carriage in which they were gathered, ticketed with the elbow of the sculptor Ski, flagged with Cottard's *Temps,* stood out in the distance like a special saloon, and rallied at the appointed station the tardy comrade. The only one who might, because of his semi-blindness, have missed these welcoming signals, was Brichot. But one of the party would always volunteer to keep a look-out for the blind man, and, as soon as his straw hat, his green umbrella and blue spectacles caught the eye, he would be gently but hastily guided towards the chosen compartment. So that it was inconceivable that one of the faithful, without exciting the gravest suspicions of his being "on the loose," or even of his not having come "by the train," should not pick up the others in the course of the journey. Sometimes the opposite process occurred: one of the faithful had been obliged to go some distance down the line during the afternoon and was obliged in consequence to make part of the journey alone before being joined by the group; but even when thus isolated, alone of his kind, he did not fail as a rule to produce a certain effect. The Future towards which he was travelling marked him out to the person on the seat opposite, who would say to himself: "That must be somebody," would discern, round the soft hat of Cottard or of the sculptor Ski, a vague aureole and would be only half-astonished when at the next station an elegant crowd, if it were their terminal point, greeted the faithful one at the carriage door and escorted him to one of the waiting carriages, all of them reverently saluted by the factotum of Douville station, or, if it were an intermediate station, invaded the compartment. This was what was done, and with precipitation, for some of them had arrived late, just as the train which was already in the station was about to start, by the troop which Cottard led at a run towards the carriage in the window of which he had seen me signalling. Brichot, who was among these faithful, had become more faithful than ever in the course of these years which had diminished the assiduity of others. As his sight became steadily weaker, he had been obliged, even in Paris, to reduce more and more his working hours after dark. Besides he was out of sympathy with the modern Sorbonne, where ideas of scientific exactitude, after the German model, were beginning to prevail over humanism. He now confined himself exclusively to his lectures and to his duties as an examiner; and so had a great deal more time to devote to social pursuits. That is to say, to evenings at the Verdurins', or to those parties that now and again were offered to the Verdurins by one of the faithful, tremulous with emotion. It is true that on two occasions love had almost succeeded in achieving what his work could no longer do, in detaching Brichot from the little clan. But Mme. Verdurin, who kept her eyes open, and moreover, having acquired the habit in the interests of her salon, had come to take a disinterested pleasure in this sort of drama and execution, had immediately brought about a coolness between him and the dangerous person, being skilled in (as she expressed it) "putting things in order" and "applying the red hot iron to the wound." This she had found all the more easy in the case of one of the dangerous persons, who was simply Brichot's laundress.

and Mme. Verdurin, having the right of entry into the Professor's fifth floor rooms, crimson with rage, when she deigned to climb his stairs, had only had to shut the door in the wretched woman's face. "What!" the Mistress had said to Brichot, "a woman like myself does you the honour of calling upon you, and you receive a creature like that?" Brichot had never forgotten the service that Mme. Verdurin had rendered him by preventing his old age from foundering in the mire, and became more and more strongly attached to her, whereas, in contrast to this revival of affection and possibly because of it, the Mistress was beginning to be tired of a too docile follower, and of an obedience of which she could be certain beforehand. But Brichot derived from his intimacy with the Verdurins a distinction which set him apart from all his colleagues at the Sorbonne. They were dazzled by the accounts that he gave them of dinner-parties to which they would never be invited, by the mention made of him in the reviews, the exhibition of his portrait in the Salon, by some writer or painter of repute whose talent the occupants of the other chairs in the Faculty of Arts esteemed, but without any prospect of attracting his attention, not to mention the elegance of the mundane philosopher's attire, an elegance which they had mistaken at first for slackness until their colleague kindly explained to them that a tall hat is naturally laid on the floor, when one is paying a call, and is not the right thing for dinners in the country, however smart, where it should be replaced by a soft hat, which goes quite well with a dinner-jacket. For the first few moments after the little group had plunged into the carriage, I could not even speak to Cottard, for he was suffocated, not so much by having run in order not to miss the train as by his astonishment at having caught it so exactly. He felt more than the joy inherent in success, almost the hilarity of an excellent joke. "Ah! That was a good one!" he said when he had recovered himself. "A minute later! 'Pon my soul, that's what they call arriving in the nick of time!" he added, with a wink intended not so much to inquire whether the expression were apt, for he was now overflowing with assurance, but to express his satisfaction. At length he was able to introduce me to the other members of the little clan. I was annoyed to see that they were almost all in the dress which in Paris is called smoking. I had forgotten that the Verdurins were beginning a timid evolution towards fashionable ways, retarded by the Dreyfus case, accelerated by the "new" music, an evolution which for that matter they denied, and continued to deny until it was complete, like those military objectives which a general does not announce until he has reached them, so as not to appear defeated if he fails. In addition to which, Society was quite prepared to go half way to meet them. It went so far as to regard them as people to whose house nobody in Society went but who were not in the least perturbed by the fact. The Verdurin salon was understood to be a Temple of Music. It was there, people assured you, that Vinteuil had found inspiration, encouragement. Now, even if Vinteuil's sonata remained wholly unappreciated, and almost unknown, his name, quoted as that of the greatest of modern composers, had an extraordinary effect. Moreover, certain young men of the Faubourg having decided that they ought to be more intellectual than the middle classes, there were three of them who had studied music, and among these Vinteuil's Sonata enjoyed an enormous vogue. They would speak of it, on returning to their homes, to the intelligent mothers who had incited them to acquire culture. And, taking an interest in what interested their sons, at a concert these mothers would gaze with a certain respect at Mme. Verdurin in her front box, following the music in the printed score. So far, this social success latent in the Verdurins was revealed by two facts only. In the first place, Mme. Verdurin would say of the Principessa di Caprarola: "Ah! She is intelligent, she is a charming woman. What I cannot endure, are the imbeciles, the people who bore me, they drive me mad." Which would have made anybody at all perspicacious realise that the Principessa di Caprarola, a woman who moved in the highest society, had called upon Mme. Verdurin. She had even mentioned her name in the course of a visit of condolence which she had paid to Mme. Swann after the death of her husband, and had asked whether she knew them. "What name did you say?" Odette had asked, with a sudden wistfulness. "Verdurin? Oh, yes, of course," she had continued in a plaintive tone, "I don't know them, or rather, I know them without really knowing them, they are people I used to meet at people's houses, years ago, they are quite nice." When the Principessa di Caprarola had gone, Odette would fain have spoken the bare truth. But the immediate falsehood was not the fruit of her calculations, but the revelation of her fears, of her desires. She denied not what it would have been adroit to deny, but what she would have liked not to have happened, even if the other person was bound to hear an hour later that it was a fact. A little later she had recovered her assurance, and would indeed anticipate questions by saying, so as not to appear to be afraid of them: "Mme. Verdurin, why, I used to know her terribly well!" with an affectation of humility, like a great lady who tells you that she has taken the tram. "There has been a great deal of talk about the Verdurins lately," said Mme. de Souvré. Odette, with the smiling disdain of a Duchess, replied: "Yes, I do seem to have heard a lot about them lately. Every now and then there are new people who arrive like that in society," without reflecting that she herself was among the newest. "The Principessa di Caprarola has dined there," Mme. de Souvré went on. "Ah!" replied Odette, accentuating her smile, "that does not surprise me. That sort of thing always begins with the Principessa di Caprarola, and then some one else follows suit, like Comtesse Molé." Odette, in saying this, appeared to be filled with a profound contempt for the two great ladies who made a habit of "house-warming" in recently established drawing-rooms. One felt from her tone that the implication was that she, Odette, was, like Mme. de Souvré, not the sort of person to let herself in for that sort of thing.

After the admission that Mme. de Verdurin had made of the Principessa di Caprarola's intelligence, the second indication that the Verdurins were conscious of their future destiny was that (without, of course, their having formally requested it) they became most anxious that people should now come to dine with them in evening dress. M. Verdurin could now have been greeted without shame by his nephew, the one who was "in the cart."

Among those who entered my carriage at Graincourt was Saniette, who long ago had been expelled from the

Verdurins' by his cousin Forcheville, but had since returned. His faults, from the social point of view, had originally been—notwithstanding his superior qualities—something like Cottard's, shyness, anxiety to please, fruitless attempts to succeed in doing so. But if the course of life, by making Cottard assume, if not at the Verdurins', where he had, because of the influence that past associations exert over us when we find ourselves in familiar surroundings, remained more or less the same, at least in his practice, in his hospital ward, at the Academy of Medicine, a shell of coldness, disdain, gravity, that became more accentuated while he rewarded his appreciative students with puns, had made a clean cut between the old Cottard and the new, the same defects had on the contrary become exaggerated in Saniette, the more he sought to correct them. Conscious that he was frequently boring, that people did not listen to him, instead of then slackening his pace as Cottard would have done, of forcing their attention by an air of authority, not only did he try by adopting a humorous tone to make them forgive the unduly serious turn of his conversation, he increased his pace, cleared the ground, used abbreviations in order to appear less long-winded, more familiar with the matters of which he spoke, and succeeded only, by making them unintelligible, in seeming interminable. His self-assurance was not like that of Cottard, freezing his patients, who, when other people praised his social graces, would reply: "He is a different man when he receives you in his consulting room, you with your face to the light, and he with his back to it, and those piercing eyes." It failed to create an effect, one felt that it was cloaking an excessive shyness, that the merest trifle would be enough to dispel it. Saniette, whose friends had always told him that he was wanting in self-confidence, and who had indeed seen men whom he rightly considered greatly inferior to himself, attain with ease to the success that was denied to him, never began telling a story without smiling at its drollery, fearing lest a serious air might make his hearers underestimate the value of his wares. Sometimes, giving him credit for the comic element which he himself appeared to find in what he was about to say, people would do him the honour of a general silence. But the story would fall flat. A fellow-guest who was endowed with a kind heart would sometimes convey to Saniette the private, almost secret encouragement of a smile of approbation, making it reach him furtively, without attracting attention, as one passes a note from hand to hand. But nobody went so far as to assume the responsibility, to risk the glaring publicity of an honest laugh. Long after the story was ended and had fallen flat, Saniette, crestfallen, would remain smiling to himself, as though relishing in it and for himself the delectation which he pretended to find adequate and which the others had not felt. As for the sculptor Ski, so styled on account of the difficulty they found in pronouncing his Polish surname, and because he himself made an affectation, since he had begun to move in a certain social sphere, of not wishing to be confused with certain relatives, perfectly respectable but slightly boring and very numerous, he had, at forty-four and with no pretension to good looks, a sort of boyishness, a dreamy wistfulness which was the result of his having been, until the age of ten, the most charming prodigal imaginable, the darling of all the ladies. Mme. Verdurin maintained that he was more of an artist than Elstir. Any resemblance that there may have been between them was, however, purely external. It was enough to make Elstir, who had met Ski once, feel for him the profound repulsion that is inspired in us less by the people who are our exact opposite than by those who resemble us in what is least good, in whom are displayed our worst qualities, the faults of which we have cured ourselves, who irritate by reminding us of how we may have appeared to certain other people before we became what we now are. But Mme. Verdurin thought that Ski had more temperament than Elstir because there was no art in which he had not a facility of expression, and she was convinced that he would have developed that facility into talent if he had not been so lazy. This seemed to the Mistress to be actually an additional gift, being the opposite of hard work which she regarded as the lot of people devoid of genius. Ski would paint anything you asked, on cuff-links or on the panels over doors. He sang with the voice of a composer, played from memory, giving the piano the effect of an orchestra, less by his virtuosity than by his vamped basses, which suggested the inability of the fingers to indicate that at a certain point the cornet entered, which, for that matter, he would imitate with his lips. Choosing his words when he spoke so as to convey an odd impression, just as he would pause before banging out a chord to say "Ping!" so as to let the brasses be heard, he was regarded as marvellously intelligent, but as a matter of fact his ideas could be boiled down to two or three, extremely limited. Bored with his reputation for whimsicality, he had set himself to shew that he was a practical, matter-of-fact person, whence a triumphant affectation of false precision, of false common sense, aggravated by his having no memory and a fund of information that was always inaccurate. The movements of his head, neck, limbs, would have been graceful if he had been still nine years old, with golden curls, a wide lace collar and little boots of red leather. Having reached Graincourt station with Cottard and Brichot, with time to spare, he and Cottard had left Brichot in the waiting-room and had gone for a stroll. When Cottard proposed to turn back, Ski had replied: "But there is no hurry. It isn't the local train to-day, it's the departmental train." Delighted by the effect that this refinement of accuracy produced upon Cottard, he added, with reference to himself: "Yes, because Ski loves the arts, because he models in clay, people think he's not practical. Nobody knows this line better than I do." Nevertheless they had turned back towards the station when, all of a sudden, catching sight of the smoke of the approaching train, Cottard, with a wild shout, had exclaimed: "We shall have to put our best foot foremost." They did as a matter of fact arrive with not a moment to spare, the distinction between local and departmental trains having never existed save in the mind of Ski. "But isn't the Princess on the train?" came in ringing tones from Brichot, whose huge spectacles, resplendent as the reflectors that laryngologists attach to their foreheads to throw a light into the throats of their patients, seemed to have taken their life from the Professor's eyes, and, possibly because of the effort that he was making to adjust his sight to them, seemed themselves, even at the most trivial moments, to be gazing at themselves with a sustained attention and an extraordinary fixity. Brichot's malady, as it gradually deprived him of his sight, had revealed to him the beauties of that sense, just as, frequently, we have to have made up our minds to part with some object, to make a present of it for instance, before we can study it, regret it, admire it. "No, no, the Princess went over to Maineville with some of Mme. Verdurin's guests who were taking the Paris train. It is within the bounds of possibility that Mme. Verdurin, who had some business at Saint-Mars. may be with her! In that case, she will be coming with us, and we shall all travel together, which will be delightful. We shall have to keep our eyes skinned at Maineville and see what we shall see! Oh, but that's nothing, you may say that we came very near to missing the bus. When I saw the train I was dumbfoundered. That's what is called arriving at the psychological moment. Can't you picture us missing the train, Mme. Verdurin seeing the carriages come back without us: Tableau!" added the doctor, who had not yet recovered from his emotion. "That would be a pretty good joke, wouldn't it? Now then, Brichot, what have you to say about our little escapade?" inquired the doctor with a note of pride. "Upon my soul," replied Brichot, "why, yes, if you had found the train gone, that would have been what the late Villemain used to call a wipe in the eye!" But I, distracted at first by these people who were strangers to me, was suddenly reminded of what Cottard had said to me in the ball-room of the little casino, and, just as though there were an invisible link uniting an organ to our visual memory, the vision of Albertine leaning her breasts against Andrée's caused my heart a terrible pain. This pain did not last: the idea of Albertine's having relations with women seemed no longer possible since the occasion, forty-eight hours earlier, when the advances that my mistress had made to Saint-Loup had excited in me a fresh jealousy which had made me forget the old. I was simple enough to suppose that one taste of necessity excludes another. At Harambouville, as the tram was full, a farmer in a blue blouse who had only a third class ticket got into our compartment. The doctor, feeling that the Princess must not be allowed to travel with such a person, called a porter, shewed his card, describing him as medical officer to one of the big railway companies, and obliged the station-master to make the farmer get out. This incident so pained and alarmed Saniette's timid spirit that, as soon as he saw it beginning, fearing already lest, in view of the crowd of peasants on the platform, it should assume the proportions of a rising, he pretended to be suffering from a stomach-ache, and, so that he might not be accused of any share in the responsibility for the doctor's violence, wandered down the corridor, pretending to be looking for what Cottard called the "water." Failing to find one, he stood and gazed at the scenery from the other end of the "twister." "If this is your first appearance at Mme. Verdurin's, Sir," I was addressed by Brichot, anxious to shew off his talents before a newcomer, "you will find that there is no place where one feels more the 'amenities of life,' to quote one of the inventors of dilettantism, of pococurantism, of all sorts of words in -ism that are in fashion among our little snobbesses, I refer to M. le Prince de Talleyrand." For, when he spoke of these great noblemen of the past, he thought it clever and "in the period" to prefix a "M." to their titles, and said "M. le Duc de La Rochefoucauld," "M. le Cardinal de Retz," referring to these also as "That struggle for lifer de Gondi," "that Boulangist de Marcillac." And he never failed to call Montesquieu, with a smile, when he referred to him: "Monsieur le Président Secondat de Montesquieu." An intelligent man of the world would have been irritated by a pedantry which reeked so of the lecture-room. But in the perfect manners of the man of the world when speaking of a Prince, there is a pedantry also, which betrays a different caste, that in which one prefixes "the Emperor" to the name "William" and addresses a Royal Highness in the third person. "Ah, now, that is a man," Brichot continued, still referring to "Monsieur le Prince de Talleyrand"—"to whom we take off our hats. He is an ancestor." "It is a charming house," Cottard told me, "you will find a little of everything, for Mme. Verdurin is not exclusive, great scholars like Brichot, the high nobility, such as the Princess Sherbatoff, a great Russian lady, a friend of the Grand Duchess Eudoxie, who even sees her alone at hours when no one else is admitted." As a matter of fact the Grand Duchess Eudoxie, not wishing Princess Sherbatoff, who for years past had been cut by everyone, to come to her house when there might be other people, allowed her to come only in the early morning, when Her Imperial Highness was not at home to any of those friends to whom it would have been as unpleasant to meet the Princess as it would have been awkward for the Princess to meet them. As, for the last three years, as soon as she came away, like a manicurist, from the Grand Duchess, Mme. Sherbatoff would go on to Mme. Verdurin, who had just awoken, and stuck to her for the rest of the day, one might say that the Princess's loyalty surpassed even that of Brichot, constant as he was at those Wednesdays, both in Paris, where he had the pleasure of fancying himself a sort of Chateaubriand at l'Abbaye-aux-Bois, and in the country, where he saw himself becoming the equivalent of what might have been in the salon of Mme. de Châtelet the man whom he always named (with an erudite sarcasm and satisfaction): "M. de Voltaire."

Her want of friends had enabled Princess Sherbatoff to shew for some years past to the Verdurins a fidelity which made her more than an ordinary member of the "faithful," the type of faithfulness, the ideal which Mme. Verdurin had long thought unattainable and which now, in her later years, she at length found incarnate in this new feminine recruit. However keenly the Mistress might feel the pangs of jealousy, it was without precedent that the most assiduous of her faithful should not have "failed" her at least once. The most stay-at-home yielded to the temptation to travel; the most continent fell from virtue; the most robust might catch influenza, the idlest be caught for his month's soldiering, the most indifferent go to close the eyes of a dying mother. And it was in vain that Mme. Verdurin told them then, like the Roman Empress, that she was the sole general whom her legion must obey, like the Christ or the Kaiser that he who loved his father or mother more than her and was not prepared to leave them and follow her was not worthy of her, that instead of slacking in bed or letting themselves be made fools of by bad women they would do better to remain in her company, by her, their sole remedy and sole delight. But destiny which is sometimes pleased to brighten the closing years of a life that has passed the mortal span had made Mme. Verdurin meet the Princess

Sherbatoff. Out of touch with her family, an exile from her native land, knowing nobody but the Baroness Putbus and the Grand Duchess Eudoxie, to whose houses, because she herself had no desire to meet the friends of the former, and the latter no desire that her friends should meet the Princess, she went only in the early morning hours when Mme. Verdurin was still asleep, never once, so far as she could remember, having been confined to her room since she was twelve years old, when she had had the measles, having on the 31st of December replied to Mme. Verdurin who, afraid of being left alone, had asked her whether she would not "shake down" there for the night, in spite of its being New Year's Eve: "Why, what is there to prevent me, any day of the year? Besides, to-morrow is a day when one stays at home, and this is my home," living in a boarding-house, and moving from it whenever the Verdurins moved, accompanying them upon their holidays, the Princess had so completely exemplified to Mme. Verdurin the line of Vigny:

> Thou only didst appear that which one seeks always,

that the Lady President of the little circle, anxious to make sure of one of her "faithful" even after death, had made her promise that whichever of them survived the other should be buried by her side. Before strangers—among whom we must always reckon him to whom we lie most barefacedly because he is the person whose scorn we should most dread: ourself—Princess Sherbatoff took care to represent her only three friendships—with the Grand Duchess, the Verdurins, and the Baroness Putbus—as the only ones, not which cataclysms beyond her control had allowed to emerge from the destruction of all the rest, but which a free choice had made her elect in preference to any other, and to which a certain love of solitude and simplicity had made her confine herself. "I see *nobody* else," she would say, insisting upon the inflexible character of what appeared to be rather a rule that one imposes upon oneself than a necessity to which one submits. She would add: "I visit only three houses," as a dramatist who fears that it may not run to a fourth announces that there will be only three performances of his play. Whether or not M. and Mme. Verdurin believed in the truth of this fiction, they had helped the Princess to instil it into the minds of the faithful. And they in turn were persuaded both that the Princess, among the thousands of invitations that were offered her, had chosen the Verdurins alone, and that the Verdurins, courted in vain by all the higher aristocracy, had consented to make but a single exception, in favour of the Princess.

In their eyes, the Princess, too far superior to her native element not to find it boring, among all the people whose society she might have enjoyed, found the Verdurins alone entertaining, while they, in return, deaf to the overtures with which they were bombarded by the entire aristocracy, had consented to make but a single exception, in favour of a great lady of more intelligence than the rest of her kind, the Princess Sherbatoff.

The Princess was very rich; she engaged for every first night a large box, to which, with the assent of Mme. Verdurin, she invited the faithful and nobody else. People would point to this pale and enigmatic person who had grown old without turning white, turning red rather like certain sere and shrivelled hedgerow fruits. They admired both her influence and her humility, for, having always with her an Academician, Brichot, a famous scientist, Cottard, the leading pianist of the day, at a later date M. de Charlus, she nevertheless made a point of securing the least prominent box in the theatre, remained in the background, paid no attention to the rest of the house, lived exclusively for the little group, who, shortly before the end of the performance, would withdraw in the wake of this strange sovereign, who was not without a certain timid, fascinating, faded beauty. But if Mme. Sherbatoff did not look at the audience, remained in shadow, it was to try to forget that there existed a living world which she passionately desired and was unable to know: the *côterie* in a box was to her what is to certain animals their almost corpselike immobility in the presence of danger. Nevertheless the thirst for novelty and for the curious which possesses people in society made them pay even more attention perhaps to this mysterious stranger than to the celebrities in the front boxes to whom everybody paid a visit. They imagined that she must be different from the people whom they knew, that a marvellous intellect combined with a discerning bounty retained round about her that little circle of eminent men. The Princess was compelled, if you spoke to her about anyone, or introduced anyone to her, to feign an intense coldness, in order to keep up the fiction of her horror of society. Nevertheless, with the support of Cottard or of Mme. Verdurin, several newcomers succeeded in making her acquaintance and such was her excitement at making a fresh acquaintance that she forget the fable of her deliberate isolation, and went to the wildest extremes to please the newcomer. If he was entirely unimportant, the rest would be astonished. "How strange that the Princess, who refuses to know anyone, should make an exception of such an uninteresting person." But these fertilising acquaintances were rare, and the Princess lived narrowly confined in the midst of the faithful.

Cottard said far more often: "I shall see him on Wednesday at the Verdurins'," than: "I shall see him on Tuesday at the Academy." He spoke, too, of the Wednesdays as of an engagement equally important and inevitable. But Cottard was one of those people, little sought-after, who make it as imperious a duty to respond to an invitation as if such invitations were orders, like a military or judicial summons. It required a call from a very important patient to make him "fail" the Verdurins on a Wednesday, the importance depending moreover rather upon the rank of the patient than upon the gravity of his complaint. For Cottard, excellent fellow as he was, would forego the delights of a Wednesday not for a workman who had had a stroke, but for a Minister's cold. Even then he would say to his wife: "Make my apologies to Mme. Verdurin. Tell her that I shall be coming later on. His Excellency might really have chosen some other day to catch cold." One Wednesday their old cook having opened a vein in her arm, Cottard, already in his dinner-jacket to go to the Verdurins', had shrugged his shoulders when his wife had timidly inquired whether he could not bandage the cut: "Of course I can't, Léontine," he had groaned; "can't you see I've got my white waistcoat on?" So as not to annoy her husband, Mme. Cottard had sent post haste for his chief dresser. He, to save time, had taken a cab, with the result that, his carriage entering the courtyard just as

Cottard's was emerging to take him to the Verdurins, five minutes had been wasted in backing to let one another pass. Mme. Cottard was worried that the dresser should see his master in evening dress. Cottard sat cursing the delay, from remorse perhaps, and started off in a villainous temper which it took all the Wednesday's pleasures to dispel.

If one of Cottard's patients were to ask him: "Do you ever see the Guermantes?" it was with the utmost sincerity that the Professor would reply: "Perhaps not actually the Guermantes, I can't be certain. But I meet all those people at the house of some friends of mine. You must, of course, have heard of the Verdurins. They know everybody. Besides, they certainly are not people who've come down in the world. They've got the goods, all right. It is generally estimated that Mme. Verdurin is worth thirty-five million. Gad, thirty-five million, that's a pretty figure. And so she doesn't make two bites at a cherry. You mentioned the Duchesse de Guermantes. Let me explain the difference. Mme. Verdurin is a great lady, the Duchesse de Guermantes is probably a nobody. You see the distinction, of course. In any case, whether the Guermantes go to Mme. Verdurin's or not, she entertains all the very best people, the d'Sherbatoffs, the d'Forchevilles, *e tutti quanti*, people of the highest flight, all the nobility of France and Navarre, with whom you would see me conversing as man to man. Of course, those sort of people are only too glad to meet the princes of science," he added, with a smile of fatuous conceit, brought to his lips by his proud satisfaction not so much that the expression formerly reserved for men like Potain and Charcot should now be applicable to himself, as that he knew at last how to employ all these expressions that were authorised by custom, and, after a long course of study, had learned them by heart. And so, after mentioning to me Princess Sherbatoff as one of the people who went to Mme. Verdurin's, Cottard added with a wink "That gives you an idea of the style of the house, if you see what I mean?" He meant that it was the very height of fashion. Now, to entertain a Russian lady who knew nobody but the Grand Duchess Eudoxie was not fashionable at all. But Princess Sherbatoff might not have known even her, it would in no way have diminished Cottard's estimate of the supreme elegance of the Verdurin salon or his joy at being invited there. The splendour that seems to us to invest the people whose houses we visit is no more intrinsic than that of kings and queens on the stage, in dressing whom it is useless for a producer to spend hundreds and thousands of francs in purchasing authentic costumes and real jewels, when a great designer will procure a far more sumptuous impression by focussing a ray of light on a doublet of coarse cloth studded with lumps of glass and on a cloak of paper. A man may have spent his life among the great ones of the earth, who to him have been merely boring relatives or tiresome acquaintances, because a familiarity engendered in the cradle had stripped them of all distinction in his eyes. The same man, on the other hand, need only have been led by some chance to mix with the most obscure people, for innumerable Cottards to be permanently dazzled by the ladies of title whose drawing-rooms they imagined as the centres of aristocratic elegance, ladies who were not even what Mme. de Villeparisis and her friends were (great ladies fallen from their greatness, whom the aristocracy that had been brought up with them no longer visited); no, those whose friendship has been the pride of so many men, if these men were to publish their memoirs and to give the names of those women and of the other women who came to their parties, Mme. de Cambremer would be no more able than Mme. de Guermantes to identify them. But what of that! A Cottard has thus his Marquise, who is to him "the Baronne," as in Marivaux, the Baronne whose name is never mentioned, so much so that nobody supposes that she ever had a name. Cottard is all the more convinced that she embodies the aristocracy—which has never heard of the lady—in that, the more dubious titles are, the more prominently coronets are displayed upon wineglasses, silver, notepaper, luggage. Many Cottards who have supposed that they were living in the heart of the Faubourg Saint-Germain have had their imagination perhaps more enchanted by feudal dreams than the men who did really live among Princes, just as with the small shopkeeper who, on Sundays, goes sometimes to look at "old time" buildings, it is sometimes from those buildings every stone of which is of our own time, the vaults of which have been, by the pupils of Viollet-le-Duc, painted blue and sprinkled with golden stars, that they derive the strongest sensation of the middle ages. "The Princess will be at Maineville. She will be coming with us. But I shall not introduce you to her at once. It will be better to leave that to Mme. Verdurin. Unless I find a loophole. Then you can rely on me to take the bull by the horns." "What were you saying?" asked Saniette, as he rejoined us, pretending to have gone out to take the air. "I was quoting to this gentleman," said Brichot, "a saying, which you will remember, of the man who, to my mind, is the first of the *fins-de-siècle* (of the eighteenth century, that is), by name Charles Maurice, Abbé de Perigord. He began by promising to be an excellent journalist. But he made a bad end, by which I mean that he became a Minister! Life has these tragedies. A far from scrupulous politician to boot who, with the lofty contempt of a thoroughbred nobleman, did not hesitate to work in his time for the King of Prussia, there are no two ways about it, and died in the skin of a 'Left Centre.'"

At Saint-Pierre-des-Ifs we were joined by a glorious girl who, unfortunately, was not one of the little group. I could not tear my eyes from her magnolia skin, her dark eyes, her bold and admirable outlines. A moment later she wanted to open a window, for it was hot in the compartment, and not wishing to ask leave of everybody, as I alone was without a greatcoat, she said to me in a quick, cool, jocular voice: "Do you mind a little fresh air, Sir?" I would have liked to say to her: "Come with us to the Verdurins?" or "Give me your name and address." I answered: "No, fresh air doesn't bother me, Mademoiselle." Whereupon, without stirring from her seat: "Do your friends object to smoke?" and she lit a cigarette. At the third station she sprang from the carriage. Next day, I inquired of Albertine, who she could be. For, stupidly thinking that people could have but one sort of love, in my jealousy of Albertine's attitude towards Robert, I was reassured so far as other women were concerned. Albertine told me, I believe quite sincerely, that she did not know. "I should so much like to see her again," I exclaimed. "Don't worry, one always sees people again," replied Albertine. In this particular instance, she was wrong; I never saw again, nor did I ever identify the pretty girl with the cigarette. We shall see, moreover, why, for a long time, I ceased to look for her. But I have not forgotten her. I find myself at times, when I think of her, seized by a wild longing. But these recurrences of desire oblige us to reflect that if we wish to rediscover these girls with the same pleasure we must also return to the year which has since been followed by ten others in the course of which her bloom has faded. We can sometimes find a person again, but we cannot abolish time. And so on until the unforeseen day, gloomy as a winter night, when we no longer seek for that girl, or for any other, when to find her would actually frighten us. For we no longer feel that we have sufficient attraction to appeal to her, or strength to love her. Not, of course, that we are, in the strict sense of the word, impotent. And as for loving, we should love her more than ever. But we feel that it is too big an undertaking for the little strength that we have left. Eternal rest has already fixed intervals which we can neither cross nor make our voice be heard across them. To set our foot on the right step is an achievement like not missing the perilous leap. To be seen in such a state by a girl we love, even if we have kept the features and all the golden locks of our youth! We can no longer undertake the strain of keeping pace with youth. All the worse if our carnal desire increases instead of failing! We procure for it a woman whom we need make no effort to attract, who will share our couch for one night only and whom we shall never see again.

"Still no news, I suppose, of the violinist," said Cottard. The event of the day in the little clan was, in fact, the failure of Mme. Verdurin's favourite violinist. Employed on military service near Doncières, he came three times a week to dine at la Raspelière, having a midnight pass. But two days ago, for the first time, the faithful had been unable to discover him on the tram. It was supposed that he had missed it. But albeit Mme. Verdurin had sent to meet the next tram, and so on until the last had arrived, the carriage had returned empty. "He's certain to have been shoved into the guard-room, there's no other explanation of his desertion. Gad! In soldiering, you know, with those fellows, it only needs a bad-tempered serjeant." "It will be all the more mortifying for Mme. Verdurin," said Brichot, "if he fails again this evening, because our kind hostess has invited to dinner for the first time the neighbours from whom she has taken la Raspelière, the Marquis and Marquise de Cambremer." "This evening, the Marquis and Marquise de Cambremer!" exclaimed Cottard. "But I knew absolutely nothing about it. Naturally, I knew like everybody else that they would be coming one day, but I had no idea that it was to be so soon. Sapristi!" he went on, turning to myself, "what did I tell you? The Princess Sherbatoff, the Marquis and Marquise de Cambremer." And, after repeating these names, lulling himself with their melody: "You see that we move in good company," he said to me. "However, as it's your first appearance, you'll be one of the crowd. It is going to be an exceptionally brilliant gathering." And, turning to Brichot, he went on: "The Mistress will be furious. It is time we appeared to lend her a hand." Ever since

Mme. Verdurin had been at la Raspelière she had pretended for the benefit of the faithful to be at once feeling and regretting the necessity of inviting her landlords for one evening. By so doing she would obtain better terms next year, she explained, and was inviting them for business reasons only. But she pretended to regard with such terror, to make such a bugbear of the idea of dining with people who did not belong to the little group that she kept putting off the evil day. The prospect did for that matter alarm her slightly for the reasons which she professed, albeit exaggerating them, if at the same time it enchanted her for reasons of snobbishness which she preferred to keep to herself. She was therefore partly sincere, she believed the little clan to be something so matchless throughout the world, one of those perfect wholes which it takes centuries of time to produce, that she trembled at the thought of seeing introduced into its midst these provincials, people ignorant of the Ring and the Meistersinger, who would be unable to play their part in the concert of conversation and were capable, by coming to Mme. Verdurin's, of ruining one of those famous Wednesdays, masterpieces of art incomparable and frail, like those Venetian glasses which one false note is enough to shatter. "Besides, they are bound to be absolutely *anti,* and militarists," M. Verdurin had said. "Oh, as for that, I don't mind, we've heard quite enough about all that business," had replied Mme. Verdurin, who, a sincere Dreyfusard, would nevertheless have been glad to discover a social counterpoise to the preponderant Dreyfusism of her salon. For, Dreyfusism was triumphant politically, but not socially. Labori, Reinach, Picquart, Zola were still, to people in society, more or less traitors, who could only keep them aloof from the little nucleus. And so, after this incursion into politics, Mme. Verdurin was determined to return to the world of art. Besides were not Indy, Debussy, on the "wrong" side in the Case? "So far as the Case goes, we need only remember Brichot," she said (the Don being the only one of the faithful who had sided with the General Staff, which had greatly lowered him in the esteem of Madame Verdurin). "There is no need to be eternally discussing the Dreyfus Case. No, the fact of the matter is that the Cambremers bore me." As for the faithful, no less excited by their unconfessed desire to make the Cambremers' acquaintance than dupes of the affected reluctance which Mme. Verdurin said she felt to invite them, they returned, day after day, in conversation with her, to the base arguments with which she herself supported the invitation, tried to make them irresistible. "Make up your mind to it once and for all," Cottard repeated, "and you will have better terms for next year, they will pay the gardener, you will have the use of the meadow. That will be well worth a boring evening. I am thinking only of yourselves," he added, albeit his heart had leaped on one occasion, when, in Mme. Verdurin's carriage, he had met the carriage of the old Mme. de Cambremer and, what was more, he had been abased in the sight of the railwaymen when, at the station, he had found himself standing beside the Marquis. For their part, the Cambremers, living far too remote from the social movement ever to suspect that certain ladies of fashion were speaking with a certain consideration of Mme. Verdurin, imagined that she was a person who could know none but Bohemians, was perhaps not even legally married, and so far as people of birth were concerned would never meet any but themselves. They had resigned themselves to the thought of dining with her only to be on good terms with a tenant who, they hoped, would return again for many seasons, especially after they had, in the previous month, learned that she had recently inherited all those millions. It was in silence and without any vulgar pleasantries that they prepared themselves for the fatal day. The faithful had given up hope of its ever coming, so often had Mme. Verdurin already fixed in their hearing a date that was invariably postponed. These false decisions were intended not merely to make a display of the boredom that she felt at the thought of this dinner-party, but to keep in suspense those members of the little group who were staying in the neighbourhood and were sometimes inclined to fail. Not that the Mistress guessed that the "great day" was as delightful a prospect to them as to herself, but in order that, having persuaded them that this dinner-party was to her the most terrible of social duties, she might make an appeal to their devotion. "You are not going to leave me all alone with those Chinese mandarins! We must assemble in full force to support the boredom. Naturally, we shan't be able to talk about any of the things in which we are interested. It will be a Wednesday spoiled, but what is one to do!"

"Indeed," Brichot explained to me, "I fancy that Mme. Verdurin, who is highly intelligent and takes infinite pains in the elaboration of her Wednesdays, was by no means anxious to see these bumpkins of ancient lineage but scanty brains. She could not bring herself to invite the dowager Marquise, but has resigned herself to having the son and daughter-in-law." "Ah! We are to see the Marquise de Cambremer?" said Cottard with a smile into which he saw fit to introduce a leer of sentimentality, albeit he had no idea whether Mme. de Cambremer were good-looking or not. But the title Marquise suggested to him fantastic thoughts of gallantry. "Ah! I know her," said Ski, who had met her once when he was out with Mme. Verdurin. "Not in the biblical sense of the word, I trust," said the doctor, darting a sly glance through his eyeglass; this was one of his favourite pleasantries. "She is intelligent," Ski informed me. "Naturally," he went on, seeing that I said nothing, and dwelling with a smile upon each word, "she is intelligent and at the same time she is not, she lacks education, she is frivolous, but she has an instinct for beautiful things. She may say nothing, but she will never say anything silly. And besides, her colouring is charming. She would be an amusing person to paint," he added, half shutting his eyes, as though he saw her posing in front of him. As my opinion of her was quite the opposite of what Ski was expressing with so many fine shades, I observed merely that she was the sister of an extremely distinguished engineer, M. Legrandin. "There, you see, you are going to be introduced to a pretty woman," Brichot said to me, "and one never knows what may come of that. Cleopatra was not even a great lady, she was a little woman, the unconscious, terrible little woman of our Meilhac, and just think of the consequences, not only to that idiot Antony, but to the whole of the ancient world." "I have already been introduced to Mme. de Cambremer," I replied. "Ah! In that case, you will find yourself on familiar ground." "I shall be all the more delighted to meet her," I answered him, "because she has promised me a book by the former curé of Combray about the place-names of this district, and I shall be able to remind her of her promise. I am interested in that priest, and also in etymologies." "Don't put any faith in the ones he gives," replied Brichot, "there is a copy of the book at la Raspelière, which I have glanced through, but without finding anything of any value; it is a mass of error. Let me give you an example. The word Bricq is found in a number of place-names in this neighbourhood. The worthy cleric had the distinctly odd idea that it comes from Briga, a height, a fortified place. He finds it already in the Celtic tribes, Latobriges, Nemetobriges, and so forth, and traces it down to such names as Briand, Brion, and so forth. To confine ourselves to the region in which we have the pleasure of your company at this moment, Bricquebose means the wood on the height, Bricqueville the habitation on the height, Bricquebec, where we shall be stopping presently before coming to Maineville, the height by the stream. Now there is not a word of truth in all this, for the simple reason that *bricq* is the old Norse word which means simply a bridge. Just as fleur, which Mme. de Cambremer's protégé takes infinite pains to connect, in one place with the Scandinavian words *floi, flo,* in another with the Irish word *ae* or *aer,* is, beyond any doubt, the *fjord* of the Danes, and means harbour. So too, the excellent priest thinks that the station of Saint-Mars-le-Vêtu, which adjoins la Raspelière, means Saint-Martin-le-Vieux (*vetus*). It is unquestionable that the word *vieux* has played a great part in the toponymy of this region. *Vieux* comes as a rule from *vadum,* and means a passage, as at the place called les Vieux. It is what the

English call *ford* (Oxford, Hereford). But, in this particular instance, Vêtu is derived not from *vetus,* but from *vastatus,* a place that is devastated and bare. You have, round about here, Sottevast, the *vast* of Setold, Brillevast, the *vast* of Berold. I am all the more certain of the curé's mistake, in that Saint-Mars-le-Vêtu was formerly called Saint-Mars du Gast and even Saint-Mars-de-Terregate. Now the *v* and the *g* in these words are the same letter. We say *dévaster,* but also *gâcher. Jâchères* and *gatines* (from the High German *wastinna*) have the same meaning: Terregate is therefore *terra vasta.* As for Saint-Mars, formerly (save the mark) Saint-Merd, it is Saint-Medardus, which appears variously as Saint-Médard, Saint-Mard, Saint-Marc, Cinq-Mars, and even Dammas. Nor must we forget that quite close to here, places bearing the name of Mars are proof simply of a pagan origin (the god Mars) which has remained alive in this country but which the holy man refuses to see. The high places dedicated to the gods are especially frequent, such as the mount of Jupiter (Jeumont). Your curé declines to admit this, but, on the other hand, wherever Christianity has left traces, they escape his notice. He has gone so far afield as to Loctudy, a barbarian name, according to him, whereas it is simply *Locus Sancti Tudeni,* nor has he in Sammarcoles divined *Sanctus Martialis.* Your curé," Brichot continued, seeing that I was interested, "derives the terminations *hon, home, holm,* from the word *holl* (*hullus*), a hill, whereas it comes from the Norse *holm,* an island, with which you are familiar in Stockholm, and which is so widespread throughout this district, la Houlme, Engohomme, Tahoume, Robehomme, Néhomme, Quettehon, and so forth." These names made me think of the day when Albertine had wished to go to Amfreville-la-Bigot (from the name of two successive lords of the manor, Brichot told me), and had then suggested that we should dine together at Robehomme. As for Maineville, we were just coming to it. "Isn't Néhomme," I asked, "somewhere near Carquethuit and Clitourps?" "Precisely; Néhomme is the *holm,* the island or peninsula of the famous Viscount Nigel, whose name has survived also in Néville. The Carquethuit and Clitourps that you mention furnish Mme. de Cambremer's protégé with an occasion for further blunders. No doubt he has seen that *carque* is a church, the *Kirche* of the Germans. You will remember Querqueville, not to mention Dunkerque. For there we should do better to stop and consider the famous word *Dun,* which to the Celts meant high ground. And that you will find over the whole of France. Your abbé was hypnotised by Duneville, which recurs in the Eure-et-Loir; he would have found Châteaudun, Dun-le-Roi in the Cher, Duneau in the Sarthe, Dun in the Ariège, Dune-les-Places in the Nièvre, and many others. This word *Dun* leads him into a curious error with regard to Douville where we shall be alighting, and shall find Mme. Verdurin's comfortable carriages awaiting us. Douville, in Latin *donvilla,* says he. As a matter of fact, Douville does lie at the foot of high hills. Your curé, who knows everything, feels all the same that he has made a blunder. He has, indeed, found in an old cartulary, the name *Domvilla.* Whereupon he retracts; Douville, according to him, is a fief belonging to the Abbot, *Domino Abbati,* of Mont Saint-Michel. He is delighted with the discovery, which is distinctly odd when one thinks of the scandalous life that, according to the Capitulary of Sainte-Claire sur Epte, was led at Mont Saint-Michel, though no more extraordinary than to picture the King of Denmark as suzerain of all this coast, where he encouraged the worship of Odin far more than that of Christ. On the other hand, the supposition that the *n* has been changed to *m* does not shock me, and requires less alteration than the perfectly correct Lyon, which also is derived from *Dun* (*Lugdunum*). But the fact is, the abbé is mistaken. Douville was never Donville, but Doville, *Eudonis villa,* the village of Eudes. Douville was formerly called Escalecliff, the steps up the cliff. About the year 1233, Eudes le Bouteiller, Lord of Escalecliff, set out for the Holy Land; on the eve of his departure he made over the church to the Abbey of Blanchelande. By an exchange of courtesies, the village took his name, whence we have Douville to-day. But I must add that toponymy, of which moreover I know little or nothing, is not an exact science; had we not this historical evidence, Douville might quite well come from Ouville, that is to say the Waters. The forms in *ai* (Aigues-Mortes), from *aqua,* are constantly changed to *eu* or *ou.* Now there were, quite close to Douville, certain famous springs, Carquethuit. You might suppose that the curé was only too ready to detect there a Christian origin, especially as this district seems to have been pretty hard to convert, since successive attempts were made by Saint Ursal, Saint Gofroi, Saint Barsanore, Saint Laurent of Brèvedent, who finally handed over the task to the monks of Beaubec. But as regards *thuit* the writer is mistaken, he sees in it a form of *toft,* a building, as in Cricquetot, Ectot, Yvetot, whereas it is the *thveit,* the clearing, the reclaimed land, as in Braquetuit, le Thuit, Regnetuit, and so forth. Similarly, if he recognises in Clitourps the Norman *thorp* which means village, he insists that the first syllable of the word must come from *clivus,* a slope, whereas it comes from *cliff,* a precipice. But his biggest blunders are due not so much to his ignorance as to his prejudices. However loyal a Frenchman one is, there is no need to fly in the face of the evidence and take Saint-Laurent en Bray to be the Roman priest, so famous at one time, when he is actually Saint Lawrence 'Toot, Archbishop of Dublin. But even more than his patriotic sentiments, your friend's religious bigotry leads him into strange errors. Thus you have not far from our hosts at la Raspelière two places called Montmartin, Montmartin-sur-Mer and Montmartin-en-Graignes. In the case of Graignes, the good curé has been quite right, he has seen that Graignes, in Latin *Grania,* in Greek *Krene,* means ponds, marshes; how many instances of Cresmays, Croen, Gremeville, Lengronne, might we not adduce? But, when he comes to Montmartin, your self-styled linguist positively insists that these must be parishes dedicated to Saint Martin. He bases his opinion upon the fact that the Saint is their patron, but does not realise that he was only adopted subsequently; or rather he is blinded by his hatred of paganism; he refuses to see that we should say Mont-Saint-Martin as we say Mont-Saint-Michel, if it were a question of Saint Martin, whereas the name Montmartin refers in a far more pagan fashion to temples consecrated to the god Mars, temples of which, it is true, no other vestige remains, but which the undisputed existence in the neighbourhood of vast Roman camps would render highly probable even without the name Montmartin, which removes all doubt. You see that the little pamphlet which you will find at la Raspelière is far from perfect." I protested that at Combray the curé had often told us interesting etymologies. "He was probably better on his own ground, the move to Normandy must have made him lose his bearings." "Nor did it do him any good," I added, "for he came here with neurasthenia and went away again with rheumatism." "Ah, his neurasthenia is to blame. He has lapsed from neurasthenia to philology, as my worthy master Pocquelin would have said. Tell us, Cottard, do you suppose that neurasthenia can have a disturbing effect on philology, philology a soothing effect on neurasthenia and the relief from neurasthenia lead to rheumatism?" "Undoubtedly, rheumatism and neurasthenia are subordinate forms of neuro-arthritism. You may pass from one to the other by metastasis." "The eminent Professor," said Brichot, "expresses himself in a French as highly infused with Latin and Greek as M. Purgon himself, of Molièresque memory! My uncle, I refer to our national Sarcey. . . ." But he was prevented from finishing his sentence. The Professor had leaped from his seat with a wild shout: "The devil!" he exclaimed on regaining his power of articulate speech, "we have passed Maineville (d'you hear?) and Renneville too." He had just noticed that the train was stopping at Saint-Mars-le-Vêtu, where most of the passengers alighted. "They can't have run through without stopping. We must have failed to notice it while we were talking about the Cambremers. Listen to me, Ski, pay attention, I am going to tell you 'a good one,'" said Cottard, who had taken a fancy to this expression, in common use in certain medical circles. "The Princess must be on the train, she can't have seen us, and will have got into another compartment. Come along and find her. Let's hope this won't land us in trouble!" And he led us all off in search of Princess Sherbatoff. He found her in the corner of an empty compartment, reading the *Revue des Deux Mondes*. She had long ago, from fear of rebuffs, acquired the habit of keeping in her place, or remaining in her corner, in life as on the train, and of not offering her hand until the other person had greeted her. She went on reading as the faithful trooped into her carriage. I recognised her immediately; this woman who might have forfeited her position but was nevertheless of exalted birth, who in any event was the pearl of a salon such as the Verdurins', was the lady whom, on the same train, I had put down, two days earlier, as possibly the keeper of a brothel. Her social personality, which had been so vague, became clear to me as soon as I learned her name, just as when, after racking our brains over a puzzle, we at length hit upon the word which clears up all the obscurity, and which, in the case of a person, is his name. To discover two days later who the person is with whom one has travelled in the train is a far more amusing surprise than to read in the next number of a magazine the clue to the problem set in the previous number. Big restaurants, casinos, local trains, are the family portrait galleries of these social enigmas. "Princess, we must have missed you at Maineville! May we come and sit in your compartment?" "Why, of course," said the Princess who, upon hearing Cottard address her, but only then, raised from her magazine a pair of eyes which, like the eyes of M. de Charlus, although gentler, saw perfectly well the people of whose presence she pretended to be unaware. Cottard, coming to the conclusion that the fact of my having been invited to meet the Cambremers was a sufficient recommendation, decided, after a momentary hesitation, to introduce me to the Princess, who bowed with great courtesy but appeared to be hearing my name for the first time. "Cré nom!" cried the doctor, "my wife has forgotten to make them change the buttons on my white waistcoat. Ah! Those women, they never remember anything. Don't you ever marry, my boy," he said to me. And as this was one of the pleasantries which he considered appropriate when he had nothing else to say, he peeped out of the corner of his eye at the Princess and the rest of the faithful, who, because he was a Professor and an Academician, smiled back, admiring his good temper and freedom from pride. The Princess informed us that the young violinist had been found. He had been confined to bed the evening before by a sick headache, but was coming that evening and bringing with him a friend of his father whom he had met at Doncières. She had learned this from Mme. Verdurin with whom she had taken luncheon that morning, she told us in a rapid voice, rolling her *r*s, with her Russian accent, softly at the back of her throat, as though they were not *r*s but *l*s. "Ah! You had luncheon with her this morning," Cottard said to the Princess; but turned his eyes to myself, the purport of this remark being to shew me on what intimate terms the Princess was with the Mistress. "You are indeed a faithful adherent!" "Yes, I love the little cirlcle, so intelligent, so agleeable, neverl spiteful, quite simple, not at all snobbish, and clevel to theirl fingle-tips." "Nom d'une pipe! I must have lost my ticket, I can't find it anywhere," cried Cottard, with an agitation that was, in the circumstances, quite unjustified. He knew that at Douville, where a couple of landaus would be awaiting us, the collector would let him pass without a ticket, and would only bare his head all the more humbly, so that the salute might furnish an explanation of his indulgence, to wit that he had of course recognised Cottard as one of the Verdurins' regular guests. "They won't shove me in the lock-up for that," the doctor concluded. "You were saying, Sir," I inquired of Brichot, "that there used to be some famous waters near here; how do we know that?" "The name of the next station is one of a multitude of proofs. It is called Fervaches." "I don't undlestand what he's talking about," mumbled the Princess, as though she were saying to me out of politeness: "He's rather a bore, ain't he?" "Why, Princess, Fervaches means hot springs. *Fervidae aquae.* But to return to the young violinist," Brichot went on, "I was quite forgetting, Cottard, to tell you the great news. Had you heard that our poor friend Dechambre, who used to be Mme. Verdurin's favourite pianist, has just died? It is terribly sad." "He was quite young," replied Cottard, "but he must have had some trouble with his liver, there must have been something sadly wrong in that quarter, he had been looking very queer indeed for a long time past." "But he was not so young as all that," said Brichot; "in the days when Elstir and Swann used to come to Mme. Verdurin's, Dechambre had already made himself a reputation in Paris, and, what is remarkable, without having first received the baptism of success abroad. Ah! He was no follower of the Gospel according to Saint Barnum, that fellow." "You are mistaken, he could not have been going to Mme. Verdurin's, at that time, he was still in the nursery." "But, unless my old memory plays me false, I was under the impression that Dechambre used to play Vinteuil's sonata for Swann, when that clubman, who had broken with the aristocracy, had still no idea that he was one day to become the embourgeoised Prince Consort of our national Odette." "It is impossible, Vinteuil's sonata was played at Mme. Verdurin's long after Swann ceased to come there," said the doctor, who, like all people who work hard and think that they remember many things which they imagine to be of use to them, forget many others, a condition which enables them to go into ecstasies over the memories of people who have nothing else to do. "You are hopelessly muddled, though your brain is as sound as ever," said the doctor with a smile. Brichot admitted that he was mistaken. The train stopped. We were at la Sogne. The name stirred my curiosity. "How I should like to know what all these names mean," I said to Cottard. "You must ask M. Brichot, he may know, perhaps." "Why, la Sogne is la Cicogne, *Siconia*," replied Brichot, whom I was burning to interrogate about many other names.

Forgetting her attachment to her "corner," Mme. Sherbatoff kindly offered to change places with me, so that I might talk more easily with Brichot, whom I wanted to ask about other etymologies that interested me, and assured me that she did not mind in the least whether she travelled with her face or her back to the engine, standing, or seated, or anyhow. She remained on the defensive until she had discovered a newcomer's intentions, but as soon as she had realised that these were friendly, she would do everything in her power to oblige. At length the train stopped at the station of Douville-Féterne, which being more or less equidistant from the villages of Féterne and Douville, bore for this reason their hyphenated name. "Saperlipopette!" exclaimed Doctor Cottard, when we came to the barrier where the tickets were collected, and, pretending to have only just discovered his loss, "I can't find my ticket, I must have lost it." But the collector, taking off his cap, assured him that it did not matter and smiled respectfully. The Princess (giving instructions to the coachman, as though she were a sort of lady in waiting to Mme. Verdurin, who, because of the Cambremers, had not been able to come to the station, as, for that matter, she rarely did) took me, and also Brichot, with herself in one of the carriages. The doctor, Saniette and Ski got into the other.

The driver, although quite young, was the Verdurins' first coachman, the only one who had any right to the title; he took them, in the daytime, on all their excursions, for he knew all the roads, and in the evening went down to meet the faithful and took them back to the station later on. He was accompanied by extra helpers (whom he selected if necessary). He was an excellent fellow, sober and capable, but with one of those melancholy faces on which a fixed stare indicates that the merest trifle will make the person fly into a passion, not to say nourish dark thoughts. But at the moment he was quite happy, for he had managed to secure a place for his brother, another excellent type of fellow, with the Verdurins. We began by driving through Douville. Grassy knolls ran down from the village to the sea, in wide slopes to which their saturation in moisture and salt gave a richness, a softness, a vivacity of extreme tones. The islands and indentations of Rivebelle, far nearer now than at Balbec, gave this part of the coast the appearance, novel to me, of a relief map. We passed by some little bungalows, almost all of which were let to painters; turned into a track upon which some loose cattle, as frightened as were our horses, barred our way for ten minutes, and emerged upon the cliff road. "But, by the immortal gods," Brichot suddenly asked, "let us return to that poor Dechambre; do you suppose Mme. Verdurin *knows?* Has anyone told *her?*" Mme. Verdurin, like most people who move in society, simply because she needed the society of other people, never thought of them again for a single day, as soon as, being dead, they could no longer come to the Wednesdays, nor to the Saturdays, nor dine without dressing. And one could not say of the little clan, a type in this respect of all salons, that it was composed of more dead than living members, seeing that, as soon as one was dead, it was as though one had never existed. But, to escape the nuisance of having to speak of the deceased, in other words to postpone one of the dinners—a thing impossible to the mistress—as a token of mourning, M. Verdurin used to pretend that the death of the faithful had such an effect on his wife that, in the interest of her health, it must never be mentioned to her. Moreover, and perhaps just because the death of other people seemed to him so conclusive, so vulgar an accident, the thought of his own death filled him with horror and he shunned any consideration that might lead to it. As for Brichot, since he was the soul of honesty and completely taken in by what M. Verdurin said about his wife, he dreaded for his friend's sake the emotions that such a bereavement must cause her. "Yes, she *knew the worst* this morning," said the Princess, "it was impossible to *keep it from her.*" "Ah! Thousand thunders of Zeus!" cried Brichot, "Ah! it must have been a terrible blow, a friend of twenty-five years standing. There was a man who was one of us." Of course, of course, what can you expect? Such incidents are bound to be painful; but Madame Verdurin is a brave woman, she is even more cerebral than emotive." "I don't altogether agree with the Doctor," said the Princess, whose rapid speech, her murmured accents, certainly made her appear both sullen and rebellious. "Mme. Verdurin, beneath a cold exterior, conceals treasures of sensibility. M. Verdurin told me that he had had great difficulty in preventing her from going to Paris for the funeral; he was obliged to let her think that it was all to be held in the country." "The devil! She wanted to go to Paris, did she? Of course, I know that she has a heart, too much heart perhaps. Poor Dechambre! As Madame Verdurin remarked not two months ago: 'Compared with him, Planté, Paderewski, Risler himself are nowhere!' Ah, he could say with better reason than that limelighter Nero, who has managed to take in even German scholarship: *Qualis artifex pereo!* But he at least, Dechambre, must have died in the fulfilment of his priesthood, in the odour of Beethovenian devotion; and gallantly, I have no doubt; he had every right, that interpreter of German music, to pass away while celebrating the Mass in D. But he was, when all is said, the man to greet the unseen with a cheer, for that inspired performer would produce at times from the Parisianised Champagne stock of which he came, the swagger and smartness of a guardsman."

From the height we had now reached, the sea suggested no longer, as at Balbec, the undulations of swelling mountains, but on the contrary the view, beheld from a mountain-top or from a road winding round its flank, of a blue-green glacier or a glittering plain, situated at a lower level. The lines of the currents seemed to be fixed upon its surface, and to have traced there for ever their concentric circles; the enamelled face of the sea which changed imperceptibly in colour, assumed towards the head of the bay, where an estuary opened, the blue whiteness of milk, in which little black boats that did not move seemed entangled like flies. I felt that from nowhere could one discover a vaster prospect. But at each turn in the road a fresh expanse was added to it and when we arrived at the Douville toll-house, the spur of the cliff which until then had concealed from us half the bay, withdrew, and all of a sudden I descried upon my left a gulf as profound as that which I had already had before me, but one that changed the proportions of the other and doubled its beauty. The air at this lofty point acquired a keenness and purity that intoxicated me. I adored the Verdurins; that they should have sent a carriage for us seemed to me a touching act of kindness. I should have liked to kiss the Princess. I told her that I had never seen anything so beautiful. She professed that she too loved this spot more than any other. But I could see that to her as to the Verdurins the thing that really mattered was not to gaze at the view like tourists, but to partake of good meals there, to entertain people whom they liked, to write letters, to read books, in short to live in these surroundings, passively allowing the beauty of the scene to soak into them rather than making it the object of their attention.

After the toll-house, where the carriage had stopped for a moment at such a height above the sea that, as from a mountain-top, the sight of the blue gulf beneath almost made one dizzy, I opened the window; the sound, distinctly caught, of each wave that broke in turn had something sublime in its softness and precision. Was it not like an index of measurement which, upsetting all our ordinary impressions, shews us that vertical distances may be coordinated with horizontal, in contradiction of the idea that our mind generally forms of them; and that, though they bring the sky nearer to us in this way, they are not great; that they are indeed less great for a sound which traverses them as did the sound of those little waves, the medium through which it has to pass being purer. And in fact if one went back but a couple of yards below the toll-house, one could no longer distinguish that sound of waves, which six hundred feet of cliff had not robbed of its delicate, minute and soft precision. I said to myself that my grandmother would have listened to it with the delight that she felt in all manifestations of nature or art, in the simplicity of which one discerns grandeur. I was now at the highest pitch of exaltation, which raised everything round about me accordingly. It melted my heart that the Verdurins should have sent to meet us at the station. I said as much to the Princess, who seemed to think that I was greatly exaggerating so simple an act of courtesy. I know that she admitted subsequently to Cottard that she found me very enthusiastic; he replied that I was too emotional, required sedatives and ought to take to knitting. I pointed out to the Princess every tree, every little house smothered in its mantle of roses, I made her admire everything, I would have liked to take her in my arms and press her to my heart. She told me that she could see that I had a gift for painting, that of course I must sketch, that she was surprised that nobody had told her about it. And she confessed that the country was indeed picturesque. We drove through, where it perched upon its height, the little village of Englesqueville (*Engleberti villa,* Brichot informed us). "But are you quite sure that there will be a party this evening, in spite of Dechambre's death, Princess?" he went on, without stopping to think that the presence at the station of the carriage in which we were sitting was in itself an answer to his question. "Yes," said the Princess, "M. Verldulin insisted that it should not be put off, simply to keep his wife from *thinking.* And besides, after never failing for all these years to entertain on Wednesdays, such a change in her habits would have been bound to upset her. Her nerves are velly bad just now. M. Verdurin was particularly pleased that you were coming to dine this evening, because he knew that it would be a great distraction for Mme. Verdurin," said the Princess, forgetting her pretence of having never heard my name before. "I think that it will be as well not to say *anything* in front of Mme. Verdurin," the Princess added. "Ah! I am glad you warned me," Brichot artlessly replied. "I shall pass on your suggestion to Cottard." The carriage stopped for a moment. It moved on again, but the sound that the wheels had been making in the village street had ceased. We had turned into the main avenue of la

Raspelière where M. Verdurin stood waiting for us upon the steps. "I did well to put on a dinner-jacket," he said, observing with pleasure that the faithful had put on theirs, "since I have such smart gentlemen in my party." And as I apologised for not having changed: "Why, that's quite all right. We're all friends here. I should be delighted to offer you one of my own dinner-jackets, but it wouldn't fit you." The handclasp throbbing with emotion which, as he entered the hall of la Raspelière, and by way of condolence at the death of the pianist, Brichot gave our host elicited no response from the latter. I told him how greatly I admired the scenery. "Ah! All the better, and you've seen nothing, we must take you round. Why not come and spend a week or two here, the air is excellent." Brichot was afraid that his handclasp had not been understood. "Ah! Poor Dechambre!" he said, but in an undertone, in case Mme. Verdurin was within earshot. "It is terrible," replied M. Verdurin lightly. "So young," Brichot pursued the point. Annoyed at being detained over these futilities, M. Verdurin replied in a hasty tone and with an embittered groan, not of grief but of irritated impatience: "Why yes, of course, but what's to be done about it, it's no use crying over spilt milk, talking about him won't bring him back to life, will it?" And, his civility returning with his joviality: "Come along, my good Brichot, get your things off quickly. We have a bouillabaisse which mustn't be kept waiting. But, in heaven's name, don't start talking about Dechambre to Madame Verdurin. You know that she always hides her feelings, but she is quite morbidly sensitive. I give you my word, when she heard that Dechambre was dead, she almost cried," said M. Verdurin in a tone of profound irony. One might have concluded, from hearing him speak, that it implied a form of insanity to regret the death of a friend of thirty years' standing, and on the other hand one gathered that the perpetual union of M. Verdurin and his wife did not preclude his constantly criticising her and her frequently irritating him. "If you mention it to her, she will go and make herself ill again. It is deplorable, three weeks after her bronchitis. When that happens, it is I who have to be sicknurse. You can understand that I have had more than enough of it. Grieve for Dechambre's fate in your heart as much as you like. Think of him, but do not speak about him. I was very fond of Dechambre, but you cannot blame me for being fonder still of my wife. Here's Cottard, now, you can ask him." And indeed he knew that a family doctor can do many little services, such as prescribing that one must not give way to grief.

The docile Cottard had said to the Mistress: "Upset yourself like that, and to-morrow you will *give me* a temperature of 102," as he might have said to the cook: "To-morrow you will give me a *riz de veau*." Medicine, when it fails to cure the sick, busies itself with changing the sense of verbs and pronouns.

M. Verdurin was glad to find that Saniette, notwithstanding the snubs that he had had to endure two days earlier, had not deserted the little nucleus. And indeed Mme. Verdurin and her husband had acquired, in their idleness, cruel instincts for which the great occasions, occurring too rarely, no longer sufficed. They had succeeded in effecting a breach between Odette and Swann, between Brichot and his mistress. They would try it again with some one else, that was understood. But the opportunity did not present itself every day. Whereas, thanks to his shuddering sensibility, his timorous and quickly aroused shyness, Saniette provided them with a whipping-block for every day in the year. And so, for fear of his failing them, they took care always to invite him with friendly and persuasive words, such as the bigger boys at school, the old soldiers in a regiment address to a recruit whom they are anxious to beguile so that they may get him into their clutches, with the sole object of flattering him for the moment and bullying him when he can no longer escape. "Whatever you do," Brichot reminded Cottard, who had not heard what M. Verdurin was saying, "mum's the word before Mme. Verdurin. Have no fear, O Cottard, you are dealing with a sage, as Theocritus says. Besides, M. Verdurin is right, what is the use of lamentations," he went on, for, being capable of assimilating forms of speech and the ideas which they suggested to him, but having no finer perception, he had admired in M. Verdurin's remarks the most courageous stoicism. "All the same, it is a great talent that has gone from the world." "What, are you still talking about Dechambre," said M. Verdurin, who had gone on ahead of us, and, seeing that we were not following him, had turned back. "Listen," he said to Brichot, "nothing is gained by exaggeration. The fact of his being dead is no excuse for making him out a genius, which he was not. He played well, I admit, and what is more, he was in his proper element here; transplanted, he ceased to exist. My wife was infatuated with him and made his reputation. You know what she is. I will go farther, in the interest of his own reputation he has died at the right moment, he is done to a turn, as the demoiselles de Caen, grilled according to the incomparable recipe of Pampilles, are going to be, I hope (unless you keep us standing here all night with your jeremiads in this Kasbah exposed to all the winds of heaven). You don't seriously expect us all to die of hunger because Dechambre is dead, when for the last year he was obliged to practise scales before giving a concert; to recover for the moment, and for the moment only, the suppleness of his wrists. Besides, you are going to hear this evening, or at any rate to meet, for the rascal is too fond of deserting his art, after dinner, for the card-table, somebody who is a far greater artist than Dechambre, a youngster whom my wife has discovered" (as she had discovered Dechambre, and Paderewski, and everybody else): "Morel. He has not arrived yet, the devil. He is coming with an old friend of his family whom he has picked up, and who bores him to tears, but otherwise, not to get into trouble with his father, he would have been obliged to stay down at Doncières and keep him company: the Baron de Charlus." The faithful entered the drawing-room. M. Verdurin, who had remained behind with me while I took off my things, took my arm by way of a joke, as one's host does at a dinner-party when there is no lady for one to take in. "Did you have a pleasant journey?" "Yes, M. Brichot told me things which interested me greatly," said I, thinking of the etymologies, and because I had heard that the Verdurins greatly admired Brichot. "I am surprised to hear that he told you anything," said M. Verdurin, "he is such a retiring man, and talks so little about the things he knows." This compliment did not strike me as being very apt. "He seems charming,"

I remarked. "Exquisite, delicious, not the sort of man you meet every day, such a light, fantastic touch, my wife adores him, and so do I!" replied M. Verdurin in an exaggerated tone, as though repeating a lesson. Only then did I grasp that what he had said to me about Brichot was ironical. And I asked myself whether M. Verdurin, since those far-off days of which I had heard reports, had not shaken off the yoke of his wife's tutelage.

The sculptor was greatly astonished to learn that the Verdurins were willing to have M. de Charlus in their house. Whereas in the Faubourg Saint-Germain, where M. de Charlus was so well known, nobody ever referred to his morals (of which most people had no suspicion, others remained doubtful, crediting him rather with intense but Platonic friendships, with behaving imprudently, while the enlightened few strenuously denied, shrugging their shoulders, any insinuation upon which some malicious Gallardon might venture), those morals, the nature of which was known perhaps to a few intimate friends, were, on the other hand, being denounced daily far from the circle in which he moved, just as, at times, the sound of artillery fire is audible only beyond a zone of silence. Moreover, in those professional and artistic circles where he was regarded as the typical instance of inversion, his great position in society, his noble origin were completely unknown, by a process analogous to that which, among the people of Rumania, has brought it about that the name of Ronsard is known as that of a great nobleman, while his poetical work is unknown there. Not only that, the Rumanian estimate of Ronsard's nobility is founded upon an error. Similarly, if in the world of painters and actors M. de Charlus had such an evil reputation, that was due to their confusing him with a certain Comte Leblois de Charlus who was not even related to him (or, if so, the connexion was extremely remote), and who had been arrested, possibly by mistake, in the course of a police raid which had become historic. In short, all the stories related of our M. de Charlus referred to the other. Many professionals swore that they had had relations with M. de Charlus, and did so in good faith, believing that the false M. de Charlus was the true one, the false one possibly encouraging, partly from an affectation of nobility, partly to conceal his vice, a confusion which to the true one (the Baron whom we already know) was for a long time damaging, and afterwards, when he had begun to go down the hill, became a convenience, for it enabled him likewise to say: "That is not myself." And in the present instance it was not he to whom the rumours referred. Finally, what enhanced the falsehood of the reports of an actual fact (the Baron's tendencies), he had had an intimate and perfectly pure friendship with an author who, in the theatrical world, had for some reason acquired a similar reputation which he in no way deserved. When they were seen together at a first night, people would say: "You see," just as it was supposed that the Duchesse de Guermantes had immoral relations with the Princesse de Parme; an indestructible legend, for it would be disproved only in the presence of those two great ladies themselves, to which the people who repeated it would presumably never come any nearer than by staring at them through their glasses in the theatre and slandering them to the occupant of the next stall. Given M. de Charlus's morals, the sculptor concluded all the more readily that the Baron's social position must be equally low, since he had no sort of information whatever as to the family to which M. de Charlus belonged, his title or his name. Just as Cottard imagined that everybody knew that the degree of Doctor of Medicine implied nothing, the title of Consultant to a Hospital meant something, so people in society are mistaken when they suppose that everybody has the same idea of the social importance of their name as they themselves and the other people of their set.

The Prince d'Agrigente was regarded as a swindler by a club servant to whom he owed twenty-five louis, and regained his importance only in the Faubourg Saint-Germain where he had three sisters who were Duchesses, for it is not among the humble people in whose eyes he is of small account, but among the smart people who know what is what, that the great nobleman creates an effect. M. de Charlus, for that matter, was to learn in the course of the evening that his host had the vaguest ideas about the most illustrious ducal families.

Certain that the Verdurins were making a grave mistake in allowing an individual of tarnished reputation to be admitted to so " select " a household as theirs, the sculptor felt it his duty to take the Mistress aside. " You are entirely mistaken, besides I never pay any attention to those tales, and even if it were true, I may be allowed to point out that it could hardly compromise *me!* " replied Mme. Verdurin, furious, for, Morel being the principal feature of the Wednesdays, the chief thing for her was not to give any offence to him. As for Cottard, he could not express an opinion, for he had asked leave to go upstairs for a moment to " do a little job " in the *buen retiro,* and after that, in M. Verdurin's bedroom, to write an extremely urgent letter for a patient.

A great publisher from Paris who had come to call, expecting to be invited to stay to dinner, withdrew abruptly, quickly, realising that he was not smart enough for the little clan. He was a tall, stout man, very dark, with a studious and somewhat cutting air. He reminded one of an ebony paper-knife.

Mme. Verdurin who, to welcome us in her immense drawing-room, in which displays of grasses, poppies, field-flowers, plucked only that morning, alternated with a similar theme painted on the walls, two centuries earlier, by an artist of exquisite taste, had risen for a moment from a game of cards which she was playing with an old friend, begged us to excuse her for just one minute while she finished her game, talking to us the while. What I told her about my impressions did not, however, seem altogether to please her. For one thing I was shocked to observe that she and her husband came indoors every day long before the hour of those sunsets which were considered so fine when seen from that cliff, and finer still from the terrace of la Raspelière, and which I would have travelled miles to see. "Yes, it's incomparable," said Mme. Verdurin carelessly, with a glance at the huge windows which gave the room a wall of glass. "Even though we have it always in front of us, we never grow tired of it," and she turned her attention back to her cards. Now my very enthusiasm made me exacting. I expressed my regret that I could not see from the drawing-room the rocks of Darnetal, which, Elstir had told me, were quite lovely at that hour, when they reflected so many colours. "Ah! You can't see them from here, you would have to go to the end of the park, to the 'view of the bay.' From the seat there, you can take in the whole panorama. But you can't go there by yourself, you will lose your way. I can take you there, if you like," she added kindly. "No, no, you are not satisfied with the illness you had the other day, you want to make yourself ill again. He will come back, he can see the view of the bay another time." I did not insist, and understood that it was enough for the Verdurins to know that this sunset made its way into their drawing-room or dining-room, like a magnificent painting, like a priceless Japanese enamel, justifying the high rent that they were paying for la Raspelière, with plate and linen, but a thing to which they rarely raised their eyes; the important thing, here, for them was to live comfortably, to take drives, to feed well, to talk, to entertain agreeable friends whom they provided with amusing games of billiards, good meals, merry tea-parties. I noticed, however, later on, how intelligently they had learned to know the district, taking their guests for excursions as "novel" as the music to which they made them listen. The part which the flowers of la Raspelière, the roads by the sea's edge, the old houses, the undiscovered churches, played in the life of M. Verdurin was so great that those people who saw him only in Paris and who, themselves, substituted for the life by the seaside and in the country the refinements of life in town could barely understand the idea that he himself formed of his own life, or the importance that his pleasures gave him in his own eyes. This importance was further enhanced by the fact that the Verdurins were convinced that la Raspelière, which they hoped to purchase, was a property without its match in the world. This superiority which their self-esteem made them attribute to la Raspelière justified in their eyes my enthusiasm which, but for that, would have annoyed them slightly, because of the disappointments which it involved (like my disappointment when long ago I had first listened to Berma) and which I frankly admitted to them.

"I hear the carriage coming back," the Mistress suddenly murmured. Let us state briefly that Mme. Verdurin, quite apart from the inevitable changes due to increasing years, no longer resembled what she had been at the time when Swann and Odette used to listen to the little phrase in her house. Even when she heard it played, she was no longer obliged to assume the air of attenuated admiration which she used to assume then, for that had become her normal expression. Under the influence of the countless neuralgias which the music of Bach, Wagner, Vinteuil, Debussy had given her, Mme. Verdurin's brow had assumed enormous proportions, like limbs that are finally crippled by rheumatism. Her temples, suggestive of a pair of beautiful, pain-stricken, milk-white spheres, in which Harmony rolled endlessly, flung back upon either side her silvered tresses, and proclaimed, on the Mistress's behalf, without any need for her to say a word: "I know what is in store for me to-night." Her features no longer took the trouble to formulate successively aesthetic impressions of undue violence, for they had themselves become their permanent expression on a countenance ravaged and superb. This attitude of resignation to the ever impending sufferings inflicted by Beauty, and of the courage that was required to make her dress for dinner when she had barely recovered from the effects of the last sonata, had the result that Mme.

Verdurin, even when listening to the most heartrending music, preserved a disdainfully impassive countenance, and actually withdrew into retirement to swallow her two spoonfuls of aspirin.

"Why, yes, here they are!" M. Verdurin cried with relief when he saw the door open to admit Morel, followed by M. de Charlus. The latter, to whom dining with the Verdurins meant not so much going into society as going into questionable surroundings, was as frightened as a schoolboy making his way for the first time into a brothel with the utmost deference towards its mistress. Moreover the persistent desire that M. de Charlus felt to appear virile and frigid was overcome (when he appeared in the open doorway) by those traditional ideas of politeness which are awakened as soon as shyness destroys an artificial attitude and makes an appeal to the resources of the subconscious. When it is a Charlus, whether he be noble or plebeian, that is stirred by such a sentiment of instinctive and atavistic politeness to strangers, it is always the spirit of a relative of the female sex, attendant like a goddess, or incarnate as a double, that undertakes to introduce him into a strange drawing-room and to mould his attitude until he comes face to face with his hostess. Thus a young painter, brought up by a godly, Protestant, female cousin, will enter a room, his head aslant and quivering, his eyes raised to the ceiling, his hands gripping an invisible muff, the remembered shape of which and its real and tutelary presence will help the frightened artist to cross without agoraphobia the yawning abyss between the hall and the inner drawing-room. Thus it was that the pious relative, whose memory is helping him to-day, used to enter a room years ago, and with so plaintive an air that one was asking oneself what calamity she had come to announce, when from her first words one realised, as now in the case of the painter, that she had come to pay an after-dinner call. By virtue of the same law, which requires that life, in the interests of the still unfulfilled act, shall bring into play, utilise, adulterate, in a perpetual prostitution, the most respectable, it may be the most sacred, sometimes only the most innocent legacies from the past, and albeit in this instance it engendered a different aspect, the one of Mme. Cottard's nephews who distressed his family by his effeminate ways and the company he kept would always make a joyous entry as though he had a surprise in store for you or were going to inform you that he had been left a fortune, radiant with a happiness which it would have been futile to ask him to explain, it being due to his unconscious heredity and his misplaced sex. He walked upon tiptoe, was no doubt himself astonished that he was not holding a cardcase, offered you his hand parting his lips as he had seen his aunt part hers, and his uneasy glance was directed at the mirror in which he seemed to wish to make certain, albeit he was bare-headed, whether his hat, as Mme. Cottard had once inquired of Swann, was not askew. As for M. de Charlus, whom the society in which he had lived furnished, at this critical moment, with different examples, with other patterns of affability, and above all with the maxim that one must, in certain cases, when dealing with people of humble rank, bring into play and make use of one's rarest graces, which one normally holds in reserve, it was with a flutter, archly, and with the same sweep with which a skirt would have enlarged and impeded his waddling motion that he advanced upon Mme. Verdurin with so flattered and honoured an air that one would have said that to be taken to her house was for him a supreme favour. One would have thought that it was Mme. de Marsantes who was entering the room, so prominent at that moment was the woman whom a mistake on the part of Nature had enshrined in the body of M. de Charlus. It was true that the Baron had made every effort to obliterate this mistake and to assume a masculine appearance. But no sooner had he succeeded than, he having in the meantime kept the same tastes, this habit of looking at things through a woman's eyes gave him a fresh feminine appearance, due this time not to heredity but to his own way of living. And as he had gradually come to regard even social questions from the feminine point of view, and without noticing it, for it is not only by dint of lying to other people, but also by lying to oneself that one ceases to be aware that one is lying, albeit he had called upon his body to manifest (at the moment of his entering the Verdurins' drawing-room) all the courtesy of a great nobleman, that body which had fully understood what M. de Charlus had ceased to apprehend, displayed, to such an extent that the Baron would have deserved the epithet "ladylike," all the attractions of a great lady. Not that there need be any connexion between the appearance of M. de Charlus and the fact that sons, who do not always take after their fathers, even without being inverts, and though they go after women, may consummate upon their faces the profanation of their mothers. But we need not consider here a subject that deserves a chapter to itself: the Profanation of the Mother.

Albeit other reasons dictated this transformation of M.

de Charlus, and purely physical ferments set his material substance "working" and made his body pass gradually into the category of women's bodies, nevertheless the change that we record here was of spiritual origin. By dint of supposing yourself to be ill you become ill, grow thin, are too weak to rise from your bed, suffer from nervous enteritis. By dint of thinking tenderly of men you become a woman, and an imaginary spirt hampers your movements. The obsession, just as in the other instance it affects your health, may in this instance alter your sex. Morel, who accompanied him, came to shake hands with me. From that first moment, owing to a two-fold change that occurred in him I formed (alas, I was not warned in time to act upon it!) a bad impression of him. I have said that Morel, having risen above his father's menial status, was generally pleased to indulge in a contemptuous familiarity. He had talked to me on the day when he brought me the photographs without once addressing me as Monsieur, treating me as an inferior. What was my surprise at Mme. Verdurin's to see him bow very low before me, and before me alone, and to hear, before he had even uttered a syllable to anyone else, words of respect, most respectful—such words as I thought could not possibly flow from his pen or fall from his lips—addressed to myself. I at once suspected that he had some favour to ask of me. Taking me aside a minute later: "Monsieur would be doing me a very great service," he said to me, going so far this time as to address me in the third person, "by keeping from Mme. Verdurin and her guests the nature of the profession that my father practised with his uncle. It would be best to say that he was, in your family, the agent for estates so considerable as to put him almost on a level with your parents." Morel's request annoyed me intensely because it obliged me to magnify not his father's position, in which I took not the slightest interest, but the wealth—the apparent wealth of my own, which I felt to be absurd. But he appeared so unhappy, so pressing, that I could not refuse him. "No, before dinner," he said in an imploring tone, "Monsieur can easily find some excuse for taking Mme. Verdurin aside." This was what, in the end, I did, trying to enhance to the best of my ability the distinction of Morel's father, without unduly exaggerating the "style," the "worldly goods" of my own family. It went like a letter through the post, notwithstanding the astonishment of Mme. Verdurin, who had had a nodding acquaintance with my grandfather. And as she had no tact, hated family life (that dissolvent of the little nucleus), after telling me that she remembered, long ago, seeing my great-grandfather, and after speaking of him as of somebody who was almost an idiot, who would have been incapable of understanding the little group, and who, to use her expression, "was not one of us," she said to me: "Families are such a bore, the only thing is to get right away from them;" and at once proceeded to tell me of a trait in my great-grandfather's character of which I was unaware, although I might have suspected it at home (I had never seen him, but they frequently spoke of him), his remarkable stinginess (in contrast to the somewhat excessive generosity of my great-uncle, the friend of the lady in pink and Morel's father's employer): "Why, of course, if your grandparents had such a grand agent, that only shews that there are all sorts of people in a family. Your grandfather's father was so stingy that, at the end of his life, when he was almost half-witted —between you and me, he was never anything very special, you are worth the whole lot of them—he could not bring himself to pay a penny for his ride on the omnibus. So that they were obliged to have him followed by somebody who paid his fare for him, and to let the old miser think that his friend M. de Persigny, the Cabinet Minister, had given him a permit to travel free on the omnibuses. But I am delighted to hear that *our* Morel's father held such a good position. I was under the impression that he had been a schoolmaster, but that's nothing, I must have misunderstood. In any case, it makes not the slightest difference, for I must tell you that here we appreciate only true worth, the personal contribution, what I call the participation. Provided that a person is artistic, provided in a word that he is one of the brotherhood, nothing else matters." The way in which Morel was one of the brotherhood was—so far as I have been able to discover—that he was sufficiently fond of both women and men to satisfy either sex with the fruits of his experience of the other. But what it is essential to note here is that as soon as I had given him my word that I would speak on his behalf to Mme. Verdurin, as soon, moreover, as I had actually done so, and without any possibility of subsequent retractation, Morel's " respect " for myself vanished as though by magic, the formal language of respect melted away, and indeed for some time he avoided me, contriving to appear contemptuous of me, so that if Mme. Verdurin wanted me to give him a message, to ask him to play something, he would continue to talk to one of the faithful, then move on to another, changing his seat if I approached him.

The others were obliged to tell him three or four times that I had spoken to him, after which he would reply, with an air of constraint, briefly, that is to say unless we were by ourselves. When that happened, he was expansive, friendly, for there was a charming side to him. I concluded all the same from this first evening that his must be a vile nature, that he would not, at a pinch, shrink from any act of meanness, was incapable of gratitude. In which he resembled the majority of mankind. But inasmuch as I had inherited a strain of my grandmother's nature, and enjoyed the diversity of other people without expecting anything of them or resenting anything that they did, I overlooked his baseness, rejoiced in his gaiety when it was in evidence, and indeed in what I believe to have been a genuine affection on his part when, having gone the whole circuit of his false ideas of human nature, he realised (with a jerk, for he shewed strange reversions to a blind and primitive savagery) that my kindness to him was disinterested, that my indulgence arose not from a want of perception but from what he called goodness; and, more important still, I was enraptured by his art which indeed was little more than an admirable virtuosity, but which made me (without his being in the intellectual sense of the word a real musician) hear again or for the first time so much good music. Moreover a manager—M. de Charlus (whom I had not suspected of such talents, albeit Mme. de Guermantes, who had known him a very different person in their younger days, asserted that he had composed a sonata for her, painted a fan, and so forth), modest in regard to his true merits, but possessing talents of the first order, contrived to place this virtuosity at the service of a versatile artistic sense which increased it tenfold. Imagine a merely skilful performer in the Russian ballet, formed, educated, developed in all directions by M. Diaghileff.

I had just given Mme. Verdurin the message with which Morel had charged me and was talking to M. de Charlus about Saint-Loup, when Cottard burst into the room announcing, as though the house were on fire, that the Cambremers had arrived. Mme. Verdurin, not wishing to appear before strangers such as M. de Charlus (whom Cottard had not seen) and myself to attach any great importance to the arrival of the Cambremers, did not move, made no response to the announcement of these tidings, and merely said to the doctor, fanning herself gracefully, and adopting the tone of a Marquise in the Théâtre-Français: "The Baron has just been telling us. . . ." This was too much for Cottard! Less abruptly than he would have done in the old days, for learning and high positions had added weight to his utterance, but with the emotion, nevertheless, which he recaptured at the Verdurins', he exclaimed: "A Baron! What Baron? Where's the Baron?" staring round the room with an astonishment that bordered on incredulity. Mme. Verdurin, with the affected indifference of a hostess when a servant has, in front of her guests, broken a valuable glass, and with the artificial, high-falutin tone of a conservatoire prize-winner acting in a play by the younger Dumas, replied, pointing with her fan to Morel's patron: "Why, the Baron de Charlus, to whom let me introduce you, M. le Professeur Cottard." Mme. Verdurin was, for that matter, by no means sorry to have an opportunity of playing the leading lady. M. de Charlus proffered two fingers which the Professor clasped with the kindly smile of a "Prince of Science." But he stopped short upon seeing the Cambremers enter the room, while M. de Charlus led me into a corner to tell me something, not without feeling my muscles, which is a German habit. M. de Cambremer bore no resemblance to the old Marquise. To anyone who had only heard of him, or of letters written by him, well and forcibly expressed, his personal appearance was startling. No doubt, one would grow accustomed to it. But his nose had chosen to place itself aslant above his mouth, perhaps the only crooked line, among so many, which one would never have thought of tracing upon his face, and one that indicated a vulgar stupidity, aggravated still further by the proximity of a Norman complexion on cheeks that were like two ripe apples. It is possible that the eyes of M. de Cambremer retained behind their eyelids a trace of the sky of the Cotentin, so soft upon sunny days when the wayfarer amuses himself in watching, drawn up by the roadside, and counting in their hundreds the shadows of the poplars, but those eyelids, heavy, bleared and drooping, would have prevented the least flash of intelligence from escaping. And so, discouraged by the meagreness of that azure glance, one returned to the big crooked nose. By a transposition of the senses, M. de Cambremer looked at you with his nose. This nose of his was not ugly, it was if anything too handsome, too bold, too proud of its own importance. Arched, polished, gleaming, brand new, it was amply prepared to atone for the inadequacy of his eyes. Unfortunately, if the eyes are sometimes the organ through which our intelligence is revealed, the nose (to leave out of account the intimate solidarity and the unsuspected repercussion of one feature upon the rest), the nose is generally the organ in which stupidity is most readily displayed.

The propriety of the dark clothes which M. de Cambremer invariably wore, even in the morning, might well reassure those who were dazzled and exasperated by the insolent brightness of the seaside attire of people whom they did not know; still it was impossible to understand why the chief magistrate's wife should have declared with an air of discernment and authority, as a person who knows far more than you about the high society of Alençon, that on seeing M. de Cambremer one immediately felt oneself, even before one knew who he was, in the presence of a man of supreme distinction, of a man of perfect breeding, a change from the sort of person one saw at Balbec, a man in short in whose company one could breathe freely. He was to her, stifled by all those Balbec tourists who did not know her world, like a bottle of smelling salts. It seemed to me on the contrary that he was one of the people whom my grandmother would at once have set down as "all wrong," and that, as she had no conception of snobbishness, she would no doubt have been stupefied that he could have succeeded in winning the hand of Mlle. Legrandin, who must surely be difficult to please, having a brother who was "so refined." At best one might have said of M. de Cambremer's plebeian ugliness that it was redolent of the soil and preserved a very ancient local tradition; one was reminded, on examining his faulty features, which one would have liked to correct, of those names of little Norman towns as to the etymology of which my friend the curé was mistaken because the peasants, mispronouncing the names, or having misunderstood the Latin or Norman words that underlay them, have finally fixed in a barbarism to be found already in the cartularies, as Brichot would have said, a wrong meaning and a fault of pronunciation. Life in these little old towns may, for all that, be pleasant enough, and M. de Cambremer must have had his good points, for if it was in a mother's nature that the old Marquise should prefer her son to her daughter-in-law, on the other hand, she, who had other children, of whom two at least were not devoid of merit, was often heard to declare that the Marquis was, in her opinion, the best of the family. During the short time he had spent in the army, his messmates, finding Cambremer too long a name to pronounce, had given him the nickname Cancan, implying a flow of chatter, which he in no way merited. He knew how to brighten a dinner-party to which he was invited by saying when the fish (even if it were stale) or the entrée came in: " I say, that looks a fine animal." And his wife, who had adopted upon entering the family everything that she supposed to form part of their customs, put herself on the level of her husband's friends and perhaps sought to please him, like a mistress, and as though she had been involved in his bachelor existence, by saying in a careless tone when she was speaking of him to officers: " You shall see Cancan presently. Cancan has gone to Balbec, but he will be back this evening." She was furious at having compromised herself by coming to the Verdurins' and had done so only upon the entreaties of her mother-in-law and husband, in the hope of renewing the lease. But, being less well-bred than they, she made no secret of the ulterior motive and for the last fortnight had been making fun of this dinner-party to her women friends. " You know we are going to dine with our tenants. That will be well worth an increased rent. As a matter of fact, I am rather curious to see what they have done to our poor old la Raspelière" (as though she had been born in the house, and would find there all her old family associations). "Our old keeper told me only yesterday that you wouldn't know the place. I can't bear to think of all that must be going on there. I am sure we shall have to have the whole place disinfected before we move in again." She arrived haughty and morose, with the air of a great lady whose castle, owing to a state of war, is occupied by the enemy, but who nevertheless feels herself at home and makes a point of shewing the conquerors that they are intruding. Mme. de Cambremer could not see me at first for I was in a bay at the side of the room with M. de Charlus, who was telling me that he had heard from Morel that Morel's father had been an "agent" in my family, and that he, Charlus, credited me with sufficient intelligence and magnanimity (a term common to himself and Swann) to forego the mean and ignoble pleasure which vulgar little idiots (I was warned) would not have failed, in my place, to give themselves by revealing to our hosts details which they might regard as derogatory. "The mere fact that I take an interest in him and extend my protection over him, gives him a pre-eminence and wipes out the past," the Baron concluded. As I listened to him and promised the silence which I would have kept even without any hope of being considered in return intelligent and magnanimous, I was looking at Mme. de Cambremer. And I had difficulty in recognising the melting, savoury morsel which I had had beside me the other afternoon at tea-time, on the terrace at Balbec, in the Norman rock-cake that I now saw, hard as a rock, in which the faithful would in vain have tried to set their teeth. Irritated in anticipation by the knowledge that her husband inherited his mother's simple kindliness, which would make him assume a flattered expression whenever one of the faithful was presented to him, anxious however to perform her duty as a leader of society, when Brichot had been named to her she decided to make him and her husband acquainted, as she had seen her more fashionable friends do, but, anger or pride prevailing over the desire to shew her knowledge of the world, she said, not, as she ought to have said: "Allow me to introduce my husband," but: "I introduce you to my husband," holding aloft thus the banner of the Cambremers, without avail, for her husband bowed as low before Brichot as she had expected. But all Mme. de Cambremer's ill humour vanished in an instant when her eye fell on M. de Charlus, whom she knew by sight. Never had she succeeded in obtaining an introduction, even at the time of her intimacy with Swann. For as M. de Charlus always sided with the woman, with his sister-in-law against M. de Guermantes's mistresses, with Odette, at that time still unmarried, but an old flame of Swann's, against the new, he had, as a stern defender of morals and faithful protector of homes, given Odette—and kept—the promise that he would never allow himself to be presented to Mme. de Cambremer. She had certainly never guessed that it was at the Verdurins' that she was at length to meet this unapproachable person. M. de Cambremer knew that this was a great joy to her, so great that he himself was moved by it and looked at his wife with an air that implied: "You are glad now you decided to come, aren't you?" He spoke very little, knowing that he had married a superior woman. "I, all unworthy," he would say at every moment, and spontaneously quoted a fable of La Fontaine and one of Florian which seemed to him to apply to his ignorance, and at the same time to enable him, beneath the outward form of a contemptuous flattery, to shew the men of science who were not members of the Jockey that one might be a sportsman and yet have read fables. The unfortunate thing was that he knew only two of them. And so they kept cropping up. Mme. de Cambremer was no fool, but she had a number of extremely irritating habits. With her the corruption of names bore absolutely no trace of aristocratic disdain. She was not the person to say, like the Duchesse de Guermantes (whom the mere fact of her birth ought to have preserved even more than Mme. de Cambremer from such an absurdity), with a pretence of not remembering the unfashionable name (albeit it is now that of one of the women whom it is most difficult to approach) of Julien de Monchâteau: "a little Madame . . . Pica della Mirandola." No, when Mme. de Cambremer said a name wrong it was out of kindness of heart, so as not to appear to know some damaging fact, and when, in her sincerity, she admitted it, she tried to conceal it by altering it. If, for instance, she was defending a woman, she would try to conceal the fact, while determined not to lie to the person who had asked her to tell the truth, that Madame So-and-so was at the moment the mistress of M. Sylvain Lévy, and would say: "No . . . I know absolutely nothing about her, I fancy that people used to charge her with having inspired a passion in a gentleman whose name I don't know, something like Cahn, Kohn, Kuhn; anyhow, I believe the gentleman has been dead for years and that there was never anything between them." This is an analogous, but contrary process to that adopted by liars who think that if they alter their statement of what they have been doing when they make it to a mistress or merely to another man, their listener will not immediately see that the expression (like her Cahn, Kohn, Kuhn) is interpolated, is of a different texture from the rest of the conversation, has a double meaning.

Mme. Verdurin whispered in her husband's ear: "Shall I offer my arm to the Baron de Charlus? As you will have Mme. de Cambremer on your right, we might divide the honours." "No," said M. Verdurin, "since the other is higher in rank" (meaning that M. de Cambremer was a Marquis), "M. de Charlus is, strictly speaking, his inferior." "Very well, I shall put him beside the Princess." And Mme. Verdurin introduced Mme. Sherbatoff to M. de Charlus; each of them bowed in silence, with an air of knowing all about the other and of promising a mutual secrecy. M. Verdurin introduced me to M. de Cambremer. Before he had even begun to speak in his loud and slightly stammering voice, his tall figure and high complexion displayed in their oscillation the martial hesitation of a commanding officer who tries to put you at your ease and says: "I have heard about you, I shall see what can be done; your punishment shall be remitted; we don't thirst for blood here; it will be all right." Then, as he shook my hand: "I think you know my mother," he said to me. The word "think" seemed to him appropriate to the discretion of a first meeting, but not to imply any uncertainty, for he went on: "I have a note for you from her." M. de Cambremer took a childish pleasure in revisiting a place where he had lived for so long. "I am at home again," he said to Mme. Verdurin, while his eyes marvelled at recognising the flowers painted on panels over the doors, and the marble busts on their high pedestals. He might, all the same, have felt himself at sea, for Mme. Verdurin had brought with her a quantity of fine old things of her own. In this respect, Mme. Verdurin, while regarded by the Cambremers as having turned everything upside down, was not revolutionary but intelligently conservative in a sense which they did not understand. They were thus wrong in accusing her of hating the old house and of degrading it by hanging plain cloth curtains instead of their rich plush, like an ignorant parish priest reproaching a diocesan architect with putting back in its place the old carved wood which the cleric had thrown on the rubbish heap, and had seen fit to replace with ornaments purchased in the Place Saint-Sulpice. Furthermore, a herb garden was beginning to take the place, in front of the mansion, of the borders that were the pride not merely of the Cambremers but of their gardener. The latter, who regarded the Cambremers as his sole masters, and groaned beneath the yoke of the Verdurins, as though the place were under occupation for the moment by an invading army, went in secret to unburden his griefs to its dispossessed mistress, grew irate at the scorn that was heaped upon his araucarias, begonias, house-leeks, double dahlias, and at anyone's daring in so grand a place to grow such common plants as camomile and maidenhair. Mme. Verdurin felt this silent opposition and had made up her mind, if she took a long lease of la Raspelière or even bought the place, to make one of her conditions the dismissal of the gardener, by whom his old mistress, on the contrary, set great store. He had worked for her without payment, when times were bad, he adored her; but by that odd multiformity of opinion which we find in the lower orders, among whom the most profound moral scorn is embedded in the most passionate admiration, which in turn overlaps old and undying grudges, he used often to say of Mme. de Cambremer who, in '70, in a house that she owned in the East of France, surprised by the invasion, had been obliged to endure for a month the contact of the Germans: "What many people can't forgive Mme. la Marquise is that during the war she took the side of the Prussians and even had them to stay in her house. At any other time, I could understand it; but in war time, she ought not to have done it. It is not right." So that he was faithful to her unto death, venerated her for her goodness, and firmly believed that she had been guilty of treason. Mme. Verdurin was annoyed that M. de Cambremer should pretend to feel so much at home at la Raspelière. "You must notice a good many changes, all the same," she replied. "For one thing there were those big bronze Barbedienne devils and some horrid little plush chairs which I packed off at once to the attic, though even that is too good a place for them." After this bitter retort to M. de Cambremer, she offered him her arm to go in to dinner. He hesitated for a moment, saying to himself: "I can't, really, go in before M. de Charlus." But supposing the other to be an old friend of the house, seeing that he was not set in the post of honour, he decided to take the arm that was offered him and told Mme. Verdurin how proud he felt to be admitted into the symposium (so it was that he styled the little nucleus, not without a smile of satisfaction at his knowledge of the term). Cottard, who was seated next to M. de Charlus, beamed at him through his glass, to make his acquaintance and to break the ice, with a series of winks far more insistent than they would have been in the old days, and not interrupted by fits of shyness. And these engaging glances, enhanced by the smile that accompanied them, were no longer dammed by the glass but overflowed on all sides. The Baron, who readily imagined people of his own kind everywhere, had no doubt that Cottard was one, and was making eyes at him. At once he turned on the Professor the cold shoulder of the invert, as contemptuous of those whom he attracts as he is ardent in pursuit of such as attract him. No doubt, albeit each one of us speaks mendaciously of the pleasure, always refused him by destiny, of being loved, it is a general law, the application of which is by no means confined to the Charlus type, that the person whom we do not love and who does love us seems to us quite intolerable. To such a person, to a woman of whom we say not that she loves us but that she bores us, we prefer the society of any other, who has neither her charm, nor her looks, nor her brains. She will recover these, in our estimation, only when she has ceased to love us. In this light, we might see only the transposition, into odd terms, of this universal rule in the irritation aroused in an invert by a man who displeases him and runs after him. And so, whereas the ordinary man seeks to conceal what he feels, the invert is implacable in making it felt by the man who provokes it, as he would certainly not make it felt by a woman, M. de Charlus for instance by the Princesse de Guermantes, whose passion for him bored him, but flattered him. But when they see another man shew a peculiar liking for them, then, whether because they fail to realise that this liking is the same as their own, or because it annoys them to be reminded that this liking, which they glorify so long as it is they themselves that feel it, is regarded as a vice, or from a desire to rehabilitate themselves by a sensational display in circumstances in which it costs them nothing, or from a fear of being unmasked which they at once recover as soon as desire no longer leads them blindfold from one imprudence to another, or from rage at being subjected, by the equivocal attitude of another person, to the injury which, by their own attitude, if that other person attracted them, they would not be afraid to inflict on him, the men who do not in the least mind following a young man for miles, never taking their eyes off him in the theatre, even if he is with friends, and there is therefore a danger of their compromising him with them, may be heard, if a man who does not attract them merely looks at them, to say: "Sir, for what do you take me?" (simply because he takes them for what they are) "I don't understand, no, don't attempt to explain, you are quite mistaken," pass if need be from words to blows, and, to a person who knows the imprudent stranger, wax indignant: "What, you know that loathsome creature. He stares at one so! . . . A fine way to behave!" M. de Charlus did not go quite so far as this, but assumed the offended, glacial air adopted, when one appears to be suspecting them, by women who are not of easy virtue, even more by women who are. Furthermore, the invert brought face to face with an invert sees not merely an unpleasing image of himself which, being purely inanimate, could at the worst only injure his self-esteem, but a second self, living, acting in the same sphere, capable therefore of injuring him in his loves. And so it is from an instinct of self-preservation that he will speak evil of the possbile rival, whether to people who are able to do him some injury (nor does invert the first mind being thought a liar when he thus denounces invert the second before people who may know all about his own case), or to the young man whom he has "picked up," who is perhaps going to be snatched away from him and whom it is important to persuade that the very things which it is to his advantage to do with the speaker would be the bane of his life if he allowed himself to do them with the other person. To M. de Charlus, who was thinking perhaps of the—wholly imaginary—dangers in which the presence of this Cottard whose smile he misinterpreted might involve Morel, an invert who did not attract him was not merely a caricature of himself, but was a deliberate rival. A tradesman, practising an uncommon trade, who, on his arrival in the provincial town where he intends to settle for life discovers that, in the same square, directly opposite, the same trade is being carried on by a competitor, is no more discomfited than a Charlus who goes down to a quiet spot to make love unobserved and, on the day of his arrival, catches sight of the local squire or the barber, whose aspect and manner leave no room for doubt. The tradesman often comes to regard his competitor with hatred; this hatred degenerates at times into melancholy, and, if there be but a sufficient strain of heredity, one has seen in small towns the tradesman begin to shew signs of insanity which is cured only by his deciding to sell his stock and goodwill and remove to another place. The invert's rage is even more agonising. He has realised that from the first moment the squire and the barber have desired his young companion. Even though he repeat to him a hundred times daily that the barber and the squire are scoundrels whose contact would dishonour him, he is obliged, like Harpagon, to watch over his treasure, and rises in the night to make sure that it is not being stolen. And it is this no doubt that, even more than desire, or the convenience of habits shared in common, and almost as much as that experience of oneself which is the only true experience, makes one invert detect another with a rapidity and certainty that are almost infallible. He may be mistaken for a moment, but a rapid divination brings him back to the truth. And so M. de Charlus's error was brief. His divine discernment shewed him after the first minute that Cottard was not of his kind, and that he need not fear his advances either for himself, which would merely have annoyed him, or for Morel, which would have seemed to him a more serious matter. He recovered his calm, and as he was still beneath the influence of the transit of Venus Androgyne, now and again, he smiled a faint smile at the Verdurins without taking the trouble to open his mouth, merely curving his lips at one corner, and for an instant kindled a coquettish light in his eyes, he so obsessed with virility, exactly as his sister-in-law the Duchesse de Guermantes might have done. "Do you shoot much, Sir?" said M. Verdurin with a note of contempt to M. de Cambremer. "Has Ski told you of the near shave we had to-day?" Cottard inquired of the mistress. "I shoot mostly in the forest of Chantepie," replied M. de Cambremer. "No, I have told her nothing," said Ski. "Does it deserve its name?" Brichot asked M. de Cambremer, after a glance at me from the corner of his eye, for he had promised me that he would introduce the topic of derivations, begging me at the same time not to let the Cambremers know the scorn that he felt for those furnished by the Combray curé. "I am afraid I must be very stupid, but I don't grasp your question," said M. de Cambremer. "I mean to say: do many pies sing in it?" replied Brichot. Cottard meanwhile could not bear Mme. Verdurin's not knowing that they had nearly missed the train. "Out with it," Mme. Cottard said to her husband encouragingly, "tell us your odyssey." "Well, really, it is quite out of the ordinary," said the doctor, and repeated his narrative from the beginning. "When I saw that the train was in the station, I stood thunderstruck. It was all Ski's fault. You are somewhat wide of the mark in your information, my dear fellow! And there was Brichot waiting for us at the station!" "I assumed," said the scholar, casting around him what he could still muster of a glance and smiling with his thin lips, "that if you had been detained at Graincourt, it would mean that you had encountered some peripatetic siren." "Will you hold your tongue, if my wife were to hear you," said the Professor. "This wife of mine, it is jealous." "Ah! That Brichot," cried Ski, moved to traditional merriment by Brichot's spicy witticism, "he is always the same;" albeit he had no reason to suppose that the university don had ever indulged in obscenity. And, to embellish this consecrated utterance with the ritual gesture, he made as though he could not resist the desire to pinch Brichot's leg. "He never changes, the rascal," Ski went on, and without stopping to think of the effect, at once tragic and comic, that the don's semi-blindness gave to his words: "Always a sharp look-out for the ladies." "You see," said M. de Cambremer, "what it is to meet with a scholar. Here have I been shooting for fifteen years in the forest of Chantepie, and I've never even thought of what the name meant." Mme. de Cambremer cast a stern glance at her husband; she did not like him to humble himself thus before Brichot. She was even more annoyed when, at every "ready-made" expression that Cancan employed, Cottard, who knew the ins and outs of them all, having himself laboriously acquired them, pointed out to the Marquis, who admitted his stupidity, that they meant nothing: "Why 'stupid as a cabbage?' Do you suppose cabbages are stupider than anything else? You say: 'repeat the same thing thirty-six times.' Why thirty-six? Why do you say: 'sleep like a top?' Why 'Thunder of Brest?' Why 'play four hundred tricks?'" But at this, the defence of M. de Cambremer was taken up by Brichot who explained the origin of each of these expressions. But Mme. de Cambremer was occupied principally in examining the changes that the Verdurins had introduced at la Raspelière, in order that she might be able to criticise some, and import others, or possibly the same ones, to Féterne. "I keep wondering what that lustre is that's hanging all crooked. I can hardly recognise my old Raspelière," she went on, with a familiarly aristocratic air, as she might have spoken of an old servant meaning not so much to indicate his age as to say that she had seen him in his cradle. And, as she was a trifle bookish in her speech: "All the same," she added in an undertone, "I can't help feeling that if I were inhabiting another person's house, I should feel some compunction about altering everything like this." "It is a pity you didn't come with them," said Mme. Verdurin to M. de Charlus and Morel, hoping that M. de Charlus was now "enrolled" and would submit to the rule that they must all arrive by the same train. "You are sure that Chantepie means the singing magpie, Chochotte?" she went on, to shew that, like the great hostess that she was, she could join in every conversation at the same time. "Tell me something about this violinist," Mme. de Cambremer said to me, "he interests me; I adore music, and it seems to me that I have heard of him before, complete my education." She had heard that Morel had come with M. de Charlus and hoped, by getting the former to come to her house, to make friends with the latter. She added, however, so that I might not guess her reason for asking, "M. Brichot, too, interests me." For, even if she was highly cultivated, just as certain persons inclined to obesity eat hardly anything, and take exercise all day long without ceasing to grow visibly fatter, so Mme. de Cambremer might in vain master, and especially at Féterne, a philosophy that became ever more esoteric, music that became ever more subtle, she emerged from these studies only to weave plots that would enable her to cut the middle-class friends of her girlhood and to form the connexions which she had originally supposed to be part of the social life of her "in laws," and had then discovered to be far more exalted and remote. A philosopher who was not modern enough for her, Leibnitz, has said that the way is long from the intellect to the heart. This way Mme. de Cambremer had been no more capable than her brother of traversing. Abandoning the study of John Stuart Mill only for that of Lachelier, the less she believed in the reality of the external world, the more desperately she sought to establish herself, before she died, in a good position in it. In her passion for realism in art, no object seemed to her humble enough to serve as a model to painter or writer. A fashionable picture or novel would have made her feel sick; Tolstoi's mujiks, or Millet's peasants, were the extreme social boundary beyond which she did not allow the artist to pass. But to cross the boundary that limited her own social relations, to raise herself to an intimate acquaintance with Duchesses, this was the goal of all her efforts, so ineffective had the spiritual treatment to which she subjected herself, by the study of great masterpieces, proved in overcoming the congenital and morbid snobbishness that had developed in her. This snobbishness had even succeeded in curing certain tendencies to avarice and adultery to which in her younger days she had been inclined, just as certain peculiar and permanent pathological conditions seem to render those who are subject to them immune to other maladies. I could not, all the same, refrain, as I listened to her, from giving her credit, without deriving any pleasure from them, for the refinement of her expressions. They were those that are used, at a given date, by all the people of the same intellectual breadth, so that the refined expression provides us at once, like the arc of a circle, with the means to describe and limit the entire circumference. And so the effect of these expressions is that the people who employ them bore me immediately, because I feel that I already know them, but are generally regarded as superior persons, and have often been offered me as delightful and unappreciated companions. " You cannot fail to be aware, Madame, that many forest regions take their name from the animals that inhabit them. Next to the forest of Chantepie, you have the wood Chantereine." "I don't know who the queen may be, but you are not very polite to her," said M. de Cambremer. "One for you, Chochotte," said Mme. de Verdurin. "And apart from that, did you have a pleasant journey?" "We encountered only vague human beings who thronged the train. But I must answer M. de Cambremer's question; *reine,* in this instance, is not the wife of a king, but a frog. It is the name that the frog has long retained in this district, as is shewn by the station, Renneville, which ought to be spelt Reineville." "I say, that seems a fine animal," said M. de Cambremer to Mme. Verdurin, pointing to a fish. (It was one of the compliments by means of which he considered that he paid his scot at a dinner-party, and gave an immediate return of hospitality. "There is no need to invite them," he would often say, in speaking of one or other couple of their friends to his wife. "They were delighted to have us. It was they that thanked me for coming.) I must tell you, all the same, that I have been going every day for years to Renneville, and I have never seen any more frogs there than anywhere else. Madame de Cambremer brought the curé here from a parish where she owns a considerable property, who has very much the same turn of mind as yourself, it seems to me. He has written a book." "I know, I have read it with immense interest," Brichot replied hypocritically. The satisfaction that his pride received indirectly from this answer made M. de Cambremer laugh long and loud. "Ah! well, the author of, what shall I say, this geography, this glossary, dwells at great length upon the name of a little place of which we were formerly, if I may say so, the Lords, and which is called Pont-à-Couleuvre. Of course I am only an ignorant rustic compared with such a fountain of learning, but I have been to Pont-à-Couleuvre a thousand times if he's been there once, and devil take me if I ever saw one of his beastly serpents there, I say beastly, in spite of the tribute the worthy La Fontaine pays them." (*The Man and the Serpent* was one of his two fables.) "You have not seen any, and you have been quite right," replied Brichot. "Undoubtedly, the writer you mention knows his subject through and through, he has written a remarkable book." "There!" exclaimed Mme. de Cambremer, "that book, there's no other word for it, is a regular Benedictine *opus*." "No doubt he has consulted various polyptychs (by which we mean the lists of benefices and cures of each diocese), which may have furnished him with the names of lay patrons and ecclesiastical collators. But there are other sources. One of the most learned of my friends has delved into them. He found that the place in question was named Pont-à-Quileuvre. This odd name encouraged him to carry his researches farther, to a Latin text in which the bridge that your friend supposes to be infested with serpents is styled *Pons cui aperit:* A closed bridge that was opened only upon due payment." "You were speaking of frogs. I, when I find myself among such learned folk, feel like the frog before the areopagus," (this being his other fable), said Cancan who often indulged, with a hearty laugh, in this pleasantry thanks to which he imagined himself to be making, at one and the same time, out of humility and with aptness, a profession of ignorance and a display of learning. As for Cottard, blocked upon one side by M. de Charlus's silence, and driven to seek an outlet elsewhere, he turned to me with one of those questions which so impressed his patients when it hit the mark and shewed them that he could put himself so to speak inside their bodies; if on the other hand it missed the mark, it enabled him to check certain theories, to widen his previous point of view. "When you come to a relatively high altitude, such as this where we now are, do you find that the change increases your tendency to choking fits?" he asked me with the certainty of either arousing admiration or enlarging his own knowledge. M. de Cambremer heard the question and smiled. "I can't tell you how amused I am to hear that you have choking fits," he flung at me across the table. He did not mean that it made him happy, though as a matter of fact it did. For this worthy man could not hear any reference to another person's sufferings without a feeling of satisfaction and a spasm of hilarity which speedily gave place to the instinctive pity of a kind heart. But his words had another meaning which was indicated more precisely by the clause that followed: "It amuses me," he explained, "because my sister has them too." And indeed it did amuse him, as it would have amused him to hear me mention as one of my friends a person who was constantly coming to their house. "How small the world is," was the reflexion which he formed mentally and which I saw written upon his smiling face when Cottard spoke to me of my choking fits. And these began to establish themselves, from the evening of this dinner-party, as a sort of interest in common, after which M. de Cambremer never failed to inquire, if only to hand on a report to his sister. As I answered the questions with which his wife kept plying me about Morel, my thoughts returned to a conversation I had had with my mother that afternoon. Having, without any attempt to dissuade me from going to the Verdurins' if there was a chance of my being amused there, suggested that it was a house of which my grandfather would not have approved, which would have made him exclaim: "On guard!" my mother had gone on to say: "Listen, Judge Toureuil and his wife told me they had been to luncheon with Mme. Bontemps. They asked me no questions. But I seemed to gather from what was said that your marriage to Albertine would be the joy of her aunt's life. I think the real reason is that they are all extremely fond of you. At the same time the style in which they suppose that you would be able to keep her, the sort of friends they more or less know that we have, all that is not, I fancy, left out of account, although it may be a minor consideration. I should not have mentioned it to you myself, because I attach no importance to it, but as I imagine that people will mention it to you, I prefer to get a word in first." "But you yourself, what do you think of her?" I asked my mother. "Well, it's not I that am going to marry her. You might certainly do a thousand times better. But I feel that your grandmother would not have liked me to influence you. As a matter of fact, I cannot tell you what I think of Albertine; I don't think of her. I shall say to you, like Madame de Sévigné: 'She has good qualities, at least I suppose so. But at this first stage I can praise her only by negatives. One thing she is not, she has not the Rennes accent. In time, I shall perhaps say, she is something else. And I shall always think well of her if she can make you happy.'" But by these very words which left it to myself to decide my own happiness, my mother had plunged me in that state of doubt in which I had been plunged long ago when, my father having allowed me to go to *Phèdre* and, what was more, to take to writing, I had suddenly felt myself burdened with too great a responsibility, the fear of distressing him, and that melancholy which we feel when we cease to obey orders which, from one day to another, keep the future hidden, and realise that we have at last begun to live in real earnest, as a grown-up person, the life, the only life that any of us has at his disposal.

Perhaps the best thing would be to wait a little longer, to begin by regarding Albertine as in the past, so as to find out whether I really loved her. I might take her, as a distraction, to see the Verdurins, and this thought reminded me that I had come there myself that evening only to learn whether Mme. Putbus was staying there or was expected. In any case, she was not dining with them. "Speaking of your friend Saint-Loup," said Mme. de Cambremer, using an expression which shewed a closer sequence in her ideas than her remarks might have led one to suppose, for if she spoke to me about music she was thinking about the Guermantes; "you know that everybody is talking about his marriage to the niece of the Princesse de Guermantes. I may tell you that, so far as I am concerned, all that society gossip leaves me cold." I was seized by a fear that I might have spoken unfeelingly to Robert about the girl in question, a girl full of sham originality, whose mind was as mediocre as her actions were violent. Hardly ever do we hear anything that does not make us regret something that we have said. I replied to Mme. de Cambremer, truthfully as it happened, that I knew nothing about it, and that anyhow I thought that the girl was still too young to be engaged. "That is perhaps why it is not yet official, anyhow there is a lot of talk about it." "I ought to warn you," Mme. Verdurin observed dryly to Mme. de Cambremer, having heard her talking to me about Morel and supposing, when Mme. de Cambremer lowered her voice to speak of Saint-Loup's engagement, that Morel was still under discussion. "You needn't expect any light music here. In matters of art, you know, the faithful who come to my Wednesdays, my children as I call them, are all fearfully advanced," she added with an air of proud terror. "I say to them sometimes: My dear people, you move too fast for your Mistress, not that she has ever been said to be afraid of anything daring. Every year it goes a little farther; I can see the day coming when they will have no more use for Wagner or Indy." "But it is splendid to be advanced, one can never be advanced enough," said Mme. de Cambremer, scrutinising as she spoke every corner of the dining-room, trying to identify the things that her mother-in-law had left there, those that Mme. Verdurin had brought with her, and to convict the latter red-handed of want of taste. At the same time, she tried to get me to talk of the subject that interested her most, M. de Charlus. She thought it touching that he should be looking after a violinist. "He seems intelligent." "Why, his mind is extremely active for a man of his age," said I. "Age? But he doesn't seem at all old, look, the hair is still young." (For, during the last three or four years, the word hair had been used with the article by one of those unknown persons who launch the literary fashions, and everybody at the same radius from the centre as Mme. de Cambremer would say "the hair," not without an affected smile. At the present day, people still say "the hair" but, from an excessive use of the article, the pronoun will be born again.) "What interests me most about M. de Charlus," she went on, "is that one can feel that he has the gift. I may tell you that I attach little importance to knowledge. Things that can be learned do not interest me." This speech was not incompatible with Mme. de Cambremer's own distinction which was, in the fullest sense, imitated and acquired. But it so happened that one of the things which one had to know at that moment was that knowledge is nothing, and is not worth a straw when compared with originality. Mme. de Cambremer had learned, with everything else, that one ought not to learn anything. "That is why," she explained to me, "Brichot, who has an interesting side to him, for I am not one to despise a certain spicy erudition, interests me far less." But Brichot, at that moment, was occupied with one thing only; hearing people talk about music, he trembled lest the subject should remind Mme. Verdurin of the death of Dechambre. He decided to say something that would avert that harrowing memory. M. de Cambremer provided him with an opportunity with the question: "You mean to say that wooded places always take their names from animals?" "Not at all," replied Brichot, proud to display his learning before so many strangers, among whom, I had told him, he would be certain to interest one at least. "We have only to consider how often, even in the names of people, a tree is preserved, like a fern in a piece of coal. One of our Conscript Fathers is called M. de Saulces de Freycinet, which means, if I be not mistaken, a spot planted with willows and ashes, *salix et fraxinetum;* his nephew M. de Selve scombines more trees still, since he is named de Selves, *de sylvis.*" Saniette was delighted to see the conversation take so animated a turn. He could, since Brichot was talking all the time, preserve a silence which would save him from being the butt of M. and Mme. Verdurin's wit. And growing even more sensitive in his joy at being set free, he had been touched when he heard M. Verdurin, notwithstanding the formality of so grand a dinner-party, tell the butler to put a decanter of water in front of M. Saniette who never drank anything else. (The generals responsible for the death of most soldiers insist upon their being well fed.) Moreover, Mme. Verdurin had actually smiled once at Saniette. Decidedly, they were kind people. He was not going to be tortured any more. At this moment the meal was interrupted by one of the party whom I have forgotten to mention, an eminent Norwegian philosopher who spoke French very well but very slowly, for the twofold reason that, in the first place, having learned the language only recently and not wishing to make mistakes (he did, nevertheless, make some), he referred each word to a sort of mental dictionary, and secondly, being a metaphysician, he always thought of what he intended to say while he was saying it, which, even in a Frenchman, causes slowness of utterance. He was, otherwise, a charming person, although similar in appearance to many other people, save in one respect. This man so slow in his diction (there was an interval of silence after every word) acquired a startling rapidity in escaping from the room as soon as he had said good-bye. His haste made one suppose, the first time one saw him, that he was suffering from colic or some even more urgent need.

"My dear—colleague," he said to Brichot, after deliberating in his mind whether colleague was the correct term, "I have a sort of—desire to know whether there are other trees in the—nomenclature of your beautiful French—Latin—Norman tongue. Madame" (he meant Madame Verdurin, although he dared not look at her) "has told me that you know everything. Is not this precisely the moment?" "No, it is the moment for eating," interrupted Mme. Verdurin, who saw the dinner becoming interminable. "Very well," the Scandinavian replied, bowing his head over his plate with a resigned and sorrowful smile. "But I must point out to Madame that if I have permitted myself this questionnaire—pardon me, this questation—it is because I have to return to-morrow to Paris to dine at the Tour d'Argent or at the Hôtel Meurice. My French—brother—M. Boutroux is to address us there about certain seances of spiritualism—pardon me, certain spirituous evocations which he has controlled." "The Tour d'Argent is not nearly as good as they make out," said Mme. Verdurin sourly. "In fact, I have had some disgusting dinners there." "But am I mistaken, is not the food that one consumes at Madame's table an example of the finest French cookery?" "Well, it is not positively bad," replied Mme. Verdurin, sweetening. "And if you come next Wednesday, it will be better." "But I am leaving on Monday for Algiers, and from there I am going to the Cape. And when I am at the Cape of Good Hope, I shall no longer be able to meet my illustrious colleague—pardon me, I shall no longer be able to meet my brother." And he set to work obediently, after offering these retrospective apologies, to devour his food at a headlong pace. But Brichot was only too delighted to be able to furnish other vegetable etymologies, and replied, so greatly interesting the Norwegian that he again stopped eating, but with a sign to the servants that they might remove his plate and help him to the next course. "One of the Forty," said Brichot, "is named Houssaye, or a place planted with hollies; in the name of a brilliant diplomat, d'Ormesson, you will find the elm, the *ulmus* beloved of Virgil, which has given its name to the town of Ulm; in the names of his colleagues, M. de la Boulaye, the birch (*bouleau*); M. d'Aunay, the alder (*aune*), M. de Buissière, the box (*buis*), M. Albaret, the sapwood (*aubier*)," (I made a mental note that I must tell this to Céleste) "M. de Cholet, the cabbage (*chou*), and the apple-tree (*pommier*) in the name of M. de la Pommeraye, whose lectures we used to attend, do you remember, Saniette, in the days when the worthy Porel had been sent to the farthest ends of the earth, as Proconsul in Odeonia?" "You said that Cholet was derived from *chou*," I remarked to Brichot. "Am I to suppose that the name of a station I passed before reaching Doncières, Saint-Frichoux, comes from *chou* also?" "No, Saint-Frichoux is *Sanctus Fructuosus*, as *Sanctus Ferreolus* gave rise to Saint-Fargeau, but that is not Norman in the least." "He knows too much, he's borling us," the Princess muttered softly. "There are so many other names that interest me, but I can't ask you everything at once." And, turning to Cottard, "Is Madame Putbus here?" I asked him. On hearing Brichot utter the name of Saniette, M. Verdurin cast at his wife and at Cottard an ironical glance which confounded their timid guest. "No, thank heaven," replied Mme. Verdurin, who had overheard my question, "I have managed to turn her thoughts in the direction of Venice, we are rid of her for this year." "I shall myself be entitled presently to two trees," said M. de Charlus, "for I have more or less taken a little house between Saint-Martin-du-Chêne and Saint-Pierre-des-Ifs." "But that is quite close to here, I hope that you will come over often with Charlie Morel. You have only to come to an arrangement with our little group about the trains, you are only a step from Doncières," said Mme. Verdurin, who hated people's not coming by the same train and not arriving at the hours when she sent carriages to meet them. She knew how stiff the climb was to la Raspelière, even if you took the zigzag path, behind Féterne, which was half-an-hour longer; she was afraid that those of her guests who kept to themselves might not find carriages to take them, or even, having in reality stayed away, might plead the excuse that they had not found a carriage at Douville-Féterne, and had not felt strong enough to make so stiff a climb on foot. To this invitation M. de Charlus responded with a silent bow. "He's not the sort of person you can talk to any day of the week, he seems a tough customer," the doctor whispered to Ski, for having remained quite simple, notwithstanding a surface-dressing of pride, he made no attempt to conceal the fact that Charlus had snubbed him. "He is doubtless unaware that at all the watering-places, and even in Paris in the wards, the physicians, who naturally regard me as their 'chief,' make it a point of honour to introduce me to all the noblemen present, not that they need to be asked twice. It makes my stay at the spas quite enjoyable," he added carelessly. "Indeed at Doncières the medical officer of the regiment, who is the doctor who attends the Colonel, invited me to luncheon to meet him, saying that I was fully entitled to dine with the General. And that General is a Monsieur *de* something. I don't know whether his title-deeds are more or less ancient than those of this Baron." "Don't you worry about him, his is a very humble coronet," replied Ski in an undertone, and added some vague statement including a word of which I caught only the last syllable, *-ast,* being engaged in listening to what Brichot was saying to M. de Charlus. "No, as for that, I am sorry to say, you have probably one tree only, for if Saint-Martin-du-Chêne is obviously *Sanctus Martinus juxta quercum,* on the other hand, the word *if* may be simply the root *ave, eve,* which means moist, as in Aveyron, Lodève, Yvette, and which you see survive in our kitchen-sinks (*éviers*). It is the word *eau* which in Breton is represented by *ster,* Stermaria, Sterlaer, Sterbouest, Ster-en-Dreuchen." I heard no more, for whatever the pleasure I might feel on hearing again the name Stermaria, I could not help listening to Cottard, next to whom I was seated, as he murmured to Ski: "Indeed! I was not aware of it. So he is a gentleman who has learned to look behind! He is one of the happy band, is he? He hasn't got rings of fat round his eyes, all the same. I shall have to keep my feet well under me, or he may start squeezing them. But I'm not at all surprised. I am used to seeing noblemen in the bath, in their birthday suits, they are all more or less degenerates. I don't talk to them, because after all I am in an official position and it might do me harm. But they know quite well who I am." Saniette, whom Brichot's appeal had frightened, was beginning to breathe again, like a man who is afraid of the storm when he finds that the lightning has not been followed by any sound of thunder, when he heard M. Verdurin interrogate him, fastening upon him a stare which did not spare the wretch until he had finished speaking, so as to put him at once out of countenance and prevent him from recovering his composure. "But you never told us that you went to those *matinées* at the Odéon, Saniette?" Trembling like a recruit before a bullying serjeant, Saniette replied, making his speech as diminutive as possible, so that it might have a better chance of escaping the blow: "Only once, to the *Chercheuse*." "What's that he says?" shouted M. Verdurin, with an air of disgust and fury combined, knitting his brows as though it was all he could do to grasp something unintelligible. "It is impossible to understand what you say, what have you got in your mouth?" inquired M. Verdurin, growing more and more furious, and alluding to Saniette's defective speech. "Poor Saniette, I won't have him made unhappy," said Mme. Verdurin in a tone of false pity, so as to leave no one in doubt as to her husband's insolent intention. "I was at the Ch... Che..." "Che, che, try to speak distinctly," said M. Verdurin, "I can't understand a word you say." Almost without exception, the faithful burst out laughing and they suggested a band of cannibals in whom the sight of a wound on a white man's skin has aroused the thirst for blood. For the instinct of imitation and absence of courage govern society and the mob alike. And we all of us laugh at a person whom we see being made fun of, which does not prevent us from venerating him ten years later in a circle where he is admired. It is in like manner that the populace banishes or acclaims its kings. "Come, now, it is not his fault," said Mme. Verdurin. "It is not mine either, people ought not to dine out if they can't speak properly." "I was at the *Chercheuse d'Esprit* by Favart." "What! It's the *Chercheuse d'Esprit* that you call the *Chercheuse?* Why, that's marvellous! I might have tried for a hundred years without guessing it," cried M. Verdurin, who all the same would have decided immediately that you were not literary, were not artistic, were not "one of us," if he had heard you quote the full title of certain works. For instance, one was expected to say the *Malade*, the *Bourgeois;* and whoso would have added *imaginaire* or *gentilhomme* would have shewn that he did not understand "shop," just as in a drawing-room a person proves that he is not in society by saying "M. de Montesquiou-Fézensac" instead of "M. de Montesquiou." "But it is not so extraordinary," said Saniette, breathless with emotion but smiling, albeit he was in no smiling mood. Mme. Verdurin could not contain herself: "Yes, indeed!" she cried with a titter. "You may be quite sure that nobody would ever have guessed that you meant the *Chercheuse d'Esprit.*" M. Verdurin went on in a gentler tone, addressing both Saniette and Brichot: "It is quite a pretty piece, all the same, the *Chercheuse d'Esprit.*" Uttered in a serious tone, this simple phrase, in which one could detect no trace of malice, did Saniette as much good and aroused in him as much gratitude as a deliberate compliment. He was unable to utter a single word and preserved a happy silence. Brichot was more loquacious. "It is true," he replied to M. Verdurin, "and if it could be passed off as the work of some Sarmatian or Scandinavian author, we might put forward the *Chercheuse d'Esprit* as a candidate for the vacant post of masterpiece. But, be it said without any disrespect to the shade of the gentle Favart, he had not the Ibsenian temperament." (Immediately he blushed to the roots of his hair, remembering the Norwegian philosopher who appeared troubled because he was seeking in vain to discover what vegetable the *buis* might be that Brichot had cited a little earlier in connexion with the name Bussière.) "However, now that Porel's satrapy is filled by a functionary who is a Tolstoist of rigorous observance, it may come to pass that we shall witness *Anna Karenina* or *Resurrection* beneath the Odeonian architrave." "I know the portrait of Favart to which you allude," said M. de Charlus. "I have seen a very fine print of it at Comtesse Molé's." The name of Comtesse Molé made a great impression upon Mme. Verdurin. "Oh! So you go to Mme. de Molé's!" she exclaimed. She supposed that people said Comtesse Molé, Madame Molé, simply as an abbreviation, as she heard people say "the Rohans" or in contempt, as she herself said: "Madame la Trémoïlle." She had no doubt that Comtesse Molé, who knew the Queen of Greece and the Principessa di Caprarola, had as much right as anybody to the particle, and for once in a way had decided to bestow it upon so brilliant a personage, and one who had been extremely civil to herself. And so, to make it clear that she had spoken thus on purpose and did not grudge the Comtesse her "de," she went on: "But I had no idea that you knew Madame de Molé!" as though it had been doubly extraordinary, both that M. de Charlus should know the lady, and that Mme. Verdurin should not know that he knew her. Now society, or at least the people to whom M. de Charlus gave that name, forms a relatively homogeneous and compact whole. And so it is comprehensible that, in the incongruous vastness of the middle classes, a barrister may say to somebody who knows one of his school friends: "But how in the world do you come to know him?" whereas to be surprised at a Frenchman's knowing the meaning of the word *temple* or *forest* would be hardly more extraordinary than to wonder at the hazards that might have brought together M. de Charlus and the Comtesse Molé. What is more, even if such an acquaintance had not been derived quite naturally from the laws that govern society, how could there be anything strange in the fact of Mme. Verdurin's not knowing of it, since she was meeting M. de Charlus for the first time, and his relations with Mme. Molé were far from being the only thing that she did not know with regard to him, about whom, to tell the truth, she knew nothing. "Who was it that played this *Chercheuse d'esprit,* my good Saniette?" asked M. Verdurin. Albeit he felt that the storm had passed, the old antiquarian hesitated before answering. "There you go," said Mme. Verdurin, "you frighten him, you make fun of everything that he says, and then you expect him to answer. Come along, tell us who played the part, and you shall have some galantine to take home," said Mme. Verdurin, making a cruel allusion to the penury into which Saniette had plunged himself by trying to rescue the family of a friend. "I can remember only that it was Mme. Samary who played the Zerbine," said Saniette. "The Zerbine? What in the world is that," M. Verdurin shouted, as though the house were on fire. "It is one of the parts in the old repertory, like

Captain Fracasse, as who should say the Fire-eater, the Pedant." "Ah, the pedant, that's yourself. The Zerbine! No, really the man's mad," exclaimed M. Verdurin. Mme. Verdurin looked at her guests and laughed as though to apologise for Saniette. "The Zerbine, he imagines that everybody will know at once what it means. You are like M. de Longepierre, the stupidest man I know, who said to us quite calmly the other day 'the Banat.' Nobody had any idea what he meant. Finally we were informed that it was a province in Serbia." To put an end to Saniette's torture, which hurt me more than it hurt him, I asked Brichot if he knew what the word Balbec meant. "Balbec is probably a corruption of Dalbec," he told me. "One would have to consult the charters of the Kings of England, Overlords of Normandy, for Balbec was held of the Barony of Dover, for which reason it was often styled Balbec d'Outre-Mer, Balbec-en-Terre. But the Barony of Dover was itself held of the Bishopric of Bayeux, and, notwithstanding the rights that were temporarily enjoyed in the abbey by the Templars, from the time of Louis d'Harcourt, Patriarch of Jerusalem and Bishop of Bayeux, it was the Bishops of that diocese who collated to the benefice of Balbec. So it was explained to me by the incumbent of Douville, a bald person, eloquent, fantastic, and a devotee of the table, who lives by the Rule of Brillat-Savarin, and who expounded to me in slightly sibylline language a loose pedagogy, while he fed me upon some admirable fried potatoes." While Brichot smiled to shew how witty it was to combine matters so dissimilar and to employ an ironically lofty diction in treating of commonplace things, Saniette was trying to find a loophole for some clever remark which would raise him from the abyss into which he had fallen. The witty remark was what was known as a "comparison," but had changed its form, for there is an evolution in wit as in literary styles, an epidemic that disappears has its place taken by another, and so forth. . . . At one time the typical "comparison" was the "height of. . . ." But this was out of date, no one used it any more, there was only Cottard left to say still, on occasion, in the middle of a game of piquet: "Do you know what is the height of absent-mindedness, it is to think that the Edict (*l'édit*) of Nantes was an Englishwoman." These "heights" had been replaced by nicknames. In reality it was still the old "comparison," but, as the nickname was in fashion, people did not observe the survival. Unfortunately for Saniette, when these "comparisons" were not his own, and as a rule were unknown to the little nucleus, he produced them so timidly that, notwithstanding the laugh with which he followed them up to indicate their humorous nature, nobody saw the point. And if on the other hand the joke was his own, as he had generally hit upon it in conversation with one of the faithful, and the latter had repeated it, appropriating the authorship, the joke was in that case known, but not as being Saniette's. And so when he slipped in one of these it was recognised, but, because he was its author, he was accused of plagiarism. "Very well, then," Brichot continued, "Bec, in Norman, is a stream; there is the Abbey of Bec, Mobec, the stream from the march (Mor or Mer meant a marsh, as in Morville, or in Bricquemar, Alvimare, Cambremer), Bricquebec the stream from the high ground coming from Briga, a fortified place, as in Bricqueville, Bricquebose, le Bric, Briand, or indeed Brice, bridge, which is the same as *bruck* in German (Innsbruck), and as the English *bridge* which ends so many place-names (Cambridge, for instance). You have moreover in Normandy many other instances of bec: Caudebec. Bolbec, le Robec, le Bec-Hellouin, Becquerel. It is the Norman form of the German *bach*, Offenbach, Anspach. Varaguebec, from the old word *varaigne*, equivalent to *warren*, preserved woods or ponds. As for Dal," Brichot went on, "it is a form of *thal*, a valley: Darnetal, Rosendal, and indeed, close to Louviers, Becdal. The river that has given its name to Balbec, is, by the way, charming. Seen from a *falaise* (*fels* in German, you have indeed, not far from here, standing on a height, the picturesque town of Falaise), it runs close under the spires of the church, which is actually a long way from it, and seems to be reflecting them." "I should think so," said I, "that is an effect that Elstir admires greatly. I have seen several sketches of it in his studio." "Elstir! You know Tiche," cried Mme. Verdurin. "But do you know that we used to be the dearest friends. Thank heaven, I never see him now. No, but ask Cottard, Brichot, he used to have his place laid at my table, he came every day. Now, there's a man of whom you can say that it has done him no good to leave our little nucleus. I shall shew you presently some flowers he painted for me; you shall see the difference from the things he is doing now, which I don't care for at all, not at all! Why! I made him do me a portrait of Cottard, not to mention all the sketches he has made of me." "And he gave the Professor purple hair," said Mme. Cottard, forgetting that at the time her husband had not been even a Fellow of the College. "I don't know, Sir, whether you find that my husband has purple hair." "That doesn't matter," said Mme. Verdurin, raising her chin with an air of contempt for Mme. Cottard and of admiration for the man of whom she was speaking, "he was a brave colourist, a fine painter. Whereas," she added, turning again to myself, "I don't know whether you call it painting, all those huge she-devils of composition, those vast structures he exhibits now that he has given up coming to me. For my part, I call it daubing, it's all so hackneyed, and besides, it lacks relief, personality. It's anybody's work." "He revives the grace of the eighteenth century, but in a modern form," Saniette broke out, fortified and reassured by my affability. "But I prefer Helleu." "He's not in the least like Helleu," said Mme. Verdurin. "Yes, he has the fever of the eighteenth century. He's a steam Watteau," and he began to laugh. "Old, old as the hills, I've had that served up to me for years," said M. Verdurin, to whom indeed Ski had once repeated the remark, but as his own invention. "It's unfortunate that when once in a way you say something quite amusing and make it intelligible, it is not your own." "I'm sorry about it," Mme. Verdurin went on, "because he was really gifted, he has wasted a charming temperament for painting. Ah! if he had stayed with us! Why, he would have become the greatest landscape painter of our day. And it is a woman that has dragged him down so low! Not that that surprises me, for he was a pleasant enough man, but common. At bottom, he was a mediocrity. I may tell you that I felt it at once. Really, he never interested me. I was very fond of him, that was all. For one thing, he was so dirty. Tell me, do you, now, really like people who never wash?" "What is this charmingly coloured thing that we are eating?" asked Ski. "It is called strawberry mousse," said Mme. Verdurin. "But it is ex-qui-site. You ought to open bottles of Château-Margaux, Château-Lafite, port wine." "I can't tell you how he amuses me, he never drinks anything but water," said Mme. Verdurin, seeking to cloak with her delight at such a flight of fancy her alarm at the thought of so prodigal an outlay. "But not to drink," Ski went on, "you shall fill all our glasses, they will bring in marvellous peaches, huge nectarines, there against the sunset; it will be as gorgeous as a fine Veronese." "It would cost almost as much," M. Verdurin murmured. "But take away those cheeses with their hideous colour," said Ski, trying to snatch the plate from before his host, who defended his gruyère with his might and main. "You can realise that I don't regret Elstir," Mme. Verdurin said to me, "that one is far more gifted. Elstir is simply hard work, the man who can't make himself give up painting when he would like to. He is the good student, the slavish competitor. Ski, now, only follows his own fancy. You will see him light a cigarette in the middle of dinner." "After all, I can't see why you wouldn't invite his wife," said Cottard, "he would be with us still." "Will you mind what you're saying, please, I don't open my doors to street-walkers, Monsieur le Professeur," said Mme. Verdurin, who had, on the contrary, done everything in her power to make Elstir return, even with his wife. But before they were married she had tried to make them quarrel, had told Elstir that the woman he loved was stupid, dirty, immoral, a thief. For once in a way she had failed to effect a breach. It was with the Verdurin salon that Elstir had broken; and he was glad of it, as converts bless the illness or misfortune that has withdrawn them from the world and has made them learn the way of salvation. "He really is magnificent, the Professor," she said. "Why not declare outright that I keep a disorderly house. Anyone would think you didn't know what Madame Elstir was like. I would sooner have the lowest street-walker at my table! Oh no, I don't stand for that sort of thing. Besides I may tell you that it would have been stupid of me to overlook the wife, when the husband no longer interests me, he is out of date, he can't even draw." "That is extraordinary in a man of his intelligence," said Cottard. "Oh, no!" replied Mme. Verdurin, "even at the time when he had talent, for he had it, the wretch, and to spare, what was tiresome about him was that he had not a spark of intelligence." Mme. Verdurin, in passing this judgment upon Elstir, had not waited for their quarrel, or until she had ceased to care for his painting. The fact was that, even at the time when he formed part of the little group, it would happen that Elstir spent the whole day in the company of some woman whom, rightly or wrongly, Mme. Verdurin considered a goose, which, in her opinion, was not the conduct of an intelligent man. "No," she observed with an air of finality, "I consider that his wife and he are made for one another. Heaven knows, there isn't a more boring creature on the face of the earth, and I should go mad if I had to spend a couple of hours with her. But people say that he finds her very intelligent. There's no use denying it, our Tiche was *extremely stupid.* I have seen him bowled over by people you can't conceive, worthy idiots we should never have allowed into our little clan. Well! He wrote to them, he argued with them, he, Elstir! That doesn't prevent his having charming qualities, oh, charming and deliciously absurd, naturally." For Mme. Verdurin was convinced that men who are truly remarkable are capable of all sorts of follies. A false idea in which there is nevertheless a grain of truth. Certainly, people's follies are insupportable. But a want of balance which we discover only in course of time is the consequence of the entering into a human brain of delicacies for which it is not regularly adapted. So that the oddities of charming people exasperate us, but there are few if any charming people who are not, at the same time, odd. "Look, I shall be able to shew you his flowers now," she said to me, seeing that her husband was making signals to her to rise. And she took M. de Cambremer's arm again. M. Verdurin tried to apologise for this to M. de Charlus, as soon as he had got rid of Mme. de Cambremer, and to give him his reasons, chiefly for the pleasure of discussing these social refinements with a gentleman of title, momentarily the inferior of those who assigned to him the place to which they considered him entitled. But first of all he was anxious to make it clear to M. de Charlus that intellectually he esteemed him too highly to suppose that he could pay any attention to these trivialities. "Excuse my mentioning so small a point," he began, "for I can understand how little such things mean to you. Middle-class minds pay attention to them, but the others, the artists, the people who are really of our sort, don't give a rap for them. Now, from the first words we exchanged, I realised that you were one of us!" M. de Charlus, who gave a widely different meaning to this expression, drew himself erect. After the doctor's oglings, he found his host's insulting frankness suffocating. "Don't protest, my dear Sir, you are one of us, it is plain as daylight," replied M. Verdurin. "Observe that I have no idea whether you practise any of the arts, but that is not necessary. It is not always sufficient. Dechambre, who has just died, played exquisitely, with the most vigorous execution, but he was not one of us, you felt at once that he was not one of us. Brichot is not one of us. Morel is, my wife is, I can feel that you are. . . ." "What were you going to tell me?" interrupted M. de Charlus, who was beginning to feel reassured as to M. Verdurin's meaning, but preferred that he should not utter these misleading remarks quite so loud. "Only that we put you on the left," replied M. Verdurin. M. de Charlus, with a comprehending, genial, insolent smile, replied: "Why! That is not of the slightest importance, *here!*" And he gave a little laugh that was all his own—a laugh that came to him probably from some Bavarian or Lorraine grandmother, who herself had inherited it, in identical form, from an ancestress, so that it had been sounding now, without change, for not a few centuries in little old-fashioned European courts, and one could relish its precious quality like that of certain old musical instruments that have now grown rare. There are times when, to paint a complete portrait of some one, we should have to add a phonetic imitation to our verbal description, and our portrait of the figure that M. de Charlus presented is liable to remain incomplete in the absence of that little laugh, so delicate, so light, just as certain compositions are never accurately rendered because our orchestras lack those "small trumpets," with a sound so entirely their own, for which the composer wrote this or that part. "But," M. Verdurin explained, stung by his laugh, "we did it on purpose. I attach no importance whatever to title of nobility," he went on, with that contemptuous smile which I have seen so many people whom I have known, unlike my grandmother and my mother, assume when they spoke of anything that they did not possess, before others who thus, they supposed, would be prevented from using that particular advantage to crow over them. "But, don't you see, since we happened to have M. de Cambremer here, and he is a Marquis, while you are only a Baron. . . ." "Pardon me," M. de Charlus replied with an arrogant air to the astonished Verdurin, "I am also Duc de Brabant, Damoiseau de Montargis, Prince d'Oléron, de Carency, de Viareggio and des Dunes. However, it is not of the slightest importance. Please do not distress yourself," he concluded, resuming his subtle smile which spread itself over these final words: "I could see at a glance that you were not accustomed to society."

Mme. Verdurin came across to me to shew me Elstir's flowers. If this action, to which I had grown so indifferent, of going out to dinner, had on the contrary, taking the form that made it entirely novel, of a journey along the coast, followed by an ascent in a carriage to a point six hundred feet above the sea, produced in me a sort of intoxication, this feeling had not been dispelled at la Raspelière. "Just look at this, now," said the Mistress, shewing me some huge and splendid roses by Elstir, whose unctuous scarlet and rich white stood out, however, with almost too creamy a relief from the flower-stand upon which they were arranged. "Do you suppose he would still have the touch to get that? Don't you call that striking? And besides, it's fine as matter, it would be amusing to handle. I can't tell you how amusing it was to watch him painting them. One could feel that he was interested in trying to get just that effect." And the Mistress's gaze rested musingly on this present from the artist in which were combined not merely his great talent but their long friendship which survived only in these mementoes of it which he had bequeathed to her; behind the flowers which long ago he had picked for her, she seemed to see the shapely hand that had painted them, in the course of a morning, in their freshness, so that, they on the table, it leaning against the back of a chair had been able to meet face to face at the Mistress's luncheon party, the roses still alive and their almost lifelike portrait. Almost only, for Elstir was unable to look at a flower without first transplanting it to that inner garden in which we are obliged always to remain. He had shewn in this water-colour the appearance of the roses which he had seen, and which, but for him, no one would ever have known; so that one might say that they were a new variety with which this painter, like a skilful gardener, had enriched the family of the Roses. "From the day he left the little nucleus, he was finished. It seems, my dinners made him waste his time, that I hindered the development of his *genius*," she said in a tone of irony. "As if the society of a woman like myself could fail to be beneficial to an artist," she exclaimed with a burst of pride. Close beside us, M. de Cambremer, who was already seated, seeing that M. de Charlus was standing, made as though to rise and offer him his chair. This offer may have arisen, in the Marquis's mind, from nothing more than a vague wish to be polite. M. de Charlus preferred to attach to it the sense of a duty which the plain gentleman knew that he owed to a Prince, and felt that he could not establish his right to this precedence better than by declining it. And so he exclaimed: "What are you doing? I beg of you! The idea!" The astutely vehement tone of this protest had in itself something typically "Guermantes" which became even more evident in the imperative, superfluous and familiar gesture with which he brought both his hands down, as though to force him to remain seated, upon the shoulders of M. de Cambremer who had not risen: "Come, come, my dear fellow," the Baron insisted, "this is too much. There is no reason for it! In these days we keep that for Princes of the Blood." I made no more effect on the Cambremers than on Mme. Verdurin by my enthusiasm for their house. For I remained cold to the beauties which they pointed out to me and grew excited over confused reminiscences; at times I even confessed my disappointment at not finding something correspond to what its name had made me imagine. I enraged Mme. de Cambremer by telling her that I had supposed the place to be more in the country. On the other hand I broke off in an ecstasy to sniff the fragrance of a breeze that crept in through the chink of the door. "I see you like draughts," they said to me. My praise of the patch of green lining-cloth that had been pasted over a broken pane met with no greater success: "How frightful!" cried the Marquise. The climax came when I said: "My greatest joy was when I arrived. When I heard my step echoing along the gallery, I felt that I had come into some village council-office, with a map of the district on the wall. This time, Mme. de Cambremer resolutely turned her back on me. "You don't think the arrangement too bad?" her husband asked her with the same compassionate anxiety with which he would have inquired how his wife had stood some painful ceremony. "They have some fine things." But, inasmuch as malice, when the hard and fast rules of sure taste do not confine it within fixed limits, finds fault with everything, in the persons or in the houses, of the people who have supplanted the critic: "Yes, but they are not in the right places. Besides, are they really as fine as all that?" "You noticed," said M. de Cambremer, with a melancholy that was controlled by a note of firmness, "there are some Jouy hangings that are worn away, some quite threadbare things in this drawing-room!" "And that piece of stuff with its huge roses, like a peasant woman's quilt," said Mme. de Cambremer whose purely artificial culture was confined exclusively to idealist philosophy, impressionist painting and Debussy's music. And, so as not to criticise merely in the name of smartness but in that of good taste: "And they have put up windscreens! Such bad style! What can you expect of such people, they don't know, where could they have learned? They must be retired tradespeople. It's really not bad for them." "I thought the chandeliers good," said the Marquis, though it was not evident why he should make an exception of the chandeliers, just as inevitably, whenever anyone spoke of a church, whether it was the Cathedral of Chartres, or of Rheims, or of Amiens, or the church at Balbec, what he would always make a point of mentioning as admirable would be: "the organ-loft, the pulpit and the misericords." "As for the garden, don't speak about it," said Mme. de Cambremer. "It's a massacre.

Those paths running all crooked." I seized the opportunity while Mme. Verdurin was pouring out coffee to go and glance over the letter which M. de Cambremer had brought me, and in which his mother invited me to dinner. With that faint trace of ink, the handwriting revealed an individuality which in the future I should be able to recognise among a thousand, without any more need to have recourse to the hypothesis of special pens, than to suppose that rare and mysteriously blended colours are necessary to enable a painter to express his original vision. Indeed a paralytic, stricken with agraphia after a seizure, and compelled to look at the script as at a drawing without being able to read it, would have gathered that Mme. de Cambremer belonged to an old family in which the zealous cultivation of literature and the arts had supplied a margin to its aristocratic traditions. He would have guessed also the period in which the Marquise had learned simultaneously to write and to play Chopin's music. It was the time when well-bred people observed the rule of affability and what was called the rule of the three adjectives. Mme. de Cambremer combined the two rules in one. A laudatory adjective was not enough for her, she followed it (after a little stroke of the pen) with a second, then (after another stroke) with a third. But, what was peculiar to herself was that, in defiance of the literary and social object at which she aimed, the sequence of the three epithets assumed in Mme. de Cambremer's notes the aspect not of a progression but of a diminuendo. Mme. de Cambremer told me in this first letter that she had seen Saint-Loup and had appreciated more than ever his "unique—rare—real" qualities, that he was coming to them again with one of his friends (the one who was in love with her daughter-in-law), and that if I cared to come, with or without them, to dine at Féterne she would be "delighted—happy—pleased." Perhaps it was because her desire to be friendly outran the fertility of her imagination and the riches of her vocabulary that the lady, while determined to utter three exclamations, was incapable of making the second and third anything more than feeble echoes of the first. Add but a fourth adjective, and, of her initial friendliness, there would be nothing left. Moreover, with a certain refined simplicity which cannot have failed to produce a considerable impression upon her family and indeed in her circle of acquaintance, Mme. de Cambremer had acquired the habit of substituting for the word (which might in time begin to ring false) "sincere," the word "true." And to shew that it was indeed by sincerity that she was impelled, she broke the conventional rule that would have placed the adjective "true" before its noun, and planted it boldly after. Her letters ended with: "*Croyez à ma mon amitié vraie.*" "*Croyez à ma sympathie vraie.*" Unfortunately, this had become so stereotyped a formula that the affectation of frankness was more suggestive of a polite fiction than the time-honoured formulas, of the meaning of which people have ceased to think. I was, however, hindered from reading her letter by the confused sound of conversation over which rang out the louder accents of M. de Charlus, who, still on the same topic, was saying to M. de Cambremer: "You reminded me, when you offered me your chair, of a gentleman from whom I received a letter this morning addressed: 'To His Highness, the Baron de Charlus,' and beginning: 'Monseigneur.'" "To be sure, your correspondent was slightly exaggerating," replied M. de Cambremer, giving way to a discreet show of mirth. M. de Charlus had provoked this; he did not partake in it. "Well, if it comes to that, my dear fellow," he said, "I may observe that, heraldically speaking, he was entirely in the right. I am not regarding it as a personal matter, you understand. I should say the same of anyone else. But one has to face the facts, history is history, we can't alter it and it is not in our power to rewrite it. I need not cite the case of the Emperor William, who at Kiel never ceased to address me as 'Monseigneur.' I have heard it said that he gave the same title to all the Dukes of France, which was an abuse of the privilege, but was perhaps simply a delicate attention aimed over our heads at France herself." "More delicate, perhaps, than sincere," said M. de Cambremer. "Ah! There I must differ from you. Observe that, personally, a gentleman of the lowest rank such as that Hohenzollern, a Protestant to boot, and one who has usurped the throne of my cousin the King of Hanover, can be no favourite of mine," added M. de Charlus, with whom the annexation of Hanover seemed to rankle more than that of Alsace-Lorraine. "But I believe the feeling that turns the Emperor in our direction to be profoundly sincere. Fools will tell you that he is a stage emperor. He is on the contrary marvellously intelligent; it is true that he knows nothing about painting, and has forced Herr Tschudi to withdraw the Elstirs from the public galleries. But Louis XIV did not appreciate the Dutch Masters, he had the same fondness for display, and yet he was, when all is said, a great Monarch. Besides, William II has armed his country from the military and naval point of view in a way that

Louis XIV failed to do, and I hope that his reign will never know the reverses that darkened the closing days of him who is fatuously styled the Roi Soleil. The Republic made a great mistake, to my mind, in rejecting the overtures of the Hohenzollern, or responding to them only in driblets. He is very well aware of it himself and says, with that gift that he has for the right expression: 'What I want is a clasped hand, not a raised hat.' As a man, he is vile; he has abandoned, surrendered, denied his best friends, in circumstances in which his silence was as deplorable as theirs was grand," continued M. de Charlus, who was irresistibly drawn by his own tendencies to the Eulenburg affair, and remembered what one of the most highly placed of the culprits had said to him: "The Emperor must have relied upon our delicacy to have dared to allow such a trial. But he was not mistaken in trusting to our discretion. We would have gone to the scaffold with our lips sealed." "All that, however, has nothing to do with what I was trying to explain, which is that, in Germany, mediatised Princes like ourselves are *Durchlaucht*, and in France our rank of Highness was publicly recognised Saint-Simon tries to make out that this was an abuse on our part, in which he is entirely mistaken. The reason that he gives, namely that Louis XIV forbade us to style him the Most Christian King and ordered us to call him simply the King, proves merely that we held our title from him, and not that we had not the rank of Prince. Otherwise, it would have to be withheld from the Duc de Lorraine and ever so many others. Besides, several of our titles come from the House of Lorraine through Thérèse d'Espinay, my great-grandmother, who was the daughter of the Damoiseau de Commercy."

Observing that Morel was listening, M. de Charlus proceeded to develop the reasons for his claim. "I have pointed out to my brother that it is not in the third part of Gotha, but in the second, not to say the first, that the account of our family ought to be included," he said, without stopping to think that Morel did not know what "Gotha" was. "But that is his affair, he is the Head of my House, and so long as he raises no objection and allows the matter to pass, I have only to shut my eyes." "M. Brichot interests me greatly," I said to Mme. de Verdurin as she joined me, and I slipped Mme. de Cambremer's letter into my pocket. "He has a cultured mind and is an excellent man," she replied coldly. "Of course what he lacks is originality and taste, he has a terrible memory. They used to say of the 'forebears' of the people we have here this evening, the *émigrés,* that they had forgotten nothing. But they had at least the excuse," she said, borrowing one of Swann's epigrams, "that they had learned nothing. Whereas Brichot knows everything, and hurls chunks of dictionary at our heads during dinner. I'm sure you know everything now about the names of all the towns and villages" While Mme. Verdurin was speaking, it occurred to me that I had determined to ask her something, but I could not remember what it was. I could not at this moment say what Mme. Verdurin was wearing that evening. Perhaps even then I was no more able to say, for I have not an observant mind. But feeling that her dress was not unambitious I said to her something polite and even admiring. She was like almost all women, who imagine that a compliment that is paid to them is a literal statement of the truth, and is a judgment impartially, irresistibly pronounced, as though it referred to a work of art that has no connexion with a person. And so it was with an earnestness which made me blush for my own hypocrisy that she replied with the proud and artless question, habitual in the circumstances: "You like it?" "I know you're talking about Brichot. Eh, Chantepie, Freycinet, he spared you nothing. I had my eye on you, my little Mistress!" "I saw you, it was all I could do not to laugh." "You are talking about Chantepie, I am certain," said M. Verdurin, as he came towards us. I had been alone, as I thought of my strip of green cloth and of a scent of wood, in failing to notice that, while he discussed etymologies, Brichot had been provoking derision. And inasmuch as the expressions which, for me, gave their value to things were of the sort which other people either do not feel or reject without thinking of them, as unimportant, they were entirely useless to me and had the additional drawback of making me appear stupid in the eyes of Mme. Verdurin who saw that I had "swallowed" Brichot, as before I had appeared stupid to Mme. de Guermantes, because I enjoyed going to see Mme. d'Arpajon. With Brichot, however, there was another reason. I was not one of the little clan. And in every clan, whether it be social, political, literary, one contracts a perverse facility in discovering in a conversation, in an official speech, in a story, in a sonnet, everything that the honest reader would never have dreamed of finding there. How many times have I found myself, after reading with a certain emotion a tale skilfully told by a learned and slightly old-fashioned Academician, on the point of saying to Bloch or to Mme. de Guermantes: "How charming this is!" when before I had opened my mouth they exclaimed, each in a different language: "If you want to be really amused, read a tale by So-and-so. Human stupidity has never sunk to greater depths." Bloch's scorn was aroused principally by the discovery that certain effects of style, pleasant enough in themselves, were slightly faded; that of Mme. de Guermantes because the tale seemed to prove the direct opposite of what the author meant, for reasons of fact which she had the ingenuity to deduce but which would never have occurred to me. I was no less surprised to discover the irony that underlay the Verdurins' apparent friendliness for Brichot than to hear, some days later, at Féterne, the Cambremers say to me, on hearing my enthusiastic praise of la Raspelière: "It's impossible that you can be sincere, after all they've done to it." It is true that they admitted that the china was good. Like the shocking windscreens, it had escaped my notice. "Anyhow, when you go back to Balbec, you will know what Balbec means," said M. Verdurin ironically. It was precisely the things Brichot had told me that interested me. As for what they called his mind, it was exactly the same mind that had at one time been so highly appreciated by the little clan. He talked with the same irritating fluency, but his words no longer carried, having to overcome a hostile silence or disagreeable echoes; what had altered was not the things that he said but the acoustics of the room and the attitude of his audience. "Take care," Mme. Verdurin murmured, pointing to Brichot. The latter, whose hearing remained keener than his vision, darted at the mistress the hastily withdrawn gaze of a short-sighted philosopher. If his bodily eyes were less good, his mind's eye on the contrary had begun to take a larger view of things. He saw how little was to be expected of human affection, and resigned himself to it. Undoubtedly the discovery pained him. It may happen that even the man who on one evening only, in a circle where he is usually greeted with joy, realises that the others have found him too frivolous or too pedantic or too loud, or too forward, or whatever it may be, returns home miserable. Often it is a difference of opinion, or of system, that has made him appear to other people absurd or old-fashioned. Often he is perfectly well aware that those others are inferior to himself. He could easily dissect the sophistries with which he has been tacitly condemned, he is tempted to pay a call, to write a letter: on second thoughts, he does nothing, awaits the invitation for the following week. Sometimes, too, these discomfitures, instead of ending with the evening, last for months. Arising from the instability of social judgments, they increase that instability further. For the man who knows that Mme. X despises him, feeling that he is respected at Mme. Y's, pronounces her far superior to the other and emigrates to her house. This however is not the proper place to describe those men, superior to the life of society but lacking the capacity to realise their own worth outside it, glad to be invited, embittered by being disparaged, discovering annually the faults of the hostess to whom they have been offering incense and the genius of her whom they have never properly appreciated, ready to return to the old love when they shall have felt the drawbacks to be found equally in the new, and when they have begun to forget those of the old. We may judge by these temporary discomfitures the grief that Brichot felt at one which he knew to be final. He was not unaware that Mme. Verdurin sometimes laughed at him publicly, even at his infirmities, and knowing how little was to be expected of human affection, submitting himself to the facts, he continued nevertheless to regard the Mistress as his best friend. But, from the blush that swept over the scholar's face, Mme. Verdurin saw that he had heard her, and made up her mind to be kind to him for the rest of the evening. I could not help remarking to her that she had not been very kind to Saniette. "What! Not kind to him! Why, he adores us, you can't imagine what we are to him. My husband is sometimes a little irritated by his stupidity, and you must admit that he has every reason, but when that happens why doesn't he rise in revolt, instead of cringing like a whipped dog? It is not honest. I don't like it. That doesn't mean that I don't always try to calm my husband, because if he went too far, all that would happen would be that Saniette would stay away; and I don't want that because I may tell you that he hasn't a penny in the world, he needs his dinners. But after all, if he does mind, he can stay away, it has nothing to do with me, when a person depends on other people he should try not to be such an idiot." "The Duchy of Aumale was in our family for years before passing to the House of France," M. de Charlus was explaining to M. de Cambremer, before a speechless Morel, for whom, as a matter of fact, the whole of this dissertation was, if not actually addressed to him, intended. "We took precedence over all foreign Princes; I could give you a hundred examples. The Princesse de Croy having attempted, at the burial of Monsieur, to fall on her knees after my great-great-grandmother, that lady reminded her sharply that she had not the privilege of the hassock, made the officer on duty remove it, and reported the matter to the King, who ordered Mme. de Croy to call upon Mme. de Guermantes and offer her apologies. The Duc de Bourgogne having come to us with ushers with raised wands, we obtained the King's authority to have them lowered. I know it is not good form to speak of the merits of one's own family. But it is well known that our people were always to the fore in the hour of danger. Our battle-cry, after we abandoned that of the Dukes of Brabant, was *Passavant!* So that it is fair enough after all that this right to be everywhere the first, which we had established for so many centuries in war, should afterwards have been confirmed to us at Court. And, egad, it has always been admitted there. I may give you a further instance, that of the Princess of Baden. As she had so far forgotten herself as to attempt to challenge the precedence of that same Duchesse de Guermantes of whom I was speaking just now, and had attempted to go in first to the King's presence, taking advantage of a momentary hesitation which my relative may perhaps have shewn (although there could be no reason for it), the King called out: 'Come in, cousin, come in; Mme. de Baden knows very well what her duty is to you.' And it was as Duchesse de Guermantes that she held this rank, albeit she was of no mean family herself, since she was through her mother niece to the Queen of Poland, the Queen of Hungary, the Elector Palatine, the Prince of Savoy-Carignano and the Elector of Hanover, afterwards King of England." "*Maecenas atavis edite regibus!*" said Brichot, addressing M. de Charlus, who acknowledged the compliment with a slight inclination of his head. "What did you say?" Mme. Verdurin asked

Brichot, anxious to make amends to him for her previous speech. "I was referring, Heaven forgive me, to a dandy who was the pick of the basket" (Mme. Verdurin winced) "about the time of Augustus," (Mme. Verdurin, reassured by the remoteness in time of this basket, assumed a more serene expression) "of a friend of Virgil and Horace who carried their sycophancy to the extent of proclaiming to his face his more than aristocratic, his royal descent, in a word I was referring to Maecenas, a bookworm who was the friend of Horace, Virgil, Augustus. I am sure that M. de Charlus knows all about Maecenas." With a gracious, sidelong glance at Mme. Verdurin, because he had heard her make an appointment with Morel for the day after next and was afraid that she might not invite him also, "I should say," said M. de Charlus, "that Maecenas was more or less the Verdurin of antiquity." Mme. Verdurin could not altogether suppress a smile of satisfaction. She went over to Morel. "He's nice, your father's friend," she said to him. "One can see that he's an educated man, and well bred. He will get on well in our little nucleus. What is his address in Paris?" Morel preserved a haughty silence and merely proposed a game of cards. Mme. Verdurin insisted upon a little violin music first. To the general astonishment, M. de Charlus, who never referred to his own considerable gifts, accompanied, in the purest style, the closing passage (uneasy, tormented, Schumannesque, but, for all that, earlier than Franck's Sonata) of the Sonata for piano and violin by Fauré. I felt that he would furnish Morel, marvellously endowed as to tone and virtuosity, with just those qualities that he lacked, culture and style. But I thought with curiosity of this combination in a single person of a physical blemish and a spiritual gift. M. de Charlus was not very different from his brother, the Duc de Guermantes. Indeed, a moment ago (though this was rare), he had spoken as bad French as his brother. He having reproached me (doubtless in order that I might speak in glowing terms of Morel to Mme. Verdurin) with never coming to see him, and I having pleaded discretion, he had replied: "But, since it is I that asks you, there is no one but I who am in a position to take offence." This might have been said by the Duc de Guermantes. M. de Charlus was only a Guermantes when all was said. But it had been enough that nature should upset the balance of his nervous system sufficiently to make him prefer to the woman that his brother the Duke would have chosen one of Virgil's shepherds or Plato's disciples, and at once qualities unknown to the Duc de Guermantes and often combined with this want of balance had made M. de Charlus an exquisite pianist, an amateur painter who was not devoid of taste, an eloquent talker. Who would ever have detected that the rapid, eager, charming style with which M. de Charlus played the Schumannesque passage of Fauré's Sonata had its equivalent—one dares not say its cause—in elements entirely physical, in the nervous defects of M. de Charlus? We shall explain later on what we mean by nervous defects, and why it is that a Greek of the time of Socrates, a Roman of the time of Augustus might be what we know them to have been and yet remain absolutely normal men, and not men-women such as we see around us to-day. Just as he had genuine artistic tendencies, which had never come to fruition, so M. de Charlus had, far more than the Duke.

loved their mother, loved his own wife, and indeed, years after her death, if anyone spoke of her to him would shed tears, but superficial tears, like the perspiration of an over-stout man, whose brow will glisten with sweat at the slightest exertion. With this difference, that to the latter we say: "How hot you are," whereas we pretend not to notice other people's tears. We, that is to say, people in society; for the humbler sort are as distressed by the sight of tears as if a sob were more serious than a hemorrhage. His sorrow after the death of his wife, thanks to the habit of falsehood, did not debar M. de Charlus from a life which was not in harmony with it. Indeed later on, he sank so low as to let it be known that, during the funeral rites, he had found an opportunity of asking the acolyte for his name and address. And it may have been true.

When the piece came to an end, I ventured to ask for some Franck, which appeared to cause Mme. de Cambremer such acute pain that I did not insist. "You can't admire that sort of thing," she said to me. Instead she asked for Debussy's *Fêtes,* which made her exclaim: "Ah! How sublime!" from the first note. But Morel discovered that he remembered the opening bars only, and in a spirit of mischief, without any intention to deceive, began a March by Meyerbeer. Unfortunately, as he left little interval and made no announcement, everybody supposed that he was still playing Debussy, and continued to exclaim "Sublime!" Morel, by revealing that the composer was that not of *Pelléas* but of *Robert le Diable* created a certain chill. Mme. de Cambremer had scarcely time to feel it, for she had just discovered a volume of Scarlatti, and had flung herself upon it with an hysterical impulse. "Oh! Play this, look, this piece, it's divine," she cried. And yet, of this composer long despised, recently promoted to the highest honours, what she had selected in her feverish impatience was one of those infernal pieces which have so often kept us from sleeping, while a merciless pupil repeats them indefinitely on the next floor. But Morel had had enough music, and as he insisted upon cards, M. de Charlus, to be able to join in, proposed a game of whist. "He was telling the Master just now that he is a Prince," said Ski to Mme. Verdurin, "but it's not true, they're quite a humble family of architects." "I want to know what it was you were saying about Maecenas. It interests me, don't you know!" Mme. Verdurin repeated to Brichot, with an affability that carried him off his feet. And so, in order to shine in the Mistress's eyes, and possibly in mine: "Why, to tell you the truth, Madame, Maecenas interests me chiefly because he is the earliest apostle of note of that Chinese god who numbers more followers in France today than Brahma, than Christ himself, the all-powerful God Ubedamd." Mme. Verdurin was no longer content, upon these occasions, with burying her head in her hands. She would descend with the suddenness of the insects called ephemeral upon Princess Sherbatoff; were the latter within reach the Mistress would cling to her shoulder, dig her nails into it, and hide her face against it for a few moments like a child playing at hide and seek. Concealed by this protecting screen, she was understood to be laughing until she cried and was as well able to think of nothing at all as people are who while saying a prayer that is rather long take the wise precaution of burying their faces in their hands. Mme. Verdurin used to imitate them when she listened to Beethoven quartets, so as at the same time to let it be seen that she regarded them as a prayer and not to let it be seen that she was asleep. "I am quite serious, Madame," said Brichot. "Too numerous, I consider, to-day is become the person who spends his time gazing at his navel as though it were the hub of the universe. As a matter of doctrine, I have no objection to offer to some Nirvana which will dissolve us in the great Whole (which, like Munich and Oxford, is considerably nearer to Paris than Asnières or Bois-Colombes), but it is unworthy either of a true Frenchman, or of a true European even, when the Japanese are possibly at the gates of our Byzantium, that socialised anti-militarists should be gravely discussing the cardinal virtues of free verse." Mme. Verdurin felt that she might dispense with the Princess's mangled shoulder, and allowed her face to become once more visible, not without pretending to wipe her eyes and gasping two or three times for breath. But Brichot was determined that I should have my share in the entertainment, and having learned, from those oral examinations which he conducted so admirably, that the best way to flatter the young is to lecture them, to make them feel themselves important, to make them regard you as a reactionary: "I have no wish to blaspheme against the Gods of Youth," he said, with that furtive glance at myself which a speaker turns upon a member of his audience whom he has mentioned by name. "I have no wish to be damned as a heretic and renegade in the Mallarmean chapel in which our new friends, like all the young men of his age, must have served the esoteric mass, at least as an acolyte, and have shewn himself deliquescent or Rosicrucian. But, really, we have seen more than enough of these intellectuals worshipping art with a big A, who, when they can no longer intoxicate themselves upon Zola, inject themselves with Verlaine. Become etheromaniacs out of Baudelairian devotion, they would no longer be capable of the virile effort which the country may, one day or another, demand of them, anaesthetised as they are by the great literary neurosis in the heated, enervating atmosphere, heavy with unwholesome vapours, of a symbolism of the opium-pipe." Feeling incapable of feigning any trace of admiration for Brichot's inept and motley tirade, I turned to Ski and assured him that he was entirely mistaken as to the family to which M. de Charlus belonged; he replied that he was certain of his facts, and added that I myself had said that his real name was Gandin, Le Gandin. "I told you," was my answer, "that Mme. de Cambremer was the sister of an engineer, M. Legrandin. I never said a word to you about M. de Charlus. There is about as much connexion between him and Mme. de Cambremer as between the Great Condé and Racine." "Indeed! I thought there was," said Ski lightly, with no more apology for his mistake than he had made a few hours earlier for the mistake that had nearly made his party miss the train. "Do you intend to remain long on this coast?" Mme. Verdurin asked M. de Charlus, in whom she foresaw an addition to the faithful and trembled lest he should be returning too soon to Paris. "Good Lord, one never knows," replied M. de Charlus in a nasal drawl. "I should like to stay here until the end of September." "You are quite right," said Mme. Verdurin; "that is the time for fine storms at sea." "To tell you the truth, that is not what would influence me. I have for some time past unduly neglected the Archangel Saint Michael, my patron, and I should like to make amends to him by staying for his feast, on the 29th of September, at the Abbey on the Mount." "You take an interest in all that sort of thing?" asked Mme. Verdurin, who might perhaps have succeeded in hushing the voice of her outraged anti-clericalism, had she not been afraid that so long an expedition might make the violinist and the Baron "fail" her for forty-eight hours. "You are perhaps afflicted with intermittent deafness," M. de Charlus replied insolently. "I have told you that Saint Michael is one of my glorious patrons." Then, smiling with a benevolent ecstasy, his eyes gazing into the distance, his voice strengthened by an excitement which seemed now to be not merely aesthetic but religious: "It is so beautiful at the offertory when Michael stands erect by the altar, in a white robe, swinging a golden censer heaped so high with perfumes that the fragrance of them mounts up to God." "We might go there in a party," suggested Mme. Verdurin, notwithstanding her horror of the clergy. "At that moment, when the offertory begins," went on M. de Charlus who, for other reasons but in the same manner as good speakers in Parliament, never replied to an interruption and would pretend not to have heard it, "it would be wonderful to see our young friend Palestrinising, indeed performing an aria by Bach. The worthy Abbot, too, would be wild with joy, and that is the greatest homage, at least the greatest public homage that I can pay to my Holy Patron. What an edification for the faithful! We must mention it presently to the young Angelico of music, a warrior like Saint Michael."

Saniette, summoned to make a fourth, declared that he

did not know how to play whist. And Cottard, seeing that there was not much time left before our train, embarked at once on a game of écarté with Morel. M. Verdurin was furious, and bore down with a terrible expression upon Saniette: "Is there anything in the world that you can play?" he cried, furious at being deprived of the opportunity for a game of whist, and delighted to have found one to insult the old registrar. He, in his terror, did his best to look clever: "Yes, I can play the piano," he said. Cottard and Morel were seated face to face. "Your deal," said Cottard. "Suppose we go nearer to the card-table," M. de Charlus, worried by the sight of Morel in Cottard's company, suggested to M. de Cambremer. "It is quite as interesting as those questions of etiquette which in these days have ceased to count for very much. The only kings that we have left, in France at least, are the kings in the pack of cards, who seem to me to be positively swarming in the hand of our young virtuoso," he added a moment later, from an admiration for Morel which extended to his way of playing cards, to flatter him also, and finally to account for his suddenly turning to lean over the young violinist's shoulder. "I-ee cut," said (imitating the accent of a cardsharper) Cottard, whose children burst out laughing, like his students and the chief dresser, whenever the master, even by the bedside of a serious case, uttered with the emotionless face of an epileptic one of his hackneyed witticisms. "I don't know what to play," said Morel, seeking advice from M. de Charlus. "Just as you please, you're bound to lose, whatever you play, it's all the same (*c'est égal*)." "*Egal* . . . Ingalli?" said the doctor, with an insinuating, kindly glance at M. de Cambremer. "She was what we call a true diva, she was a dream, a Carmen such as we shall never see again. She was wedded to the part. I used to enjoy too listening to Ingalli—married." The Marquis drew himself up with that contemptuous vulgarity of well-bred people who do not realise that they are insulting their host by appearing uncertain whether they ought to associate with his guests, and adopt English manners by way of apology for a scornful expression: "Who is that gentleman playing cards, what does he do for a living, what does he *sell?* I rather like to know whom I am meeting, so as not to make friends with any Tom, Dick or Harry. But I didn't catch his name when you did me the honour of introducing me to him." If M. Verdurin, availing himself of this phrase, had indeed introduced M. de Cambremer to his fellow-guests, the other would have been greatly annoyed. But, knowing that it was the opposite procedure that was observed, he thought it gracious to assume a genial and modest air, without risk to himself. The pride that M. Verdurin took in his intimacy with Cottard had increased if anything now that the doctor had become an eminent professor. But it no longer found expression in the artless language of earlier days. Then, when Cottard was scarcely known to the public, if you spoke to M. Verdurin of his wife's facial neuralgia: "There is nothing to be done," he would say, with the artless self-satisfaction of people who assume that anyone whom they know must be famous, and that everybody knows the name of their family singing-master. "If she had an ordinary doctor, one might look for a second opinion, but when that doctor is called Cottard" (a name which he pronounced as though it were Bouchard or Charcot) "one has simply to bow to the inevitable."

Adopting a reverse procedure, knowing that M. de Cambremer must certainly have heard of the famous Professor Cottard, M. Verdurin adopted a tone of simplicity. "He's our family doctor, a worthy soul whom we adore and who would let himself be torn in pieces for our sakes; he is not a doctor, he is a friend, I don't suppose you have ever heard of him or that his name would convey anything to you, in any case to us it is the name of a very good man, of a very dear friend, Cottard." This name, murmured in a modest tone, took in M. de Cambremer who supposed that his host was referring to some one else. "Cottard? You don't mean Professor Cottard?" At that moment one heard the voice of the said Professor who, at an awkward point in the game, was saying as he looked at his cards: "This is where Greek meets Greek." "Why, yes, to be sure, he is a professor," said M. Verdurin. "What! Professor Cottard! You are not making a mistake! You are quite sure it's the same man! The one who lives in the Rue du Bac!" "Yes, his address is 43, Rue du Bac. You know him?" "But everybody knows Professor Cottard. He's at the top of the tree! You might as well ask me if I knew Bouffe de Saint-Blaise or Courtois-Suffit. I could see when I heard him speak that he was not an ordinary person, that is why I took the liberty of asking you." "Come now, what shall I play, trumps?" asked Cottard. Then abruptly, with a vulgarity which would have been offensive even in heroic circumstances, as when a soldier uses a coarse expression to convey his contempt for death, but became doubly stupid in the safe pastime of a game of cards, Cottard, deciding to play a trump, assumed a sombre, suicidal air, and, borrowing the language of people who are risking their skins, played his card as though it were his life, with the exclamation: "There it is, and be damned to it!" It was not the right card to play, but he had a consolation. In the middle of the room, in a deep armchair, Mme. Cottard, yielding to the effect, which she always found irresistible, of a good dinner, had succumbed after vain efforts to the vast and gentle slumbers that were overpowering her. In vain might she sit up now and again, and smile, whether at her own absurdity or from fear of leaving unanswered some polite speech that might have been addressed to her, she sank back, in spite of herself, into the clutches of the implacable and delicious malady. More than the noise, what awakened her thus for an instant only was the glance (which, in her wifely affection she could see even when her eyes were shut, and foresaw, for the same scene occurred every evening and haunted her dreams like the thought of the hour at which one will have to rise), the glance with which the Professor drew the attention of those present to his wife's slumbers. To begin with, he merely looked at her and smiled, for if as a doctor he disapproved of this habit of falling asleep after dinner (or at least gave this scientific reason for growing annoyed later on, but it is not certain whether it was a determining reason, so many and diverse were the views that he held about it), as an all-powerful and teasing husband, he was delighted to be able to make a fool of his wife, to rouse her only partly at first, so that she might fall asleep again and he have the pleasure of waking her afresh.

By this time, Mme. Cottard was sound asleep. "Now then, Léontine, you're snoring," the professor called to her. "I am listening to Mme. Swann, my dear," Mme.

Cottard replied faintly, and dropped back into her lethargy. "It's perfect nonsense," exclaimed Cottard, "she'll be telling us presently that she wasn't asleep. She's like the patients who come to consult us and insist that they never sleep at all." "They imagine it, perhaps," said M. de Cambremer with a laugh. But the doctor enjoyed contradicting no less than teasing, and would on no account allow a layman to talk medicine to him. "People do not imagine that they never sleep," he promulgated in a dogmatic tone. "Ah!" replied the Marquis with a respectful bow, such as Cottard at one time would have made. "It is easy to see," Cottard went on, "that you have never administered, as I have, as much as two grains of trional without succeeding in provoking somnolescence." "Quite so, quite so," replied the Marquis, laughing with a superior air, "I have never taken trional, or any of those drugs which soon cease to have any effect but ruin your stomach. When a man has been out shooting all night, like me, in the forest of Chantepie, I can assure you he doesn't need any trional to make him sleep." "It is only fools who say that," replied the Professor. "Trional frequently has a remarkable effect on the nervous tone. You mention trional. have you any idea what it is?" "Well . . . I've heard people say that it is a drug to make one sleep." "You are not answering my question," replied the Professor, who, thrice weekly, at the Faculty, sat on the board of examiners. "I don't ask you whether it makes you sleep or not, but what it is. Can you tell me what percentage it contains of amyl and ethyl?" "No," replied M. de Cambremer with embarrassment. "I prefer a good glass of old brandy or even 345 Port." "Which are ten times as toxic," the Professor interrupted. "As for trional," M. de Cambremer ventured, "my wife goes in for all that sort of thing, you'd better talk to her about it." "She probably knows just as much about it as yourself. In any case, if your wife takes trional to make her sleep, you can see that mine has no need of it. Come along, Léontine, wake up, you're getting ankylosed, did you ever see me fall asleep after dinner? What will you be like when you're sixty, if you fall asleep now like an old woman? You'll go and get fat, you're arresting the circulation. She doesn't even hear what I'm saying." "They're bad for one's health, these little naps after dinner, ain't they, Doctor?" said M. de Cambremer, seeking to rehabilitate himself with Cottard. "After a heavy meal one ought to take exercise." "Stuff and nonsense!" replied the Doctor. "We have taken identical quantities of food from the stomach of a dog that has lain quiet and from the stomach of a dog that has been running about, and it is in the former that digestion is more advanced." "Then it is sleep that stops digestion." "That depends upon whether you mean oesophagic digestion, stomachic digestion, intestinal digestion; it is useless to give you explanations which you would not understand since you have never studied medicine. Now then, Léontine, quick march, it is time we were going." This was not true, for the doctor was going merely to continue his game, but he hoped thus to cut short in a more drastic fashion the slumbers of the deaf mute to whom he had been addressing without a word of response the most learned exhortations. Whether a determination to remain awake survived in Mme. Cottard, even in the state of sleep, or because the armchair offered no support to her head, it was jerked mechanically from left to right, and up and down, in the empty air, like a lifeless object, and Mme. Cottard, with her nodding poll, appeared now to be listening to music, now to be in the last throes of death. Where her husband's increasingly vehement admonitions failed of their effect, her sense of her own stupidity proved successful: "My bath is nice and hot," she murmured, "but the feathers in the dictionary . . ." she exclaimed as she sat bolt upright. "Oh! Good lord, what a fool I am. Whatever have I been saying, I was thinking about my hat, I'm sure I said something silly, in another minute I should have been asleep, it's that wretched fire." Everybody began to laugh, for there was no fire in the room.[1]

[1] In the French text of Sodome et Gomorrhe, Volume II ends at this point.

"You are making fun of me," said Mme. Cottard, herself laughing, and raising her hand to her brow to wipe away, with the light touch of a hypnotist and the sureness of a woman putting her hair straight, the last traces of sleep, "I must offer my humble apologies to dear Mme. Verdurin and ask her to tell me the truth." But her smile at once grew sorrowful, for the Professor who knew that his wife sought to please him and trembled lest she should fail, had shouted at her: "Look at yourself in the glass, you are as red as if you had an eruption of acne, you look just like an old peasant." "You know, he is charming," said Mme. Verdurin, "he has such a delightfully sarcastic side to his character. And then, he snatched my husband from the jaws of death when the whole Faculty had given him up. He spent three nights by his bedside, without ever lying down. And so Cottard to me, you know," she went on, in a grave and almost menacing tone, raising her hand to the twin spheres, shrouded in white tresses, of her musical temples, and as though we had wished to assault the doctor, "is sacred! He could ask me for anything in the world! As it is, I don't call him Doctor Cottard, I call him Doctor God! And even in saying that I am slandering him, for this God does everything in his power to remedy some of the disasters for which the other is responsible." "Play a trump," M. de Charlus said to Morel with a delighted air. "A trump, here goes," said the violinist. "You ought to have declared your king first," said M. de Charlus, "you're not paying attention to the game, but how well you play!" "I have the king," said Morel. "He's a fine man," replied the Professor. "What's all that business up there with the sticks?" asked Mme. Verdurin, drawing M. de Cambremer's attention to a superb escutcheon carved over the mantelpiece. "Are they your *arms?*" she added with an ironical disdain. "No, they are not ours," replied M. de Cambremer. "We bear, *barry of five, embattled counterembattled or and gules, as many trefoils countercharged.* No, those are the arms of the Arrachepels, who were not of our stock, but from whom we inherited the house, and nobody of our line has ever made any changes here. The Arrachepels (formerly Pelvilains, we are told) bore *or five piles couped in base gules.* When they allied themselves with the Féterne family, their blazon changed, but remained *cantoned within twenty cross crosslets fitchee in base or, a dexter canton ermine.*" "That's one for her!" muttered Mme. de Cambremer. "My great-grandmother was a d'Arrachepel or de Rachepel, as you please, for both forms are found in the old charters," continued M. de Cambremer, blushing vividly, for only then did the idea for which his wife had given him credit occur to him, and he was afraid that Mme. Verdurin might have applied to herself a speech which had been made without any reference to her. "The history books say that, in the eleventh century, the first Arrachepel, Macé, named Pelvilain, shewed a special aptitude, in siege warfare, in tearing up piles. Whence the name Arrachepel by which he was ennobled, and the piles which you see persisting through the centuries in their arms. These are the piles which, to render fortifications more impregnable, used to be driven, plugged, if you will pardon the expression, into the ground in front of them, and fastened together laterally. They are what you quite rightly called sticks, though they had nothing to do with the floating sticks of our good Lafontaine. For they were supposed to render a stronghold unassailable. Of course, with our modern artillery, they make one smile. But you must bear in mind that I am speaking of the eleventh century." "It is all rather out of date," said Mme. Verdurin, "but the little campanile has a character." "You have," said Cottard, "the luck of . . . turlututu," a word which he gladly repeated to avoid using Molière's. "Do you know why the king of diamonds was turned out of the army?" "I shouldn't mind being in his shoes," said Morel, who was tired of military service. "Oh! What a bad patriot," exclaimed M. de Charlus, who could not refrain from pinching the violinist's ear. "No, you don't know why the king of diamonds was turned out of the army," Cottard pursued, determined to make his joke, "it's because he has only one eye." "You are up against it, Doctor," said M. de Cambremer, to shew Cottard that he knew who he was. "This young man is astonishing," M. de Charlus interrupted innocently. "He plays like a god." This observation did not find favour with the doctor, who replied: "Never too late to mend. Who laughs last, laughs longest." "Queen, ace," Morel, whom fortune was favouring, announced triumphantly. The doctor bowed his head as though powerless to deny this good fortune, and admitted, spellbound: "That's fine." "We are so pleased to have met M. de Charlus," said Mme. de Cambremer to Mme. Verdurin. "Had you never met him before? He is quite nice, he is unusual, he is *of a period*" (she would have found it difficult to say which), replied Mme. Verdurin with the satisfied smile of a connoisseur, a judge and a hostess. Mme. de Cambremer asked me if I was coming to Féterne with Saint-

Loup. I could not suppress a cry of admiration when I saw the moon hanging like an orange lantern beneath the vault of oaks that led away from the house. "That's nothing, presently, when the moon has risen higher and the valley is lighted up, it will be a thousand times better." "Are you staying any time in this neighbourhood, Madame?" M. de Cambremer asked Mme. Cottard, a speech that might be interpreted as a vague intention to invite and dispensed him for the moment from making any more precise engagement. "Oh, certainly, Sir, I regard this annual exodus as most important for the children. Whatever you may say, they must have fresh air. The Faculty wanted to send me to Vichy; but it is too stuffy there, and I can look after my stomach when those big boys of mine have grown a little bigger. Besides, the Professor, with all the examinations he has to hold, has always got his shoulder to the wheel, and the hot weather tires him dreadfully. I feel that a man needs a thorough rest after he has been on the go all the year like that. Whatever happens we shall stay another month at least." "Ah! In that case we shall meet again." "Besides, I shall be all the more obliged to stay her as my husband has to go on a visit to Savoy, and won't be finally settled here for another fortnight." "I like the view of the valley even more than the sea view," Mme. Verdurin went on. "You are going to have a splendid night for your journey." "We ought really to find out whether the carriages are ready, if you are absolutely determined to go back to Balbec to-night," M. Verdurin said to me, "for I see no necessity for it myself. We could drive you over to-morrow morning. It is certain to be fine. The roads are excellent." I said that it was impossible. "But in any case it is not time yet," the Mistress protested. "Leave them alone, they have heaps of time. A lot of good it will do them to arrive at the station with an hour to wait. They are far happier here. And you, my young Mozart," she said to Morel, not venturing to address M. de Charlus directly, "won't you stay the night. We have some nice rooms facing the sea." "No, he can't," M. de Charlus replied on behalf of the absorbed card-player who had not heard. "He has a pass until midnight only. He must go back to bed like a good little boy, obedient, and well-behaved," he added in a complaisant, mannered, insistent voice, as though he derived some sadic pleasure from the use of this chaste comparison and also from letting his voice dwell, in passing, upon any reference to Morel, from touching him with (failing his fingers) words that seemed to explore his person.

From the sermon that Brichot had addressed to me, M. de Cambremer had concluded that I was a Dreyfusard. As he himself was as anti-Dreyfusard as possible, out of courtesy to a foe, he began to sing me the praises of a Jewish colonel who had always been very decent to a cousin of the Chevregny and had secured for him the promotion he deserved. "And my cousin's opinions were the exact opposite," said M. de Cambremer; he omitted to mention what those opinions were, but I felt that they were as antiquated and misshapen as his own face, opinions which a few families in certain small towns must long have entertained. "Well, you know, I call that really fine!" was M. de Cambremer's conclusion. It is true that he was hardly employing the word "fine" in the aesthetic sense in which it would have suggested to his wife and mother different works, but works, anyhow, of art. M. de Cambremer often made use of this term, when for instance he was congratulating a delicate person who had put on a little flesh. "What, you have gained half-a-stone in two months. I say, that's fine!" Refreshments were set out on a table. Mme. Verdurin invited the gentlemen to go and choose whatever drinks they preferred. M. de Charlus went and drank his glass and at once returned to a seat by the card-table from which he did not stir. Mme. Verdurin asked him: "Have you tasted my orangeade?" Upon which M. de Charlus, with a gracious smile, in a crystalline tone which he rarely sounded and with endless motions of his lips and body, replied: "No, I preferred its neighbour, it was strawberry-juice, I think, it was delicious." It is curious that a certain order of secret actions has the external effect of a manner of speaking or gesticulating which reveals them. If a gentleman believes or disbelieves in the Immaculate Conception, or in the innocence of Dreyfus, or in a plurality of worlds, and wishes to keep his opinion to himself, you will find nothing in his voice or in his movements that will let you read his thoughts. But on hearing M. de Charlus say in that shrill voice and with that smile and waving his arms: "No, I preferred its neighbour, the strawberry-juice," one could say: "There, he likes the stronger sex," with the same certainty as enables a judge to sentence a criminal who has not confessed, a doctor a patient suffering from general paralysis who himself is perhaps unaware of his malady but has made some mistake in pronunciation from which one can deduce that he will be dead in three years. Perhaps the people who conclude from a man's way of saying: "No,

I preferred its neighbour, the strawberry-juice," a love of the kind called unnatural, have no need of any such scientific knowledge. But that is because there is a more direct relation between the revealing sign and the secret. Without saying it in so many words to oneself, one feels that it is a gentle, smiling lady who is answering and who appears mannered because she is pretending to be a man and one is not accustomed to seeing men adopt such mannerisms. And it is perhaps more pleasant to think that for long years a certain number of angelic women have been included by mistake in the masculine sex where, in exile, ineffectually beating their wings towards men in whom they inspire a physical repulsion, they know how to arrange a drawing-room, compose "interiors." M. de Charlus was not in the least perturbed that Mme. Verdurin should be standing, and remained installed in his armchair so as to be nearer to Morel. "Don't you think it criminal," said Mme. Verdurin to the Baron, "that that creature who might be enchanting us with his violin should be sitting there at a card-table. When anyone can play the violin like that!" "He plays cards well, he does everything well, he is so intelligent," said M. de Charlus, keeping his eye on the game, so as to be able to advise Morel. This was not his only reason, however, for not rising from his chair for Mme. Verdurin. With the singular amalgam that he had made of the social conceptions at once of a great nobleman and of an amateur of art, instead of being polite in the same way that a man of his world would be, he would create a sort of tableau-vivant for himself after Saint-Simon; and at that moment was amusing himself by impersonating the Maréchal d'Uxelles, who interested him from other aspects also, and of whom it is said that he was so proud as to remain seated, with a pretence of laziness, before all the most distinguished persons at court. "By the way, Charlus," said Mme. Verdurin, who was beginning to grow familiar, "you don't know of any ruined old nobleman in your Faubourg who would come to me as porter?" "Why, yes . . . why, yes," replied M. de Charlus with a genial smile, "but I don't advise it." "Why not?" "I should be afraid for your sake, that your smart visitors would call at the lodge and go no farther." This was the first skirmish between them. Mme. Verdurin barely noticed it. There were to be others, alas, in Paris. M. de Charlus remained glued to his chair. He could not, moreover, restrain a faint smile, seeing how his favourite maxims as to aristocratic prestige and middle-class cowardice were confirmed by the so easily won submission of Mme. Verdurin. The Mistress appeared not at all surprised by the Baron's posture, and if she left him it was only because she had been perturbed by seeing me taken up by M. de Cambremer. But first of all, she wished to clear up the mystery of M. de Charlus's relations with Comtesse Molé. "You told me that you knew Mme. de Molé. Does that mean, you go there?" she asked, giving to the words "go there" the sense of being received there, of having received authority from the lady to go and call upon her. M. de Charlus replied with an inflexion of disdain, an affectation of precision and in a sing-song tone: "Yes, sometimes." This "sometimes" inspired doubts in Mme. Verdurin, who asked: "Have you ever met the Duc de Guermantes there?" "Ah! That I don't remember." "Oh!" said Mme. Verdurin, "you don't know the Duc de Guermantes?" "And how should I not know him?" replied M. de Charlus, his lips curving in a smile. This smile was ironical; but as the Baron was afraid of letting a gold tooth be seen, he stopped it with a reverse movement of his lips, so that the resulting sinuosity was that of a good-natured smile. "Why do you say: 'How should I not know him?'" "Because he is my brother," said M. de Charlus carelessly, leaving Mme. Verdurin plunged in stupefaction and in the uncertainty whether her guest was making fun of her, was a natural son, or a son by another marriage. The idea that the brother of the Duc de Guermantes might be called Baron de Charlus never entered her head. She bore down upon me. "I heard M. de Cambremer invite you to dinner just now. It has nothing to do with me, you understand. But for your own sake, I do hope you won't go. For one thing, the place is infested with bores. Oh! If you like dining with provincial Counts and Marquises whom nobody knows, you will be supplied to your heart's content." "I think I shall be obliged to go there once or twice. I am not altogether free, however, for I have a young cousin whom I cannot leave by herself" (I felt that this fictitious kinship made it easier for me to take Albertine about). "But as for the Cambremers, as I have been introduced to them. . . ." "You shall do just as you please. One thing I can tell you: it's extremely unhealthy; when you have caught pneumonia, or a nice little chronic rheumatism, you'll be a lot better off!" "But isn't the place itself very pretty?" "Mmmmyesss. . . . If you like. For my part, I confess frankly that I would a hundred times rather have the view from here over this valley. To begin with, if they'd paid us I wouldn't have taken the other house because the sea air is fatal to M. Verdurin. If your cousin suffers at all from nerves. . . . But you yourself have bad nerves, I think . . . you have choking fits. Very well! You shall see. Go there once, you won't sleep for a week after it; but it's not my business." And without thinking of the inconsistency with what she had just been saying: "If it would amuse you to see the house, which is not bad, pretty is too strong a word, still it is amusing with its old moat, and the old drawbridge, as I shall have to sacrifice myself and dine there once, very well, come that day, I shall try to bring all my little circle, then it will be quite nice. The day after to-morrow we are going to Harambouville in the carriage. It's a magnificent drive, the cider is delicious. Come with us. You, Brichot, you shall come too. And you too, Ski. That will make a party which, as a matter of fact, my husband must have arranged already. I don't know whom all he has invited, Monsieur de Charlus, are you one of them?" The Baron, who had not heard the whole speech, and did not know that she was talking of an excursion to Harambouville, gave a start. "A strange question," he murmured in a mocking tone by which Mme. Verdurin felt hurt. "Anyhow," she said to me, "before you dine with the Cambremers, why not bring her here, your cousin? Does she like conversation, and clever people? Is she pleasant? Yes, very well then. Bring her with you. The Cambremers aren't the only people in the world. I can understand their being glad to invite her, they must find it difficult to get anyone. Here she will have plenty of fresh air, and lots of clever men. In any case, I am counting on you not to fail me next Wednesday. I heard you were having a tea-party at Rivebelle with your cousin, and M. de Charlus, and I forget who' else. You must arrange to bring the whole lot on here, it would be nice if you all came in a body. It's the easiest thing in the world to get here, the roads are charming; if you like I can send down for you. I can't imagine what you find attractive in Rivebelle, it's infested with mosquitoes. You are thinking perhaps of the reputation of the rock-cakes. My cook makes them far better. I can let you have them, here, Norman rock-cakes, the real article, and shortbread; I need say no more. Ah! If you like the filth they give you at Rivebelle, that I won't give you, I don't poison my guests, Sir, and even if I wished to, my cook would refuse to make such abominations and would leave my service. Those rock-cakes you get down there, you can't tell what they are made of. I knew a poor girl who got peritonitis from them, which carried her off in three days. She was only seventeen. It was sad for her poor mother," added Mme. Verdurin with a melancholy air beneath the spheres of her temples charged with experience and suffering. "However, go and have tea at Rivebelle, if you enjoy being fleeced and flinging money out of the window. But one thing I beg of you, it is a confidential mission I am charging you with, on the stroke of six, bring all your party here, don't allow them to go straggling away by themselves. You can bring whom you please. I wouldn't say that to everybody. But I am sure that your friends are nice, I can see at once that we understand one another. Apart from the little nucleus, there are some very pleasant people coming on Wednesday. You don't know little Madame de Longpont. She is charming, and so witty, not in the least a snob, you will find, you'll like her immensely. And she's going to bring a whole troop of friends too," Mme. Verdurin added to shew me that this was the right thing to do and encourage me by the other's example. "We shall see which has most influence and brings most people, Barbe de Longpont or you. And then I believe somebody's going to bring Bergotte," she added with a vague air, this meeting with a celebrity being rendered far from likely by a paragraph which had appeared in the papers that morning, to the effect that the great writer's health was causing grave anxiety. "Anyhow, you will see that it will be one of my most successful Wednesdays, I don't want to have any boring women. You mustn't judge by this evening, it has been a complete failure. Don't try to be polite, you can't have been more bored than I was, I thought myself it was deadly. It won't always be like to-night, you know! I'm not thinking of the Cambremers, who are impossible, but I have known society people who were supposed to be pleasant, well, compared with my little nucleus, they didn't exist. I heard you say that you thought Swann clever. I must say, to my mind, his cleverness was greatly exaggerated, but without speaking of the character of the man, which I have always found fundamentally antipathetic, sly, underhand, I have often had him to dinner on Wednesdays. Well, you can ask the others, even compared with Brichot, who is far from being anything wonderful, a good assistant master, whom I got into the Institute, Swann was simply nowhere. He was so dull!" And, as I expressed a contrary opinion: "It's the truth. I don't want to say a word against him to you, since he was your friend, indeed he was very fond of you, he has spoken to me about you in the most charming way, but ask the others here if he ever said anything interesting, at our dinners. That, after all, is the supreme test. Well, I don't know why it was, but Swann, in my house, never seemed to come off, one got nothing out of him. And yet anything there ever was in him he picked up here." I assured her that he was highly intelligent. "No, you only think that, because you haven't known him as long as I have. One got to the end of him very soon. I was always bored to death by him." (Which may be interpreted: "He went to the La Trémoïlles and the Guermantes and knew that I didn't.") "And I can put up with anything, except being bored. That, I cannot and will not stand!" Her horror of boredom was now the reason upon which Mme. Verdurin relied to explain the composition of the little group. She did not yet entertain duchesses because she was incapable of enduring boredom, just as she was unable to go for a cruise, because of sea-sickness. I thought to myself that what Mme. Verdurin said was not entirely false, and, whereas the Guermantes would have declared Brichot to be the stupidest man they had ever met, I remained uncertain whether he were not in reality superior, if not to Swann himself, at least to the other people endowed with the wit of the Guermantes who would have had the good taste to avoid and the modesty to blush at his pedantic pleasantries; I asked myself the question as though a fresh light might be thrown on the nature of the intellect by the answer that I should make, and with the earnestness of a Christian influenced by Port-Royal when he considers the problem of Grace. "You will see," Mme. Verdurin continued, "when one has society people together with people of real intelligence, people of our set, that's where one has to see them, the society man who is brilliant in the kingdom of the blind, is only one-eyed here. Besides, the others don't feel at home any longer. So much so that I'm inclined to ask myself whether, instead of attempting mixtures that spoil everything, I shan't start special evenings confined to the bores so as to have the full benefit of my little nucleus. However: you are coming again with your cousin. That's settled. Good. At any rate you will both find something to eat here. Féterne is starvation corner. Oh, by the way, if you like rats, go there at once, you will get as many as you want. And they will keep you there as long as you are prepared to stay. Why, you'll die of hunger. I'm sure, when I go there, I shall have my dinner before I start. The more the merrier, you must come here first and escort me. We shall have high tea, and supper when we get back. Do you like apple-tarts? Yes, very well then, our chef makes the best in the world. You see, I was quite right when I told you that you were meant to live here. So come and stay. You know, there is far more room in the house than people think. I don't speak of it, so as not to let myself in for bores. You might bring your cousin to stay. She would get a change of air from Balbec. With this air here, I maintain I can cure incurables. I have cured them, I may tell you, and not only this time. For I have stayed quite close to here before, a place I discovered and got for a mere song, a very different style of house from their Raspelière. I can shew you it if we go for a drive together. But I admit that even here the air is invigorating. Still, I don't want to say too much about it, the whole of Paris would begin to take a fancy to my little corner. That has always been my luck. Anyhow, give your cousin my message. We shall put you in two nice rooms looking over the valley, you ought to see it in the morning, with the sun shining on the mist! By the way, who is this Robert de Saint-Loup of whom you were speaking?" she said with a troubled air, for she had heard that I was to pay him a visit at Doncières, and was afraid that he might make me fail her. "Why not bring him here instead, if he's not a bore. I have heard of him from Morel; I fancy he's one of his greatest friends," said Mme. Verdurin with entire want of truth, for Saint-Loup and Morel were not even aware of one another's existence. But having heard that Saint-Loup knew M. de Charlus, she supposed that it was through the violinist, and wished to appear to know all about them. "He's not taking up medicine, by any chance, or literature? You know, if you want any help about examinations, Cottard can do anything, and I make what use of him I please. As for the Academy later on, for I suppose he's not old enough yet, I have several votes in my pocket. Your friend would find himself on friendly soil here, and it might amuse him perhaps to see over the house. Life's not very exciting at Doncières. But you shall do just what you please, then you can arrange what you think best," she concluded, without insisting, so as not to appear to be trying to know people of noble birth, and because she always maintained that the system by which she governed the faithful, to wit despotism, was named liberty. "Why, what's the matter with you," she said, at the sight of M. Verdurin who, with gestures of impatience, was making for the wooden terrace that ran along the side of the drawing-room above the valley, like a man who is bursting with rage and must have fresh air. "Has Saniette been annoying you again? But you know what an idiot he is, you have to resign yourself to him, don't work yourself up into such a state. I dislike this sort of thing," she said to me, "because it is bad for him, it sends the blood to his head. But I must say that one would need the patience of an angel at times to put up with Saniette, and one must always remember that it is a charity to have him in the house. For my part I must admit that he's so gloriously silly, I can't help enjoying him. I dare say you heard what he said after dinner: 'I can't play whist, but I can the piano.' Isn't it superb? It is positively colossal, and incidentally quite untrue, for he knows nothing at all about either. But my husband, beneath his rough exterior, is very sensitive, very kind-hearted, and Saniette's self-centred way of always thinking about the effect he is going to make drives him crazy. Come, dear, calm yourself, you know Cottard told you that it was bad for your liver. And it is I that will have to bear the brunt of it all," said Mme. Verdurin. "To-morrow Saniette will come back all nerves and tears. Poor man, he is very ill indeed. Still, that is no reason why he should kill other people. Besides, even at times when he is in pain, when one would like to be sorry for him, his silliness hardens one's heart. He is really too stupid. You have only to tell him quite politely that these scenes make you both ill, and he is not to come again, since that's what he's most afraid of, it will have a soothing effect on his nerves," Mme. Verdurin whispered to her husband.

One could barely make out the sea from the windows

on the right. But those on the other side shewed the valley, now shrouded in a snowy cloak of moonlight. Now and again one heard the voices of Morel and Cottard. "You have a trump?" "Yes." "Ah! You're in luck, you are," said M. de Cambremer to Morel, in answer to his question, for he had seen that the doctor's hand was full of trumps. "Here comes the lady of diamonds," said the doctor. "That's a trump, you know? My trick. But there's isn't a Sorbonne any longer," said the doctor to M. de Cambremer; "there's only the University of Paris." M. de Cambremer confessed his inability to understand why the doctor made this remark to him. "I thought you were talking about the Sorbonne," replied the doctor. "I heard you say: *tu nous la sors bonne*," he added, with a wink, to shew that this was meant for a pun. "Just wait a moment," he said, pointing to his adversary, "I have a Trafalgar in store for him." And the prospect must have been excellent for the doctor, for in his joy his shoulders began to shake rapturously with laughter, which in his family, in the "breed" of the Cottards, was an almost zoological sign of satisfaction. In the previous generation the gesture of rubbing the hands together as though one were soaping them used to accompany this movement. Cottard himself had originally employed both forms simultaneously, but one fine day, nobody ever knew by whose intervention, wifely, professorial perhaps, the rubbing of the hands had disappeared. The doctor, even at dominoes, when he got his adversary on the run, and made him take the double six, which was to him the keenest of pleasures, contented himself with shaking his shoulders. And when—which was as seldom as possible—he went down to his native village for a few days, and met his first cousin, who was still at the hand-rubbing stage, he would say to Mme. Cottard on his return: "I thought poor René very common." "Have you the little dee-ar?" he said, turning to Morel. "No? Then I play this old David." "Then you have five, you have won!" "That's a great victory, Doctor," said the Marquis. "A Pyrrhic victory," said Cottard, turning to face the Marquis and looking at him over his glasses to judge the effect of his remark. "If there is still time," he said to Morel, "I give you your revenge. It is my deal. Ah! no, here come the carriages, it will have to be Friday, and I shall shew you a trick you don't see every day." M. and Mme. Verdurin accompanied us to the door. The Mistress was especially coaxing with Saniette so as to make certain of his returning next time. "But you don't look to me as if you were properly wrapped up, my boy," said M. Verdurin, whose age allowed him to address me in this paternal tone. "One would say the weather had changed." These words filled me with joy, as though the profoundly hidden life, the uprising of different combinations which they implied in nature, hinted at other changes, occurring these in my own life, and created fresh possibilities in it. Merely by opening the door upon the park, before leaving, one felt that a different "weather" had, at that moment, taken possession of the scene; cooling breezes, one of the joys of summer, were rising in the fir plantation (where long ago Mme. de Cambremer had dreamed of Chopin) and almost imperceptibly, in caressing coils, capricious eddies, were beginning their gentle nocturnes. I declined the rug which, on subsequent evenings, I was to accept when Albertine was with me, more to preserve the secrecy of my pleasure than to avoid the risk of cold. A vain search was made for the Norwegian philosopher. Had he been seized by a colic? Had he been afraid of missing the train? Had an aeroplane come to fetch him? Had he been carried aloft in an Assumption? In any case he had vanished without anyone's noticing his departure, like a god. "You are unwise," M. de Cambremer said to me, "it's as cold as charity." "Why charity?" the doctor inquired. "Beware of choking," the Marquis went on. "My sister never goes out at night. However, she is in a pretty bad state at present. In any case you oughtn't to stand about bare-headed, put your tile on at once." "They are not frigorific chokings," said Cottard sententiously. "Oh, indeed!" M. de Cambremer bowed. "Of course, if that's your opinion. . . ." "Opinions of the press!" said the doctor, smiling round his glasses. M. de Cambremer laughed, but, feeling certain that he was in the right, insisted: "All the same," he said, "whenever my sister goes out after dark, she has an attack." "It's no use quibbling," replied the doctor, regardless of his want of manners. "However, I don't practise medicine by the seaside, unless I am called in for a consultation. I am here on holiday." He was perhaps even more on holiday than he would have liked. M. de Cambremer having said to him as they got into the carriage together: "We are fortunate in having quite close to us (not on your side of the bay, on the opposite side, but it is quite narrow at that point) another medical celebrity, Doctor du Boulbon," Cottard, who, as a rule, from "deontology," abstained from criticising his colleagues, could not help exclaiming, as he had exclaimed to me on the fatal day when we had visited the little casino: "But he is not a doctor. He practises a literary medicine, it is all fantastic therapeutics, charlatanism. All the same, we are on quite good terms. I should take the boat and go over and pay him a visit, if I weren't leaving." But, from the air which Cottard assumed in speaking of du Boulbon to M. de Cambremer, I felt that the boat which he would gladly have taken to call upon him would have greatly resembled that vessel which, in order to go and ruin the waters discovered by another literary doctor, Virgil (who took all their patients from them as well), the doctors of Salerno had chartered, but which sank with them on the voyage. "Good-bye, my dear Saniette, don't forget to come to-morrow, you know how my husband enjoys seeing you. He enjoys your wit, your intellect; yes indeed, you know quite well, he takes sudden moods, but he can't live without seeing you. It's always the first thing he asks me: 'Is Saniette coming? I do so enjoy seeing him.'" "I never said anything of the sort," said M. Verdurin to Saniette with a feigned frankness which seemed perfectly to reconcile what the Mistress had just said with the manner in which he treated Saniette. Then looking at his watch, doubtless so as not to prolong the leave-taking in the damp night air, he warned the coachmen not to lose any time, but to be careful when going down the hill, and assured us that we should be in plenty of time for our train. This was to set down the faithful, one at one station, another at another, ending with myself, for no one else was going as far as Balbec, and beginning with the Cambremers. They, so as not to bring their horses all the way up to la Raspelière at night, took the train with us at Douville-Féterne. The station nearest to them was indeed not this, which, being already at some distance from the village, was farther still from the mansion, but la Sogne. On arriving at the station of Douville-Féterne, M. de Cambremer made a point of giving a "piece," as Françoise used to say, to the Verdurins' coachman (the nice, sensitive coachman, with melancholy thoughts), for M. de Cambremer was generous, and in that respect took, rather, "after his mamma." But, possibly because his "papa's" strain intervened at this point, he felt a scruple, or else that there might be a mistake—either on his part, if, for instance, in the dark, he were to give a sou instead of a franc, or on the recipient's who might not perceive the importance of the present that was being given him. And so he drew attention to it: "It is a franc I'm giving you, isn't it?" he said to the coachman, turning the coin until it gleamed in the lamplight, and so that the faithful might report his action to Mme. Verdurin. "Isn't it? Twenty sous is right, as it's only a short drive." He and Mme. de Cambremer left us at la Sogne. "I shall tell my sister," he repeated to me, "that you have choking fits, I am sure she will be interested." I understood that he meant: "will be pleased." As for his wife, she employed, in saying good-bye to me, two abbreviations which, even in writing, used to shock me at that time in a letter, although one has grown accustomed to them since, but which, when spoken, seem to me to-day even to contain in their deliberate carelessness, in their acquired familiarity, something insufferably pedantic: "Pleased to have met you," she said to me: "greetings to Saint-Loup, if you see him." In making this speech, Mme. de Cambremer pronounced the name "Saint-Loupe." I have never discovered who had pronounced it thus in her hearing, or what had led her to suppose that it ought to be so pronounced. However it may be, for some weeks afterwards, she continued to say "Saint-Loupe" and a man who had a great admiration for her and echoed her in every way did the same. If other people said "Saint-Lou," they would insist, would say emphatically "Saint-Loupe," whether to teach the others an indirect lesson or to be different from them. But, no doubt, women of greater brilliance than Mme. de Cambremer told her, or gave her indirectly to understand that this was not the correct pronunciation, and that what she regarded as a sign of originality was a mistake which would make people think her little conversant with the usages of society, for shortly afterwards Mme. de Cambremer was again saying "Saint-Lou," and her admirer similarly ceased to hold out, whether because she had lectured him, or because he had noticed that she no longer sounded the final consonant, and had said to himself that if a woman of such distinction, energy and ambition had yielded, it must have been on good grounds. The worst of her admirers was her husband. Mme. de Cambremer loved to tease other people in a way that was often highly impertinent. As soon as she began to attack me, or anyone else, in this fashion, M. de Cambremer would start watching her victim, laughing the while. As the Marquis had a squint—a blemish which gives an effect of wit to the mirth even of imbeciles—the effect of this laughter was to bring a segment of pupil into the otherwise complete whiteness of his eye. So a sudden rift brings a patch of blue into an otherwise clouded sky. His monocle moreover protected, like the glass over a valuable picture, this delicate operation. As for the actual intention of his laughter, it was hard to say whether it was friendly: "Ah! You rascal! You're in an enviable position, aren't you. You have won the favour of a lady who has a pretty wit!" Or coarse: "Well, Sir, I hope you'll learn your lesson, you've got to eat a slice of humble pie." Or obliging: "I'm here, you know, I take it with a laugh because it's all pure fun, but I shan't let you be ill-treated." Or cruelly accessory: "I don't need to add my little pinch of salt, but you can see, I'm revelling in all the insults she is showering on you. I'm wriggling like a hunchback, therefore I approve, I, the husband. And so, if you should take it into your head to answer back, you would have me to deal with, my young Sir. I should first of all give you a pair of resounding smacks, well aimed, then we should go and cross swords in the forest of Chantepie."

Whatever the correct interpretation of the husband's merriment, the wife's whimsies soon came to an end. Whereupon M. de Cambremer ceased to laugh, the temporary pupil vanished and as one had forgotten for a minute or two to expect an entirely white eyeball, it gave this ruddy Norman an air at once anaemic and ecstatic, as though the Marquis had just undergone an operation, or were imploring heaven, through his monocle, for the palms of martyrdom.

CHAPTER III

The sorrows of M. de Charlus.—His sham duel.—The stations on the "Transatlantic."—Weary of Albertine, I decide to break with her.

I WAS dropping with sleep. I was taken up to my floor not by the lift-boy, but by the squinting page, who to make conversation informed me that his sister was still with the gentleman who was so rich, and that, on one occasion, when she had made up her mind to return home instead of sticking to her business, her gentleman friend had paid a visit to the mother of the squinting page and of the other more fortunate children, who had very soon made the silly creature return to her protector. "You know, Sir, she's a fine lady, my sister is. She plays the piano, she talks Spanish. And you would never take her for the sister of the humble employee who brings you up in the lift, she denies herself nothing; Madame has a maid to herself, I shouldn't be surprised if one day she keeps her carriage. She is very pretty, if you could see her, a little too high and mighty, but, good lord, you can understand that. She's full of fun. She never leaves a hotel without doing something first in a wardrobe or a drawer, just to leave a little keepsake with the chambermaid who will have to wipe it up. Sometimes she does it in a cab, and after she's paid her fare, she'll hide behind a tree, and she doesn't half laugh when the cabby finds he's got to clean his cab after her. My father had another stroke of luck when he found my young brother that Indian Prince he used to know long ago. It's not the same style of thing, of course. But it's a superb position. The travelling by itself would be a dream. I'm the only one still on the shelf. But you never know. We're a lucky family; perhaps one day I shall be President of the Republic. But I'm keeping you talking" (I had not uttered a single word and was beginning to fall asleep as I listened to the flow of his). "Good-night, Sir. Oh! Thank you, Sir. If everybody had as kind a heart as you, there wouldn't be any poor people left. But, as my sister says, 'there will always have to be the poor so that now that I'm rich I can s—t on them.' You'll pardon the expression. Good-night, Sir."

Perhaps every night we accept the risk of facing, while we are asleep, sufferings which we regard as unreal and unimportant because they will be felt in the course of a sleep which we suppose to be unconscious. And indeed on these evenings when I came back late from la Raspelière I was very sleepy. But after the weather turned cold I could not get to sleep at once, for the fire lighted up the room as though there were a lamp burning in it. Only it was nothing more than a blazing log, and—like a lamp too, for that matter, like the day when night gathers—its too bright light was not long in fading; and I entered a state of slumber which is like a second room that we take, into which, leaving our own room, we go when we want to sleep. It has noises of its own and we are sometimes violently awakened by the sound of a bell, perfectly heard by our ears, although nobody has rung. It has its servants, its special visitors who call to take us out so that we are ready to get up when we are compelled to realise, by our almost immediate transmigration into the other room, the room of overnight, that it is empty, that nobody has called. The race that inhabits it is, like that of our first human ancestors, androgynous. A man in it appears a moment later in the form of a woman. Things in it shew a tendency to turn into men, men into friends and enemies. The time that elapses for the sleeper, during these spells of slumber, is absolutely different from the time in which the life of the waking man is passed. Sometimes its course is far more rapid, a quarter of an hour seems a day, at other times far longer, we think we have taken only a short nap, when we have slept through the day. Then, in the chariot of sleep, we descend into depths in which memory can no longer overtake it, and on the brink of which the mind has been obliged to retrace its steps. The horses of sleep, like those of the sun, move at so steady a pace, in an atmosphere in which there is no longer any resistance, that it requires some little aerolith extraneous to ourselves (hurled from the azure by some Unknown) to strike our regular sleep (which otherwise would have no reason to stop, and would continue with a similar motion world without end) and to make it swing sharply round, return towards reality, travel without pause, traverse the regions bordering on life in which presently the sleeper will hear the sounds that come from life, quite vague still, but already perceptible, albeit corrupted—and come to earth suddenly and awake. Then from those profound slumbers we awake in a dawn, not knowing who we are, being nobody, newly born, ready for anything, our brain being emptied of that past which was previously our life. And perhaps it is more pleasant still when our landing at the waking-point is abrupt and the thoughts of our sleep, hidden by a cloak of oblivion, have not time to return to us in order, before sleep ceases. Then, from the black tempest through which we seem to have passed (but we do not even say *we*), we emerge prostrate, without a thought, a *we* that is void of content. What hammer-blow has the person or thing that is lying there received to make it unconscious of anything, stupefied until the moment when memory, flooding back, restores to it consciousness or personality? Moreover, for both these kinds of awakening, we must avoid falling asleep, even into deep slumber, under the law of habit. For everything that habit ensnares in her nets, she watches closely, we must escape her, take our sleep at a moment when we thought we were doing anything else than sleeping, take, in a word, a sleep that does not dwell under the tutelage of foresight, in the company, albeit latent, of reflexion. At least, in these awakenings which I have just described, and which I experienced as a rule when I had been dining overnight at la Raspelière, everything occurred as though by this process, and I can testify to it, I the strange human being who, while he waits for death to release him, lives behind closed shutters, knows nothing of the world, sits motionless as an owl, and like that bird begins to see things a little plainly only when darkness falls. Everything occurs as though by this process, but perhaps only a layer of wadding has prevented the sleeper from taking in the internal dialogue of memories and the incessant verbiage of sleep. For (and this may be equally manifest in the other system, vaster, more mysterious, more astral) at the moment of his entering the waking state, the sleeper hears a voice inside him saying: "Will you come to this dinner to-night, my dear friend, it would be such fun?" and thinks: "Yes, what fun it will be, I shall go"; then, growing wider awake, he suddenly remembers: "My grandmother has only a few weeks to live, the Doctor assures us." He rings, he weeps at the thought that it will not be, as in the past, his grandmother, his dying grandmother, but an indifferent waiter that will come in answer to his summons. Moreover, when sleep bore him so far away from the world inhabited by memory and thought, through an ether in which he was alone, more than alone; not having that companion in whom we perceive things, ourself, he was outside the range of time and its measures. But now the footman is in the room, and he dares not ask him the time, for he does not know whether he has slept, for how many hours he has slept (he asks himself whether it should not be how many days, returning thus with weary body and mind refreshed, his heart sick for home, as from a journey too distant not to have taken a long time). We may of course insist that there is but one time, for the futile reason that it is by looking at the clock that we have discovered to have been merely a quarter of an hour what we had supposed a day. But at the moment when we make this discovery we are a man awake, plunged in the time of waking men, we have deserted the other time. Perhaps indeed more than another time: another life. The pleasures that we enjoy in sleep, we do not include them in the list of the pleasures that we have felt in the course of our existence. To allude only to the most grossly sensual of them all, which of us, on waking, has not felt a certain irritation at having experienced in his sleep a pleasure which, if he is anxious not to tire himself, he is not, once he is awake, at liberty to repeat indefinitely during the day. It seems a positive waste. We have had pleasure, in another life, which is not ours

Sufferings and pleasures of the dream-world (which generally vanish soon enough after our waking), if we make them figure in a budget, it is not in the current account of our life.

Two times, I have said; perhaps there is only one after all, not that the time of the waking man has any validity for the sleeper, but perhaps because the other life, the life in which he sleeps, is not—in its profounder part—included in the category of time. I came to this conclusion when on the mornings after dinners at la Raspelière I used to lie so completely asleep. For this reason. I was beginning to despair, on waking, when I found that, after I had rung the bell ten times, the waiter did not appear. At the eleventh ring he came. It was only the first after all. The other ten had been mere suggestions in my sleep which still hung about me, of the peal that I had been meaning to sound. My numbed hands had never even moved. Well, on those mornings (and this is what makes me say that sleep is perhaps unconscious of the law of time) my effort to awaken consisted chiefly in an effort to make the obscure, undefined mass of the sleep in which I had just been living enter into the scale of time. It is no easy task; sleep, which does not know whether we have slept for two hours or two days, cannot provide any indication. And if we do not find one outside, not being able to re-enter time, we fall asleep again, for five minutes which seem to us three hours.

I have always said—and have proved by experiment—that the most powerful soporific is sleep itself. After having slept profoundly for two hours, having fought against so many giants, and formed so many lifelong friendships, it is far more difficult to awake than after taking several grammes of veronal. And so, reasoning from one thing to the other, I was surprised to hear from the Norwegian philosopher, who had it from M. Boutroux, "my eminent colleague—pardon me, my brother," what M. Bergson thought of the peculiar effects upon the memory of soporific drugs. "Naturally," M. Bergson had said to M. Boutroux, if one was to believe the Norwegian philosopher, "soporifics, taken from time to time in moderate doses, have no effect upon that solid memory of our every-day life which is so firmly established within us. But there are other forms of memory, loftier, but also more unstable. One of my colleagues lectures upon ancient history. He tells me that if, overnight, he has taken a tablet to make him sleep, he has great difficulty, during his lecture, in recalling the Greek quotations that he requires. The doctor who recommended these tablets assured him that they had no effect upon the memory. 'That is perhaps because you do not have to quote Greek,' the historian answered, not without a note of derisive pride."

I cannot say whether this conversation between M. Bergson and M. Boutroux is accurately reported. The Norwegian philosopher, albeit so profound and so lucid, so passionately attentive, may have misunderstood. Personally, in my own experience I have found the opposite result. The moments of oblivion that come to us in the morning after we have taken certain narcotics have a resemblance that is only partial, though disturbing, to the oblivion that reigns during a night of natural and profound sleep. Now what I find myself forgetting in either case is not some line of Baudelaire, which on the other hand keeps sounding in my ear, it is not some concept of one of the philosophers above-named, it is the actual reality of the ordinary things that surround me—if I am asleep—my non-perception of which makes me an idiot; it is, if I am awakened and proceed to emerge from an artificial slumber, not the system of Porphyry or Plotinus, which I can discuss as fluently as at any other time, but the answer that I have promised to give to an invitation, the memory of which is replaced by a universal blank. The lofty thought remains in its place; what the soporific has put out of action is the power to act in little things, in everything that demands activity in order to seize at the right moment, to grasp some memory of every-day life. In spite of all that may be said about survival after the destruction of the brain, I observe that each alteration of the brain is a partial death. We possess all our memories, but not the faculty of recalling them, said, echoing M. Bergson, the eminent Norwegian philosopher whose language I have made no attempt to imitate in order not to prolong my story unduly. But not the faculty of recalling them. But what, then, is a memory which we do not recall? Or, indeed, let us go farther. We do not recall our memories of the last thirty years; but we are wholly steeped in them; why then stop short at thirty years, why not prolong back to before our birth this anterior life? The moment that I do not know a whole section of the memories that are behind me, the moment that they are invisible to me, that I have not the faculty of calling them to me, who can assure me that in that *mass* unknown to me there are not some that extend back much farther than my human life. If I can have in me and round me so many memories which I do not remember, this oblivion (a *de facto* oblivion, at least, since

I have not the faculty of seeing anything) may extend over a life which I have lived in the body of another man, even upon another planet. A common oblivion effaces all. But what, in that case, signifies that immortality of the soul the reality of which the Norwegian philosopher affirmed? The person that I shall be after death has no more reason to remember the man whom I have been since my birth than the latter to remember what I was before it.

The waiter came in. I did not mention to him that I had rung several times, for I was beginning to realise that hitherto I had only dreamed that I was ringing. I was alarmed nevertheless by the thought that this dream had had the clear precision of experience. Experience would, reciprocally, have the irreality of a dream.

Instead I asked him who it was that had been ringing so often during the night. He told me: "Nobody," and could prove his statement, for the bell-board would have registered any ring. And yet I could hear the repeated, almost furious peals which were still echoing in my ears and were to remain perceptible for several days. It is however seldom that sleep thus projects into our waking life memories that do not perish with it. We can count these aeroliths. If it is an idea that sleep has forged, it soon breaks up into slender, irrecoverable fragments. But, in this instance, sleep had fashioned sounds. More material and simpler, they lasted longer. I was astonished by the relative earliness of the hour, as told me by the waiter. I was none the less refreshed. It is the light sleeps that have a long duration, because, being an intermediate state between waking and sleeping, preserving a somewhat faded but permanent impression of the former, they require infinitely more time to refresh us than a profound sleep, which may be short. I felt quite comfortable for another reason. If remembering that we are tired is enought to make us feel our tiredness, saying to oneself: "I am refreshed," is enough to create refreshment. Now I had been dreaming that M. de Charlus was a hundred and ten years old, and had just boxed the ears of his own mother, Madame Verdurin, because she had paid five thousand millions for a bunch of violets; I was therefore assured that I had slept profoundly, had dreamed the reverse of what had been in my thoughts overnight and of all the possibilities of life at the moment; this was enough to make me feel entirely refreshed.

I should greatly have astonished my mother, who could not understand M. de Charlus's assiduity in visiting the Verdurins, had I told her whom (on the very day on which Albertine's toque had been ordered, without a word about it to her, in order that it might come as a surprise) M. de Charlus had brought to dine in a private room at the Grand Hotel, Balbec. His guest was none other than the footman of a lady who was a cousin of the Cambremers. This footman was very smartly dressed, and, as he crossed the hall, with the Baron, "did the man of fashion" as Saint-Loup would have said in the eyes of the visitors. Indeed, the young page-boys, the Levites who were swarming down the temple steps at that moment because it was the time when they came on duty, paid no attention to the two strangers, one of whom, M. de Charlus, kept his eyes lowered to shew that he was paying little if any to them. He appeared to be trying to carve his way through their midst. "Prosper, dear hope of a sacred nation," he said, recalling a passage from Racine, and applying to it a wholly different meaning. "Pardon?" asked the footman, who was not well up in the classics. M. de Charlus made no reply, for he took a certain pride in never answering questions and in marching straight ahead as though there were no other visitors in the hotel, or no one existed in the world except himself, Baron de Charlus. But, having continued to quote the speech of Josabeth: "Come, come, my children," he felt a revulsion and did not, like her, add: "Bid them approach," for these young people had not yet reached the age at which sex is completely developed, and which appealed to M. de Charlus. Moreover, if he had written to Madame de Chevregny's footman, because he had had no doubt of his docility, he had hoped to meet some one more virile. On seeing him, he found him more effeminate than he would have liked. He told him that he had been expecting some one else, for he knew by sight another of Madame de Chevregny's footmen, whom he had noticed upon the box of her carriage. This was an extremely rustic type of peasant, the very opposite of him who had come, who, on the other hand, regarding his own effeminate ways as adding to his attractiveness, and never doubting that it was this man-of-the-world air that had captivated M. de Charlus, could not even guess whom the Baron meant. "But there is no one else in the house, except one that you can't have given the eye to, he is hideous, just like a great peasant." And at the thought that it was perhaps this rustic whom the Baron had seen, he felt his self-esteem wounded. The Baron guessed this, and, widening his quest: "But I have not taken a vow that I will know only Mme. de Chevregny's men," he said. "Surely there are plenty of fellows in one house or another here or in Paris, since you are leaving soon, that you could introduce to me?" "Oh, no!" replied the footman, "I never go with anyone of my own class. I only speak to them on duty. But there is one very nice person I can make you know." "Who?" asked the Baron. "The Prince de Guermantes." M. de Guermantes was vexed at being offered only a man so advanced in years, one, moreover, to whom he had no need to apply to a footman for an introduction. And so he declined the offer in a dry tone and, not letting himself be discouraged by the menial's social pretensions, began to explain to him again what he wanted, the style, the type, a jockey, for instance, and so on. . . . Fearing lest the solicitor, who went past at that moment, might have heard them, he thought it cunning to shew that he was speaking of anything in the world rather than what his hearer might suspect, and said with emphasis and in ringing tones, but as though he were simply continuing his conversation: "Yes, in spite of my age, I still keep up a passion for collecting, a passion for pretty things, I will do anything to secure an old bronze, an early lustre. I adore the Beautiful." But to make the footman understand the change of subject he had so rapidly executed, M. de Charlus laid such stress upon each word, and what was more, to be heard by the solicitor, he shouted his words so loud that this charade should in itself have been enough to reveal what it concealed from ears more alert than those of the officer of the court. He suspected nothing, any more than any of the other residents in the hotel, all of whom saw a fashionable foreigner in the footman so smartly attired. On the other hand, if the gentlemen were deceived and took him for a distinguished American, no sooner did he appear before the servants than he was spotted by them, as one convict recognises another. indeed scented afar off, as certain animals scent one another. The head waiters raised their eyebrows. Aimé cast a suspicious glance. The wine waiter, shrugging his shoulders, uttered behind his hand (because he thought it polite) an offensive expression which everybody heard. And even our old Françoise, whose sight was failing and who went past at that moment at the foot of the staircase to dine with the *courriers*, raised her head, recognised a servant where the hotel guests never suspected one—as the old nurse Euryclea recognises Ulysses long before the suitors seated at the banquet—and seeing, arm in arm with him, M. de Charlus, assumed an appalled expression, as though all of a sudden slanders which she had heard repeated and had not believed had acquired a heartrending probability in her eyes. She never spoke to me, nor to anyone else, of this incident, but it must have caused a considerable commotion in her brain, for afterwards, whenever in Paris she happened to see "Julien," to whom until then she had been so greatly attached, she still treated him with politeness, but with a politeness that had cooled and was always tempered with a strong dose of reserve. This same incident led some one else to confide in me: this was Aimé. When I encountered M. de Charlus, he, not having expected to meet me, raised his hand and called out "Good evening" with the indifference—outwardly, at least—of a great nobleman who believes that everything is allowed him and thinks it better not to appear to be hiding anything. Aimé who at that moment was watching him with a suspicious eye and saw that I greeted the companion of the person in whom he was certain that he detected a servant, asked me that same evening who he was. For, for some time past, Aimé had shewn a fondness for talking, or rather, as he himself put it, doubtless in order to emphasise the character—philosophical, according to him—of these talks, "discussing" with me. And as I often said to him that it distressed me that he should have to stand beside the table while I ate instead of being able to sit down and share my meal, he declared that he had never seen a guest shew such "sound reasoning." He was talking at that moment to two waiters. They had bowed to me, I did not know why their faces were unfamiliar, albeit their conversation sounded a note which seemed to me not to be novel. Aimé was scolding them both because of their matrimonial engagements, of which he disapproved. He appealed to me, I said that I could not have any opinion on the matter since I did not know them. They told me their names, reminded me that they had often waited upon me at Rivebelle. But one had let his moustache grow, the other had shaved his off and had had his head cropped; and for this reason, albeit it was the same head as before that rested upon the shoulders of each of them (and not a different head as in the faulty restorations of Notre-Dame), it had remained almost as invisible to me as those objects which escape the most minute search and are actually staring everybody in the face where nobody notices them, on the mantelpiece. As soon as I knew their names, I recognised exactly the uncertain music of their voices because I saw once more the old face which made it clear. "They want to get married and they haven't even learned English!" Aimé said to me, without reflecting that I was little versed in the ways of hotel service, and could not be aware that a person who does not know foreign languages cannot be certain of getting a situation. I, who supposed that he would have no difficulty in finding out that the newcomer was M. de Charlus, and indeed imagined that he must remember him, having waited upon him in the dining-room when the Baron came, during my former visit to Balbec, to see Mme. de Villeparisis, I told him his name. Not only did Aimé not remember the Baron de Charlus, but the name appeared to make a profound impression upon him. He told me that he would look for a letter next day in his room which I might perhaps be able to explain to him. I was all the more astonished in that M. de Charlus, when he had wished to give me one of Bergotte's books, at Balbec, the other year, had specially asked for Aimé, whom he must have recognised later on in that Paris restaurant where I had taken luncheon with Saint-Loup and his mistress and where M. de Charlus had come to spy upon us. It is true that Aimé had not been able to execute these commissions in person, being on the former occasion in bed, and on the latter engaged in waiting. I had nevertheless grave doubts as to his sincerity, when he pretended not to know M. de Charlus. For one thing, he must have appealed to the Baron. Like all the upstairs waiters of the Balbec Hotel, like several of the Prince de Guermantes's footmen, Aimé belonged to a race more ancient than that of the Prince, therefore more noble. When you asked for a sitting-room, you thought at first that you were alone. But presently, in the service-room you caught sight of a sculptural waiter, of that ruddy Etruscan kind of which Aimé was typical, slightly aged by excessive consumption of champagne and seeing the inevitable hour approach for Contrexéville water. Not all the visitors asked them merely to wait upon them. The underlings who were young, conscientious, busy, who had mistresses waiting for them outside, made off. Whereupon Aimé reproached them with not being serious. He had every right to do so. He himself was serious. He had a wife and children, and was ambitious on their behalf. And so the advances made to him by a strange lady or gentleman he never repulsed, though it meant his staying all night. For business must come before everything. He was so much of the type that attracted M. de Charlus that I suspected him of falsehood when he told me that he did not know him. I was wrong. The page had been perfectly truthful when he told the Baron that Aimé (who had given him a dressing-down for it next day) had gone to bed (or gone out), and on the other occasion was busy waiting. But imagination outreaches reality. And the page-boy's embarrassment had probably aroused in M. de Charlus doubts as to the sincerity of his excuses that had wounded sentiments of which Aimé had no suspicion. We have seen moreover that Saint-Loup had prevented Aimé from going out to the carriage in which M. de Charlus, who had managed somehow or other to discover the waiter's new address, received a further disappointment. Aimé, who had not noticed him, felt an astonishment that may be imagined when, on the evening of that very day on which I had taken luncheon with Saint-Loup and his mistress, he received a letter sealed with the Guermantes arms, from which I shall quote a few passages here as an example of unilateral insanity in an intelligent man addressing an imbecile endowed with sense. "Sir, I have been unsuccessful, notwithstanding efforts that would astonish many people who have sought in vain to be greeted and welcomed by myself, in persuading you to listen to certain explanations which you have not asked of me but which I have felt it to be incumbent upon my dignity and your own to offer you. I am going therefore to write down here what it would have been more easy to say to you in person. I shall not conceal from you that, the first time that I set eyes upon you at Balbec, I found your face frankly antipathetic." Here followed reflexions upon the resemblance—remarked only on the following day—to a deceased friend to whom M. de Charlus had been deeply attached. "The thought then suddenly occurred to me that you might, without in any way encroaching upon the demands of your profession, come to see me and, by joining me in the card games with which his mirth used to dispel my gloom, give me the illusion that he was not dead. Whatever the nature of the more or less fatuous suppositions which you probably formed, suppositions more within the mental range of a servant (who does not even deserve the name of servant since he has declined to serve) than the comprehension of so lofty a sentiment, you probably thought that you were giving yourself importance, knowing not who I was nor what I was, by sending word to me, when I asked you to fetch me a book, that you were in bed; but it is a mistake to imagine that impolite behaviour ever adds to charm, in which you moreover are entirely lacking. I should have ended matters there had I not, by chance, the following morning, found an opportunity of speaking to you. Your resemblance to my poor friend was so accentuated, banishing even the intolerable protuberance of your too prominent chin, that I realised that it was the deceased who at that moment was lending you his own kindly expression so as to permit you to regain your hold over me and to prevent you from missing the unique opportunity that was being offered you. Indeed, although I have no wish, since there is no longer any object and it is unlikely that I shall meet you again in this life, to introduce coarse questions of material interest, I should have been only too glad to obey the prayer of my dead friend (for I believe in the Communion of Saints and in their deliberate intervention in the destiny of the living), that I should treat you as I used to treat him, who had his carriage, his servants, and to whom it was quite natural that I should consecrate the greater part of my fortune since I loved him as a father loves his son. You have decided otherwise. To my request that you should fetch me a book you sent the reply that you were obliged to go out. And this morning when I sent to ask you to come to my carriage, you then, if I may so speak without blasphemy, denied me for the third time. You will excuse my not enclosing in this envelope the lavish gratuity which I intended to give you at Balbec and to which it would be too painful to me to restrict myself in dealing with a person with whom I had thought for a moment of sharing all that I possess. At least you might spare me the trouble of making a fourth vain attempt to find you at your restaurant, to which my patience will not extend." (Here M. de Charlus gave his address, stated the hours at which he would be at home, etc.) "Farewell, Sir. Since I assume that, resembling so strongly the friend whom I have lost, you cannot be entirely stupid, otherwise physiognomy would be a false science, I am convinced that if, one day, you think of this incident again, it will not be without feeling some regret and some remorse. For my part, believe that I am quite sincere in saying that I retain no bitterness. I should have preferred that we should part with a less unpleasant memory than this third futile endeavour. It will soon be forgotten. We are like those vessels which you must often have seen at Balbec, which have crossed one another's course for a moment; it might have been to the advantage of each of them to stop; but one of them has decided otherwise; presently they will no longer even see one another on the horizon and their meeting is a thing out of mind; but, befcre this final parting, each of them salutes the other, and so at this point, Sir, wishing you all good fortune, does

THE BARON DE CHARLUS."

Aimé had not even read this letter through, being able to make nothing of it and suspecting a hoax. When I had explained to him who the Baron was, he appeared to be lost in thought and to be feeling the regret that M. de Charlus had anticipated. I would not be prepared to swear that he would not at that moment have written a letter of apology to a man who gave carriages to his friends. But in the interval M. de Charlus had made Morel's acquaintance. It was true that, his relations with Morel being possibly Platonic, M. de Charlus occasionally sought to spend an evening in company such as that in which I had just met him in the hall. But he was no longer able to divert from Morel the violent sentiment which, at liberty a few years earlier, had asked nothing better than to fasten itself upon Aimé and had dictated the letter which had distressed me, for its writer's sake, when the head waiter shewed me it. It was, in view of the anti-social nature of M. de Charlus's love, a more striking example of the insensible, sweeping force of these currents of passion by which the lover, like a swimmer, is very soon carried out of sight of land. No doubt the love of a normal man may also, when the lover, by the successive invention of his desires, regrets, disappointments, plans, constructs a whole romance about a woman whom he does not know, allow the two legs of the compass to gape at a quite remarkably wide angle. All the same, such an angle was singularly enlarged by the character of a passion which is not generally shared and by the difference in social position between M. de Charlus and Aimé.

Every day I went out with Albertine. She had decided to take up painting again and had chosen as the subject of her first attempts the church of Saint-Jean de la Haise which nobody ever visited and very few had even heard of, a spot difficult to describe, impossible to discover without a guide, slow of access in its isolation, more than half an hour from the Epreville station, after one had long left behind one the last houses of the village of Quetteholme. As to the name Epreville I found that the curé's book and Brichot's information were at variance. According to one, Epreville was the ancient Sprevilla; the other derived the name from Aprivilla. On our first visit we took a little train in the opposite direction from Féterne, that is to say towards Grattevast. But we were in the dog days and it had been a terrible strain simply to go out of doors immediately after luncheon. I should have preferred not to start so soon; the luminous and burning air provoked thoughts of indolence and cool retreats. It filled my mother's room and mine, according to their exposure, at varying temperatures, like rooms in a Turkish bath. Mamma's dressing-room, festooned by the sun with a dazzling, Moorish whiteness, appeared to be sunk at the bottom of a well, because of the four plastered walls on which it looked out, while far above, in the empty space, the sky, whose fleecy white waves one saw slip past, one behind another, seemed (because of the longing that one felt), whether built upon a terrace or seen reversed in a mirror hung above the window, a tank filled with blue water, reserved for bathers. Notwithstanding this scorching temperature, we had taken the one o'clock train. But Albertine had been very hot in the carriage, hotter still in the long walk across country, and I was afraid of her catching cold when she proceeded to sit still in that damp hollow where the sun's rays did not penetrate. Having, on the other hand, as long ago as our first visits to Elstir, made up my mind that she would appreciate not merely luxury but even a certain degree of comfort of which her want of money deprived her, I had made arrangements with a Balbec jobmaster that a carriage was to be sent every day to take us out. To escape from the heat we took the road through the forest of Chantepie. The invisibility of the innumerable birds, some of them almost sea-birds, that conversed with one another from the trees on either side of us, gave the same impression of repose that one has when one shuts one's eyes. By Albertine's side, enchained by her arms within the carriage, I listened to these Oceanides. And when by chance I caught sight of one of these musicians as he flitted from one leaf to the shelter of another, there was so little apparent connexion between him and his songs that I could not believe that I beheld their cause in the little body, fluttering, humble, startled and unseeing. The carriage could not take us all the way to the church. I stopped it when we had passed through Quetteholme and bade Albertine good-bye. For she had alarmed me by saying to me of this church as of other buildings, of certain pictures: "What a pleasure it would be to see that with you!" This pleasure was one that I did not feel myself capable of giving her. I felt it myself in front of beautiful things only if I was alone or pretended to be alone and did not speak. But since she supposed that she might, thanks to me, feel sensations of art which are not communicated thus—I thought it more prudent to say that I must leave her, would come back to fetch her at the end of the day, but that in the mean time I must go back with the carriage to pay a call on Mme. Verdurin or on the Cambremers, or even spend an hour with Mamma at Balbec, but never farther afield. To begin with, that is to say. For, Albertine having once said to me petulantly: "It's a bore that Nature has arranged things so badly and put Saint-Jean de la Haise in one direction, la Raspelière in another, so that you're imprisoned for the whole day in the part of the country you've chosen;" as soon as the toque and veil had come I ordered, to my eventual undoing, a motor-car from Saint-Fargeau (*Sanctus Ferreolus,* according to the curé's book). Albertine, whom I had kept in ignorance and who had come to call for me, was surprised when she heard in front of the hotel the purr of the engine, delighted when she learned that this motor was for ourselves. I made her come upstairs for a moment to my room. She jumped for joy. "We are going to pay a call on the Verdurins." "Yes, but you'd better not go dressed like that since you are going to have your motor. There, you will look better in these." And I brought out the toque and veil which I had hidden. "They're for me? Oh! You are an angel," she cried, throwing her arms round my neck. Aimé who met us on the stairs, proud of Albertine's smart attire and of our means of transport, for these vehicles were still comparatively rare at Balbec, gave himself the pleasure of coming downstairs behind us. Albertine, anxious to display herself in her new garments, asked me to have the car opened, as we could shut it later on when we wished to be more private. "Now then," said Aimé to the driver, with whom he was not acquainted and who had not stirred, "don't you (*tu*) hear, you're to open your roof?" For Aimé, sophisticated by hotel life, in which moreover he had won his way to exalted rank, was not as shy as the cab driver to whom Françoise was a "lady"; notwithstanding the want of any formal introduction, plebeians whom he had never seen before he addressed as *tu*, though it was hard to say whether this was aristocratic disdain on his part or democratic fraternity. "I am engaged," replied the chauffeur, who did not know me by sight. "I am ordered for Mlle. Simonet. I can't take this gentleman." Aimé burst out laughing: "Why, you great pumpkin," he said to the driver, whom he at once convinced, "this is Mademoiselle Simonet, and Monsieur, who tells you to open the roof of your car, is the person who has engaged you." And as Aimé, although personally he had no feeling for Albertine, was for my sake proud of the garments she was wearing, he whispered to the chauffeur: "Don't get the chance of driving a Princess like that every day, do you?" On this first occasion it was not I alone that was able to go to la Raspelière as I did on other days, while Albertine painted; she decided to go there with me. She did indeed think that we might stop here and there on our way, but supposed it to be impossible to start by going to Saint-Jean de la Haise. That is to say in another direction, and to make an excursion which seemed to be reserved for a different day. She learned on the contrary from the driver that nothing could be easier than to go to Saint-Jean, which he could do in twenty minutes, and that we might stay there if we chose for hours, or go on much farther, for from Quetteholme to la Raspelière would not take more than thirty-five minutes. We realised this as soon as the vehicle, starting off, covered in one bound twenty paces of an excellent horse. Distances are only the relation of space to time and vary with that relation. We express the difficulty that we have in getting to a place in a system of miles or kilometres which becomes false as soon as that difficulty decreases. Art is modified by it also, when a village which seemed to be in a different world from some other village becomes its neighbour in a landscape whose dimensions are altered. In any case the information that there may perhaps exist a universe in which two and two make five and the straight line is not the shortest way between two points would have astonished Albertine far less than to hear the driver say that it was easy to go in a single afternoon to Saint-Jean and la Raspelière, Douville and Quetteholme, Saint-Mars le Vieux and Saint-Mars le Vêtu, Gourville and Old Balbec, Tourville and Féterne, prisoners hitherto as hermetically confined in the cells of distinct days as long ago were Méséglise and Guermantes, upon which the same eyes could not gaze in the course of one afternoon, delivered now by the giant with the seven-league boots, came and clustered about our tea-time their towers and steeples, their old gardens which the encroaching wood sprang back to reveal.

Coming to the foot of the cliff road, the car took it in its stride, with a continuous sound like that of a knife being ground, while the sea falling away grew broader beneath us. The old rustic houses of Montsurvent ran towards us, clasping to their bosoms vine or rose-bush; the firs of la Raspelière, more agitated than when the evening breeze was rising, ran in every direction to escape from us and a new servant whom I had never seen before came to open the door for us on the terrace, while the gardener's son, betraying a precocious bent, devoured the machine with his gaze. As it was not a Monday we did not know whether we should find Mme. Verdurin, for except upon that day, when she was at home, it was unsafe to call upon her without warning. No doubt she was "principally" at home, but this expression, which Mme. Swann employed at the time when she too was seeking to form her little clan, and to draw visitors to herself without moving towards them, an expression which she interpreted as meaning "on principle," meant no more than "as a general rule," that is to say with frequent exceptions. For not only did Mme. Verdurin like going out, but she carried her duties as a hostess to extreme lengths, and when she had had people to luncheon, immediately after the coffee, liqueurs and cigarettes (notwithstanding the first somnolent effects of the heat and of digestion in which they would have preferred to watch through the leafy boughs of the terrace the Jersey packet passing over the enamelled sea), the programme included a series of excursions in the course of which her guests, installed by force in carriages, were conveyed, willy-nilly, to look at one or other of the views that abound in the neighbourhood of Douville. This second part of the entertainment was, as it happened (once the effort to rise and enter the carriage had been made), no less satisfactory than the other to the guests, already prepared by the succulent dishes, the vintage wines or sparkling cider to let themselves be easily intoxicated by the purity of the breeze and the magnificence of the views. Mme. Verdurin used to make strangers visit these rather as though they were portions (more or less detached) of her property, which you could not help going to see the moment you came to luncheon with her and which conversely you would never have known had you not been entertained by the Mistress. This claim to arrogate to herself the exclusive right over walks and drives, as over Morel's and formerly Dechambre's playing, and to compel the landscapes to form part of the little clan was not for that matter so absurd as it appears at first sight. Mme. Verdurin deplored the want of taste which, according to her, the Cambremers shewed in the furnishing of la Raspelière and the arrangement of the garden, but still more their want of initiative in the excursions that they took or made their guests take in the surrounding country. Just as, according to her, la Raspelière was only beginning to become what it should always have been now that it was the asylum of the little clan, so she insisted that the Cambremers, perpetually exploring in their barouche, along the railway line, by the shore, the one ugly road that there was in the district, had been living in the place all their lives but did not know it. There was a grain of truth in this assertion. From force of habit, lack of imagination, want of interest in a country which seemed hackneyed because it was so near, the Cambremers when they left their home went always to the same places and by the same roads. To be sure they laughed heartily at the Verdurins' offer to shew them their native country. But when it came to that, they and even their coachman would have been incapable of taking us to the splendid, more or less secret places, to which M. Verdurin brought us, now forcing the barrier of a private but deserted property upon which other people would not have thought it possible to venture, now leaving the carriage to follow a path which was not wide enough for wheeled traffic, but in either case with the certain recompense of a marvellous view. Let us say in passing that the garden at la Raspelière was in a sense a compendium of all the excursions to be made in a radius of many miles. For one thing because of its commanding position, overlooking on one side the valley, on the other the sea, and also because, on one and the same side, the seaward side for instance, clearings had been made through the trees in such a way that from one point you embraced one horizon, from another another. There was at each of these points of view a bench; you went and sat down in turn upon the bench from which there was the view of Balbec, or Parville, or Douville. Even to command a single view one bench would have been placed more or less on the edge of the cliff, another farther back. From the latter you had a foreground of verdure and a horizon which seemed already the vastest imaginable, but which became infinitely larger if, continuing along a little path, you went to the next bench from which you scanned the whole amphitheatre of the sea. There you could make out exactly the sound of the waves which did not penetrate to the more secluded parts of the garden, where the sea was still visible but no longer audible. These resting-places bore at la Raspelière among the occupants of the house the name of "views." And indeed they assembled round the mansion the finest views of the neighbouring places, coastline or forest, seen greatly diminished by distance, as Hadrian collected in his villa reduced models of the most famous monuments of different countries. The name that followed the word "view" was not necessarily that of a place on the coast, but often that of the opposite shore of the bay which you could make out, standing out in a certain relief notwithstanding the extent of the panorama. Just as you took a book from M. Verdurin's library to go and read for an hour at the "view of Balbec," so if the sky was clear the liqueurs would be served at the "view of Rivebelle," on condition however that the wind was not too strong, for, in spite of the trees planted on either side, the air up there was keen. To come back to the carriage parties that Mme. Verdurin used to organise for the afternoons, the Mistress, if on her return she found the cards of some social butterfly "on a flying visit to the coast," would pretend to be overjoyed, but was actually broken-hearted at having missed his visit and (albeit people at this date came only to "see the house" or to make the acquaintance for a day of a woman whose artistic salon was famous, but outside the pale in Paris) would at once make M. Verdurin invite him to dine on the following Wednesday. As the tourist was often obliged to leave before that day, or was afraid to be out late, Mme. Verdurin had arranged that on Mondays she was always to be found at teatime. These teaparties were not at all large, and I had known more brilliant gatherings of the sort in Paris, at the Princesse de Guermantes's, at Mme. de Gallifet's or Mme. d'Arpajon's. But this was not Paris, and the charm of the setting enhanced, in my eyes, not merely the pleasantness of the party but the merits of the visitors. A meeting with some social celebrity, which in Paris would have given me no pleasure, but which at la Raspelière, whither he had come from a distance by Féterne or the forest of Chantepie, changed in character, in importance, became an agreeable incident. Sometimes it was a person whom I knew quite well and would not have gone a yard to meet at the Swanns. But his name sounded differently upon this cliff, like the name of an actor whom one has constantly heard in a theatre, printed upon the announcement, in a different colour, of an extraordinary and gala performance, where his notoriety is suddenly multiplied by the unexpectedness of the rest. As in the country people behave without ceremony, the social celebrity often took it upon him to bring the friends with whom he was staying, murmuring the excuse in Mme. Verdurin's ear that he could not leave them behind as he was living in their house; to his hosts on the other hand he pretended to offer, as a sort of courtesy, the distraction, in a monotonous seaside life, of being taken to a centre of wit and intellect, of visiting a magnificent mansion and of making an excellent tea. This composed at once an assembly of several persons of semi-distinction; and if a little slice of garden with a few trees, which would seem shabby in the country, acquires an extraordinary charm in the Avenue Gabriel or let us say the Rue de Monceau, where only multi-millionaires can afford such a luxury, inversely gentlemen who are of secondary importance at a Parisian party stood out at their full value on a Monday afternoon at la Raspelière. No sooner did they sit down at the table covered with a cloth embroidered in red, beneath the painted panels, to partake of the rock cakes, Norman puff pastry, tartlets shaped like boats filled with cherries like beads of coral, "diplomatic" cakes, than these guests were subjected, by the proximity of the great bowl of azure upon which the window opened, and which you could not help seeing when you looked at them, to a profound alteration, a transmutation which changed them into something more precious than before. What was more, even before you set eyes on them, when you came on a Monday to Mme. Verdurin's, people who in Paris would scarcely turn their heads to look, so familiar was the sight of a string of smart carriages waiting outside a great house, felt their hearts throb at the sight of the two or three broken-down dog-carts drawn up in front of la Raspelière, beneath the tall firs. No doubt this was because the rustic setting was different, and social impressions thanks to this transposition regained a kind of novelty. It was also because the broken-down carriage that one hired to pay a call upon Mme. Verdurin called to mind a pleasant drive and a costly bargain struck with a coachman who had demanded "so much" for the whole day. But the slight stir of curiosity with regard to fresh arrivals, whom it was still impossible to distinguish, made everybody ask himself: "Who can this be?" a question which it was difficult to answer, when one did not know who might have come down to spend a week with the Cambremers or elsewhere, but which people always enjoy putting to themselves in rustic, solitary lives where a meeting with a human creature whom one has not seen for a long time ceases to be the tiresome affair that it is in the life of Paris, and forms a delicious break in the empty monotony of lives that are too lonely, in which even the postman's knock becomes a pleasure. And on the day on which we arrived in a motor-car at la Raspelière, as it was not Monday, M. and Mme. Verdurin must have been devoured by that craving to see people which attacks men and women and inspires a longing to throw himself out of the window in the patient who has been shut up away from his family and friends, for a cure of strict isolation. For the new and more swift-footed servant, who had already made himself familiar with these expressions, having replied that "if Madame has not gone out she must be at the view of Douville," and that he would go and look for her, came back immediately to tell us that she was coming to welcome us. We found her slightly dishevelled, for she came from the flower beds, farmyard and kitchen garden, where she had gone to feed her peacocks and poultry, to hunt for eggs, to gather fruit and flowers to "make her table-centre," which would suggest her park in miniature; but on the table it conferred the distinction of making it support the burden of only such things as were useful and good to eat; for round those other presents from the garden which were the pears, the whipped eggs, rose the tall stems of bugloss, carnations, roses and coreopsis, between which one saw, as between blossoming boundary posts, move from one to another beyond the glazed windows, the ships at sea. From the astonishment which M. and Mme. Verdurin, interrupted while arranging their flowers to receive the visitors that had been announced, shewed upon finding that these visitors were merely Albertine and myself, it was easy to see that the new servant, full of zeal but not yet familiar with my name, had repeated it wrongly and that Mme. Verdurin, hearing the names of guests whom she did not know, had nevertheless bidden him let them in, in her need of seeing somebody, no matter whom. And the new servant stood contemplating this spectacle from the door in order to learn what part we played in the household. Then he made off at a run, taking long strides, for he had entered upon his duties only the day before. When Albertine had quite finished displaying her toque and veil to the Verdurins, she gave me a warning look to remind me that we had not too much time left for what we meant to do. Mme. Verdurin begged us to stay to tea, but we refused, when all of a sudden a suggestion was mooted which would have made an end of all the pleasures that I promised myself from my drive with Albertine: the Mistress, unable to face the thought of tearing herself from us, or perhaps of allowing a novel distraction to escape, decided to accompany us. Accustomed for years past to the experience that similar offers on her part were not well received, and being probably dubious whether this offer would find favour with us, she concealed beneath an excessive assurance the timidity that she felt when addressing us and, without even appearing to suppose that there could be any doubt as to our answer, asked us no question, but said to her husband, speaking of Albertine and myself, as though she were conferring a favour on us: "I shall see them home, myself." At the same time there hovered over her lips a smile that did not belong to them, a smile which I had already seen on the faces of certain people when they said to Bergotte with a knowledgeable air: "I have bought your book, it's not bad," one of those collective, universal smiles which, when they feel the need of them—as we make use of railways and removal vans—individuals borrow, except a few who are extremely refined, like Swann or M. de Charlus on whose lips I have never seen that smile settle. From that moment my visit was poisoned. I pretended not to have understood. A moment later it became evident that M. Verdurin was to be one of the party. "But it will be too far for M. Verdurin," I objected. "Not at all," replied Mme. Verdurin with a condescending, cheerful air, "he says it will amuse him immensely to go with you young people over a road he has travelled so many times; if necessary, he will sit beside the engineer, that doesn't frighten him, and we shall come back quietly by the train like a good married couple. Look at him, he's quite delighted." She seemed to be speaking of an aged and famous painter full of friendliness, who, younger than the youngest, takes a delight in scribbling figures on paper to make his grandchildren laugh. What added to my sorrow was that Albertine seemed not to share it and to find some amusement in the thought of dashing all over the countryside like this with the Verdurins. As for myself, the pleasure that I had vowed that I would take with her was so imperious that I refused to allow the Mistress to spoil it; I invented falsehoods which the irritating threats of Mme. Verdurin made excusable, but which Albertine alas, contradicted. "But we have a call to pay," I said. "What call?" asked Albertine. "You shall hear about it later, there's no getting out of it." "Very well, we can wait outside," said Mme. Verdurin, resigned to anything. At the last minute my anguish at seeing wrested from me a happiness for which I had so longed gave me the courage to be impolite. I refused point blank, alleging in Mme. Verdurin's ear that because of some trouble which had befallen Albertine and about which she wished to consult me, it was absolutely necessary that I should be alone with her. The Mistress appeared vexed: "All right, we shan't come," she said to me in a voice tremulous with rage. I felt her to be so angry that, so as to appear to be giving way a little: "But we might perhaps . . ." I began. "No," she replied, more furious than ever, "when I say no, I mean no." I supposed that I was out of favour with her, but she called us back at the door to urge us not to "fail" on the following Wednesday, and not to come with that contraption, which was dangerous at night, but by the train with the little group, and she made me stop the car, which was moving down hill across the park, because the footman had forgotten to put in the hood the slice of tart and the shortbread which she had had made into a parcel for us. We started off, escorted for a moment by the little houses that came running to meet us with their flowers. The face of the countryside seemed to us entirely changed, so far, in the topographical image that we form in our minds of separate places, is the notion of space from being the most important factor. We have said that the notion of time segregates them even farther. It is not the only factor either. Certain places which we see always in isolation seem to us to have no common measure with the rest, to be almost outside the world, like those people whom we have known in exceptional periods of our life, during our military service, in our childhood, and whom we associate with nothing. In my first year at Balbec there was a piece of high ground to which Mme. de Villeparisis liked to take us because from it you saw only the water and the woods, and which was called Beaumont. As the road that she took to approach it, and preferred to other routes because of its old trees, went up hill all the way, her carriage was obliged to go at a crawling pace and took a very long time. When we reached the top we used to alight, stroll about for a little, get into the carriage again, return by the same road, without seeing a single village, a single country house. I knew that Beaumont was something very special, very remote, very high, I had no idea of the direction in which it was to be found, having never taken the Beaumont road to go anywhere else; besides, it took a very long time to get there in a carriage. It was obviously in the same Department (or in the same Province) as Balbec, but was situated for me on another plane, enjoyed a special privilege of extraterritoriality. But the motor-car respects no mystery, and, having passed beyond Incarville, whose houses still danced before my eyes, as we were going down the cross road that leads to Parville (*Paterni villa*), catching sight of the sea from a natural terrace over which we were passing, I asked the name of the place, and before the chauffeur had time to reply recognised Beaumont, close by which I passed thus unconsciously whenever I took the little train, for it was within two minutes of Parville. Like an officer of my regiment who might have seemed us me a creature apart, too kindly and simple to be of a great family, too remote already and mysterious to be simply of a great family, and of whom I was afterwards to learn that he was the brother-in-law, the cousin of people with whom I was dining, so Beaumont, suddenly brought in contact with places from which I supposed it to be so distinct, lost its mystery and took its place in the district, making me think with terror that Madame Bovary and the Sanseverina might perhaps have seemed to me to be like ordinary people, had I met them elsewhere than in the close atmosphere of a novel. It may be thought that my love of magic journeys by train ought to have prevented me from sharing Albertine's wonder at the motor-car which takes even the invalid wherever he wishes to go and destroys our conception—which I had held hitherto—of position in space as the individual mark, the irreplaceable essence of irremovable beauties. And no doubt this position in space was not to the motor-car, as it had been to the railway train, when I came from Paris to Balbec, a goal exempt from the contingencies of ordinary life, almost ideal at the moment of departure, and, as it remains so at that of arrival, at our arrival in that great dwelling where no one dwells and which bears only the name of the town, the station, seeming to promise at last the accessibility of the town, as though the station were its materialisation. No, the motor-car did not convey us thus by magic into a town which we saw at first in the whole that is summarised by its name, and with the illusions of a spectator in a theatre. It made us enter that theatre by the wings which were the streets, stopped to ask the way of an inhabitant. But, as a compensation for so familiar a progress one has the gropings of the chauffeur uncertain of his way and retracing his course, the "general post" of perspective which sets a castle dancing about with a hill, a church and the sea, while one draws nearer to it, in spite of its vain efforts to hide beneath its primeval foliage; those ever narrowing circles which the motor-car describes round a spellbound town which darts off in every direction to escape it and upon which finally it drops down, straight, into the heart of the valley where it lies palpitating on the ground; so that this position in space, this unique point, which the motor-car seems to have stripped of the mystery of express trains, it gives us on the contrary the impression of discovering, of determining for ourselves as with a compass, of helping us to feel with a more fondly exploring hand, with a finer precision, the true geometry, the fair measure of the earth.

What unfortunately I did not know at that moment and did not learn until more than two years later was that one of the chauffeur's patrons was M. de Charlus, and that Morel, instructed to pay him and keeping part of the money for himself (making the chauffeur triple and quintuple the mileage), had become very friendly with him (while pretending not to know him before other people) and made use of his car for long journeys. If I had known this at the time, and that the confidence which the Verdurins were presently to feel in this chauffeur came, unknown to them, from that source, perhaps many of the sorrows of my life in Paris, in the year that followed, much of my trouble over Albertine would have been avoided, but I had not the slightest suspicion of it. In themselves M. de Charlus's excursions by motor-car with Morel were of no direct interest to me. They were more over confined as a rule to a luncheon or dinner in some restaurant along the coast where M. de Charlus was regarded as an old and penniless servant and Morel, whose duty it was to pay the bill, as a too kind-hearted gentleman. I report the conversation at one of these meals, which may give an idea of the others. It was in a restaurant of elongated shape at Saint-Mars-le-Vêtu. "Can't you get them to remove this thing?" M. de Charlus asked Morel, as though appealing to an intermediary without having to address the staff directly. "This thing" was a vase containing three withered roses with which a well-meaning head waiter had seen fit to decorate the table. "Yes . . ." said Morel in embarrassment. "You don't like roses?" "My request ought on the contrary to prove that I do like them, since there are no roses here" (Morel appeared surprised) "but as a matter of fact I do not care much for them. I am rather sensitive to names; and whenever a rose is at all beautiful, one learns that it is called Baronne de Rothschild or Maréchale Niel, which casts a chill. Do you like names? Have you found beautiful titles for your little concert numbers?" "There is one that is called *Poème triste*." "That is horrible," replied M. de Charlus in a shrill voice that rang out like a blow. "But I ordered champagne?" he said to the head waiter who had supposed he was obeying the order by placing by the diners two glasses of foaming liquid. "Yes, Sir." "Take away that filth, which has no connexion with the worst champagne in the world. It is the emetic known as *cup*, which consists, as a rule, of three rotten strawberries swimming in a mixture of vinegar and soda-water. Yes," he went on, turning again to Morel, "you don't seem to know what a title is. And even in the interpretation of the things you play best, you seem not to be aware of the mediumistic side." "You mean to say?" asked Morel, who, not having understood one word of what the Baron had said, was afraid that he might be missing something of importance, such as an invitation to luncheon. M. de Charlus having failed to regard "You mean to say?" as a question, Morel, having in consequence received no answer, thought it best to change the conversation and to give it a sensual turn: "There, look at the fair girl selling the flowers you don't like; I'm certain she's got a little mistress. And the old woman dining at the table at the end, too." "But how do you know all that?" asked M. de Charlus, amazed at Morel's intuition. "Oh! I can spot them in an instant. If we went out together in a crowd, you would see that I never make a mistake." And anyone looking at Morel at that moment, with his girlish air enshrined in his masculine beauty, would have understood the obscure divination which made him no less obvious to certain women than them to him. He was anxious to supplant Jupien, vaguely desirous of adding to his regular income the profits which, he supposed, the tailor derived from the Baron. "And with boys I am surer still, I could save you from making any mistake. We shall be having the fair soon at Balbec, we shall find lots of things there. And in Paris too, you'll see, you'll have a fine time." But the inherited caution of a servant made him give a different turn to the sentence on which he had already embarked. So that M. de Charlus supposed that he was still referring to girls. "Listen," said Morel, anxious to excite in a fashion which he considered less compromising for himself (albeit it was actually more immoral) the Baron's senses, "what I should like would be to find a girl who was quite pure, make her fall in love with me, and take her virginity." M. de Charlus could not refrain from pinching Morel's ear affectionately, but added innocently: "What good would that be to you? If you took her maidenhead, you would be obliged to marry her." "Marry her?" cried Morel, guessing that the Baron was fuddled, or else giving no thought to the man, more scrupulous in reality than he supposed, to whom he was speaking. "Marry her? Balls! I should promise, but once the little operation was performed, I should clear out and leave her." M. de Charlus was in the habit, when a fiction was capable of causing him a momentary sensual pleasure, of believing in its truth, while keeping himself free to withdraw his credulity altogether a minute later, when his pleasure was at an end. "You would really do that?" he said to Morel with a laugh, squeezing him more tightly still. "And why not?" said Morel, seeing that he was not shocking the Baron by continuing to expound to him what was indeed one of his desires. "It is dangerous," said M. de Charlus. "I should have my kit packed and ready, and buzz off and leave no address." "And what about me?" asked M. de Charlus. "I should take you with me, of course," Morel made haste to add, never having thought of what would become of the Baron who was the least of his responsibilities. "I say, there's a kid I should love to try that game on, she's a little seamstress who keeps a shop in M. le Duc's *hôtel*." "Jupien's girl," the Baron exclaimed, as the wine-waiter entered the room. "Oh! Never," he added, whether because the presence of a third person had cooled his ardour, or because even in this sort of black mass in which he took a delight in defiling the most sacred things, he could not bring himself to allow the mention of people to whom he was bound by ties of friendship. "Jupien is a good man, the child is charming, it would be a shame to make them unhappy." Morel felt that he had gone too far and was silent, but his gaze continued to fix itself in imagination upon the girl for whose benefit he had once begged me to address him as "dear great master" and from whom he had ordered a waistcoat. An industrious worker, the child had not taken any holiday, but I learned afterwards that while the violinist was in the neighbourhood of Balbec she never ceased to think of his handsome face, ennobled by the accident that having seen Morel in my company she had taken him for a "gentleman."

"I never heard Chopin play," said the Baron, "and yet I might have done so, I took lessons from Stamati. but he forbade me to go and hear the Master of the Nocturnes at my aunt Chimay's." "That was damned silly of him," exclaimed Morel. "On the contrary," M. de Charlus retorted warmly, in a shrill voice. "He shewed his intelligence. He had realised that I had a 'nature' and that I would succumb to Chopin's influence. It made no difference, because when I was quite young I gave up music, and everything else, for that matter. Besides one can more or less imagine him," he added in a slow, nasal, drawling tone, "there are still people who did hear him, who can give you an idea. However, Chopin was only an excuse to come back to the mediumistic aspect which you are neglecting."

The reader will observe that, after an interpolation of common parlance, M. de Charlus had suddenly become as precious and haughty in his speech as ever. The idea of Morel's " dropping " without compunction a girl whom he had outraged had given him a sudden and entire pleasure. From that moment his sensual appetites were satisfied for a time and the sadist (a true medium, he, if you like) who had for a few moments taken the place of M. de Charlus had fled, leaving a clear field for the real M. de Charlus, full of artistic refinement, sensibility, goodness. " You were playing the other day the transposition for the piano of the Fifteenth Quartet, which is absurd in itself because nothing could be less pianistic. It is meant for people whose ears are hurt by the too highly strained chords of the glorious Deaf One. Whereas it is precisely that almost bitter mysticism that is divine. In any case you played it very badly and altered all the movements. You ought to play it as though you were composing it: the young Morel, afflicted with a momentary deafness and with a non-existent genius stands for an instant motionless. Then, seized by the divine frenzy, he plays, he composes the opening bars. After which, exhausted by this initial effort, he gives way, letting droop his charming forelock to please Mme. Verdurin, and, what is more, gives himself time to recreate the prodigious quantity of grey matter which he has commandeered for the Pythian objectivation. Then, having regained his strength, seized by a fresh and overmasternig inspiration, he flings himself upon the sublime, imperishable phrase which the virtuoso of Berlin " (we suppose M. de Charlus to have meant by this expression Mendelssohn) " was to imitate without ceasing. It is in this, the only really transcendent and animating fashion, that I shall make you play in Paris." When M. de Charlus gave him advice of this sort, Morel was far more alarmed than when he saw the head waiter remove his scorned roses and "cup," for he asked himself with anxiety what effect it would create among his "class." But he was unable to dwell upon these reflexions, for M. de Charlus said to him imperiously: "Ask the head waiter if he has a Bon Chrétien." "A good christian, I don't understand." "Can't you see we've reached the dessert, it's a pear. You may be sure, Mme. de Cambremer has them in her garden, for the Comtesse d'Escarbagnas whose double she is had them. M. Thibaudier sends her them, saying: 'Here is a Bon Chrétien which is worth tasting.'" "No, I didn't know." "I can see that you know nothing. If you have never even read Molière. . . . Oh, well, since you are no more capable of ordering food than of anything else, ask simply for a pear which is grown in this neighbourhood, the Louise-Bonne d'Avranches." "The?" "Wait a minute, since you are so stupid, I shall ask him myself for others, which I prefer. Waiter, have you any Doyennée des Comices? Charlie, you must read the exquisite passage about that pear by the Duchesse Emilie de Clermont-Tonnerre." "No, Sir, there aren't any." Have you Triomphe de Jodoigne?" "No, Sir." "Any Virginie-Dallet? Or Passe-Colmar? No? Very well, since you've nothing, we may as well go. The Duchesse d'Angoulême is not in season yet, come along, Charlie." Unfortunately for M. de Charlus, his want of common sense, perhaps too the chastity of what were probably his relations with Morel, made him go out of his way at this period to shower upon the violinist strange bounties which the other was incapable of understanding, and to which his nature, impulsive in its own way, but mean and ungrateful, could respond only by a harshness or a violence that were steadily intensified and plunged M. de Charlus—formerly so proud, now quite timid—in fits of genuine despair. We shall see how, in the smallest matters, Morel, who fancied himself a M. de Charlus a thousand times more important, completely misunderstood, by taking them literally, the Baron's arrogant information with regard to the aristocracy. Let us for the moment say simply this, while Albertine waits for me at Saint-Jean de la Haise, that if there was one thing which Morel set above nobility (and this was in itself distinctly noble, especially in a person whose pleasure was to pursue little girls—on the sly—with the chauffeur), it was his artistic reputation and what the others might think of him in the violin class. No doubt it was an ugly trait in his character that because he felt M. de Charlus to be entirely devoted to him he appeared to disown him, to make fun of him, in the same way as, when I had promised not to reveal the secret of his father's position with my great-uncle, he treated me with contempt. But on the other hand his name, as that of a recognised artist, Morel, appeared to him superior to a "name." And when M. de Charlus, in his dreams of Platonic affection, tried to make him adopt one of his family titles, Morel stoutly refused.

When Albertine thought it better to remain at Saint-Jean de la Haise and paint, I would take the car, and it was not merely to Gourville and Féterne, but to Saint-Mars le Vêtu and as far as Criquetot that I was able to penetrate before returning to fetch her. While pretending to be occupied with anything rather than herself, and to be obliged to forsake her for other pleasures, I thought only of her. As often as not I went no farther than the great plain which overlooks Gourville, and as it resembles slightly the plain that begins above Combray, in the direction of Méséglise, even at a considerable distance from Albertine, I had the joy of thinking that if my gaze could not reach her, still, travelling farther than my vision, that strong and gentle sea breeze which was sweeping past me must be flowing down, without anything to arrest it as far as Quetteholme, until it stirred the branches of the trees that bury Saint-Jean de la Haise in their foliage, caressing the face of my mistress, and must thus be extending a double tie between her and myself in this retreat indefinitely enlarged, but without danger, as in those games in which two children find themselves momentarily out of sight and earshot of one another, and yet, while far apart, remain together. I returned by those roads from which there is a view of the sea, and on which in the past, before it appeared among the branches, I used to shut my eyes to reflect that what I was going to see was indeed the plaintive ancestress of the earth, pursuing as in the days when no living creature yet existed its lunatic, immemorial agitation. Now, these roads were no longer simply the means of rejoining Albertine; when I recognised each of them in their uniformity, knowing how far they would run in a straight line, where they would turn, I remembered that I had followed them while I thought of Mlle. de Stermaria, and also that this same eagerness to find Albertine I had felt in Paris as I walked the streets along which Mme. de Guermantes might pass; they assumed for me the profound monotony, the moral significance of a sort of ruled line that my character must follow. It was natural, and yet it was not without importance; they reminded me that it was my fate to pursue only phantoms, creatures whose reality existed to a great extent in my imagination; there are people indeed—and this had been my case from my childhood—for whom all the things that have a fixed value, assessable by others, fortune, success, high positions, do not count; what they must have, is phantoms. They sacrifice all the rest, leave no stone unturned, make everything else subservient to the capture of some phantom. But this soon fades away; then they run after another, prepared to return later on to the first. It was not the first time that I had gone in quest of Albertine, the girl I had seen that first year outlined against the sea. Other women, it is true, had been interposed between the Albertine whom I had first loved and her from whom I was scarcely separated at this moment; other women, notably the Duchesse de Guermantes. But, the reader will say, why give yourself so much anxiety with regard to Gilberte, take so much trouble over Madame de Guermantes, if, when you have become the friend of the latter, it is with the sole result of thinking no more of her, but only of Albertine? Swann, before his own death, might have answered the question, he who had been a lover of phantoms. Of phantoms pursued, forgotten, sought afresh sometimes for a single meeting and in order to establish contact with an unreal life which at once escaped, these Balbec roads were full. When I thought that their trees, pear trees, apple trees, tamarisks, would outlive me, I seemed to receive from them the warning to set myself to work at last, before the hour should strike of rest everlasting.

I left the carriage at Quetteholme, ran down the sunken

path, crossed the brook by a plank and found Albertine painting in front of the church all spires and crockets, thorny and red, blossoming like a rose bush. The lantern alone shewed an unbroken front; and the smiling surface of the stone was abloom with angels who continued, before the twentieth century couple that we were, to celebrate, taper in hand, the ceremonies of the thirteenth. It was they that Albertine was endeavouring to portray on her prepared canvas, and, imitating Elstir, she was laying on the paint in sweeping strokes, trying to obey the noble rhythm set, the great master had told her, by those angels so different from any that he knew. Then she collected her things. Leaning upon one another we walked back up the sunken path, leaving the little church, as quiet as though it had never seen us, to listen to the perpetual sound of the brook. Presently the car started, taking us home by a different way. We passed Marcouville l'Orgueilleuse. Over its church, half new, half restored, the setting sun spread its patina as fine as that of centuries. Through it the great bas-reliefs seemed to be visible only through a floating layer, half liquid, half luminous; the Blessed Virgin, Saint Elizabeth, Saint Joachim swam in the impalpable tide, almost on dry land, on the water's or the sunlight's surface. Rising in a warm dust, the many modern statues reached, on their pillars, halfway up the golden webs of sunset. In front of the church a tall cypress seemed to be in a sort of consecrated enclosure. We left the car for a moment to look at it and strolled for a little. No less than of her limbs, Albertine was directly conscious of her toque of Leghorn straw and of the silken veil (which were for her the source of no less satisfaction), and derived from them, as we strolled round the church, a different sort of impetus, revealed by a contentment which was inert but in which I found a certain charm; veil and toque which were but a recent, adventitious part of my friend, but a part that was already dear to me, as I followed its trail with my eyes, past the cypress in the evening air. She herself could not see it, but guessed that the effect was pleasing, for she smiled at me, harmonising the poise of her head with the headgear that completed it: "I don't like it, it's restored," she said to me, pointing to the church and remembering what Elstir had said to her about the priceless, inimitable beauty of old stone. Albertine could tell a restoration at a glance. One could not help feeling surprised at the sureness of the taste she had already acquired in architecture, as contrasted with the deplorable taste she still retained in music. I cared no more than Elstir for this church, it was with no pleasure to myself that its sunlit front had come and posed before my eyes, and I had got out of the car to examine it only out of politeness to Albertine. I found, however, that the great impressionist had contradicted himself; why exalt this fetish of its objective architectural value, and not take into account the transfiguration of the church by the sunset? "No, certainly not," said Albertine, "I don't like it; I like its name *orgueilleuse*. But what I must remember to ask Brichot is why Saint-Mars is called *le Vêtu*. We shall be going there next, shan't we?" she said, gazing at me out of her black eyes over which her toque was pulled down, like her little polo cap long ago. Her veil floated behind her. I got back into the car with her, happy in the thought that we should be going next day to Saint-Mars, where, in this blazing weather when one could think only of the delights of a bath, the two ancient steeples, salmon-pink, with their lozenge-shaped tiles, gaping slightly as though for air, looked like a pair of old, sharp-snouted fish, coated in scales, moss-grown and red, which without seeming to move were rising in a blue, transparent water. On leaving Marcouville, to shorten the road, we turned aside at a crossroads where there is a farm. Sometimes Albertine made the car stop there and asked me to go alone to fetch, so that she might drink it in the car, a bottle of calvados or cider, which the people assured me was not effervescent, and which proceeded to drench us from head to foot. We sat pressed close together. The people of the farm could scarcely see Albertine in the closed car, I handed them back their bottles; we moved on again, as though to continue that private life by ourselves, that lovers' existence which they might suppose us to lead, and of which this halt for refreshment had been only an insignificant moment; a supposition that would have appeared even less far-fetched if they had seen us after Albertine had drunk her bottle of cider; she seemed then positively unable to endure the existence of an interval between herself and me which as a rule did not trouble her; beneath her linen skirt her legs were pressed against mine, she brought close against my cheeks her own cheeks which had turned pale, warm and red over the cheekbones, with something ardent and faded about them such as one sees in girls from the slums. At such moments, almost as quickly as her personality, her voice changed also, she forsook her own voice to adopt another, raucous, bold, almost dissolute. Night began to fall. What a pleasure to feel her leaning against me, with her toque and her veil, reminding me that it is always thus, seated side by side, that we meet couples who are in love. I was perhaps in love with Albertine, but as I did not venture to let her see my love, although it existed in me, it could only be like an abstract truth, of no value until one has succeeded in checking it by experiment; as it was, it seemed to me unrealisable and outside the plane of life. As for my jealousy, it urged me to leave Albertine as little as possible, although I knew that it would not be completely cured until I had parted from her for ever. I could even feel it in her presence, but would then take care that the circumstances should not be repeated which had aroused it. Once, for example, on a fine morning, we went to luncheon at Rivebelle. The great glazed doors of the dining-room and of that hall in the form of a corridor in which tea was served stood open revealing the sunlit lawns beyond, of which the huge restaurant seemed to form a part. The waiter with the flushed face and black hair that writhed like flames was flying from end to end of that vast expanse less rapidly than in the past, for he was no longer an assistant but was now in charge of a row of tables; nevertheless, owing to his natural activity, sometimes far off, in the dining-room, at other times nearer, but out of doors, serving visitors who had preferred to feed in the garden, one caught sight of him, now here, now there, like successive statues of a young god running, some in the interior, which for that matter was well lighted, of a mansion bounded by a vista of green grass, others beneath the trees, in the bright radiance of an open air life. For a moment he was close to ourselves. Albertine replied absent-mindedly to what I had just said to her. She was gazing at him with rounded eyes. For a minute or two I felt that one may be close to the person whom one loves and yet not have her with one. They had the appearance of being engaged in a mysterious conversation, rendered mute by my presence, and the sequel possibly of meetings in the past of which I knew nothing, or merely of a glance that he had given her—at which I was the *terzo incomodo,* from whom the others try to hide things. Even when, forcibly recalled by his employer, he had withdrawn from us, Albertine while continuing her meal seemed to be regarding the restaurant and its gardens merely as a lighted running-track, on which there appeared here and there amid the varied scenery the swift-foot god with the black tresses. At one moment I asked myself whether she was not going to rise up and follow him, leaving me alone at my table. But in the days that followed I began to forget for ever this painful impression, for I had decided never to return to Rivebelle, I had extracted a promise from Albertine, who assured me that she had never been there before and would never return there. And I denied that the nimble-footed waiter had had eyes only for her, so that she should not believe that my company had deprived her of a pleasure. It happened now and again that I would revisit Rivebelle, but alone, and drink too much, as I had done there in the past. As I drained a final glass I gazed at a round pattern painted on the white wall, concentrated upon it the pleasure that I felt. It alone in the world had any existence for me; I pursued it, touched it and lost it by turns with my wavering glance, and felt indifferent to the future, contenting myself with my painted pattern like a butterfly circling about a poised butterfly with which it is going to end its life in an act of supreme consummation.

The moment was perhaps particularly well chosen for giving up a woman whom no very recent or very keen suffering obliged me to ask for this balm for a malady which they possess who have caused it. I was calmed by these very drives, which, even if I did not think of them at the moment save as a foretaste of a morrow which itself, notwithstanding the longing with which it filled me, was not to be different from to-day, had the charm of having been torn from the places which Albertine had frequented hitherto and where I had not been with her, her aunt's house, those of her girl friends. The charm not of a positive joy, but only of the calming of an anxiety, and quite strong nevertheless. For at an interval of a few days, when my thoughts turned to the farm outside which we had sat drinking cider, or simply to the stroll we had taken round Saint-Mars le Vêtu, remembering that Albertine had been walking by my side in her toque, the sense of her presence added of a sudden so strong a virtue to the trivial image of the modern church that at the moment when the sunlit front came thus of its own accord to pose before me in memory, it was like a great soothing compress laid upon my heart. I dropped Albertine at Parville, but only to join her again in the evening and lie stretched out by her side, in the darkness, upon the beach. No doubt I did not see her every day, still I could say to myself: "If she were to give an account of how she spent her time, of her life, it would still be myself that played the largest part in it;" and we spent together long hours on end which brought into my days so sweet an intoxication that even when, at Parville, she jumped from the car which I was to send to fetch her an hour later, I no more felt myself to be alone in it than if before leaving me she had strewn it with flowers. I might have dispensed with seeing her every day; I was going to be happy when I left her, and I knew that the calming effect of that happiness might be prolonged over many days. But at that moment I heard Albertine as she left me say to her aunt or to a girl friend: "Then to-morrow at eight-thirty. We mustn't be late, the others will be ready at a quarter past." The conversation of a woman one loves is like the soil that covers a subterranean and dangerous water; one feels at every moment beneath the words the presence, the penetrating chill of an invisible pool; one perceives here and there its treacherous percolation, but the water itself remains hidden. The moment I heard these words of Albertine, my calm was destroyed. I wanted to ask her to let me see her the following morning, so as to prevent her from going to this mysterious rendezvous at half-past eight which had been mentioned in my presence only in covert terms. She would no doubt have begun by obeying me, while regretting that she had to give up her plans; in time she would have discovered my permanent need to upset them; I should have become the person from whom one hides everything. Besides, it is probable that these gatherings from which I was excluded amounted to very little, and that it was perhaps from the fear that I might find one of the other girls there vulgar or boring that I was not invited to them. Unfortunately this life so closely involved with Albertine's had a reaction not only upon myself; to me it brought calm; to my mother it caused an anxiety, her confession of which destroyed my calm. As I entered the hotel happy in my own mind, determined to terminate, one day soon, an existence the end of which I imagined to depend upon my own volition, my mother said to me, hearing me send a message to the chauffeur to go and fetch Albertine: "How you do waste your money." (Françoise in her simple and expressive language said with greater force: "That's the way the money goes.") "Try," Mamma went on, "not to become like Charles de Sévigné, of whom his mother said: 'His hand is a crucible in which money melts.' Besides, I do really think you have gone about quite enough with Albertine. I assure you, you're overdoing it, even to her it may seem ridiculous. I was delighted to think that you found her a distraction, I am not asking you never to see her again, but simply that it may not be impossible to meet one of you without the other." My life with Albertine, a life devoid of keen pleasures—that is to say of keen pleasures that I could feel—that life which I intended to change at any moment, choosing a calm interval, became once again suddenly and for a time necessary to me when, by these words of Mamma's, it found itself threatened. I told my mother that what she had just said would delay for perhaps two months the decision for which she asked, which otherwise I would have reached before the end of that week. Mamma began to laugh (so as not to depress me) at this instantaneous effect of her advice, and promised not to speak of the matter to me again so as not to prevent the rebirth of my good intentions. But, since my grandmother's death, whenever Mamma allowed herself to laugh, the incipient laugh would be cut short and would end in an almost heartbroken expression of sorrow, whether from remorse at having been able for an instant to forget, or else from the recrudescence which this brief moment of oblivion had given to her cruel obsession. But to the thoughts aroused in her by the memory of my grandmother, which was rooted in my mother's mind, I felt that on this occasion there were added others, relative to myself, to what my mother dreaded as the sequel of my intimacy with Albertine; an intimacy to which she dared not, however, put a stop, in view of what I had just told her. But she did not appear convinced that I was not mistaken. She remembered all the years in which my grandmother and she had refrained from speaking to me of my work, and of a more wholesome rule of life which, I said, the agitation into which their exhortations threw me alone prevented me from beginning, and which, notwithstanding their obedient silence, I had failed to pursue. After dinner the car brought Albertine back; there was still a glimmer of daylight; the air was not so warm, but after a scorching day we both dreamed of strange and delicious coolness; then to our fevered eyes the narrow slip of moon appeared at first (as on the evening when I had gone to the Princesse de Guermantes's and Albertine had telephoned to me) like the slight, fine rind, then like the cool section of a fruit which an invisible knife was beginning to peel in the sky. Sometimes too, it was I that went in search of my mistress, a little later in that case; she would be waiting for me before the arcade of the market at Maineville. At first I could not make her out; I would begin to fear that she might not be coming, that she had misunderstood me. Then I saw her in her white blouse with blue spots spring into the car by my side with the light bound of a young animal rather than a girl. And it was like a dog too that she began to caress me interminably. When night had fallen and, as the manager of the hotel remarked to me, the sky was all "studied" with stars, if we did not go for a drive in the forest with a bottle of champagne, then, without heeding the strangers who were still strolling upon the faintly lighted front, but who could not have seen anything a yard away on the dark sand, we would lie down in the shelter of the dunes; that same body in whose suppleness abode all the feminine, marine and sportive grace of the girls whom I had seen for the first time pass before a horizon of waves, I held pressed against my own, beneath the same rug, by the edge of the motionless sea divided by a tremulous path of light; and we listened to the sea without tiring and with the same pleasure, both when it held its breath, suspended for so long that one thought the reflux would never come, and when at last it gasped out at our feet the long awaited murmur. Finally I took Albertine back to Parville. When we reached her house, we were obliged to break off our kisses for fear lest some one should see us; not wishing to go to bed she returned with me to Balbec, from where I took her back for the last time to Parville; the chauffeurs of those early days of the motor-car were people who went to bed at all hours. And as a matter of fact I returned to Balbec only with the first dews of morning, alone this time, but still surrounded with the presence of my mistress, gorged with an inexhaustible provision of kisses. On my table I would find a telegram or a postcard. Albertine again! She had written them at Quetteholme when I had gone off by myself in the car, to tell me that she was thinking of me. I got into bed as I read them over. Then I caught sight, over the curtains, of the bright streak of daylight and said to myself that we must be in love with one another after all, since we had spent the night in one another's arms. When next morning I caught sight of Albertine on the front, I was so afraid of her telling me that she was not free that day, and could not accede to my request that we should go out together, that I delayed as long as possible making the request. I was all the more uneasy since she wore a cold, preoccupied air; people were passing whom she knew; doubtless she had made plans for the afternoon from which I was excluded. I looked at her, I looked at that charming body, that blushing head of Albertine, rearing in front of me the enigma of her intentions, the unknown decision which was to create the happiness or misery of my afternoon. It was a whole state of the soul, a whole future existence that had assumed before my eyes the allegorical and fatal form of a girl. And when at last I made up my mind, when with the most indifferent air that I could muster, I asked: "Are we to go out together now, and again this evening?" and she replied: "With the greatest pleasure," then the sudden replacement, in the rosy face, of my long uneasiness by a delicious sense of ease made even more precious to me those outlines to which I was perpetually indebted for the comfort, the relief that we feel after a storm has broken. I repeated to myself: "How sweet she is, what an adorable creature!" in an excitement less fertile than that caused by intoxication, scarcely more profound than that of friendship, but far superior to the excitement of social life. We cancelled our order for the car only on the days when there was a dinner-party at the Verdurins' and on those when, Albertine not being free to go out with me, I took the opportunity to inform anybody who wished to see me that I should be remaining at Balbec. I gave Saint-Loup permission to come on these days, but on these days only. For on one occasion when he had arrived unexpectedly, I had preferred to forego the pleasure of seeing Albertine rather than run the risk of his meeting her, than endanger the state of happy calm in which I had been dwelling for some time and see my jealousy revive. And I had been at my ease only after Saint-Loup had gone. And so he pledged himself, with regret, but with scrupulous observance, never to come to Balbec unless summoned there by myself. In the past, when I thought with longing of the hours that Mme. de Guermantes passed in his company, how I valued the privilege of seeing him! Other people never cease to change places in relation to ourselves. In the imperceptible but eternal march of the world, we regard them as motionless in a moment of vision, too short for us to perceive the motion that is sweeping them on. But we have only to select in our memory two pictures taken of them at different moments, close enough together however for them not to have altered in themselves —perceptibly, that is to say—and the difference between the two pictures is a measure of the displacement that they have undergone in relation to us. He alarmed me dreadfully by talking to me of the Verdurins, I was afraid that he might ask me to take him there, which would have been quite enough, what with the jealousy that I should be feeling all the time, to spoil all the pleasure that I found in going there with Albertine. But fortunately Robert assured me that, on the contrary, the one thing he desired above all others was not to know them. "No," he said to me, "I find that sort of clerical atmosphere maddening." I did not at first understand the application of the adjective clerical to the Verdurins, but the end of Saint-Loup's speech threw a light on his meaning, his concessions to those fashions in words which one is often astonished to see adopted by intelligent men. "I mean the houses," he said, "where people form a tribe, a religious order, a chapel. You aren't going to tell me that they're not a little sect; they're all butter and honey to the people who belong, no words bad enough for those who don't. The question is not, as for Hamlet, to be or not to be, but to belong or not to belong. You belong, my uncle Charlus belongs. I can't help it, I never have gone in for that sort of thing, it isn't my fault."

I need hardly say that the rule which I had imposed upon Saint-Loup, never to come and see me unless I had expressly invited him, I promulgated no less strictly for all and sundry of the persons with whom I had gradually begun to associate at la Raspelière, Féterne, Montsurvent, and elsewhere; and when I saw from the hotel the smoke of the three o'clock train which in the anfractuosity of the cliffs of Parville left its stable plume which long remained hanging from the flank of the green slopes, I had no hesitation as to the identity of the visitor who was coming to tea with me and was still, like a classical deity, concealed from me by that little cloud. I am obliged to confess that this visitor, authorised by me beforehand to come, was hardly ever Saniette, and I have often reproached myself for this omission. But Saniette's own consciousness of his being a bore (far more so, naturally, when he came to pay a call than when he told a story) had the effect that, albeit he was more learned, more intelligent and a better man all round than most people, it seemed impossible to feel in his company, I do not say any pleas ure, but anything save an almost intolerable irritation which spoiled one's whole afternoon. Probably if Saniette had frankly admitted this boredom which he was afraid of causing, one would not have dreaded his visits. Boredom is one of the least of the evils that we have to endure, his boringness existed perhaps only in the imagination of other people, or had been inoculated into him by them by some process of suggestion which had taken root in his charming modesty. But he was so anxious not to let it be seen that he was not sought after, that he dared not offer himself. Certainly he was right in not behaving like the people who are so glad to be able to raise their hats in a public place, that when, not having seen you for years, they catch sight of you in a box with smart people whom they do not know, they give you a furtive but resounding good-evening, seeking an excuse in the pleasure, the emotion that they felt on seeing you, on learning that you are going about again, that you are looking well, etc. Saniette, on the contrary, was lacking in courage. He might, at Mme. Verdurin's or in the little tram, have told me that it would give him great pleasure to come and see me at Balbec, were he not afraid of disturbing me. Such a suggestion would not have alarmed me. On the contrary, he offered nothing, but with a tortured expression on his face and a stare as indestructible as a fired enamel, into the composition of which, however, there entered, with a passionate desire to see one—provided he did not find some one else who was more entertaining—the determination not to let this desire be manifest, said to me with a detached air: " You don't happen to know what you will be doing in the next few days, because I shall probably be somewhere in the neighbourhood of Balbec? Not that it makes the slightest difference, I just thought I would ask you." This air deceived nobody, and the inverse signs whereby we express our sentiments by their opposites are so clearly legible that we ask ourselves how there can still be people who say, for instance: "I have so many invitations that I don't know where to lay my head" to conceal the fact that they have been invited nowhere. But what was more, this detached air, probably on account of the heterogeneous elements that had gone to form it, gave you, what you would never have felt in the fear of boredom or in a frank admission of the desire to see you, that is to say that sort of distaste, of repulsion, which in the category of relations of simple social courtesy corresponds to—in that of love—the disguised offer made to a lady by the lover whom she does not love to see her on the following day, he protesting the while that it does not really matter, or indeed not that offer but an attitude of false coldness. There emanated at once from Saniette's person something or other which made you answer him in the tenderest of tones: "No, unfortunately, this week, I must explain to you. . . ." And I allowed to call upon me instead people who were a long way his inferiors but had not his gaze charged with melancholy or his mouth wrinkled with all the bitterness of all the calls which he longed, while saying nothing about them, to pay upon this person and that. Unfortunately it was very rarely that Saniette did not meet in the "crawler" the guest who was coming to see me, if indeed the latter had not said to me at the Verdurins': "Don't forget, I'm coming to see you on Thursday," the very day on which I had just told Saniette that I should not be at home. So that he came in the end to imagine life as filled with entertainments arranged behind his back, if not actually at his expense. On the other hand, as none of us is ever a single person, this too discreet of men was morbidly indiscreet. On the one occasion on which he happened to come and see me uninvited, a letter, I forget from whom, had been left lying on my table. After the first few minutes, I saw that he was paying only the vaguest attention to what I was saying. The letter, of whose subject he knew absolutely nothing, fascinated him and at every moment I expected his glittering eyeballs to detach themselves from their sockets and fly to the letter which, of no importance in itself, his curiosity had made magnetic. You would have called him a bird about to dash into the jaws of a serpent. Finally he could restrain himself no longer, he began by altering its position, as though he were trying to tidy my room. This not sufficing him, he took it up, turned it over, turned it back again, as though mechanically. Another form of his indiscretion was that once he had fastened himself to you he could not tear himself away. As I was feeling unwell that day, I asked him to go back by the next train, in half-an-hour's time. He did not doubt that I was feeling unwell, but replied: "I shall stay for an hour and a quarter, and then I shall go." Since then I have regretted that I did not tell him, whenever I had an opportunity, to come and see me. Who knows? Possibly I might have charmed away his ill fortune, other people would have invited him for whom he would immediately have deserted myself, so that my invitations would have had the twofold advantage of giving him pleasure and ridding me of his company.

On the days following those on which I had been "at

home," I naturally did not expect any visitors and the motor-car would come to fetch us, Albertine and myself. And, when we returned, Aimé, on the lowest step of the hotel, could not help looking, with passionate, curious, greedy eyes, to see what tip I was giving the chauffeur. It was no use my enclosing my coin or note in my clenched fist, Aimé's gaze tore my fingers apart. He turned his head away a moment later, for he was discreet, well bred, and indeed was himself content with relatively small wages. But the money that another person received aroused in him an irrepressible curiosity and made his mouth water. During these brief moments, he wore the attentive, feverish air of a boy reading one of Jules Verne's tales, or of a diner seated at a neighbouring table in a restaurant who, seeing the waiter carving for you a pheasant which he himself either could not afford or would not order, abandons for an instant his serious thoughts to fasten upon the bird a gaze which love and longing cause to smile.

And so, day after day, these excursions in the motor-car followed one another. But once, as I was being taken up to my room, the lift-boy said to me: "That gentleman has been, he gave me a message for you." The lift-boy uttered these words in an almost inaudible voice, coughing and expectorating in my face. "I haven't half caught cold!" he went on, as though I were incapable of perceiving this for myself. "The doctor says it's whooping-cough," and he began once more to cough and expectorate over me. "Don't tire yourself by trying to speak," I said to him with an air of kindly interest, which was feigned. I was afraid of catching the whooping-cough which, with my tendency to choking fits, would have been a serious matter to me. But he made a point of honour, like a virtuoso who refuses to let himself be taken to hospital, of talking and expectorating all the time. "No, it doesn't matter," he said ("Perhaps not to you," I thought, "but to me it does"). "Besides, I shall be returning soon to Paris" ("Excellent, provided he doesn't give it to me first"). "It seems," he went on, "that Paris is quite superb. It must be even more superb than here or Monte-Carlo, although pages, in fact visitors, and even head waiters who have been to Monte-Carlo for the season have often told me that Paris was not so superb as Monte-Carlo. They were cheated, perhaps, and yet, to be a head waiter, you've got to have your wits about you; to take all the orders, reserve tables, you need a head! I've heard it said that it's even more terrible than writing plays and books." We had almost reached my landing when the lift-boy carried me down again to the ground floor because he found that the button was not working properly, and in a moment had put it right. I told him that I preferred to walk upstairs, by which I meant, without putting it in so many words, that I preferred not to catch whooping-cough. But with a cordial and contagious burst of coughing the boy thrust me back into the lift. "There's no danger now, I've fixed the button." Seeing that he was not ceasing to talk, preferring to learn the name of my visitor and the message that he had left, rather than the comparative beauties of Balbec, Paris and Monte-Carlo, I said to him (as one might say to a tenor who is wearying one with Benjamin Godard, "Won't you sing me some Debussy?") "But who is the person that called to see me?" "It's the gentleman you went out with yesterday. I am going to fetch his card, it's with my porter." As, the day before, I had dropped Robert de Saint-Loup at Doncières station before going to meet Albertine, I supposed that the lift-boy was referring to him, but it was the chauffeur. And by describing him in the words: "The gentleman you went out with," he taught me at the same time that a working man is just as much a gentleman as a man about town. A lesson in the use of words only. For in point of fact I had never made any distinction between the classes. And if I had felt, on hearing a chauffeur called a gentleman, the same astonishment as Comte X who had only held that rank for a week and whom, by saying: "the Comtesse looks tired," I made turn his head round to see who it was that I meant, it was simply because I was not familiar with that use of the word; I had never made any difference between working men, professional men and noblemen, and I should have been equally ready to make any of them my friends. With a certain preference for the working men, and after them for the noblemen, not because I liked them better, but because I knew that one could expect greater courtesy from them towards the working men than one finds among professional men, whether because the great nobleman does not despise the working man as the professional man does or else because they are naturally polite to anybody, as beautiful women are glad to bestow a smile which they know to be so joyfully received. I cannot however pretend that this habit that I had of putting people of humble station on a level with people in society, even if it was quite understood by the latter, was always entirely satisfactory to my mother. Not that, humanly speaking, she made any difference between one person and another, and if Françoise was ever in sorrow or in pain she was comforted and tended by Mamma with the same devotion as her best friend. But my mother was too much my grandmother's daughter not to accept, in social matters, the rule of caste. People at Combray might have kind hearts, sensitive natures, might have adopted the most perfect theories of human equality, my mother, when a footman became emancipated, began to say "you" and slipped out of the habit of addressing me in the third person, was moved by these presumptions to the same wrath that breaks out in Saint-Simon's *Memoirs*, whenever a nobleman who is not entitled to it seizes a pretext for assuming the style of "Highness" in an official document, or for not paying dukes the deference he owes to them and is gradually beginning to lay aside. There was a "Combray spirit" so refractory that it will require centuries of good nature (my mother's was boundless), of theories of equality, to succeed in dissolving it. I cannot swear that in my mother certain particles of this spirit had not remained insoluble. She would have been as reluctant to give her hand to a footman as she would have been ready to give him ten francs (which for that matter he was far more glad to receive). To her, whether she admitted it or not, masters were masters, and servants were the people who fed in the kitchen. When she saw the driver of a motor-car dining with me in the restaurant, she was not altogether pleased, and said to me: "It seems to me you might have a more suitable friend than a mechanic," as she might have said, had it been a question of my marriage: "You might find somebody better than that." This particular chauffeur (fortunately I never dreamed of inviting him to dinner) had come to tell me that the motor-car company which had sent him to Balbec for the season had ordered him to return to Paris on the following day. This excuse, especially as the chauffeur was charming and expressed himself so simply that one would always have taken anything he said for Gospel, seemed to us to be most probably true. It was only half so. There was as a matter of fact no more work for him at Balbec. And in any case, the Company being only half convinced of the veracity of the young Evangelist, bowed over the consecration cross of his steering-wheel, was anxious that he should return as soon as possible to Paris. And indeed if the young Apostle wrought a miracle in multiplying his mileage when he was calculating it for M. de Charlus, when on the other hand it was a matter of rendering his account to the Company, he divided what he had earned by six. In consequence of which the Company, coming to the conclusion either that nobody wanted a car now at Balbec, which, so late in the season, was quite probable, or that it was being robbed, decided that, upon either hypothesis, the best thing was to recall him to Paris, not that there was very much work for him there. What the chauffeur wished was to avoid, if possible, the dead season. I have said—though I was unaware of this at the time, when the knowledge of it would have saved me much annoyance—that he was on intimate terms (without their ever shewing any sign of acquaintance before other people) with Morel. Starting from the day on which he was ordered back, before he realised that there was still a way out of going, we were obliged to content ourselves for our excursions with hiring a carriage, or sometimes, as an amusement for Albertine and because she was fond of riding, a pair of saddle-horses. The carriages were unsatisfactory. "What a rattle-trap," Albertine would say. I would often, as it happened, have preferred to be driving by myself. Without being ready to fix a date, I longed to put an end to this existence which I blamed for making me renounce not so much work as pleasure. It would happen also, however, that the habits which bound me were suddenly abolished, generally when some former self, full of the desire to live a merry life, took the place of what was my self at the moment. I felt this longing to escape especially strong one day when, having left Albertine at her aunt's, I had gone on horseback to call on the Verdurins and had taken an unfrequented path through the woods the beauty of which they had extolled to me. Clinging to the outline of the cliffs, it alternately climbed and then, hemmed in by dense woods on either side, dived into savage gorges. For a moment the barren rocks by which I was surrounded, the sea visible in their jagged intervals, swam before my eyes, like fragments of another universe: I had recognised the mountainous and marine landscape which Elstir had made the scene of those two admirable water colours: "Poet meeting a Muse," "Young Man meeting a Centaur" which I had seen at the Duchesse de Guermantes's. The thought of them transported the place in which I was so far beyond the world of to-day that I should not have been surprised if, like the young man of the prehistoric age that Elstir painted, I had in the course of my ride come upon a mythological personage. Suddenly, my horse gave a start; he had heard a strange sound; it was all I could do to hold him and remain in the saddle, then I raised in the direction from which the sound seemed to come my eyes filled with tears and saw, not two hundred feet above my head, against the sun, between two great wings of flashing metal which were carrying him on, a creature whose barely visible face appeared to me to resemble that of a man. I was as deeply moved as a Greek upon seeing for the first time a demi-god. I cried also, for I was ready to cry the moment I realised that the sound came from above my head—aeroplanes were still rare in those days—at the thought that what I was going to see for the first time was an aeroplane. Then, just as when in a newspaper one feels that one is coming to a moving passage, the mere sight of the machine was enough to make me burst into tears. Meanwhile the airman seemed to be uncertain of his course; I felt that there lay open before him—before me, had not habit made me a prisoner—all the routes in space, in life itself; he flew on, let himself glide for a few moments, over the sea, then quickly making up his mind, seeming to yield to some attraction the reverse of gravity, as though returning to his native element, with a slight movement of his golden wings, rose sheer into the sky.

To come back to the mechanic, he demanded of Morel that the Verdurins should not merely replace their break by a motor-car (which, granted their generosity towards the faithful, was comparatively easy), but, what was less easy, replace their head coachman, the sensitive young man who was inclined to dark thoughts, by himself, the chauffeur. This change was carried out in a few days by the following device. Morel had begun by seeing that the coachman was robbed of everything that he needed for the carriage. One day it was the bit that was missing, another day the curb. At other times it was the cushion of his box-seat that had vanished, or his whip, his rug, his hammer, sponge, chamois-leather. But he always managed to borrow what he required from a neighbour; only he was late in bringing round the carriage, which put him in M. Verdurin's bad books and plunged him in a state of melancholy and dark thoughts. The chauffeur, who was in a hurry to take his place, told Morel that he would have to return to Paris. It was time to do something desperate. Morel persuaded M. Verdurin's servants that the young coachman had declared that he would set a trap for the lot of them, boasting that he could take on all six of them at once, and assured them that they could not overlook such an insult. He himself could not take any part in the quarrel, but he warned them so that they might be on their guard. It was arranged that while M. and Mme. Verdurin and their guests were out walking the servants should fall upon the young man in the coach house. I may mention, although it was only the pretext for what was bound to happen, but because the people concerned interested me later on, that the Verdurins had a friend staying with them that day whom they had promised to take for a walk before his departure, which was fixed for that same evening.

What surprised me greatly when we started off for our walk was that Morel, who was coming with us, and was to play his violin under the trees, said to me: "Listen, I have a sore arm, I don't want to say anything about it to Mme. Verdurin, but you might ask her to send for one of her footmen, Howsler for instance, he can carry my things." "I think you ought to suggest some one else," I replied. "He will be wanted here for dinner." A look of anger passed over Morel's face. "No, I'm not going to trust my violin to any Tom, Dick or Harry." I realised later on his reason for this selection. Howsler was the beloved brother of the young coachman, and, if he had been left at home, might have gone to his rescue. During our walk, dropping his voice so that the elder Howsler should not overhear: "What a good fellow he is," said Morel. "So is his brother, for that matter. If he hadn't that fatal habit of drinking. . . ." "Did you say drinking?" said Mme. Verdurin, turning pale at the idea of having a coachman who drank. "You've never noticed it. I always say to myself it's a miracle that he's never had an accident while he's been driving you." "Does he drive anyone else, then?" "You can easily see how many spills he's had, his face to-day is a mass of bruises. I don't know how he's escaped being killed, he's broken his shafts." "I haven't seen him to-day," said Mme. Verdurin, trembling at the thought of what might have happened to her, "you appal me." She tried to cut short the walk so as to return at once, but Morel chose an aria by Bach with endless variations to keep her away from the house. As soon as we got back she went to the stable, saw the new shaft and Howsler streaming with blood. She was on the point of telling him, without making any comment on what she had seen, that she did not require a coachman any longer, and of paying him his wages, but of his own accord, not wishing to accuse his fellow-servants, to whose animosity he attributed retrospectively the theft of all his saddlery, and seeing that further patience would only end in his being left for dead on the ground, he asked leave to go at once, which made everything quite simple. The chauffeur began his duties next day and, later on, Mme. Verdurin (who had been obliged to engage another) was so well satisfied with him that she recommended him to me warmly, as a man on whom I might rely. I, knowing nothing of all this, used to engage him by the day in Paris, but I am anticipating events, I shall come to all this when I reach the story of Albertine. At the present moment we are at la Raspelière, where I have just been dining for the first time with my mistress, and M. de Charlus with Morel, the reputed son of an "Agent" who drew a fixed salary of thirty thousand francs annually, kept his carriage, and had any number of majordomos, subordinates, gardeners, bailiffs and farmers at his beck and call. But, since I have so far anticipated, I do not wish to leave the reader under the impression that Morel was entirely wicked. He was, rather, a mass of contradictions, capable on certain days of being genuinely kind.

I was naturally greatly surprised to hear that the coachman had been dismissed, and even more surprised when I recognised his successor as the chauffeur who had been taking Albertine and myself in his car. But he poured out a complicated story, according to which he had thought that he was summoned back to Paris, where an order had come for him to go to the Verdurins, and I did not doubt his word for an instant. The coachman's dismissal was the cause of Morel's talking to me for a few minutes, to express his regret at the departure of that worthy fellow. However, even apart from the moments when I was alone, and he literally bounded towards me beaming with joy, Morel, seeing that everybody made much of me at la Raspelière and feeling that he was deliberately cutting himself off from the society of a person who could in no way imperil him, since he had made me burn my boats and had destroyed all possibility of my treating him with an air of patronage (which I had never, for that matter, dreamed of adopting), ceased to hold aloof from me. I attributed his change of attitude to the influence of M. de Charlus, which as a matter of fact did make him in certain respects less limited, more of an artist, but in others, when he interpreted literally the eloquent, insincere, and moreover transient formulas of his master, made him stupider than ever. That M. de Charlus might have said something to him was as a matter of fact the only thing that occurred to me. How was I to have guessed then what I was told afterwards (and have never been certain of its truth, Andrée's assertions as to everything that concerned Albertine, especially later on, having always seemed to me to be statements to be received with caution, for, as we have already seen, she was not genuinely fond of my mistress and was jealous of her), a thing which in any event, even if it was true, was remarkably well concealed from me by both of them: that Albertine was on the best of terms with Morel? The novel attitude which, about the time of the coachman's dismissal, Morel adopted with regard to myself, enabled me to change my opinion of him. I retained the ugly impression of his character which had been suggested by the servility which this young man had shewn me when he needed my services, followed, as soon as the service had been rendered, by a scornful aloofness as though he did not even see me. I still lacked evidence of his venal relations with M. de Charlus, and also of his bestial and purposeless instincts, the non-gratification of which (when it occurred) or the complications that they involved, were the cause of his sorrows; but his character was not so uniformly vile and was full of contradictions. He resembled an old book of the middle ages, full of mistakes, of absurd traditions, of obscenities; he was extraordinarily composite. I had supposed at first that his art, in which he was really a past-master, had given him superiorities that went beyond the virtuosity of the mere performer. Once when I spoke of my wish to start work "Work, become famous," he said to me. "Who said that?" I inquired. "Fontanes, to Chateaubriand." He also knew certain love letters of Napoleon. Good, I thought to myself, he reads. But this phrase which he had read I know not where was doubtless the only one that he knew in the whole of ancient or modern literature, for he repeated it to me every evening. Another which he quoted even more frequently to prevent me from breathing a word about him to anybody, was the following, which he considered equally literary, whereas it is barely grammatical, or at any rate makes no kind of sense, except perhaps to a mystery-loving servant: "Beware of the wary." As a matter of fact, if one cast back from this stupid maxim to what Fontanes had said to Chateaubriand, one explored a whole side, varied but less contradictory than one might suppose, of Morel's character. This youth who, provided there was money to be made by it, would have done anything in the world, and without remorse—perhaps not without an odd sort of vexation, amounting to nervous excitement, to which however the name remorse could not for a moment be applied—who would, had it been to his advantage, have plunged in distress, not to say mourning, whole families, this youth who set money above everything, above, not to speak of unselfish kindness, the most natural sentiments of common humanity, this same youth nevertheless set above money his certificate as first prize-winner at the Conservatoire and the risk of there being anything said to his discredit in the flute or counterpoint class. And so his most violent rages, his most sombre and unjustifiable fits of ill-temper arose from what he himself (generalising doubtless from certain particular cases in which he had met with spiteful people) called universal treachery. He flattered himself that he escaped from this fault by never speaking about anyone, by concealing his tactics, by distrusting everybody. (Alas for me, in view of what was to happen after my return to Paris, his distrust had not "held" in the case of the Balbec chauffeur, in whom he had doubtless recognised a peer, that is to say, in contradiction of his maxim, a wary person in the good sense of the word, a wary person who remains obstinately silent before honest folk and at once comes to an understanding with a blackguard.) It seemed to him—and he was not absolutely wrong—that his distrust would enable him always to save his bacon, to slip unscathed out of the most perilous adventures, without anyone's being able not indeed to prove but even to suggest anything against him, in the institution in the Rue Bergère. He would work, become famous, would perhaps be one day, with his respectability still intact, examiner in the violin on the Board of that great and glorious Conservatoire.

But it is perhaps crediting Morel's brain with too much logic to attempt to discriminate between these contradictions. As a matter of fact his nature was just like a sheet of paper that has been folded so often in every direction that it is impossible to straighten it out.

He seemed to act upon quite lofty principles, and in a magnificent hand, marred by the most elementary mistakes in spelling, spent hours writing to his brother that he had behaved badly to his sisters, that he was their elder, their natural support, etc., and to his sisters that they had shewn a want of respect for himself.

Presently, as summer came to an end, when one got out of the train at Douville, the sun dimmed by the prevailing mist had ceased to be anything more in a sky that was uniformly mauve than a lump of redness. To the great peace which descends at nightfall over these tufted saltmarshes, and had tempted a number of Parisians, painters mostly, to spend their holidays at Douville, was added a moisture which made them seek shelter early in their little bungalows. In several of these the lamp was already lighted. Only a few cows remained out of doors gazing at the sea and lowing, while others, more interested in humanity, turned their attention towards our carriages. A single painter who had set up his easel where the ground rose slightly was striving to render that great calm, that hushed luminosity. Perhaps the cattle were going to serve him unconsciously and kindly as models, for their contemplative air and their solitary presence when the human beings had withdrawn, contributed in their own way to enhance the strong impression of repose that evening conveys. And, a few weeks later, the transposition was no less agreeable when, as autumn advanced, the days became really short, and we were obliged to make our journey in the dark. If I had been out anywhere in the afternoon, I had to go back to change my clothes, at the latest, by five o'clock, when at this season the round, red sun had already sunk half way down the slanting sheet of glass, which formerly I had detested, and, like a Greek fire, was inflaming the sea in the glass fronts of all my book-cases. Some wizard's gesture having revived, as I put on my dinner-jacket, the alert and frivolous self that was mine when I used to go with Saint-Loup to dine at Rivebelle and on the evening when I looked forward to taking Mme. de Stermaria to dine on the island in the Bois, I began unconsciously to hum the same tune that I had hummed then; and it was only when I realised this that by the song I recognised the resurrected singer, who indeed knew no other tune. The first time that I sang it, I was beginning to be in love with Albertine, but I imagined that I would never get to know her. Later on, in Paris, it was when I had ceased to be in love with her and some days after I had enjoyed her for the first time. Now it was when I was in love with her again and on the point of going out to dinner with her, to the great regret of the manager who supposed that I would end by staying at la Raspelière altogether and deserting his hotel, and assured me that he had heard that fever was prevalent in that neighbourhood, due to the marshes of the Bac and their "stagnous" water. I was delighted by the multiplicity in which I saw my life thus spread over three planes; and besides, when one becomes for an instant one's former self, that is to say different from what one has been for some time past, one's sensibility, being no longer dulled by habit, receives the slightest shocks of those vivid impressions which make everything that has preceded them fade into significance, and to which, because of their intensity, we attach ourselves with the momentary enthusiasm of a drunken man. It was already night when we got into the omnibus or carriage which was to take us to the station where we would find the little train. And in the hall the chief magistrate was saying to us: "Ah! You are going to la Raspelière! Sapristi, she has a nerve, your Mme. Verdurin, to make you travel an hour by train in the dark, simply to dine with her. And then to start off again at ten o'clock at night, with a wind blowing like the very devil. It is easy to see that you have nothing else to do," he added, rubbing his hands together. No doubt he spoke thus from annoyance at not having been invited, and also from the satisfaction that people feel who are "busy"—though it be with the most idiotic occupation—at "not having time" to do what you are doing.

Certainly it is only right that the man who draws up reports, adds up figures, answers business letters, follows the movements of the stock exchange, should feel when he says to you with a sneer: "It's all very well for you; you have nothing better to do," an agreeable sense of his own superiority. But this would be no less contemptuous, would be even more so (for dining out is a thing that the busy man does also) were your recreation writing *Hamlet* or merely reading it. Wherein busy men shew a want of reflexion. For the disinterested culture which seems to them a comic pastime of idle people at the moment when they find them engaged in it is, they ought to remember, the same that in their own profession brings to the fore men who may not be better magistrates or administrators than themselves but before whose rapid advancement they bow their heads, saying: "It appears he's a great reader, a most distinguished individual." But above all the chief magistrate did not take into account that what pleased me about these dinners at la

Raspelière was that, as he himself said quite rightly, though as a criticism, they "meant a regular journey," a journey whose charm appeared to me all the more thrilling in that it was not an object in itself, and no one made any attempt to find pleasure in it—that being reserved for the party for which we were bound, and greatly modified by all the atmosphere that surrounded it. It was already night now when I exchanged the warmth of the hotel—the hotel that had become my home—for the railway carriage into which I climbed with Albertine, in which a glimmer of lamplight on the window shewed, at certain halts of the panting little train, that we had arrived at a station. So that there should be no risk of Cottard's missing us, and not having heard the name of the station, I opened the door, but what burst headlong into the carriage was not any of the faithful, but the wind, the rain, the cold. In the darkness I could make out fields, I could hear the sea, we were in the open country. Albertine, before we were engulfed in the little nucleus, examined herself in a little mirror, extracted from a gold bag which she carried about with her. The fact was that on our first visit, Mme. Verdurin having taken her upstairs to her dressing-room so that she might make herself tidy before dinner, I had felt, amid the profound calm in which I had been living for some time, a slight stir of uneasiness and jealousy at being obliged to part from Albertine at the foot of the stair, and had become so anxious while I was by myself in the drawing-room, among the little clan, and asking myself what my mistress could be doing, that I had sent a telegram the next day, after finding out from M. de Charlus what the correct thing was at the moment, to order from Cartier's a bag which was the joy of Albertine's life and also of mine. It was for me a guarantee of peace of mind, and also of my mistress's solicitude. For she had evidently seen that I did not like her to be parted from me at Mme. Verdurin's and arranged to make in the train all the toilet that was necessary before dinner.

Included in the number of Mme. Verdurin's regular frequenters, and reckoned the most faithful of them all, had been, for some months now, M. de Charlus. Regularly, thrice weekly, the passengers who were sitting in the waiting-rooms or standing upon the platform at Doncières-Ouest used to see that stout gentleman go past with his grey hair, his black moustaches, his lips reddened with a salve less noticeable at the end of the season than in summer when the daylight made it more crude and the heat used to melt it. As he made his way towards the little train, he could not refrain (simply from force of habit, as a connoisseur, since he now had a sentiment which kept him chaste, or at least, for most of the time, faithful) from casting at the labourers, soldiers, young men in tennis flannels, a furtive glance at once inquisitorial and timorous, after which he immediately let his eyelids droop over his half-shut eyes with the unction of an ecclesiastic engaged in telling his beads, with the modesty of a bride vowed to the one love of her life or of a well brought up girl. The faithful were all the more convinced that he had not seen them, since he got into a different compartment from theirs (as, often enough, did Princess Sherbatoff also), like a man who does not know whether people will be pleased or not to be seen with him and leaves them the option of coming and joining him if they choose. This option had not been taken, at first, by the Doctor, who had asked us to leave him by himself in his compartment. Making a virtue of his natural hesitation now that he occupied a great position in the medical world, it was with a smile, throwing back his head, looking at Ski over his glasses, that he said, either from malice or in the hope of eliciting the opinion of the " comrades ": " You can understand that if I was by myself, a bachelor, but for my wife's sake I ask myself whether I ought to allow him to travel with us after what you have told me," the Doctor whispered. " What's that you're saying? " asked Mme. Cottard. " Nothing, it doesn't concern you, it's not meant for ladies to hear," the Doctor replied with a wink, and with a majestic self-satisfaction which held the balance between the dryly malicious air he adopted before his pupils and patients and the uneasiness that used in the past to accompany his shafts of wit at the Verdurins', and went on talking in a lowered tone. Mme. Cottard could make out only the words " one of the brotherhood " and " *tapette*," and as in the Doctor's vocabulary the former expression denoted the Jewish race and the latter a wagging tongue, Mme. Cottard concluded that M. de Charlus must be a garrulous Israelite. She could not understand why people should keep aloof from the Baron for that reason, felt it her duty as the senior lady of the clan to insist that he should not be left alone, and so we proceeded in a body to M. de Charlus's compartment, led by Cottard who was still perplexed. From the corner in which he was reading a volume of Balzac, M. de Charlus observed this hesitation; and yet he had not raised his eyes. But just as deaf-mutes detect, from a movement of the air imperceptible to other people, that some one is standing behind them, so he had, to warn him of other people's coldness towards him, a positive hyperaesthesia. This had, as it habitually does in every sphere, developed in M. de Charlus imaginary sufferings. Like those neuropaths who, feeling a slight lowering of the temperature, induce from this that there must be a window open on the floor above, become violently excited and start sneezing, M. de Charlus, if a person appeared preoccupied in his presence, concluded that somebody had repeated to that person a remark that he had made about him. But there was no need even for the other person to have a distracted, or a sombre, or a smiling air, he would invent them. On the other hand, cordiality completely concealed from him the slanders of which he had not heard. Having begun by detecting Cottard's hesitation, if, greatly to the surprise of the faithful who did not suppose that their presence had yet been observed by the reader's lowered gaze, he held out his hand to them when they were at a convenient distance, he contented himself with a forward inclination of his whole person which he quickly drew back for Cottard, without taking in his own gloved hand the hand which the Doctor had held out to him. "We felt we simply must come and keep you company, Sir, and not leave you alone like that in your little corner. It is a great pleasure to us," Mme. Cottard began in a friendly tone to the Baron. "I am greatly honoured," the Baron intoned, bowing coldly. "I was so pleased to hear that you have definitely chosen this neighbourhood to set up your taber. . . ." She was going to say "tabernacle" but it occurred to her that the word was Hebraic and discourteous to a Jew who might see an allusion in it. And so she paused for a moment to choose another of the expressions that were familiar to her, that is to say a consecrated expression: "to set up, I should say, your *penates*." (It is true that these deities do not appertain to the Christian religion either, but to one which has been dead for so long that it no longer claims any devotees whose feelings one need be afraid of hurting.) "We, unfortunately, what with term beginning, and the Doctor's hospital duties, can never choose our domicile for very long in one place." And glancing at a cardboard box: "You see too how we poor women are less fortunate than the sterner sex, to go only such a short distance as to our friends the Verdurins', we are obliged to take a whole heap of impedimenta." I meanwhile was examining the Baron's volume of Balzac. It was not a paper-covered copy, picked up on a bookstall, like the volume of Bergotte which he had lent me at our first meeting. It was a book from his own library, and as such bore the device: "I belong to the Baron de Charlus," for which was substituted at times, to shew the studious tastes of the Guermantes: "In proeliis non semper," or yet another motto: "Non sine labore." But we shall see these presently replaced by others, in an attempt to please Morel. Mme. Cottard, a little later, hit upon a subject which she felt to be of more personal interest to the Baron. "I don't know whether you agree with me, Sir," she said to him presently, "but I hold very broad views, and, to my mind, there is a great deal of good in all religions. I am not one of the people who get hydrophobia at the sight of a . . . Protestant." "I was taught that mine is the true religion," replied M. de Charlus. "He's a fanatic," thought Mme. Cottard, "Swann, until recently, was more tolerant; it is true that he was a converted one." Now, so far from this being the case, the Baron was not only a Christian, as we know, but pious with a mediaeval fervour. To him as to the sculptors of the middle ages, the Christian church was, in the living sense of the word, peopled with a swarm of beings, whom he believed to be entirely real, Prophets, Apostles, Angels, holy personages of every sort, surrounding the Incarnate Word, His Mother and Her Spouse, the Eternal Father, all the Martyrs and Doctors of the Church, as they may be seen carved in high relief, thronging the porches or lining the naves of the cathedrals. Out of all these M. de Charlus had chosen as his patrons and intercessors the Archangels Michael, Gabriel and Raphael, to whom he made frequent appeals that they would convey his prayers to the Eternal Father, about Whose Throne they stand. And so Mme. Cottard's mistake amused me greatly.

To leave the religious sphere, let us mention that the Doctor, who had come to Paris meagrely equipped with the counsels of a peasant mother, and had then been absorbed in the almost purely materialistic studies to which those who seek to advance in a medical career are obliged to devote themselves for a great many years, had never become cultured, had acquired increasing authority but never any experience, took the word "honoured" in its literal meaning and was at once flattered by it because he was vain and distressed because he had a kind heart. "That poor de Charlus," he said to his wife that evening, "made me feel sorry for him when he said he was honoured by travelling with us. One feels, poor devil, that he knows nobody, that he has to humble himself."

But presently, without any need to be guided by the

charitable Mme. Cottard, the faithful had succeeded in overcoming the qualms which they had all more or less felt at first, on finding themselves in the company of M. de Charlus. No doubt in his presence they were incessantly reminded of Ski's revelations, and conscious of the sexual abnormality embodied in their travelling companion. But this abnormality itself had a sort of attraction for them. It gave for them to the Baron's conversation, remarkable in itself but in ways which they could scarcely appreciate, a savour which made the most interesting conversation, that of Brichot himself, appear slightly insipid in comparison. From the very outset, moreover, they had been pleased to admit that he was intelligent. "The genius that is perhaps akin to madness," the Doctor declaimed, and albeit the Princess, athirst for knowledge, insisted, said not another word, this axiom being all that he knew about genius and seeming to him less supported by proof than our knowledge of typhoid fever and arthritis. And as he had become proud and remained ill-bred: "No questions, Princess, do not interrogate me, I am at the seaside for a rest. Besides, you would not understand, you know nothing about medicine." And the Princess held her peace with apologies, deciding that Cottard was a charming man and realising that celebrities were not always approachable. In this initial period, then, they had ended by finding M. de Charlus an agreeable person notwithstanding his vice (or what is generally so named). Now it was, quite unconsciously, because of that vice that they found him more intelligent than the rest. The most simple maxims to which, adroitly provoked by the sculptor or the don, M. de Charlus gave utterance concerning love, jealousy, beauty, in view of the experience, strange, secret, refined and monstrous, upon which he founded them, assumed for the faithful that charm of unfamiliarity with which a psychology analogous to that which our own dramatic literature has always offered us bedecks itself in a Russian or Japanese play performed by native actors. One might still venture, when he was not listening, upon a malicious witticism at his expense. "Oh!" whispered the sculptor, seeing a young railwayman with the sweeping eyelashes of a dancing girl at whom M. de Charlus could not help staring, "if the Baron begins making eyes at the conductor, we shall never get there, the train will start going backwards. Just look at the way he's staring at him, this is not a steam-tram we're on, it's a funicular." But when all was said, if M. de Charlus did not appear, it was almost a disappointment to be travelling only with people who were just like everybody else, and not to have by one's side this painted, paunchy, tightly-buttoned personage, reminding one of a box of exotic and dubious origin from which escapes the curious odour of fruits the mere thought of tasting which stirs the heart. From this point of view, the faithful of the masculine sex enjoyed a keener satisfaction in the short stage of the journey between Saint-Martin du Chêne, where M. de Charlus got in, and Doncières, the station at which Morel joined the party. For so long as the violinist was not there (and provided the ladies and Albertine, keeping to themselves so as not to disturb our conversation, were out of hearing), M. de Charlus made no attempt to appear to be avoiding certain subjects and did not hesitate to speak of "what it is customary to call degenerate morals." Albertine could not hamper him, for she was always with the ladies, like a well-bred girl who does not wish her presence to restrict the freedom of grown-up conversation. And I was quite resigned to not having her by my side, on condition however that she remained in the same carriage. For I, who no longer felt any jealousy and scarcely any love for her, never thought of what she might be doing on the days when I did not see her; on the other hand, when I was there, a mere partition which might at a pinch be concealing a betrayal was intolerable to me, and if she retired with the ladies to the next compartment, a moment later, unable to remain in my seat any longer, at the risk of offending whoever might be talking, Brichot, Cottard or Charlus, to whom I could not explain the reason for my flight, I would rise, leave them without ceremony, and, to make certain that nothing abnormal was going on, walk down the corridor. And, till we came to Doncières, M. de Charlus, without any fear of shocking his audience, would speak sometimes in the plainest terms of morals which, he declared, for his own part he did not consider either good or evil. He did this from cunning, to shew his breadth of mind, convinced as he was that his own morals aroused no suspicion in the minds of the faithful. He was well aware that there did exist in the world several persons who were, to use an expression which became habitual with him later on, "in the know" about himself. But he imagined that these persons were not more than three or four, and that none of them was at that moment upon the coast of Normandy. This illusion may appear surprising in so shrewd, so suspicious a man. Even in the case of those whom he believed to be more or less well informed, he flattered himself that their information was all quite vague, and hoped, by telling them this or that fact about anyone, to clear the person in question from all suspicion on the part of a listener who out of politeness pretended to accept his statements. Indeed, being uncertain as to what I might know or guess about him, he supposed that my opinion, which he imagined to be of far longer standing than it actually was, was quite general, and that it was sufficient for him to deny this or that detail to be believed, whereas on the contrary, if our knowledge of the whole always precedes our knowledge of details, it makes our investigation of the latter infinitely easier and having destroyed his cloak of invisibility no longer allows the pretender to conceal what he wishes to keep secret. Certainly when M. de Charlus, invited to a dinner-party by one of the faithful or of their friends, took the most complicated precautions to introduce among the names of ten people whom he mentioned that of Morel, he never imagined that for the reasons, always different, which he gave for the pleasure or convenience which he would find that evening in being invited to meet him, his hosts, while appearing to believe him implicitly, substituted a single reason, always the same, of which he supposed them to be ignorant, namely that he was in love with him. Similarly, Mme. Verdurin, seeming always entirely to admit the motives, half artistic, half charitable, with which M. de Charlus accounted to her for the interest that he took in Morel, never ceased to thank the Baron with emotion for his kindness—his touching kindness, she called it—to the violinist. And how astonished M. de Charlus would have been, if, one day when Morel and he were delayed and had not come by the train, he had heard the Mistress say: "We're all here now except the young ladies." The

Baron would have been all the more stupefied in that, going hardly anywhere save to la Raspelière, he played the part there of a family chaplain, like the abbé in a stock company, and would sometimes (when Morel had 48 hours' leave) sleep there for two nights in succession. Mme. Verdurin would then give them communicating rooms and, to put them at their ease, would say: "If you want to have a little music, don't worry about us, the walls are as thick as a fortress, you have nobody else on your floor, and my husband sleeps like lead." On such days M. de Charlus would relieve the Princess of the duty of going to meet strangers at the station, apologise for Mme. Verdurin's absence on the grounds of a state of health which he described so vividly that the guests entered the drawing-room with solemn faces, and uttered cries of astonishment on finding the Mistress up and doing and wearing what was almost a low dress.

For M. de Charlus had for the moment become for Mme. Verdurin the faithfullest of the faithful, a second Princess Sherbatoff. Of his position in society she was not nearly so certain as of that of the Princess, imagining that if the latter cared to see no one outside the little nucleus it was out of contempt for other people and preference for it. As this pretence was precisely the Verdurin's own, they treating as bores everyone to whose society they were not admitted, it is incredible that the Mistress can have believed the Princess to possess a heart of steel, detesting what was fashionable. But she stuck to her guns, and was convinced that in the case of the great lady also it was in all sincerity and from a love of things intellectual that she avoided the company of bores. The latter were, as it happened, diminishing in numbers from the Verdurins' point of view. Life by the seaside robbed an introduction of the ulterior consequences which might be feared in Paris. Brilliant men who had come down to Balbec without their wives (which made everything much easier) made overtures to la Raspelière and, from being bores, became too charming. This was the case with the Prince de Guermantes, whom the absence of his Princess would not, however, have decided to go " as a bachelor " to the Verdurins', had not the lodestone of Dreyfusism been so powerful as to carry him in one stride up the steep ascent to la Raspelière, unfortunately upon a day when the Mistress was not at home. Mme. Verdurin as it happened was not certain that he and M. de Charlus moved in the same world. The Baron had indeed said that the Duc de Guermantes was his brother, but this was perhaps the untruthful boast of an adventurer. Man of the world as he had shewn himself to be, so friendly, so " faithful " to the Verdurins, the Mistress still almost hesitated to invite him to meet the Prince de Guermantes. She consulted Ski and Brichot: " The Baron and the Prince de Guermantes, will they be all right together? " " Good gracious, Madame, as to one of the two I think I can safely say." " What good is that to me? " Mme. Verdurin had retorted crossly. " I asked you whether they would mix well together." " Ah! Madame, that is one of the things that it is hard to tell." Mme. Verdurin had been impelled by no malice. She was certain of the Baron's morals, but when she expressed herself in these terms had not been thinking about them for a moment, but had merely wished to know whether she could invite the Prince and M. de Charlus on the same evening, without their clashing. She had no malevolent intention when she employed these ready-made expressions which are popular in artistic "little clans." To make the most of M. de Guermantes, she proposed to take him in the afternoon, after her luncheon-party, to a charity entertainment at which sailors from the neighbourhood would give a representation of a ship setting sail. But, not having time to attend to everything, she delegated her duties to the faithfullest of the faithful, the Baron. "You understand, I don't want them to hang about like mussels on a rock, they must keep moving, we must see them weighing anchor, or whatever it's called. Now you are always going down to the harbour at Balbec-Plage, you can easily arrange a dress rehearsal without tiring yourself. You must know far more than I do, M. de Charlus, about getting hold of sailors. But after all, we're giving ourselves a great deal of trouble for M. de Guermantes. Perhaps he's only one of those idiots from the Jockey Club. Oh! Heavens, I'm running down the Jockey Club, and I seem to remember that you're one of them. Eh, Baron, you don't answer me, are you one of them? You don't care to come out with us? Look, here is a book that has just come, I think you'll find it interesting. It is by Roujon. The title is attractive: "*Life among men.*"

For my part, I was all the more glad that M. de Charlus often took the place of Princess Sherbatoff, inasmuch as I was thoroughly in her bad books, for a reason that was at once trivial and profound. One day when I was in the little train, paying every attention, as was my habit, to Princess Sherbatoff, I saw Mme. de Villeparisis get in. She had as a matter of fact come down to spend some weeks with the Princesse de Luxembourg, but, chained to the daily necessity of seeing Albertine, I had never replied to the repeated invitations of the Marquise and her royal hostess. I felt remorse at the sight of my grandmother's friend, and, purely from a sense of duty (without deserting Princess Sherbatoff), sat talking to her for some time. I was, as it happened, entirely unaware that Mme. de Villeparisis knew quite well who my companion was but did not wish to speak to her. At the next station, Mme. de Villeparisis left the carriage, indeed I reproached myself with not having helped her on to the platform; I resumed my seat by the side of the Princess. But one would have thought—a cataclysm frequent among people whose position is far from stable and who are afraid that one may have heard something to their discredit, and may be looking down upon them—that the curtain had risen upon a fresh scene. Buried in her *Revue des Deux Mondes,* Madame Sherbatoff barely moved her lips in reply to my questions and finally told me that I was making her head ache. I had not the faintest idea of the nature of my crime. When I bade the Princess good-bye, the customary smile did not light up her face, her chin drooped in a dry acknowledgment, she did not even offer me her hand, nor did she ever speak to me again. But she must have spoken—though what she said I cannot tell—to the Verdurins; for as soon as I asked them whether I ought not to say something polite to Princess Sherbatoff, they replied in chorus: "No! No! No! Nothing of the sort! She does not care for polite speeches!" They did not say this to effect a breach between us, but she had succeeded in making them believe that she was unmoved by civilities, that hers was a spirit unassailed by the vanities of this world.

One needs to have seen the politician who was reckoned the most single-minded, the most uncompromising, the most unapproachable, so long as he was in office, one must have seen him in the hour of his disgrace, humbly soliciting, with a bright, affectionate smile, the haughty greeting of some unimportant journalist, one must have seen Cottard (whom his new patients regarded as a rod of iron) draw himself erect, one must know out of what disappointments in love, what rebuffs to snobbery were built up the apparent pride, the universally acknowledged anti-snobbery of Princess Sherbatoff, in order to grasp that among the human race the rule—which admits of exceptions, naturally—is that the reputedly hard people are weak people whom nobody wants, and that the strong, caring little whether they are wanted or not, have alone that meekness which the common herd mistake for weakness.

However, I ought not to judge Princess Sherbatoff severely. Her case is so common! One day, at the funeral of a Guermantes, a distinguished man who was standing next to me drew my attention to a slim person with handsome features. "Of all the Guermantes," my neighbour informed me, "that is the most astonishing, the most singular. He is the Duke's brother." I replied imprudently that he was mistaken, that the gentleman in question, who was in no way related to the Guermantes, was named Journier-Sarlovèze. The distinguished man turned his back upon me, and has never even bowed to me since.

A great musician, a member of the Institute, occupying a high official position, who was acquainted with Ski, came to Harambouville, where he had a niece staying, and appeared at one of the Verdurins' Wednesdays. M. de Charlus was especially polite to him (at Morel's request), principally in order that on his return to Paris the Academician might enable him to attend various private concerts, rehearsals and so forth, at which the violinist would be playing. The Academician, who was flattered, and was naturally a charming person, promised, and kept his promise. The Baron was deeply touched by all the consideration which this personage (who, for his own part, was exclusively and passionately a lover of women) shewed him, all the facilities that he procured to enable him to see Morel, in those official quarters which the profane world may not enter, all the opportunities by which the celebrated artist secured that the young virtuoso might shew himself, might make himself known, by naming him in preference to others of equal talent for auditions which were likely to make a special stir. But M. de Charlus never suspected that he ought to be all the more grateful to the maestro in that the latter, doubly deserving, or, if you prefer it, guilty twice over, was completely aware of the relations between the young violinist and his noble patron. He favoured them, certainly without any sympathy for them, being unable to comprehend any other love than that for the woman who had inspired the whole of his music, but from moral indifference, a professional readiness to oblige, social affability, snobbishness. As for his doubts as to the character of those relations, they were so scanty that, at his first dinner at la Raspelière, he had inquired of Ski, speaking of M. de Charlus and Morel, as he might have spoken of a man and his mistress: "Have they been long together?" But, too much the man of the world to let the parties concerned see what was in his mind, prepared, should any gossip arise among Morel's fellow-students, to rebuke them, and to reassure Morel by saying to him in a fatherly tone: "One hears that sort of thing about everybody nowadays," he did not cease to load the Baron with civilities which the latter thought charming, but quite natural, being incapable of suspecting the eminent maestro of so much vice or of so much virtue. For the things that were said behind M. de Charlus's back, the expressions used about Morel, nobody was ever base enough to repeat to him. And yet this simple situation is enough to shew that even that thing universally decried, which would find no defender anywhere: the breath of scandal, has itself, whether it be aimed at us and so become especially disagreeable to us, or inform us of something about a third person of which we were unaware, a psychological value of its own. It prevents the mind from falling asleep over the fictitious idea that it has of what it supposes things to be when it is actually no more than their outward appearance. It turns this appearance inside out with the magic dexterity of an idealist philosopher and rapidly presents to our gaze an unsuspected corner of the reverse side of the fabric. How could M. de Charlus have imagined the remark made of him by a certain tender relative: "How on earth can you suppose that Memé is in love with me, you forget that I am a woman!" And yet she was genuinely, deeply attached to M. de Charlus. Why then need we be surprised that in the case of the Verdurins, whose affection and goodwill he had no title to expect, the remarks which they made behind his back (and they did not, as we shall see, confine themselves to remarks), were so different from what he imagined them to be, that is to say from a mere repetition of the remarks that he heard when he was present? The latter alone decorated with affectionate inscriptions the little ideal tent to which M. de Charlus retired at times to dream by himself, when he introduced his imagination for a moment into the idea that the Verdurins held of him. Its atmosphere was so congenial, so cordial, the repose it offered so comforting, that when M. de Charlus, before going to sleep, had withdrawn to it for a momentary relief from his worries, he never emerged from it without a smile. But, for each one of us, a tent of this sort has two sides: as well as the side which we suppose to be the only one, there is the other which is normally invisible to us, the true front, symmetrical with the one that we know, but very different, whose decoration, in which we should recognise nothing of what we expected to see, would horrify us, as being composed of the hateful symbols of an unsuspected hostility. What a shock for M. de Charlus, if he had found his way into one of these enemy tents, by means of some piece of scandal as though by one of those service stairs where obscene drawings are scribbled outside the back doors of flats by unpaid tradesmen or dismissed servants. But, just as we do not possess that sense of direction with which certain birds are endowed, so we lack the sense of our own visibility as we lack that of distances, imagining as quite close to us the interested attention of the people who on the contrary never give us a thought, and not suspecting that we are at the same time the sole preoccupation of others. And so M. de Charlus lived in a state of deception like the fish which thinks that the water in which it is swimming extends beyond the glass wall of its aquarium which mirrors it, while it does not see close beside it in the shadow the human visitor who is amusing himself by watching its movements, or the all-powerful keeper who, at the unforeseen and fatal moment, postponed for the present in the case of the Baron (for whom the keeper, in Paris, will be Mme. Verdurin), will extract it without compunction from the place in which it was happily living to cast it into another. Moreover, the races of mankind, in so far as they are not merely collections of individuals, may furnish us with examples more vast, but identical in each of their parts, of this profound, obstinate and disconcerting blindness. Up to the present, if it was responsible for M. de Charlus's discoursing to the little clan remarks of a wasted subtlety or of an audacity which made his listeners smile at him in secret, it had not yet caused him, nor was it to cause him at Balbec any serious inconvenience. A trace of albumen, of sugar, of cardiac arythmia, does not prevent life from remaining normal for the man who is not even conscious of it, when only the physician sees in it a prophecy of catastrophes in store. At presence the fondness—whether Platonic or not—that M. de Charlus felt for Morel merely led the Baron to say spontaneously in Morel's absence that he thought him very good looking, supposing that this would be taken in all innocence, and thereby acting like a clever man who when summoned to make a statement before a Court of Law will not be afraid to enter into details which are apparently to his disadvantage but for that very reason are more natural and less vulgar than the conventional protestations of a stage culprit. With the same freedom, always between Saint-Martin du Chêne and Doncières-Ouest—or conversely on the return journey—M. de Charlus would readily speak of men who had, it appeared, very strange morals, and would even add: "After all, I say strange, I don't know why, for there's nothing so very strange about that," to prove to himself how thoroughly he was at his ease with his audience. And so indeed he was, provided that it was he who retained the initiative, and that he knew his gallery to be mute and smiling, disarmed by credulity or good manners.

When M. de Charlus was not speaking of his admiration for Morel's beauty, as though it had no connexion with an inclination—called a vice—he would refer to that vice, but as though he himself were in no way addicted to it. Sometimes indeed he did not hesitate to call it by its name. As after examining the fine binding of his volume of Balzac I asked him which was his favourite novel in the *Comédie Humaine*, he replied, his thoughts irresistibly attracted to the same topic: "Either one thing or the other, a tiny miniature like the *Curé de Tours* and the *Femme abandonnée*, or one of the great frescoes like the series of *Illusions perdues*. What! You've never read *Illusions perdues?* It's wonderful. The scene where Carlos Herrera asks the name of the château he is driving past, and it turns out to be Rastignac, the home of the young man he used to love. And then the abbé falls into a reverie which Swann once called, and very aptly, the *Tristesse d'Olimpio* of paederasty. And the death of Lucien! I forget who the man of taste was who, when he was asked what event in his life had most distressed him, replied: 'The death of Lucien de Rubempré in *Splendeurs et Misères*.'" "I know that Balzac is all the rage this year, as pessimism was last," Brichot interrupted. "But, at the risk of distressing the hearts that are smitten with the Balzacian fever, without laying any claim, damme, to being a policeman of letters, or drawing up a list of offences against the laws of grammar, I must confess that the copious improviser whose alarming lucubrations you appear to me singularly to overrate, has always struck me as being an insufficiently meticulous scribe. I have read these *Illusions perdues* of which you are telling us, Baron, flagellating myself to attain to the fervour of an initiate, and I confess in all simplicity of heart that those serial instalments of bombastic balderdash, written in double Dutch—and in triple Dutch: *Esther heureuse, Où mènent les mauvais chemins, A combien l'amour revient aux vieillards*, have always had the effect on me of the *Mystères de Rocambole*, exalted by an inexplicable preference to the precarious position of a masterpiece." "You say that because you know nothing of life," said the Baron, doubly irritated, for he felt that Brichot would not understand either his aesthetic reasons or the other kind. "I quite realise," replied Brichot, "that, to speak like Master François Rabelais, you mean that I am *moult sorbonagre, sorbonicole et sorboniforme*. And yet, just as much as any of the comrades, I like a book to give an impression of sincerity and real life, I am not one of those clerks. . . ." "The *quart d'heure de Rabelais*," the Doctor broke in, with an air no longer of uncertainty but of assurance as to his own wit. ". . . who take a vow of literature following the rule of the Abbaye-aux-Bois, yielding obedience to M. le Vicomte de Chateaubriand, Grand Master of common form, according to the strict rule of the humanists. M. le Vicomte de Chateaubriand's mistake. . . ." "With fried potatoes?" put in Dr. Cottard. "He is the patron saint of the brotherhood," continued Brichot, ignoring the wit of the Doctor, who, on the other hand, alarmed by the don's phrase, glanced anxiously at M. de Charlus. Brichot had seemed wanting in tact to Cottard, whose pun had brought a delicate smile to the lips of Princess Sherbatoff. "With the Professor, the mordant irony of the complete sceptic never forfeits its rights," she said kindly, to shew that the scientist's witticism had not passed unperceived by herself. "The sage is of necessity sceptical," replied the Doctor. "It's not my fault. *Gnothi seauton,* said Socrates. He was quite right, excess in anything is a mistake. But I am dumbfoundered when I think that those words have sufficed to keep Socrates's name alive all this time. What is there in his philosophy, very little when all is said. When one reflects that Charcot and others have done work a thousand times more remarkable, work which moreover is at least founded upon something, upon the suppression of the pupillary reflex as a syndrome of general paralysis, and that they are almost forgotten. After all, Socrates was nothing out of the common. They were people who had nothing better to do, and spent their time strolling about and splitting hairs. Like Jesus Christ: 'Love one another!' it's all very pretty." "My dear," Mme. Cottard implored. "Naturally my wife protests, women are all neurotic." "But, my dear Doctor, I am not neurotic," murmured Mme. Cottard. "What, she is not neurotic! When her son is ill, she exhibits phenomena of insomnia. Still, I quite admit that Socrates, and all the rest of them, are necessary for a superior culture, to acquire the talent of exposition. I always quote his *gnothi seauton* to my pupils at the beginning of the course. Père Bouchard, when he heard of it, congratulated me." "I am not one of those who hold to form for form's sake, any more than I should treasure in poetry the rhyme millionaire," replied Brichot. "But all the same the *Comédie Humaine*—which is far from human—is more than the antithesis of those works in which the art exceeds the matter, as that worthy hack Ovid says. And it is permissible to choose a middle course, which leads to the presbytery of Meudon or the hermitage of Ferney, equidistant from the Valley of Wolves, in which René superbly performed the duties of a merciless pontificate, and from les Jardies, where Honoré de Balzac, browbeaten by the bailiffs, never ceased voiding upon paper to please a Polish woman, like a zealous apostle of balderdash."

"Chateaubriand is far more alive now than you say, and Balzac is, after all, a great writer," replied M. de Charlus, still too much impregnated with Swann's tastes not to be irritated by Brichot, "and Balzac was acquainted with even those passions which the rest of the world ignores, or studies only to castigate them. Without referring again to the immortal *Illusions perdues; Sarrazine, La Fille aux yeux d'or, Une passion dans le désert,* even the distinctly enigmatic *Fausse Maîtresse* can be adduced in support of my argument. When I spoke of this 'unnatural' aspect of Balzac to Swann, he said to me: 'You are of the same opinion as Taine.' I never had the honour of knowing Monsieur Taine," M. de Charlus continued, with that irritating habit of inserting an otiose "Monsieur" to which people in society are addicted, as though they imagine that by styling a great writer "Monsieur" they are doing him an honour, perhaps keeping him at his proper distance, and making it evident that they do not know him personally. "I never knew Monsieur Taine, but I felt myself greatly honoured by being of the same opinion as he." However, in spite of these ridiculous social affectations, M. de Charlus was extremely intelligent, and it is probable that if some remote marriage had established a connexion between his family and that of Balzac, he would have felt (no less than Balzac himself, for that matter) a satisfaction which he would have been unable to help displaying as a praiseworthy sign of condescension.

Now and again, at the station after Saint-Martin du Chêne, some young men would get into the train. M. de Charlus could not refrain from looking at them, but as he cut short and concealed the attention that he was paying them, he gave it the air of hiding a secret, more personal even than his real secret; one would have said that he knew them, allowed his acquaintance to appear in spite of himself, after he had accepted the sacrifice, before turning again to us, like children who, in consequence of a quarrel among their respective parents, have been forbidden to speak to certain of their schoolfellows, but who when they meet them cannot forego the temptation to raise their heads before lowering them again before their tutor's menacing cane.

At the word borrowed from the Greek with which M. de Charlus in speaking of Balzac had ended his comparison of the *Tristesse d'Olympio* with the *Splendeurs et Misères,* Ski, Brichot and Cottard had glanced at one another with a smile perhaps less ironical than stamped with that satisfaction which people at a dinner-party would shew who had succeeded in making Dreyfus talk about his own case, or the Empress Eugénie about her reign. They were hoping to press him a little farther upon this subject, but we were already at Doncières, where Morel joined us. In his presence, M. de Charlus kept a careful guard over his conversation and, when Ski tried to bring it back to the love of Carlos Herrera for Lucien de Rubempré, the Baron assumed the vexed, mysterious, and finally (seeing that nobody was listening to him) severe and judicial air of a father who hears people saying something indecent in front of his daughter. Ski having shewn some determination to pursue the subject, M. de Charlus, his eyes starting out of his head, raised his voice and said, in a significant tone, looking at Albertine, who as a matter of fact could not hear what we were saying, being engaged in conversation with Mme. Cottard and Princess Sherbatoff, and with the suggestion of a double meaning of a person who wishes to teach ill bred people a lesson: "I think it is high time we began to talk of subjects that are likely to interest this young lady." But I quite realised that, to him, the young lady was not Albertine but Morel; he proved, as it happened, later on, the accuracy of my interpretation by the expressions that he employed when he begged that there might be no more of such conversation in front of Morel. "You know," he said to me, speaking of the violinist, "that he is not at all what you might suppose, he is a very respectable youth who has always behaved himself, he is very serious." And one gathered from these words that M. de Charlus regarded sexual inversion as a danger as menacing to young men as prostitution is to women, and that if he employed the epithet "respectable," of Morel it was in the sense that it has when applied to a young shop-girl. Then Brichot, to change the conversation, asked me whether I intended to remain much longer at Incarville. I had pointed out to him more than once, but in vain, that I was staying not at Incarville but at Balbec, he always repeated the mistake, for it was by the name of Incarville or Balbec-Incarville that he described this section of the coast. There are people like that, who speak of the same things as ourselves but call them by a slightly different name. A certain lady of the Faubourg Saint-Germain used invariably to ask me, when she meant to refer to the Duchesse de Guermantes, whether I had seen Zénaïde lately, or Oriane-Zénaïde, the effect of which was that at first I did not understand her. Probably there had been a time when, some relative of Mme. de Guermantes being named Oriane, she herself, to avoid confusion, had been known as Oriane-Zénaïde. Perhaps, too, there had originally been a station only at Incarville, from which one went in a carriage to Balbec. "Why, what have you been talking about?" said Albertine, astonished at the solemn, paternal tone which M. de Charlus had suddenly adopted. "About Balzac," the Baron hastily replied, "and you are wearing this evening the very same clothes as the Princesse de Cadignan, not her first gown, which she wears at the dinner-party, but the second." This coincidence was due to the fact that, in choosing Albertine's clothes, I sought inspiration in the taste that she had acquired thanks to Elstir, who greatly appreciated a sobriety which might have been called British, had it not been tempered with a gentler, more flowing grace that was purely French. As a rule the garments that he chose offered to the eye a harmonious combination of grey tones like the dress of Diane de Cadignan. M. de Charlus was almost the only person capable of appreciating Albertine's clothes at their true value; at a glance, his eye detected what constituted their rarity, justified their price; he would never have said the name of one stuff instead of another, and could always tell who had made them. Only he preferred—in women—a little more brightness and colour than Elstir would allow. And so this evening she cast a glance at me half smiling, half troubled, wrinkling her little pink cat's nose. Indeed, meeting over her skirt of grey crêpe de chine, her jacket of grey cheviot gave the impression that Albertine was dressed entirely in grey. But, making a sign to me to help her, because her puffed sleeves needed to be smoothed down or pulled up, for her to get into or out of her jacket, she took it off, and as her sleeves were of a Scottish plaid in soft colours, pink, pale blue, dull green, pigeon's breast, the effect was as though in a grey sky there had suddenly appeared a rainbow. And she asked herself whether this would find favour with M. de Charlus. "Ah!" he exclaimed in delight, "now we have a ray, a prism of colour. I offer you my sincerest compliments." "But it is this gentleman who has earned them," Albertine replied politely, pointing to myself, for she liked to shew what she had received from me. "It is only women who do not know how to dress that are afraid of colours," went on M. de Charlus. "A dress may be brilliant without vulgarity and quiet without being dull. Besides, you have not the same reasons as Mme. de Cadignan for wishing to appear detached from life, for that was the idea which she wished to instil into d'Arthez by her grey gown." Albertine, who was interested in this mute language of clothes, questioned M. de Charlus about the Princesse de Cadignan. "Oh! It is a charming tale," said the Baron in a dreamy tone. "I know the little garden in which Diane de Cadignan used to stroll with M. d'Espard. It belongs to one of my cousins." All this talk about his cousin's garden," Brichot murmured to Cottard, "may, like his pedigree, be of some importance to this worthy Baron. But what interest can it have for us who are not privileged to walk in it, do not know the lady, and possess no titles of nobility?" For Brichot had no suspicion that one might be interested in a gown and in a garden as works of art, and that it was in the pages of Balzac that M. de Charlus saw, in his mind's eye, the garden paths of Mme. de Cadignan. The Baron went on: "But you know her," he said to me, speaking of this cousin, and, by way of flattering me, addressing himself to me as to a person who, exiled amid the little clan, was to M. de Charlus, if not a citizen of his world, at any rate a visitor to it. "Anyhow you must have seen her at Mme. de Villeparisis's." "Is that the Marquise de Villeparisis who owns the château at Baucreux?" asked Brichot with a captivated air. "Yes, do you know her?" inquired M. de Charlus dryly. "No, not at all," replied Brichot, "but our colleague Norpois spends part of his holidays every year at Baucreux. I have had occasion to write to him there." I told Morel, thinking to interest him, that M. de Norpois was a friend of my father. But not a movement of his features shewed that he had heard me, so little did he think of my parents, so far short did they fall in his estimation of what my great-uncle had been, who had employed Morel's father as his valet, and, as a matter of fact, being, unlike the rest of the family, fond of giving trouble, had left a golden memory among his servants. "It appears that Mme. de Villeparisis is a superior woman; but I have never been allowed to judge of that for myself, nor for that matter has any of my colleagues. For Norpois, who is the soul of courtesy and affability at the Institute, has never introduced any of us to the Marquise. I know of no one who has been received by her except our friend Thureau-Dangin, who had an old family connexion with her, and also Gaston Boissier, whom she was anxious to meet because of an essay which interested her especially. He dined with her once and came back quite enthralled by her charm. Mme. Boissier, however, was not invited." At the sound of these names, Morel melted in a smile. "Ah! Thureau-Dangin," he said to me with an air of interest as great as had been his indifference when he heard me speak of the Marquis de Norpois and my father. "Thureau-Dangin; why, he and your uncle were as thick as thieves. Whenever a lady wanted a front seat for a reception at the Academy, your uncle would say: 'I shall write to Thureau-Dangin.' And of course he got the ticket at once, for you can understanding that M. Thureau-Dangin would never have dared to refuse anything to your uncle, who would have been certain to pay him out for it afterwards if he had. I can't help smiling, either, when I hear the name Boissier, for that was where your uncle ordered all the presents he used to give the ladies at the New Year. I know all about it, because I knew the person he used to send for them." He had not only known him, the person was his father. Some of these affectionate allusions by Morel to my uncle's memory were prompted by the fact that we did not intend to remain permanently in the Hôtel Guermantes, where we had taken an apartment only on account of my grandmother. Now and again there would be talk of a possible move. Now, to understand the advice that Charlie Morel gave me in this connexion, the reader must know that my great-uncle had lived, in his day, at 40*bis* Boulevard Malesherbes. The consequence was that, in the family, as we were in the habit of frequently visiting my uncle Adolphe until the fatal day when I made a breach between my parents and him by telling them the story of the lady in pink, instead of saying "at your uncle's" we used to say "at 40*bis*." If I were going to call upon some kinswoman, I would be warned to go first of all "to 40*bis*," in order that my uncle might not be offended by my not having begun my round with him. He was the owner of the house and was, I must say, very particular as to the choice of his tenants, all of whom either were or became his personal friends. Colonel the Baron de Vatry used to look in every day and smoke a cigar with him in the hope of making him consent to pay for repairs. The carriage entrance was always kept shut. If my uncle caught sight of a cloth or a rug hanging from one of the windowsills he would dash into the room and have it removed in less time than the police would take to do so nowadays. All the same, he did let part of the house, reserving for himself only two floors and the stables. In spite of this, knowing that he was pleased when people praised the house, we used always to talk of the comfort of the "little mansion" as though my uncle had been its sole occupant, and he allowed us to speak, without uttering the formal contradiction that might have been expected. The "little mansion" was certainly comfortable (my uncle having installed in it all the most recent inventions). But there was nothing extraordinary about it. Only, my uncle, while saying with a false modesty "my little hovel," was convinced, or in any case had instilled into his valet, the latter's wife, the coachman, the cook, the idea that there was no place in Paris to compare, for comfort, luxury, and general attractiveness, with the little mansion. Charles Morel had grown up in this belief. Nor had he outgrown it. And so, even on days when he was not talking to me, if in the train I mentioned to anyone else the possibility of our moving, at once he would smile at me and, with a wink of connivance, say: "Ah! What you want is something in the style of 40*bis!* That's a place that would suit you down to the ground! Your uncle knew what he was about. I am quite sure that in the whole of Paris there's nothing to compare with 40*bis.*"

The melancholy air which M. de Charlus had assumed in speaking of the Princesse de Cadignan left me in no doubt that the tale in question had not reminded him only of the little garden of a cousin to whom he was not particularly attached. He became lost in meditation, and, as though he were talking to himself: "The secrets of the Princesse de Cadignan!" he exclaimed, "What a masterpiece! How profound, how heartrending the evil reputation of Diane, who is afraid that the man she loves may hear of it. What an eternal truth, and more universal than might appear, how far it extends!" He uttered these words with a sadness in which nevertheless one felt that he found a certain charm. Certainly M. de Charlus, unaware to what extent precisely his habits were or were not known, had been trembling for some time past at the thought that when he returned to Paris and was seen there in Morel's company, the latter's family might intervene and so his future happiness be jeopardised. This eventuality had probably not appeared to him hitherto save as something profoundly disagreeable and painful. But the Baron was an artist to his finger-tips. And now that he had begun to identify his own position with that described by Balzac, he took refuge, in a sense, in the tale, and for the calamity which was perhaps in store for him and did not in any case cease to alarm him, he had the consolation of finding in his own anxiety what Swann and also Saint-Loup would have called something "quite Balzacian." This identification of himself with the Princesse de Cadignan had been made easy for M. de Charlus by virtue of the mental transposition which was becoming habitual with him and of which he had already furnished several examples. It was enough in itself, moreover, to make the mere conversion of a woman, as the beloved object, into a young man immediately set in motion about him the whole sequence of social complications which develop round a normal love affair. When, for any reason, we introduce once and for all time a change in the calendar, or in the daily time-table, if we make the year begin a few weeks later, or if we make midnight strike a quarter of an hour earlier, as the days will still consist of twenty-four hours and the months of thirty days, everything that depends upon the measure of time will remain unaltered. Everything may have been changed without causing any disturbance, since the ratio of the figures is still the same. So it is with lives which adopt Central European time, or the Eastern calendar. It seems even that the gratification a man derives from keeping an actress played a part in these relations.

When, after their first meeting, M. de Charlus had made inquiries as to Morel's actual position, he must certainly have learned that he was of humble extraction, but a girl with whom we are in love does not forfeit our esteem because she is the child of poor parents. On the other hand, the well known musicians to whom he had addressed his inquiries, had—and not even from any personal motive, unlike the friends who, when introducing Swann to Odette, had described her to him as more difficult and more sought after than she actually was—simply in the stereotyped manner of men in a prominent position overpraising a beginner, answered the Baron: "Ah! Great talent, has made a name for himself, of course he is still quite young, highly esteemed by the experts, will go far." And, with the mania which leads people who are innocent of inversion to speak of masculine beauty: "Besides, it is charming to watch him play; he looks better than anyone at a concert; he has lovely hair, holds himself so well; his head is exquisite, he reminds one of a violinist in a picture." And so M. de Charlus, raised to a pitch of excitement moreover by Morel himself, who did not fail to let him know how many offers had been addressed to him, was flattered by the prospect of taking him home with him, of making a little nest for him to which he would often return. For during the rest of the time he wished him to enjoy his freedom, which was necessary to his career, which M. de Charlus meant him, however much money he might feel bound to give him, to continue, either because of the thoroughly "Guermantes" idea that a man ought to do something, that he acquires merit only by his talent, and that nobility or money is simply the additional cypher that multiplies a figure, or because he was afraid lest, having nothing to do and remaining perpetually in his company, the violinist might grow bored. Moreover he did not wish to deprive himself of the pleasure which he found, at certain important concerts, in saying to himself: "The person they are applauding at this moment is coming home with me to-night." Fashionable people, when they are in love and whatever the nature of their love, apply their vanity to anything that may destroy the anterior advantages from which their vanity would have derived satisfaction.

Morel, feeling that I bore him no malice, being sincerely attached to M. de Charlus, and at the same time absolutely indifferent physically to both of us, ended by treating me with the same display of warm friendship as a courtesan who knows that you do not desire her and that her lover has a sincere friend in you who will not attempt to part him from her. Not only did he speak to me exactly as Rachel, Saint-Loup's mistress, had spoken to me long ago, but what was more, to judge by what M. de Charlus reported to me, he used to say to him about me in my absence the same things that Rachel had said about me to Robert. In fact M. de Charlus said to me: "He likes you so much," as Robert had said: "She likes you so much." And just as the nephew on behalf of his mistress, so it was on Morel's behalf that the uncle often invited me to come and dine with them. There were, for that matter, just as many storms between them as there had been between Robert and Rachel. To be sure, after Charlie (Morel) had left us, M. de Charlus would sing his praises without ceasing, repeating—the thought of it was flattering to him—that the violinist was so good to him. But it was evident nevertheless that often

Charlie, even in front of all the faithful, wore an irritated expression, instead of always appearing happy and submissive as the Baron would have wished. This irritation became so violent in course of time, owing to the weakness which led M. de Charlus to forgive Morel his want of politeness, that the violinist made no attempt to conceal, if he did not even deliberately assume it. I have seen M. de Charlus, on entering a railway carriage in which Morel was sitting with some of his soldier friends, greeted with a shrug of the musician's shoulders, accompanied by a wink in the direction of his comrades. Or else he would pretend to be asleep, as though this incursion bored him beyond words. Or he would begin to cough, and the others would laugh, derisively mimicking the affected speech of men like M. de Charlus; would draw Charlie into a corner, from which he would return, as though under compulsion, to sit by M. de Charlus, whose heart was pierced by all these cruelties. It is inconceivable how he can have put up with them; and these ever varied forms of suffering set the problem of happiness in fresh terms for M. de Charlus, compelled him not only to demand more, but to desire something else, the previous combination being vitiated by a horrible memory. And yet, painful as these scenes came to be, it must be admitted that at first the genius of the humble son of France traced for Morel, made him assume charming forms of simplicity, of apparent frankness, even of an independent pride which seemed to be inspired by disinterestedness. This was not the case, but the advantage of this attitude was all the more on Morel's side since, whereas the person who is in love is continually forced to return to the charge, to increase his efforts, it is on the other hand easy for him who is not in love to proceed along a straight line, inflexible and graceful. It existed by virtue of the privilege of the race in the face —so open—of this Morel whose heart was so tightly shut, that face indued with the neo-Hellenic grace which blooms in the basilicas of Champagne. Notwithstanding his affectation of pride, often when he caught sight of M. de Charlus at a moment when he was not expecting to see him, he would be embarrassed by the presence of the little clan, would blush, lower his eyes, to the delight of the Baron, who saw in this an entire romance. It was simply a sign of irritation and shame. The former sometimes found expression; for, calm and emphatically decent as Morel's attitude generally was, it was not without frequent contradictions. Sometimes, indeed, at something which the Baron said to him, Morel would come out, in the harshest tone, with an insolent retort which shocked everybody. M. de Charlus would lower his head with a sorrowful air, make no reply, and with that faculty which doting fathers possess of believing that the coldness, the rudeness of their children has passed unnoticed, would continue undeterred to sing the violinist's praises. M. de Charlus was not, indeed, always so submissive, but as a rule his attempts at rebellion proved abortive, principally because, having lived among people in society, in calculating the reactions that he might provoke he made allowance for the baser instincts, whether original or acquired. Now, instead of these, he encountered in Morel a plebeian tendency to spells of indifference. Unfortunately for M. de Charlus, he did not understand that, with Morel, everything else must give place when the Conservatoire (and the good reputation of the Conservatoire, but with this, which was to be a more serious matter, we are not at present concerned) was in question. Thus, for instance, people of the middle class will readily change their surnames out of vanity, noblemen for personal advantage. To the young violinist, on the contrary, the name Morel was inseparably linked with his first prize for the violin, and so impossible to alter. M. de Charlus would have liked Morel to take everything from himself, including a name. Going upon the facts that Morel's other name was Charles, which resembled Charlus, and that the place where they were in the habit of meeting was called les Charmes, he sought to persuade Morel that, a pleasant name, easy to pronounce, being half the battle for artistic fame, the virtuoso ought without hesitation to take the name Charmel, a discreet allusion to the scene of their intimacy. Morel shrugged his shoulders. As a conclusive argument, M. de Charlus was unfortunately inspired to add that he had a footman of that name. He succeeded only in arousing the furious indignation of the young man. "There was a time when my ancestors were proud of the title of groom, of butler to the King." "There was also a time," replied Morel haughtily, "when my ancestors cut off your ancestors' heads." M. de Charlus would have been greatly surprised had he been told that even if, abandoning the idea of "Charmel," he made up his mind to adopt Morel and to confer upon him one of the titles of the Guermantes family which were at his disposal but which circumstances, as we shall see, did not permit him to offer the violinist, the other would decline, thinking of the artistic reputation attached to the name Morel, and of the things that would be said about him in "the class." So far above the Faubourg Saint-Germain did he place the Rue Bergère. And so M. de Charlus was obliged to content himself with having symbolical rings made for Morel, bearing the antique device: PLVS VLTRA CAR'LVS. Certainly, in the face of an adversary of a sort with which he was unfamiliar, M. de Charlus ought to have changed his tactics. But which of us is capable of that? Moreover, if M. de Charlus made blunders, Morel was not guiltless of them either. Far more than the actual circumstance which brought about the rupture between them, what was destined, provisionally, at least (but this provisional turned out to be final), to ruin him with M. de Charlus was that his nature included not only the baseness which made him lie down under harsh treatment and respond with insolence to kindness. Running parallel to this innate baseness, there was in him a complicated neurasthenia of ill breeding, which, roused to activity on every occasion when he was in the wrong or was becoming a nuisance, meant that at the very moment when he had need of all his politeness, gentleness, gaiety, to disarm the Baron, he became sombre, petulant, tried to provoke discussions on matters where he knew that the other did not agree with him, maintained his own hostile attitude with a weakness of argument and a slashing violence which enhanced that weakness. For, very soon running short of arguments, he invented fresh ones as he went along, in which he displayed the full extent of his ignorance and folly. These were barely noticeable when he was in a friendly mood and sought only to please. On the contrary, nothing else was visible in his fits of sombre humour, when, from being inoffensive, they became odious. Whereupon M. de Charlus felt that he could endure no more, that his only hope lay in a brighter morrow, while Morel, forgetting that the Baron was enabling him to live in the lap of luxury, gave an ironical smile, of condescending pity, and said: "I have never taken anything from anybody. Which means that there is nobody to whom I owe a word of thanks."

In the mean time, and as though he had been dealing with a man of the world, M. de Charlus continued to give vent to his rage, whether genuine or feigned, but in either case ineffective. It was not always so, however. Thus one day (which must be placed, as a matter of fact, subsequent to this initial period) when the Baron was returning with Charlie and myself from a luncheon party at the Verdurins', and expecting to spend the rest of the afternoon and the evening with the violinist at Doncières, the latter's dismissal of him, as soon as we left the train, with: "No, I've an engagement," caused M. de Charlus so keen a disappointment, that in spite of all his attempts to meet adversity with a brave face, I saw the tears trickling down and melting the paint beneath his eyes, as he stood helpless by the carriage door. Such was his grief that, since we intended, Albertine and I, to spend the rest of the day at Doncières, I whispered to her that I would prefer that we did not leave M. de Charlus by himself, as he seemed, I could not say why, to be unhappy. The dear girl readily assented. I then asked M. de Charlus if he would not like me to accompany him for a little. He also assented, but declined to put my "cousin" to any trouble. I found a certain charm (and one, doubtless, not to be repeated, since I had made up my mind to break with her), in saying to her quietly, as though she were my wife: "Go back home by yourself, I shall see you this evening," and in hearing her, as a wife might, give me permission to do as I thought fit, and authorise me, if M. de Charlus, to whom she was attached, needed my company, to place myself at his disposal. We proceeded, the Baron and I, he waddling obesely, his jesuitical eyes downcast, and I following him, to a café where we were given beer. I felt M. de Charlus's eyes turning uneasily towards the execution of some plan. Suddenly he called for paper and ink, and began to write at an astonishing speed. While he covered sheet after sheet, his eyes glittered with furious fancies. When he had written eight pages: "May I ask you to do me a great service?" he said to me. "You will excuse my sealing this note. I am obliged to do so. You will take a carriage, a motor-car if you can find one, to get there as quickly as possible. You are certain to find Morel in his quarters, where he has gone to change his clothes. Poor boy, he tried to bluster a little when we parted, but you may be sure that his heart is fuller than mine. You will give him this note, and, if he asks you where you met me, you will tell him that you stopped at Doncières (which, for that matter, is the truth) to see Robert, which is not quite the truth perhaps, but that you met me with a person whom you do not know, that I seemed to be extremely angry, that you thought you heard something about sending seconds (I am, as a matter of fact, fighting a duel to-morrow). Whatever you do, don't say that I am asking for him, don't make any effort to bring him here, but if he wishes to come with you, don't prevent him from doing so. Go, my boy, it is for his good, you may be the means of averting a great tragedy. While you are away, I am going to write to my seconds. I have prevented you from spending the afternoon with your cousin. I hope that she will bear me no ill will for that, indeed I am sure of it. For her's is a noble soul, and I know that she is one of the people who are strong enough not to resist the greatness of circumstances. You must thank her on my behalf. I am personally indebted to her, and I am glad that it should be so." I was extremely sorry for M. de Charlus; it seemed to me that Charlie might have prevented this duel, of which he was perhaps the cause, and I was revolted, if that were the case, that he should have gone off with such indifference, instead of staying to help his protector. My indignation was increased when, on reaching the house in which Morel lodged, I recognised the voice of the violinist, who, feeling the need of an outlet for his happiness, was singing boisterously: "Some Sunday morning, when the wedding-bells rrring!" If poor M. de Charlus had heard him, he who wished me to believe, and doubtless believed himself that Morel's heart at that moment was full! Charlie began to dance with joy when he caught sight of me. "Hallo, old boy! (excuse me, addressing you like that; in this damned military life, one picks up bad habits) what luck, seeing you. I have nothing to do all evening. Do let's go somewhere together. We can stay here if you like, or take a boat if you prefer that, or we can have some music, it's all the same to me." I told him that I was obliged to dine at Balbec, he seemed anxious that I should invite him to dine there also, but I refrained from doing so. "But if you're in such a hurry, why have you come here?" "I have brought you a note from M. de Charlus." At that moment all his gaiety vanished; his face contracted. "What! He can't leave me alone even here. So I'm a slave, am I? Old boy, be a sport. I'm not going to open his letter. You can tell him that you couldn't find me." "Wouldn't it be better to open it, I fancy it contains something serious." "No, certainly not, you don't know all the lies, the infernal tricks that old scoundrel's up to. It's a dodge to make me go and see him. Very well! I'm not going, I want to have an evening in peace." "But isn't there going to be a duel tomorrow?" I asked Morel, whom I supposed to be equally well informed. "A duel?" he repeated with an air of stupefaction. "I never heard a word about it. After all, it doesn't matter a damn to me, the dirty old beast can go and get plugged in the guts if he likes. But wait a minute, this is interesting, I'm going to look at his letter after all. You can tell him that you left it here for me, in case I should come in." While Morel was speaking to me, I was looking with amazement at the beautiful books which M. de Charlus had given him, and which littered his room. The violinist having refused to accept those labelled: "I belong to the Baron" etc., a device which he felt to be insulting to himself, as a mark of vassalage, the Baron, with the sentimental ingenuity in which his ill-starred love abounded, had substituted others, originated by his ancestors, but ordered from the binder according to the circumstances of a melancholy friendship. Sometimes they were terse and confident, as *Spes mea* or *Expectata non eludet*. Sometimes merely resigned, as *J'attendrai*. Others were gallant: *Mesmes plaisir du mestre*, or counselled chastity, such as that borrowed from the family of Simiane, sprinkled with azure towers and lilies, and given a fresh meaning: *Sustendant lilia turres*. Others, finally, were despairing, and appointed a meeting in heaven with him who had spurned the donor upon earth: *Manet ultima caelo,* and (finding the grapes which he had failed to reach too sour, pretending not to have sought what he had not secured) M. de Charlus said in one: *Non mortale quod opto.* But I had not time to examine them all.

If M. de Charlus, in dashing this letter down upon paper had seemed to be carried away by the demon that was inspiring his flying pen, as soon as Morel had broken the seal (a leopard between two roses gules, with the motto: *atavis et armis*) he began to read the letter as feverishly as M. de Charlus had written it, and over those pages covered at breakneck speed his eye ran no less rapidly than the Baron's pen. "Good God!" he exclaimed, "this is the last straw! But where am I to find him? Heaven only knows where he is now." I suggested that if he made haste he might still find him perhaps at a tavern where he had ordered beer as a restorative. "I don't know whether I shall be coming back," he said to his landlady, and added *in petto,* "it will depend on how the cat jumps." A few minutes later we reached the café. I remarked M. de Charlus's expression at the moment when he caught sight of me. When he saw that I did not return unaccompanied, I could feel that his breath, his life were restored to him. Feeling that he could not get on that evening without Morel, he had pretended that somebody had told him that two officers of the regiment had spoken evil of him in connexion with the violinist and that he was going to send his seconds to call upon them. Morel had foreseen the scandal, his life in the regiment made impossible, and had hastened to the spot. In doing which he had not been altogether wrong.

For to make his falsehood more plausible, M. de Charlus had already written to two of his friends (one was Cottard) asking them to be his seconds. And, if the violinist had not appeared, we may be certain that, in the frantic state in which M. de Charlus then was (and to change his sorrow into rage), he would have sent them with a challenge to some officer or other with whom it would have been a relief to him to fight. During the interval, M. de Charlus, remembering that he came of a race that was of purer blood than the House of France, told himself that it was really very good of him to take so much trouble over the son of a butler whose employer he would not have condescended to know. On the other hand, if his only amusement, almost, was now in the society of disreputable persons, the profoundly ingrained habit which such persons have of not replying to a letter, of failing to keep an appointment without warning you beforehand, without apologising afterwards, aroused in him, since, often enough, his heart was involved, such a wealth of emotion and the rest of the time caused him such irritation, inconvenience and anger, that he would sometimes begin to regret the endless letters over nothing at all, the scrupulous exactitude of Ambassadors and Princes, who, even if, unfortunately, their personal charms left his cold, gave him at any rate some sort of peace of mind. Accustomed to Morel's ways, and knowing how little hold he had over him, how incapable he was of insinuating himself into a life in which friendships that were vulgar but consecrated by force of habit occupied too much space and time to leave a stray hour for the great nobleman, evicted, proud, and vainly imploring, M. de Charlus was so convinced that the musician was not coming, was so afraid of losing him for ever if he went too far, that he could barely repress a cry of joy when he saw him appear. But feeling himself the victor, he felt himself bound to dictate the terms of peace and to extract from them such advantages as he might. "What are you doing here?" he said to him. "And you?" he went on, gazing at myself, "I told you, whatever you did, not to bring him back with you." "He didn't want to bring me," said Morel, turning upon M. de Charlus, in the artlessness of his coquetry, a glance conventionally mournful and languorously old-fashioned, with an air, which he doubtless thought to be irresistible, of wanting to kiss the Baron and to burst into tears. "It was I who insisted on coming in spite of him. I come, in the name of our friendship, to implore you on my bended knees not to commit this rash act." M. de Charlus was wild with joy. The reaction was almost too much for his nerves; he managed, however, to control them. "The friendship to which you appeal at a somewhat inopportune moment," he replied in a dry tone, "Ought, on the contrary, to make you support me when I decide that I cannot allow the impertinences of a fool to pass unheeded. However, even if I chose to yield to the prayers of an affection which I have known better inspired, I should no longer be in a position to do so, my letters to my seconds have been sent off and I have no doubt of their consent. You have always behaved towards me like a little idiot and, instead of priding yourself, as you had every right to do, upon the predilection which I had shewn for you, instead of making known to the mob of serjeants or servants among whom the law of military service compels you to live, what a source of incomparable satisfaction a friendship such as mine was to you, you have sought to make excuses for yourself, almost to make an idiotic merit of not being grateful enough. I know that in so doing," he went on, in order not to let it appear how deeply certain scenes had humiliated him, "you are guilty merely of having let yourself be carried away by the jealousy of others. But how is it that at your age you are childish enough (and a child ill-bred enough) not to have seen at once that your election by myself and all the advantages that must result for you from it were bound to excite jealousies, that all your comrades while they egged you on to quarrel with me were plotting to take your place? I have not thought it necessary to tell you of the letters that I have received in that connexion from all the people in whom you place most confidence. I scorn the overtures of those flunkeys as I scorn their ineffective mockery. The only person for whom I care is yourself, since I am fond of you, but affection has its limits and you ought to have guessed as much." Harsh as the word flunkey might sound in the ears of Morel, whose father had been one, but precisely because his father had been one, the explanation of all social misadventures by "jealousy," an explanation fatuous and absurd, but of inexhaustible value, which with a certain class never fails to "catch on" as infallibly as the old tricks of the stage with a theatrical audience or the threat of the clerical peril in a parliament, found in him an adherence hardly less solid than in Françoise, or the servants of Mme. de Guermantes, for whom jealousy was the sole cause of the misfortunes that beset humanity. He had no doubt that his comrades had tried to oust him from his position and was all the more wretched at the thought of this disastrous, albeit imaginary duel. "Oh!

How dreadful," exclaimed Charlie. "I shall never hold up my head again. But oughtn't they to see you before they go and call upon this officer?" "I don't know, I suppose they ought. I've sent word to one of them that I shall be here all evening and can give him his instructions." "I hope that before he comes I can make you listen to reason; you will, anyhow, let me stay with you," Morel asked him tenderly. This was all that M. de Charlus wanted. He did not however yield at once. "You would do wrong to apply in this case the 'Whoso loveth well, chasteneth well' of the proverb, for it is yourself whom I loved well, and I intend to chasten even after our parting those who have basely sought to do you an injury. Until now, their inquisitive insinuations, when they dared to ask me how a man like myself could mingle with a boy of your sort, sprung from the gutter, I have answered only in the words of the motto of my La Rochefoucauld cousins: ''Tis my pleasure.' I have indeed pointed out to you more than once that this pleasure was capable of becoming my chiefest pleasure, without there resulting from your arbitrary elevation any degradation of myself." And in an impulse of almost insane pride he exclaimed, raising his arms in the air: "*Tantus ab uno splendor!* To condescend is not to descend," he went on in a calmer tone, after this delirious outburst of pride and joy. "I hope at least that my two adversaries, notwithstanding their inferior rank, are of a blood that I can shed without reproach. I have made certain discreet inquiries in that direction which have reassured me. If you retained a shred of gratitude towards me, you ought on the contrary to be proud to see that for your sake I am reviving the bellicose humour of my ancestors, saying like them in the event of a fatal issue, now that I have learned what a little rascal you are: 'Death to me is life.'" And M. de Charlus said this sincerely, not only because of his love for Morel, but because a martial instinct which he quaintly supposed to have come down to him from his ancestors filled him with such joy at the thought of fighting that this duel, which he had originally invented with the sole object of making Morel come to him, he could not now abandon without regret. He had never engaged in any affair of the sort without at once imagining himself the victor, and identifying himself with the illustrious Constable de Guermantes, whereas in the case of anyone else this same action of taking the field appeared to him to be of the utmost insignificance. "I am sure it will be a fine sight," he said to us in all sincerity, dwelling upon each word. "To see Sarah Bernhardt in *L'Aiglon,* what is that but tripe? Mounet-Sully in *Oedipus,* tripe! At the most it assumes a certain pallid transfiguration when it is performed in the Arena of Nîmes. But what is it compared to that unimaginable spectacle, the lineal descendant of the Constable engaged in battle." And at the mere thought of such a thing, M. de Charlus, unable to contain himself for joy, began to make passes in the air which recalled Molière, made us take the precaution of drawing our glasses closer, and fear that, when the swords crossed, the combatants, doctor and seconds would at once be wounded. "What a tempting spectacle it would be for a painter. You who know Monsieur Elstir," he said to me," you ought to bring him." I replied that he was not in the neighbourhood. M. de Charlus suggested that he might be summoned by telegraph. "Oh! I say it in his interest," he added in response to my silence. "It is always interesting for a master—which he is, in my opinion—to record such an instance of racial survival. And they occur perhaps once in a century."

But if M. de Charlus was enchanted at the thought of a duel which he had meant at first to be entirely fictitious, Morel was thinking with terror of the stories that might be spread abroad by the regimental band and might, thanks to the stir that would be made by this duel, penetrate to the holy of holies in the Rue Bergère. Seeing in his mind's eye the "class" fully informed, he became more and more insistent with M. de Charlus, who continued to gesticulate before the intoxicating idea of a duel. He begged the Baron to allow him not to leave him until the day after the next, the supposed day of the duel, so that he might keep him within sight and try to make him listen to the voice of reason. So tender a proposal triumphed over M. de Charlus's final hesitations. He said that he would try to find a way out of it, that he would postpone his final decision for two days. In this fashion, by not making any definite arrangement at once, M. de Charlus knew that he could keep Charlie with him for at least two days, and make use of the time to fix future engagements with him in exchange for his abandoning the duel, an exercise, he said, which in itself delighted him and which he would not forego without regret. And in saying this he was quite sincere, for he had always enjoyed taking the field when it was a question of crossing swords or exchanging shots with an adversary. Cottard arrived at length, although extremely late, for, delighted to act as second but even more upset by the prospect, he had been obliged to halt at all the cafés or farms by the way, asking the occupants to be so kind as to shew him the way to "No. 100" or "a certain place." As soon as he arrived, the Baron took him into another room, for he thought it more correct that Charlie and I should not be present at the interview, and excelled in making the most ordinary room serve for the time being as throne-room or council chamber. When he was alone with Cottard he thanked him warmly, but informed him that it seemed probable that the remark which had been repeated to him had never really been made, and requested that, in view of this, the Doctor would be so good as let the other second know that, barring possible complications, the incident might be regarded as closed. Now that the prospect of danger was withdrawn, Cottard was disappointed. He was indeed tempted for a moment to give vent to anger, but he remembered that one of his masters, who had enjoyed the most successful medical career of his generation, having failed to enter the Academy at his first election by two votes only, had put a brave face on it and had gone and shaken hands with his successful rival. And so the Doctor refrained from any expression of indignation which could have made no difference, and, after murmuring, he the most timorous of men, that there were certain things which one could not overlook, added that it was better so, that this solution delighted him. M. de Charlus, desirous of shewing his gratitude to the Doctor, just as the Duke his brother would have straightened the collar of my father's greatcoat or rather as a Duchess would put her arm round the waist of a plebeian lady, brought his chair close to the Doctor's, notwithstanding the dislike that he felt for the other. And, not only without any physical pleasure, but having first to overcome a physical repulsion, as a Guermantes, not as an invert, in taking leave of the Doctor, he clasped his hand and caressed it for a moment with the affection of a rider rubbing his horse's nose and giving it a lump of sugar. But Cottard, who had never allowed the Baron to see that he had so much as heard the vaguest rumours as to his morals, but nevertheless regarded him in his private judgment as one of the class of "abnormals" (indeed, with his habitual inaccuracy in the choice of terms, and in the most serious tone, he said of one of M. Verdurin's footmen: "Isn't he the Baron's mistress?"), persons of whom he had little personal experience; imagined that this stroking of his hand was the immediate prelude to an act of violence in anticipation of which, the duel being a mere pretext, he had been enticed into a trap and led by the Baron into this remote apartment where he was about to be forcibly outraged. Not daring to stir from his chair, to which fear kept him glued, he rolled his eyes in terror, as though he had fallen into the hands of a savage who, for all he could tell, fed upon human flesh. At length M. de Charlus, releasing his hand and anxious to be hospitable to the end, said: "Won't you come and take something with us, as the saying is, what in the old days used to be called a *mazagran* or a *gloria*, drinks that are no longer to be found, as archaeological curiosities, except in the plays of Labiche and the cafés of Doncières. A *gloria* would be distinctly suitable to the place, eh?, and to the occasion, what do you say?" "I am President of the Anti-Alcohol League," replied Cottard. "Some country sawbones has only got to pass, and it will be said that I do not practise what I preach. *Os homini sublime dedit coelumque tueri,*" he added, not that this had any bearing on the matter, but because his stock of Latin quotations was extremely limited, albeit sufficient to astound his pupils. M. de Charlus shrugged his shoulders and led Cottard back to where we were, after exacting a promise of secrecy which was all the more important to him since the motive for the abortive duel was purely imaginary. It must on no account reach the ears of the officer whom he had arbitrarily selected as his adversary. While the four of us sat there drinking, Mme. Cottard, who had been waiting for her husband outside, where M. de Charlus could see her quite well, though he had made no effort to summon her, came in and greeted the Baron, who held out his hand to her as though to a housemaid, without rising from his chair, partly in the manner of a king receiving homage, partly as a snob who does not wish a woman of humble appearance to sit down at his table, partly as an egoist who enjoys being alone with his friends, and does not wish to be bothered. So Mme. Cottard remained standing while she talked to M. de Charlus and her husband. But, possibly because politeness, the knowledge of what "ought to be done," is not the exclusive privilege of the Guermantes, and may all of a sudden illuminate and guide the most uncertain brains, or else because, himself constantly unfaithful to his wife, Cottard felt at odd moments, as a sort of compensation, the need to protect her against anyone else who failed in his duty to her, the Doctor quickly frowned, a thing I had never seen him do before, and, without consulting M. de Charlus, said in a tone of authority: "Come, Léontine, don't stand about like that, sit down." "But are you sure I'm not disturbing you?" Mme. Cottard inquired timidly of M. de Charlus, who, surprised by the Doctor's tone, had made no observation. Whereupon, without giving him a second chance, Cottard repeated with authority: "I told you to sit down."

Presently the party broke up, and then M. de Charlus said to Morel: "I conclude from all this business, which has ended more happily than you deserved, that you are incapable of looking after yourself and that, at the expiry of your military service, I must lead you back myself to your father, like the Archangel Raphael sent by God to the young Tobias." And the Baron began to smile with an air of grandeur, and a joy which Morel, to whom the prospect of being thus led home afforded no pleasure, did not appear to share. In the exhilaration of comparing himself to the Archangel, and Morel to the son of Tobit, M. de Charlus no longer thought of the purpose of his speech which had been to explore the ground and see whether, as he hoped, Morel would consent to come with him to Paris. Intoxicated with his love or with his self-love, the Baron did not see or pretended not to see the violinist's wry grimace, for, leaving him by himself in the café, he said to me with a proud smile: "Did you notice how, when I compared him to the son of Tobit, he became wild with joy? That was because, being extremely intelligent, he at once understood that the Father in whose company he was henceforth to live was not his father after the flesh, who must be some horrible valet with moustaches, but his spiritual father, that is to say Myself. What a triumph for him! How proudly he reared his head! What joy he felt at having understood me. I am sure that he will now repeat day by day: 'O God Who didst give the blessed Archangel Raphael as *guide* to thy servant Tobias, upon a long journey, grant to us,

Thy servants, that we may ever be protected by him and armed with his succour.' I had no need even," added the Baron, firmly convinced that he would one day sit before the Throne of God, "to tell him that I was the heavenly messenger, he realised it for himself, and was struck dumb with joy!" And M. de Charlus (whom his joy, on the contrary, did not deprive of speech), regardless of the passers-by who turned to stare at him, supposing that he must be a lunatic, cried out by himself and at the top of his voice raising his hands in the air: "Alleluia!"

This reconciliation gave but a temporary respite to M. de Charlus's torments; often, when Morel had gone out on training too far away for M. de Charlus to be able to go and visit him or to send me to talk to him, he would write the Baron desperate and affectionate letters, in which he assured him that he was going to put an end to his life because, owing to a ghastly affair, he must have twenty-five thousand francs. He did not mention what this ghastly affair was, and had he done so, it would doubtless have been an invention. As far as the money was concerned, M. de Charlus would willingly have sent him it, had he not felt that it would make Charlie independent of him and free to receive the favours of some one else. And so he refused, and his telegrams had the dry, cutting tone of his voice. When he was certain of their effect, he hoped that Morel would never forgive him, for, knowing very well that it was the contrary that would happen, he could not help dwelling upon all the drawbacks that would be revived with this inevitable tie. But, if no answer came from Morel, he lay awake all night, had not a moment's peace, so great is the number of the things of which we live in ignorance, and of the interior and profound realities that remain hidden from us. And so he would form every conceivable supposition as to the enormity which put Morel in need of twenty-five thousand francs, gave it every possible shape, labelled it with, one after another, many proper names. I believe that at such moments M. de Charlus (in spite of the fact that his snobbishness, which was now diminishing, had already been overtaken if not outstripped by his increasing curiosity as to the ways of the lower orders) must have recalled with a certain longing the lovely, many-coloured whirl of the fashionable gatherings at which the most charming men and women sought his company only for the disinterested pleasure that it afforded them, where nobody would have dreamed of "doing him down," of inventing a "ghastly affair," on the strength of which one is prepared to take one's life, if one does not at once receive twenty-five thousand francs. I believe that then, and perhaps because he had after all remained more "Combray" at heart than myself, and had grafted a feudal dignity upon his Germanic pride, he must have felt that one cannot with impunity lose one's heart to a servant, that the lower orders are by no means the same thing as society, that in short he did not "get on" with the lower orders as I have always done.

The next station upon the little railway, Maineville, reminds me of an incident in which Morel and M. de Charlus were concerned. Before I speak of it, I ought to mention that the halt of the train at Maineville (when one was escorting to Balbec a fashionable stranger who, to avoid giving trouble, preferred not to stay at la Raspelière) was the occasion of scenes less painful than that which I am just about to describe. The stranger, having his light luggage with him in the train, generally found that the Grand Hotel was rather too far away, but, as there was nothing until one came to Balbec except small bathing places with uncomfortable villas, had, yielding to a preference for comfortable surroundings, resigned himself to the long journey when, as the train came to a standstill at Maineville, he saw the Palace staring him in the face, and never suspected that it was a house of ill fame. "But don't let us go any farther," he would invariably say to Mme. Cottard, a woman well-known for her practical judgment and sound advice. "There is the very thing I want. What is the use of going on to Balbec, where I certainly shan't find anything better. I can tell at a glance that it has all the modern comforts; I can quite well invite Mme. Verdurin there, for I intend, in return for her hospitality, to give a few little parties in her honour. She won't have so far to come as if I stay at Balbec. This seems to me the very place for her, and for your wife, my dear Professor. There are bound to be sitting rooms, we can have the ladies there. Between you and me, I can't imagine why Mme. Verdurin didn't come and settle here instead of taking la Raspelière. It is far healthier than an old house like la Raspelière, which is bound to be damp, and is not clean either, they have no hot water laid on, one can never get a wash. Now, Maineville strikes me as being far more attractive. Mme. Verdurin would have played the hostess here to perfection. However, tastes differ; I intend, anyhow, to remain here. Mme. Cottard, won't you come along with me; we shall have to be quick, for the train will be starting again in a minute. You can pilot me through that house, which you must know inside out, for you must often have visited it. It is the ideal setting for you." The others would have the greatest difficulty in making the unfortunate stranger hold his tongue, and still more in preventing him from leaving the train, while he, with the obstinacy which often arises from a blunder, insisted, gathered his luggage together and refused to listen to a word until they had assured him that neither Mme. Verdurin nor Mme. Cottard would ever come to call upon him there. "Anyhow, I am going to make my headquarters there. Mme. Verdurin has only to write, if she wishes to see me."

The incident that concerns Morel was of a more highly specialised order. There were others, but I confine myself at present, as the train halts and the porter calls out "Doncières," "Grattevast," "Maineville" etc., to noting down the particular memory that the watering-place or garrison town recalls to me. I have already mentioned Maineville (*media villa*) and the importance that it had acquired from that luxurious establishment of women which had recently been built there, not without arousing futile protests from the mothers of families. But before I proceed to say why Maineville is associated in my memory with Morel and M. de Charlus, I must make a note of the disproportion (which I shall have occasion to examine more thoroughly later on) between the importance that Morel attached to keeping certain hours free, and the triviality of the occupations to which he pretended to devote them, this same disproportion recurring amid the explanations of another sort which he gave to M. de Charlus. He, who played the disinterested artist for the Baron's benefit (and might do so without risk, in view of the generosity of his protector), when he wished to have the evening to himself, in order to give a lesson, etc., never failed to add to his excuse the following words, uttered with a smile of cupidity: "Besides, there may be forty francs to be got out of it. That's always something. You will let me go, for, don't you see, it's all to my advantage. Damn it all, I haven't got a regular income like you, I have my way to make in the world, it's a chance of earning a little money." Morel, in professing his anxiety to give his lesson, was not altogether insincere. For one thing, it is false to say that money has no colour. A new way of earning them gives a fresh lustre to coins that are tarnished with use. Had he really gone out to give a lesson, it is probable that a couple of louis handed to him as he left the house by a girl pupil would have produced a different effect on him from a couple of louis coming from the hand of M. de Charlus. Besides, for a couple of louis the richest of men would travel miles, which become leagues when one is the son of a valet. But frequently M. de Charlus had his doubts as to the reality of the violin lesson, doubts which were increased by the fact that often the musician pleaded excuses of another sort, entirely disinterested from the material point of view, and at the same time absurd. In this Morel could not help presenting an image of his life, but one that deliberately, and unconsciously too, he so darkened that only certain parts of it could be made out. For a whole month he placed himself at M. de Charlus's disposal, on condition that he might keep his evenings free, for he was anxious to put in a regular attendance at a course of algebra. Come and see M. de Charlus after the class? Oh, that was impossible, the classes went on, sometimes, very late. "Even after two o'clock in the morning?" the Baron asked. "Sometimes." "But you can learn algebra just as easily from a book." "More easily, for I don't get very much out of the lectures." "Very well, then! Besides, algebra can't be of any use to you." "I like it. It soothes my nerves." "It cannot be algebra that makes him ask leave to go out at night," M. de Charlus said to himself. "Can he be working for the police?" In any case Morel, whatever objection might be made, reserved certain evening hours, whether for algebra or for the violin. On one occasion it was for neither, but for the Prince de Guermantes who, having come down for a few days to that part of the coast, to pay the Princesse de Luxembourg a visit, picked up the musician, without knowing who he was or being recognised by him either, and offered him fifty francs to spend the night with him in the brothel at Maineville; a twofold pleasure for Morel, in the profit received from M. de Guermantes and in the delight of being surrounded by women whose sunburned breasts would be visible to the naked eye. In some way or other M. de Charlus got wind of what had occurred and of the place appointed, but did not discover the name of the seducer. Mad with jealousy, and in the hoping of finding out who he was, he telegraphed to Jupien, who arrived two days later, and when, early in the following week, Morel announced that he would again be absent, the Baron asked Jupien if he would undertake to bribe the woman who kept the establishment, and make her promise to hide the Baron and himself in some place where they could witness what occurred. "That's all right. I'll see to it, dearie," Jupien assured the Baron. It is hard to imagine to what extent this anxiety was agitating, and by so doing had momentarily enriched the mind of M. de Charlus. Love is responsible in this way for regular volcanic upheavals of the mind. In his, which, a few days earlier, resembled a plain so uniform that as far as the eye could reach it would have been impossible to make out an idea rising above the level surface, there had suddenly sprung into being, hard as stone, a chain of mountains, but mountains as elaborately carved as if some sculptor, instead of quarrying and carting his marble from them, had chiselled it on the spot, in which there writhed in vast titanic groups Fury, Jealousy, Curiosity, Envy, Hatred, Suffering, Pride, Terror and Love.

Meanwhile the evening on which Morel was to be absent had come. Jupien's mission had proved successful. He and the Baron were to be there about eleven o'clock, and would be put in a place of concealment. When they were still three streets away from this gorgeous house of prostitution (to which people came from all the fashionable resorts in the neighborhood), M. de Charlus had begun to walk upon tiptoe, to disguise his voice, to beg Jupien not to speak so loud, lest Morel should hear them from inside. Whereas, on creeping stealthily into the entrance hall, M. de Charlus, who was not accustomed to places of the sort, found himself, to his terror and amazement, in a gathering more clamorous than the Stock Exchange or a sale room. It was in vain that he begged the girls who gathered round him to moderate their voices; for that matter their voices were drowned by the stream of announcements and awards made by an old "assistant matron" in a very brown wig, her face crackled with the gravity of a Spanish attorney or priest, who kept shouting at every minute in a voice of thunder, ordering the doors to be alternately opened and shut, like a policeman regulating the flow of traffic: "Take this gentleman to twenty-eight, the Spanish room." "Let no more in." "Open the door again, these gentlemen want Mademoiselle Noémie. She's expecting them in the Persian parlour." M. de Charlus was as terrified as a countryman who has to cross the boulevards; while, to take a simile infinitely less sacrilegious than the subject represented on the capitals of the porch of the old church of Corleville, the voices of the young maids repeated in a lower tone, unceasingly, the assistant matron's orders, like the catechisms that we hear school-children chanting beneath the echoing vault of a parish church in the country. However great his alarm, M. de Charlus who, in the street, had been trembling lest he should make himself heard, convinced in his own mind that Morel was at the window, was perhaps not so frightened after all in the din of those huge staircases on which one realised that from the rooms nothing could be seen. Coming at length to the end of his calvary, he found Mlle. Noémie, who was to conceal him with Jupien, but began by shutting him up in a sumptuously furnished Persian sitting-room from which he could see nothing at all. She told him that Morel had asked for some orangeade, and that as soon as he was served the two visitors would be taken to a room with a transparent panel. In the mean time, as some one was calling for her, she promised them, like a fairy godmother, that to help them to pass the time she was going to send them a "clever little lady." For she herself was called away. The clever little lady wore a Persian wrapper, which she proposed to remove. M. de Charlus begged her to do nothing of the sort, and she rang for champagne which cost 40 francs a bottle. Morel, as a matter of fact, was, during this time, with the Prince de Guermantes; he had, for form's sake, pretended to go into the wrong room by mistake, had entered one in which there were two women, who had made haste to leave the two gentlemen undisturbed. M. de Charlus knew nothing of this, but was fidgeting with rage, trying to open the doors, sent for Mlle. Noémie, who, hearing the clever little lady give M. de Charlus certain information about Morel which was not in accordance with what she herself had told Jupien, banished her promptly, and sent presently, as a substitute for the clever little lady, a "dear little lady" who exhibited nothing more but told them how respectable the house was and called, like her predecessor, for champagne. The Baron, foaming with rage, sent again for Mlle. Noémie, who said to them: "Yes, it is taking rather long, the ladies are doing poses, he doesn't look as if he wanted to do anything." Finally, yielding to the promises, the threats of the Baron, Mlle. Noémie went away with an air of irritation, assuring them that they would not be kept waiting more than five minutes. The five minutes stretched out into an hour, after which Noémie came and tiptoed in front of M. de Charlus, blind with rage, and Jupien plunged in misery, to a door which stood ajar, telling them: "You'll see splendidly from here. However, it's not very interesting just at present, he is with three ladies, he is telling them about life in his regiment." At length the Baron was able to see through the cleft of the door and also the reflexion in the mirrors beyond. But a deadly terror forced him to lean back against the wall. It was indeed Morel that he saw before him, but, as though the pagan mysteries and Enchantments still existed, it was rather the shade of Morel, Morel embalmed, not even Morel restored to life like Lazarus, an apparition of Morel, a phantom of Morel, Morel "walking" or "called up" in that room (in which the walls and couches everywhere repeated the emblems of sorcery), that was visible a few feet away from him, in profile. Morel had, as though he were already dead, lost all his colour; among these women, with whom one might have expected him to be making merry, he remained livid, fixed in an artificial immobility; to drink the glass of champagne that stood before him, his arm, sapped of its strength, tried in vain to reach out, and dropped back again. One had the impression of that ambiguous state implied by a religion which speaks of immortality but means by it something that does not exclude annihilation. The women were plying him with questions: "You see," Mlle. Noémie whispered to the Baron, "they are talking to him about his life in the regiment, it's amusing, isn't it?"—here she laughed—"You're glad you came? He is calm, isn't he," she added, as though she were speaking of a dying man. The women's questions came thick and fast, but Morel, inanimate, had not the strength to answer them. Even the miracle of a whispered word did not occur. M. de Charlus hesitated for barely a moment before he grasped what had really happened, namely that, whether from clumsiness on Jupien's part when he had called to make the arrangements, or from the expansive power of a secret lodged in any breast, which means that no secret is ever kept, or from the natural indiscretion of these ladies, or from their fear of the police, Morel had been told that two gentlemen had paid a large sum to be allowed to spy on him, unseen hands had spirited away the Prince de Guermantes, metamorphosed into three women, and had placed the unhappy Morel, trembling, paralysed with fear, in such a position that if M. de Charlus had but a poor view of him, he, terrorised, speechless, not daring to lift his glass for fear of letting it fall, had a perfect view of the Baron.

The story moreover had no happier ending for the Prince de Guermantes. When he had seen sent away, so that M. de Charlus should not see him, furious at his disappointment, without suspecting who was responsible for it, he had implored Morel, still without letting him know who he was, to make an appointment with him for the following night in the tiny villa which he had taken and which, despite the shortness of his projected stay in it, he had, obeying the same insensate habit which we have already observed in Mme. de Villeparisis, decorated with a number of family keepsakes, so that he might feel more at home. And so, next day, Morel, turning his head every moment, trembling with fear of being followed and spied upon by M. de Charlus, had finally, having failed to observe any suspicious passer-by, entered the villa. A valet shewed him into the sitting-room, telling him that he would inform "Monsieur" (his master had warned him not to utter the word "Prince" for fear of arousing suspicions). But when Morel found himself alone, and went to the mirror to see that his forelock was not disarranged, he felt as though he were the victim of a hallucination. The photographs on the mantelpiece (which the violinist recognised, for he had seen them in M. de Charlus's room) of the Princesse de Guermantes, the Duchesse de Luxembourg, Mme. de Villeparisis, left him at first petrified with fright. At the same moment he caught sight of the photograph of M. de Charlus, which was placed a little behind the rest. The Baron seemed to be concentrating upon Morel a strange, fixed glare. Mad with terror, Morel, recovering from his first stupor, never doubting that this was a trap into which M. de Charlus had led him in order to put his fidelity to the test, sprang at one bound down the steps of the villa and set off along the road as fast as his legs would carry him, and when the Prince (thinking he had kept a casual acquaintance waiting sufficiently long, and not without asking himself whether it were quite prudent and whether the person might not be dangerous) entered the room, he found nobody there. In vain did he and his valet, afraid of burglary, and armed with revolvers, search the whole house, which was not large, every corner of the garden, the basement; the companion of whose presence he had been certain had completely vanished. He met him several times in the course of the week that followed. But on each occasion it was Morel, the dangerous person, who turned tail and fled, as though the Prince were more dangerous still. Confirmed in his suspicions, Morel never outgrew them, and even in Paris the sight of the Prince de Guermantes was enough to make him take to his heels. Whereby M. de Charlus was protected from a betrayal which filled him with despair, and avenged without ever having imagined such a thing, still less how it came about.

But already my memories of what I have been told about all this are giving place to others, for the B. A. G., resuming its slow crawl, continues to set down or take up passengers at the following stations.

At Grattevast, where his sister lived with whom he had been spending the afternoon, there would sometimes appear M. Pierre de Verjus, Comte de Crécy (who was called simply the Comte de Crécy), a gentleman without means but of the highest nobility, whom I had come to know through the Cambremers, although he was by no means intimate with them. As he was reduced to an extremely modest, almost a penurious existence, I felt that a cigar, a "drink" were things that gave him so much pleasure that I formed the habit, on the days when I could not see Albertine, of inviting him to Balbec. A man of great refinement, endowed with a marvellous power of self-expression, snow-white hair, and a pair of charming blue eyes, he generally spoke in a faint murmur, very delicately, of the comforts of life in a country house, which he had evidently known from experience, and also of pedigrees. On my inquiring what was the badge engraved on his ring, he told me with a modest smile: "It is a branch of verjuice." And he added with a relish, as though sipping a vintage: "Our arms are a branch of verjuice—symbolic, since my name is Verjus—slipped and leaved vert." But I fancy that he would have been disappointed if at Balbec I had offered him nothing better to drink than verjuice. He liked the most expensive wines, because he had had to go without them, because of his profound knowledge of what he was going without, because he had a palate, perhaps also because he had an exorbitant thirst. And so when I invited him to dine at Balbec, he would order the meal with a refinement of skill, but ate a little too much, and drank copiously, made them warm the wines that needed warming, place those that needed cooling upon ice. Before dinner and after he would give the right date or number for a port or an old brandy, as he would have given the date of the creation of a marquisate which was not generally known but with which he was no less familiar.

As I was in Aimé's eyes a favoured customer, he was delighted that I should give these special dinners and would shout to the waiters: "Quick, lay number 25;" he did not even say "lay" but "lay me," as though the table were for his own use. And, as the language of head waiters is not quite the same as that of sub-heads, assistants, boys, and so forth, when the time came for me to ask for the bill he would say to the waiter who had served us, making a continuous, soothing gesture with the back of his hand, as though he were trying to calm a horse that was ready to take the bit in its teeth: "Don't go too fast" (in adding up the bill), "go gently, very gently." Then, as the waiter was retiring with this guidance, Aimé, fearing lest his recommendations might not be carried out to the letter, would call him back: "Here, let me make it out." And as I told him not to bother: "It's one of my principles that we ought never, as the saying is, to sting a customer." As for the manager, since my guest was attired simply, always in the same clothes, which were rather threadbare (albeit nobody would so well have practised the art of dressing expensively, like one of Balzac's dandies, had he possessed the means), he confined himself, out of respect for me, to watching from a distance to see that everything was all right, and ordering, with a glance, a wedge to be placed under one leg of the table which was not steady. This was not to say that he was not qualified, though he concealed his early struggles, to lend a hand like anyone else. It required some exceptional circumstance nevertheless to induce him one day to carve the turkey-poults himself. I was out, but I heard afterwards that he carved them with a sacerdotal majesty, surrounded, at a respectful distance from the service-table, by a ring of waiters who were endeavouring thereby not so much to learn the art as to make themselves conspicuously visible, and stood gaping in open-mouthed admiration. Visible to the manager, for that matter (as he plunged a slow gaze into the flanks of his victims, and no more removed his eyes, filled with a sense of his exalted mission, from them than if he had been expected to read in them some augury), they were certainly not. The hierophant was not conscious of my absence even. When he heard of it, he was distressed: "What, you didn't see me carving the turkey-poults myself?" I replied that having failed, so far, to see Rome, Venice, Siena, the Prado, the Dresden gallery, the Indies, Sarah in *Phèdre*, I had learned to resign myself, and that I would add his carving of turkey-poults to my list. The comparison with the dramatic art (Sarah in *Phèdre*) was the only one that he seemed to understand, for he had already been told by me that on days of gala performances the elder Coquelin had accepted a beginner's parts, even that of a character who says but a single line or nothing at all. "It doesn't matter, I am sorry for your sake. When shall I be carving again? It will need some great event, it will need a war." (It did, as a matter of fact, need the armistice.) From that day onwards, the calendar was changed, time was reckoned thus: "That was the day after the day I carved the turkeys myself." "That's right, a week after the manager carved the turkeys himself." And so this prosectomy furnished, like the Nativity of Christ or the Hegira, the starting point for a calendar different from the rest, but neither so extensively adopted nor so long observed.

The sadness of M. de Crécy's life was due, just as much as to his no longer keeping horses and a succulent table, to his mixing exclusively with people who were capable of supposing that Cambremers and Guermantes were one and the same thing. When he saw that I knew that Legrandin, who had now taken to calling himself Legrand de Méséglise, had no sort of right to that name, being moreover heated by the wine that he was drinking, he broke out in a transport of joy. His sister said to me with an understanding air: "My brother is never so happy as when he has a chance of talking to you." He felt indeed that he was alive now that he had discovered somebody who knew the unimportance of the Cambremers and the greatness of the Guermantes, somebody for whom the social universe existed. So, after the burning of all the libraries on the face of the globe and the emergence of a race entirely unlettered, an old Latin scholar would recover his confidence in life if he heard somebody quoting a line of Horace. And so, if he never left the train without saying to me: "When is our next little gathering?", it was not so much with the hunger of a parasite as with the gluttony of a savant, and because he regarded our symposia at Balbec as an opportunity for talking about subjects which were precious to him and of which he was never able to talk to anyone else, and analogous in that way to those dinners at which assemble on certain specified dates, round the particularly succulent board of the Union Club, the Society of Bibliophiles. He was extremely modest, so far as his own family was concerned, and it was not from M. de Crécy that I learned that it was a very great family indeed, and a genuine branch transplanted to France of the English family which bears the title of Crecy. When I learned that he was a true Crécy, I told him that one of Mme. de Guermantes's nieces had married an American named Charles Crecy, and said that I did not suppose there was any connexion between them. "None," he said. "Any more than—not, of course, that my family is so distinguished—heaps of Americans who call themselves Montgomery, Berry, Chandos or Capel have with the families of Pembroke, Buckingham or Essex, or with the Duc de Berry." I thought more than once of telling him, as a joke, that I knew Mme. Swann, who as a courtesan had been known at one time by the name Odette de Crécy; but even if the Duc d'Alençon had shewn no resentment when people mentioned in front of him Émilienne d'Alençon, I did not feel that I was on sufficiently intimate terms with M. de Crécy to carry a joke so far. "He comes of a very great family," M. de Montsurvent said to me one day. "His family name is Saylor." And he went on to say that on the wall of his old castle above Incarville, which was now almost uninhabitable and which he, although born to a great fortune, was now too much impoverished to put in repair, was still to be read the old motto of the family. I thought this motto very fine, whether applied to the impatience of a predatory race niched in that eyrie from which its members must have swooped down in the past, or at the present day, to its contemplation of its own decline, awaiting the approach of death in that towering, grim retreat. It is, indeed, in this double sense that this motto plays upon the name Saylor, in the words: "*Ne sçais l'heure.*"

At Hermenonville there would get in sometimes M. de Chevregny, whose name, Brichot told us, signified like that of Mgr. de Cabrières, a place where goats assemble. He was related to the Cambremers, for which reason, and from a false idea of what was fashionable, the latter often invited him to Féterne, but only when they had no other guests to dazzle. Living all the year round at Beausoleil, M. de Chevregny had remained more provincial than they. And so when he went for a few weeks to Paris, there was not a moment to waste if he was to " see everything " in the time; so much so that occasionally, a little dazed by the number of spectacles too rapidly digested, when he was asked if he had seen a particular play he would find that he was no longer sure. But this uncertainty was rare, for he had that detailed knowledge of Paris only to be found in people who seldom go there. He advised me which of the " novelties " I ought to see (" It's worth your while "), regarding them however solely from the point of view of the pleasant evening that they might help to spend, and so completely ignoring the aesthetic point of view as never to suspect that they might indeed constitute a " novelty " occasionally in the history of art. So it was that, speaking of everything in the same tone, he told us: " We went once to the Opéra-Comique, but the show there is nothing much. It's called *Pelléas et Mélisande*. It's rubbish. Périer always acts well, but it's better to see him in something else. At the Gymnase, on the other hand, they're doing *La Châtelaine*. We went again to it twice; don't miss it, whatever you do, it's well worth seeing; besides, it's played to perfection; you have Frévalles, Marie Magnier, Baron fils; " and he went on to quote the names of actors of whom I had never heard, and without prefixing Monsieur, Madame or Mademoiselle, like the Duc de Guermantes, who used to speak in the same ceremoniously contemptuous tone of the "songs of Mademoiselle Yvette Guilbert" and the "experiments of Monsieur Charcot." This was not M. de Chevregny's way, he said "Cornaglia and Dehelly," as he might have said "Voltaire and Montesquieu." For in him, with regard to actors as to everything that was Parisian, the aristocrat's desire to shew his scorn was overcome by the desire to appear on familiar terms of the provincial.

Immediately after the first dinner-party that I had attended at la Raspelière with what was still called at Féterne "the young couple," albeit M. and Mme. de Cambremer were no longer, by any means, in their first youth, the old Marquise had written me one of those letters which one can pick out by their handwriting from among a thousand. She said to me: "Bring your delicious—charming—nice cousin. It will be a delight, a pleasure," always avoiding, and with such unerring dexterity, the sequence that the recipient of her letter would naturally have expected, that I finally changed my mind as to the nature of these diminuendoes, decided that they were deliberate, and found in them the same corruption of taste—transposed into the social key—that drove Sainte-Beuve to upset all the normal relations between words, to alter any expression that was at all conventional. Two methods, taught probably by different masters, came into conflict in this epistolary style, the second making Mme. de Cambremer redeem the monotony of her multiple adjectives by employing them in a descending scale, by avoiding an ending upon the perfect chord. On the other hand, I was inclined to see in these inverse gradations, not an additional refinement, as when they were the handiwork of the Dowager Marquise, but an additional clumsiness whenever they were employed by the Marquis her son or by his lady cousins. For throughout the family, to quite a remote degree of kinship and in admiring imitation of aunt Zélia, the rule of the three adjectives was held in great honour, as was a certain enthusiastic way of catching your breath when you were talking. An imitation that had passed into the blood, moreover; and whenever, in the family circle, a little girl, while still in the nursery, stopped short while she was talking to swallow her saliva, her parents would say: "She takes after aunt Zélia," would feel that as she grew up, her upper lip would soon tend to hide itself beneath a faint moustache, and would make up their minds to cultivate her inherited talent for music. It was not long before the Cambremers were on less friendly terms with Mme. Verdurin than with myself, for different reasons. They felt, they must invite her to dine. The "young" Marquise said to me contemptuously: "I don't see why we shouldn't invite that woman, in the country one meets anybody, it needn't involve one in anything." But being at heart considerably impressed, they never ceased to consult me as to the way in which they should carry out their desire to be polite. I thought that as they had invited Albertine and myself to dine with some friends of Saint-Loup, smart people of the neighbourhood, who owned the château of Gourville, and represented a little more than the cream of Norman society, for which Mme. Verdurin, while pretending never to look at it, thirsted, I advised the Cambremers to invite the Mistress to meet them. But the lord and lady of Féterne, in their fear (so timorous were they) of offending their noble friends, or (so simple were they) that M. and Mme. Verdurin might be bored by people who were not intellectual, or yet again (since they were impregnated with a spirit of routine which experience had not fertilised) of mixing different kinds of people, and making a social blunder, declared that it would not be a success, and that it would be much better to keep Mme. Verdurin (whom they would invite with all her little group) for another evening. For this coming evening—the smart one, to meet Saint-Loup's friends—they invited nobody from the little nucleus but Morel, in order that M. de Charlus might indirectly be informed of the brilliant people whom they had in their house, and also that the musician might help them to entertain their guests, for he was to be asked to bring his violin. They threw in Cottard as well, because M. de Cambremer declared that he had "a go" about him, and would be a success at the dinner-table; besides, it might turn out useful to be on friendly terms with a doctor, if they should ever have anybody ill in the house. But they invited him by himself, so as not to "start any complications with the wife." Mme. Verdurin was furious when she heard that two members of the little group had been invited without herself to dine at Féterne "quite quietly." She dictated to the doctor, whose first impulse had been to accept, a stiff reply in which he said: "*We* are dining that evening with Mme. Verdurin," a plural which was to teach the Cambremers a lesson, and to shew them that he was not detachable from Mme. Cottard. As for Morel, Mme. Verdurin had no need to outline a course of impolite behaviour for him, he found one of his own accord, for the following reason. If he preserved, with regard to M. de Charlus, in so far as his pleasures were concerned, an independence which distressed the Baron, we have seen that the latter's influence was making itself felt more and more in other regions, and that he had for instance enlarged the young virtuoso's knowledge of music and purified his style. But it was still, at this point in our story, at least, only an influence. At the same time there was one subject upon which anything that M. de Charlus might say was blindly accepted and put into practice by Morel. Blindly and foolishly, for not only were M. de Charlus's instructions false, but, even had they been justifiable in the case of a great gentleman, when applied literally by Morel they became grotesque. The subject as to which Morel was becoming so credulous and obeyed his master with such docility was that of social distinction. The violinist, who, before making M. de Charlus's acquaintance, had had no conception of society, had taken literally the brief and arrogant sketch of it that the Baron had outlined for him: "There are a certain number of outstanding families," M. de Charlus had told him, "first and foremost the Guermantes, who claim fourteen alliances with the House of France, which is flattering to the House of France if anything, for it was to Aldonce de Guermantes and not to Louis the Fat, his consanguineous but younger brother, that the Throne of France should have passed. Under Louis XIV, we 'draped' at the death of Monsieur, as having the same grandmother as the king; a long way below the Guermantes, one may however mention the families of La Trémoïlle, descended frcm the Kings of Naples and the Counts of Poitiers; of d'Uzès, scarcely old as a family, but the premier peers; of Luynes, who are of entirely recent origin, but have distinguished themselves by good marriages; of Choiseul, Harcourt, La Rochefoucauld. Add to these the family of Noailles (notwithstanding the Comte de Toulouse), Montesquiou and Castellane, and, I think I am right in saying, those are all. As for all the little people who call themselves Marquis de Cambremerde or de Vatefairefiche, there is no difference between them and the humblest private in your regiment. It doesn't matter whether you go and p— at Comtesse S—t's or s—t at Baronne P—'s, it's exactly the same, you will have compromised yourself and have used a dirty rag instead of toilet paper. Which is not nice." Morel had piously taken in this history lesson, which was perhaps a trifle cursory, and looked upon these matters as though he were himself a Guermantes and hoped that he might some day have an opportunity of meeting the false La Tour d'Auvergnes in order to let them see, by the contemptuous way in which he shook hands, that he did not take them very seriously. As for the Cambremers, here was his very chance to prove to them that they were no better than "the humblest private in his regiment." He did not answer their invitation, and on the evening of the dinner declined at the last moment by telegram, as pleased with himself as if he had behaved like a Prince of the Blood. It must be added here that it is impossible to imagine how intolerable and interfering M. de Charlus could be, in a more general fashion, and even, he who was so clever, how stupid, on all occasions when the flaws in his character came into play. We may say indeed that these flaws are like an intermittent malady of the mind. Who has not observed the fact among women, and even among men, endowed with remarkable intelligence but afflicted with nerves, when they are happy, calm, satisfied with their surroundings, we cannot help admiring their precious gifts, the words that fall from their lips are the literal truth. A touch of headache, the slightest injury to their self-esteem is enough to alter everything. The luminous intelligence, become abrupt, convulsive and narrow, reflects nothing but an irritated, suspicious, teasing self, doing everything that it can to give trouble. The Cambremers were extremely angry; and in the interval other incidents brought about a certain tension in their relations with the little clan. As we were returning, the Cottards, Charlus, Brichot, Morel and I, from a dinner at la Raspelière, one evening after the Cambremers who had been to luncheon with friends at Harambouville had accompanied us for part of our outward journey: "You who are so fond of Balzac, and can find examples of him in the society of to-day," I had remarked to M. de Charlus, "you must feel that those Cambremers come straight out of the *Scènes de la Vie de Province.*" But M. de Charlus, for all the world as though he had been their friend, and I had offended him by my remark, at once cut me short: "You say that because the wife is superior to the husband," he informed me in a dry tone. "Oh, I wasn't suggesting that she was the *Muse du département,* or Mme. de Bargeton, although. . . ." M. de Charlus again interrupted me: "Say rather, Mme. de Mortsauf." The train stopped and Brichot got out. "Didn't you see us making signs to you? You are incorrigible." "What do you mean?" "Why, have you never noticed that Brichot is madly in love with Mme. de Cambremer?" I could see from the attitude of Cottard and Charlie that there was not a shadow of doubt about this in the little nucleus. I felt that it shewed a trace of malice on their part. "What, you never noticed how distressed he became when you mentioned her," went on M. de Charlus, who liked to shew that he had experience of women, and used to speak of the sentiment which they inspire with a natural air and as though this were the sentiment which he himself habitually felt. But a certain equivocally paternal tone in addressing all young men—notwithstanding his exclusive affection for Morel—gave the lie to the views of a woman-loving man which he expressed. "Oh! These children," he said in a shrill, mincing, sing-song voice, "one has to teach them everything, they are as innocent as a newborn babe, they can't even tell when a man is in love with a woman. I wasn't such a chicken at your age," he added, for he liked to use the expressions of the underworld, perhaps because they appealed to him, perhaps so as not to appear, by avoiding them, to admit that he consorted with people whose current vocabulary they were. A few days later, I was obliged to yield to the force of evidence, and admit that Brichot was enamoured of the Marquise. Unfortunately he accepted several invitations to luncheon with her. Mme. Verdurin decided that it was time to put a stop to these proceedings. Quite apart from the importance of such an intervention to her policy in controlling the little nucleus, explanations of this sort and the dramas to which they gave rise caused her an ever increasing delight which idleness breeds just as much in the middle classes as in the aristocracy. It was a day of great emotion at la Raspelière when Mme. Verdurin was seen to disappear for a whole hour with Brichot, whom (it was known) she proceeded to inform that Mme. de Cambremer was laughing at him, that he was the joke of her drawing-room, that he would end his days in disgrace, having forfeited his position in the teaching world. She went so far as to refer in touching terms to the laundress with whom he was living in Paris, and to their little girl. She won the day, Brichot ceased to go to Féterne, but his grief was such that for two days it was thought that he would lose his sight altogether, while in any case his malady increased at a bound and held the ground it had won. In the mean time, the Cambremers, who were furious with Morel, invited M. de Charlus on one occasion, deliberately, without him. Receiving no reply from the Baron, they began to fear that they had committed a blunder, and, deciding that malice made an evil counsellor, wrote, a little late in the day, to Morel, an ineptitude which made M. de Charlus smile, as it proved to him the extent of his power. "You shall answer for us both that I accept," he said to Morel. When the evening of the dinner came, the party assembled in the great drawing-room of Féterne. In reality, the Cambremers were giving this dinner for those fine flowers of fashion M. and Mme. Féré. But they were so much afraid of displeasing M. de Charlus, that although she had got to know the Férés through M. de Chevregny, Mme. de Cambremer went into a fever when, on the afternoon before the dinner, she saw him arrive to pay a call on them at Féterne. She made every imaginable excuse for sending him back to Beausoleil as quickly as possible, not so quickly, however, that he did not pass, in the courtyard, the Férés, who were as shocked to see him dismissed like this as he himself was ashamed. But, whatever happened, the Cambremers wished to spare M. de Charlus the sight of M. de Chevregny, whom they judged to be provincial because of certain little points which are overlooked in the family circle and become important only in the presence of strangers, who are the last people in the world to notice them. But we do not like to display to them relatives who have remained at the stage which we ourselves have struggled to outgrow. As for M. and Mme. Féré, they were, in the highest sense of the words, what are called "really nice people." In the eyes of those who so defined them, no doubt the Guermantes, the Rohans and many others were also really nice people, but their name made it unnecessary to say so. As everybody was not aware of the exalted birth of Mme. Féré's mother, and the extraordinarily exclusive circle in which she and her husband moved, when you mentioned their name, you invariably added by way of explanation that they were "the very best sort." Did their obscure name prompt them to a sort of haughty reserve? However that may be, the fact remains that the Férés refused to know people on whom a La Trémoïlle would have called. It needed the position of queen of her particular stretch of coast, which the old Marquise de Cambremer held in the Manche, to make the Férés consent to come to one of her afternoons every year. The Cambremers had invited them to dinner and were counting largely on the effect that would be made on them by M. de Charlus. It was discreetly announced that he was to be one of the party. As it happened, Mme. Féré had never met him. Mme. de Cambremer, on learning this, felt a keen satisfaction, and the smile of the chemist who is about to bring into contact for the first time two particularly important bodies hovered over her face. The door opened, and Mme. de Cambremer almost fainted when she saw Morel enter the room alone. Like a private secretary charged with apologies for his Minister, like a morganatic wife who expresses the Prince's regret that he is unwell (so Mme. de Clinchamp used to apologise for the Duc d'Aumale), Morel said in the airiest of tones: "The Baron can't come. He is not feeling very well, at least I think that is why, I haven't seen him this week," he added, these last words completing the despair of Mme. de Cambremer, who had told M. and Mme. Féré that Morel saw M. de Charlus at every hour of the day. The Cambremers pretended that the Baron's absence gave an additional attraction to their party and, without letting Morel hear them, said to their other guests: "We can do very well without him, can't we, it will be all the better." But they were furious, suspected a plot hatched by Mme. Verdurin, and, tit for tat, when she invited them again to la Raspelière, M. de Cambremer, unable to resist the pleasure of seeing his house again and of mingling with the little group, came, but came alone, saying that the Marquise was so sorry, but her doctor had ordered her to stay in her room. The Cambremers hoped by this partial attendance at once to teach M. de Charlus a lesson, and to shew the Verdurins that they were not obliged to treat them with more than a limited politeness, as Princesses of the Blood used in the old days to "shew out" Duchesses, but only to the middle of the second saloon. After a few weeks, they were scarcely on speaking terms. M. de Cambremer explained this to me as follows: "I must tell you that with M. de Charlus it was rather difficult. He is an extreme

Dreyfusard. . . ." "Oh, no!" "Yes. . . . Anyhow his cousin the Prince de Guermantes is, they've come in for a lot of abuse over that. I have some relatives who are very particular about that sort of thing. I can't afford to mix with those people, I should quarrel with the whole of my family." "Since the Prince de Guermantes is a Dreyfusard, that will make it all the easier," said Mme. de Cambremer, "for Saint-Loup, who is said to be going to marry his niece, is one too. Indeed, that is perhaps why he is marrying her." "Come now, my dear, you mustn't say that Saint-Loup, who is a great friend of ours, is a Dreyfusard. One ought not to make such allegations lightly," said M. de Cambremer. "You would make him highly popular in the army!" "He was once, but he isn't any longer," I explained to M. de Cambremer. "As for his marrying Mlle. de Guermantes-Brassac, is there any truth in that?" "People are talking of nothing else, but you should be in a position to know." "But I repeat that he told me himself, he was a Dreyfusard," said Mme. de Cambremer. "Not that there isn't every excuse for him, the Guermantes are half German." "The Guermantes in the Rue de Varenne, you can say, are entirely German," said Cancan. "But Saint-Loup is a different matter altogether; he may have any amount of German blood, his father insisted upon maintaining his title as a great nobleman of France, he rejoined the service in 1871 and was killed in the war in the most gallant fashion. I may take rather a strong line about these matters, but it doesn't do to exaggerate either one way or the other. *In medio . . . virtus*, ah, I forget the exact words. It's a remark Doctor Cottard made. Now, there's a man who can always say the appropriate thing.

You ought to have a small Larousse in the house." To avoid having to give an opinion as to the Latin quotation, and to get away from the subject of Saint-Loup, as to whom her husband seemed to think that she was wanting in tact, Mme. de Cambremer fell back upon the Mistress whose quarrel with them was even more in need of an explanation. "We were delighted to let la Raspelière to Mme. Verdurin," said the Marquise. "The only trouble is, she appears to imagine that with the house, and everything else that she has managed to tack on to it, the use of the meadow, the old hangings, all sorts of things which weren't in the lease at all, she should also be entitled to make friends with us. The two things are entirely distinct. Our mistake lay in our not having done everything quite simply through a lawyer or an agency. At Féterne it doesn't much matter, but I can just imagine the face my aunt de Ch'nouville would make if she saw old mother Verdurin come marching in, on one of my days, with her hair streaming. As for M. de Charlus, of course, he knows some quite nice people, but he knows some very nasty people too." I asked for details. Driven into a corner, Mme. de Cambremer finally admitted: "People say that it was he who maintained a certain Monsieur Moreau, Morille, Morue, I don't remember. Nothing to do, of course, with Morel, the violinist," she added, blushing. "When I realised that Mme. Verdurin imagined that because she was our tenant in the Manche, she would have the right to come and call upon me in Paris, I saw that it was time to cut the cable."

Notwithstanding this quarrel with the Mistress, the Cambremers were on quite good terms with the faithful, and would readily get into our carriage when they were travelling by the train. Just before we reached Douville, Albertine, taking out her mirror for the last time, would sometimes feel obliged to change her gloves, or to take off her hat for a moment, and, with the tortoiseshell comb which I had given her and which she wore in her hair, would smooth the plaits, pull out the puffs, and if necessary, over the undulations which descended in regular valleys to the nape of her neck, push up her chignon. Once we were in the carriages which had come to meet us, we no longer had any idea where we were; the roads were not lighted; we could tell by the louder sound of the wheels that we were passing through a village, we thought we had arrived, we found ourselves once more in the open country, we heard bells in the distance, we forgot that we were in evening dress, and had almost fallen asleep when, at the end of this wide borderland of darkness which, what with the distance we had travelled and the incidents characteristic of all railway journeys, seemed to have carried us on to a late hour of the night and almost half way back to Paris, suddenly after the crunching of the carriage wheels over a finer gravel had revealed to us that we had turned into the park, there burst forth, reintroducing us into a social existence, the dazzling lights of the drawing-room, then of the dining-room where we were suddenly taken aback by hearing eight o'clock strike, that hour which we supposed to have so long since passed, while the endless dishes and vintage wines followed one another round men in black and women with bare arms, at a dinner-party ablaze with light like any real dinner-party, surrounded only, and thereby changing its character, by the double veil, sombre and strange, that was woven for it, with a sacrifice of their first solemnity to this social purpose, by the nocturnal, rural, seaside hours of the journey there and back. The latter indeed obliged us to leave the radiant and soon forgotten splendour of the lighted drawing-room for the carriages in which I arranged to sit beside Albertine so that my mistress might not be left with other people in my absence, and often for another reason as well, which was that we could both do many things in a dark carriage, in which the jolts of the downward drive would moreover give us an excuse, should a sudden ray of light fall upon us, for clinging to one another. When M. de Cambremer was still on visiting terms with the Verdurins, he would ask me: "You don't think that this fog will bring on your choking fits? My sister was terribly bad this morning. Ah! You have been having them too," he said with satisfaction. "I shall tell her that to-night. I know that, as soon as I get home, the first thing she will ask will be whether you have had any lately." He spoke to me of my sufferings only to lead up to his sister's, and made me describe mine in detail simply that he might point out the difference between them and hers. But notwithstanding these differences, as he felt that his sister's choking fits entitled him to speak with authority, he could not believe that what "succeeded" with hers was not indicated as a cure for mine, and it irritated him that I would not try these remedies, for if there is one thing more difficult than submitting oneself to a regime it is refraining from imposing it upon other people. "Not that I need speak, a mere outsider, when you are here before the areopagus, at the fountainhead of wisdom. What does Professor Cottard think about them?" I saw his wife once again, as a matter of fact, because she had said that my " cousin " had odd habits, and I wished to know what she meant by that. She denied having said it, but finally admitted that she had been speaking of a person whom she thought she had seen with my cousin. She did not know the person's name and said faintly that, if she was not mistaken, it was the wife of a banker, who was called Lina, Linette, Lisette, Lia, anyhow something like that. I felt that " wife of a banker " was inserted merely to put me off the scent. I decided to ask Albertine whether this were true. But I preferred to speak to her with an air of knowledge rather than of curiosity. Besides Albertine would not have answered me at all, or would have answered me only with a " no " of which the " n " would have been too hesitating and the " o " too emphatic. Albertine never related facts that were capable of injuring her, but always other facts which could be explained only by them, the truth being rather a current which flows from what people say to us, and which we apprehend, invisible as it may be, than the actual thing that they say. And so when I assured her that a woman whom she had known at Vichy had a bad reputation, she swore to me that this woman was not at all what I supposed, and had never attempted to make her do anything improper. But she added, another day, when I was speaking of my curiosity as to people of that sort, that the Vichy lady had a friend, whom she, Albertine, did not know, but whom the lady had "*promised* to introduce to her." That she should have promised her this, could only mean that Albertine wished it, or that the lady had known that by offering the introduction she would be giving her pleasure. But if I had pointed this out to Albertine, I should have appeared to be depending for my information upon her, I should have put an end to them at once, I should never have learned anything more, I should have ceased to make myself feared. Besides, we were at Balbec, the Vichy lady and her friend lived at Menton; the remoteness, the impossibility of the danger made short work of my suspicions. Often when M. de Cambremer hailed me from the station I had been with Albertine making the most of the darkness, and with all the more difficulty as she had been inclined to resist, fearing that it was not dark enough. "You know, I'm sure Cottard saw us, anyhow, if he didn't, he must have noticed how breathless we were from our voices, just when they were talking about your other kind of breathlessness," Albertine said to me when we arrived at the Douville station where we were to take the little train home. But this homeward, like the outward journey, if, by giving me a certain poetical feeling, it awakened in me the desire to travel, to lead a new life, and so made me decide to abandon any intention of marrying Albertine, and even to break off our relations finally, also, and by the very fact of their contradictory nature, made this breach more easy. For, on the homeward journey just as much as on the other, at every station there joined us in the train or greeted us from the platform people whom we knew; the furtive pleasures of the imagination were outweighed by those other, continual pleasures of sociability which are so soothing, so soporific. Already, before the stations themselves, their names (which had suggested so many fancies to me since the day on which I first heard them, the evening on which I travelled down to Balbec with my grandmother), had grown human, had lost their strangeness since the evening when Brichot, at Albertine's request, had given us a more complete account of their etymology. I had been charmed by the "flower" that ended certain names, such as Fiquefleur, Honfleur, Flers, Barfleur, Harfleur, etc., and amused by the "beef" that comes at the end of Bricquebœuf. But the flower vanished, and also the beef, when Brichot (and this he had told me on the first day in the train) informed us that *fleur* means a harbour (like *fiord*), and that *bœuf,* in Norman *budh,* means a hut. As he cited a number of examples, what had appeared to me a particular instance became general, Bricquebœuf took its place by the side of Elbeuf, and indeed in a name that was at first sight as individual as the place itself, like the name Pennedepie, in which the obscurities most impossible for the mind to elucidate seemed to me to have been amalgamated from time immemorial in a word as coarse, savoury and hard as a certain Norman cheese, I was disappointed to find the Gallic *pen* which means mountain and is as recognisable in Pennemarck as in the Apennines. As at each halt of the train I felt that we should have friendly hands to shake if not visitors to receive in our carriage, I said to Albertine: "Hurry up and ask Brichot about the names you want to know. You mentioned to me Marcouville l'Orgueilleuse." "Yes, I love that *orgueil,* it's a proud village," said Albertine. "You would find it," Brichot replied, "prouder still if, instead of turning it into French or even adopting a low Latinity, as we find in the Cartulary of the Bishop of Bayeux, *Marcouvilla superba,* you were to take the older form, more akin to the Norman, *Marculplinvilla superba,* the village, the domain of Merculph. In almost all these names which end in *ville*, you might see still marshalled upon this coast, the phantoms of the rude Norman invaders. At Hermenonville, you had, standing by the carriage door, only our excellent Doctor, who, obviously, has nothing of the Nordic chief about him. But, by shutting your eyes, you might have seen the illustrious Herimund (*Herimundivilla*). Although I can never understand why people choose those roads, between Loigny and Balbec-Plage, rather than the very picturesque roads that lead from Loigny to old Balbec, Mme. Verdurin has perhaps taken you out that way in her carriage. If so, you have seen Incarville, or the village of Wiscar; and Tourville, before you come to Mme. Verdurin's, is the village of Turold. And besides, there were not only the Normans. It seems that the Germans (*Alemanni*) came as far as here: Aumenancourt, *Alemanicurtis*—don't let us speak of it to that young officer I see there; he would be capable of refusing to visit his cousins there any more. There were also Saxons, as is proved by the springs of Sissonne" (the goal of one of Mme. Verdurin's favourite excursions, and quite rightly), "just as in England you have Middlesex, Wessex. And what is inexplicable, it seems that the Goths, miserable wretches as they are said to have been, came as far as this, and even the Moors, for Mortagne comes from *Mauretania*. Their trace has remained at Gourville—*Gothorunvilla*. Some vestige of the Latins subsists also, Lagny (*Latiniacum*)." "What I should like to have is an explanation of Thorpehomme," said M. de Charlus. "I understand *homme*," he added, at which the sculptor and Cottard exchanged significant glances. "But *Thorpe?*" "*Homme* does not in the least mean what you are naturally led to suppose, Baron," replied Brichot, glancing maliciously at Cottard and the sculptor. *Homme* has nothing to do, in this instance, with the sex to which I am not indebted for my mother. *Homme* is *holm* which means a small island, etc. . . . As for *Thorpe,* or village, we find that in a hundred words with which I have already bored our young friend. Thus in Thorpehomme there is not the name of a Norman chief, but words of the Norman language. You see how the whole of this country has been Germanised." "I think that is an exaggeration," said M. de Charlus. "Yesterday I was at Orgeville." "This time I give you back the man I took from you in Thorpehomme, Baron. Without wishing to be pedantic, a Charter of Robert I gives us, for Orgeville, *Otgervilla,* the domain of Otger. All these names are those of ancient lords. Octeville la Venelle is a corruption of l'Avenel. The Avenels were a family of repute in the middle ages. Bourguenolles, where Mme. Verdurin took us the other day, used to be written Bourg de Môles, for that village belonged in the eleventh century to Baudoin de Môles, as also did la Chaise-Baudoin, but here we are at Doncières." "Heavens, look at all these subalterns trying to get in," said M. de Charlus with feigned alarm. "I am thinking of you, for it doesn't affect me, I am getting out here." "You hear, Doctor? " said Brichot. "The Baron is afraid of officers passing over his body. And yet they have every right to appear here in their strength, for Doncières is precisely the same as Saint-Cyr, *Dominus Cyriacus.* There are plenty of names of towns in which *Sanctus* and *Sancta* are replaced by *Dominus* and *Domina.* Besides, this peaceful military town has sometimes a false air of Saint-Cyr, of Versailles, and even of Fontainebleau."

During these homeward (as on the outward) journeys I used to tell Albertine to put on her things, for I knew very well that at Aumenancourt, Doncières, Epreville, Saint-Vast we should be receiving brief visits from friends. Nor did I at all object to these, when they took the form of (at Hermenonville—the domain of Herimund) a visit from M. de Chevregny, seizing the opportunity, when he had come down to meet other guests, of asking me to come over to luncheon next day at Beausoleil, or (at Doncières) the sudden irruption of one of Saint-Loup's charming friends sent by him (if he himself was not free) to convey to me an invitation from Captain de Borodino, from the officers' mess at the Cocq-Hardi, or the serjeants' at the Faisan Doré. If Saint-Loup often came in person, during the whole of the time that he was stationed there, I contrived, without attracting attention, to keep Albertine a prisoner under my own watch and ward, not that my vigilance was of any use. On one occasion however my watch was interrupted. When there was a long stop, Bloch, after greeting us, was making off at once to join his father, who, having just succeeded to his uncle's fortune, and having leased a country house by the name of La Commanderie, thought it befitting a country gentleman always to go about in a post chaise, with postilions in livery. Bloch begged me to accompany him to the carriage. "But make haste, for these quadrupeds are impatient, come, O man beloved of the gods, thou wilt give pleasure to my father." But I could not bear to leave Albertine in the train with Saint-Loup; they might, while my back was turned, get into conversation, go into another compartment, smile at one another, touch one another; my eyes, glued to Albertine, could not detach themselves from her so long as Saint-Loup was there. Now I could see quite well that Bloch, who had asked me, as a favour, to go and say how d'ye do to his father, in the first place thought it not very polite of me to refuse when there was nothing to prevent me from doing so, the porters having told us that the train would remain for at least a quarter of an hour in the station, and almost all the passengers, without whom it would not start, having alighted; and, what was more, had not the least doubt that it was because quite decidedly—my conduct on this occasion furnished him with a definite proof of it—I was a snob. For he was well aware of the names of the people in whose company I was. In fact M. de Charlus had said to me, some time before this and without remembering or caring that the introduction had had been made long ago: "But you must introduce your friend to me, you are shewing a want of respect for myself," and had talked to Bloch, who had seemed to please him immensely, so much so that he had gratified him with an: "I hope to meet you again." "Then it is irrevocable, you won't walk a hundred yards to say how d'ye do to my father, who would be so pleased," Bloch said to me. I was sorry to appear to be wanting in good fellowship, and even more so for the reason for which Bloch supposed that I was wanting, and to feel that he imagined that I was not the same towards my middle class friends when I was with people of "birth." From that day he ceased to shew me the same friendly spirit and, what pained me more, had no longer the same regard for my character. But, in order to undeceive him as to the motive which made me remain in the carriage, I should have had to tell him something —to wit, that I was jealous of Albertine—which would have distressed me even more than letting him suppose that I was stupidly worldly. So it is that in theory we find that we ought always to explain ourselves frankly, to avoid misunderstandings. But very often life arranges these in such a way that, in order to dispel them, in the rare circumstances in which it might be possible to do so, we must reveal either—which was not the case here— something that would annoy our friend even more than the injustice that he imputes to us, or a secret the disclosure of which—and this was my predicament—appears to us even worse than the misunderstanding. Besides, even without my explaining to Bloch, since I could not, my reason for not going with him, if I had begged him not to be angry with me, I should only have increased his anger by shewing him that I had observed it. There was nothing to be done but to bow before the decree of fate which had willed that Albertine's presence should prevent me from accompanying him, and that he should suppose that it was on the contrary the presence of people of distinction, the only effect of which, had they been a hundred times more distinguished, would have been to make me devote my attention exclusively to Bloch and reserve all my civility for him. It is sufficient that accidentally, absurdly, an incident (in this case the juxtaposition of Albertine and Saint-Loup) be interposed between two destinies whose lines have been converging towards one another, for them to deviate, stretch farther and farther apart, and never converge again. And there are friendships more precious than Bloch's for myself which have been destroyed without the involuntary author of the offence having any opportunity to explain to the offended party what would no doubt have healed the injury to his self-esteem and called back his fugitive affection.

Friendships more precious than Bloch's is not, for that matter, saying very much. He had all the faults that most annoyed me. It so happened that my affection for Albertine made them altogether intolerable. Thus in that brief moment in which I was talking to him, while keeping my eye on Robert, Bloch told me that he had been to luncheon with Mme. Bontemps and that everybody had spoken about me with the warmest praise until the "decline of Helios." "Good," thought I, "as Mme. Bontemps regards Bloch as a genius, the enthusiastic support that he must have given me will do more than anything that the others can have said, it will come round to Albertine. Any day now she is bound to learn, and I am surprised that her aunt has not repeated it to her already, that I am a 'superior person.'" "Yes," Bloch went on, "everybody sang your praises. I alone preserved a silence as profound as though I had absorbed, in place of the repast (poor, as it happened) that was set before us, poppies, dear to the blessed brother of Thanatos and Lethe, the divine Hypnos, who enwraps in pleasant bonds the body and the tongue. It is not that I admire you less than the band of hungry dogs with whom I had been bidden to feed. But I admire you because I understand you, and they admire you without understanding you. To tell the truth, I admire you too much to speak of you thus in public, it would have seemed to me a profanation to praise aloud what I carry in the profoundest depths of my heart. In vain might they question me about you, a sacred Pudor, daughter of Kronion, made me remain mute." I had not the bad taste to appear annoyed, but this Pudor seemed to me akin—far more than to Kronion—to the modesty that prevents a critic who admires you from speaking of you because the secret temple in which you sit enthroned would be invaded by the mob of ignorant readers and journalists—to the modesty of the statesman who does not recommend you for a decoration because you would be lost in a crowd of people who are not your equals, to the modesty of the academician who refrains from voting for you in order to spare you the shame of being the colleague of X—— who is devoid of talent, to the modesty in short, more respectable and at the same time more criminal, of the sons who implore us not to write about their dead father who abounded in merit, so that we shall not prolong his life and create a halo of glory round the poor deceased who would prefer that his name should be borne upon the lips of men to the wreaths, albeit laid there by pious hands, upon his tomb.

If Bloch, while he distressed me by his inability to understand the reason that prevented me from going to speak to his father, had exasperated me by confessing that he had depreciated me at Mme. Bontemps's (I now understood why Albertine had never made any allusion to this luncheon-party and remained silent when I spoke to her of Bloch's affection for myself), the young Israelite had produced upon M. de Charlus an impression that was quite the opposite of annoyance.

Certainly Bloch now believed not only that was I unable to remain for a second out of the company of smart people, but that, jealous of the advances that they might make to him (M. de Charlus, for instance), I was trying to put a spoke in his wheel and to prevent him from making friends with them; but for his part the Baron regretted that he had not seen more of my friend. As was his habit, he took care not to betray this feeling. He began by asking me various questions about Bloch, but in so casual a tone, with an interest that seemed so assumed, that one would have thought he did not hear the answers. With an air of detachment, an intonation that expressed not merely indifference but complete distraction, and as though simply out of politeness to myself: "He looks intelligent, he said he wrote, has he any talent?" I told M. de Charlus that it had been very kind of him to say that he hoped to see Bloch again. The Baron made not the slightest sign of having heard my remark, and as I repeated it four times without eliciting a reply, I began to wonder whether I had not been the dupe of an acoustic mirage when I thought I heard M. de Charlus utter those words. "He lives at Balbec?" intoned the Baron, with an air so far from questioning that it is a nuisance that the written language does not possess a sign other than the mark of interrogation with which to end these speeches which are apparently so little interrogative. It is true that such a sign would scarcely serve for M. de Charlus. "No, they have taken a place near here, La Commanderie." Having learned what he wished to know, M. de Charlus pretended to feel a contempt for Bloch. "How appalling," he exclaimed, his voice resuming all its clarion strength. "All the places or properties called La Commanderie were built or owned by the Knights of the Order of Malta (of whom I am one), as the places called Temple or Cavalerie were by the Templars. That I should live at La Commanderie would be the most natural thing in the world. But a Jew! However, I am not surprised; it comes from a curious instinct for sacrilege, peculiar to that race. As soon as a Jew has enough money to buy a place in the country he always chooses one that is called Priory, Abbey, Minster, Chantry. I had some business once with a Jewish official, guess where he lived: at Pont-l'Evêque. When he came to grief, he had himself transferred to Brittany, to Pont-l'Abbé. When they perform in Holy Week those indecent spectacles that are called "the Passion," half the audience are Jews, exulting in the thought that they are going to hang Christ a second time on the Cross, at least in effigy. At one of the Lamoureux concerts, I had a wealthy Jewish banker sitting next to me. They played the *Boyhood of Christ* by Berlioz, he was quite shocked. But he soon recovered his habitually blissful expression when he heard the Good Friday music. So your friend lives at the Commanderie, the wretch! What sadism! You shall shew me the way to it," he went on, resuming his air of indifference, "so that I may go there one day and see how our former domains endure such a profanation. It is unfortunate, for he has good manners, he seems to have been well brought up. The next thing I shall hear will be that his address in Paris is Rue du Temple!" M. de Charlus gave the impression, by these words, that he was seeking merely to find a fresh example in support of his theory; as a matter of fact he was aiming at two birds with one stone, his principal object being to find out Bloch's address. "You are quite right," put in Brichot, "the Rue du Temple used to be called Rue de la Chevalerie-du-Temple. And in that connexion will you allow me to make a remark, Baron?" said the don. "What? What is it?" said M. de Charlus tartly, the proffered remark preventing him from obtaining his information. "No, it's nothing," replied Brichot in alarm. "It is with regard to the etymology of Balbec, about which they were asking me. The Rue du Temple was formerly known as the Rue Barre-du-Bac, because the Abbey of Bac in Normandy had its Bar of Justice there in Paris." M. de Charlus made no reply and looked as if he had not heard, which was one of his favourite forms of insolence. "Where does your friend live, in Paris? As three streets out of four take their name from a church or an abbey, there seems every chance of further sacrilege there. One can't prevent Jews from living in the Boulevard de la Madeleine, Faubourg Saint-Honoré or Place Saint-Augustin. So long as they do not carry their perfidy a stage farther, and pitch their tents in the Place du Parvis Notre-Dame, Quai de l'Archevêché, Rue Chanoinesse or Rue de l'Avemaria, we must make allowance for their difficulties." We could not enlighten M. de Charlus, not being aware of Bloch's address at the time. But I knew that his father's office was in the Rue des Blancs-Manteaux. "Oh! Is not that the last word in perversity?" exclaimed M. de Charlus, who appeared to find a profound satisfaction in his own cry of ironical indignation. "Rue des Blancs-Manteaux!" he repeated, dwelling with emphasis upon each syllable and laughing as he spoke. "What sacrilege! Imagine that these White Mantles polluted by M. Bloch were those of the mendicant brethren, styled Serfs of the Blessed Virgin, whom Saint Louis established there. And the street has always housed some religious Order. The profanation is all the more diabolical since within a stone's-throw of the Rue des Blancs-Manteaux there is a street whose name escapes me, which is entirely conceded to the Jews, there are Hebrew characters over the shops, bakeries for unleavened bread, kosher butcheries, it is positively the Judengasse of Paris. That is where M. Bloch ought to reside. Of course," he went on in an emphatic, arrogant tone, suited to the discussion of aesthetic matters, and giving, by an unconscious strain of heredity, the air of an old musketeer of Louis XIII to his backward tilted face, "I take an interest in all that sort of thing only from the point of view of art. Politics are not in my line, and I cannot condemn wholesale, because Bloch belongs to it, a nation that numbers Spinoza among its illustrious sons. And I admire Rembrandt too much not to realise the beauty that can be derived from frequenting the synagogue. But after all a ghetto is all the finer, the more homogeneous and complete it is. You may be sure, moreover, so far are business instincts and avarice mingled in that race with sadism, that the proximity of the Hebraic street of which I was telling you, the convenience of having close at hand the fleshpots of Israel will have made your friend choose the Rue des Blancs-Manteaux. How curious it all is! It was there, by the way, that there lived a strange Jew who used to boil the Host, after which I think they boiled him, which is stranger still, since it seems to suggest that the body of a Jew can be equivalent to the Body of Our Lord. Perhaps it might be possible to arrange with your friend to take us to see the church of the White Mantles. Just think that it was there that they laid the body of Louis d'Orléans after his assassination by Jean sans Peur, which unfortunately did not rid us of the Orléans. Personally, I have always been on the best of terms with my cousin the Duc de Chartres; still, after all, they are a race of usurpers who caused the assassination of Louis XVI and dethroned Charles X and Henri V. One can see where they get that from, when their ancestors include Monsieur, who was so styled doubtless because he was the most astounding old woman, and the Regent and the rest of them. What a family!" This speech, anti-Jew or pro-Hebrew—according as one regards the outward meaning of its phrases or the intentions that they concealed—had been comically interrupted for me by a remark which Morel whispered to me, to the fury of M. de Charlus. Morel, who had not failed to notice the impression that Bloch had made, murmured his thanks in my ear for having "given him the push," adding cynically: "He wanted to stay, it's all jealousy, he would like to take my place. Just like a yid!" "We might have taken advantage of this halt, which still continues, to ask your friend for some explanations of his ritual. Couldn't you fetch him back?" M. de Charlus asked me, with the anxiety of uncertainty. "No, it's impossible, he has gone away in a carriage, and besides, he is vexed with me." "Thank you, thank you," Morel breathed. "Your excuse is preposterous, one can always overtake a carriage, there is nothing to prevent your taking a motor-car," replied M. de Charlus, in the tone of a man accustomed to see everyone yield before him. But, observing my silence: "What is this more or less imaginary carriage?" he said to me insolently, and with a last ray of hope. "It is an open post chaise which must by this time have reached la Commanderie." Before the impossible, M. de Charlus resigned himself and made a show of jocularity. "I can understand their recoiling from the idea of a new brougham. It might have swept them clean." At last we were warned that the train was about to start, and Saint-Loup left us. But this was the only day when by getting into our carriage he, unconsciously, caused me pain, when I thought for a moment of leaving him with Albertine in order to go with Bloch. The other times his presence did not torment me. For of her own accord Albertine, to save me from any uneasiness, would upon some pretext or other place herself in such a position that she could not even unintentionally brush against Robert, almost too far away to have to hold out her hand to him, and turning her eyes away from him would plunge, as soon as he appeared, into ostentatious and almost affected conversation with any of the other passengers, continuing this make-believe until Saint-Loup had gone. So that the visits which he paid us at Doncières, causing me no pain, no inconvenience even, were in no way discordant from the rest, all of which I found pleasing because they brought me so to speak the homage and invitation of this land. Already, as the summer drew to a close, on our journey from Balbec to Douville, when I saw in the distance the watering-place at Saint-Pierre des Ifs where, for a moment in the evening, the crest of the cliffs glittered rosy pink as the snow upon a mountain glows at sunset, it no longer recalled to my mind, I do not say the melancholy which the sight of its strange, sudden elevation had aroused in me on the first evening, when it filled me with such a longing to take the train back to Paris instead of going on to Balbec, but the spectacle that in the morning, Elstir had told me, might be enjoyed from there, at the hour before sunrise, when all the colours of the rainbow are refracted from the rocks, and when he had so often wakened the little boy who had served him, one year, as model, to paint him, nude, upon the sands. The name Saint-Pierre des Ifs announced to me merely that there would presently appear a strange, intelligent, painted man of fifty with whom I should be able to talk about Chateaubriand and Balzac. And now in the mists of evening, behind that cliff of Incarville, which had filled my mind with so many dreams in the past, what I saw, as though its old sandstone wall had become transparent, was the comfortable house of an uncle of M. de Cambremer in which I knew that I should always find a warm welcome if I did not wish to dine at la Raspelière or to return to Balbec. So that it was not merely the place-names of this district that had lost their initial mystery, but the places themselves. The names, already half-stripped of a mystery which etymology had replaced by reason, had now come down a stage farther still. On our homeward journeys, at Hermenonville, at Incarville, at Harambouville, as the train came to a standstill, we could make out shadowy forms which we did not at first identify, and which Brichot, who could see nothing at all, might perhaps have mistaken in the darkness for the phantoms of Herimund, Wiscar and Herimbald. But they came up to our carriage. It was merely M. de Cambremer, now completely out of touch with the Verdurins, who had come to see off his own guests and, as ambassador for his wife and mother, came to ask me whether I would not let him "carry me off" to keep me for a few days at Féterne where I should find successively a lady of great musical talent, who would sing me the whole of Gluck, and a famous chess-player, with whom I could have some splendid games, which would not interfere with the fishing expeditions and yachting trips on the bay, nor even with the Verdurin dinner-parties, for which the Marquis gave me his word of honour that he would "lend" me, sending me there and fetching me back again, for my greater convenience and also to make sure of my returning. "But I cannot believe that it is good for you to go so high up. I know my sister could never stand it. She would come back in a fine state! She is not at all well just now. Indeed, you have been as bad as that! To-morrow you won't be able to stand up!" And he shook with laughter, not from malevolence but for the same reason which made him laugh whenever he saw a lame man hobbling along the street, or had to talk to a deaf person. "And before this? What, you haven't had an attack for a fortnight. Do you know, that is simply marvellous. Really, you ought to come and stay at Féterne, you could talk about your attacks to my sister." At Incarville it was the Marquis de Montpeyroux who, not having been able to go to Féterne, for he had been away shooting, had come "to meet the train" in top boots, with a pheasant's feather in his hat, to shake hands with the departing guests and at the same time with myself, bidding me expect, on the day of the week that would be most convenient to me, a visit from his son, whom he thanked me for inviting, adding that he would be very glad if I would make the boy read a little; or else M. de Crécy, come out to digest his dinner, he explained, smoking his pipe, accepting a cigar or indeed more than one, and saying to me: "Well, you haven't named a day for our next Lucullus evening? We have nothing to discuss? Allow me to remind you that we left unsettled the question of the two families of Montgomery. We really must settle it. I am relying upon you." Others had come simply to buy newspapers. And many others came and chatted with us who, I have often suspected, were to be found upon the platform of the station nearest to their little mansion simply because they had nothing better to do than to converse for a moment with people of their acquaintance. A scene of social existence like any other, in fact, these halts on the little railway. The train itself appeared conscious of the part that had devolved upon it, had contracted a sort of human kindliness; patient, of a docile nature, it waited as long as they pleased for the stragglers, and even after it had started would stop to pick up those who signalled to it; they would then run after it panting, in which they resembled itself, but differed from it in that they were running to overtake it at full speed whereas it employed only a wise slowness. And so Hermenonville, Harambouville, Incarville no longer suggested to me even the rugged grandeurs of the Norman Conquest, not content with having entirely rid themselves of the unaccountable melancholy in which I had seen them steeped long ago in the moist evening air. Doncières! To me, even after I had come to know it and had awakened from my dream, how much had long survived in that name of pleasantly glacial streets, lighted windows, succulent flesh of birds. Doncières! Now it was nothing more than the station at which Morel joined the train, Egleville (*Aquilae villa*) that at which we generally found waiting for us Princess Sherbatoff, Maineville, the station at which Albertine left the train on fine evenings, when, if she was not too tired, she felt inclined to enjoy a moment more of my company, having, if she took a footpath, little if any farther to walk than if she had alighted at Parville (*Paterni villa*). Not only did I no longer feel the anxious dread of isolation which had gripped my heart the first evening, I had no longer any need to fear its reawakening, nor to feel myself a stranger or alone in this land productive not only of chestnut trees and tamarisks, but of friendships which from beginning to end of the journey formed a long chain, interrupted like that of the blue hills, hidden here and there in the anfractuosity of the rock or behind the lime trees of the avenue, but delegating at each stage an amiable gentleman who came to interrupt my course with a cordial handclasp, to prevent me from feeling it too long, to offer if need be to continue the journey with me. Another would be at the next station, so that the whistle of the little tram parted us from one friend only to enable us to meet others. Between the most isolated properties and the railway which skirted them almost at the pace of a person who is walking fast, the distance was so slight that at the moment when, from the platform, outside the waiting-room, their owners hailed us, we might almost have imagined that they were doing so from their own doorstep, from their bedroom window, as though the little departmental line had been merely a street in a country town and the isolated mansion-house the town residence of a family; and even at the few stations where no "good evening" sounded, the silence had a nourishing and calming fulness, because I knew that it was formed from the slumber of friends who had gone to bed early in the neighbouring manor, where my arrival would have been greeted with joy if I had been obliged to arouse them to ask for some hospitable office. Not to mention that a sense of familiarity so fills up our time that we have not, after a few months, a free moment in a town where on our first arrival the day offered us the absolute disposal of all its twelve hours, if one of these had by any chance fallen vacant, it would no longer have occurred to me to devote it to visiting some church for the sake of which I had come to Balbec in the past, nor even to compare a scene painted by Elstir with the sketch that I had seen of it in his studio, but rather to go and play one more game of chess at M. Féré's. It was indeed the degrading influence, as it was also the charm that this country round Balbec had had, that it should become for me in the true sense a friendly country; if its territorial distribution, its sowing, along the whole extent of the coast, with different forms of cultivation, gave of necessity to the visits which I paid to these different friends the form of a journey, they also reduced that journey to nothing more than the social amusement of a series of visits. The same place-names, so disturbing to me in the past that the mere Country House Year Book, when I turned over the chapter devoted to the Department of the Manche, caused me as keen an emotion as the railway time-table, had become so familiar to me that, in the time-table itself, I could have consulted the page headed: *Balbec to Douville via Doncières,* with the same happy tranquility as a directory of addresses. In this too social valley, along the sides of which I felt assembled, whether visible or not, a numerous company of friends, the poetical cry of the evening was no longer that of the owl or frog, but the "How goes it?" of M. de Criquetot or the

" Chaire! " of Brichot. Its atmosphere no longer aroused any anguish, and, charged with effluvia that were purely human, was easily breathable, indeed unduly soothing. The benefit that I did at least derive from it was that of looking at things only from a practical point of view. The idea of marrying Albertine appeared to me to be madness.

CHAPTER IV

Sudden revulsion in favour of Albertine. Agony at sunrise. I set off at once with Albertine for Paris.

I WAS only waiting for an opportunity for a final rupture. And, one evening, as Mamma was starting next day for Combray, where she was to attend the deathbed of one of her mother's sisters, leaving me behind so that I might get the benefit, as my grandmother would have wished, of the sea air, I had announced to her that I had irrevocably decided not to marry Albertine and would very soon stop seeing her. I was glad to have been able, by these words, to give some satisfaction to my mother on the eve of her departure. She had not concealed from me that this satisfaction was indeed extreme. I had also to come to an understanding with Albertine. As I was on my way back with her from la Raspelière, the faithful having alighted, some at Saint-Mars le Vêtu, others at Saint-Pierre des Ifs, others again at Doncières, feeling particularly happy and detached from her, I had decided, now that there were only our two selves in the carriage, to embark at length upon this subject. The truth, as a matter of fact, is that the girl of the Balbec company whom I really loved, albeit she was absent at that moment, as were the rest of her friends, but who was coming back there (I enjoyed myself with them all, because each of them had for me, as on the day when I first saw them, something of the essential quality of all the rest, as though they belonged to a race apart), was Andrée. Since she was coming back again, in a few days' time, to Balbec, it was certain that she would at once pay me a visit, and then, to be left free not to marry her if I did not wish to do so, to be able to go to Venice, but at the same time to have her, while she was at Balbec, entirely to myself, the plan that I would adopt would be that of not seeming at all eager to come to her, and as soon as she arrived, when we were talking together, I would say to her: "What a pity it is that I didn't see you a few weeks earlier. I should have fallen in love with you; now my heart is bespoke. But that makes no difference, we shall see one another frequently, for I am unhappy about my other love, and you will help to console me." I smiled inwardly as I thought of this conversation, by this strategem I should be giving Andrée the impression that I was not really in love with her; and so she would not grow tired of me and I should take a joyful and pleasant advantage of her affection. But all this only made it all the more necessary that I should at length speak seriously to Albertine, so as not to behave indelicately, and, since I had decided to consecrate myself to her friend, she herself must be given clearly to understand that I was not in love with her. I must tell her so at once, as Andrée might arrive any day. But as we were getting near Parville, I felt that we should not have time that evening and that it was better to put off until the morrow what was now irrevocably settled. I confined myself, therefore, to discussing with her our dinner that evening at the Verdurins'. As she put on her cloak, the train having just left Incarville, the last station before Parville, she said to me: "To-morrow then, more Verdurin, you won't forget that you are coming to call for me." I could not help answering rather sharply: "Yes, that is if I don't 'fail' them, for I am beginning to find this sort of life really stupid. In any case, if we go there, so that my time at la Raspelière may not be absolutely wasted, I must remember to ask Mme. Verdurin about something that may prove of great interest to myself, provide me with a subject for study, and give me pleasure as well, for I have really had very little this year at Balbec." "You are not very polite to me, but I forgive you, because I can see that your nerves are bad. What is this pleasure?" "That Mme. Verdurin should let me hear some things by a musician whose work she knows very well. I know one of his things myself, but it seems there are others and I should like to know if the rest of his work is printed, if it is different from what I know." "What musician?" "My dear child, when I have told you that his name is Vinteuil, will you be any the wiser?" We may have revolved every possible idea in our minds, and yet the truth has never occurred to us, and it is from without, when we are least expecting it, that it gives us its cruel stab and wounds us for all time. "You can't think how you amuse me," replied Albertine as she rose, for the train was slowing down. "Not only does it mean a great deal more to me than you suppose, but even without Mme. Verdurin I can get you all the information that you require. You remember my telling you about a friend older than myself, who has been a mother, a sister to me, with whom I spent the happiest years of my life at Trieste, and whom for that matter I am expecting to join in a few weeks at Cherbourg, when we shall start on our travels together (it sounds a little odd, but you know how I love the sea), very well, this friend (oh! not at all the type of woman you might suppose!), isn't this extraordinary, she is the dearest and most intimate friend of your

Vinteuil's daughter, and I know Vinteuil's daughter almost as well as I know her. I always call them my two big sisters. I am not sorry to let you see that your little Albertine can be of use to you in this question of music, about which you say, and quite rightly for that matter, that I know nothing at all." At the sound of these words, uttered as we were entering the station of Parville, so far from Combray and Montjouvain, so long after the death of Vinteuil, an image stirred in my heart, an image which I had kept in reserve for so many years that even if I had been able to guess, when I stored it up, long ago, that it had a noxious power, I should have supposed that in the course of time it had entirely lost it; preserved alive in the depths of my being—like Orestes whose death the gods had prevented in order that, on the appointed day, he might return to his native land to punish the murderer of Agamemnon—as a punishment, as a retribution (who can tell?) for my having allowed my grandmother to die, perhaps; rising up suddenly from the black night in which it seemed for ever buried, and striking, like an Avenger, in order to inaugurate for me a novel, terrible and merited existence, perhaps also to making dazzlingly clear to my eyes the fatal consequences which evil actions indefinitely engender, not only for those who have committed them, but for those who have done no more, have thought that they were doing no more than look on at a curious and entertaining spectacle, like myself, alas, on that afternoon long ago at Montjouvain, concealed behind a bush where (as when I complacently listened to an account of Swann's love affairs), I had perilously allowed to expand within myself the fatal road, destined to cause me suffering, of Knowledge. And at the same time, from my bitterest grief I derived a sentiment almost of pride, almost joyful, that of a man whom the shock he has just received has carried at a bound to a point to which no voluntary effort could have brought him. Albertine the friend of Mlle. Vinteuil and of her friend, a practising and professional Sapphist, was, compared to what I had imagined when I doubted her most, as are, compared to the little acousticon of the 1889 Exhibition with which one barely hoped to be able to transmit sound from end to end of a house, the telephones that soar over streets, cities, fields, seas, uniting one country to another. It was a terrible terra incognita this on which I had just landed, a fresh phase of undreamed-of sufferings that was opening before me. And yet this deluge of reality that engulfs us, if it is enormous compared with our timid and microscopic suppositions, was anticipated by them. It was doubtless something akin to what I had just learned, something akin to Albertine's friendship with Mlle. Vinteuil, something which my mind would never have been capable of inventing, but which I obscurely apprehended when I became uneasy at the sight of Albertine and Andrée together. It is often simply from want of the creative spirit that we do not go to the full extent of suffering. And the most terrible reality brings us, with our suffering, the joy of a great discovery, because it merely gives a new and clear form to what we have long been ruminating without suspecting it. The train had stopped at Parville, and, as we were the only passengers in it, it was in a voice lowered by a sense of the futility of his task, by the force of habit which nevertheless made him perform it, and inspired in him simultaneously exactitude and indolence, and even more by a longing for sleep, that the porter shouted: "Parville!" Albertine, who stood facing me, seeing that she had arrived at her destination stepped across the compartment in which we were and opened the door. But this movement which she was making to alight tore my heart unendurably, just as if, notwithstanding the position independent of my body which Albertine's body seemed to be occupying a yard away from it, this separation in space, which an accurate draughtsman would have been obliged to indicate between us, was only apparent, and anyone who wished to make a fresh drawing of things as they really were would now have had to place Albertine, not at a certain distance from me, but inside me. She distressed me so much by her withdrawal that, overtaking her, I caught her desperately by the arm. "Would it be materially impossible," I asked her, "for you to come and spend the night at Balbec?" "Materially, no. But I'm dropping with sleep." "You would be doing me an immense service. . . ." "Very well, then, though I don't in the least understand; why didn't you tell me sooner? I'll come, though." My mother was asleep when, after engaging a room for Albertine on a different floor, I entered my own. I sat down by the window, suppressing my sobs, so that my mother, who was separated from me only by a thin partition, might not hear me. I had not even remembered to close the shutters, for at one moment, raising my eyes, I saw facing me in the sky that same faint glow as of a dying fire which one saw in the restaurant at Rivebelle in a study that Elstir had made of a sunset effect. I remembered how thrilled I had been when I had seen from the railway on the day of my first arrival at Balbec, this same image of an evening which preceded not the night but a new day. But no day now would be new to me any more, would arouse in me the desire for an unknown happiness; it would only prolong my sufferings, until the point when I should no longer have the strength to endure them. The truth of what Cottard had said to me in the casino at Parville was now confirmed beyond a shadow of doubt. What I had long dreaded, vaguely suspected of Albertine, what my instinct deduced from her whole personality and my reason controlled by my desire had gradually made me deny, was true! Behind Albertine I no longer saw the blue mountains of the sea, but the room at Montjouvain where she was falling into the arms of Mlle. Vinteuil with that laugh in which she gave utterance to the strange sound of her enjoyment. For, with a girl as pretty as Albertine, was it possible that Mlle. Vinteuil, having the desires she had, had not asked her to gratify them? And the proof that Albertine had not been shocked by the request but had consented, was that they had not quarrelled, indeed their intimacy had steadily increased. And that graceful movement with which Albertine laid her chin upon Rosemonde's shoulder, gazed at her smilingly, and deposited a kiss upon her throat, that movement which had reminded me of Mlle. Vinteuil, in interpreting which I had nevertheless hesitated to admit that an identical line traced by a gesture must of necessity be due to an identical inclination, for all that I knew, Albertine might simply have learned it from Mlle. Vinteuil. Gradually, the lifeless sky took fire. I who until them had never awakened without a smile at the humblest things, the bowl of coffee and milk, the sound of the rain, the thunder of the wind, felt that the day which in a moment was to dawn, and all the days to come would never bring me any more the hope of an unknown happiness, but only the prolongation of my martyrdom. I clung still to life; I knew that I had nothing now that was not cruel to expect from it. I ran to the lift, regardless of the hour, to ring for the lift-boy who acted as night watchman, and asked him to go to Albertine's room, and to tell her that I had something of importance to say to her, if she could see me there. "Mademoiselle says she would rather come to you," was his answer. "She will be here in a moment." And presently, sure enough, in came Albertine in her dressing-gown. "Albertine," I said to her in a whisper, warning her not to raise her voice so as not to arouse my mother, from whom we were separated only by that partition whose thinness, to-day a nuisance, because it confined us to whispers, resembled in the past, when it so clearly expressed my grandmother's intentions, a sort of musical transparency, "I am ashamed to have disturbed you. Listen. To make you understand, I must tell you something which you do not know. When I came here, I left a woman whom I ought to have married, who was ready to sacrifice everything for me. She was to start on a journey this morning, and every day for the last week I have been wondering whether I should have the courage not to telegraph to her that I was coming back. I have had that courage, but it made me so wretched that I thought I would kill myself. That is why I asked you last night if you could not come and sleep at Balbec. If I had to die, I should have liked to bid you farewell." And I gave free vent to the tears which my fiction rendered natural. "My poor boy, if I had only known, I should have spent the night beside you," cried Albertine, to whom the idea that I might perhaps marry this woman, and that her own chance of making a "good marriage" was thus vanishing, never even occurred, so sincerely was she moved by a grief the cause of which I was able to conceal from her, but not its reality and strength. "Besides," she told me, "last night, all the time we were coming from la Raspelière, I could see that you were nervous and unhappy, I was afraid there must be something wrong." As a matter of fact my grief had begun only at Parville, and my nervous trouble, which was very different but which fortunately Albertine identified with it, arose from the boredom of having to spend a few more days in her company. She added: "I shan't leave you any more, I am going to spend all my time here." She was offering me, in fact—and she alone could offer me—the sole remedy for the poison that was burning me, a remedy akin, as it happened, to the poison, for, though one was sweet, the other bitter, both were alike derived from Albertine. At that moment, Albertine—my malady—ceasing to cause me to suffer, left me—she, Albertine the remedy—as weak as a convalescent. But I reflected that she would presently be leaving Balbec for Cherbourg, and from there going to Trieste. Her old habits would be reviving. What I wished above all things was to prevent Albertine from taking the boat, to make an attempt to carry her off to Paris. It was true that from Paris, more easily even than from Balbec, she might, if she wished, go to Trieste, but at Paris we should see; perhaps I might ask Mme. de Guermantes to exert her influence indirectly upon Mlle. Vinteuil's friend so that she should not remain at Trieste, to make her accept a situation elsewhere, perhaps with the Prince de ——, whom I had met at Mme. de Villeparisis's and, indeed, at Mme. de Guermantes's. And he, even if Albertine wished to go to his house to see her friend, might, warned by Mme. de Guermantes, prevent them from meeting. Of course I might have reminded myself that in Paris, if Albertine had those tastes, she would find many other people with whom to gratify them. But every impulse of jealousy is individual and bears the imprint of the creature—in this instance Mlle. Vinteuil's friend—who has aroused it. It was Mlle. Vinteuil's friend who remained my chief preoccupation. The mysterious passion with which I had thought in the past about Austria because it was the country from which Albertine came (her uncle had been a Counsellor of Embassy there), because its geographical peculiarities, the race that inhabited it, its historical buildings, its scenery, I could study, as in an atlas, as in an album of photographs, in Albertine's smile, her ways; this mysterious passion I still felt but, by an inversion of symbols, in the realm of horror. Yes, it was from there that Albertine came. It was there that, in every house, she could be sure of finding, if not Mlle. Vinteuil's friend, others of the sort. The habits of her childhood would revive, they would be meeting in three months' time for Christmas, then for the New Year, dates which were already painful to me in themselves, owing to an instinctive memory of the misery that I had felt on those days when, long ago, they separated me, for the whole of the Christmas holidays, from Gilberte. After the long dinner-parties, after the midnight revels, when everybody was joyous, animated, Albertine would adopt the same attitudes with her friends there that I had seen her adopt with Andrée, albeit her friendship for Andrée was innocent, the same attitudes, possibly, that I had seen Mlle. Vinteuil adopt, pursued by her friend, at Montjouvain. To Mlle. Vinteuil, while her friend titillated her desires before subsiding upon her, I now gave the inflamed face of Albertine, of an Albertine whom I heard utter as she fled, then as she surrendered herself, her strange, deep laugh. What, in comparison with the anguish that I was now feeling, was the jealousy that I might have felt on the day when Saint-Loup had met Albertine with myself at Doncières and she had made teasing overtures to him, or that I had felt when I thought of the unknown initiator to whom I was indebted for the first kisses that she had given me in Paris, on the day when I was waiting for a letter from Mlle. de Stermaria? That other kind of jealousy provoked by Saint-Loup, by a young man of any sort, was nothing. I should have had at the most in that case to fear a rival over whom I should have attempted to prevail. But here the rival was not similar to myself, bore different weapons, I could not compete upon the same ground, give Albertine the same pleasures, nor indeed conceive what those pleasures might be. In many moments of our life, we would barter the whole of our future for a power that in itself is insignificant. I would at one time have foregone all the good things in life to make the acquaintance of Mme. Blatin, because she was a friend of Mme. Swann. To-day, in order that Albertine might not go to Trieste, I would have endured every possible torment, and if that proved insufficient, would have inflicted torments upon her, would have isolated her, kept her under lock and key, would have taken from her the little money that she had so that it should be materially impossible for her to make the journey. Just as long ago, when I was anxious to go to Balbec, what urged me to start was the longing for a Persian church, for a stormy sea at daybreak, so what was now rending my heart as I thought that Albertine might perhaps be going to Trieste, was that she would be spending the night of Christmas there with Mlle. Vinteuil's friend: for imagination, when it changes its nature and turns to sensibility, does not for that reason acquire control of a larger number of simultaneous images. Had anyone told me that she was not at that moment either at Cherbourg or at Trieste, that there was no possibility of her seeing Albertine, how I should have wept for joy. How my whole life and its future would have been changed! And yet I knew quite well that this localisation of my jealousy was arbitrary, that if Albertine had these desires, she could gratify them with other girls. And perhaps even these very girls, if they could have seen her elsewhere, would not have tortured my heart so acutely. It was Trieste, it was that unknown world in which I could feel that Albertine took a delight, in which were her memories, her friendships, her childish loves, that exhaled that hostile, inexplicable atmosphere, like the atmosphere that used to float up to my bedroom at Combray, from the dining-room in which I could hear talking and laughing with strangers, amid the clatter of knives and forks, Mamma who would not be coming upstairs to say good-night to me; like the atmosphere that had filled for Swann the houses to which Odette went at night in search of inconceivable joys. It was no longer as of a delicious place in which the people were pensive, the sunsets golden, the church bells melancholy, that I thought now of Trieste, but as of an accursed city which I should have liked to see go up in flames, and to eliminate from the world of real things. That city was embedded in my heart as a fixed and permanent point. The thought of letting Albertine start presently for Cherbourg and Trieste filled me with horror; as did even that of remaining at Balbec. For now that the revelation of my mistress's intimacy with Mlle. Vinteuil became almost a certainty, it seemed to me that at every moment when Albertine was not with me (and there were whole days on which, because of her aunt, I was unable to see her), she was giving herself to Bloch's sister and cousin, possibly to other girls as well. The thought that that very evening she might be seeing the Bloch girls drove me mad. And so, after she had told me that for the next few days she would stay with me all the time, I replied: "But the fact is, I want to go back to Paris. Won't you come with me? And wouldn't you like to come and stay with us for a while in Paris?" At all costs I must prevent her from being by herself, for some days at any rate, I must keep her with me, so as to be certain that she could not meet Mlle. Vinteuil's friend. She would as a matter of fact be alone in the house with myself, for my mother, taking the opportunity of a tour of inspection which my father had to make, had taken it upon herself as a duty, in obedience to my grandmother's wishes, to go down to Combray and spend a few days there with one of my grandmother's sisters. Mamma had no love for her aunt, because she had not been to my grandmother, who was so loving to her, what a sister should be. So, when they grow up, children remember with resentment the people who have been unkind to them. But Mamma, having become my grandmother, was incapable of resentment; her mother's life was to her like a pure and innocent childhood from which she would extract those memories whose sweetness or bitterness regulated her actions towards other people. Our aunt might have been able to furnish Mamma with certain priceless details, but now she would have difficulty in obtaining them, her aunt being seriously ill (they spoke of cancer), and she reproached herself for not having gone sooner, to keep my father company, found only an additional reason for doing what her mother would have done, just as she went on the anniversary of the death of my grandmother's father, who had been such a bad parent, to lay upon his grave the flowers which my grandmother had been in the habit of taking there. And so, to the side of the grave which was about to open, my mother wished to convey the kind words which my aunt had not come to offer to my grandmother. While she was at Combray, my mother would busy herself with certain things which my grandmother had always wished to be done, but only if they were done under her daughter's supervision. So that they had never yet been begun, Mamma not wishing, by leaving Paris before my father, to make him feel too keenly the burden of a grief in which he shared, but which could not afflict him as it afflicted her. "Ah! That wouldn't be possible just at present," Albertine assured me. "Besides, why should you need to go back to Paris so soon, if the lady has gone?" "Because I shall feel more at my ease in a place where I have known her than at Balbec, which she has never seen and which I have begun to loathe." Did Albertine realise later on that this other woman had never existed, and that if that night I had really longed for death, it was because she had stupidly revealed to me that she had been on intimate terms with Mlle. Vinteuil's friend? It is possible. There are moments when it appears to me probable. Anyhow, that morning, she believed in the existence of this other woman. "But you ought to marry this lady," she told me, "my dear boy, it would make you happy, and I'm sure it would make her happy as well." I replied that the thought that I might be making the other woman happy had almost made me decide; when, not long since, I had inherited a fortune which would enable me to provide my wife with ample luxury and pleasures, I had been on the point of accepting the sacrifice of her whom I loved. Intoxicated by the gratitude that I felt for Albertine's kindness, coming so soon after the atrocious suffering that she had caused me, just as one would think nothing of promising a fortune to the waiter who pours one out a sixth glass of brandy, I told her that my wife would have a motor-car, a yacht, that from that point of view, since Albertine was so fond of motoring and yachting, it was unfortunate that she was not the woman I loved, that I should have been the perfect husband for her, but that we should see, we should no doubt be able to meet on friendly terms. After all, as even when we are drunk we refrain from addressing the passers-by, for fear of blows, I was not guilty of the imprudence (if such it was) that I should have committed in Gilberte's time, of telling her that it was she, Albertine, whom I loved. "You see, I came very near to marrying her. But I did not dare do it, after all, I should not like to make a young woman live with anyone so sickly and troublesome as myself." "But you must be mad, anybody would be delighted to live with you, just look how people run after you. They're always talking about you at Mme. Verdurin's, and in high society too, I'm told. She can't have been at all nice to you, that lady, to make you lose confidence in yourself like that. I can see what she is, she's a wicked woman, I detest her. I'm sure, if I were in her shoes!" "Not at all, she is very kind, far too kind. As for the Verdurins and all that, I don't care a hang. Apart from the woman I love, whom moreover I have given up, I care only for my little Albertine, she is the only person in the world who, by letting me see a great deal of her—that is, during the first few days," I added, in order not to alarm her and to be able to ask anything of her during those days, "—can bring me a little consolation." I made only a vague allusion to the possibility of marriage, adding that it was quite impracticable since we should never agree. Being, in spite of myself, still pursued in my jealousy by the memory of Saint-Loup's relations with "Rachel, when from the Lord," and of Swann's with Odette, I was too much inclined to believe that, from the moment that I was in love, I could not be loved in return, and that pecuniary interest alone could attach a woman to me. No doubt it was foolish to judge Albertine by Odette and Rachel. But it was not she; it was myself; it was the sentiments that I was capable of inspiring that my jealousy made me underestimate. And from this judgment, possibly erroneous, sprang no doubt many of the calamities that were to overwhelm us. "Then you decline my invitation to Paris?" "My aunt would not like me to leave just at present. Besides, even if I can come, later on, wouldn't it look rather odd, my staying with you like that? In Paris everybody will know that I'm not your cousin." "Very well, then. We can say that we're practically engaged. It can't make any difference, since you know that it isn't true." Albertine's throat which emerged bodily from her nightgown, was strongly built, sunburned, of coarse grain. I kissed her as purely as if I had been kissing my mother to charm away a childish grief which as a child I did not believe that I would ever be able to eradicate from my heart. Albertine left me, in order to go and dress. Already, her devotion was beginning to falter; a moment ago she had told me that she would not leave me for a second. (And I felt sure that her resolution would not last long, since I was afraid, if we remained at Balbec, that she would that very evening, in my absence, be seeing the Bloch girls.) Now, she had just told me that she wished to call at Maineville and that she would come back and see me in the afternoon. She had not looked in there the evening before, there might be letters lying there for her, besides, her aunt might be anxious about her. I had replied: "If that is all, we can send the lift-boy to tell your aunt that you are here and to call for your letters." And, anxious to shew herself obliging but annoyed at being tied down, she had wrinkled her brow, then, at once, very sweetly, said: "All right" and had sent the lift-boy. Albertine had not been out of the room a moment before the boy came and tapped gently on my door. I had not realised that, while I was talking to Albertine, he had had time to go to Maineville and return. He came now to tell me that Albertine had written a note to her aunt and that she could, if I wished, come to Paris that day. It was unfortunate that she had given him this message orally, for already, despite the early hour, the manager was about, and came to me in a great state to ask me whether there was anything wrong, whether I was really leaving; whether I could not stay just a few days longer, the wind that day being rather "tiring" (trying). I did not wish to explain to him that the one thing that mattered to me was that Albertine should have left Balbec before the hour at which the Bloch girls took the air, especially since Andrée, who alone might have protected her, was not there, and that Balbec was like one of those places in which a sick man who has difficulty in breathing is determined, should he die on the journey, not to spend another night. I should have to struggle against similar entreaties, in the hotel first of all, where the eyes of Marie Gineste and Céleste Albaret were red. (Marie, moreover, was giving vent to the swift sob of a mountain torrent. Céleste, who was gentler, urged her to keep calm; but, Marie having murmured the only poetry that she knew: "Down here the lilacs die," Céleste could contain herself no longer, and a flood of tears spilled over her lilac-hued face; I dare say they had forgotten my existence by that evening.) After which, on the little local railway, despite all my precautions against being seen, I met M. de Cambremer who, at the sight of my boxes, turned pale, for he was counting upon me for the day after the next; he infuriated me by trying to persuade me that my choking fits were caused by the change in the weather, and that October would do them all the good in the world, and asked me whether I could not "postpone my departure by a week," an expression the fatuity of which enraged me perhaps only because what he was suggesting to me made me feel ill. And while he talked to me in the railway carriage, at each station I was afraid of seeing, more terrible than Heribald or Guiscard, M. de Crécy imploring me to invite him, or, more dreadful still, Mme. Verdurin bent upon inviting me. But this was not to happen for some hours. I had not got there yet. I had to face only the despairing entreaties of the manager. I shut the door on him, for I was afraid that, although he lowered his voice, he would end by disturbing Mamma. I remained alone in my room, that room with the too lofty ceiling in which I had been so wretched on my first arrival, in which I had thought with such longing of Mlle. de Stermaria, had watched for the appearance of Albertine and her friends, like migratory birds alighting upon the beach, in which I had enjoyed her with so little enjoyment after I had sent the lift-boy to fetch her, in which I had experienced my grandmother's kindness, then realised that she was dead; those shutters at the foot of which the morning light fell, I had opened the first time to look out upon the first ramparts of the sea (those shutters which Albertine made me close in case anybody should see us kissing). I became aware of my own transformations as I compared them with the identity of my surroundings. We grow accustomed to these as to people and when, all of a sudden, we recall the different meaning that they used to convey to us, then, after they had lost all meaning, the events very different from those of to-day which they enshrined, the diversity of actions performed beneath the same ceiling, between the same glazed bookshelves, the change in our heart and in our life that diversity implies, seem to be increased still further by the unalterable permanence of the setting, reinforced by the unity of scene.

Two or three times it occurred to me, for a moment, that the world in which this room and these bookshelves were situated and in which Albertine counted for so little, was perhaps an intellectual world, which was the sole reality, and my grief something like what we feel when we read a novel, a thing of which only a madman would make a lasting and permanent grief that prolonged itself through his life; that a tiny movement of my will would suffice, perhaps, to attain to that real world, to re-enter it, passing through my grief, as one breaks through a paper hoop, and to think no more about what Albertine had done than we think about the actions of the imaginary heroine of a novel after we have finished reading it. For that matter, the mistresses whom I have loved most passionately have never coincided with my love for them. That love was genuine, since I subordinated everything else to the need of seeing them, of keeping them to myself, and would weep aloud if, one evening, I had waited for them in vain. But it was more because they had the faculty of arousing that love, of raising it to a paroxysm, than because they were its image. When I saw them, when I heard their voices, I could find nothing in them which resembled my love and could account for it. And yet my sole joy lay in seeing them, my sole anxiety in waiting for them to come. One would have said that a virtue that had no connexion with them had been attached to them artificially by nature, and that this virtue, this quasi-electric power had the effect upon me of exciting my love, that is to say of controlling all my actions and causing all my sufferings. But from this, the beauty, or the intelligence, or the kindness of these women was entirely distinct. As by an electric current that gives us a shock, I have been shaken by my love affairs, I have lived them, I have felt them: never have I succeeded in arriving at the stage of seeing or thinking them. Indeed I am inclined to believe that in these love affairs (I leave out of account the physical pleasure which is their habitual accompaniment but is not enough in itself to constitute them), beneath the form of the woman, it is to those invisible forces which are attached to her that we address ourselves as to obscure deities. It is they whose goodwill is necessary to us, with whom we seek to establish contact without finding any positive pleasure in it. With these goddesses, the woman, during our assignation with her, puts us in touch and does little more. We have, by way of oblation, promised jewels, travels, uttered formulas which mean that we adore and, at the same time, formulas which mean that we are indifferent. We have used all our power to obtain a fresh assignation, but on condition that no trouble is involved. Now would the woman herself, if she were not completed by these occult forces, make us give ourselves so much trouble, when, once she has left us, we are unable to say how she was dressed and realise that we never even looked at her?

As our vision is a deceiving sense, a human body, even when it is loved as Albertine's was, seems to us to be at a few yards', at a few inches' distance from us. And similarly with the soul that inhabits it. But something need only effect a violent change in the relative position of that soul to ourself, to shew us that she is in love with others and not with us, then by the beating of our dislocated heart we feel that it is not a yard away from us but within us that the beloved creature was. Within us, in regions more or less superficial. But the words:

"That friend is Mlle. Vinteuil" had been the *Open, sesame* which I should have been incapable of discovering by myself, which had made Albertine penetrate to the depths of my shattered heart. And the door that had closed behind her, I might seek for a hundred years without learning how it might be opened.

I had ceased for a moment to hear these words ringing in my ears while Albertine was with me just now. While I was kissing her, as I used to kiss my mother, at Combray, to calm my anguish, I believed almost in Albertine's innocence, or at least did not think continuously of the discovery that I had made of her vice. But now that I was alone the words began to sound afresh like those noises inside the ear which we hear as soon as the other person stops talking. Her vice now seemed to me to be beyond any doubt. The light of the approaching sunrise, by altering the appearance of the things round me, made me once again, as though it shifted my position for a moment, and even more painfully conscious of my suffering. I had never seen the dawn of so beautiful or so painful a morning. And thinking of all the nondescript scenes that were about to be lighted up, scenes which, only yesterday, would have filled me simply with the desire to visit them, I could not repress a sob when, with a gesture of oblation mechanically performed which appeared to me to symbolise the bloody sacrifice which I should have to make of all joy, every morning, until the end of my life, a solemn renewal, celebrated as each day dawned, of my daily grief and of the blood from my wound, the golden egg of the sun, as though propelled by the breach of equilibrium brought about at the moment of coagulation by a change of density, barbed with tongues of flame as in a painting, came leaping through the curtain behind which one had felt that it was quivering with impatience, ready to appear on the scene and to spring aloft, the mysterious, ingrained purple of which it flooded with waves of light. I heard the sound of my weeping. But at that moment, to my astonishment, the door opened and, with a throbbing heart, I seemed to see my grandmother standing before me, as in one of those apparitions that had already visited me, but only in my sleep. Was all this but a dream, then? Alas, I was wide awake. "You see a likeness to your poor grandmother," said Mamma, for it was she, speaking gently to calm my fear, admitting moreover the resemblance, with a fine smile of modest pride which had always been innocent of coquetry. Her dishevelled hair, the grey locks in which were not hidden and strayed about her troubled eyes, her ageing cheeks, my grandmother's own dressing-gown which she was wearing, all these had for a moment prevented me from recognising her and had made me uncertain whether I was still asleep or my grandmother had come back to life. For a long time past my mother had resembled my grandmother, far more than the young and smiling Mamma that my childhood had known. But I had ceased to think of this resemblance. So, when we have long been sitting reading, our mind absorbed, we have not noticed how the time was passing, and suddenly we see round about us the sun that shone yesterday at the same hour call up the same harmonies, the same effects of colour that precede a sunset. It was with a smile that my mother made me aware of my mistake, for it was pleasing to her that she should bear so strong a resemblance to her mother. "I came," said my mother, "because when I was asleep I thought I heard some one crying. It wakened me. But how is it that you aren't in bed? And your eyes are filled with tears. What is the matter?" I took her head in my arms: "Mamma, listen, I'm afraid you'll think me very changeable. But first of all, yesterday I spoke to you not at all nicely about Albertine; what I said was unfair." "But what difference can that make?" said my mother, and, catching sight of the rising sun, she smiled sadly as she thought of her own mother, and, so that I might not lose the benefit of a spectacle which my grandmother used to regret that I never watched, she pointed to the window. But beyond the beach of Balbec, the sea, the sunrise, which Mamma was pointing out to me, I saw, with movements of despair which did not escape her notice, the room at Montjouvain where Albertine, rosy and round like a great cat, with her rebellious nose, had taken the place of Mlle. Vinteuil's friend and was saying amid peals of her voluptuous laughter: "Well! If they do see us, it will be all the better. I? I wouldn't dare to spit upon that old monkey?" It was this scene that I saw, beyond the scene that was framed in the open window and was no more than a dim veil drawn over the other, super-imposed upon it like a reflexion. It seemed indeed almost unreal, like a painted view. Facing us, where the cliff of Parville jutted out, the little wood in which we had played "ferret" thrust down to the sea's edge, beneath the varnish, still all golden, of the water, the picture of its foliage, as at the hour when often, at the close of day, after I had gone there to rest in the shade with Albertine, we had risen as we saw the sun sink in the sky. In the confusion of the night mists which still hung in rags of pink and blue over the water littered with the pearly fragments of the dawn, boats were going past smiling at the slanting light which gilded their sails and the point of their bowsprits as when they are homeward bound at evening: a scene imaginary, chilling and deserted, a pure evocation of the sunset which did not rest, as at evening, upon the sequence of the hours of the day which I was accustomed to see precede it, detached, interpolated, more unsubstantial even than the horrible image of Montjouvain which it did not succeed in cancelling, covering, concealing—a poetical, vain image of memory and dreams. "But come," my mother was saying, "you said nothing unpleasant about her, you told me that she bored you a little, that you were glad you had given up the idea of marrying her. There is no reason for you to cry like that. Remember, your Mamma is going away to-day and can't bear to leave her big baby in such a state. Especially, my poor boy, as I haven't time to comfort you. Even if my things are packed, one has never any time on the morning of a journey." "It is not that." And then, calculating the future, weighing well my desires, realising that such an affection on Albertine's part for Mlle. Vinteuil's friend, and one of such long standing, could not have been innocent, that Albertine had been initiated, and, as every one of her instinctive actions made plain to me, had moreover been born with a predisposition towards that vice which in my uneasiness I had only too often dreaded, in which she could never have ceased to indulge (in which she was indulging perhaps at that moment, taking advantage of an instant in which I was not present), I said to my mother, knowing the pain that I was causing her, which she did not shew, and which revealed itself only by that air of serious preoccupation which she wore when she was weighing the respective seriousness of making me unhappy or making me unwell, that air which she had assumed at Combray for the first time when she had resigned herself to spending the night in my room, that air which at this moment was extraordinarily like my grandmother's when she allowed me to drink brandy, I said to my mother: "I know how what I am going to say will distress you. First of all, instead of remaining here as you wished, I want to leave by the same train as you. But that is nothing. I am not feeling well here, I would rather go home. But listen to me, don't make yourself too miserable. This is what I want to say. I was deceiving myself, I deceived you in good faith, yesterday, I have been thinking over it all night. It is absolutely necessary, and let us decide the matter at once, because I am quite clear about it now in my own mind, because I shall not change again, and I could not live without it, it is absolutely necessary that I marry Albertine."